HOUSE NAME

HOUSE NAME

A Novel of *The House War*

MICHELLE WEST

DAW BOOKS, INC.

DONALD A. WOLLHEIM, FOUNDER

375 Hudson Street, New York, NY 10014

ELIZABETH R. WOLLHEIM

SHEILA E. GILBERT

PUBLISHERS

www.dawbooks.com

First Printing January 2011
1   2   3   4   5   6   7   8   9

This is for Sheila Gilbert, who cares for these books almost as much as I do. Without her unflagging support, I'm not sure they'd exist at all, and I am profoundly grateful.

Acknowledgments

My home team—John, Kristen, Gary, Ayami—continues to impress with their patience and, sometimes, their unfortunate mockery. My family—Thomas, Daniel and Ross—do the same, although perhaps the oldest son has become immune to the glamour and mystery of life as a writer of fiction. For some reason, he thinks that writers are not *entirely* objective. I can't imagine why. Terry Pearson continues to alpha read, and given the stretches of book that induce despair during the initial drafts, this says something about his monumental patience. My mother and father hold the fort, feed the kids, and provide comfort and encouragement, although on my mother's part it's not always silent.

Jody Lee continues to grace my books with covers that make me squeal when I first see them; when I'm feeling discouraged, I grab them and set them up beside the computer as incentive to work through the difficulties—because when you have a Jody cover, you want the book to be worthy of it.

Publishers often get a lot of annoyed mail, and not so much love, and I think this is a shame, because DAW is my away team; it's my extended family. Sheila, Betsy, Marsha, Debra and Joshua keep everything running, and make so many of the decisions I'd have no clue about if they were left up to me. Words—mine—are only a part of what goes into making a book. All of the rest of the work done on the book that is now in your hands was theirs.

Prologue

THE RUINS OF THE ANCIENT CITY lay undisturbed in almost unbroken darkness. Sunlight did not trouble its roads, and the moons, with their scant silver light, were likewise invisible; the sky was a thing of curved, uneven rock.

Great stone slabs and the bases of statues lined empty streets; crevices, created by the slow shift of the earth beneath those streets, had widened into a darkness so complete that even demon eyes could not easily penetrate it. But in the ruins, there was a silent, funereal majesty that demanded, and held, the attention. Echoes of voices that had perished centuries ago existed in some of the small statues and maker's works that still adorned deserted buildings—rotting floors in the dry, dark air notwithstanding.

There were gardens in this city that had been swallowed, at once, by the abiding earth, but they were not living gardens; no one tended them. Nor had they any need; they were creations of stone that suggested the fragile and enduring beauty of memory, not life. That they were modeled on living things signified little; they were not, and had never been, alive. Which is why they endured.

Lord Isladar wandered through the subtle pathways of this garden, slowly examining flowers, delicate trailing ivy, shrubs, and the stone legs of benches; the actual seats had long since rotted away. Everything here had been carved in stone by the hand of the maker-born, but the stone seemed to move and breathe and grow; it was an artful and pleasing illusion.

He was alone not because it was safest—although in the Hells of his experience this was often the case—but because he had no desire for the company of his kin; the world had opened, had allowed him entry, and he had accepted it. He had forced from it a shape of his choosing, neither too tall nor too short; it was slender and seemed much like the form that had been his when he had first left childhood behind.

Childhood.

He bent, his fingers brushing dust and webs from the delicate curl of open petals before he rose. He admired what remained of this hidden city, but it was not for the city that he had been summoned from the side of the Lord of the Hells by the ambitious, and surprisingly competent, Sor Na Shannen so many years past.

No, Lord Isladar had been chosen because he was one of the few who understood the men who had made gardens such as these; who had watched and encouraged them, in his fashion, during the ages when the gods had walked the world. It was for his curiosity, his observation, and his ability to predict what the merely mortal would say—or do—when placed in a difficult position.

The kin understood pain. They understood how to break things. Even cities as glorious as this one at its height had not been immune. But mortals, especially those born to the gods in their ethereal Between, were still capable of posing a threat, and if not mortals, then the others, firstborn and hidden.

Mortals.

Isladar smiled. Regardless of the danger or the consequence of the summoning, mortals played their fraught games of demonology. They did not, of course, understand what lay at the base of those games; they merely understood that it was both forbidden and powerful. Could he but choose one avenue to open up the world to the demonic kin, again and again, it would be that one. It was convenient, then, that the men and women charged with guarding against just such uses of magic understood their own kin so poorly.

This time, a mortal mage, sequestered in the relative solitude of a rich man's manse, had taken forbidden texts and cobbled together just enough knowledge that he might begin the summoning of lesser creatures. He understood the spells and protections but, again, did not understand that what he was opening was a small door through which something might walk. Yes, demons—but as relevant to the *Kialli* lords as rats might be to mortals—came at his call, and they danced his cautious tune until they were returned to the Hells.

There, they made their way—as all denizens of the Hells must—to the foot of the mountain upon which the Lord of the Hells ruled, in the heat and the sway of the charnel winds, beneath the angry sky. They were expected to make the climb on their own, and they were expected to survive it; not all would, but this was not considered a loss.

In Isladar's opinion, it was; because word of a possible mage, a possible entry into the world that was ever on his Lord's mind, would thus escape detection for many years, and by the time the existence of such a mortal reached his Lord's ears, the mortal would likely be dead—of the consequences of his own ambition or of age.

If the mage was foolish or of middling will, he would escape detection completely; if the lesser kin escaped that mage's control in mortal lands, they would seek vengeance and cause inestimable pain—and death—before they were apprehended by other, less foolish mages and sent back to the Hells as dust.

But their vengeance would open no doors, and it was a single such door that was required.

And so it went. Here and there, the promise of a particular mage's name would be whispered in the throne room upon the peaks, and Isladar would listen and nod. He would take the measure of the kin who made his enraged report—for who among their kind willingly submitted the whole of their will to another and, at that, a *lesser*, being?—and in so doing, would gain some measure of the summoner. But the powerful were not summoned often, and if they were, they did not return to the Lord in a way that provided useful information.

Instead, they lived in the mortal world, evading both detection and the absolute grip of the Lord's rule. It was as close to freedom as the *Kialli* could now come.

Time passed in the Hells, as it passed everywhere: slowly. The screams of the damned, or their whimpers, were sedating and soothing; they brought comfort and peace to the kin. Not so Lord Isladar, although he, like any of the kin, felt the call strongly. What he wanted, what he had wanted from the moment he had first set foot upon the plains of the Hells and understood just what his service had brought him, was more complicated.

To his surprise—and he, like any of the *Kialli*, abhorred surprise, because it was so often the final emotion in a powerful existence—Sor Na Shannen, a cunning but ultimately insignificant demon, had been summoned by an enterprising and ambitious mage. It was not the first time she had been summoned, and it was unlikely to be the last, for even mages had their base desires, and she had littered her name across the ancient texts and reliquaries with deliberate malice; it was not hard to find. She had not returned, but in her captivity she had found the privacy and the time to call her Lord's name across the divide. He heard.

He heard, and he informed Isladar of both her captivity and her master: Davash AMarkham, a mage-born mortal in the city over which the god-born now ruled in relative peace. It was not the ideal geographic location; it was too close to the most dangerous of their enemies and far too close to those who might detect such summoning and end it abruptly before larger work could be done.

It was Isladar's suggestion that she subtly provide the mage enough information to summon one of the *Kialli* lords in stead of a less powerful creature. Only the lords—and even then, not all—had the power and knowledge to open gates and to struggle with the names and the will of those they summoned, binding them.

But Sor Na Shannen had, again, proved clever and resourceful, and perhaps it was a gift that she was not a significant power in the Hells, for she was accustomed to both the loss of dignity and the cunning indirection necessary for those who could not contest power in any direct fashion. She had captivated the mage, reducing him, over the course of months, into a willing servant, transferring lust for power to a more malleable lust. What she could not do, she was not willing to summon a greater Lord to do; she now demanded the mage give her the knowledge she lacked, and she *learned*.

Over the months, molding her power and her understanding of the mortal world in which she increasingly moved freely, she studied, practiced, swallowed her pride—such as it was—and became one of the few of the kin who might summon her kind to the mortal plane.

The Lord of the Hells had bid her summon Lord Isladar. Had he not, had Isladar not witnessed the command himself, he would have destroyed Sor Na Shannen for her arrogance and her hubris the moment he reasserted his existence in the lands of the living. As it was, it was close, far closer than he cared to admit—for she had attempted to control him, to subvert his ancient and unfaltering will to her own.

She had, of course, failed. He played at subservience, thinking it was useful; he had played at the contest, allowing her some sense of her own worth. But it was never in doubt; only she could assume as much, if vanity dictated such an assumption. It did, of course, and he allowed it.

After Isladar, she had summoned—again at the behest of the Lord—Karathis. She did not even attempt to control him; the only compulsion Karathis felt at all was the compulsion to travel to the point at which she stood, and even prepared for it, he was enraged. But he was also well apprised of the Lord's growing regard for the resourcefulness and the knowledge of this singular lesser kin; he held his hand.

Holding it, he had watched Isladar. Isladar had said nothing, indicated nothing; he observed, no more, no less.

I will kill her for her presumption, Karathis had whispered.

Yes. But not now. Not yet. She is needed. Come, brother, let us open the ways; we will disinter the oldest of our cities, and we will find what we need there. Do you not wish to walk its streets? Do you not wish to see what remains of its glory?

Karathis had not replied.

Nor had he need; the only one of the *Kialli* who might openly express such a foreign desire to see the site of their greatest failure was, indeed, Lord Isladar.

But there was beauty in failure. It was an understated, attenuated beauty; it could be seen only if all pride could be cast aside. Isladar alone of his kin had both the memory of the city in its living glory and the ability to cast aside the rage and the fury caused by its fall, so it was Isladar who walked these streets, guided by memory, even when that memory failed to unearth the map of what now remained. It was Isladar who could see the promise of the city as it had once been; it was Isladar who could remember the beauty of its heights, could hear the echoes of the whisper of the wild wind as it drove them to those heights at their command; Isladar who could see the ghosts of the great statuary erected in reverence and fear of Allasakar.

It was Isladar who could see the beauty not in defeat but in the strange dignity of defeat, in the effort to grab and hold what little remained. There, he thought, fell Siandoria, who could not—would not—bow to the will of the conquering gods. He could mark the spot, although it now lay shadowed by fallen rock and natural darkness.

Siandoria, bloodied but calm, his face white, his hands mailed, his eyes a flashing silver gray. His armor had been rent as if it were cloth, and the wild wind no longer heard his voice, but these were simple, calculable losses from which he might recover in time. His shield had been riven and his sword, broken, their light forever guttered.

Yet without them, he fought.

Siandoria understood that he faced death; he had no hope of survival and needed—at that moment—none. As if memory were stone, Siandoria's expression was now chiseled, in just the same way the garden had been, into the hollows of Isladar's mind. He could look and see its exact likeness, and feel *life* in it, although it spoke only of, always of, death. Not for Siandoria surrender; not for Siandoria the choice to follow or abandon Allasakar in his defeat.

Siandoria, we will not see your like again. There was pain in that. But in pain, there was also beauty; no architect of the Hells could deny that. He bowed his head a moment before he continued to traverse these empty streets.

They had worked to open the ways, and the work was long and arduous. It was not work that Sor Na Shannen could sustain for long; indeed, it was work that, in its entirety, depended upon the powers of Lord Isladar and Lord Karathis—and it was not to Karathis' liking to be sent to dig in the dirt like the least of human slaves. Karathis was quick to show displeasure, and Isladar intervened in his subtle fashion to ensure the survival of Sor Na Shannen.

But if Karathis had the arrogance and the power of a Duke of the Hells, he also had wisdom and cunning; he understood that she was necessary. It chafed. But any form of dependence on others always did.

The first such labor undertaken by Karathis and Isladar had nearly destroyed the Cordufar manse, for Lord Karathis had attempted to leash the Old Earth in their service. It was a mistake he would make only once, for that was the nature of mistakes: If one survived, one learned. Many did not survive, but that, as well, was the nature of the Hells.

Isladar could still hear the echoes of the Old Earth's voice; it was angry. Slow to wake, it was also slow to sleep, and the rumble of its anger, its sense of betrayal and loss—had they not, in the end, chosen to disavow it, to leave forever the lands under which the Earth held dominion, in its fashion?—lingered for weeks.

So the excavations under Cordufar were undertaken the arduous, slow way, and Karathis did not suggest, then or ever, that the Old Earth be invoked. *Do you feel the loss, brother?* Isladar thought, and had thought. If he did, he did not expose it.

Those excavations were the most complete; they were the most heavily guarded. The first door opened, foot by onerous foot, into the most ancient of cities.

Even Sor Na Shannen, not notable for her tact or her self-control, fell silent when they had first set foot not into dank tunnel or new earth but into the streets of the city itself. Only the lesser buildings now remained, and of those, only the ones that had relied less heavily on wooden beams and supports. Facades, however, stood in the black day of the city. Glimmers of ancient magic, contained by stone shapes, statues, gargoyles, could be felt or detected, but it was not for these that they had come.

No.

They had come for one thing and one thing alone, and although it took weeks, they finally found it: the coliseum. "Here," Isladar told them softly. "We will build here."

The stone, of course, had proved problematic. To build the arch, to enchant the stone, to inscribe it in the necessary fashion, had been both difficult and costly. In this impoverished, mortal world, there were no great quarries; the mortal quarries were simple things of dead stone, and it was not dead stone that they required. Even so, Lord Isladar had traveled to several quarries to the east of Averalaan; he had inspected both the visible rock and the rock that had not yet been broken, seeking some hint of the ancient in their sleeping forms.

It was not to be found, not there.

Sor Na Shannen was ill-pleased. Karathis might have been as ill-pleased, but her foul humor often amused him. *What, then, shall we do, brother?* he asked.

I will retreat, Isladar replied gravely, *to the Deepings, if they even remain. If not, we will work with what we can obtain.*

It is too much of a risk.

It is a risk, he agreed. *But if we have no choice, we will take it. The arch will either hold, or it will not, and it is my suspicion that we will know before the long summoning begins. If you desire, begin your construction and your invocation now; I will search while you . . . experiment.*

That had been to Sor Na Shannen's liking. Although she, like the rest of the kin, did not age, she was nonetheless impatient. Such impatience had often been their downfall; Isladar had no intention of allowing it to run unchecked here.

Isladar had then traveled south, past the borders of the Empire in which the god-born ruled, and he had found, again, a travesty of power, a mockery of its substance, in the rulers there. But there, at least, without the god-born to hamper them, the rules of power were clearer and cleaner.

He spent some years in the South, traveling; he observed the differences in custom between the Northern Empire and the Southern Dominion. When at last he was satisfied that he understood these diminished people well enough, he encountered his first danger: the Voyani.

They were both of the South and entirely separate from it, and they had the knowledge and power of their ancient ancestors, albeit in shreds and tatters. They did not own land, and for this reason, he had missed them during his first sojourn in the courts of the powerful. No, they traveled in their wagons, led by their Matriarchs.

And their Matriarchs? They knew him. Understood what he was, what his presence might presage. He had been forced to flee, for the power to destroy them, while his, would not guarantee his survival. Lord Isladar had very little pride when it came to displays of power; he did not care whether or not the merely mortal held him in contempt.

But he took note of the Matriarchs and the Voyani caravans, and when he was quit of them, some hundreds of miles away, he endeavored to learn what he could. He accepted—as Karathis did not—that the mortals, the *mere* mortals, could be a threat to the plans of the Lord, and as such, some caution and knowledge were required.

He made his way to the Green Deepings. They were bounded on all sides by either mountains or the ferocious superstition of Southern slaves in their small enclaves and villages. He was *Kialli*; he understood fear in all its nuances, and he understood, as well, that the *only* people who dared the Old Forests were the Voyani themselves. It was, of course, a warning.

Accepting the warning with the cool grace of a powerful, free man— albeit a stranger to these villages—he had smiled. He did not ride, and free men of any power were expected to take to horseback as if born there, but the slaves were cautious, regardless. It was not their position to question the identity of strange men of rank; that was the responsibility of their lords and owners. He accepted their warnings with gravity.

But of course, he entered the Old Forest, as they'd called it.

There, he found the elder trees, preserved somehow against the graying and dwindling of mortality. He walked among them, as he had not walked among them for years beyond count, and he whispered their names. They could not—or would not—hear him, and this was bitter, but it was not unexpected, for there were older and darker things than even Lord Isladar in these forests. Some slumbered, some did not.

But it was here, for the first time, that he touched the hidden paths. They were not obvious, and they were not visible in a way that mortal vision could easily discern; nor, apparently, immortal vision. But between one step and another, the wind changed, and the sunlight; even the color of the leaves above and the forest growth beneath his feet changed. He heard the wind's voice so clearly he could call it—and he did, for a moment, speaking its endless litany of names, and asking from it no task but response.

Wind, of the wild elements, was quickest: quick to anger and quick to forgive. It carried dead leaves in its folds with as much grace and force as it tickled the living, pulling them from their branches. It was not the Earth. And it was willing, on this hidden path, to converse as wind did.

He walked the path and understood at last the heart of the Old Forest, for the forest's roots touched this path, this narrow road in which the Green Deepings lived and breathed. The mortal slaves feared the powerful—with reason—and they therefore found only fear in the lee of the forest's edge.

Isladar did not fear power, and he did not fear the unknown—for in the end, very little *was* unknown to him. He found rivers upon the hidden path, and they spoke with the voice of wild water, although water, like earth, was not his friend, and it rose in fury at the sound of his voice. But what it would not willingly give, he could force from it, for he had the time. He did not find fire here, but fire alone welcomed the *Kialli* to their ancient home.

And so it went. He was almost foolish in his desire to explore, and it was a sentimental folly—this had once been *home*.

But he had abandoned home for the love of the Lord, and it was no longer his. He found the first signs of the Wild Hunt while he followed this path, tracing its curving and unpredictable lines toward the distant mountains. He did not encounter the Hunt itself, for it was not Scarran, nor close, but the wind whispered the name of the Queen of the Hunt, the Queen of the Hidden Court: Ariane. Hoof prints had been stamped into the very rock that adorned the side of one river, as if stags had been driven up the face of cliffs in search of prey.

Yet even this reminder of ancient enemies, ancient enmity, filled him with yearning. It was Winter in these lands. The Hunt rode only in Winter.

Yes, the trees seemed to whisper, and he understood then why they did not speak or listen or grow enraged—as water and earth did—by the sound of his voice: it was Winter in the forest. Winter. How long? How long had it been since the forest had seen Summer?

The forest itself did not reply. Later, he would seek the answer in more unobtrusive ways, but the task of the moment demanded his attention. He did not, however, stray from the hidden path, and it traveled from the Green Deepings to the farthest edges of the Northern Wastes, land of brilliant, biting light, howling winds, desolate beauty. It traveled to hidden oases, to endless caverns, to vistas that had not been touched by either god or man since the gods last walked the world, and it almost pained him to leave them, so stricken was he by the visceral desire for *home*.

He did not speak of this; not then, when there were no witnesses, and not later. The home of that longing, the brief and unexpected pain, was long, long lost. What existed now was the Hells and, if he was ultimately successful, the whole of the mortal plane.

To this end, he continued, with more caution and less curiosity, until he at last found the remnants of the Stone Deepings. He did not delve there long, nor could he; magics had been wrought there, and if he did not recognize the caster, he recognized the power: They were ancient, and they barred the way. But they were subtle as well; he could not discern the whole of their purpose, and it both troubled and irritated.

It signified little. He had found the living stone, and he carved it with care, piece by piece, each of a size and shape that might support the magics that must be worked upon it. It was not quick work, and it required a raw power that he seldom used, but this far beneath all that was human he did not fear detection; he feared, instead, to somehow set off the strange and unidentifiable magic that hid all but a small part of the Deepings from view. The mountains rumbled in their slow and thunderous way, and he spoke in their ancient tongue. But they, kin to the earth, resisted.

Had he been any other Lord, he might have died and returned, lessened, to the foothills of the Hells.

But he was Isladar, and although time was short, he took the time he needed, not to defy the living stone but to soothe it.

Only then, the first arduous steps taken toward relearning an ancient tongue made foreign by his departure from the plane and his sojourn in the realm of the Lord, did he make his return to Averalaan.

There he gave the stones into the keeping of Lord Karathis, and together they began to build the arch, imbuing it, at each iteration of pillar, each placement of stone, with the power of the *Kialli*. Only once it was finished, only once they had spent the three days in the long invocations, sacrificing the mortals they had scrounged for that purpose from the streets of the city above, did the long journey of Allasakar at last begin.

And they watched, joined by Sor Na Shannen in her wild impatience. Centuries had passed since the Lord to whom they had dedicated the whole of their existence while they lived had walked this world. He would walk it again, but this time—ah, this time, there would be no gods to hinder him. Sor Na Shannen had, centuries past, destroyed the worship of the only one who *might*.

So it stood, day by day. Lord Karathis assumed the form and shape of Lord Cordufar in the manse above, and Lord Isladar spent time traversing the plane. He spent some years in the Southern Dominion, witnessing the wars of the Tyrs and Tors, as the nobles there were called, as they struggled for supremacy against both their northern neighbors and their internal rivals.

He traveled, as well, to the far North, before returning to Averalaan. And everywhere he went, he assessed the powerful, and he examined the colors of their souls, judging them, searching for those among their number who might be both competent and malleable under the right circumstances.

But he returned, always, to venture to the standing arch, with its single runed keystone; he knelt not two feet away from where it stood, and he bowed in complete subservience to the heart of the gate. He had often stood by the side of the Lord's throne in the Hells, and of the *Kialli* who had done so, Isladar was the only one who had survived either his Lord's attention or the suspicion of the rest of the *Kialli* Court.

The Court was distant now, but if those who currently labored within the confines of the Empire of Essalieyan had success, it would not remain so; only the surroundings would change. And the souls, he thought; those, too, would change. The Shining City would once again rise, as if from slumber, with the Lord upon the throne.

But he returned to the undercity when he desired privacy or silence, and he walked among the ruins there, conjuring the ghosts of their former grandeur as clearly as only the *Kialli* could.

On one such excursion, Isladar discovered, alone among the notable and powerful buildings, one that he did not recognize. It was not—could not—be of any recent construction, for it was here, beneath the earth and the sullen mortal streets above. It must have been erected *after* the fall, for the plummet of the city into the waiting, ancient earth had not destroyed or marred it.

He approached it with a suspicion that hardened almost to certainty by the time his feet touched the first of the large, carved symbols perfectly laid in stone, for the lights in this building cast his shadow against the ground so sharply they might have been sun. He felt, for a moment, the touch of the gods upon the stone; saw the dim impression of their finger-prints upon the walls; saw their work in each carved symbol.

It had been so long since he had seen even a hint of their language, for not even the Lord of the Hells spoke it now—what use had he for a tongue meant for communication among the gods? He was, and had always been, solitary. He spoke to destroy and to render to those who were worthy of his respect an epitaph. To the gods, the god-tongue.

Isladar had chosen to follow only one, but he was aware that, follower of the one or no, he was not immune to the presence of even his sworn enemies, be they but gods. They were like the heart of the wild elements, like the tallest of mountain precipices, like the most savage of coastal storms. They existed as a force beyond comprehension and control, and they inspired awe; something as petty as envy could not touch them.

And so he had approached this new building, this edifice that had never been touched by memory. In size and shape it was a lesser archi-tectural work, but the grandest of buildings that adorned the Shining City had required the living power of Allasakar to sustain its impossible heights.

Isladar had walked the length and breadth of the streets of Averalaan above. He had glanced at the many so-called cathedrals, and he had looked for some sign that power—that beauty—existed within the mean streets; he had found none.

Therefore even this lesser work, this lesser edifice, fanned the dying embers of wonder and awe in him. He was surprised at how those embers could burn, but he was *Kialli*. He remembered, and memory was painful. It was their art.

Alone, he traversed the terra-cotta floors, his feet skirting the deep grooves the circular runic forms made. He did not touch them, but he read their meaning slowly and with care. He understood that the sigils were meant as a warning and as a lament, and he cursed, in silence, his partial ignorance. But none of the *Kialli* spoke the tongue of gods, not even the most learned.

Lights had been wrought here, in crystal, in glass, in gold, each warm and luminescent. Even fallen, even buried, the gods did not choose to accept the fact of endless Night. The gods, like the firstborn and the lesser mortals who had followed, were proud. He considered destroying that light, but in the end, he held his hand. He could not say why.

The long, wide halls, broken with runes that told the story of the fall of the Shining City and the desertion of this world by its gods, he traversed for days. He spent hours studying each glyph, learning its shape and its pattern; its sound was lost to him forever, for matters of such a simple thing as pronunciation were not the type of question he could ask of the only god he now knew. It frustrated him bitterly, but he accepted his ignorance, galling though it was.

He did not accept that he would always be ignorant, however; who, in the end, could predict what might or might not occur in the future of this world? So, he walked, and stopped, and studied; he consigned shape and height and texture, as well as positioning, of each such sigil to memory.

Was it any wonder, then, that he took days? He required no sleep and no sustenance, and the hours and days and months of the long unfolding of the Lord's plan left him little to do in the darkness; he considered the study a worthy endeavor, even if he suspected where the end of the tale they told must lead, and why. He let it unfold, in its mystery, its partial glimpses of ancient history, as if, at the tale's end, he must once more emerge into darkness and the gray world of mortals, riven from even the hints of ancient magic and majesty and true wilderness.

Thus it was that Isladar finally came upon the Sleepers in their chamber of eternal repose. And Isladar, in the glory of the light they shed, paid them the respect that was their due; for in the end, were it not for the treachery of the Sleepers, the Lord of the Hells might now be dead, his body scattered ash, his followers riven from both himself and each other.

He had seen them ride in the full glory of the Winter Hunt, by the side of their cold Queen, and he had seen them fight, and kill. No matter that they fought his own kin; the *Kialli* might curse them or taunt them in the heat of battle, but they respected power, and the Sleepers had been powerful. He knew their names, but he did not speak them, not aloud.

They had faltered once; they had failed once. This was the result of their failure, this deathlike sleep, the splendor of this dream.

At the behest of the Winter Queen, they had ridden to war at the side of Moorelas; they had ridden to war with the godslayer. Yet Moorelas was no *Arianni*, no *Allasianni*; he had been born to mortals, and he had aged greatly in the mere handful of years he had wielded the sword that alone might strike a fatal blow against Allasakar. Moorelas did not comprehend the wonder and the savage beauty of the gods—how could he? He was mortal.

No more did he understand the light and the brilliance of the princes of the Queen's realm. They were his allies, and they were necessary, but he did not revere them, and he did not fully trust them. In such a way, he proved himself exceptionally wise for one of his mean origins.

Isladar understood the treachery of the Sleepers. Had they not been princes of Ariane's realm? Had they not been the strength and the pride of both Winter and Summer Courts? Had they not ridden at the head of her grim and ancient host to stand against the very gods themselves? They had experienced all the glory of the world, of the gods, of the wars that rearranged mountains and plains and rivers before one side or the other might at last claim victory.

They, like the *Kialli*, had been born in blood, raised to war, trained to attain the heights of its savage glory, to see the beauty in the death that followed in its wake; it was their truest test. They did not raise livestock and cut firewood and shear sheep for rough, poor fabric; nor did they trundle with battered wagons and poor guards to deliver these pathetic goods. They were the princes of the firstborn.

And were they to strike to diminish and humble the whole of their known world for the sake of the merely mortal? Were they to bleed the numinous and the eternal from the world until all that remained was the essence of mortal soul? Nor did the mortals fight and struggle and craft these souls, these shards of the eternal; they were born wrapped around them and lived in ignorance of their existence, all but a few.

They would have welcomed the ride, he thought. The four against Allasakar. They would have risked their own oblivion, without the host of the Queen, for just such a battle. But for the sake of the *mortals*?

They could not do it.

Perhaps there were other reasons for their treachery; he was certain there must have been. But driving them to it, the anger, the love, the desire for things that were not beholden to the weak, the short lived, the pathetic.

Now, they slept. Their shields were defaced and blank, their swords sheathed. Their armor, of course, was finely crafted, ornate, a statement in and of itself; no easy death by spear or arrow or fire or magery would take them unaware. Their hair was the white of their kin, and their eyes, closed; they were tall, and fair, and, even in their slumber, proud scions of a lost age.

He bowed again. He could not say for certain how long he remained within that chamber, although he knew why: Here again was youth, some evidence that memory was true. Could he but wake them, he might know battle and death—his or theirs—and feel again the quickening of the ancient in his veins. He desired it greatly—desired it even more than he hungered for the momentary satisfaction of the fear and the pain of dying mortals.

But he had understood just enough of what he had so carefully memorized to understand the warning laid in wall and floor: When the Sleepers wakened to the world again, gods would—gods *must*—perish. Allasakar would be, once again, upon the mortal plane, if Isladar's long game were to at last begin in earnest.

He had therefore set his wards upon the building itself; were it disturbed, were it entered by so much as a bat, he would know. No one must disturb the Sleepers, for even the *Kialli* now knew what their waking presaged.

That done, he waited. He had waited for millennia; he was capable of patience. He heard his Lord's voice more clearly as the mortal years passed. Time, he thought. It would be time, and soon.

But he did not smile. Not yet.

Chapter One

22nd of Scaral, 410 A.A.
Undercity, Averalaan

SOR NA SHANNEN was incandescent with rage; had light been required for the kin to see by, she would have nonetheless been visible in the night of the ruins, so potent was her fury. Stray strands of ebony hair flew, limned in blue and red.

"Sor Na Shannen." It was Lord Isladar who spoke. Even Karathis was silent.

She wheeled, her hands now shaped in fists, the perfect length of her nails also glittering with traces of dark light. She waited for his anger, his accusation, or the cool tones of his mockery; failure, if it did not destroy, had other consequences. She was not of a mind to accept them with grace.

But he was Lord Isladar, the least predictable of the *Kialli* lords. "We have been prepared for discovery for some time. It has come later, rather than earlier." He glanced at Lord Karathis, who nodded.

"Ariane has . . . disturbed the gate; she is now aware of what she faces. Whether or not she can intervene again remains to be seen—but it is my suspicion that she cannot." He knelt; the marble into which she had driven her sword was cracked, and the crack ran the length of the polished stone from one side of the coliseum to the other. "We have failed in our attempt to take House Terafin, but it was never necessary; it would have been convenient, no more."

"It would have given us the opportunity," Karathis cut in, his voice rumbling and crackling, "to destroy the god-born in the heart of their own domain. With their destruction, the Empire would have been in chaos just as the Lord emerged."

Isladar nodded; that had, indeed, been the plan. It was not, however, the first time a plan would be frustrated; nor was it likely to be the last. Individually, mortals were beneath notice. This was an acknowledged truth. But in the aggregate? They were powerful and capable. This second truth, however, was less acknowledged, and when it was, in however reluctant a way, it was qualified: The god-born were mortal, but they bore the blood of gods.

"We will not now have that opportunity," Isladar continued softly. "But it was never required." He tendered the enraged demon a brief nod. "We have what we require, if we are *careful*, and if your servitors can be kept in check.

"We will begin, Karathis and I, to close the ways."

"We will not now have Scarran," she said, grudging the slower burn of her rage.

"We will. The damage done by the Winter Queen will require the whole of the darkest night to repair. Can you do it?" he asked. It was a challenge.

But it was, as well, a gift, and it mollified her. "Yes."

"Then stay; we must go in haste. Tell us only what you know of the entrances that Ararath once used to wander these streets; it is there we will go first."

"Does it matter? If they are found, we will merely add to the numbers of sacrifices required to dedicate the standing ground at the ceremony's close."

Isladar's silence was not gratifying. But, inasmuch as a *Kialli* lord could be, he had been gracious. She waited. "It matters," he finally said. "If, by unforeseen circumstance, one such mortal should escape, the Kings will know."

"They will *know now*," she snarled.

Isladar chuckled. "You have been decades in your dance among mortals of power," he pointed out. "But you have not observed The Ten or their relationship with the Kings closely. I do not believe that it is so simple an affair as that. I believe that The Terafin will ask for—will indeed *require*—proof, before she approaches the Kings. Yes, if she chooses to do so without proof, they will hear her, and they will listen. But it might be politically costly for Terafin to do so.

"It is therefore urgent that we find, and seal off, all entrances that Ararath used before his death. Or," he added, "all of the entrances gleaned from his thoughts before his death. They will be the most common, I think, and will also be the first searched.

"We must give them nothing."

22nd of Scaral, 410 A.A.
Healerie, House Terafin, Averalaan Aramarelas

Arann woke in the late afternoon.

The slightly rounded ceiling of the healerie was the first thing he expected to see, and when he opened his eyes, it was there.

Although he'd never been in this room before, he knew it almost as well as he knew the den's apartment. He knew where the beds were laid out; he knew, as well, what the cupboards, recessed along the far wall, contained. He knew the women—and men—who had learned their craft from Alowan. He knew that Alowan, almost revered in Terafin, had steadfastly refused to take the House Name, and he even knew why: A House Name was a political statement, a statement of allegiance. Alowan's allegiance was to life, in all its forms, and more, to the preservation of life. Healer-born, and scarred by his talent—more than most—he had nonetheless chosen to serve. But service to The Terafin was not, in the end, service to the House. It was, in its entirety, service to the woman. Amarais Handernesse ATerafin.

Alowan had healed her, just as he had healed Arann. And he had left her, just as he had left Arann, bereft and on the shoals of life, as if life were an unexpected burden.

But *she* had borne it. She had accepted the gift, and in return, she had offered Alowan the healerie for as long as he was willing to stay within her walls. She had offered him the House Name, but she had never expected him to accept it. And he had not disappointed, in the end.

Arann knew Alowan's life.

Alowan knew Arann's.

"Arann?"

He glanced down from the curve of a ceiling beyond which the sun shone cool in the coming Scaral evening. Finch was seated beside his bed, her face pale, her hair clean and bound above her face. She wasn't Jay; tendrils didn't escape to cover her eyes.

She wore a pale cream dress with a simple belt; he couldn't see her feet, but it didn't matter. He reached for her with his left hand, and she met him halfway with both of hers. He tried not to crush her fingers.

She tried not to notice when he failed.

"Finch."

She nodded. "Jay told me to tell you—" she hesitated. "There was trouble, in the House." Her voice dropped to a whisper. "A mage came. There was magic. And Jay says . . . something tried to kill The Terafin."

"Something?"

She nodded. "It looked like Rath." She glanced around the empty room. "I'm not supposed to upset you. Or talk much, really."

He nodded. Waited. Neither of them had ever been big talkers, and it was always awkward when two quiet people had no loud buffers between them.

"We're not sure what happened. Jay's going to talk with The Terafin tonight." Drawing a breath, she added, "The Terafin's given us rooms here. Big rooms. And our own kitchen. And an old guy, Ellerson. I think he's one of the servants." She hesitated and then added, "But his only job right now is us."

Arann nodded again.

"Jay will come later if Alowan lets her in."

"He will."

She hesitated and then asked, "Should I stay?"

He nodded again and closed his eyes. After a few minutes, he said, "I think this is a good place."

"The healerie?"

"The House."

"Why?"

He shook his head. "The Terafin."

"Why?"

"What she wants isn't that different from what Jay wants."

"Jay wants to protect the rest of us."

"She wants to protect the things she loves. Right now, that's only us." Arann opened his eyes. "But it won't *always* be only us." He glanced at the ceiling again, at the small cracks there. "Jay thinks she failed," he said quietly. "Because of Lefty."

Finch didn't mention the others by name, but he felt the small accusation in her silence. "What do you think?"

Coming from Finch, the question surprised him enough that he pushed himself up the headboard into a seated position. He didn't, however, let go of Finch's hand, so the shift in position dragged her half out of her chair.

"I think she failed," he said, after a long pause. "She failed Lefty."

Before Finch could find words—and it was pretty clear she was searching for them—he added, "But it wasn't her fault. All of us failed him. He's gone," he added.

"He's—"

"Dead."

She didn't ask him how he knew. She knew where he had almost gone.

"I was so angry, Finch. I was *so angry*. At myself. At Jay. At everything." He forced himself to release her hand, to lay his, white and trembling, against the coverlet across his lower body. "But we don't fail if we don't try. Jay will always try. She won't always succeed."

"Arann—"

"It's better to try. Because she won't always fail, either." He looked at Finch, then. Finch, who, like Arann, was still alive.

"Yes," a new voice said, and Finch turned to see Alowan, standing in the arch that separated the arboretum from the beds. "She will not always fail."

Arann tensed. He couldn't help that. But he didn't try to stand; he didn't try to go to the old healer.

"Tell me about your Jay," Alowan said quietly. His voice carried; there was nothing to break it. Even breath was almost silent in this place.

Finch glanced at Arann.

Arann said, "He knows what *I* know. He's not asking me."

Alowan grimaced slightly but nodded. "Tell me, Finch, about the first time you met Jay."

Finch hesitated. But Alowan's age and the peaceful wisdom he radiated couldn't be reduced to simple threat; it couldn't be ignored as distant authority. "Why?" she asked, at last.

"She reminds me of someone, I think. And I would like to know what you see in her."

Finch spread her hands. "She's Jay. She saved my life."

"And you stayed with her?"

"I had nowhere else to go." She hesitated again and then added, "But even if I had, I would have wanted to stay with her."

"Why?"

"Because she's Jay. She knows things. She believes in things. I think she wants to change the world. I know I can't, not by myself—but if I stay with her, I might be able to help."

"Does she know this?"

"I don't know. It's never seemed important to her. Why we stay, I mean. I don't know if she really questions it."

Alowan nodded, as if that answer satisfied him. "She doesn't question it; she is young, and she is not yet what she will be. But it is there."

It was dark, and the moon's light filtered through the arboretum, silvering leaves and hanging plants, by the time Teller came to relieve Finch.

"Jay's back," he whispered. He glanced at Arann, who was sleeping.

"He sleeps a lot," Finch told him, as she vacated her chair. "But so does Alowan."

"Alowan's old."

She nodded. "But . . . I like him."

Teller smiled. He took Arann's hand from hers and settled in. "Jay'll come in the morning. She's cleared the kitchen," he added, with just the hint of a smile.

"How did Ellerson take it?"

"About as well as she expected."

Finch's grimace was delicate.

"Did she speak with The Terafin?"

Teller nodded. "The Terafin offered her two solarii a day."

Finch couldn't whistle, and she seldom regretted the lack. She did make the attempt, now, and it fell into a quiet huff of breath, as it always did. "For what?" She was wary, but she wasn't entirely suspicious. Just a little. They would always have that "little" when dealing with the powerful.

"Work." Teller hesitated. "We're not entirely certain *what* she wants, but she said—" he glanced at Finch. "Maybe you should go back to the wing and let Jay explain."

"She won't say anything you don't." They both knew that Teller's memory was better. He was, as far as they had one, a keeper of records, a mini-historian. It was Teller who transcribed Jay's dreams.

"Jay says The Terafin wants proof that the undercity exists. She—The Terafin—sent people out to explore Rath's place and the subbasement. They found *nothing*."

Finch frowned. "In the basement?"

He nodded. "Nothing at all."

"But we've *used* that entrance—"

"About a hundred times. They couldn't find it."

"Maybe they—"

"Jay thinks it wasn't there."

"How could a hole that size just—just disappear?"

Teller shrugged. He reached over and touched Arann's forehead with the back of his hand before nodding and returning to his chair. "Probably magic," he told her, still gazing at Arann's sleeping face. "We almost lost him."

Finch touched his shoulder gently.

"We lost Duster."

She had saved Finch's life. Finch said nothing, waiting.

"Jay wants to find the body if she can."

"Why?"

"Bury it. Have a funeral. She says we'll never find the others."

"Did she say when?"

Teller shook his head. "But she's serious about the work for The Terafin. Because The Terafin promised two things in exchange for the work. The money."

"And?"

"We get to stay. Here, in the wing, while Jay works."

"And when she's done?"

"If she can prove her value to the House and to The Terafin, we—" He swallowed. "We get to stay."

"Stay?"

"She'll offer Jay the House Name."

Silence then. Of all the things they'd been foolish enough to hope for, to dream of, in the streets of the twenty-fifth, in an apartment that was smaller than their single rooms, becoming *ATerafin* wasn't one of them. "Jay won't look for Duster," Finch said quietly.

Teller nodded. Even in the gentle dark, his face was expressionless.

"She's practical," he said softly. "While there's *any* chance that she can do this, that she can prove she's useful, she'll concentrate on that to the exclusion of almost everything else."

"What does she want us to do?"

"She hasn't said. Angel's biting through walls," he added, "because Jay's going to be searching—on her own—with the mage. He asked to go, and she said no."

"Did she take Carver?"

"She's taking *no one*."

"So . . . we're supposed to sit around in our rooms and wait?"

Teller nodded.

"We've done worse."

"I told Angel that."

"He wasn't impressed."

"Not much." Teller hesitated again and then added, "She's lost too much. She can't stop, and she can't think about it. This is better, for her."

Finch agreed. But the presence of a mage—a known mage—made her uneasy. "I'll go back," she told him and turned toward the arch.

"Finch?"

She paused.

"Talk to the others. Talk to Ellerson."

"What should I—" she stopped. "I will. Watch Arann. He's really, really lonely," she added, searching for words and finding all of them inadequate.

"It's the healing," Teller replied softly.

She wanted to ask him how he knew. But she didn't; he was Teller.

"Rath told me once." He paused and then added, "Rath's dead."

So much death. So much death to bring them to the edge of House Terafin, upon the Isle.

She surprised herself when she spoke. "Let's make it mean something." Looking back, she saw that she had his attention. "The deaths," she said. "Let's make them count."

"For what?"

"For anything, Teller. Duster died so the rest of us could live. Let's make it count."

"You sound like Jay."

"There are worse things to sound like." They both smiled, and she turned then and left the room, pausing for a moment to dip her fingers into ripples of moon-dappled water in the arboretum's fountain.

*   *   *

She would have gotten lost on the way to the West Wing, but a servant was lingering in the halls when she pushed the heavy door open and stepped outside of Alowan's domain. He bowed once and then smiled at her slightly rounded eyes.

"Burton ATerafin," he told her, with just the hint of pride.

"ATerafin?"

He nodded. "I led Teller to the healerie, and I thought you might want to return to your wing." He carried a small lamp in one hand; it swayed as he stood.

"Do you know your way around the entire manse?" she asked as she fell into step beside him. He was much taller than she was, and he was also older—although not as old as Torvan ATerafin, and not quite so intimidating.

He nodded, his smile deepening. It was not an unkind smile; it had the faint air of pride but none of its edge. "I got lost a lot for the first two weeks, though."

She gazed at the height of the ceilings as they turned into one of the large galleries. "I think it will take us a lot longer than two weeks not to get lost," she admitted quietly. And then, because he seemed friendly and the prospect of Terafin was so daunting, she asked, "Is there anywhere in the House we shouldn't go?"

"Probably not the kitchen; the cook is a bit of a bear."

"Which kitchen?"

He smiled. "You can, of course, do whatever what you want in the kitchen in your wing; I spoke of the main kitchen, in which The Terafin's meals—and the meals of the rest of the House—are prepared."

"Anywhere else?"

"You can go anywhere you want. If there's an area you shouldn't be in, someone will tell you."

"I'd like not to offend whoever that someone is."

"They won't take offense. You're new here, and everyone pretty much knows it."

The idea that the den was being talked about by this nebulous "everyone" didn't bring much comfort. "What else do they know?"

He laughed. She liked the sound of it, realizing that in the past few days, or weeks, they'd laughed so very little at home. "They know your names and your general descriptions. They know that a domicis was hired for the West Wing and its guests. They know that The Terafin opened up the West Wing for your personal use."

"That doesn't happen often?"

He raised a brow. It was an orange bronze in the lamplight and the softer, nocturnal glow of magelights. She could almost pretend she was walking in a street—but the facades of buildings had been replaced by shadowed paintings and tapestries, and the round, hard cobbles, often cracked, by the flat slats of finely oiled and waxed wood. And rugs.

"It hasn't happened in the years I've served the house."

"Oh."

He laughed again. "They know that your den leader—that's what you call her, isn't it?" He waited until she nodded before continuing, " . . . saved The Terafin's life. Believe that that has made her very popular."

"But—but how—"

"If she didn't tell you, I shouldn't," he said. But he didn't seem terribly afraid of doing so.

"But how did you hear?"

"Servants have ears," he replied with a grin. "Just the way walls do in this place. You see one of the Chosen marching down the halls at speed, and word carries; people watch where he's going and with whom.

"But be that as it may, your den leader went and got the Chosen, and the Chosen summoned the mage. We didn't know why until later—but apparently there was a mage of some sort who meant to assassinate The Terafin; if not for the summoning, he would have succeeded. The Terafin is loved in this House, and your Jewel Markess has done us all a service, whether she knew it at the time or not.

"She cares about you," he added, the smile dropping away from all but the corners of his lips. "And she knows damn well you're *all* out of place here. What we can do to make your stay easier, we will do.

"So get out of the West Wing when you can, and wander about the House; look at it, meet people. Most of them will be friendly." He paused and then added, "I'll try to send a rough floor plan to your domicis. I'll mark the rooms of the House Council and the members of the House who are a little on the frosty side; you can avoid those."

She smiled at him, hesitantly, and then said, "Thank you, Burton." Extending a hand, she added, "I'm Finch."

He hesitated for just a moment and then grinned again, accepting the offered hand.

"Did I do something wrong?"

"Technically, yes. Ask your domicis. I'm sure he'll tell you."

"I'd rather not." She grimaced. "I *think* he's nice enough, but he's got so many rules."

"We all have rules; I've just broken at least three of them." He shrugged. "But some of the rules come into conflict, and then we're left with a choice."

"And shaking my hand was bad?"

"Technically," he repeated. "I know your name, of course; I have to. I've been assigned to keep an eye on the West Wing. But you're not here as a servant. I'm supposed to be invisible."

He was rather tall and rather well dressed for an invisible man. "Why?"

"Good servants always are. We keep the place clean. Impeccably clean," he added, with a mock severity that indicated he was mimicking someone. "It's hard, however, to be an invisible guide. You'll see less of me as the days go by—and if you don't, I'd ask that you at least *pretend* to see less of me." His grin was broad.

She stared at him. "You know that you're better dressed than I've ever been, until now?"

He nodded. "We know you're from the old holdings. They don't generally have dens in the new ones."

"And it doesn't bother you to be told to serve the likes of us?"

"I told you, Finch—your den leader saved The Terafin. Obviously The Terafin had some inkling of her abilities, or she would never have opened that wing. We don't question." His smile gentled. "I like what I do. I know it's not what people daydream of doing with their lives—but I like the order, the tidiness, the sense of purpose.

"I'm never going to lead. I never want to lead. I want to do what I'm doing now, for as long as House Terafin stands. One day, I'll train men and women to do as I'm doing. That's the whole of my ambition." He glanced at her.

"I don't know what I want," she confessed. "Mostly, not to starve."

"Your leader's earned that, at least. But you should think about it. What you want defines what you do, at least in this life. And the Houses—The Ten—prove that it's not just birth that counts. I wasn't born to a family that served a grand House like this one, but I'm here."

She nodded and smiled again, following Burton ATerafin to her den.

*   *   *

There was a small commotion in the wing when it came time to bed down. Jay came out of her room and started a frenzied search of the dining room and the kitchen, looking for "nothing," as she very curtly put it. Five minutes of intense and testy questioning reduced "nothing" to "magestone." They were all silently horrified, and they all joined her in her fruitless search.

Finch almost sent Jester to relieve Teller, because Teller was *good* at finding things. Angel stopped her and shook his head, gesturing in densign while Jay was crawling under the table for the fifteenth time. Finch responded in kind, but den-sign wasn't designed for difficult conversations, and by the time they'd negotiated their way through half of this one, Jay emerged on her hands and knees, flyaway strands of her hair hanging, as usual, across her eyes.

An hour later, she shoved that hair out of her eyes and glanced out the windows. The windows here were glassed, and although they could be opened—and not simply with warped shutters you had to tie to keep closed—they were shut and barred; it was Scaral. It was also, by the rise of the bright moon, late.

Jay's shoulders sagged as she turned to the wall. She punched it. Hard.

Finch thought she heard bones crack, and she winced in sympathy. She knew why Jay had searched for so long. They all did. But they were silent, and they let her retreat to her cavernous room. Only when the door slammed—and it did—did Angel slump against a wall, pausing to kick Carver on the way down.

Carver, who had not quite given up, threw something at Angel's head, and Angel's spire of hair caught it. Jester leaned up against the wall to one side of the large window, folding his arms across his slender chest.

"Mage'll be here in the morning," he said.

"Yeah. And Jay'll meet him on next to no sleep."

They shared another glance. Jay never went to sleep without light. If Carver and Duster were out, they took the stone, and Jay worked in the kitchen until they were back, burning candles until there were no more candles to burn.

But she slept with the light when it returned, taking it from Carver's palm and walking it into the bedroom she shared with Duster, Finch, and Teller. There, she'd drop it into the pedestal Rath had given her, and she'd tuck in, in any weather; Jay hated to sleep exposed. Even in the grim humidity of the worst summer nights, she covered herself with blankets and sweated a lot.

The light was gone.

"It's not just that," Finch said softly, trying to be fair. "Rath gave her the magestone. It was one of the first things he gave her."

Angel nodded.

"Maybe it won't be so bad," Jester said. "There are guards all over the damn place. Maybe she'll be able to sleep without it."

Finch glanced at Carver. Carver shrugged. She sighed and headed toward the kitchen. After a moment, the others picked themselves up off the floor and followed her.

Ellerson watched in silence. He watched from the back corner of the dining room until the last of the den—Angel—disappeared from view, and then he stepped lightly and briskly across the expanse of rug toward the kitchen's swinging double doors. Before he reached them, he heard the clatter of dishes—pots and pans, by the sound, and not very carefully handled.

He did not rush in but waited for the din to cease. When it did, he pushed the doors open a crack and slid between them. Not all of the domicis chose this sort of subtlety in their approach to their masters; one chose the methods that worked, after all.

The den was now seated around the large, wood-block table that was meant for food preparation. They had removed some of the hanging pots and pans that overlooked the table's surface, and Ellerson surmised that this was because neither Carver nor Angel could stand without hitting them.

They had pulled stools and chairs from beneath counters also situated for kitchen work, and they had arrayed these around the table. He made a mental note to ask for suitable chairs; this type of untidiness, if the den sought to make use of the kitchen as a meeting space, was unacceptable to Ellerson's organized soul.

Finch was speaking. Her voice was low and, to Ellerson's ear, gentle; she and Teller had this in common. "No, Arann's fine. The healer didn't hurt him."

"He healed him. Why won't they let him come back to us?" Carver was leaning precariously back on the rear legs of his chair.

"I don't really understand all of what happened," she replied carefully, "but he's safe in the healerie for now. Teller's with him. You're up next," she added to Carver. "Because Teller needs to get *some* sleep."

Carver nodded.

"And we need to figure out what we do while Jay is with the mage."

"It's only going to be a day."

But Angel shook his head. "You were eating, not listening, idiot. She said The Terafin sent men to Rath's, and they *couldn't find* the maze. Jay's not going to be a day. If she's damn lucky, she'll only be a week."

Finch nodded. "We're not going with her. We'll be here. But we don't have to do nothing while we're here."

"What can we do here?"

Finch shrugged. "Learn."

"Learn?"

"Learn how the House operates. Learn who's in charge of what. Learn who thinks they're in charge of everything else. Just—learn. We can keep an ear to the ground here. She has to prove she's worthy to The Terafin, but she won't be here—she'll be with the mage. *We'll* be here. We'll learn what she can't, and we'll tell her about it."

Angel nodded. "I hate that she can't take any of us with her," he added. It was perhaps the fiftieth time he had said it. "Even Carver would be better than nothing."

"Hey!"

But Ellerson nodded quietly, watching them. Listening to them. Gone were the discussions about what might be stolen and secreted from the manse.

"Let's just hope she sleeps," Carver said quietly.

"She can do without much sleep for a week or two," Angel replied. "And even at her pay, we can't afford to replace that stone anytime soon."

There was a moment of silence, but it was a silence filled with the daydreams of the hopeful; Ellerson was certain that each and every one of this den was thinking of ways in which they might find—or replace—what Jewel had lost. They were surprising, these children.

But he could work with them. What they brought to the table—even as inappropriate a table as this one—he could not have supplied. The finishes, however, he could, and if it was not to be easy, and in Ellerson's opinion, their age and their set ways would be very difficult to overcome, that was acceptable; he dealt not in easy but in possible.

23rd of Scaral, 410 A.A.
Twenty-fifth Holding, Averalaan

"This," Meralonne APhaniel said, with the rise of a single brow, "is where he lived?"

Jewel, standing by his side in Rath's admittedly dingy basement rooms, nodded. They were not, obviously, the first people to come through the apartment, although they were possibly the only people who had the keys. "It wasn't usually this messy," she added.

Which was true. The contents of his room had been scattered across the floor; even the ancient trunk he had tucked away beneath the bed had been removed and opened, its contents upended.

Whoever had done this was clearly not in need of money; a sword in an old scabbard lay half-buried by Rath's many jackets and shirts. "Is it all right to touch things now?" she asked as she knelt.

Meralonne nodded absently. "You can hardly," he said, "do any more harm."

Thanks. She managed to keep the sarcasm—and the word—behind tightly closed lips. It had been a single day since she had last set foot in these rooms. It felt like weeks. Or months.

The pedestal that held Rath's magestone was on his desk. The magestone, however, was not. Jewel stopped for a moment in front of the table across which the maps she had once rescued—or stolen, depending on your viewpoint—from an illegal brothel usually lay. It was bare.

Meralonne could be the world's most irritating man. "What," he asked, although she had said nothing, and hadn't moved, "is the problem now?"

You need him, she reminded herself. It was funny just how hard it was to cling to that reminder; she'd only been partnered with him for all of a very damn long morning. He even managed to make smoking a pipe irritating, and Jewel generally found the familiarity of the smoke's smell a comfort. *You need his good opinion, because The Terafin is going to listen to him.*

She took a deep breath and turned to face the mage, with his disconcerting gray eyes and his habitual irritation. "Something's missing," she told him flatly.

"I gathered that. What, exactly, is missing?"

"Maps."

He crossed the room, by some minor miracle not stepping on anything that lay strewn across the floor. It must have been a miracle, because he sure as hell didn't look as if he cared enough to avoid anything. "Maps of what?"

She took another breath, held it, and exhaled. "Maps," she said quietly, "of the undercity."

He stared at her as if she were speaking in Torra, or at least in a language he didn't understand.

"Ararath made maps?"

"No, Rath didn't make these. He didn't need maps," she added, "and as he'd no intention of ever letting anyone else know about the maze, he didn't want to make it easier for anyone who might steal things."

"Jewel, I realize you've had little sleep, and you've had a long day. I also realize that you are not well taught. I am therefore being as patient as I can, but my patience is limited. If Ararath did not devise these maps, who did?"

"I don't know. We found them," she added. "We saved them from a— from a house fire."

He stared at her for a long moment and then drew his pipe from his sleeve. "Jewel," he said, as he lined the bowl, "Ararath is dead. If he had any plans for you, he fulfilled those when he sent you to House Terafin. There is nothing you can say or do that will protect his memory. I do not know what he told you," he added, as the leaves burst into sudden flame, "but at this point, it is imperative that you tell us what you know."

What she knew was that the entrance to the maze was gone. She had believed The Terafin when The Terafin had told her that no trace of the entrance could be found, of course—but it was still a shock to see the landscape so utterly changed. "They were magical maps," she finally told the mage.

He raised a pale brow. "Magical?"

"They had writing on them—and yes, I know that writing doesn't make them magical—that neither Rath nor I could read."

He didn't think much of her ability to read, but the fact that Rath couldn't seemed somehow significant. "Did he recognize the tongue?"

"No. It wasn't Old Weston, and it wasn't any form of Torra."

Meralonne frowned. "Continue."

"We could touch any two points on the map, and lines—usually blue lines, but some were brighter than others—would travel between them, following the streets."

His eyes widened.

"There were three maps. Rath thought they were in sections," she added. "I think the—I think they used them."

"Before they fell into your hands."

She nodded.

"And you used them, after?"

"Rath did. I couldn't really make sense of them; I could see some familiar landmarks, and the main streets, but there was too much there that doesn't exist anymore."

Meralonne removed the stem of the pipe from the corner of his mouth and walked over to the desk. He searched there a moment and then, cursing, bent to the floor to retrieve scraps of paper. These, he placed on the empty table. "Find me an inkwell in this mess," he added.

When she did, he took it from her hands, opened it, and then cursed again. She handed him the quill she'd found as well.

In spite of herself, she watched with fascination as he slid carelessly into Rath's working chair. His fingers were long, but smoke hadn't stained them; they looked almost delicate as he took the quill and began to write.

What he wrote, she couldn't say—he didn't write the characters in Weston letterforms, if they were letters at all. But something about the bold lines he'd scribed was nagging in its familiarity.

"Was this the language?"

"I—I don't know." She frowned. "I don't think so." She looked up at the shelf above the mantel without much hope; it, like the tabletop, was empty.

"What do you see here?"

She forgot to look at his face or his expression; instead, as if he were an echo of Rath, she looked at what he'd written, at the small, precise shapes that were more like geometry than any language she'd learned.

"They look familiar to you," he said. It wasn't a question. She nodded hesitantly, because they did. "Where did you see these runes?"

"Not these ones," she finally said. "But ones that were similar in shape. In the undercity," she added. "But they were much larger. One of them was carved into the floor."

He was utterly silent for a long moment. Then he left the chair. Blue smoke wafted from his compressed lips.

"What does it mean?" she asked quietly.

"It means, Jewel Markess, that we must work—quickly—to find this undercity of which you've spoken." He shook his head. "I confess I don't understand the timing."

She waited, and after a moment, he said, "It was Scarran last night. Anything that happened should have happened then. Perhaps Ararath bought time in some unexpected way; we will likely never know."

"You knew him, didn't you?"

The mage raised a silver brow. "I did not know him as you knew him, but yes, we were acquainted, and yes, I was aware of some of his activities. I was not, however, aware of *where* those activities occurred, and had I been, much might have been prevented."

"Would he still be alive?" She hadn't meant to ask the question, but it left her lips of its own volition, shadowed by, of all things, a twinge of guilt.

Meralonne met her gaze and held it. He doused his pipe. "I cannot say. He played a game that I would have said was beyond him, and in the end, he won."

"It killed him," she replied, her voice steady and flat.

"Yes. But victory is not always defined by survival."

Jewel shook her head. "For Rath, it was."

"Perhaps. Perhaps not. If he hid things from you, he had his reasons for doing so, and I will respect his implicit wishes in this. But more than that, I cannot do. Come, Jewel. We must find this maze."

Jewel nodded and once again glanced at the debris strewn across the floor. At the velvet jacket that had once seemed so fine to her, at the shirts, the various jars of color, lids cracked, contents spilled. But her eyes returned to the sword in its scabbard. Bending, she retrieved it in shaking hands.

"You have use for a sword?"

"No. Not me. But . . . it was important to him. It was from his old life, and I think it's the only thing he couldn't make himself throw away. He almost never wore it—but he did; I saw him use it once." To save Arann, she thought, when Lefty had come at a desperate run to their home.

Lefty.

"I can take this?"

"I think it fair to say you can take anything at all that is left here. If you do not, the landlord no doubt will."

She hesitated again and then, making a decision, asked, "Can you help me carry the books?"

*   *   *

Jay came in just before the middle dinner hour, and she looked both dirty and exhausted.

"We saved you food," Finch began, but Ellerson cleared his throat. Jay, weary and pale, looked up at a man who was starched and perfectly clean.

"Bath," he said firmly. "Everyone else has."

"But not quietly," Teller added, glancing at Carver. Carver shrugged; it was his only response. Finch watched as Jay glanced at the table. Saving food in this case didn't mean much; Angel couldn't eat his way through half of what was left on a good day.

"Bath," Jay said, forlornly, and headed down the hall.

After dinner, they gathered in the kitchen. It had gone past the middle and into the late dinner hour, but as they had no guests—and the den privately thought the idea of having guests when they *were* guests was ridiculous—Ellerson made little comment. He did, however, join them in the kitchen.

Finch noted that there were actual chairs—matching chairs—around the butcher-block table, and she glanced at Ellerson's completely neutral expression before she took a seat.

"I'll keep it short," Jay told them, as she shoved her hair away from her eyes. The weather was cool and dry enough that it almost stayed that way; it certainly didn't have the springy quality it adopted in the humidity of the summer months. "I spent the day with a very irritating mage."

"Member APhaniel may be many things," Ellerson said, clearing his throat slightly, "but simply irritating would not be among them."

"He can be whatever he wants—he can clearly get away with it," Jay snapped back. "But he *is* damn irritating." She folded her fingers together and cracked her knuckles, which caused the domicis to frown.

"Did he do anything magical?" Teller asked. They all wanted to know, but only Teller was willing to risk the question.

"Yes. He lit his pipe."

Silence, followed by a disappointed, "That's it?"

"Pretty much. He's got eagle eyes, though. He notices everything."

Meaning, of course, that he noticed things she wasn't happy to have noticed. Finch glanced at Angel, and Angel nodded.

"We went by Rath's place first. Meralonne wanted to see it."

Ellerson cleared his throat, and Jay glanced up at him; he stood by the doors. "What?"

"Member APhaniel is what he is most frequently called."

"He told me to call him Meralonne." Her expression made clear that it was a lot better than anything else she might have called him.

"Be that as it may," Ellerson replied, "it is possible your familiarity will draw more attention to you than you would ideally like at this stage in your career."

"My what?"

He didn't blink. "Your career. Your performance will be evaluated, and while it is unlikely that the mage will consider the use of his personal name to be of note, others who are not as familiar might."

All of the den were staring at him now.

After a long moment, Jay spoke. "It might not matter," she told them softly, staring at the tabletop, and the glow of lamplight against it.

"How so?"

"What The Terafin said was true. There is no entrance to the maze from Rath's place."

"But—but where did it go?" Finch asked.

"We don't know. Meralonne—Member APhaniel—examined the basement for an hour, and he found nothing."

"Nothing?"

"Dirt. Rock. Old, rotten wooden boards. Nothing else."

"But—"

"He said none of it seemed new, either. It's not like they covered over the hole—it's just not there anymore."

A thought occurred to everyone—except possibly Jester—at more or less the same time. "Do they think you were lying?"

Jay's shoulders sagged. "No one's said that," she told them, placing her hands flat against the surface of the table. "But it's got to damn well look that way."

"It's only one entrance," Carver began.

Jay nodded, but it wasn't a particularly good nod. "The entrance by Bronson's is gone, as well."

"What, the chute?"

"Yeah. We pulled up the boards; we went down into the basement. We even pulled up the trap that led down. It led to dirt and the stone foundation."

"Where else did you go?"

"There and the entrance by the edge of the thirty-second."

No one asked her what she'd found. They didn't have to.

Jay still stared at the tabletop. Then she rose, restless, and shoved hair that wasn't in her eyes out of them. "It's got to be there," she told them all, spreading her hands. "And we've got to find it. If it weren't for the—the creature that tried to kill her, she'd probably have us bouncing off our asses in the high streets by now."

They weren't yet up to the task of showing gratitude for a creature that graced their nightmares.

"We just need to find entrances that Rath didn't use much," Jay added. "Meralonne—the mage, I mean—"

"Member APhaniel."

"Member APhaniel thinks they're somehow closing the entrances that Rath knew about. He thinks they knew a lot of what Rath knew. But they obviously didn't know it all," she added.

"Why?" Ellerson asked.

"Because if they had, I'd never have come to Terafin. They'd have known about the letter. They'd have known what it told me to do." She rubbed her eyes with the backs of her hands. "I'm beat," she told them. "And I have nothing else to say. I'm going to bed."

Finch opened her mouth to speak and closed it again, aware of Ellerson's presence in the room. "Go," she said, instead. "We'll clean up here."

"No," Ellerson told her quietly, "you will not."

"But the dining room—"

"It is already cleared."

"But—"

"Finch, there are servants whose sole duties are to this wing. If you attempt to do their work, one of two things will happen. Either they will take it as a criticism of their work, and they will be somewhat justifiably aggrieved, or they will be judged by the quality of *your* work, with the same result."

Finch stared at Ellerson.

He waited a beat. "You are here, for the moment, as The Terafin's guests. The servants take their duties to her guests seriously; it is a matter of House pride. If you feel you must be considerate of these servants, do your best not to make too much of a mess. Anything else would be interference.

"It cannot have escaped your notice that many of the servants have the House Name. They did not come to that name by extraordinary acts of heroism; they achieved their names by diligent service in *her* name. Do not deprive the servants here of their ability to earn that rank."

Carver snorted. "Rath was right," he muttered. "The patriciate is insane."

"Even their servants," Jester added.

Jay didn't sleep well. Even a room away, Finch could hear her cries as she woke from sleep into an unfamiliar darkness. The third time it happened, she woke, found the robe hanging by the bedside table, and put it on. Then she dragged herself out of her room, pausing only long enough to pull the counterpane and one pillow from her own bed. Teller's door was slightly ajar. She went to knock on it and nearly shrieked as it opened.

"You too?" he asked quietly.

She nodded.

They walked over to Jay's door. It was closed. Finch pushed it open and walked in. The room was huge; it was bigger than any of the others. It seemed empty, although there was furniture to navigate in the darkness that was alleviated only by moonlight through the unshuttered glass.

They made their way to the bedside, and they arranged their blankets and pillows in a familiar way. The blankets were much finer, and the pillows were thick and heavy with down; the floor was flat, and it didn't creak much beneath the carpets.

They bedded down on the same side of the bed, nearest the window, placing their blankets at the same distance they'd been in their old home. The edges were touching.

"I don't know if it'll help," Finch told Teller.

"It can't hurt," he replied. She couldn't tell whether or not he smiled as he said it, but it didn't matter; it was comforting to know that, absent starvation and the fear of street dens and cold, they could still worry about the same things and come to the same conclusions.

Not everything had to change.

When Jewel woke in the morning, the first thing she saw was Finch, and the second, Teller. They were sleeping in blankets far finer than the ones they'd owned back home, but they were curled on a stretch of floor as if bound by invisible walls. She knew why they were there, and she felt two things at once: gratitude and guilt. She struggled with the latter as she slipped out of bed and walked toward the closet—which was a large room—that Ellerson had been slowly filling.

They knew about her nightmares. They knew she always had them. They also knew that she was sleeping, or trying to sleep, in the dark. Teller had hesitantly—and privately—suggested that she tell Ellerson that she needed a lamp, at the very least, when she slept, and she almost bit his head off. *I can't be seen as a child who's afraid of the dark*, she said between clenched teeth, when she'd managed to rein in a very frayed temper.

Teller, however, had endured her anger. *You can't go without sleep and do what you need to do. Ellerson won't tell.*

But *she'd* know, damn it.

So Teller and Finch—who both finally had beds, *real* beds, of their own, and gods only knew for how long—were sleeping on her floor. She should have been angry. She should have felt humiliated by the need for their company and its familiarity.

Instead, she made every effort to move quietly as she approached her second day of work for The Terafin. Even if things didn't work out well here, it didn't matter—the solarii Jewel earned would see them through the hard times. They could find their own place in the holdings again. They could take back their life.

Because her duties lay in the dark and damp basements of the old holdings, Ellerson hadn't insisted she immediately learn to dress, as he put it, properly; he'd allowed, and requisitioned—his word—practical clothing that was nonetheless of matching, rather than clashing, colors. This practical clothing didn't feature skirts, and it did boast large pockets in several places.

He'd allowed her to keep her boots because on her return from the holdings they'd been encrusted with dirt and dust. The boots she would have insisted on keeping, in any case; they were good. She knew they were good. They'd certainly cost enough.

She slid into an undershirt, covered it with a heavy shirt, and then did the same with the wide pants; she selected a jacket as well, a heavy blue fabric that seemed too fine or soft to be wool. Ellerson, however, assured her that it was.

She didn't argue with him.

When she slid out of her door, he was waiting for her in the hall. He bowed, ignoring her sharp intake of breath.

"Make noise," she told him sharply.

"As you wish," he replied. "Breakfast is waiting."

"Is anything else?" she asked as she followed him down the hall.

"The rest of your den appear to be sleeping."

She shrugged. "There's not much for them to wake up to," she pointed out.

"That might be a concern."

She hesitated. Shrugged. "We usually head out to the Common in the morning and to the well; we do laundry once a week in rotation."

He nodded, as if this were somehow relevant.

"But in the past few weeks, any real work we've done, we've done in the evening."

He didn't ask, and she didn't elaborate. But when he led her into the breakfast room—which was a much smaller version of the dining room with a table that wasn't so insanely long—it wasn't empty. Meralonne APhaniel was seated in front of a plate, smoking.

The plate was covered with food he hadn't touched. Jewel recognized most of it—bread, cheese, some sort of soft fish. "Am I late?" she asked, struggling to keep anxiety out of her voice.

"No."

"Then why are you here?"

"I'm endeavoring to make certain that you are not. Late," he added, blowing rings into the still air.

Jewel opened her mouth and snapped it shut again. She glanced at Ellerson who stood, impassive, by the wall.

"I would like, if possible, to make a list of the entrances that Ararath showed you, starting at the most commonly used and ending with the least common. We can compose this list while you eat," he added. "With luck, we'll have more success today than we had yesterday."

With her luck, Jewel thought, scraping a chair across the floor and sitting heavily in it, success was not in the cards. Breakfast, apparently, was not in the cards, either, at least not according to her appetite. But she ate. Her Oma had never liked to see food wasted, and Jewel had a lifetime of ingrained habit, against which lack of appetite counted for little; she chewed, she swallowed, and she made her way through whatever was on her plate.

As she did, she began to do what the mage had asked. It wasn't hard. During the long bouts of sleeplessness, she'd been mentally composing the list he'd asked her to make.

"I don't know all of the entrances he knew about," she admitted. "I know which ones we found on our own."

The mage nodded. "Are you certain you found exits—or entrances—that Ararath didn't know?" He sounded dubious.

Jewel shrugged. "We didn't compare notes, if that's what you're asking. Not after we left his place."

The mage raised a silver brow. Smoke wreathed his face.

She knew what he was asking. She didn't feel like answering. Instead, she said, grudging every word, "He showed us how to get into the maze; he showed us how to search it. He showed us a little of what to search for, but he didn't particularly like to see us in there on our own.

"He knew we went; he handled the sale of anything we found."

"You . . . sold . . . things from the undercity."

She nodded. She shouldn't have been pleased to get a rise out of the mage, but, perversely, she was. "They weren't useful to us in any other way."

"To whom did you sell these things? And what things, exactly, did you find?"

She shrugged. "Useless things, mostly. Candlesticks. Old bowls. Bits of things with writing on them. And I have no idea who we sold them to—Rath did all the selling. I told you."

Meralonne removed the pipe stem from very compressed lips. "He never mentioned his clientele?"

She shrugged. "Some of it went to the Order of Knowledge. Well, to people in the Order."

"He didn't mention names."

"No. He wouldn't let us try to sell anything on our own, and we didn't want to cross the bridge."

But the mage nodded, and his usual irritable expression shifted into something that, while smoother, was vastly less comfortable. "It's possible that's how he was detected," he finally said. "There can't have been many men who offered antiques of that particular nature for sale in the Empire." He rose. "I see," he told her, pausing to empty the ashes from his pipe's bowl onto the nearest clean plate, "that you've finished. You *have* finished?"

"Yes." She stood as well.

"Then let us depart. If we are not successful within the next few days, we will in all likelihood no longer be working alone."

Jewel nodded. But as she pushed her chair back, she asked, "Have you told the Kings?"

He frowned. "About what?"

Her eyes widened. "About the—the creature—and the attempt on The Terafin's *life*."

"Ah. No, I'm afraid I have not. I have been instructed," he added, glancing at the domicis whom Jewel herself had almost forgotten, "to keep my own counsel in this affair until we have found adequate proof."

"Of *what*? There were *witnesses*—one of them was The Terafin!"

Ellerson cleared his throat, and she turned. "What?"

"The Terafin is a woman who understands politics well."

"What does politics have to do with what *we all saw*?"

"She is The Terafin. Her death, no matter how it arrives, will have deep political consequences for both her House, and given its import, the Empire. Anyone—anything—that attempts to bring about that death in an untimely fashion is motivated, in the end, by things political."

"Ellerson, it wasn't even human!"

"So you've said. But The Terafin will be cautious. Unless there is a catastrophe of a greater nature, she will approach the Kings with care, if at all. She cannot afford to be seen as weak."

Jewel just stared at him for a long moment. "Rath was right," she muttered.

"Oh?" Meralonne said.

"You're all insane."

As conversations went, it was perhaps not the most politically adept Ellerson had ever heard. It was not, however, the least. Jewel Markess' hopes for the safety of her den, and her own future in House Terafin, did not appear to cause obsequious deference to the mage. Nor, from Ellerson's vantage, did the mage seem unduly upset by her lack of finesse, her inability to hold a fork in the correct hand, or her weary lack of guile.

The guild of the domicis had an unusual relationship with the Order of Knowledge. Among those who served as members of the Halls of the Domicis, which was treated as a guild and often called one—although Ellerson was aware that there were articles that were not entirely in keeping with general guild charter—were those who were talent-born. Some had spent some time training with the Order's mages, before deciding that their temperament and their inclinations did not lend themselves to a lifetime's seclusion in the Towers.

The Order, of course, tracked those who had learned in their halls and, in particular, those who had evinced some power. Meralonne APhaniel was reputed to be a First Circle mage of the highest order. He did not, however, seem to care a great deal about the nicety of title when he worked; Jewel Markess' marked lack of respect—where in this case respect meant some mixture of fear and groveling—did not seem to annoy him.

He did not, in fact, seem to notice it at all.

Ellerson watched as Jewel started to walk away from the table. She stumbled slightly, righted herself, and stopped moving.

"Jewel?" Member APhaniel said quietly.

She didn't appear to hear him, and time passed as she stared straight ahead, her eyes slightly widened and entirely unfocused. When the mage spoke her name for the third time, she shook herself. She had paled.

Ellerson watched her with care, and he marked the moment her expression snapped into place. He expected her to speak, but he was surprised at what she said when she did.

"The Kings need to know," she told the mage, although she didn't appear to be *seeing* him. "The Kings need to know before—"

"Before?"

She shook her head again, and her flyaway curls fell into a loose drape over her eyes. She did not, however, push them away with her characteristic impatience. "It's—it's nothing," she told the mage. "I was just—I was just thinking out loud."

She was also, Ellerson realized, lying.

Chapter Two

MARGARET WAS HOPPING AROUND like a little neckless bird in the lee of winter. Arann, who had spent a week in the healerie, understood instantly what this meant. He wasn't entirely certain if the understanding was his own familiarity with her daily routine, or if it was Alowan's, but it didn't really matter. Folding his arms across his chest, he stood by the bed that had grown increasingly confining as the days wore on, waiting.

Teller was standing just inside the arch that led from the arboretum, watching, the lines of his face stretched in mild concern.

Arann lifted his hand, signed *all clear*, and Teller nodded, relaxing.

"I'm sorry," Margaret repeated, in a tone of voice that failed to convey regret in any way, "but you are *not* leaving the healerie wearing *that* clothing. I should have had it burned," she added, "but I'm a sentimental old woman."

She was not entirely old. Arann failed to point this out.

He glanced at Teller, and Teller grimaced.

Teller was no longer wearing the sturdy but mismatched colors that Helen saved from her various jobs as a seamstress in order to clothe the den as cheaply as possible, as she had for so many years. Instead, he wore a pale blue tunic over much darker leggings. It was plain, and the fabric was a fine wool; it was also one of the few things that Teller had ever worn that wasn't a shade too large. Helen, aware of the den's fortunes, had always sewn things with "room to grow in."

Arann said, patiently, "I don't have anything else to wear." That he'd look the fool running through the halls stark naked, he also failed to mention. It was, however, tiring to have to talk so much.

"It's only as far as our rooms," Teller told her, his voice quieter than Arann's. "Alowan told Ellerson that Arann wasn't to be disturbed over something as trivial as clothing measurements, so nothing's been made for him yet."

Margaret opened her mouth, and Teller quickly added, "and it won't be made for him, either, if he can't leave."

Arann, arms still folded across his chest, continued to wait.

Margaret argued for a few minutes longer—as if Arann's clothing would somehow be blamed on the healerie, and on Alowan in particular. Arann couldn't see exactly how this blame could be placed, but Margaret seemed so certain, he didn't argue. At least not with that point.

But in the end, she was—as were all of Alowan's assistants—practical enough to agree. She fussed, however, all the way to the door, and Arann had no doubt at all that she would have continued had Torvan ATerafin not been standing in the doorway.

He wasn't in armor, and he didn't carry a sword, but Margaret clearly recognized him anyway.

The part of Arann that was Alowan—that would always be Alowan, no matter how many years passed—recognized him as well. Alowan liked and approved of Torvan. He also liked and approved of the rest of The Terafin's Chosen, a fact that Alowan found mildly surprising whenever he thought about it.

Arann had never spent much time thinking about people, and most of the real thought had gone into ways of avoiding their notice. He'd paid attention to Lefty.

"Arann?"

Arann shook his head. Lifted a hand. *It's nothing.*

Teller's gaze shifted slightly toward the floor; he knew. But he was Teller. He wouldn't say anything else.

Torvan ATerafin stepped away from the door. "I came with Teller," he told Arann.

Arann nodded.

"We're to take you off Alowan's hands and return you to the rest of your kin."

Arann glanced once over his shoulder; the arboretum was green and peaceful. Alowan wasn't here, and Alowan wouldn't come; not yet. He'd spoken with Arann three times in the past week, but Alowan had never come alone, and he'd stayed by the arch to the fountain and its surrounding plants as if they were his anchor.

Arann knew why. He knew, but it still pained him.

He looked at Torvan. He was the only one of the den who didn't have to look up. Nodding, he began to walk down the hall; Teller's hand caught his sleeve and gently steered him in the right direction.

The halls, at this hour in the morning, were surprisingly busy—but then again, up to this point, Arann had seen only his den-kin and the healerie's assistants, and none of them moved around a lot. Except Jester. You could nail Jester's feet to the floor and it wouldn't keep him still. Or quiet.

Torvan ATerafin said very little as they walked, but he walked slowly, allowing Arann to appreciate the long, light-filled galleries, with their detailed carpets, their dark-stained floors, their wide, long windows, and their tapestries, hangings, and paintings.

"You're not wearing your armor," Arann said hesitantly, the words tailing up at the end as if it were a question.

"I'm off duty."

"But you're here?"

"I live in the manse." Torvan's smile was slow, but genuine. "All of the Chosen do."

"You live where you work?"

"As you can see, it's a very large place."

It was. Alowan seldom left the healerie, and when he did, it was always with cause, and it was almost always because of an emergency. The exceptions were his visits to the Houses of Healing on the Isle, a place at which he had both taught and been taught in his youth.

Consequently, Arann's knowledge of the House was colored by the healer's; he knew he would recognize some of the rooms. None of those rooms, however, were the galleries.

"I know you've had visitors," Torvan said, when Arann didn't speak. "So you're aware of the rooms the den occupies."

Arann nodded; he was aware of that and more. He hesitated, and then he said, "Thanks."

Torvan could have pretended to misunderstand; he didn't. "If I did you a favor," he told Arann, his expression momentarily grave, "your den leader repaid it a hundredfold." He hesitated and then added, "I'm not certain, by the end of this, she won't repay it a thousandfold. She's an unusual girl."

Arann nodded, and Teller smiled. He seemed younger, in his new clothing.

They walked, in silence, to a large set of double doors; the wood was thick and unpainted, but it gleamed in the magelights that adorned either side of the wall. Torvan stopped there and nodded to both Arann and Teller.

Before he left, however, he turned to face Arann and spoke again.

"You're large for your age. And you don't seem to have much of either an ego or a temper. If things work out here, and I hope they will, consider applying to the House Guard."

Arann said, "I'm not much good with a sword."

"No, I imagine you've not had much training. And if you were expecting a berth to the Kings' Challenge, the lack of early training would be a serious detriment. It will not be an impediment for the House Guard of Terafin. You will, however, have to learn.

"Think about it," he added quietly. "I'm not the Captain of the House Guard; the decision is not in my hands. What I offer is opinion—an informed opinion—not a promise."

"But—but—why?"

Torvan exhaled. "I don't know how you came to be injured," he told Arann, glancing at Teller as he spoke. "And I won't ask if you don't want to speak about it. But I've a hunch you were injured in the line of duty, and you accepted that. You didn't run, you didn't hide, and you didn't abandon your leader." He bowed, briefly, to both boys.

Arann was still shaking his head when Teller opened the doors.

Ellerson heard the shouting from the small waiting room he habitually occupied when his services were not required by the den. The definition of required was, in this case, elastic; it was not the more formal scheduling and care that one would normally find in a House of any quality. It therefore demanded a certain discretion.

This discretion, he now exercised, rising from the tea that Finch had prepared for him. Any attempt to tell her that this was not an acceptable definition of master and servant had been politely ignored, and in the end, Ellerson was well aware that this group of almost-children would have to be eased into a more formal future. He did, however, insist on instructing her in the proper preparation of tea.

Her reaction? Laughter.

"You could have just skipped the part about master and servant and gone right to 'you make bad tea,' you know."

He'd raised a brow but had allowed himself a small smile; it was difficult to refrain when her laughter—at her own expense—was offered so openly.

He heard that laughter as he entered the hall that led to the greeting rooms and narrowly avoided a collision as Finch rounded the corner at a run. She passed him, skidded to a halt, grabbed the wall with the flat of her palms, and spun.

"Finch," he said, in his most severe voice. "The walls are not meant to be used as brakes."

"My hands are clean, honest," she replied, removing them instantly. "I was just coming to get you," she added. "Arann's back."

"I believe I did tell you he would be."

"You did. He took a bit of time convincing someone in the healerie that he needed to wear his old clothes."

"Of course. Has he eaten?"

"He says he's not hungry."

"Which would, in the parlance of Finch or Teller, mean no. Angel does not, I believe, understand what those words signify. In any language he speaks. What does it mean for Arann?"

"You probably want to meet him," she replied.

"Oh, indeed."

Arann was not quite what Ellerson had expected, but then again, none of the den were. The boy was larger than he had imagined a scant living on the streets would allow, and he was quiet. When he spoke, there was always a marked hesitation before words, as if he were sifting through them and painstakingly removing the offensive ones.

None of his den-kin seemed to find his size intimidating; he carried himself like a much smaller person.

"Is Jay here?" Arann asked Finch.

Finch's expression lost a bit of its sparkle. "No. She's out."

"Out?"

Finch nodded. "With the mage. They had a screaming fight in the breakfast nook this morning. I thought the guards would break the doors down."

"They did not have a screaming fight," Ellerson said, pinching the bridge of his nose.

"What would *you* call it?"

"If I were to discuss it at all—and it is inadvisable in the extreme to discuss it outside of these rooms—I would say they had a heated discussion."

"A . . . heated discussion."

"Indeed."

Finch shook her head.

"A fight generally has a less positive outcome."

"You call that positive?" Carver cut in. "Jay was in a *foul* mood."

"Mage wasn't much better," Angel added.

"It is positive in that neither the young lady nor the *very respected* Member of the Order of Knowledge were injured; it is positive in that they both left—on time, I might add—with the same goals as they had evinced before their discussion." He frowned. "The mage did not quit," he said severely, "and neither did Jewel."

Arann listened to this as if picking meaning from syllables that only barely made sense. When he seemed to have found enough of it, he turned to Finch. "She hasn't found anything, then."

Finch grimaced. "Not yet."

"It's been a week. Why aren't the rest of us—" he broke off, and glanced at Ellerson.

Ellerson expected the boy to raise his hands in the crude, but silent, hand language the den used.

Before he could, Teller said, "You know why."

"Carver knows the maze at least as well as Jay," Arann said. Teller seemed slightly surprised, which told Ellerson that Arann seldom argued.

"Better," Carver said. "I know it *better*."

Of the den, Carver was the most flamboyant. Jester's noise was different; it required a crowd, and it demanded attention. But it was not the attention that many young men often sought. Angel, whose hair was arresting, was of a height with Carver, and they were often together—but Angel and Carver were not the same.

Angel listened for Jewel. He waited up, just as Finch and Teller did, although he didn't join them in their inexplicable nocturnal pilgrimage to Jewel's room. If the rest of the den grumbled or worried about Jewel's long daily absence, only Angel chafed under it. He wanted to be with her.

To Ellerson's eye, Angel was not ignorant. The very real possibility of danger—or death—did not undermine that desire. Angel had been the most resistant to the change in the den's clothing, and while he ate well—and often—the week had done nothing for either his color or his demeanor. He was not at home in the wing.

Finch and Teller, however, were. Through them, the rest of the den found ways of making themselves comfortable. Were it not for the quiet way in which they claimed space and remade what they could of it, Angel might not have stayed.

Into this, the last of the den had now been introduced.

"Arann?"

Arann glanced down at Finch.

"Sorry, I forgot—this is Ellerson. He's our domicis. I told you about him the other day."

"He's like a servant, but scarier?"

"Exactly." She glanced at Ellerson, her lips curving in a slight smile. "But he's scary the way Jay is. Well, sort of—he's on our side."

"Do we need sides here?"

Finch hesitated. "We probably need sides everywhere. The Terafin didn't become The Terafin without a lot of fighting and bloodshed—all of it inside the House."

"The servants aren't scary," Teller added, changing the somewhat delicate political subject. "I think Burton might come by later, before Jay gets back. You'll like him."

Arann nodded.

"Come into the kitchen," Finch added, grabbing Arann's sleeve. "You have to see it."

He followed, and Ellerson retreated to his room to find the tape measure and the ruler. The clothing that had been the subject of discussion in the healerie was in far worse condition than the clothing the rest of the den had worn on the first day he'd met them; it would definitely have to go.

9th of Mistral, 410 A.A.
Terafin Manse, Averalaan Aramarelas

Jewel had often heard silence described as stony, but she had rarely seen a better example of why. Meralonne, who had started to stuff leaves into the bowl of his pipe, a sure sign of his irritation, sat opposite The Terafin. Behind her were four of her Chosen, including Torvan ATerafin.

It had taken some time to get used to the fact that he looked right through her whenever he was on duty. She'd seen a lot of guards on duty by this point—admittedly mostly in the streets of the holdings, both lower and middle—and none of them were as stiff and unfriendly as The Terafin's personal guard.

But because Torvan had taken the time to find her when he was off duty, and to carefully explain what his duty was and why she suddenly appeared to be invisible while he was in the presence of his Lord, she understood that it wasn't personal. She also understood that it wasn't because she'd been born in the poor holdings.

Even had she not been so informed, she wouldn't have taken it personally this time. Meralonne's knuckles were white. The Terafin's lips were compressed in the type of line that also whitened them. This, Jewel thought, was why white was one of the colors of mourning in the Empire.

The silence stretched.

It was, not surprisingly, Meralonne who broke it. "We cannot proceed with caution at this point," he said, curtly. It was a variant on what had begun this morning's grim silence, which had been broken by equally clipped and short phrases on the other side of the table. Jewel looked at the floor and wished it would swallow her and spit her out anywhere else.

The day had *not* gone well. Like any of the previous fourteen or fifteen days, they had crawled through chutes and basements, searching without luck for any of the entrances that Jewel *knew* had been there a few weeks—or months—ago. The mage, give him this, did not question her knowledge; he didn't appear to doubt her word.

And in his position, she knew damn well she would have. Either that or doubt her sanity. When he wasn't actively castigating her for some imagined wrong or, worse, ordering her about as if she were a barely competent flunky, she remembered to feel grateful for it.

"You've not yet finished your search," The Terafin said, after another long moment.

"No, but I doubt at this point that the search will turn up what we need. We must go to the Kings with the information we have in hand."

"Oh?" Her voice was cool. "May I remind you—again—that you are employed *by* House Terafin?"

"Please do."

Two minutes, this time. Meralonne blew concentric rings of smoke into the air above the table. They narrowly missed drifting toward the austere and stony face of the House ruler.

"Very well. You are employed by *my* House. Matters political—"

"Demons cannot be considered merely political—"

"Matters *political*, such as assassination attempts, are *internal affairs*."

"Demons care little for the politics of the merely mortal. If they attempted to assassinate you, it was certainly in keeping with larger goals—goals that I won't hesitate to point out threaten the *whole* of the Empire and not merely a single House."

"If I doubted that, I would not—at my own expense—continue with a search that has proved fruitless up to this point. Suspicion, however, is *not* fact. I cannot call the Council of The Ten with something as tenuous as the suspicions of the magi. It would be too costly for my House."

"Terafin, while you play your political games with the other Ten Houses, our time shortens."

"You have not yet said what you suspect the demons' goal is, Member APhaniel."

"I am not, regardless of what is said about me, a demon. How should I know?"

Kalliaris, Jewel thought, edging toward the wall as quietly as possible. *Please, Lady, smile. Smile.*

Not today.

The Terafin turned to look at her. If she noted that Jewel was now about ten feet farther away from the table than she had been when the discussion had started, she overlooked the display of raw cowardice. Jewel struggled not to add to it.

Her den was eating, and eating well. They had a safe, warm place to sleep. They had clothing that Helen would never have been able to produce at a price they could afford; they even had new shoes *and* new boots. An indoor pair and an outdoor pair, the latter of which saw no use.

And they had all this until the moment The Terafin decided Jewel

Markess was no longer of use. Jewel's hands were shaking, and she clasped them behind her back. No one liked a coward.

"Jewel."

Jewel, mindful of Ellerson's brief but ferocious lessons, fell instantly to one knee, bending the whole of her spine as she lowered her head. If The Terafin noticed, she said nothing. Instead, she waited until Jewel rose.

"Terafin," Jewel said, as she lifted her head. "How may I be of service?"

The Terafin's eyes were dark. But her lips lost the thin ring of white as she met, and held, Jewel's gaze.

"The Member of the Order says you've had little success in your search to date."

Jewel nodded.

"Will you have success if you continue?"

"I—I don't know, Terafin."

The Terafin nodded. She turned her attention once more to the mage, who sat idly smoking. "I am certain, Member APhaniel, that you are conducting your own—private—inquiries within the Order of Knowledge. Demons imply rogue mages, and rogue mages *are* considered a threat."

"We are hampered," he replied coldly. His glance at Jewel was less friendly than The Terafin's, but it didn't sting; she was used to it.

"Will you fail?" The Terafin said, into the silence that followed Meralonne's words.

"*No.*" Jewel's jaw snapped shut.

But The Terafin seemed to relax. "You are certain, Jewel?"

This time, she was. She let her hands slide to her lap; her knee against the floor was beginning to go numb. "Yes, Terafin."

"Very well. Member APhaniel, your request is provisionally denied."

"Provisionally?"

"We will revisit it at a later point in time. Until that point, I require your services, as offered, to continue to search the holdings." She rose. "I regret that I have other appointments; please don't let me detain you."

When Meralonne APhaniel and Jewel Markess had been escorted from the room, The Terafin turned. Morretz came to her, from a side chamber.

"You were listening?" she asked him quietly.

He nodded, and added, "Member APhaniel was well aware of my presence."

"As expected. And?"

"His concern is genuine, and it is in keeping with the current leader of the Order of Knowledge."

"Sigurne Mellifas."

Morretz nodded gravely. "There is no way you could halt a private inquiry from that quarter, and if it is of any consolation, the pressure being brought to bear by Member APhaniel almost certainly originates with the guildmaster."

Amarais nodded. She sat in the chair she had abandoned.

"Your concern, Terafin?"

"I know Sigurne, and I have some passing familiarity with Member APhaniel."

"He *is* the House Mage."

She ignored this. "If he—or Sigurne—is worried enough to continue to press this case, it is likely that his suspicions are not unfounded." She looked up, her eyes dark and ringed with circles. She had not, he knew, slept well. "How much can we risk without risking the lives of people who have no say and no political power?"

Morretz understood that this was rhetorical. He made no reply.

"It sits ill with me."

"The governance of a powerful House seldom sits easily."

"I must decide," she said softly. "How much do I trust the instincts of a girl who was born to old-stock Voyani in the streets of the holdings?"

No one answered; the answer was evident in the decision she had handed down. She rose again, straightening her shoulders as she did. The moment of obvious doubt, shared only by her domicis and the utterly silent Chosen, passed.

But she had not quite finished, and the question she asked surprised her domicis. It was not asked of him, and she seldom conversed with the Chosen when they were on duty.

"Torvan," she said quietly, "how does Jewel's den fare in the House?"

Torvan ATerafin didn't blink or in any way betray surprise. And perhaps, Morretz thought, just perhaps, he was not.

"They fare as well as can be expected. Perhaps better. The domicis," he added, inclining his head briefly in Morretz's direction, "has taken the task of their instruction in House behavior very seriously."

"And they listen to him?"

"As much," Torvan replied, with just the trace of hesitation, "as one could expect, given their circumstances."

The Terafin nodded. "Very well. Please keep an eye on them, and alert me to any difficulty they either cause or suffer."

He saluted.

16th of Mistral, 410 A.A.
Terafin Manse, Averalaan Aramarelas

Ellerson would never have said a kitchen was a suitable place for work that did not involve meal preparation. It was, however, the only place in which the den habitually gathered, if one didn't include the end of meal sloth that kept them glued to their seats in the various meal rooms. They still ate like starving children, and that sloth was not feigned; after a meal was not the time to grab or hold their attention.

Carver was often absent after the first week had passed. He would slip into the wing and then out again after a brief pause to speak with either Finch or Angel. Teller and Finch seldom strayed far from the wing.

Jester sometimes went with Carver and sometimes left on his own.

Arann, however, to Finch's surprise, would also leave, often for hours. She worried.

It was during a period of extended worry that she explained the den's past to Ellerson, who listened with the brisk efficiency that marked his training. He had heard similar stories from students in the Hall of the Domicis in the past, and it was therefore a simple matter to both contain reaction, and choose what he let show.

But Finch spoke in such a matter-of-fact way that it was difficult to offer sympathy; she wanted none. She described the facts of her life with the delicate hesitation of one who is uncertain whether or not the audience will be bored, and if she felt any sense of the injustice of the universe in those spare facts, she was far better at hiding it than most.

Given the den's leader, however, he doubted it was an act.

"But it was when we lost Lefty," she finally said, "that things unraveled for Arann." She glanced past him, to the uncluttered wooden surface of the table, with its now-matching chairs. "You didn't know him, before. Actually," she added, thinking through the words, her expression still distant, which was oddly disconcerting in her otherwise friendly face, "he's a bit more like he was. But . . . he's not the same, not quite."

"The healing often has a striking effect, when the healed are otherwise dead."

Finch nodded, more to indicate she'd heard him than that his words had any resonant meaning. Perhaps, in time. "He was always big. It's the first thing you notice about him. That he's big. But he's always been quiet, and he's never been one of the fighters. He didn't like to fight. But after Lefty disappeared, he would. He'd just—he would."

"He didn't seem to care, anymore?"

"No, it was worse than that. He was so angry. He didn't think. He didn't seem to feel pain—to feel anything that wasn't anger. Jay stopped letting him leave the apartment. We were afraid he'd kill someone. Or die."

The latter, Ellerson thought, was the more pressing concern to the den leader.

"But he didn't mind. Being at home." She glanced at the kitchen door. "I wonder what he's doing."

"So," Arann said quietly. "Your job is protecting people."

"Strictly speaking, my job is to obey The Terafin," Torvan replied.

They cast middling shadows against the cropped grass of the grounds. Torvan had led Arann into the gardens; they were almost empty at this time of year. The pavilion, which saw so much use in the summer months, was closed, its decorative boards latched down, its flags and banners in the safety of the groundskeepers' many sheds.

Arann didn't seem to notice. "But she orders you to protect people?"

"To protect The Terafin, yes." Torvan hesitated. "I'm not sure what you're asking," he said at last, coming to rest by the pavilion's stairs.

Arann shrugged. He wasn't moody; there was no irritation or youthful boredom in his expression. Torvan was painfully familiar with both, although the years had dulled them enough that he could wince when he thought of his life at Arann's age.

He'd never had the boy's size, on the other hand; not so young.

"I never cared much for fighting," Arann said. "Can I sit here?"

Torvan chuckled. "You can sit anywhere you like. At this time of year, no one's likely to come and chase you off the grass." Wincing slightly, he added, "In the summer months, when The Terafin and the House Council are expected to entertain dignitaries of note, it's different. Not even the Chosen are exempt from the groundskeepers' rules."

Arann sat, predictably, on the steps below Torvan. The steps ran the circumference of the pavilion.

"Some of the people I used to know figured they'd find a den, and they'd live with the den until they could join the Kings' armies."

Torvan nodded. Intended or not, it was often the fate of the young men who lived by some mixture of wit and brawn in the holdings. "It's not a bad life," he said quietly. "And you've a chance to learn what you're capable of."

Arann's silences were extended punctuation, and it had taken Torvan some little while to accustom himself to them.

"Do you have brothers?" Arann asked now.

"Two."

"Do you like them?"

"Well enough. They're younger," he added. "One of them by several years."

"They're both still alive?"

Ah.

"They're both still alive. No thanks to me, according to our mother," he added wryly.

"I don't. Have brothers." Arann looked down at his hands. "I had Lefty. He was like a brother to me. A younger brother," he added. "He was hurt bad one time. Everything spooked him but me. And Jay, eventually. But he was afraid of Jay at the beginning."

Lefty, thought Torvan, was dead. He didn't ask; instead, he waited through another of Arann's silences, knowing that this particular conversation was not yet at an end. It was Torvan's way to let the den lead discussion, both in the beginning, and at the end, however abrupt that end might be.

"We lost him," Arann said quietly. "In the maze. The one Jay's searching for with that mage." He paused and then added, "I don't think she likes him much."

This didn't surprise Torvan. "Most people don't like mages."

"But she's not afraid of him. They shout a lot."

"If she has no success, her position within the House is insecure. And if the mage has no success, *he* feels the Empire is in danger. They'll shout."

"She doesn't care about her position."

"No?"

"Well, she does, but not because it's a position. We—things were bad. For us. They're not bad, here. She wants here *for us*. And we're letting her do it on her own."

"One of the hardest things to learn—possibly *the* hardest thing—is that. When to let others do the work they *can* do, while you sit on your hands and wait."

Arann looked up at Torvan. "I didn't care about being able to fight. I didn't need it. I looked after Lefty." He swallowed, and looked away. "But we lost him." Looking back, Torvan saw his expression had shifted, or perhaps cracked. What was there now was painful to look at. "I failed him."

"Arann—"

Arann lifted his hand, and Torvan stopped speaking. "I failed him."

"Could fighting—could knowing *how* to fight—have prevented that?"

"I don't know." Arann closed his eyes. "Part of me thinks no. Part of me isn't sure. But all of me is sure of one thing: He's gone. I didn't kill him. It's not my fault he's dead. But I didn't *save* him, either, and he trusted me.

"I want to be able to protect the people I care about. All of them. I don't want to hide from the fighting anymore. Look at me. I'm big. I've always been big. It's the only thing anyone ever notices. My size. My strength. But it didn't *do any good*, back then. And I want to be able to do something now. If this is what I have, I want to be able to use it.

"And I thought maybe a guard—a House Guard, even—did that. Protected people."

His words trailed off into his more familiar silence.

Torvan said, "It's at the heart of what the House Guards do. Let me tell you a bit about them."

"So this is how you work?"

The maid shrieked. In the narrow, windowless servants' halls, the sound *bounced*. Carver covered his ears in mock pain.

"Carver," the girl hissed, "you shouldn't *be* here."

He shrugged, and leaned up against the wall, which should have looked ridiculous. "I wanted to see where you worked."

"Why? You *know* where I work. At the moment, my duties are in the West Wing. So," she added, tilting her head to the side, "are yours."

He had to admit that he liked that particular tilting expression. She wasn't skinny the way Finch was, but something about her reminded him of Finch. Except for her hair, which reminded him of Jay's, except that the curls were darker and fuller. Everything about her was.

"I never see you leave the wing, and I never—almost never—see you arrive," he added.

"You're not *supposed* to see me," she hissed. "And if anyone sees *you*, I'll be in trouble."

"How much trouble?"

"Have you met the Master of the Household staff?"

"What, the white-haired, grouchy old woman?"

Merry looked shocked. She probably was. She smacked his chest, dead center, and not lightly either. "She's *not* old."

He shrugged. "I notice you didn't argue about the grouchy part."

"She will be beyond something as petty as grouchy if she sees *you* here. These halls aren't used by anyone but the servants. And for good damn reason," she added. "The servants who serve in the main house—The Terafin's manse—are mostly ATerafin. I'm new," she added. "And young for it. And I don't want them to strip me of the name—my parents are over the moon, and my aunt brags about it every chance she gets. I swear she talks about it more than she breathes.

"They'd be heartbroken, and I'd be out of the best job I'm ever going to find. Do you understand?"

He nodded. He did not, however, leave. "So," he said, looking around the narrow hall, "these halls—how far in do they go?"

"They're between the outer and inner walls of most of the manse's residential rooms. The large state rooms don't have them; when they're open, the servants are expected to be visible. Silent, perfectly mannered, and visible."

"So, no swearing."

She had the grace to redden. "No. No swearing." She heaved a sigh, which was an entirely physical act, and then grimaced. "We were told your wing was an exceptional case, and we were to tread with care."

"On what?"

She stepped somewhat heavily on his toes, which made him laugh, a sound that also bounced off the walls. He was not particularly fond of the sound of his own laughter; it reminded him too much of Jester.

"Come on. If we don't get out of here soon, we'll cause a traffic jam, and then I really *will* be in trouble."

"You're going back to the West Wing?"

"What do you think?"

"I think playing dumb around you is suicidal."

"Smart boy. I am just finished cleaning—and I have to say, we all thought there'd be a lot more mess—and I have forty-five minutes of break. I'm heading to lunch," she added.

"Can I join you?"

"Not if you're going to eat."

He laughed.

She looked up at him for a moment and then shook her head. "You're impossible," she told him, with just a glimpse of dimple to soften the tone. She did not, however, step on him again, and he followed her.

The halls, as Merry implied, did seem to go everywhere. There were stairs and the occasional cross hall, all of which were precisely cut, and all of which were narrow. The floors were, for the most part, stone, as were the low ceilings, but here and there, small doors could be glimpsed. They were the size of the closet doors in the West Wing, if that. They certainly weren't the large, peaked doors or the doubled doors that fronted many of the rooms.

"Carver, did I mention you're not supposed to be here?"

"About a dozen times."

"And did I mention that *only* the servants are supposed to use these halls?"

"About the same number."

"Then *why* do you keep asking me questions every time we turn a corner or pass a door?"

"Because I want to know where they go? I mean, if you're supposed to slip into—and out of—a room without being seen, they can't all enter into rooms."

"Some of them enter into the supply rooms," she replied. "Some of them enter into the attendants' chambers."

"The what?"

"The nobles who lived here, at one point in time, surrounded themselves with nobles of lesser stature—daughters and sons of other nobles, for instance—and they were called attendants. They were considered the right sort of company, and they waited on—not served—the ruler of the House."

"But you don't have those anymore."

"No, but the rooms are still there. They're used," she added. "But not the same way. In your wing, Ellerson occupies the attendant's room for most of the day. He has quarters in which he sleeps and changes, but for the most part, the attendant's room is his. It's where he works."

Carver nodded. "So . . . all of the guest wings have them?"

"I know what you're doing."

"Humor me?"

"I am. You're still breathing, and you're still following me."

He grinned. "Sorry," he told her. It wasn't perhaps his most sincere apology.

But it stopped her for a moment, and her expression went from mild irritation to serious. He wasn't certain he liked the change.

"I know this is all hard for you," she told him quietly.

He shrugged, suddenly ill at ease.

"But you can't inflict your boredom on all of the servants. You certainly can't inflict it on all the maids. Most of us know that Jewel Markess did something that saved The Terafin's life, and that's your leeway here. But it won't last, and you can push it too far."

"Am I?"

"You probably can't push it too far with me, and I'm going to hate myself in an hour for saying that," she told him, still serious. "The servants assigned to your wing were chosen for a reason."

"What's that?"

"What's what?"

"The reason."

"Oh, that. We can carry ourselves as if we're the scions of the gods' own servants. We know when to be serious and when to relax. We won't embarrass the House, and we won't allow ourselves to be embarrassed. Not easily," she added, reddening slightly.

"I haven't stolen anything while I've been here."

"No. And you won't, either, until you're told to leave."

This surprised him, and his obvious discomfort made her laugh. "I am going to starve to death if I don't get out of these halls. Come on. You can watch me eat. It can't," she added, "be worse than watching your den eat. And don't repeat *that* to anyone, or I'll be scrubbing floors in the main dining hall for six months."

He didn't. But he did wheedle information out of her as they walked, which was, he told himself, the entire point of the exercise.

18th of Misteral, 410 A.A.
Port Authority, Averalaan

Angel left The Terafin manse only once in the weeks that Jewel worked alongside the mage. He told Finch he was going out for the morning. She didn't ask where he was going, and he didn't volunteer the information.

He did, however, ask Ellerson how to get to the port from the Isle. Ellerson, like Finch, didn't question him about anything, except for his possible presence, or absence, at lunch and dinner.

Angel made his way down to the Port Authority, abandoning Ellerson's crisp directions as soon as he had cleared the footbridge to the Isle. He wasn't required to actually pay the tolls back, Ellerson had informed him. As a guest of House Terafin, those tolls would be covered. Therefore, instead of coin, he had given Angel a letter, which clearly stated—and in almost the exact words—what Ellerson had just said. It had, however, the full Terafin seal beneath the words, which made it a lot more official.

The port wasn't busy at this time of year, but the heavy rains had yet to fall. It was therefore still open, and it would remain so. The winds were brisk, and when they hit, they were cold, but the air was clear, and it lacked the torpid humidity of high summer. Flags flew along the poles of the dock and atop the Port Authority itself. The Authority's doors were still jammed open, still guarded, and still traversed by people who were in a hurry. Angel slid out of their way without noticing much else about them.

Terrick was behind his customary wicket when Angel entered the building. He was leafing through the paperwork the Port Authority seemed to specialize in generating, and standing in front of him, shoulders touching, were a man and a woman. They were dressed for cold weather, and their jackets were stained with the salty powder so often seen in travelers.

Angel took his place in the short line and waited. When he finally reached the wicket, Terrick looked up and nodded. It made Angel smile; his father would have noticed Angel the minute he entered the building, and he would have failed to acknowledge his presence in exactly the same way. He could think about his father most days without pain, now.

This wasn't one of them.

"Lunch is in forty minutes, give or take a few," Terrick told him, without preamble.

Angel nodded. "I'm not starving at the moment," he added.

"Good. I'd like to be able to say the same after lunch." Terrick's Northern grin was broad and brief.

Angel sat in the back room of Terrick's office and felt, for a moment, as though he'd never truly left it. The tension eased out of his shoulders and jaw as he watched Terrick break bread and fill mug.

"You're not eating?" Terrick asked.

"No. I'm expected back for dinner, and I ate everything at breakfast."

Terrick raised a brow. "I haven't seen you in a little while."

Angel shrugged. "There's not a lot of work at the port in Scaral. Or Misteral."

"You didn't get that tunic doing 'not a lot of work' And given the living you can make hand to mouth on the streets, you didn't get it cutting purses, either."

Angel's face reddened, but he kept his words firmly behind his lips until the urge to say them passed. He had nothing to reply with, in any case; if *he* hadn't cut pursestrings, Carver and Duster certainly had, and he'd lived off what they managed to get away with. As a child, he would have said he would never stoop to theft. Hunger was a harsh teacher, and he'd learned quickly.

Terrick, watching Angel, put his bread down. "What's happened?" he asked, slipping into Rendish, his smooth, Imperial accent giving way to the harsher, Northern bark.

Angel looked across the table for a long moment and then took out the letter Ellerson had given him for dodging tolls. He placed it on top of the stack of neat papers that occupied the right-hand corner of Terrick's desk.

The seal caught Terrick's eye. He frowned as he lifted it. He read it—once, judging by the speed with which he looked back at Angel—and asked, quietly, "Do you know what this says?"

"More or less. I can read it, it just takes time."

"You're a guest of possibly the most powerful woman in the Empire."

"I'm not."

"Then you haven't read the document carefully enough."

"I'm staying there," Angel said, frowning. "But not through anything I've said or done. I'm ballast. My den leader—my friend—" he added, catching the word just after it left his lips, rather than before, "is the real guest."

"Den leader."

Angel grimaced. "Den leader."

"And he has something of value to offer The Terafin?"

"She, and obviously."

Terrick lifted a hand. "I mean no criticism of your den leader," he said quietly, each syllable so heavily pronounced the words sounded like ritual, rather than conversation.

Angel met his gaze and then folded his arms across his chest. "She's what she is," he said, his voice as quiet, and exact, as Terrick's had been. "She *is* a den leader. She leads a den. I'm part of it."

"So."

"When she went to House Terafin, she took us with her. All of us."

"And The Terafin allowed this."

Angel glanced pointedly at the paper.

"Who is this den leader?"

"Jewel. Jewel Markess." It wasn't what she liked to be called, but Angel held the den-name back; no one else used it. It belonged to no one else. He realized, then, that Terrick's quiet disclaimer had even been a necessary one. "I'm the newest of her den. The others, she's had with her for three years. Maybe a bit more, or a bit less. She found them, rescued them, made them as much of a home as orphans with nothing can have in this city."

"And she found you."

Angel nodded. "She does what she has to, to survive. She doesn't do more."

"Fair enough. Why did you come here today?"

Angel rose; the chair was suddenly too confining. The chair, he thought, and Terrick's keen, sharp gaze. Northern steel, there.

"I'm in House Terafin," he replied. "And *if* everything works out, Jewel Markess will *earn* the House Name."

Terrick, whose views on The Ten, with their strict disavowal of blood ties, Angel knew well, said nothing for a moment. The moment passed, and Terrick picked words gingerly, offering them in the most neutral of tones.

"The Terafin will grant the House Name—a name that many men and women of rank and power would pay to possess—to a girl who commands a handful of orphans in the poor holdings of Averalaan?"

Angel nodded. "If you'd met The Terafin, you'd understand. She could offer us money, and we'd take it in return for the same work. Or the same lack of work."

"What do you do while you're there?"

"Nothing," Angel replied, flatly.

Terrick grimaced. "Pardon. Continue."

"She could have offered money. She *is* paying Jewel. But—" He drew breath. "She offered something else instead, and Jewel wants it badly. Not for her own sake. Or not for her own sake alone; she wants it for us."

"There's more to this story."

"There always is."

"Are you free to tell me, or are you honor bound to withhold?"

"I—" Angel sat again. "We've always done what we thought best. Jay—Jewel, I mean—lives with it. Yes. I'm free to tell you." He hesitated, then asked, "Have you ever heard the word *demon* before?"

The pause that followed the question was long, profound. It was also entirely Terrick's. The Northerner watched Angel, in his new and obviously fine tunic, his darker leggings. He was thinner than he had been when he'd first hit port, but in truth, not by much, and some of that lankiness might be due to the height he'd also gained. At this age, boys grew like weeds.

But slimmer, better dressed—these were illusory things to Terrick. Beneath them, he could see that Garroc's son was both restless and worried. The desperation, the fury at the universe and its gods, had all but deserted him. It had been hard to watch his decline into wildness, and harder still to wait it out; to wonder, as any parent does in the silence of an empty apartment, whether the boy would find the death on the streets he seemed to be so frantically searching for.

When the boy had entered the Port Authority, Terrick had seen him. He knew Angel was aware of this. He had been both curious and almost content, which was rare.

That contentment now left him in its entirety. What remained was the Weston word at the heart of Angel's question.

"Aye," he said at last. "I know the word."

Angel nodded, as if this had not surprised him. But he hesitated. "Are you going to eat that?"

Terrick snorted. He lifted the bread and cheese, wedged sausage between them, and lifted it all to his mouth, although he knew it would taste like ash.

Angel took the letter back and folded it, putting it carefully into an interior pocket. "I live at House Terafin," he told Terrick quietly.

Terrick, chewing, nodded.

"I don't understand all of what happened," he continued, "but Jewel's old teacher was The Terafin's blood brother, before he abandoned Handernesse. They were estranged," he added, "but in the end? He sent Jewel to The Terafin—with a letter."

"And The Terafin, after reading it, chose to house us all."

Terrick nodded again.

"I wouldn't have come just for that," Angel continued. "But . . . there was a demon. He not only looked like a man, he looked exactly like The Terafin's brother. He tried to kill The Terafin," Angel added, "and he failed." Angel leaned back into his chair, attempting to look relaxed and achieving the opposite effect.

"What Weyrdon said—to me—the day I met him—"

Terrick lifted a hand in warning. "I remember, Angel," he said quietly.

Angel nodded. "I've spent two weeks thinking about it. They're connected. The House, the demon, and Garroc's duty."

There was no doubt in the boy's voice, and perhaps because of this, there was no doubt in Terrick. When Angel spoke with that quiet confidence, he was most like the man Terrick had served; Terrick wondered if he knew.

"The *Ice Wolf* will not come to port in Misteral," Terrick told him. "It will not come to the port at all until well after Veral; the seas to the north will be impassable."

Angel shrugged. "It's not Weyrdon I wanted to speak with," he told Terrick.

Terrick stared at the boy, seeing again some semblance to Garroc in his youthful, quiet features. "I've no counsel to offer," Terrick told him, after a pause.

"You always have an opinion."

In spite of himself, Terrick chuckled. The shadow of the word *demon* shortened that sound but could not quell it entirely. He lifted water toward Angel's chest, and Angel shook his head. Terrick drank. "I'd ask, first, how you know the word *demon* and how you knew the assassin was one."

"Oh. There was a mage," Angel replied. "A magus. From the Order of Knowledge. He stopped the demon from killing The Terafin."

"And he recognized the creature for what it was?"

"By the end, everyone did. When the demon realized he was cornered, he shed the appearance of humanity." Angel hesitated, and then added, "I think he may have been wearing the actual body; Jay—Jewel, I mean—said there was skin and hair left behind. But what was left after he stopped looking human wasn't human in any way."

"Left behind?"

"He turned to ash when he died. There was no body."

Terrick lifted his hands, briefly, to his face. "Aye, boy," he said wearily. "I know the word, and the legends. Demon, then. Garroc's duty."

"Garroc's duty was to find a worthy leader," Angel said, grimmer now. "At this time and in this place."

"You said you weren't concerned with fulfilling his quest."

"I wasn't."

"And now?"

"Demons."

Endless night. Neither of them spoke the words; neither of them needed to do so.

"Is The Terafin a worthy ruler?"

"I don't know. I've seen her once. But . . . Jay thinks so."

It was clear that the opinion of this den leader, this Jewel or this Jay, carried a great deal of weight for Angel. Other things, however, were also clear to Terrick.

"And this Jewel," he asked softly. "Is she worthy of fealty?"

Angel grimaced as if in pain and pulled himself up from the chair. He began to pace around it, tracing a very flat oval across the plank surface of the back office floors.

"She's not my lord," Angel said, as he walked, avoiding Terrick's gaze. "She's—she's not my boss. She's a friend, Terrick. She doesn't tell me what to do, not often."

"But she does on occasion?"

Angel shrugged, staring at his feet as they moved. "Yeah. But when she does, she's telling *everyone* what to do—and when she does, everyone listens." He hesitated, and then added, "She'd be like an aunt or a mother if she were older. She—she makes sure things get done."

"Angel."

Angel looked across the room at Terrick, on the curve of the irregular oval he was tracing as he paced.

"Do you think I bent knee to Garroc?"

"You served him."

"Yes. I did. And would, were he still alive. But I don't think you understand, yet, what that means. To either Garroc or Terrick." He looked at Angel, refused to let him look away. "Weyrdon was a worthy lord. A worthy man. It would have been an honor to serve him."

"But you didn't even—"

Terrick lifted a hand. "Garroc served Weyrdon. Garroc bent knee. Garroc listened, counseled, and warred in his name. I did none of those things in Garroc's. I understand the wyrd placed upon your shoulders, and believe, boy, that I understand the significance of demons in this place."

Something about the way he spoke the last sentence stilled Angel's pacing. "What do you mean, in this place?"

Terrick listened to the sounds of the outer office. "My time grows short," he said.

If Angel hadn't known him well, he would have said that Terrick was stalling. He wasn't fool enough to make the accusation. Instead, he found his chair again and sat heavily on its hard surface. "There's one other thing," he told Terrick, watching the Northerner's lined face with caution.

"Speak. You could not say worse."

"When I met Jewel, when I met the den, we weren't stealing. We were—foraging. We found things that no one was using—I mean *no one*—and we took them to Rath. He sold them for us and gave us a cut of the money."

Terrick waited.

"There's a city under this city," Angel told him quietly. "It's a dead place. Old stone, broken roads, sheared walls, remnants of statues. There's no light there but the light we bring, and it goes on for miles in all directions." Watching now. Seeing in the sudden stillness of Terrick's expression some hint of recognition, of suspicion, and yes—something that bordered on fear. Never open fear, never from Terrick.

"They're in the holdings now, my den leader and the magus, looking for that damn city. She knows every way into it," he added, "but she can't find an entrance anymore. It's as if they're all being destroyed, or unmade."

"By . . . demons," Terrick said. His voice was quiet enough to be a whisper; it wasn't. His turn, now, to rise, to shed the comfort of solid chair, to seek movement to still his restlessness, mask his concern.

"Boy," he said at last, although he did not look at Angel, "in the North, there are stories. Legends. The North feared the South for a long time. They distrusted the ease and the beauty, the magic, the craftsmanship, the supposed indolence of the Imperials.

"But they did so because of those stories and legends. We speak, in Arrend, of the time when the gods walked the world. They do not walk it now, and they do not speak to the golden-eyed of those ancient journeys; what we have, we have kept for ourselves.

"And what we have, in fragments, is not the truth. I have lived here for years, and I understand the Empire as well as any from Arrend can; it is full of people, no more or less human than those that live in our cities. But here, boy, overlooking the bay, they say that one god once lived. His city was called the Shining City, and it was fair beyond reckoning.

"The . . . Shining City."

"Yes. For the Lord of the dark."

Endless night.

"They do not speak of the Shining City here. There are no legends or stories save those that involve Moorelas, who rode into the city's heart and faced the god with a weapon crafted by the god's kin. But they do not speak the name except in bardic lay.

"They called it, in the oldest of styles, *Vexusa*." Terrick bowed his head. "And if you have walked its streets, and they are now denied you, the time Weyrdon feared is almost come."

Angel rose in the silence Terrick's word's left. The lunch's end had not yet sounded, but it was over. Terrick did not resume his seat, and Angel did not speak.

But as he turned toward the door that led to the wickets, Terrick cleared his throat. Angel turned a little too quickly.

"It's hard to search for something when you have no idea what you hope to find," he told Angel quietly. "I don't envy you your task."

"And you've no advice for me, either."

"Actually, it happens I do." Terrick's smile was slight, but it was there, changing the contours of his weathered lips. "If they—if Weyrdon and his Alaric—knew for certain what you must achieve, believe they would tell you, and at length. They *don't know*."

"I don't, either."

"No. But it's yours to find, Angel, Garroc's son. A worthy leader," he added, "means many, many things. A man's definition of worth says everything about the man himself. For some, it is purely based on power, and for some, on the obvious trappings of power. For some, it is based on kinship.

"For Terrick," Terrick added, "it was complicated. But it was also simple. Had I been told what you were told, it wouldn't have changed a damn thing. I think you heard the word demon, and you understood what it might mean.

"But you've heard the word leader, and you don't. You hear not what the word might mean but only what the failure to fulfill Garroc's quest might. Leave the fear. The only person who can define that word is you. Angel."

"My father failed," Angel said, the words soft and stark.

"Aye, he did. And he lived with that failure. But I think it was not yet time, and I think, in the end, it was not *his* burden. It was yours."

"Terrick—"

"Garroc was of Weyrdon and of Arrend. He was too much of both. You are neither but are informed by them."

"But—"

Terrick lifted a broad hand. "You want to ask me why I think this. Very well. You have met demons. You have seen the ruins of the darkest city of the past. You are here, now, and you have walked a path that none of Weyrdon has walked.

"Walk it farther, boy. See it to its end."

"How will I know?" Angel asked, laying at last all fear bare.

"You will, I think, know. In the end, you'll know."

The horn lowed the end of the discussion.

"And when you know, come back and tell me." He paused, and then added, "You think that your job will be done if you somehow find this mythical leader. But I think that it will, only then, begin in earnest."

Chapter Three

2nd of Corvil, 410 A. A.
Terafin Manse, Averalaan Aramarelas

JEWEL HAD BEEN COOPED UP in the Terafin manse for the whole of the day. It was her first "day off," but it felt like either a punishment or a long-delayed judgment. She had searched for the under-city every day since she had first accepted The Terafin's offer, and she had returned each time with nothing but a frustrated, tired mage.

Today, for the first time, the mage had not come in the morning. Instead, he had sent a message with his firm but brusque regret; he would be absent. No other partner had been chosen for Jewel. No other help was offered. She could, of course, have taken to the streets on her own—but that would prove nothing. Even if she managed to find her way back into the maze, she would do it without witnesses.

So she paced in the dining room, and when that provided no comfort, she moved herself to the kitchen—the kitchen that was larger in its entirety than the whole of the den's apartment had been. It was her room of choice.

For one, it was practical. It *looked* like a kitchen, even given its size. The table looked like a huge cutting board, and suspended above that table, on hanging chains, were various pots and utensils. They also lined the walls, their dented and scratched surfaces an indication that they had been, and would be, used. That they served some purpose.

The dining room, the breakfast nook, the meeting rooms—they were always so clean and so utterly tidy they looked unfinished somehow, as if the people who were meant to make them a home hadn't yet arrived. Or never would. The furniture made her feel dirty and awkward just by the difference in their respective states; Jewel came home covered in dirt and dust and smelling more than a bit rank, even though it wasn't summer.

No matter what the hour, Ellerson was waiting by the front doors of the wing, and he ushered her firmly toward the bath. She was surprised at how accustomed she'd grown to the hot water, the clean towels, the scent of the water; it was one of the few places in which she now relaxed.

But she didn't even wash her own clothing anymore. It was taken and replaced, each evening, by Ellerson.

Around her, the den hovered. They knew better than to ask about her work for The Terafin. But that didn't leave them much to talk about in the end—it was *all* she did. She listened to them speak about their own days, about the people they'd met—mostly servants—and the things they'd discovered about the manse. Some of it was interesting—the servants' hidden hallways, for one.

Jewel didn't tell them what to do here. She didn't hold the pursestrings; she didn't arrange outings to the Common, or to the river, or to the wells. She didn't break up any arguments about whose turn it was to cook or clean—they no longer had those duties.

What *did* they have now?

She shook her head. She was obviously going crazy. They had a roof over their heads—one that didn't, and wouldn't, leak. They had enough food to feed the entire twenty-fifth holding. They had better clothing than they'd ever had and access to both the old city and the breadth of the Isle, courtesy of House Terafin.

What else did they need?

Restless, nervous, she shoved her hair out of her eyes, pacing in tighter circles. They needed nothing—right up until the moment The Terafin decided Jewel's search was pointless. Then they'd have the money she'd made to date—and it wasn't a small sum—and the streets of the twenty-fifth, or the thirtieth, or any other holding in the old city, would open up to swallow them again.

In those streets, and beneath them, she'd lost *so many* of her den-kin. She'd lose more, she thought bitterly. She'd lose them.

Gods, where were the damn tunnels? Where was the damn maze?

If the demons—and the mage used the word so often it had become a fact of life, like street thieves loitering outside the Common—were some-how destroying the entrances, they were doing it with Rath's help. With the help of his memories. And while Jewel had gone searching the maze without Rath so often in the past three years she was certain she'd seen things he hadn't, there wasn't any *damn* evidence of it.

Someone cleared his throat. "You called?" Ellerson said.

"You know damn well I didn't call," she snapped. "So you can stop that stuffy, polite act."

"As you wish," he replied, in exactly the same even tone of voice. "But may I point something out to the young lady?"

"Like I could stop you if I wanted to."

"It is unkind—and inaccurate in some cases—to assume that the mannerisms and gestures of another person are assumed, rather than genuine. While you will never develop the same style that I have developed, you were also never exposed to the same influences. I do not assume that your behavior is an act."

She snorted. "If I were going to act, I'd probably choose something different to act like."

"Agreed."

"Ellerson, don't you have something to do?"

"I am your domicis."

It was what he always said. Jewel was convinced that she could grab a random knife and try to cut his arms off, and he would still come up with the same phrase. "I forgot."

"As you say."

Grinding her teeth, and aware that she was behaving like a spoiled, tired child, she asked, "Did you come here for a reason?"

"Indeed. Appropriate attire has arrived for you and your companions. I thought you might want to have your old clothing removed, as you will be representing The Terafin and will therefore be expected to dress appropriately."

She did what she usually did when he used that tone of voice: She nodded. It bought her a bit of time and space as Ellerson vacated the kitchen. Which lasted until Carver entered. In his House tunic.

"Carver, go tell Ellerson I've changed my mind about the clothing."

"Right, sir," he replied, his jaunty sarcasm so at odds with Ellerson's crisp correctness it was almost a comfort. "But I'll trade."

"Trade what?"

"The Terafin's looking for you. Torvan's outside."

She should have known Ellerson wouldn't have insisted on laying out new clothing—for her—without cause. "Why? We don't have another meeting scheduled for two days." Still, the thought of a meeting without the icy silence of either the mage or the House ruler was very, very tempting.

"Teller says he saw the mage with a group of people. Three men, a really scrubby woman, and a bunch of dogs."

Just like that the floor fell out from under her; her knees wobbled at the sudden seismic shift. "They've called someone else in?"

He failed to meet her gaze. "Looks like," he said, shrugging. The shrug, in the new clothing, managed to look the same as it always had: irritating.

For the first time ever, Ellerson insisted that they *dress appropriately*. She knew he'd already had the run of the den, but she'd squeaked clear of the fancy, expensive clothing for the most part because even Ellerson could be practical; rooting about in dirty basements and crawlspaces did not require the same attention to detail as walking across the grand galleries.

If it weren't for Torvan's steady presence, she would have gotten lost. Again. The rest of her den had managed, over the last several weeks, to learn the ins and outs of the manse; they knew it about as well as they knew the Common—or any other place they hadn't called home.

Under the cut-glass light of one of the multitudes of chandeliers, she stopped, gripped by a homesickness that made her throat tighten. Had you asked her—ever—she would have said that *this* was her dream life. And it was.

But the problem with dreams was they were never complete. In her dreams of future glory, it had never occurred to her that she would spend *weeks* away from the side of Farmer Hanson's stalls; that she would miss the way he shouted at his good-humored sons. He'd known, of course, that things had gotten bad, and he'd taken to slipping her more food than she'd paid for. She'd taken to accepting it in silence.

He'd worry, now. It had been weeks since she'd gone.

Weeks since she'd even thought of going. She wondered if Teller or Finch had left the grounds at all. They weren't with her; she couldn't ask.

"Jewel?"

She glanced at Torvan, took a deep breath—or as deep a breath as she could in this dress, with its mile-long sash wound so tightly around her middle—and nodded. The stray curls that characterized her hair in any season had been pulled back so tightly it made her teeth hurt.

Torvan led her down the public galleries, ignoring the people who were gathered there in twos and threes. They didn't entirely ignore Torvan, but none of them spoke; Jewel tried to hold her head up high and to walk as if she belonged here.

Her clothing did. She didn't. And the only way she would *ever* belong here was if she found the undercity, miles and miles of streets and deserted buildings that she couldn't even reach anymore. So she made her silent list of the entrances and exits they'd tracked, ticking them off, one at a time.

She was at the tail end of this process when she noticed that Torvan had stopped walking. Turning, she looked at the doors in front of which he'd come to stand. "Isn't this where—"

"Yes. But the repairs have been done, and well. Except for scoring in the stone, you would not know that a battle of any sort took place here." He nodded toward the doors.

"Aren't you coming?"

"I wasn't summoned. There are other guests."

"Which means I've got to be on good behavior, right?"

"The choice," he replied, with a very slight smile, "is always yours."

"Not much of a choice," she replied as she caught the handles of the closed door. "Starve or jump through hoops."

"Welcome to the adult world." But again, he smiled, to take the edge off words she knew damn well were true. She'd gotten so used to Torvan it was hard to remember, sometimes, that he belonged in House Terafin.

If Jewel wasn't exactly comfortable in The Terafin's presence by this time, she was no longer terrified. The Terafin wasn't friendly and would probably *never* be friendly, but they had grief in common, and they were both used to hiding grief; The Terafin was just better at it.

Jewel, however, was unaccustomed to other visitors, and she froze a moment in the open door.

Three men sat in chairs around a long, low table, only one of whom she recognized. Meralonne. He was either not annoyed at the moment—which was a minor miracle in and of itself—or he was on good behavior because he didn't really know the other two strangers that well. There was a silvered jug, with appropriate cups around it, on a tray that also shone with reflected light; there was food of some sort, but Jewel was not yet adept at recognizing the ways in which ingredients were disguised in a fine House.

If she had been stuffed into a dress—with a full skirt, and a sash that cut off breath—the two strangers had not. But they wore clothing that even the dirt of the road could not make common. That clothing was not in Averalaan colors; it was a deep, deep green, with some flashings of brown on the full sleeves and in the gathers of the breast.

One of the two men looked as bored as Carver could get. His hair was a dark brown, and his eyes, in this light, dark as well. The other man, who gave him a glance that clearly said *pay attention*, was blond; his hair was long but not braided, and his eyes were lighter; she couldn't tell, at this distance, what color they were. They were both older than she was but significantly younger than The Terafin.

In and of themselves, they would have been a bit unsettling, because they were clearly foreigners. Jewel wasn't certain how she knew, but she *knew*. But seated quietly—and on the ground—to one side of the dark-haired stranger, was a young woman. Her hair was matted and lank; it hung in clumped strands all about her face, and she took no trouble to brush it out of her eyes. She wasn't lovely, although possibly if Ellerson had been allowed to take her into hand—and more important, into the baths—she might have been.

Something about her was . . . wrong. She looked up at Jewel when Jewel entered, but she didn't rise, didn't nod, didn't otherwise seem to notice.

The two men, however, left their seats and offered Jewel bows, which was awkward, because Jewel had no idea what to offer them in return. As she hesitated, The Terafin spoke.

"Jewel. Good. Please join us." The Terafin sat behind her desk. It was new; the old one had been scored and burned. But new or no, it was elegant and clearly well crafted.

"This is Lord Elseth of the Kingdom of Breodanir," she said, indicating the very bored, dark-haired man. "And this is his companion, Stephen. The young woman," she continued, as if said young woman weren't seated on the carpets across the floor, "is called Espere. She is, unfortunately, mute—and they have traveled this distance to find a cure for her condition."

Mute. Jewel glanced at the two men. Mute was not the girl's problem. *Oh? And what is?*

She ignored the inner question; she didn't know. Had they been guests in her own home—or even in the wing the den now occupied—she would have questioned them. But this was The Terafin's domain, and what The Terafin accepted, Jewel was forced to accept. Besides which, it was nice to have something be someone else's problem, for a change. Her only problem, and her only fear at the moment, was that these foreigners might somehow take from her the only job she'd ever had.

She took a chair. If The Terafin noticed that she'd chosen the chair as far from the strangers as possible, she made no comment. Jewel looked at the cups laid out on the table and glanced at the food. But as the guests had touched little, she couldn't. Even without the benefit of a House's wealth and tutors, she had *some* manners.

"Gentlemen, this is Jewel Markess. She is one of three people that I've personally appointed to investigate the unusual occurrences in the inner holdings." A brief, but distinct, knock interrupted her, and she glanced at the door. Jewel heard the knock, but she was having trouble with the "three"; as far as she knew, neither she nor Meralonne counted as two.

"Enter."

Jewel, to her embarrassment, hadn't bothered to knock.

The doors opened, and a man she had never seen before entered the room. He was Torvan's age, but aside from gender, he had very little in common with the House Guard; his hair was dark but sprinkled, faintly, with silver; his eyes were darker than the foreign lord's. He could walk, and did, silently and gracefully. He wore House colors, and they suited him.

He took the chair closest to the foreigners, nodding briefly at Meralonne APhaniel as if they were more than passing acquaintances—and not entirely comfortable ones, at that.

"I'm sorry I'm late, Terafin."

"I'd prefer that you were less sorry and more often on time," she replied, but the words were too wry to be a reprimand. "Very well. You know Meralonne, more or less. The two gentlemen are visitors from beyond the Empire. This is Lord Elseth of Breodanir, and this, his companion, is Stephen. The young woman to your right is Jewel Markess; it is she whom you will be advising.

"Devon ATerafin has been a member of my House for almost twenty years. He is absolutely trustworthy."

Lord Elseth turned to his companion; his companion shrugged. It was brief, but it might as well have been den-sign.

"Although his duties are to the Trade Commission, he has agreed to aid us in this difficult time."

Jewel attempted to accept this news with grace; she managed silence. She had no idea what the Trade Commission actually was, but she could hazard a guess, given the name. She couldn't figure out why the Trade Commission's advice was supposed to help *her*. That The Terafin felt she needed advice from anyone besides the mage was nerve-wracking. And, she thought, given her total failure to date, it was also deserved.

The fair-haired companion now rose and offered Devon ATerafin a perfect and correct bow. It was a little on the stiff side. His lord rose a few seconds later, and performed a bow that was, surprisingly, just as good. Jewel would have sworn he'd had to be dragged to his feet, and she'd seen no glance, no look, no hand signal, that might have accomplished this.

She heard growling and looked up in surprise. She must be damn nervous, she thought. There were dogs lying against the far wall, massive triangular heads resting against their forepaws, and she'd missed them. She'd never seen anything larger than a cat—well, nothing alive at any rate—inside the manse before. Two of these dogs had lifted their heads; they hadn't gained their feet, but the growling was the steady, low thrum of noise that made barking seem safe.

They didn't appear to like Devon ATerafin.

For his part, Devon ATerafin was aware of this at once, but he didn't seem particularly bothered—or surprised—by it. He glanced at the dogs briefly and then turned a pleasant smile upon the visitors.

"Isn't it unusual for Hunter Lords to travel?" he asked.

Hunter Lord. *Hunter* Lord. Jewel froze a moment as the words sunk in.

"It is very unusual," the man The Terafin had introduced as Stephen replied. "And we must not tarry; by the first of Veral, we must be in Breodanir, in the King's city."

"Or?" Devon asked. He knew the answer, Jewel thought. She wasn't sure why she thought it, but she didn't doubt the certainty.

"There is no or," Stephen said gravely. "We are Hunters, and we abide by the Hunter's Oath. If we cannot achieve our goal—or yours, Terafin—by that date, we must set aside the goal until the passing of the Sacred Hunt."

Devon nodded as if the response was entirely the one he expected.

Silence now descended upon the room; it wasn't a comfortable silence. Rather, it was the silence of strangers with too many duties and too little time to accomplish any of them. Jewel knew the silence well; it was partly her own.

But it wasn't her job—thank the gods—to alleviate it.

"Devon," said the woman whose job it was, "I must ask you one question. Do you know who holds the seventeenth, the thirty-second, and the thirty-fifth?"

His face lost its friendly, easy smile as he raised a brow. "Pardon?" It clearly wasn't the question he'd been expecting. Fair enough; Jewel found it confusing as well. Before The Terafin could repeat the question, he lifted a hand. "My apologies, Terafin. I heard the question."

"And?"

"I must confess that I leave that for the record keepers and the treasury. It's easy enough to find the three names if you require them."

"It's not necessary," she replied. "Meralonne?"

The mage didn't have a pipe in his hands. The expression on his face made clear that this lack was onerous. "They are not three names; they are one. Those holdings, as well as the seventh and the fifty-ninth, are in the care of Lord Cordufar."

"Two of the richest and three of the poorest," Devon said, lifting his hand to his chin a moment and staring into the space above the tabletop.

"The two richest and the three poorest," The Terafin replied.

"That is . . . unusual."

Jewel was at sea in the discussion. She had just managed to understand that the numbers referred to five of the hundred holdings. She didn't know the latter two, but knew the former three quite well. It had never occurred to her to think of them as lands *held* or *owned* by the patriciate; the patriciate, with their fabled mansions and their obvious wealth, seemed to have nothing in common with her old life.

They certainly wouldn't be caught dead crossing any of the streets.

Devon said what Jewel was thinking but would never have dared to say. "Why is this of significance to this problem?" He gestured briefly around the room.

Since Jewel was entirely uncertain how any of the others, with the exception of the mage, had anything to do with the problem, she listened carefully.

"We believe that the magisterial courts have been corrupted within those holdings."

Devon's brows rose again; this time they rose higher and were slower to descend. If the abrupt turn in the conversation had given him pause, The Terafin's last statement had been a figurative slap in the face. She knew the expression, even if he mastered it far better than any of her den would.

"Oh? By whom?"

She didn't even pause, this woman who ruled the House. "Either by Patris Cordufar, who heads one of the richest of the noble families in the Empire, or by those who have managed to take advantage of him. Devon, you've met Cordufar."

He nodded. He was on his guard, even though he bore her House Name and in doing so, the implied duty to serve her. "I realize that you would never make such a statement without proof, but I must nevertheless ask why you've reached that conclusion."

"Of course," she replied, as if the almost-question was expected. She leaned over to the corner of the desk and lifted a small pile of papers from it. "These are the names of people who have been reported as missing throughout the holdings in the last decade." She set those down and picked up another document. "These are a list of people who have gone missing within the three poorer holdings that Cordufar holds during that same time."

He stood, walked to the desk, and retrieved both of the items she'd referenced so crisply. He read them both, and if he read quickly, he read carefully; Jewel could see his eyes moving as they scanned names. He frowned. He lifted the second document, the one that referred specifically to the three poor holdings.

"If these were not reported, how do you know they've gone missing?"

Jewel was frustrated; she wanted to read what he'd read.

"We have reason to believe that they *were* reported, at least initially. You'll want, of course, to read this as well." She added a third report to the two that still remained in his hands.

He took it and read it as well. Jewel sat on her hands. Literally.

"You suspect," he said, his voice quieter, "that whoever has been suppressing these reports is also involved with the disappearances." The words were flat, more of a statement than a question.

Everyone else in the room, even the foreigners, seemed to follow his logic. Jewel struggled to keep up.

"Why?" Lord Elseth asked. He turned to glare at his companion and fell silent.

"Because," Meralonne replied, "It's perfectly clear that whoever has been suppressing this information knows which disappearances he, she, or they are responsible for and which are random acts of violence."

Devon ATerafin put all three of the reports back on the desk. He did not, however, return to his seat. Instead, he faced The Terafin as if she were the only other person in the room.

"Terafin, I do not believe that this is House business alone. To imply that a lord of the patriciate has somehow managed to subvert the magisterial courts is a grave accusation, and possibly worse. A matter of this nature should be reported at once to the appropriate—"

"Be seated, Devon."

He sat.

"There is more, and I trust that you will understand why I say what I say when you have heard it."

"Terafin, please. I—"

"You will stand down! And," she added, her voice losing the sudden raw edge of power, "you will listen." She stood, then, and abandoned the separation provided by her desk.

"Have you heard stories of the demon-kin?"

Devon's expression was quiet, shorn of smile. He nodded, his eyes never leaving her face.

"Good. Because we believe that the people responsible for the destruction of the unreported missing persons are either demons or those in league with them. Meralonne can attest to the fact that many of the kin feel a need to . . . feed. If a mage—or more likely a House—has a collection of these creatures, it is quite likely that they will require some physical sacrifice."

"The Terafin is correct," Meralonne said quietly. He spoke without apparent concern, and although he glanced at Devon, his gaze shifted to the foreigners.

"Further," The Terafin continued, when Devon asked no questions, "we know for a fact that some of the demon-kin can assume not only the shape of a man, but also much of his identity and much of his memory. This is, of course, at the cost of the life of the one so imitated." She paused as if for breath, her voice cool and even.

Jewel flinched for both of them, but she didn't speak. She wanted to, though. Rath deserved better from her. From both of them.

"This is no illusion, Devon. Such an assumption is not magical in nature, and when looked for, no magic will be found."

Devon ATerafin, the man whose job was with the Trade Commission, paled. He had become completely still as the words faded into silence. "Reymaris' Sword," he whispered.

The Terafin did not appear to hear him. Given how she could fail to hear Meralonne at his loudest, Jewel knew it was deliberate.

"We do not know at which level the ranks of the Cordufar family have been infiltrated—but we know that upon the staff of the magisterial truthseekers, there was one who was no longer seeking truth." Her glance strayed, briefly, to Lord Elseth and his companion. She did not, to Jewel's regret, elaborate.

"Then we must find the summoner of these creatures," Devon said.

"Yes, we must. And we must do so with care and caution. I have already sent word, through all the channels that I have access to, that an assassination attempt was carried out, by magical means, against me. I have made it clear that there was a summoning of some sort, and I have offered the usual reward for information about the mage who accepted the job."

"In other words, you've done everything you can to appear as ignorant as possible."

"Yes. But I'm not at all sure that it will work."

"Why?"

"Because the man they killed and replaced—the man whose partial memories they own—was once my brother. We did not love each other overmuch in our later years, but we knew each other well."

"Ararath," Devon said softly.

The Terafin's bitter smile cut Jewel. She looked at Devon again, and this time, she looked closely. He *knew* who Rath was. No one else in the House seemed to have really heard of him before, but Devon *knew*.

Who was he?

"Meralonne APhaniel is one of a suspected half dozen of the mage-born who can easily detect these creatures for what they are. But he must be looking for it. Needless to say, most people will not.

"We cannot allow this information to be known; if people know of it, and know that they cannot detect these creatures easily, there will be panic. And the panic will be twofold." She turned, then, to look at Jewel, at Meralonne, and at the foreigners.

"First, people will begin to look for demons where none exist, and I fear that the innocent may well suffer in such a hunt, and second—and most important—if the kin are involved in higher levels of our own councils, they may feel the need to prematurely move against us, our House, and our supporters. We must leak information, and that information must be true; we must let them know that we are stymied in our search and that we suspect only the mage-born.

"I have begun a 'private' investigation into the mage-born members of the Order of Knowledge, to this end. I have also sent my operatives into the lower holdings to search for foreign mages who may have been involved in this black art."

"And why do we need to involve our foreign guests in our internal matters?"

"Because," The Terafin replied, "it seems that Stephen of Elseth—unlike Meralonne or any of the mage-born—can see the demon-kin without resorting to the use of spell. He does not need to search for the signs; if he can see the creature, we believe he will know it for what it is."

"What proof do you have of this?"

Jewel almost cringed at the question; Devon *must* be important in the House. No one else spoke to The Terafin in that tone of voice. But The Terafin didn't appear to notice.

Meralonne, however, replied. "For reasons that are not clear to me or to any of us, the demons are searching for Stephen and Lord Elseth. They were waiting at the western demi-wall for their arrival."

"Waiting? That implies they knew they would be here."

Stephen nodded and joined the conversation quietly. "We met them first in Breodanir. At the time, they were hunting Espere," he added, nodding quietly to the girl who sat on the floor. "She is not quite right, and we hoped to find both the answer to the question of why the demons hunted her and the cure to her condition—if it can be cured—here."

"And instead you have found that these creatures are here and hunting for you?"

"Yes."

"I see," Devon said softly. His gaze drifted to the center of the table, his expression shuttered and neutral.

The Terafin didn't give him much time to think. "The demon they met here wore the guise of a magisterial truthseeker. We have been able to ascertain which truthseeker; he has been in service to the courts for more than fifteen years." She returned to the chair behind her desk and sat slowly, watching Devon ATerafin. "Devon?"

"Yes," he told her, after a brief pause. "I understand it."

"And you understand that no word of this is to leave the House?"

"Are you so sure that this is a House affair?"

Jewel winced, certain of what was to follow.

"It does not matter if I am not," she said severely, as Meralonne grimaced in Devon's direction. "I gave you an order."

Devon was utterly silent, but to Jewel's surprise, so was Meralonne. It was rare; by this point in any discussion—most of which came down to the question of external information—he would have at least broken out his pipe and raised his voice a few notches.

"Devon, Patris Cordufar owes his loyalty to which House?"

"Darias."

"Indeed. Do you see?"

Jewel wanted to weep with frustration, because Devon nodded, and his silent nod brought her no closer to understanding. Darias was one of The Ten. This much she knew from Rath's lessons—the lessons that had seemed such a pointless waste of time.

The Terafin continued to speak. "It may indeed be that this matter is not solely a difficulty that my House must face. But to bring it to the attention of Kings, in the light of the assassination attempt, will cost us more than I wish to pay upon the Council. If it comes to that, it is a decision I will make."

Devon was silent for a long moment. Jewel couldn't understand why. When he finally spoke, his words—given The Terafin's—made almost no sense. "I will remain ATerafin if you judge me worthy."

Her expression made clear that she didn't value any questioning of her judgment; she did not relieve him of the House Name, however.

"As a member of your House of little rank and merit, I must ask a boon."

"Ask, then," she replied, as if she had expected—and prepared—for this much.

"It is not, unfortunately, of you that that favor must be asked." But he nodded to his lord before he turned his attention, and his gravity, toward the foreigners. "At court," he told Stephen, "there are two women, Lady Morgan and Lady Faergif; they are of the Breodani, and they traveled here when their sons inherited the responsibilities of their demesnes. They are sharp and canny in defense of the interests of your kingdom, and they have become accustomed to all things Essalieyanese. But if they learn that a

Hunter Lord has left Breodanir to travel to the Empire, they will wish to meet that lord—and, of course, his Huntbrother."

"You want us to go to Court?" Lord Elseth spoke with such obvious discomfort that Jewel felt a twinge of genuine sympathy; had she been asked the same thing, her horror would have been silent, but it would have been the same. In the stories she'd heard as a child, and admittedly ones that involved Court were rare, the nobles *belonged* there. She didn't. This man, however, *was* a noble.

Stephen shot him a look; it was dire. Lord Elseth failed to acknowledge it. "What he means, to say, Lord ATerafin—"

"Devon will do."

"Devon, then. What he means to say is that we are not attired or prepared for a court so complicated and unique as that of the Twin Kings, and he does not wish to insult."

Devon did smile at that. Jewel almost snorted.

"But he would come?"

"Yes, we would both *be happy* to accept your invitation."

"Good." Devon rose. "I must prepare for your dogs—they will be properly kenneled and cared for in the style to which they are accustomed." He bowed, and the bow was deep and formal—but it was entirely the wrong bow. Jewel had never seen its like before.

As if to underscore the foreign gesture, Devon then turned to The Terafin, and brought his arm to chest in a crisp salute. "Terafin."

"ATerafin," she replied, with a nod that acknowledged his respect. "We will speak again. You may have your day in the two courts, and then we must have your day in the streets of the city. We need to conceal what we do."

Devon ATerafin escorted Lord Elseth and his Huntbrother out of the room. Jewel watched them go, but only when the doors had closed did she relax.

She was troubled. She wasn't certain why, and it gnawed at her. Devon had called Stephen a Huntbrother; he had called Lord Elseth a Hunter Lord. She had seen neither of the two men in a vision or in the nightmares she sometimes called dreams.

But she had seen forest, and in that primal, dreaming vision, she had heard the desperate winding of horns. She had seen what emerged from those ancient trees: not men, but something larger, darker, something that defined bestial. Was *this* what that dream had referred to? These two men?

"Jewel, your report." The Terafin's tone of voice reminded Jewel that it wasn't only the future she had to fear.

She swallowed and forced her shoulders to straighten. Then she recounted the previous two days' worth of failure, trying to make it sound brisk, efficient, and busy. Trying to make it sound as if it were worth two solarii a day, plus fancier room and board than she had ever dreamed of.

"You work well, Jewel. I understand the difficulty you labor under, and I must add to it. We will no longer send out crews to the various sites that Ararath also mentioned in his letter."

Jewel stiffened; she hadn't been aware that anyone else was working on this at all. But she didn't question The Terafin. "Instead, I will send you out with Devon, and only Devon.

"You are to follow his commands in all things; if you feel that his command exceeds my wishes, you are nonetheless obligated to carry out his word. I will take your reports in my chambers, and I will entertain any concerns that you may have at that time. Do I make myself clear?"

When Jewel left The Terafin's official reception rooms, Torvan was in the hall. He was not loitering, not exactly; he stood as if he were on duty. But there were already guards on duty, and one of the things she had noticed about the guards was that they operated in pairs. He was a fifth.

As she passed through the four who did not apparently notice her departure, Torvan fell into step beside her, shortening his stride. He made a lot more noise just walking than she did, and if she were being fair, his armor didn't look more comfortable than the dress with its pinched sash. She wanted to head straight to her rooms to dump it, preferably in the nearest fireplace. Ellerson, on the other hand, would probably have volumes to say about that.

They made it halfway to the West Wing before Torvan cleared his throat quietly.

Jewel exhaled. "I didn't embarrass her," she told him curtly.

He winced.

"And yes, it was that obvious," she added. But she couldn't manage to walk ten yards nursing that particular annoyance; it was what she'd been terrified she'd do, after all.

"Torvan, do you know Devon ATerafin?" She glanced at his face when his silence had gone on just that little bit too long. "You do."

"I am acquainted in passing with most of the members of House Terafin," he replied.

"You must have seen him enter the room."

"I did."

"And you must have seen him leave."

"Indeed."

"What is he to The Terafin?"

"He is a member of her House," Torvan replied.

"He works in the Trade Commission?"

Torvan nodded. "He works in the offices of the Royal Trade Commission."

She hesitated. Her silence stretched out for at least as long as his had, but hopefully for different reasons; she was not supposed to discuss what she did at the behest of The Terafin with anyone *but* The Terafin and her mage.

But . . . the Chosen were often present when some of those discussions took place; they *had* to know.

As if he could hear the thought in the pleasant and oddly warm light of the gallery, Torvan said, "You are not to discuss your work."

"Can I discuss his, instead?"

"Not if it coincides with yours." Torvan grimaced. "Yes, we're aware of what you do, Jewel. We're not deaf. But we're The Terafin's Chosen; what we're permitted to know, we keep to ourselves. It's treason to do otherwise, and The Chosen are subject to the Laws of The Ten, and not the courts of the Empire."

"The Laws of the Ten?"

He glanced at her. "How much of our history do you understand?"

Because it was Torvan, she didn't bridle.

"You know that The Ten occupy a special position in the Empire."

Since *everyone* knew that, given the holidays, she allowed herself to grind her teeth a bit. She did, however, manage to nod.

"What we're told at the Gathering of the Ten is that they were granted special privileges by the Twin Kings because of their choice to war, alongside the first Kings, against the Blood Barons. In and of itself, this is true—but it's less clear which came first: the agreements or the service." His smile was slight, and wry. "House Law is, in its entirety, separate from Imperial Law, as long as no members outside of the House are involved.

"This allows, among other things, House Wars," he added, his voice dropping, the words trailing off. "Inasmuch as the victims of the struggle for succession are Terafin, their deaths are not investigated by the magisterial guards or courts without the express request of the ruler of the House.

"If, however, the House Lord requests such an intervention, the discoveries made during the investigation are *all* subject to Imperial Law. I've heard—we've *all* heard—Member APhaniel's many arguments with The Terafin. Understand that there is a reason she has not yet taken this to the Kings.

"She *is* the House, to us."

Jewel knew he meant the Chosen.

"And there has been no contest of her rule since she became The Terafin. But should she weaken the House by allowing the Kings access to all of its internal affairs, there would be." He shook himself. "I wander. What I meant to say is that the Chosen who break her confidence or her edict commit treason against the House, and at her discretion, they suffer the same penalties that treason against the Crowns incurs."

"That's not why you don't do it."

"No."

"And that's got nothing to do with Devon."

He exhaled. "Devon ATerafin specializes in the minutiae of the Trade Commission and its various grants; he is considered something of an expert."

"And why exactly would an expert in trade law be dragging me through the city streets?" She reddened. "Hypothetically."

"It is not all that he does. Understand that the House strength is measured by the competence of its members. Its members serve in various capacities in many of the guilds and in the Order of Knowledge; they are also merchants and craftsmen. As men and women with jobs external to the House and its politics, their loyalties are of necessity split between two duties.

"In some cases, those duties are very, very difficult to navigate." He paused. "We are at your rooms," he told her quietly. It was true. He hesitated for just a moment, and then said, "Ask Ellerson about the Astari."

She nodded.

"The Astari?"

Jewel almost took a step back at the tone of Ellerson's voice; the single word was sharp and harsh, and his eyebrows had flexed, both rising and falling in ways that were almost unseen on his face.

"Why are you asking about the Astari?"

Torvan told me to ask you. She did not, however, say this out loud. "I heard the word in passing."

He lifted one gray brow in open disbelief, and she had the grace to redden and look at the carpets, which had the advantage of actually being visually interesting.

"Do not, if you have any choice in the matter, become involved with the Astari."

"Why? What or who are they?"

He shook his head. She had come upon him in the rooms that he generally occupied when he wasn't herding the den from one place to another, and he now lifted an obviously used rag and began to polish a silver goblet. "I like to keep busy," he said, by way of explanation. "And the servants have not yet complained about my work."

"I don't think they're allowed to."

"They are absolutely not allowed to complain to *you*," he replied firmly. "I, however, am almost one of their number."

She highly doubted it, but she kept that to herself. "The Astari?"

"They are the personal guards of the Twin Kings."

"You mean, like the Chosen?"

"No, they are nothing like the Chosen."

"But—"

"Guard is a euphemism. You are familiar with that word?"

"Maybe."

He frowned. "They serve the Kings, and they protect them. The protection they provide is seldom the simple protection of sword and shield; the Kings' Swords are in *Avantari* for that purpose."

"So . . . what do they do?"

He set his work aside and pinched the bridge of his nose. "They watch. They spy, where they can, upon people of power within the Empire, most of whom are concentrated within Averalaan, but not all. When it becomes necessary, they are rumored to remove possible threats."

"Remove?"

"Assassinate."

Her brows rose. "But—but that's—"

"They distrust everyone," Ellerson continued, with a slight nod as

Jewel failed to come up with the appropriate word. "They owe loyalty only to their duties and to the Kings, and even the word of the Kings does not always supercede those duties; they have some discretion in their pursuits.

"They are very, very ill-loved," he added.

"And if—if I were to be . . . introduced . . . to a member of the Astari, what would it mean?"

Ellerson watched her carefully. "Have you been?"

She was silent.

"If you were to be called upon or questioned by the Astari, you would meet only one man. The head of the Astari, and its only public face: Duvari. You would not be allowed to speak with him alone," Ellerson said softly. "The Terafin would not allow it, and the Kings could not overrule her."

Jewel frowned. "She wouldn't have that jurisdiction."

His frown deepened.

"I'm not ATerafin."

"Then avoid them, while you can."

"Ellerson—"

"But if you do not meet Duvari, the Astari will ask you no obvious questions. It is why you *must* learn to guard your tongue."

"Not in the House—"

"In the House. On the street. In parlors. In taverns. In the Common and in the High Market."

She fell silent, considering the full weight of his words. "Here?" she asked, at last.

"No. Here, oddly enough, it is safe to dissemble. No domicis has ever served as Astari. No man can serve two masters."

She hesitated. "You're certain?"

He said nothing, and after a minute, she apologized. He nodded. "Very well. Let us pretend, for the sake of discussion, that you will have some contact with the Astari. If the contact you have is not Duvari, you will not know."

"But—"

"But it is likely that The Terafin will suspect. Jewel, I have heard your many and varied arguments with Member APhaniel of the Order of Knowledge. It is a constant surprise to me that most of the House has not heard them. And I am using the word 'varied' kindly in this instance."

"Sorry, Ellerson. But he—"

"If you say, 'He started it,' I shall be disappointed."

"Yes, Ellerson."

"If, however, The Terafin is aware of the possibility that she has introduced you to one who serves the Astari, and she accepts the risk, there is one clear reason for taking it."

She waited.

"And I want you to tell me what you think it is."

She hated these questions and almost regretted asking him for the information. But his expression was serious, and she realized that in *this* place, even speaking was probably a test. A test that, if she wanted to stay here, she couldn't afford to fail.

So she thought. If there were an outsider in her den, and he was, essentially, spying on it, why would The Terafin want him there at all?

"If The Terafin thinks that what we're looking for is a threat to the Empire, and not just the House," she said quietly, "and she can't take this information directly to the people who would use it, she could let them find out for themselves."

Ellerson graced her with a genuine smile. "Indeed," he said. His voice didn't match his expression. It was grave.

"I don't understand the politics."

"Not yet, but you're learning. Jewel—"

"How big is this going to get?"

"You're searching for demons," he replied.

"I'm searching for the undercity."

He said nothing.

"You think finding one will be finding the other."

He nodded. "Be wary," he told her.

Chapter Four

3rd of Corvil, 410 A.A.
Order of Knowledge, Averalaan Aramarelas

SIGURNE MELLIFAS, the presiding ruler of the Order of Knowledge, felt her age keenly in the stuffy and quiet rooms of her chilly tower. She sat behind a well-worn desk, and although the usual piles of official paperwork girded its sides, she was concerned with a single, spare document that lay directly between her still hands. It awaited only her seal and the magical identification that would indicate that it was genuine.

She had yet to apply either, and she rose. The tower had windows, but while tall, they were narrow, and she found them as confining as her desk, her chair, and the duty that she had made her life. No matter how vigilant she was, no matter how carefully she observed, she would be unequal to that duty; the proof of that lay before her now, its spare, austere, and formal words all the accusation required.

So much had happened in the last month.

Ararath Handernesse's death cast a long shadow. She had known he would face death. Had even gone so far as to warn him, time and again; he would not be moved. And because he would not be moved, she had used his rage and his cunning, and he had given her the information she desired.

But he had given her, as well, information that she could not have known existed: the brief and mysterious vision of gods in the streets of Averalaan. She was by nature a skeptical and pragmatic woman; she could hold fear at bay as she worked, because fear in the end was not practical.

But the Hunter Lords had come to the city, and in their wake, the demons had revealed themselves. Rath's vision, or rather, the vision that he had shared, had spoken of two: the Hunter God and the Lord of the Hells.

What part has the Order played, in ignorance? What did we foster here? What knowledge of ours, what ancient writings, have brought us to this pass?

When the delicate lattice just above her door began to glow, she welcomed the interruption. The welcome was unusual. She was not Meralonne; she did not snap, snarl, or on occasion open herself up to reprimand for inappropriate displays of magic. But she did not precisely enjoy a steady stream of interruptions, because for the most part anyone who was willing to engage in them did so for the slightest of reasons.

She rose and went to the door, choosing, as she most often did, to open it by hand. Some of the younger mages felt this simple—and decidedly unmagical—act was beneath her dignity. They did not, however, complain about this to her; she heard it from other sources and often diverted those discussions into minor complaints about the attitude of the young and inexperienced.

It was not the young and inexperienced that she now faced.

She opened the door to Meralonne APhaniel, glanced at his grim expression, and stepped to one side to allow him to enter. She then retreated to her desk, and he took one of the two chairs that faced it, placing both feet firmly upon the other.

"Have you any word about our rogue mage?" he asked her, coming directly to what she assumed was the point. Word had, no doubt, escaped since the full council meeting at which the writ was demanded. Word, she thought grimly, of the Hunter Lords, their claim of demons, and their accusations of forbidden magic in the hands of a member of the Order of Knowledge stationed in the Kingdom of Breodanir, was even now filtering, in distorted whispers, throughout the Order's halls.

She could not put a stop to rumor, and even at her most bored, she would have hesitated to try. All she could do now lay on her desk awaiting only her signature.

She shook her head. "None. We have ascertained that Krysanthos was indeed in Breodanir, as the Hunter Lord claimed; he was there as part of the research team."

Meralonne's opinion of such teams—which were often comprised of simple scholars as well as the mage-born—was low. And commonly known. "Did he leave behind anything that might give us some hint of the identity of his allies?"

"We are working on it now. There were, however, deaths."

Meralonne shrugged. Death did not disturb him. But unlike many with such a cavalier attitude toward life—one that Sigurne did not, and would never, share—he had no particular attachment to his own; she thought he might run toward death with gravity and a strange, uncanny joy, possibly because he was powerful, and so certain of his power that death was always a gamble, never a certainty, no matter what form it took.

He glanced at the writ that lay in the center of her desk. Meralonne, unlike most of the magi who came to her tower, did not pretend he could not read words when they were upside down. She found it refreshing. "Krysanthos." He frowned. "I am not entirely familiar with the member."

"He was not a First Circle mage."

"Second?"

"It is irrelevant. He was not considered a great power."

"I do not consider him one, now. But we have witnesses to his culpability. I consider them credible."

"We would hardly have the writ," she said, her voice cool and dry, "if the witnesses were not deemed credible."

"It is of interest to me that Krysanthos' activity was confined to the Western Kingdoms; he did not do his work at the heart of the Empire."

She raised a brow. "No. He did not. Why is this of interest to you? The Breodani?"

Meralonne nodded.

"Meralonne?"

He reached into the folds of his robes and drew out his pipe. She did not tell him to set it aside, but it was tempting; it had already been a long and difficult day, and these games of petty annoyance were wearing.

"The Terafin will not allow us to openly approach the Kings."

"No. But you did not expect her acquiescence."

"And when the games were smaller, Sigurne—or when my understanding of their possible significance was—I was willing to bide my time. I believe," he continued, "that the time we now have is very, very short." He paused. "She has, however, opened both an investigation and the possibility of censure in the Council Hall against Lord Cordufar. I believe some discreet inquiries are now ongoing within the Magisterium."

Sigurne nodded. "How discreet?"

"I do not think, in the end, it will matter; the Magisterium is not directly connected with The Terafin. Were we able to find some proof that demons exist within their ranks, and that magisterial guards in the three holdings have been subverted, we would have what we need to move openly and quickly."

"The Terafin grants what she can," Sigurne replied.

"She is, at the moment, our only unimpeachable witness. What she saw, the Kings will not doubt, either privately or in public. But," he added, grudgingly, "she specifically instructed Devon ATerafin to convey the foreigners to the Twin Courts."

"The Hunter Lord and his Huntbrother?"

Meralonne nodded. As this was what they had hoped for, Sigurne found his lack of any satisfaction troubling.

He lined the bowl of his pipe with care, but he did not light it. "The Hunter Lord, the Huntbrother, and the wild girl, who is at the heart of this mystery. Teos, Lord of Knowledge, told one of his sons that she was god-born." He paused, and then added, "Hunter-born. She is the living daughter of the Hunter God."

"The Breodani god."

"Yes. You see the difficulty?"

She did. Despite many, many decades of study in the Western Kingdom of Breodanir, no proof, no solid proof, that the Hunter God *was* a god had been found. His worship was strong, but so, too, was the worship of the Southern Lady; people's beliefs and the truth often failed to coincide.

Yet if Teos, a true god, claimed that the Hunter God, who did not in theory exist, had fathered a living child, they had miscalculated. She glanced more sharply at Meralonne APhaniel. "There is more," she said.

"There is more." He was silent for a long moment, and when at last he spoke, he lifted the unlit pipe to his lips, waiting. The pipe, today, was not a red flag; it was meant as a comfort. The day, which had been long and stressful, suddenly darkened.

"Smoke, if it eases you."

"Thank you." The leaves burned, brief and orange, cupped in his hand. "The Huntbrother can, indeed, see the kin without recourse to ancient magics."

"So you've said." And his role in the Twin Court, as envoy, was the only apolitical way they might inspect the Court for the possibility of demonic presence.

"I do not know how or why, but I can guess." He raised his head; smoke came in a thin stream from his lips, but he did not blow rings; his thought was upon his words, and their choice. She had never labored under the illusion that he spoke all of what he knew.

"The Huntbrother is oathbound, Sigurne."

She frowned. "I do not think I know the term."

"I forget myself. You have a great understanding of ancient and lost arts, but it is narrowly focused." He rose, still clutching his pipe. "The gods of the Empire *are* gods; as proof, we have their children, and their children can bespeak them when it is needful.

"This can only happen because the gods exist in the half-world, between our two lands. It is there that the children go, and there that we are summoned. That has been our test of gods for as long as the Empire has studied them."

She nodded.

"But the wild girl is Hunter-born."

"There was never, in the history of the gods, a Hunter God."

"No."

"Meralonne—"

"But there was a God of Oaths, Sigurne, in the time before the gods chose to depart these lands."

She did not ask him how he knew. The gods themselves were remarkably reticent about speaking of the world that had existed before they had chosen to withdraw from it.

"The God of Oaths was called Bredan, in the Old Weston style. The Hunter Lords call themselves the Breodani." Meralonne hesitated for a moment and then set his pipe's stem between his lips. He was silent, as if lost in thought, and she found it oddly comforting. So much about this man was, to her.

But when he spoke again, all comfort was lost. "Bredan was the God of the Covenant," he said quietly.

The Covenant.

"When the gods agreed to leave this world to the living, they undertook one last task; they remade the world, and they sundered its ability to easily sustain them. But this was not enough.

"Bredan took the oaths of the gods, and he bound them into the Covenant. They cannot, with ease, return to the world while he holds their oaths, and if he is aware of their passage, he can prevent it." He paused.

"But it is said that at least three gods did not agree to the oath-binding, although they, like the others, drifted from the world.

"Bredan, the Keeper. Neamis, who is called Mystery or Destiny, and about whom very little is known."

She lifted a hand, as if to ward off the last name, the last god. She knew well who it must be.

He nodded, acknowledging both her gesture and her sudden, visceral fear. But he was Meralonne. "Teos offered one other warning to the Hunter Lords and his son.

"The Lord of the Hells is no longer upon his throne."

She closed her eyes.

"But there is hope, if it is dim," he said, when the silence had continued for just long enough. "I said, and will say again, that the Huntbrother, Stephen of Elseth, is oathbound. He could not be so if the god himself had not accepted his oath."

"What oath?" she whispered. She rose. The chair was small and confining, the tower room too dark. She felt trapped by his words, by the weight of what they presaged.

"I am not entirely certain," he replied. "But I have done some reading and some research; I have visited the Twin Courts and spent some time with the Breodani envoys. They are all, without exception, women; the men, it seems, do not leave the borders of Breodanir."

"These two have."

"Yes. Lady Faergif was suitably shocked. As she is a somewhat canny—and suspicious—woman, it was difficult to engage her in conversation. However, when it became clear to her that the only information I was interested in was, in fact, information that even a Breodani peasant knows, she was willing to speak."

"And that information?"

"The Hunter Lords choose a Huntbrother for their sons. They choose a boy of the same age as their son, and they choose him from farms, or the streets of the city, or even the orphanages; they adopt these boys. The Huntbrother is therefore not noble by birth, but when the family adopts him, he is raised as one. He is, in all ways except blood, brother to the Hunter. He will have some say in his Hunter's marriage, and he will hunt by his side until one or the other fails."

She nodded.

"The Hunter Lords do not travel, and they do not travel at this time of year; it is too close, Lady Faergif said, to the Sacred Hunt."

"This is a . . . ritual?"

"It is more than that, Sigurne. But how much more, I do not think any of us has clearly understood, until now. The Sacred Hunt is called, in the Sacred Grove in the King's city, once a year. It is called upon the first day of Veral. All Hunter Lords who wish to retain their titles and their lands must travel to the King's city at this time, and all Hunter Lords must participate in this Hunt.

"She had much to say about the horn calls and the rituals that mark the beginning of the Sacred Hunt, about the drums and the hunted beasts themselves and what they signify. I did not interrupt her, because I did not want to alarm her; I will, however, spare you the grueling details.

"During this Sacred Hunt, one man will die. He will face what the Breodani call the Hunter's Death. It is, by all accounts, not a pleasant death, but when the death itself is discovered, it signals the end of the Sacred Hunt. The fallen man is honored, and he is returned to his lands by a contingent of Breodani Hunter Lords.

"He is honored," Meralonne added, "because he has fulfilled the Breodani oath—the ancient oath—to their god. Once a year, the Hunter God hunts his own. For the rest of the year, he protects and succors them."

"It sounds barbaric," she said at length. "A human sacrifice."

"It is."

"And it continues, even now?"

"This is the interesting part," he replied, carefully tapping ash out of his pipe and then lining it again. "One King, influenced by foreigners, decided to forego the Sacred Hunt. For three years, he refused to call it. The land withered slowly. The crops failed.

"And when the Sacred Hunt was finally called, there were not three simple deaths—there were a hundred. It was a slaughter. There are stories from that hunt that speak of the Hunter's Death as a giant, fearsome beast, a ravening, hungry god with claw and fang and fur; there is nothing remotely human about the description. Nor, apparently, about those deaths." He paused and then said, "But after those deaths, the land once again became fecund, and after those deaths, the Kings—for the old King, I believe, perished—have called the Sacred Hunt without fail."

"So the Huntbrother is oathbound? But not the Hunter Lord?"

He lifted a hand, and a thin stream of smoke trailed from between his lips. "Yes. To both questions. But this story does have a point, though a long and winding one.

"The Huntbrothers swear an oath when they take the title of Huntbrother. I do not have the exact oath to hand," he added, "but the gist of it, buried among all the *other* vows a boy of eight or ten is expected to make to his adoptive family, is that he will face death in the place of his Hunter.

"During the Sacred Hunt, if the Hunter Lord dies at the hands of the Hunter's Death—and hands, in this case, is entirely figurative, I assure you—the Huntbrother always follows. He dies a wasting, consumptive death. There has, as far as the members of the Order in Breodanir are aware, been no exception."

"This is known?"

"It is not entirely clear that the Hunters understand the significance." He inhaled pipe smoke and blew it out in a thin, focused stream. "Because there is a bond between Hunter Lord and Huntbrother that not even the magi understand. It is more than simple empathy. In the history of the Breodani, *many* Hunter Lords and *many* Huntbrothers have died following the loss of their brother in many hunts, not only the Sacred Hunt. The dogs," he added, "frequently refuse to eat as well."

"Dogs?"

"Ah. Yes. They treat their hunting dogs as valued personal retainers, and they expect them to be treated that way when they travel. Which is probably the other reason they don't travel outside their borders. There was a brief incident in the dining hall when the Hunters arrived here; if you have not heard about it yet, you no doubt will. But I digress.

"The fact that the death of one is frequently followed by the death of the other buries the significance of the Sacred Hunt to those who have no knowledge of gods, of convenants, and of the ways in which a world that once existed for the amusement of the gods now defies the gods' will." Smoke became a thickening veil in the confines of the room as he hesitated.

"It is my suspicion—and it is only a suspicion, based as it is on little fact—that the god of the Breodani *is* Bredan. In few other ways could the Huntbrother be oathbound. If the Huntbrothers *are* oathbound, as I suspect they are, and they wither and die if they fail their oath, then their god is Bredan, long absent from the heavens."

She waited. Meralonne APhaniel was not a mage known for his patience or his humility, and with just cause. Exposing ignorance—when it was his own—was not a thing that came easily; not for Meralonne the dissembling and the feigned forgetfulness Sigurne often found it convenient to adopt.

"We do not know how the changes in this world affect the gods," he finally said. "There has been no clear way to study it, and only the ancient—and long dead—mages wasted their time on such theories. The gods were gone; there was no practical reason to attempt such a study." He inhaled again, and again he hesitated. It was unusual.

"However, one of those theoreticians—and if you have any pressing interest, I believe I can find some of his work in the library, but it would take some time—felt that the world itself was bled, in some way, of some essential divinity. Whether this occurred because the gods left or before they left, he was not entirely certain.

"But you are aware of the long game of the *Kialli* and their Lord. The last of that divinity, the last of the eternal, exists *within* mortals, passing from lifetime to lifetime until it, too, sunders ties with this plane.

"What the gods require to function upon this world, they must take," he continued, still musing, still quiet. "And I believe it is just possible that *if* Bredan had made the long and difficult journey to return to this world—and it would be an act of decades, not of hours or days—he would have found that the world was hostile.

"The gods do not think, or dream, or live as you live," he added, softly. "And I think—again, without substantive proof—that *if* Breodanir is Bredan, he might have had to consume, or devour, the living souls, the small shards of divinity, within mortals in order to be able to think, to live, and to act *here*.

"Once a year, without fail, Sigurne."

"The Sacred Hunt," she whispered.

"Even so." He paused. "I do not think he intended to remain in this world. But . . . if the wild girl is in truth his daughter, then he is here."

"And if he is here—"

"The Lord of the Hells is not upon his throne."

She closed her eyes.

"It is theory," he said, and she heard his soft words at a distance.

"And do you feel it to be the truth?"

"I?"

She opened her eyes slowly and sat heavily on her desk; for the moment, even walking around it to the comfort of her chair felt beyond her. "There is no one else in this room," she told him.

"Yes."

"Meralonne—"

"The Sacred Hunt," he continued, as if there had been no pause, no shadowed silence, "is called without fail in the Western Kingdoms, where the Breodani reside. Krysanthos showed an interest in the wild girl, and in all things Breodani, long before this hidden city came to light.

"But here, and now, when word of Allasakar has reached us, and the shadowed mention of a fallen city haunts House Terafin and possibly far more of the city than anyone could guess, I think the Hunter Lord—and, far more significant, his Huntbrother—have arrived for a reason."

She watched him.

"That reason?"

"I am not entirely certain, not yet." The familiar lines of frustration now etched themselves into his brow and the corners of his mouth. "But I will know more." He glanced at the desk. "The writ of execution remains unsigned, Sigurne."

She returned, then, to her chair. "I do not understand men who seek power," she told him, lighting a candle with a simple twist of her hand. "Can they not see that in the end, all power they are granted in such a fashion diminishes them?"

"No. Of course they can't. They daydream their way to death."

"If it were only their own deaths," she said, heating and melting wax, "I would not mind nearly so much." She laid it against the writ and then pressed her seal into it.

"No," he replied. "You would not. It says much about you, Sigurne. Even when you betrayed your teacher in the Northern Wastes, you were prepared to die for what you knew. For what you had done."

"I am prepared to die now," she told him grimly. But her expression was dark, her color pale.

"Yes. But in both cases, Sigurne Mellifas, your death would be a waste." He smiled then. It was a cool smile, but it held as much approval as he ever showed. "If you face your death, it will be because the city has fallen."

"And you?"

He nodded, his lips curved in a strange, fey smile.

*   *   *

The lattice above the door shifted, breaking the moment. Meralonne, always sensitive to the warp and weft of her protective spells, raised a brow.

"Word," she told him softly, gazing a moment at the patterns.

He approached the closed door. "May I?"

"Please," she said, with genuine gratitude, "do."

He opened the door, and his shoulders stiffened. But he said, "I suppose you will be excused any interruption; Sigurne is far too indulgent." He stepped out of the way, and as he did, she saw that Matteos stood in the door's frame, looking grim.

There had already been little joy in the day; she could not imagine what he could possibly say that could make it worse—but his expression indicated that he meant to try.

"What news, Matteos?" she asked.

He had known her for many years, and she saw that her tone, which she had made as gentle and neutral as she possibly could, had conveyed something to him; he hesitated. But after a moment, he entered the tower room and waved the door shut.

"This is not official news," he told her quietly.

They were not promising first words. "Continue."

"Official word may travel, but it may not; we're not sure how much will leave *Avantari*."

"*Avantari?*"

Matteos nodded.

"The Kings?"

"No. The Kings were not harmed."

"What happened?"

"There was some sort of attack—magical in nature—that involved the Breodani lord and his retainer. They were not the perpetrators," he added, seeing her expression, "but the intended victims."

"What magic, Matteos?"

"Fire," he replied. "The Hunters survived. The would-be assassin did not."

"Good."

"Duvari of the Astari was seen."

Bad. She did not, however, feel the need to state this clearly.

4th of Corvil, 410 A.A.
Terafin Manse, Averalaan Aramarelas

The Terafin manse did not boast large front grounds; on the Isle, where land was expensive and much coveted, it was not practical. What land there was, and it was extensive, was reserved for the use of The Terafin, and in it resided her many gardens, her pavilions, and her summer stage.

Nestled within the gardens, the path almost obscured by the careful placement of trees, was the Terafin House shrine. It was not the only shrine within the garden; that would be an act of arrogance. Nor was it the first; to come to the Terafin shrine, one must pass the three others: the shrine of the Mother, the shrine of Reymaris, Lord of Justice, and the shrine of Cormaris, Lord of Wisdom.

Each of these shrines quartered the garden of contemplation, but the last of these—unless one wished to enrage the gardeners by ignoring the carefully laid stones of the path—one arrived at by first paying respects to the other three.

He waited in silence. It was not a patient silence, but there was no one to note it, no one to criticize. The moons were high, and the air was cool. Would she come?

Ah, patience, patience. She was new, and she was young; the grounds, she had barely touched. Which was appropriate; she was a guest here, a visitor; she did not feel secure enough to wander. He knew. He had waited in silence in the evening hours for almost a fortnight, and if it was necessary, he would wait longer.

It was not, after all, the first time he had waited in this fashion.

He glanced at the small altar beneath the rounded dome of the dais that formed the Terafin House shrine. The stone was flat and cool; it was not adorned by gold or jewels. The dome itself was simple, if curved, and lamps—not magelights—flickered above it, evenly spaced along the circular rim.

He stood behind it.

This evening, however, the waiting bore fruit.

He felt her presence upon the path of the garden of contemplation. He knew, by her movement and by the cessation of that movement, when she had reached the Mother's shrine. She paused there for minutes. What she offered, he did not know; nor did he care. It was not for show that she stopped; there were no witnesses, here.

She started to walk again, and he could almost time the steps, could almost mark the moment when they would stop again. The second shrine. Reymaris, Lord of Justice. Here, too, she paused. What she offered Reymaris, he also did not know, but he could guess. So many people offered their pain, their anger, and their outrage to a god who understood justice. Sometimes they forgot that Justice and Vengeance were not the same; he wondered if this girl would likewise forget. She was young.

It did not surprise him that her pause at the third shrine, the one that honored the Lord of Wisdom, was so brief. It was, on the other hand, The Terafin's most sought shrine.

A life could be marked, and the changes in it noted, simply by the length of time one spent at each shrine, for it changed with the passage of years; one sought different things from the gods one worshiped as one aged. Here and now, she marked herself as young.

But she continued past the three shrines, as he had hoped she would, coming at last to this one: the shrine of House Terafin. Very few were the House members who came here. The Chosen, of course, at least once, but beyond that? It was a private, quiet place.

He watched her face as she approached, for she approached hesitantly at first, looking at the round, concentric circles that were the steps; the marble, pale and almost reflective in the lamplight caught and reflected her wavering form. She looked up to the dome, as if seeking the symbols that girded it; there were none.

She came closer, and closer still; he looked at her slightly freckled face, her pale skin, the hair that sun had tinted red. It was an auburn that would fade to brown without the touch of light. She pushed it out of her eyes now, and it fell back almost instantly.

Mounting the stairs, she came to stand to one side of the altar itself, searching for some mark that would identify it. She would, of course, find none.

But as her search yielded nothing, her frown deepened, and at last she reached out to touch the smooth, flat stone, as if her palms could force it to surrender the identity of its god.

He spoke then, in a measured, quiet voice. "Do not touch it unless you have something to offer."

She startled at the sound of his voice, jumping back until her heels skirted the edge of the round dais and, therefore, the top of the stairs.

He stepped out of his perpetual shadow, carrying a raised torch, as if he might signal a distant, watchful god with its light.

When she saw his face, she relaxed. Interesting, that; the armor that he wore, with its stylized, raised helm, its polished plate breast and greaves, did not seem to discomfit her at all. But she seemed to recognize him, and as that had been his intent, he made no comment.

"If I had something to offer, who would I be offering it to?"

Bold child. He smiled. "You would be offering it to the spirit that guards Terafin."

She snorted and even started to chuckle, but he had no like mirth to offer her, and his gravity leeched the laughter from her voice. "What spirit?"

"Well, rumor has it that the founder of Terafin watches over it still."

"Bet that's news to Mandaros."

He cringed, but inwardly; outwardly, this unfamiliar face smiled down at her. "Perhaps, perhaps not. What we know of the gods and the life beyond is not perfect, Jewel." What he had denied her, he now did himself; he walked to the altar until he rested against its familiar stone edge. "Every guard that is Chosen places his arms and armor here; they offer their service and possibly their lives to protect Terafin. If the spirit exists, he grants them his blessing in return."

She frowned. "Why would he?"

It was not entirely the question he had expected. "Why would he what?"

"Why would he want to stay here and watch?"

"I don't know," he said quietly. It was even, in some part, the truth, although truth, like any ancient thing, was complicated and often contradictory. He looked beyond her slender shoulders for a moment, to the grounds; they had changed much in his tenure, and no doubt, they would change again. Even the manse was different; it was much, much larger than it had once been, although the heart of it remained.

"If you died, would you not want to watch over your den?"

If her question had been unexpected, his was both that and unwelcome; he saw that instantly in the way she retreated while standing in place. "I don't know," she said, voice thick. "I haven't done that good a job so far."

This, he understood. "You brought them here to safety, and you protect them while they are here. What more could you do?"

"I didn't bring them all," she said, after a pause in which he feared her silence would remain unbroken. "I lost Duster. And before that—before I even knew what was going on—I lost Lefty and Fisher. Even when I had suspicions, I still lost Lander." She reached out and touched the altar, and this time he did not stop her.

What she offered in the gesture, he could—barely—accept.

"Do you think that people in your service shouldn't die?"

"They don't *serve* me."

He raised a brow, then. "They do. They follow you, they obey you, and they trust you." The middle was perhaps a bit of a stretch, but they obeyed her to the best of their stunted abilities, and she was wise enough—or perhaps canny enough, or perhaps even just lucky enough—that she did not push them for more.

"All right! Yes, I think they shouldn't die." She lifted her hand from the stone surface and shoved it, and the other, into the belt that encircled her tunic. This act of defiance did not comfort her, and she turned away from his watchful eyes. "If I deserved their trust, they wouldn't have. I hate it. I hate that they trust me, and I hate that I failed."

"Then let them go."

She stilled. The anger had not fled, but it had been shunted, briefly, to one side by, of all things, surprise. "What?"

"Send them away. Refuse to take their service. Cast them off."

"I can't do that—what would they do?"

"What did they do without you? They survived, and I imagine that they will survive again."

The anger that had clung to her from the moment she set foot in the garden of contemplation now died. "I know what you're trying to do," she said softly. "And you don't have to do it."

"No? Jewel, do you think they hold you responsible for the deaths of their den-mates?"

"No."

"Good. But you hold yourself responsible."

Wearily she met his gaze and held it. "Yes." The single word was almost inaudible, but he would have heard it in the winter gales. For a moment, in his vision, the altar was limned in a light that traveled its perimeter; it waited only a dedication.

But that, he thought, would not come yet.

"Good. You aren't, and you are. You did not kill them, but had you not chosen them from the streets—and chosen, I think, well—they would not have died at the hands of demon-kin."

"Thanks." Her lips twisted in a bitter grimace that did not suit the youth of her face.

"Remember this feeling because to The Terafin, the House *is* her den. You don't understand her—or so you think—but you have more in common than you know."

He watched her struggle with what she assumed was a simple compliment; she had nothing to offer in return, but it took her some minutes to accept this.

"Why did you come here tonight?"

She glanced at the altar, at the domed ceiling, and at his face. "I'm having nightmares. I've been having them a lot recently. All of my dead come back to me; they surround me and try to take me with them."

"Ghosts?"

"No. Walking corpses. Ghosts, I think I could live with."

"Corpses?"

"Yes."

"You are certain that they are dead?" For he understood the precarious nature of her dreams.

"Look, they're *my* dreams."

"Interesting. Do you always have such morbid nightmares?"

"Only when I've lost over a third of my kin," she snapped. She stopped, relaxing the fists her hands had become. "I'm sorry, Torvan. I know you're trying to help, and I know what you've told me is true—but it—it makes it harder."

"I know." He did not speak again of the altar; nor did he speak of what she might, in the end, offer at it. "Stay at the shrine, if you will. Don't let me disturb you. But Jewel: Trust your instincts."

5th of Corvil, 410 A.A.
The Common, Averalaan

Devon ATerafin was *not* Meralonne APhaniel, a fact that should have brought Jewel joy, given how often she and the mage disagreed. But the mage was so obviously irritable, so obviously bored, or so obviously annoyed, you *knew* where you stood with him. With Devon ATerafin? You knew precisely what he wanted you to know, and for the better part of two days, that had been exactly *nothing*. He could be charming to a fault, but he clearly didn't feel that charm was necessary for her sake; she only saw it when it was applied to other people.

He was well spoken, polite, and attractive in the way that men who are utterly certain of their own power are. It was not a character trait that Jewel found compelling.

But to be fair, she didn't find the mage-born all that compelling anymore, either. Working with Meralonne—and the occasional member of Terafin called in to examine, of all things, the *dirt* in the various entrances to the undercity that had once—and no longer—existed—magic had lost its mystery. If Meralonne was anything to go by, mages used magic to light their bloody pipes.

Devon didn't smoke.

He had fumed, however, when she told him where she intended to take him. They had discussed it the previous afternoon, on their return from his first outing, and he had—politely—declined. She had—much less politely—pointed out that there weren't a lot of other places left, and most of those involved the ancient cathedrals that stood in the hundred holdings.

She'd intended to let him choose. She honestly had.

And she wasn't certain why, in the end, she had insisted on the Merchant Authority—because she didn't actually want to be here. It was far too crowded, for one, and it had too damn many guards. They couldn't easily approach it in the dark, after hours, so the possibility of witnesses was high.

But although she told him he could pick the site, in the end, she had withdrawn the offer; she would take him to the Merchant Authority, and its old basement entrance. Or she'd stay home.

He'd raised one brow, where Meralonne would have raised both his voice and his pipe. But after five minutes of cold, measured silence, he had inclined his head.

"Be ready early," he told her. "We'll have to prepare."

That should have been a clue.

She grimaced and adjusted her dress. She didn't even like dresses, and she found this one annoying; it was the Northern idea of what Southern commoners dressed like. It wasn't actually *real*. Added to that indignity were the large earrings—which didn't actually sit on her lobes because, unlike many of the women of Devon's acquaintance, Jewel didn't have holes in her ears—a scarf around her head, and gold-plated chain loops for a "belt" around her waist. It wasn't much of a belt, in her opinion; it certainly wasn't there to hold anything up.

Although she had to grudgingly admit that the hooks that fell from the chain links were convenient; they carried a waterskin and a couple of empty pouches. Beneath these, she wore a dagger. It was not her usual dagger; she wore that on the other side, refusing to be parted from it.

But Devon had given her a knife, and he had told her not to draw or use it unless they were cornered. By what, he had failed to specify. But his failure, the quality of his silence, had almost frightened her, and she had taken the dagger—which seemed awkward and unbalanced—without further comment.

Her hair, which was flyaway on the best of days, was loose; had it been summer, it would have been a standing mass of dense curls. As it was, it was irritating. Almost everything was today.

It was *hard* to be here.

She knew the Common. The den knew it. Even this close to the Merchant Authority, she was aware of the way the streets turned and aware of the gates, the guards, and the placement of the various stalls and storefronts. She knew which part of the Common had High Market pretensions, but she avoided those; she knew which parts were reserved for people who sold their services as fortune-tellers, a practice that had galled and infuriated her Oma.

But she also knew which parts housed the farmers, and in particular, could trace an exact path to Farmer Hanson. Devon had not been at all pleased when she had entered the Common and started to head that way, her feet carrying her on a familiar route while her thoughts were elsewhere.

She was not here to speak with Farmer Hanson. It had been weeks since she'd seen him at all, and she knew he'd be worse than worried. But Devon had been quite clear: She could come to the Common on her own time.

Of course, her own time started after the Common, and in particular Farmer Hanson, was closed for the day. Every day. Without fail.

It was probably, she thought pensively, a good thing. He'd take one look at the outlandish way she was dressed, and he'd give Devon the suspicious once-over. She couldn't explain anything, either.

But . . . it wasn't just to quell his worry that she wanted to go; she wanted to see *him*. She wanted to look over his food and listen to his sons grumble in their good-natured way; she wanted to see his daughter's severe face. She wanted just a little bit of *normal*.

What she had instead?

The looming Merchant Authority. And a partner who was, like the Authority's stone face, cool and austere. She wondered what the hell he was thinking.

Devon glanced at Jewel ATerafin, and grimaced. The girl looked outlandish, which had been the intent; Devon had spared his dignity no injury in the process of transforming them both into something that suited the public's image of Southern wanderers. Only a very few made their way across the borders and into the Empire, and of those, none returned to the Dominion of Annagar. They made their homes in the tightly packed buildings of the poorest holdings; he did not know if they counted those homes a blessing.

Jewel had never traveled in the South; she could speak like a native, but only if one didn't actually *know* any natives. Her Torra was shaded with Weston words and oddities, changing, as most street language did, into something not wholly one thing or the other.

He had done what he could with her hair and with the lines of her face; he had done what he could to harshen them, to draw out the appearance of age. But none of it, in spite of his best efforts, was visible now; she looked young, to him. Young, apprehensive, and prickly in the way girls of her age could be. She was also, he thought, exhausted; even in the darker complexion of her skin, her eyes were shadowed by gray circles.

He could not afford to treat her as a child. He wanted to, but he was not a man who indulged such a whim with any frequency.

And he understood, although the understanding was oblique, that she was special; she was not here entirely because of any knowledge she claimed to have. Had it just been knowledge or familiarity with the so-called undercity that was required, any of the other den members would do, and at least one of them seemed, to Devon, to be more certain. Admittedly he'd had little chance to observe them in the last few days.

The incident in *Avantari* had devoured most of his time, his attention, and, yes—his fear. The Huntbrother, Stephen, had indeed found demons within *Avantari*. Or, to be more precise, the demons had found *him*. Had found the Hunter Lord, his cursed inconvenient dogs, and the almost bestial wild girl. Fire had started in *Avantari*, behind the backs of the Kings' Swords; there was anger and resentment and humiliation in the ranks, much of it exacerbated by Duvari's contempt at their failure to apprehend a danger.

Duvari, Lord of the Astari. Devon grimaced.

He, too, was tired.

He was caught between the demands of the Astari, whom he served and to whom he had sworn his life in defense of the Twin Kings, and The Terafin, whose name he bore and whose House he also served, when service to the House and service to the Kings did not come into conflict.

In her name, he woke early, after the scant hours of sleep that had followed Duvari's cold debriefing; in her name, he had taken a girl barely out of childhood into the streets of the hundred holdings, to dark basements and damp tunnels, in search of something that could not, it appeared, be found.

You will take the lead, of course, The Terafin had told him. *But Jewel is unusual, Devon, as you will no doubt become aware. I ask—but I do not command— that you trust her instincts when you are together. If she speaks with certainty—not with petulance and not with anger, but with true certainty—I would advise you to heed her words.*

She had said no more.

But Devon, accustomed to the nuances of the powerful, understood two things. She was offering him this opportunity to observe the girl and to find what the girl herself had not yet found.

The demons existed, and that knowledge was burning its way through the Kings' Palace; no mouth in *Avantari* would be still, given the dramatic attempt on a guest's life within the palace itself. The Terafin sought some way of making their possible danger clearer without committing herself to the Kings before the Council of The Ten.

He understood why.

And he understood as well that she had given him the opportunity to discover information that might—discreetly—be used in the defense of the Kings should the need arise. But the assassins had gone nowhere near the Kings, the Queens, or the patriciate of Essalieyan; instead, they had found the foreign lords.

He was grateful for at least one thing: It was not he who would convey the news to Lady Faergif.

The girl was not afraid of crowds. She was, after the initial argument about her clothing and what it was meant to achieve, not afraid of being noticed; for all her blunt words and her inability to dissemble, she knew how to move through a crowd. She collided with no one; had she wanted to, however, she was more than capable of arranging it.

She did not have the casual disregard for property that marked the few known thieves of Devon's acquaintance; nor did she have their easy, fluid grace or their dramatic sense of a challenge. But he thought, observing her, that she had some of their skill. Even now, she was casually scanning the crowded steps that led into the Merchant Authority for any sign of difficulty.

The guards were, to a man, somewhat bored. It wasn't clear by their posture or their expressions; the Merchant Authority could afford to hire men with self-discipline. Devon, however, had done his share of interminable observation, and he knew the signs well. There had been no trouble here, and they expected none.

She stopped at the base of those stairs, and waited. He nodded and made his way up them. When she did not follow immediately, he turned to see that she was still standing by the stairs, her hands on the polished brass rails. Her color, which had by no means been good at the start of the day, was now almost gray. Her eyes were wide; he wondered what she had seen that had panicked her. The guards did indeed look at her, but not with any suspicion.

Whatever it was, she overcame it with effort and began to follow through the stream of people moving in either direction. She walked, he thought, as if she owned the stairs. Or as if her temper did. All objections to the clothing itself aside, she was capable of wearing it as if it were her natural garb. An odd child.

He made his way onto the crowded, and very loud, floor, passing the familiar livery of House Guards and the less familiar chain shirts of private guards. Magisterial guards quartered the floor; they were not in the uniform of the Merchant Authority, and they were clearly bored. Above them, a second tier of open offices overlooked the floor, and above those, another. Guards could be seen from any vantage and could also *see* from any vantage.

He noted that at least three Houses were present, which always caused some congestion in foot traffic in the Common; in the Authority, it caused more. But no one who came here expected to spend less than an hour waiting.

He turned; Jewel was no longer behind him.

This, he thought, was why he disliked amateurs. Had he a clearer idea of where they were going, he would have left her in the relative safety of the enclosed, multistory trading center.

He found her, approaching her as she stood, back to one side of the central support pillar in the north half of the open hall. It stretched to the ceiling, dwarfing her, but because it was in the way, she had few people to contend with.

Frowning, he walked slowly toward her; the girl who had so artfully, and perhaps gracelessly, navigated her way through the crowds was eclipsed now by fear. He approached her silently and frowned as her hand fell to her dagger and gripped its hilt tightly. He had seen her angry— with some frequency—and frustrated; had seen her intimidated, and also hungry, cold, and miserable.

But afraid? No. Casting a glance around the Authority floor, he could see no one—no guards, no merchants—near her; nothing that could account for her whitening knuckles, her pale face. He therefore took care to make noise as he approached the pillar from the side.

"I've been waiting for you," he said lightly. "Come on."

Fear gave way to the customary annoyance; she did not like being treated like a child. But the expression was cosmetic; her hand still remained on her dagger. This time, however, she nodded toward the large, open doors that led to the stairs and the rest of the Common.

"We don't have time for this." He kept his tone businesslike and cool, hoping to draw her from the floor and the crowd quickly.

She didn't move. "Something's wrong."

He would have asked her what, but she lifted one hand and pressed it firmly against his lips; her fingers were shaking.

But he kissed her fingers, pressing his lips against them, and her eyes rounded as she hastily withdrew her hand. It afforded him some amusement; nothing else about her did. The Terafin's words came back to him, and he smiled a lazy smile through their warning.

Taking her into his arms, he bent his head to her ear, ignoring the stiffening and the tension that took her whole body. "Should we leave?" he asked quietly, the tone entirely at odds with the gesture.

He drew her back, toward an alcove in the wall; it wasn't private, and the open familiarity of his embrace had drawn its share of attention, some of it harried, some amused, and some scornful. None of it was suspicious, however.

He turned her as he moved, his arms around her, until she faced his chest—and the wall—and he, the doors.

And then, as he watched them, he cursed, quietly and efficiently, in her ear.

"Patris Cordufar."

Chapter Five

DEVON BENT HIS HEAD AGAIN, brushing his cheek against Jewel's as he pulled her farther along the wall—and farther away from the doors. Patris Cordufar traveled with a small guard of four men and at least one attendant; he surveyed the Authority floor with the bored air of a man who does not require its services.

For the most part, this was not true. But the Cordufar family was wealthy. He did not expect Jewel to know the man on sight; he did expect her to recognize his name. She had been in Council with The Terafin when some part of the Cordufar affair had been discussed.

Devon was ill at ease, however. While it was not unusual to find Lord Cordufar in the Authority itself, it was disturbing to find his presence and Jewel's inexplicable fear linked in this fashion.

But that fear seemed to travel in only one direction; Cordufar did not turn or look; he did not appear to be aware of her existence at all. Devon released the girl and stepped toward the safety of the wicket as the danger passed beyond view.

He grimaced. This, this was to be a test of sorts.

Jewel watched Devon approach the wicket, and drawing a breath, straightening her shoulders, she joined him there. The crowd was thick and suffocating, and although Devon had relaxed when Patris Cordufar had departed the building, she hadn't. She couldn't.

"We need a distraction," Devon had told her.

She was used to this. What she *wasn't* used to was Devon's idea of distraction. He told her what they would do at the money changer's wicket, and she had gaped at him. "Are you *crazy?*"

He'd simply raised a brow.

"Everyone in the building will be staring at us!"

"Yes. But there will be some mild discomfort, and they will not question what they see."

And somehow, she'd agreed.

She wished he could meet Haval. Haval might like him.

Then again, Haval might dislike him intensely; with Haval, it was hard to tell. All she had to do was to walk out those doors and around the Common, and she'd know, one way or the other.

But, like Farmer Hanson, Haval wasn't in the cards today. So much of her life was gone.

Devon and the money changer were bartering; the money changer—a man from the South, or at least born to Southern parents—looked bored.

She waited until they had almost agreed upon a sum and then drew breath, remembering as she did, her Oma at the market.

"That isn't even an offer," she broke in, and for just a moment, the memories clung. "That's theft. Or isn't our gold good enough for the likes of you?"

They did, of course, carry Annagarian gold, some of which was now spread out on the counter before the money changer. To Jewel, it looked no different than Imperial gold, if you ignored the stamping. On the other hand, it was only very recently that she'd had any experience with the gold coins of either nation. She didn't much like gold; there wasn't any place you could spend it in safety if you didn't want every den streetside in miles to relieve you of its burden. Word traveled.

None of which was relevant right now. She felt her Oma's fingers pinch her wrist. Some memories, she could live without.

"You're Annagarian," she said, as if it were an accusation.

The wicketeer nodded.

"And you would do this to your own? Have you so forgotten yourself that you've sold all your honor to these foreign lapdogs?"

His pallid face went red beneath his dark hair.

"My love," Devon said, attempting to draw her from the wicket. She saw one eyebrow rise; this was not exactly what he'd planned. Then again, most of his so-called plan had involved starting an argument. "I think you react a little strongly. It's not as if—"

She yanked her hand free; it was what she wanted to do anyway. Haval had taught her to use her natural reactions, rather than fighting them. She did so, now. "So you start this again?" Before he could answer, she slapped him, hard. "What kind of a man are you, that you choose him over me? You've done nothing but bow and scrape since we crossed the cursed border!"

She spoke in Torra, of course.

She spoke in Torra, which at least every working wicketeer and half the people on the floor would understand. It was street Torra, but they wouldn't expect better from her.

It was hard to feel so many eyes on her, to know that it was because of her flamboyant and uncontrolled behavior. Turning, she stormed away from Devon, heading anywhere, clearly furious. And she *was* angry. Angry and frightened.

Haval's words guided her, here. *Use what you have. Show it. Let other people make assumptions.*

And, as Devon had said they would, people got out of her way.

She couldn't hear what he said to the money changer, and it didn't matter. The only thing that did was that she get off this floor. She pulled off the earcuffs, and any other hanging bits that could catch on stone in the near dark, shoving them out of the way and hoping she didn't destroy them.

But when Devon caught up with her in the small hall that led to stairs that traveled both up toward the small offices that didn't front the trading square and down and toward the storerooms that any building of any size maintained, she caught his hand.

"We don't have time," she told him, her words coming out so shakily they were almost a whisper.

She saw him open—and close—his mouth; whatever questions he wanted to ask, and clearly, they were there, he held in abeyance. But his fingers tightened in hers, and she pulled his hand and began to run.

She let go of his hands when they reached the sheltered wagon docks in which merchants parked cargo that required careful inspection. The outer docks, which were used at the height of the traveling season, were open but sparsely occupied; the inner docks were not.

In spite of her often surly delivery, he had listened to most of the words that left her mouth; it was helpful, now, because her lips were so tightly compressed, they were white. She was, he thought, as she freed her hand, afraid. No, she was more than afraid. She was terrified.

But in terror's grasp, she still moved, and she moved with purpose, as if that purpose had walls, like a tunnel, that she could follow, ignoring what lay without. He knew what she was searching for: a trapdoor, some way down through the old floors. These floors were well tended, unlike the chutes in the buildings that he had inspected, some at her side and some entirely alone; the seams of the wood were not so visible as to draw attention.

But she'd said she had come up here at least once, and he believed her. It was hard, even absent evidence for her claims, not to believe Jewel Markess; she radiated the outraged earnestness of youth. *She* believed.

She skirted the walls and paused behind large crates when they were near at hand; her gaze trailed wood grain as she searched. She often paused and turned that little bit too quickly, but whatever she was looking for— whatever she was so afraid of—failed to materialize.

He watched her. Her fear was not contagious, not quite, but he was alert regardless.

She found the hatch and signaled, but it was some while before Devon could slip into place to open it; an inspector and a merchant had engaged in a somewhat heated argument directly over the door, and while they drew attention—with the exchange of incrementally heated and veiled insults, it would be hard for them to do much else—it was not useful attention in this case.

But at length, Authority guards were summoned, and the merchant stormed away, while the much smaller inspector grimaced and bit the heads off of anyone less senior who wasn't busy enough to avoid staring. Which would be, Devon thought wryly, most of them.

And then he slid in beside Jewel, pulled up the trap just enough to allow her entry. He listened, and to his surprise, he heard her drop, heard the heaviness of her landing. That implied distance, and also, a harder surface. Eyes slightly narrowed, he slid in behind her, into the darkness.

In that darkness, she reached for his hand—and missed. He wasn't, in the end, one of hers, and the instinctive reach, adjusted without thought for her den, did not yet exist for Devon. With Meralonne, it had never been an issue; with Meralonne, they had never *found* anything that was truly dark. That, and he required no light; he simply waved his hands, in that bored, indolent way of his, and light came.

The ground here was uneven, and it was hard, almost rocky. The dirt that often characterized the first level of basement was absent; whatever the Merchant Authority was built on, it had never been soft. Rath had explained the importance of foundations to her on their early runs through the undercity, and she knew that these were too uneven to be those foundations, although they might be in the right place.

She pulled a small, thin rope from her tunic and fastened it quickly around her waist; her hands were shaking, and quickly today was damn slow. Then she reached for Devon, and this time she found his hand. "Come on," she told him, struggling to keep her voice calm and measured, both things he seemed to value. She tied the other end of the rope around him.

It wouldn't help them if they hit a crevice or a drop; it wouldn't support their weight. But it would allow them to move without losing each other, if the need arose. And if, she thought, he meant to move in the darkness.

Had her hair not been standing on end on both neck and arms, she might have asked for a magestone; she was certain he had one. But she was afraid of the light, here. She had never been afraid of light in this darkness before.

Devon didn't argue with the rope. But after she'd finished tying it—in a knot that would have caused Rath to frown for half an hour—he pulled out a magestone. It was not like the pebbles that Jewel's den had used; it was a glass, or a crystal, the heart of which was a soft, pale gold that shaded into white.

It figured. Even in the dank and uncomfortable rock, Devon ATerafin exuded his aura of wealth. She started to tell him to douse the light, but before the words came out, he enclosed it in his palm, and it dimmed; she could see the orange glow light his veins, no more.

"Lead," he whispered softly, opening his hand again.

She nodded. The trap was here, and the tunnels would lead to the sub-basement, and from there, to the undercity. She was almost certain that she would find what she'd spent weeks looking for. She should have felt the profound relief that comes with vindication.

But she felt fear instead. It grew as she began to move, the darkness hemming her in, the path ahead growing less and less accessible as her knees faltered. The tunnel here widened. It was tall enough at this point to accommodate Devon; it was easily taller than Jewel.

Glancing, briefly, at Devon, she straightened her shoulders and walked. "We're under the main hall," she told him softly.

He nodded, glancing up, and she turned once again toward the tunnel, toward the darkness ahead, beyond which lay the undercity with its familiar streets and its painful, inexplicable losses. She took a step. Took another, while Devon almost ran into her. Her knees locked, and then she felt it: certainty, knowledge, something that she had no words for, it was so sudden.

"The light!" she hissed, turning back, running half into his chest. She pushed them both against the closest wall and then pulled them along its uneven surface, dropping to her knees, grabbing his shirt in a silent indication that she needed him to do the same.

His eyes narrowed; she saw that much before his hand once again guttered brilliance, denying these tunnels illumination.

He didn't speak a word. Not a word, and she was absurdly grateful at the moment that Meralonne APhaniel was not here; Meralonne did not skulk or hide, and she thought—had he been her partner now—he might have moved to stand in the tunnel's center, pausing only to give her a withering glance.

Not Devon. Devon tugged the rope very lightly, and he found a natural recess in the stone; he dropped to the tunnel floor and crawled along it, gently guiding Jewel so that she was forced to follow. Devon drew her back, and he pulled her into his arms.

She stiffened once, and he froze. It helped. The fear helped, as well. She retreated into it, past the reflexive desire to be free of any entrapment, and she sank, silent, against his chest, listening to his breath, his heartbeat, the soft sound of cloth rubbing against cloth.

Her own breath, she held; it came and went when she needed air.

"Jewel—"

Lifting her hand, she covered his lips. He fell silent, and as the preternaturally loud syllables of her name faded, they were replaced by the distant sound of voices. Footsteps.

He did not try to speak again.

She heard the voices grow louder, but they spoke in a language she didn't know or didn't recognize. She didn't dare ask Devon if he did, and not for the usual reason; here, dignity was forgotten. But with the voices came footsteps.

What didn't follow either was *light*. She heard no cursing, no stumbling, no interruptions in the fall of feet that spoke of hesitance. Whoever was coming didn't need light to see in the darkness. She tried not to burrow into Devon. If they didn't need light to see, they could, if they were careful, see Jewel.

They would kill her.

She *knew* it. They would kill Jewel, they would kill Devon, and the gods only knew where their bodies would eventually be found.

Oh, she prayed. She prayed to Kalliaris, to the goddess of whim and fortune. *Smile, Lady.* She couldn't even barter here; she could think of nothing she had to offer. *Smile, please, please, Lady.*

The footsteps drew no closer. They didn't pause, but space between the beats changed slightly as they began to recede. Jewel almost wept with relief. Devon relaxed beneath her, and his arms loosened their hold on her back. They only had to wait until those steps were silent again, and then they could bolt for the trapdoor, and freedom.

But Devon rose, his back pressed against the uneven abutments, and he pulled Jewel to her feet as well. He stayed there as the unfamiliar language grew distant.

When he spoke, however, he didn't speak of flight. "They are going where we wish to go."

The last words rose, as if the statement contained some hint of doubt; she nodded. She didn't trust herself to speak. The basement—if you could call this wide, flat place a basement, was all on a level; there was, beneath it, a subbasement, one flat and low enough that not even Jewel could stand in it. This crawl space was not easily found, but it extended well beneath the Merchant Authority in a small web, and if you followed it south—at least she thought it was south—it came to the collapsed ruin of a door's arch, another hole—an entrance into the undercity itself.

It was obvious. In fact, it seemed to Jewel that the basement had been built above the subbasement, and the floor had collapsed over the years, slowly sinking into the maze the way glass, over centuries, pooled toward the bottom of the Churches' lead frames. At that, it had only sunk in the one spot, and it was not a large one: big enough for one person, maybe two. If it were in an area that was used at all, it might have been pursued; instead, it was tucked away in a moldy corner like a forgotten secret. There were boards above the hole, but they had been eaten away by time and moisture—it was these slats, hoisted out of place by Carver's slender shoulders, that had signaled the exit from the crawl space into a larger building.

"Then we must follow." He started forward, toward the opposite wall, moving silently. The thin rope that bound them tautened, and he paused; it was either that or drag her, risking the sound of her fall.

"We can't," she whispered.

"We can. Or I can."

"Devon—"

"That's not a request. But if you fear to go, I will go alone."

"We can't see what they're doing." She heard the fear and the plea in her words; later, she might hate them. But right now? Kalliaris had smiled, and Devon was going to spit in her face. "They travel in darkness. They work in darkness." All of this, now, she *knew* as truth. "If we bring light, they'll know who we are, and they'll destroy us." This, too, was true.

But she knew, as the words left her lips, that he would be unmoved. *This* was what he needed to see and to know. She stood frozen for a moment, as the voices at last traveled beyond the range of her hearing.

This was how she had lost Lefty and Fisher. She knew it.

This was how they had disappeared.

Why it was Lefty and Fisher alone, she didn't know; they could have taken the entire den. Instead, they had let them live and crawl about the suddenly strange streets of their undercity like desperate, terrified insects.

She should have felt anger. Or fury. Or hatred. She should have desired vengeance—or justice.

But she felt the cold and the dark as if it would never, ever leave her. It left no room for anything else.

Devon pulled on the thin rope again, and this time she surrendered to the inevitable. He would not return, and she knew better than to leave him.

He had never seen Jewel so still. Gesture and movement punctuated all of her conversation; she fidgeted when she was not allowed to speak, as if the words themselves were energy that must be expended.

But here and now? He felt her presence as a tug in the dark at his waist, no more. He did not dare to let the light play out more than an inch or two, and their progress was agonizingly slow, and not without some minor pain.

But the T-junction itself, she navigated with care. And it was, by feel, the T-junction he had assumed it must be. The ground was flat for most of their travel; he paused once or twice, signaling by two tugs that she do the same, to listen for any sounds of movement ahead. He heard none, and what she feared, she kept to herself.

But the floor at last began to slope ever so slightly. She tugged the rope twice and inched ahead until it was taut; he followed only when she gave it a single tug. They moved this way until she signaled a halt with a tug that was sharper and more definitive.

Her fear was—almost—a contagion. He felt the tension of it in his arms and his shoulders; he was braced as if to leap, either to or from danger, depending on what that danger might be. His hand slid down to the daggers he carried. They were a gift—if gift was the word for something demanded—from the Exalted of Cormaris. How, exactly, the Exalted of Cormaris had known that such a demand might be forthcoming had given him pause, for the dagger had to be consecrated, and the consecration required a ceremony that was not mere minutes in the enacting.

But that question was both Duvari's concern and Duvari's problem; of the Astari, only Duvari was capable of the sustained suspicion necessary to investigate the god-born son of the Lord of Wisdom.

Darkness. Damp, cold. The only light that touched it at all came from the fragments Devon allowed between the fingers of the fist that held his expensive magestone. Jewel had always thought she feared the dark; she understood, now, what fear was. It was hard to move; it was hard to breath. She did both, her mouth dry.

She needed some light to navigate, but she didn't want it, and every time some small ray illuminated the floor, she had to bite her lip; she wanted Devon to gutter it entirely because light—any light—increased their danger.

But she knew that a fall here would be bad; if she fell, if she lost that much control, they would hear it. They would know. Who they were no longer mattered; death was death. Had she faced this fear, this visceral, terrible panic, she would never have searched for her lost kin. She wouldn't have been able to.

Now, without the hope of finding and saving them, it was so much harder. She knew that this was what she'd been searching for for almost a month; she hadn't known it, then. If she had, she might not have tried so hard.

But . . . her den was safe. For now, it was safe. She *had to do this*.

It was easier when the incline grew steep enough that she had to flatten herself completely against the fallen surface of rock; it was solid and cool against her chest, and it removed at least the fear of tripping or falling. She inched forward along the surface to the edge of the entrance. There, slats, broken boards, added splinters to her fingers.

She'd found it. Here was her proof.

But she felt no triumph; had she been on her own, she would have gained her feet and backed away, moving as quickly and silently as she could. She tugged the rope twice, and Devon joined her. His breath was even and regular; it was almost calming.

But it shifted slightly when he saw what she'd touched: The slats, the broken boards, had been pulled up. This was where they had to go, yes—but it was also where the unknown others had gone. They were in the subbasement.

Normally, this wasn't a bad drop; because of the way the floor sloped, it wasn't hard to get back up, but Jewel had only done it twice. What had made this particular exit so hazardous was the timing and the crowds above it. Then? She'd been worried about discovery; about what Rath would say—or do—if he found out that she'd revealed the existence of the undercity.

Rath was dead.

She didn't want to join him. Taking a breath to steady herself, she lifted her body from the comfort of its connection with solid ground and crouched on bent knees just above the exposed entrance. Devon tugged the rope once, and then, to make his point clearer, he caught her shoulder in one hand, pushing her gently away.

She understood what he was offering her, and she wanted to take it so badly it was hard to speak. But what she said, instead, and in a voice so faint she hardly knew it as her own, was, "Devon, I have to go first. I know the tunnels."

He shifted his hand from her shoulder to her arm and tightened it briefly. This, too, she understood. She lowered herself into the crawl space, and his hand never left. It should have been awkward, but it was the only warmth she felt—at all—and she couldn't bring herself to tell him to let her go.

The ground was solid, and the drop was so slight she could land without making noise; it was the only good thing about the slow sinking of the upper floor. Devon slid the magestone into his shirt; from here on, they would be navigating entirely by touch. Jewel's memory was not as good as either Duster's or Carver's, and she'd not come this way often—but she remembered no gaps, no sudden crevices, no sharp and deadly drops. If she moved slowly, she could make it out and into the streets of the undercity.

If she moved silently, she'd survive.

She did both, now.

The crawl space was not tall enough for Devon to stand in; Jewel could have, but she chose to stay close to the ground. She inched forward, following the tunnel's path; Devon was behind her, and he was a comfortable shadow in this place that cast none; he moved when she moved and stopped when she stopped; she didn't even need to tug at the rope to give him direction. He touched her calf to navigate, and she was tense enough in this darkness that it didn't make things worse; it was, for once, a simple touch. A way of speaking without words or sight.

She listened for him.

She listened for other things: movement, voices.

But she had not expected to be stopped by something she could *see*. And when she stopped, her stillness was so complete and so sudden that Devon bumped into her.

She could *see* the darkness. And she felt, as she rested on her hands and her knees, that if she were not careful, if she were not utterly silent, the darkness would see her. It moved. It was—she knew this—watching, alive. It had a voice, and if there was one mercy in these tunnels at this moment it was this: She couldn't hear it. But she could feel it, and that was enough.

She reached out, reached back, connected with the curve of Devon's shoulder, and held tight. It was meant to be a warning, but it came out wrong; her hand was shaking. He didn't speak, didn't move.

Unseen voices broke the silence, if not the stillness.

"I said *all* life."

"It is done, Lord."

"You are certain?"

"As certain as I can be."

"Good. Your existence depends on it. Now, stand out of my way."

"Lord."

No movement of bodies indicated who had spoken. But she didn't need those now. She saw the darkness unfold, black against black, illuminated by movement, as if that were the whole of the illumination it knew. She saw it reach out, one flat sweep in all directions, and for a moment, she saw the jagged entrance that led to—and from—the undercity.

Her breath came sharp, short, as if she were in pain; she felt Devon's hand tense, and then she felt the cool absence of his hand on her calf. That hand now traveled in the darkness, touching her shoulder, the side of her neck, reading the lines of her face, her slightly open mouth. She said and did nothing; she didn't even flinch. All of his touch was a silent question, and here silence was survival.

But it helped that he touched lightly, and his fingers never closed, never pressed; that the answers he sought were not, in the end, the response to demands.

The world enfolded in darkness shifted, as if it were being devoured. No, as if infinitely thin layers of it were being peeled off, one at a time, like onion skin and heart. She saw the jagged hole shift, the edges sharpening, and then she saw them change, and she understood on some level that what was being peeled away was time, the effects of time: A door stood where the hole had been, and it was not a small door, not a thin, cheap one; it was runed and engraved, and it sat astride a rectangular stone frame.

And then, even that was gone, and the stone itself lost its definition, lost its structure, vanished as if it were slowly being eaten away.

She had been so disappointed with Meralonne APhaniel and his use of magic; only once had he shown both power and majesty, and on that day? She'd been watching The Terafin and the parody of Rath.

But today she wanted to see small fires and pipe smoke and hear his indolent and arrogant tones of bored frustration. She wanted to see no more magic, no more power, no more of the ancient and the mysterious. Ever.

She knew what had happened to the entrances to the undercity: They had been unmade, unraveled, the slow march of time absorbed and destroyed.

She knew when it had ended and knew, in that instant, that she was too damn close; they were too damn close. Rocking back on her knees, her hands suddenly seeking purchase in stone, she felt Devon's hand in the small of her back, and she rested there a moment, as if she could somehow absorb his calm, his detachment.

She turned, and he turned as well, both of them still close to ground.

"Jewel," he whispered. Her name, in the stillness. She wanted to tell him to shut up. She lifted her hands in the flat imperative of den-sign. But he couldn't see it, and she couldn't force the words past her lips. She held onto them as if her life depended on it.

He pushed her forward, past him; he took the rear, as he had on the crawl toward the entrance. She moved past him, aware of the way her clothing scraped against the ground. She held her breath until her lungs gave out and then forced herself to breathe as evenly as she possibly could; it was what Devon was doing.

But it was hard to move *quickly.*

They're not coming yet. They're not coming yet.

But they would be, and soon. No time, no time. They would walk as slowly as they had when they arrived, and she could almost hear the first of those careless steps; they would carry no light, but they needed none.

When she crawled in the dark, stones cut her knees, and her palms were scored; she bit her lip more than once to stop from crying out or cursing. She knew she was moving too slowly. And she knew that in this darkness, there was no other way to move; standing or attempting to run would only leave her on the ground again, but with far less control.

She prayed. It was almost wordless, it was so incoherent. But the fear had to go somewhere, and prayer was silent. She felt Devon's hand in the darkness, not as a threat or an encroachment but as an anchor. His breathing never changed, and the silence of his movements told her that even on his hands and knees, he was graceful. She wanted that grace.

But want it or no, she moved, biting her lip, ignoring the small sting of stone in her palms and her knees; she bruised her elbow at least once when the tunnel walls crimped.

Kalliaris smiled for a second time that day; they reached the entrance into the basement. The footsteps had grown slightly louder, but they were not yet close; she still had time.

Her knees had practically locked into their cramped position; she felt her muscles tense and stretch as she rose. They were shaking; she was shaking. She ignored it and reached above her head until her palms hit the warped, old surface of unfinished planking. Drawing breath, she tensed and pushed.

The planks creaked. In the still darkness, the sound echoed like the cry of gulls in the early morning. It was too much. They were heavy, and she couldn't move them without making noise; she'd drop them, or she'd failed to push them aside in time—

Devon's hand closed on her shoulder. She almost screamed, but his hand's weight was now familiar. He pushed her, firmly, to one side, and this time, when the planks creaked again, they scraped stone; she heard them move. It was not the only movement she heard.

Devon's hand touched her knee, and then her foot; she nodded, although he couldn't see it, and instead of speaking, she tugged the rope twice, lifting one foot. Felt his hands lock beneath that foot. He gave her the boost she needed to get her arms over the jagged but damp wood, and she scrabbled out of the hole.

Devon followed far more quickly. She heard the movement of cloth, felt the slight tug of rope, and then saw, briefly, the dim glow of magelight. It was harsh, now, and it was brief. She stared at it, blinking, both fearing it and wanting it. Light. Vision.

Devon grabbed her hand. She saw the magelight beneath his fingers; it turned his flesh orange. He didn't speak a word. Instead, he began to run, and she had no choice but to follow. Maybe that was the idea. She didn't know. Didn't care.

From the moment she had seen the perfect arch simply vanish into dirt, her entire body had wanted nothing more than to do as she was doing now: run. It wasn't a fast run; in these tunnels, in the very scant light that Devon's barely revealed stone let out, it couldn't be. But it was movement, and compared to the long and agonizingly slow crawl, it was speed itself.

He no longer let her lead; it was no longer necessary. He knew where he was going. He retraced their halting steps without any marked hesitation and came to the T-junction in the tunnel.

Her hair rose along her arms and the back of her neck as it sometimes did when the storms in the harbor were fierce. She turned to look over her shoulder and stumbled; Devon didn't let go of her hand, and a stumble was all he allowed her. He didn't let her fall.

But she cried out, tried to cry out, in warning. She could see over her shoulder, spreading across the tunnel at their back, far faster than their feet had traveled, even at a run, a lattice of livid, red light. No words escaped—just sound.

He heard her. He didn't pause, didn't ask her what she'd seen. Tightening his grip on her hand, he yanked her around the corner of the junction.

At their back, the light they'd all but denied themselves erupted across the stone, and with it, red and white and orange heat. Fire. It lingered, bouncing off walls, and if the intent had been something as quick as a painful, burning death, its effect was momentary illumination.

Jewel could see the trapdoor that led to the interior yards of the Merchant Authority. She could see a hint of a light that wasn't death, and she wanted to weep because it seemed so damn far away.

They ran. The fire that still lit the junction at their back burned in a silence that was so cold it almost denied heat. But the cold didn't last, couldn't last; it was broken by fire, and this fire, unlike the last, didn't end at wall; it lapped at feet, at legs, it singed hair. The air grew hot and breath burned.

She heard Devon curse. For the first time since she'd met him, his breath was as labored as hers, but his hands, when they pushed her roughly to one side of the rocky wall, were steady.

She pushed up at the trapdoor; her curses were louder than his, wasting air. Her hands felt thick and heavy, but they did what she needed them to do: They shoved the trap up, and she heard it skitter against the floor.

She rose when Devon lifted her; he wasn't gentle. It didn't matter. She hit the ground with elbow and knee, and rising, she threw herself the rest of the way clear, leaving space for Devon.

Devon. Turning as if, for a moment, he was one of her own, she saw his fingers at the edge of the trapdoor, and she saw him rise, vaulting into the air, feet over head. He hadn't learned *that* at the Trade Commission.

His fingers were still gripping the edge of the opening when fire gouted up from below, and she saw it envelop both air and his hands. Devon grunted. Just that. But his hands were blistered, the skin dark and raw, as he forced them to let go. He rolled back, controlling his fall; he landed on his feet in a defensive crouch, his hands up and in front of his curved body. She reached out and caught his shoulder to steady him, and he stiffened.

He did not, however, hit her. Releasing his shoulder, she grabbed not his hand but his elbow, and she dragged him—inasmuch as she could, given their disparate weight and height—to his feet; he followed the motion, adding momentum to it.

They ran, deserting the docks. It was coming on early evening; she saw that clearly from the slanting light. The Merchant Authority would not—yet—be closed for the day, although it would be much less crowded.

The crowds might have been a blessing; it was hard to tell. How many people would their pursuers be willing to kill? How many people had they already destroyed?

She made it down the long and narrow halls that led to the main trading floor, and only when she was in sight of the heart of Averalaan's commerce did she pause. She was practical, had always been practical, and she now drew her dagger, releasing Devon's elbow. He didn't seem to see it, which was bad.

But she wasn't going to stab him, after all; maybe he only noticed the details that had some chance of killing him. She bent, grabbed a fold of the voluminous and much disliked skirt, and ran her knife along its lower seamed ruffle; she came up with a yard of torn and jagged cloth.

She wound it around his hands, working quickly.

They were bleeding.

Blood, she thought, would leave far more of a trail than witnesses. She repeated this process, shortening the skirt, until both of his hands were bound. They wouldn't be useful, but they didn't have to be; there was nothing to fight. If they were discovered, if they were caught, they'd be dead.

He nodded at her once, his face slightly gray, his lips so pale they seemed almost white. Then she darted forward, into the sparse crowd, and he followed. She didn't take care not to be seen, not here; there was no point. She didn't know what Devon was doing, but she knew he didn't shout and didn't correct her; that was good enough.

They reached the outer stairs, the wide, flat marbled surface now reflecting some hint of pink and the pale purple that blue goes when the sun sets. She turned to look over her shoulder, and he shook his head. "Go."

And really, what else did he have to say? She started to run; she'd wanted to run since the moment she'd set foot in the tunnels. The Common was made unfamiliar by the urgency. She had no desire, now, to visit the old friends in those areas she knew well; she had no desire to lead their pursuers to them.

Devon was in pain, but he had fought through pain before; he ran, slightly slowed, in Jewel's wake. He had seen none of what she had seen, but the fire had been unmistakable; magic, there. Magery. It was not slight.

What disturbed him now, besides the burns that had made his hands so instantly raw, was the fact that that magery was confined in the hands of men who had no need at all for even the simplest of light. They had walked those tunnels in utter darkness, and they had not—from the sounds of their strides—scrupled to walk them with care; they had never misstepped, never taken a wrong turn, and if they touched walls for guidance, it had not slowed them at all.

He wondered whether she was aware of it. Aware or not—and he thought she might not be, not yet—she had done well here. Better than many and better, if he was honest, than he would have said she would, had anyone asked. He flexed his fingers, grimaced, and let them be; she had bound his hands, and that was smart. Even pursued, she had taken only enough time to reach something resembling safety, and she had done just enough to lessen immediate danger.

Nor had she run and left him behind.

Amarais Handernesse ATerafin had always been an impressive woman; she balanced the wisdom of experience with the impulse of instinct. What she had seen in Jewel Markess, Devon now understood, and he let that thought guide him as he followed her through the city streets to the footbridge that led to the Isle.

She did not, however, slow until the Terafin manse was in sight, although he told her, as often as she looked, that there was no pursuit.

Their only argument was in the foyer of the Terafin manse itself. Jewel's hands, dusty and lined with dirt, now folded themselves onto her almost nonexistent hips for emphasis. "Where do you think you're going?" she said, her tone so sharp he raised a brow.

"We must report to The Terafin. At once."

"We must report," she replied, mimicking his quiet force, "to the *healerie*. At once." She glared at his hands. Blood had seeped through her bindings, but not enough to fall upon either stone or earth.

"I will see Alowan, in all haste, the minute we've made our report."

"I've made reports to The Terafin. You are *not* standing in her rooms for three hours while your hands are like that. And Alowan doesn't have appointments running from here until the end of the world."

He was torn between the desire to snap at her and the desire to laugh. Neither was particularly useful, and he discarded both with an obvious grimace. "You are not my lord," he told her, quietly. "And if The Terafin feels that the report can wait, I will attend Alowan. Will that suffice?"

She glared. She was, Devon thought, with enough amusement that it dulled the pain, quite good at it. She accepted defeat with poor grace, but she did accept it.

*   *   *

The debriefing did not go well. It started out with the tense and formal stiffness that Jewel disliked. She hadn't been allowed time to return to her wing—or, more important, to Ellerson—and was aware of how dirty and underdressed she was. The Terafin, of course, looked perfect, if perfection had that slightly grim and pale cast to it, and Morretz hovered in silence like a shadow that couldn't quite stay attached as much as it would like. Devon was not in any shape to meander his way through an explanation, and he'd come directly to the point: The tunnels of the undercity *did* exist, but they were being unmade.

He had not, unfortunately, been able to see what had unmade them and therefore couldn't actually answer the questions his statement provoked; he'd left that to Jewel. She didn't appreciate the privilege, but she was tired enough at that point to stumble her way through an answer. The fear that had driven her flight from the holdings to the Isle had deserted her, but with it had gone the nervous tension that had kept her awake and aware.

She wanted to go home.

Instead, she stood and answered the questions. She tried to describe what she'd seen in the darkness. No one asked her *how*, mind. They accepted what she offered at face value. She was too tired to be nervous or worried about this fact. Rath would have been angry.

But Rath, damn him, wasn't here. He hadn't listened.

She tried to pull back from that thought, because she knew where it went: to her father. To the day she had finally become an orphan in the streets of the city.

Meralonne's unexpected appearance, and his quiet assertion that what she had seen was impossible, helped. For a value of help that was not entirely easy to appreciate. Instead of pulling out his pipe and smoking it in a way that irritated everyone present, he'd pulled out a chair in front of one of the smaller tables, and he had had Jewel describe exactly what she'd seen.

Then he'd recreated it, in miniature, across the table's surface. How, she wasn't certain, and she wasn't in any position to ask—but had she not been so tired, she would have been fascinated. As it was, the magical display—an illusion of some sort—had done what her words alone couldn't; they had made clear what she'd seen.

His "impossible" had been repeated, but softly; Jewel was aware of some shift, quiet and subtle, in his expression—it slid from absolute certainty to the desire for a certainty that was slipping away. But even that hadn't caused as much of a stir as what he did next; he had stood, swayed, and collapsed.

And now, she thought grimly, he was here, in the same healerie to which she'd practically dragged Devon. Devon was ATerafin, and accustomed to Alowan; he allowed Alowan to examine his hands. He also allowed Alowan to escort him to one of the beds in the heart of the healerie, and after a half-hearted attempt to excuse himself from using it, lay down. The healer then pulled a large chair up to the bedside.

Jewel, her daggers deposited in the wooden box to one side of the outer door, watched, trying not to flinch as the healer peeled back her makeshift bandages.

Alowan glanced at her, his gaze briefly marking the ragged hem of a skirt that was composed of exactly the same material as those bandages, albeit without the blood. "Well done," he told her softly.

Her smile was tired, but it was genuine. It was impossible not to like Alowan, and therefore impossible not to feel a little bit of pride when he offered her the acknowledgment she was almost afraid to admit she wanted. He didn't bother with ointments or dressing, not for these burns; instead, he took both of Devon's hands in his and closed his eyes.

Devon kept his open, and he grimaced in obvious distaste. Which meant he was really, really uncomfortable being healed—he usually had a face that was about as expressive as brickwork. It made no sense to Jewel; he wasn't dying. The healing couldn't be as intrusive or emotionally painful as it had been for Arann, who had been.

But Meralonne APhaniel gave her perspective, because the mage refused to be healed. In fact, he refused to be *approached* by the healer.

Alowan raised both of his frail hands, and exposed his palms. "I mean you no harm," he told the mage.

Meralonne, who was shuddering enough that he had difficulty speaking clearly, said, "You mean more harm than you know. I am in the throes of the fevers. I am not injured."

"I have some experience with the—"

"Keep your distance!"

Alowan's hands didn't move. Nor did he take a step forward; he simply waited for silence. Devon started to rise, and Alowan, as if he had eyes in the back of the head he didn't even turn a fraction of an inch, said, "ATerafin, remain in your bed."

Devon subsided at once.

"I don't understand," Jewel whispered, moving slightly closer to where the mage lay.

"No."

"What's wrong with him? Why did he collapse?"

"He's mage-born. Talent-born," he added. "But there's a reason they're often called mage fevers."

When she didn't appear to look enlightened, he grimaced. "We each have abilities and limitations. In the case of the magi, the limitations aren't obvious—but they exist. If mages tax their power beyond those limitations, they pay."

"But—the illusion—"

"No. It was not the illusion. Don't even think it. He could do something like that for four days on end without sleep; this has nothing to do with you. The fevers come when the mage has been unwise in his use of power. If the mage is spectacularly unwise, the fevers can consume him.

"Only in that case is a healer actually useful; the healing cannot in any way stem the course of the fevers, but it *can* heal any damage the fevers cause to the body."

"Do you think he'll—" She stiffened.

A bright, orange globe suddenly flared to life around the bed in which Meralonne so angrily lay.

"Devon?"

"What?"

"If it's *because* he used his power that he's now suffering, shouldn't it be impossible for him to use any more of it?"

Devon swore. Alowan, defeated, retreated and gave orders to his assistants to do the same.

"He is powerful, Jewel," Devon told her softly. "Never doubt it."

"And arrogant," she added quietly. "And really, really grouchy."

"Luckily, he is not *your* problem." Devon reached out and caught her hand. "Go back to your rooms," he told her gently. "Eat. Try to sleep. I think it highly unlikely that you will be called upon to search for the undercity again."

Chapter Six

5th of Corvil, 410 A. A.
Terafin Manse, Averalaan Aramarelas

WHEN JEWEL WOKE for the third time that night, she bitterly regretted sending Teller and Finch scuttling for cover from the floor of her room. It was easy to feel self-conscious during the day; it was easy to worry—to know—that the ability to sleep in the dark without crying like a child was damned important if she wanted to *stay* in this house.

At night, though, with the sky moon-dark, and the air slightly chilly, it was much, much harder. She glanced at the floor upon which her den-kin had slept, keeping watch, as if the very fine beds in their individual rooms counted for nothing, and she missed them fiercely. The fact that she could leave her room and enter theirs without walking outside on a bitter stretch of holding street meant nothing; she wouldn't do it. She knew herself that well.

But she missed them.

Shaking herself, she slipped out of her bed, grabbing a robe that was hanging over the nearest chair. There were more chairs in this room, she thought, than they'd had at home. It wasn't precisely true, but there was certainly more *space*. All of her den could live here, and it wouldn't be crowded. She rose and left her room; she'd had enough of what lay waiting in sleep to want to avoid it.

*　　*　　*

Teller heard her door open; he heard it close. He'd heard, from the safety of his bed, her cries through the open door. He heard the floor creak slightly as Jewel walked past, and he almost rose. But he knew she would tell him to go back to sleep, and he knew that his presence wouldn't comfort her at all.

Here, without the cold and the lack of food hanging over them all like a threat, the den had not grown comfortable; they had simply paused, holding breath. They were waiting. He was waiting. For what, he couldn't say. He liked the Terafin servants, or at least the ones that saw to the wing; he liked the old healer and visited him frequently, taking care not to interfere with his work. He liked Torvan, and Arrendas, the two Chosen who stopped by every so often to see how the den was doing.

But he wasn't comfortable with The Terafin. The fact that they never saw her probably helped. Or didn't. He turned over onto his side, pulling the blankets around himself. Trying to sleep.

Thinking of Jewel in the kitchen, because he knew that's where she would go.

It was not Teller—or Finch—who interrupted Jewel's silent vigil; it was Ellerson. And he did not interrupt it immediately; he stood like shadow in the space left by a door that was partially open, watching her slumped back, the curved line of her shoulders. This was not the first night that she had walked in relative silence to the large, enclosed kitchen; it would no doubt not be the last. But tonight she stayed longer, and she seemed, in the flickering of lamplight, to be almost defeated.

Her hands, however, were in motion, and if he listened with care, he could hear the scratch of chalk across the surface of slate. Beside her, lid open, was a blackened iron box; she glanced at it every so often.

He was aware of the circumstances surrounding her return from her outing with Devon ATerafin; he was also aware that Devon ATerafin and Meralonne APhaniel had both subsequently been sent to Alowan. Jewel, however, had not been required to surrender to the healer's ministrations. She had been sent to the West Wing, instead.

He watched her work for a few minutes more. *They drive you too hard.* Frowning, he entered the room.

"That is not," he told her quietly, "a wise use of oil."

She didn't startle at the sound of his voice; that much, time and familiarity had given him.

"I'm studying."

He lifted the lamp in his hand as she continued to write and saw that her eyes were half-closed. "To bed."

She rose, slowly, but managed not to sway. "I—"

"To bed. Now."

She was so transparent to a man of Ellerson's varied experiences. He saw the desire to argue come and go on her face as she turned and lifted her own lamp, as if it were a shield. Or as if the light it cast were.

"It is not often," he told her, lowering his lamp in turn, "that a domicis finds his master in a kitchen."

She shrugged. Of all her gestures, it was the most common, and it was shared across the den. "Back at the den, it was the only empty room. Wasn't even a full room." Her lamp's light moved as she turned, surveying the kitchen. "Our whole place was smaller than this."

Her voice was low and soft, and in it he heard nothing that surprised him. Gentling his own, he said, "But you miss it."

Denial came and went, just as argument had; she looked up and met his steady gaze. "Yes. I miss it. It was mine. I knew how much it cost, I knew when I had to pay rent, I knew how to clean it and break into it when I had to." She turned back toward the slate and the box. "It's stupid. I couldn't dream of a better place than this."

So dreams went. He said nothing as she struggled with words. The desire to speak them and the desire to deny their truth was evident in the gaunt lines of her face.

"But I don't see my den-kin anymore. I go out early, I come in late, and I'm forbidden to speak about anything I do in The Terafin's service. It's not what I thought it'd be."

"No. It never is. Come, Jewel. It is time to sleep."

She looked young, then. She never looked old, but it was easy to forget that she was so close to childhood. He led her down the hall and back to the door of her room, which was ajar. She hesitated only once, at the threshold.

Ellerson knew about her nightmares. Both Finch and Teller had taken care to inform him. He knew, also, that some were significant. Those, however, she was not self-conscious about; she woke the den. But the others? She tried to keep them to herself, shouldering them with the guilt and resentment of someone who yearns to be strong but doubts, always, that she will ever achieve that state.

"Jewel, I am a domicis. I have been trained for most of my life to serve. I take pride in it; all of our number do. I was brought here to serve you; it seems that you did not—or do not—understand this." He held out his hand for the lamp she carried. Her fingers caused the light—and its cast shadow—to shake. But she did as he silently demanded, surrendering light into his keeping. "Come. It is time for you to sleep."

He placed her lamp on one side of her bed and placed his own on the other. She stared at them in confusion.

That confusion did not ease much when he pulled the closest chair to her bedside and sat in it. "I will watch the lamps," he told her quietly. "When they are low, I will fill them."

"But the oil—the cost—"

"Sleep, Jewel. You are not the master that I envisioned when I was called to serve—but I understand now why it was I who was sent."

He watched her crawl between the covers and watched as her head sank into the pillows. Her eyes were circled and dark, and her skin was almost sallow, but her hair was the same wild mess it always was.

He was not entirely certain that his presence would calm her, but it did, and he took some small satisfaction from the knowledge; her face lost its tired, stretched lines as she surrendered wakefulness.

She looked young then.

6th of Corvil, 410 A. A.
Terafin Manse, Averalaan Aramarelas

Night. Again. Jewel woke not to darkness but to light; Ellerson, however, was nodding off quietly in his chair. She felt a twinge of guilt, watching him; he was not by any stretch of the imagination a young man, and instead of sleeping in a bed—and she assumed he had one, although it occurred to her that she had never, ever seen his rooms—he sat awkwardly in an armchair.

She had not, apparently, screamed.

But even moving as quietly as she could while sliding her legs off the edge of her bed, she woke him. One white brow rose as she cringed.

"Where are you going?" he asked, in his usual starched voice.

She glanced at her clothing. The desire to be curt came and went; he was here because of her nightmares, no more and no less. "I'm going," she told him softly, "to the Terafin shrine." She didn't ask his permission.

In turn, he didn't ask her why she'd awakened. He glanced at her nightdress.

"Yes," she told him, "I'm going to get changed first." She paused, and then said, "Thank you."

He didn't ask her why; he nodded in his usual brisk way.

But when he had turned from the door she had just exited, he did not immediately make his way back to the small suite of sparsely furnished rooms he occupied; instead, he waited by the door until the shadows moved.

They resolved themselves, almost hesitantly, into the spiral-haired Angel, who stood, arms stiff by his sides. "You saw me," he said.

Ellerson nodded.

"Jay didn't."

"She is much occupied at the moment with The Terafin's concerns."

Angel's nod was as unlike Ellerson's as a nod could be. He was not, precisely, belligerent, but he was not entirely comfortable. Of the den, the House seemed to suit him the least. The others had found some role for themselves among the servants or in the unexpected tedium of their daily routine—but Angel had yet to surrender to that comfort.

He was not Carver; he was often silent, and in Ellerson's opinion, unusual hair aside, he was not a boy who cared greatly for the regard of others.

"Did you wish to speak with me?" Ellerson asked him quietly.

Angel hesitated again and almost turned to leave, but the unadorned question forced another nod.

"Then come, Angel. Join me in the kitchen."

Angel bridled, but he didn't argue. The kitchen, however, was Jay's, and in the end, Ellerson chose to lead him to the outer chambers of what had once been attendant rooms. The long benches that girded two walls were habitually empty; the only attendant who used them was Ellerson himself.

He carried a lamp, which added a trace of orange gold to everything its light touched; this he set to one side. Indicating that Angel should sit, Ellerson offered him water. Angel accepted, glancing around the sparse and simple room, its benches and its counter, overlooked by closed cup-boards, the only adornments.

Ellerson poured water for himself and leaned against the cupboard wall. "You wished to speak with me," he said quietly.

Angel nodded. After a long pause, he asked, "What is a domicis?"

It was not the question Ellerson expected, but he had long since given up demanding predictability of life. "An unusual question. What do you think it is?"

"I don't know."

"And you will not chance an answer?"

"You do know. I thought I'd ask you instead."

At that, the older man smiled. "Some would call me a servant."

Angel nodded. "Servants don't have guilds."

"Not generally, no."

"Torvan said you were hired especially for this wing."

"I was. The guildmaster understood the nature of the request far better than I, at the time I chose to accept employment here."

"You serve Jay."

Ellerson nodded.

"But you're paid to serve her."

Ah. "I am not her leige, no. I have accepted a contract with House Terafin for my responsibilities to Jewel Markess; it remains in force for two years, or until the situation markedly changes."

"So . . . it's a job."

"It is a vocation," Ellerson replied with quiet dignity. "Understand that the Guild of Domicis encompasses service. Not all who apply to learn the art of the domicis are accepted, and not all who are accepted, in the end, are deemed worthy of offering that service. The domicis are, of course, free to decide where their services are best put to use."

"So it's up to you."

"It is. When we serve, we bend the whole of our thought and our will to our master, or masters. We give them advice, yes, but we do not expect all of that advice to be followed; they take the lead, we merely attempt to guide. We are not—as you may have noticed—mute and obedient; fear of having no roof over our head does not determine our future in the way it often determines the future of others.

"But we value our service, and we do not give it lightly. In the end, it is not," he added softly, "a life that recommends itself to everyone."

"Did you never dream of leading?"

"Or ruling? Perhaps when I was four; I admit that I am so far from that age that I cannot honestly recall." He hesitated, aware that more was wanted but unaware of precisely what the more entailed. "Angel, I am proud of what I have achieved in my life. It will not be written about; there will be no songs sung in my honor, and if I fall in the line of duty, my body is not the body that will be borne home upon a shield."

That struck a mark.

"Is it the money that disturbs you? The existence of a contract?"

That, too, struck home. Angel's eyes were darker in the orange light. After a moment, he nodded. "It makes it seem like a job."

"It *is* a job," Ellerson replied with care. "I am not a political man; that was never my strength. Nor am I content to serve where I am not needed—and that, perhaps, has been my one vanity. What is it you desire?"

But Angel was not yet ready to answer that question. Instead, he said, "Why don't you serve The Terafin?"

"The Terafin has a domicis."

"You know what I mean."

Ellerson nodded. "I do. You wonder why it is that a man of my years and experience does not serve a lord of power."

Angel nodded, losing at last the hesitance that had marred all of his questions.

"I have never desired to serve the powerful," Ellerson replied. "Not all of the powerful make a difference in this world. I have been content to serve those who need what I offer, and this will always be the case. Men of power—women of power—require a knowledge and a state of mind that is not mine; I do not protect in the ways that a domicis who serves such a lord must be able to.

"Power doesn't define worthiness," he added softly. "Or rather, it is not the only definition that counts; perhaps it counts for the young. Perhaps. There are those among my peers who have served rulers all of their lives."

"But—but why did you decide—"

Ellerson smiled. It was a worn smile. "I observed," he said quietly. "And for me? It is the street musician's song that speaks more strongly than the orchestra." His answer made little sense to the boy; he saw that.

"You must understand what it is that you admire," he told Angel quietly. "You must also understand what it is that *you* require of a leader or a ruler."

"And if I'm wrong?"

"There is no wrong, or rather, no wrong that is not the product of deceit."

It was not the answer that the boy wanted. And the boy was not entirely his charge, but in spite of this, he gentled his voice and tried again.

"What you trust, what you respect, and what you consider worthy will define your service—but it is tied to what *you* know and what you understand. Service and worship are not, in the end, the same thing; you can offer your service to something you respect and even love—but you offer much less to something you worship and hold in awe. Worship is a burden," Ellerson added softly, "and in the end, it is a burden that men are not capable of shouldering well, or for long, no matter how much they might think they desire otherwise.

"You ask me why I don't serve a lord of power? Why don't you?"

The lights that flickered in sconces at the shrine never seemed to gutter or dim; they weren't magical. They were tended. Jewel half expected to see the person who maintained them, but there were no gardeners in the night garden; nothing but the breeze seemed to move the grass. Even the birds were all but silent.

It was the silence that she found difficult at times. In the holdings, there wasn't much of it. Certainly not at home; several people sleeping almost on top of each other still made noise. Arann especially. But in the early morning, even before the den made its way out of the front doors, there'd been movement and noise in the streets below.

People needed to eat, after all, and food didn't grow on their counters.

Here? It might as well have. It appeared on their table as if by magic, and there was so damn much of it, they didn't really need more than one meal a day. Ellerson, however, insisted.

Most of the den had stopped their packrat habits; they'd had weeks to get used to things. But Finch often squirreled away the leftovers, and Ellerson overlooked this. Loudly.

Jewel touched the altar with her palm.

Torvan, however, failed to emerge, and after a moment, she dropped to her knees and rested her head against the cool stone. She was awake, yes, but she was so damn tired. Not sleepy; sleep had been riven from her, and she didn't yet wish to return to it. But she wanted company, even his.

Talk to your den, idiot.

I can't. I can't talk about anything I'm doing. I can't talk about my fear and my guilt; it's not like they don't have enough of their own.

She closed her eyes and saw only darkness behind her lids.

Please, she thought, resting there. *Please. Don't take them away from me. Don't let me lose anyone else.*

But the undercity, its passages closing one by one, now loomed large in her thoughts and fears. It was there they'd lost Lefty, Fisher, and Lander, and she *knew* that whatever had taken them had been nothing as simple and merciful as a fall. She would have to tell the others that, and she couldn't face them now.

What would she say, after all? *I'm sorry.* Yes. Just that. And maybe she'd wait there for their forgiveness. It was almost too much.

She was unprepared for the sound of footsteps here. They were wrong for Ellerson, and they were definitely far too quiet for Torvan, whose feet fell like steel thunder wherever he walked.

Maybe, she thought, as she turned, it was the unseen servants who tended the shrine. She took a breath, struggling with her sense of invaded privacy because she was aware that she had no right to it.

But it wasn't a servant.

"T-Terafin."

"Jewel," The Terafin replied. She looked at the altar at which Jewel had been kneeling. "We have come here, no doubt, for the same reason—although I confess I'm surprised that you found the shrine so readily."

Jewel could think of nothing to say, and sometimes silence—although it was often hard—was best. Her Oma had said that a lot, but then again, her Oma had never been silent.

"What troubles you, Jewel?"

Jewel turned back to the altar, bowing her head a moment as if in prayer. And wasn't she, in the end? She brought her hands briefly up to her face and then let them fall. "I don't know how you do it," she said softly. "I don't know how you can be responsible for so many people. I don't know how you can choose your Chosen. It's not *their* oath—I understand that—it's that they uphold it at all. Torvan says they die. For you."

"They die," The Terafin said, in a perfect, regal voice, "for Terafin."

But it was late, and Jewel was tired. Too tired to be cautious or political. "They die for *you*." It was the truth. Anyone with two eyes, or at least one open one, could see that.

And hadn't her own died for just the same thing, in the end? Hadn't Duster died in the open streets, with no chance at all, for some of the same reason Torvan would, if the need arose?

"We don't even have the bodies. I mean, not that they'd've meant much in the twenty-fifth—but here, here where everything's decent and we've got anything we ever wanted—here, it matters."

"Jewel, you cannot continue to think about the dead. Think about the living."

"I do," Jewel told the woman who ruled the House she wanted for her den. For herself, if she were honest. What would it be like, to know that things were in the hands of this powerful, intelligent, and completely confident woman? The Terafin could make the decisions. She already did. She would know what to do, unlike Jewel, who stumbled from mistake to loss and back again. "I think about them all the time. Because if I make a mistake, they might not be alive to regret it."

"Then if you have ever desired rulership, remember this."

I never desired it, Jewel thought. She glanced at The Terafin, pushing her hair out of her eyes so that they could see each other clearly.

"How do they haunt you?" The Terafin asked.

Jewel examined the words for a criticism she did not, in the end, find. Instead, more dangerous than she had ever thought possible, she saw a glimmer of the compassion that comes from understanding.

"At night. It's always at night. I haven't had a single night's sleep in the last three weeks where I didn't see them." Her voice grew that shade of distant that spoke of memory. "They're dead. They rise out of the ground, out of the stone—they reach for me, and there's nothing in their eyes but death. They blame me." She tried to hide pain and fear behind laughter; it worked. Sort of.

"Are your dreams usually significant?"

Jewel glanced, again, at the woman who was the master of her fate. There was an edge to the question that spoke of certain knowledge. For a moment she tightened, her body gathering in on itself.

Best begin as you mean to continue, her Oma said quietly, no softness in the words. It was almost a comfort. It was like permission.

"If they happen all the time. They aren't—they aren't the wyrd, though. These dreams," she added. "They're different enough each time."

"Raising the dead in such a fashion is an art long lost," The Terafin told her quietly, as if it were meant to comfort. The words were unexpected enough that they did. Jewel hadn't taken the dreams literally. She understood them as the accusation they were, and it was not the first time she had failed the people she loved.

It would not, she thought, be the last. But . . . she had all but promised them safety.

"Jewel, how long have you been coming to the shrine?"

"I don't know. A week, maybe a little more." Jewel hesitated, and then asked, "Why?"

"Who taught you the customs of the Terafin shrine?"

Her next hesitation was shorter. "Torvan."

"Oh?"

"He was on duty in the gardens the night—the first night—that I came here. He said I wasn't allowed to touch the altar unless I had something to offer the House. And I do," she added, forcing herself to speak firmly. "Myself and my service."

"I see." The Terafin glanced at the altar and then nodded. "And that, in the end, is all any one of us has to offer, no more and no less. Come; if you take comfort from this, then join me. For I, too, have had my nightmares. This force that we are searching for—it is not the province of Terafin alone; I do not have the resources to combat the kin wherever we may find them and to uncover the source of their summoning."

"But . . . you're part of the Kings' Council. You have the ears of the Kings. You can go to them and tell them and they'll *listen* to you."

"Yes. But it would be much as if you went to the magisterial guards when you had difficulties with your rivals in the twenty-fifth."

Jewel snorted; she couldn't help herself. The Terafin, who saw so much so clearly, could sometimes be so wrong. The fact was both unsettling and strangely comforting. "No. They'd never listen to me."

"Then it's not the same," The Terafin replied, accepting Jewel's assertion without argument. "But there are similarities. The Ten are not like brothers and sisters; they do not serve the same House or the same purpose, although they all serve Essalieyan in their particular ways.

"Among The Ten, there is a heirarchy, an understood measure of power and influence. Terafin is a seat that holds power. And I will weaken Terafin in the eyes of The Ten if I go to the Kings for aid, no matter how justified that request might be. Among The Ten are two who are our enemy, and they are close enough in rank to take advantage of any sign of weakness.

"But if I do not go to the Kings, there may be, in the end, a far greater price to pay than momentary political power. I don't know what form that price will take, but I believe it has already started." Her lids closed over her eyes, and she bowed her head forward.

She was silent for a long moment, and that moment was the time it took Jewel to understand that The Terafin was praying.

We're not so different, she thought, almost in wonder. *We're afraid of the same things, it's just that hers are so much bigger*. And again, she felt awe for this woman and for what she carried in silence behind the perfectly schooled lines of her expression.

She started to speak, and then the world shifted as she gazed at this woman's face. Saw it whiten, go pale and gray, saw it lose the patina of control and power that was so damn compelling.

Saw, she knew, death.

She cried out, all words, all attempt at them, momentarily swamped by the sudden, certain knowledge that hit her like a blow to the gut. She fell back, her hands striking the hard, cold marble of gleaming stairs before she managed to catch herself, hold herself in.

"Jewel!" The Terafin rose, prayer broken, and turned in Jewel's direction.

"Don't do it," Jewel told her, managing to get her elbows behind her and lever herself off the ground. "Don't do it or they'll kill you."

It was not the answer that Amarais had come to the Terafin shrine to receive, but she had asked, and she accepted what was given.

She offered Jewel Markess her hand, and the girl stared at it, as if still seeing death. But Amarais did not withdraw that hand; she simply held it steady in front of the girl's dark eyes until the peculiar distance in them receded.

Jewel took the offered help; her hand was shaking. But she did not plead with The Terafin; she did not further add to the stark and certain words.

"You have offered me an answer." She rose. "But you, Jewel Markess, what answers did you seek at the House shrine?"

Jewel realized, then, that she would never understand the powerful. But the vision's grip loosened, and she shed it as she rose, her elbows aching at the contact with cold marble. She would have brushed the question aside had it been asked for the sake of politeness, for she'd come to understand the casual question that desired no answer that wasn't a verbal translation of a nod or a wave.

Instead, she glanced at the altar. It steadied her.

"I need my den," she said quietly.

Any other woman might have chosen to misunderstand the reply; any other woman might have found it confusing, for Jewel's den was here, in House Terafin, under the watchful and expert eye of both handpicked servants and the Chosen, not to mention Ellerson.

But . . . this woman was The Terafin. She drew breath, considering the words. "What do you need of them?" she finally asked.

Jewel exhaled, because she could. "I need them to be what they were." Shaking her head, she added, "No, they are what they were—but they're not *doing* anything. I can't talk to them," she added, spreading her hands until her fingers were taut and almost white. "I can't talk about any of the stuff I do. I don't know what you talk to your Council about. I don't know what you say to your Chosen when I'm not with you. Maybe you tell them nothing.

"Maybe that's because there's nothing they can tell *you*. But I'm not like that. I—" she struggled again with words, with the certainty of her inadequacy in the face of this woman's experience and knowledge—and with the uncertainty of what that admission might cost her den. "But my den—they're not my servants. I don't *pay* them. I can't really tell them what to do."

"You lead them."

"Yes." She faced that clearly. "Yes. I lead them. They follow me." She turned back to the altar, to its gleaming, cool surface, and imagined for a moment that she could lay her forehead against it and find peace. "But I follow them, as well. I'm led *by* them. What they worry about, what they say—even what they choose not to say—it guides me.

"Here, in this place, they have nothing to say, nothing to offer me. It makes them feel useless, and it makes me feel blind."

She raised her face to meet The Terafin's. The older woman had said nothing, but that nothing was not in her gaze; Jewel felt measured. She couldn't tell if she was being found wanting. "What do you need them to know?" The question didn't give much away.

But it didn't matter.

She faced the woman who ruled the House, letting her fear and anxiety drop away for a moment. It wasn't gone forever; she knew that. Knew that she would pick it up and shoulder it as the burden it was in probably less than an hour. But she needed to set it aside right now.

"I want this House for them. I want it," she added, speaking cleanly and clearly, "for myself. I know I have to earn it. I know the decision to give the House Name is yours in its entirety.

"But Rath sent me here. And he sent me here, to you, for a reason. I don't know if it killed him," she added. "Because I don't know, in the end, what killed him. I knew he would die. I told him he would die. He chose what he chose. They always do," she added, with a trace of bitterness.

"But I'm here now. I've seen the House. I've seen *you*. And I trust you enough to give my den to the House. They're worthy of it," she added. "I know that now. I've seen your servants. Your guards. Even your Chosen. My den are worthy to be numbered among them." She lifted a hand. "But I know that what *I* think doesn't matter. I know they have to prove themselves, as well.

"But they *can't*. Not in silence. Not in ignorance. They huddle in the West Wing because—yes—I tell them to huddle there. But they'll never know enough to be part of this House if they continue to do that. And I'll never know enough to be part of this House because I'm almost never *in it*."

"And how much, in the end, do you think you are all required to know?" Measured words. Cool words.

"I don't know. But it's not enough to know which halls lead to the healerie and which halls lead to your offices—all of them. It's not enough to know how to get to the garden or even how to get to this shrine. We don't know enough about how anything works here. We knew how things worked in the twenty-fifth."

"What, then, would you have me to do to alleviate this ignorance?"

Jewel's answer was slow in coming. She hadn't planned this conversation, because she hadn't foreseen this meeting; that was the problem with her talent. You couldn't count on it to do anything subtle. Swallowing, she said, "I want Arann to spend some time in the House Guard."

It was hard to tell who the words had surprised more. But Jewel's surprise, she could manage to contain; she'd said them, after all. "I want Teller and Finch to be employed—I mean, to be stationed—with one of the merchants."

"They can read and write?"

"Yes." The question bit, and Jewel let it. "They can read and write. Teller is our best, but Finch isn't much worse. They're not as good yet with numbers, but they're working on what I know."

"And you?"

"I'm only good enough to keep a roof over our head and food in our stomachs."

"Good enough, then. And what, in this theoretical education, would you do with the others?"

Jewel grimaced. *Kick at least one of them in the butt.* She did not, however, share this bit of humor. "The others have probably already made a few friends.

"But . . . I need to be able to talk to them. I don't have to tell them everything—but I can't keep telling them *nothing*. They have nothing to say to me, nothing to offer, if I do. You don't tell the House Council everything you're thinking—but if you told them nothing, what would be the point?"

"And if I allow this? If I allow you to discuss your work and its circumstances with your den at your own discretion?"

"It'll help. It'll help them. It'll help me." Keeping anxiety at bay, she added, "It'll help the House, in the end. I swear it."

The Terafin glanced at the altar, and her lips curved in a very odd, very slight smile. "Very well, Jewel Markess. I will consider your request for the deployment of the three, and I will exercise my own judgment here. You may discuss, in general, the difficulties that you now face, with your den. It is to go no further."

Jewel felt, then, the shift of the weight that she had almost unconsciously shouldered since she had first crossed the Terafin threshold.

It must have shown on her face, because The Terafin said, "No, do not thank me; you do not yet understand how what you ask will change both yourself and your den. But it is an interesting request, and a thoughtful one.

"Now, I must leave you. I have other things to consider."

"What things?"

The smile left The Terafin's face, but a frown did not replace it; instead, distance did. "A letter," she replied softly. "To the Kings."

She left Jewel with the ghost of a vision and the slow return of fear, her skirts trailing above the shorn edges of grass like a delicate, cloth cloud.

*   *   *

After she'd gone, and only then, Jewel rose. She knelt, briefly, by the side of the House altar, and she bowed her head into the cool stone as if that stone were a hand, and she were fevered. Here, now, she needed to *think*. She needed to have a plan. But it was hard; everything was too damn big.

No.

Think.

The world had always been too damn big; she'd lived—*they'd* lived—by focusing on the parts of it they could handle. What did she know? That The Terafin would be in danger. That someone would try to kill her. But she wasn't dead yet.

And what could she do about it?

Forehead against stone, she ceased to pray; she needed more than fear right now. Eyes closed, she struggled, as she had often struggled, silent and immobile.

Oh, hells with it. *I'll give you my service,* she told the Terafin altar. *I'll give you the service of my den. In the name of your House. How do I protect her?*

The answer came not from the shrine and not from the nameless deity to whom she'd prayed—after all, what House had its own god?—but from memory. Standing in front of Devon ATerafin, as if he were a mirror, both of them dressed in foolish, embarrassing clothing, his hands holding the ornate and decorative scabbard of a dagger that looked as if it were meant to be used in street plays.

Take this, he told her, grim, the words he offered so sparse each syllable might have been solid gold, and he as poor as she. Something in his voice had stopped her, and she'd turned to look at his face, his shuttered expression.

Don't draw it unless we're cornered. You'll know when to use it; you can only use it once.

She wondered, then, if he meant her to use it on herself, and she opened her mouth to tell him she couldn't. The words didn't leave her mouth. Instead, she nodded.

She nodded now as she lifted her head from the altar's surface. She still had the dagger; he hadn't asked for it back, and to be fair, watching his blistered, bleeding hands hadn't left much room for any other thought. Rising, she drew the sheath from under the folds of her robe. It was a stupid dagger, but she carried it anyway because of Devon's conviction.

In the fire's light, she drew it from its scabbard. It was, as it looked, ungainly; it couldn't be thrown. It couldn't be used to cut anything harder or thicker than paper or cloth, in her opinion; the metal was a soft one that took no tarnish and kept very little in the way of edge. You could probably point it and stab.

But she frowned as the blade caught the light, reflecting it and absorbing it at the same time. Runes were carved in its flat on both sides, and they glowed faintly as she turned it. She thought it the light's reflection at first, but while shards of scattered light hit the underside of the shrine, she saw that the light in the runnels of those runes didn't falter.

Magic.

"It is a consecrated blade."

She turned at the sound of Torvan's voice. Only his voice; she'd been so deep in thought she hadn't even heard his steps approaching.

"Consecrated?"

"Generally by the Three. There are ancient spells that were once used against the Lord of the Hells and his servants. Those runes hold some trace of that magic and that conflict." He glanced at her face and then smiled. It was a weary smile.

"We need this," she told him softly. "No, we need more. How do we get them?"

He raised a brow. "I don't know. I imagine that you petition the Exalted of Cormaris, Reymaris, or the Mother."

"And wait a lot?"

The smile deepened. "And wait, yes."

"And if we don't have time?" She hesitated. Torvan was Chosen; the safety of The Terafin was almost literally in his hands. What could she offer as aid that wouldn't somehow be insulting? Once, it wouldn't have mattered. She understood that this hesitation was the effect of Ellerson's constant, quiet lecturing, and she didn't even resent it.

"If you don't have time, you generally do without."

"Can we?"

His gaze was measured. "Jewel," he finally said, "this is The Terafin's battle. It is not yet yours."

"It *is*," she replied, with more heat than she'd intended. She turned from him and slid the dagger back into its sheath. The sheath itself was old, and it was also runed; at one time, she would have kept it because it might be worth something on the open market.

On Rath's open market. He was gone. If she was ever to fence things again, she would have to build her own.

"What have you seen?" he asked softly.

He knew. She'd told him the first day she'd crossed his threshold, trusting him in the end because he'd carried Arann all the way from the guardhouse to the literal feet of The Terafin. "They're going to try to kill her," Jewel whispered.

He knew instantly who she meant. "Who will?"

"The demons. I think. It's fuzzy, Torvan. It's not clear enough."

"The Chosen will be prepared."

"Of course they will." She hesitated again. "But I want *us* to be prepared, too. We're here because, in the end, Rath died."

"He knew he would die?"

"I told him. I told him, and he sent us here." She drew a sharp breath. "I see things you don't see," she said quietly. "I tell her what I see, but—I can't always tell her in time. Sometimes I know things a second before they happen." Not often, but she wasn't lying. Lying here would do her no good. "But everything here—it's so complicated and it's so damn *slow*. She won't keep me under her feet—I wouldn't, if I were her—but it's under her feet that I'll probably do the most good if—if something happens."

"Where did you get this dagger?"

"Devon gave it to me, the day we went to the Merchant Authority."

He nodded.

After a moment, gazing into the distance, he spoke.

And after that, he escorted her to the edge of the garden. "Be careful, Jewel," he told her softly. "Whether or not you attempt to do things in service to the House, if you are caught, understand that you will be judged only by the action."

She nodded. It didn't matter. He'd told her, obliquely, where many of the important members of House Terafin lived, worked, or slept. It was a long list, and she did pay attention, but the name that stood out at this moment was Devon ATerafin.

Chapter Seven

TELLER GAZED AT THE WALLS of Gabriel ATerafin's office. He was, by this time, accustomed to the sheer finery, the size of the rooms, and the height of the ceilings; the entire Terafin manse boasted these. But Gabriel's office, unlike the galleries and the public areas, reminded him most of the spare rooms in which The Terafin worked.

Gabriel was in the inner office, behind a closed door.

Teller glanced at the Chosen who stood to either side of that door; as usual, they failed to notice that he—or anyone else in the room—was present. He wondered how they could be such good guards when they failed to notice so much.

But the man seated at the desk to one side of those closed doors looked up. He set both quill and paper aside, and rose.

"You," he said, glancing at something on the surface of the desk, "are Teller . . ." He frowned.

"Just Teller," Teller told him quickly.

"Just Teller, then." The frown didn't ease. "Please be seated and remain there. The right-kin should be with you shortly; his appointment has run long." He made his way to the closed doors, ignoring the guards that flanked them as easily as they ignored him. He knocked once, and then he opened the doors and slid between them.

Teller glanced at the chairs. They were positioned in one row against the wall, and while they looked comfortable, they were also expensive and empty. He felt more comfortable standing. He felt less comfortable disobeying what was barely a request. Eventually, he sat.

When the doors opened, they revealed the man behind the desk, who had failed to introduce himself. He looked far less composed as he made his way out, but he glanced at Teller, seated, and nodded, regaining his lost composure as he took the chair behind his desk. He didn't speak. Teller didn't ask him what was wrong; instead, he gazed at the walls again.

At the painting, the single painting, that adorned them.

It was a quiet painting, a seascape by day. Senniel College adorned the skyline, and little else. What made it unusual was that the central figure was not a building, not a man—or several men—not a ship; it was a bird, wings catching some hint of sunlight. It wasn't a gull; those, anyone who lived in the city could recognize. This was the wrong shape, the wrong color, possibly the wrong size—it was flying high enough over the sea and Senniel that there was nothing to compare it to.

But its wings were stretched, tip to tip, in a long glide.

"It was painted by Haveros," someone said.

Teller looked up, surprised to see that it was the unidentified man behind the desk. He knew instantly that the name should mean something to him, and he knew as well that it didn't.

The man, however, did not seem ruffled by his ignorance; indeed, he now seemed to expect it, which was safest. "It's called *Freedom*."

"Did the right-kin choose it?"

"Yes. It is in his personal possession, not the possession of the House."

Teller turned back to the painting. Freedom? What freedom, in the end, did a bird know? It flew, yes, but it flew the way the rest of the living world drew breath. If it was hungry, it tried to find food. If it was tired, it slept. If it was hunted—and what would hunt it?—it tried to escape.

The door opened, and Teller turned.

A young man—not the right-kin—stood for a moment in its frame, his face a shade of red that suggested anger. Or fury. Were it not for his expression, he might have been handsome; his hair was auburn, and the magelights—the ever present source of illumination throughout the manse—caught the red highlights, brightening them. His eyes were dark. Even in this light, they were dark enough that his pupils couldn't be seen.

The man at the desk hadn't moved an inch, nor did he look up; the guards, however, now turned to face each other.

This time, they were obviously aware.

And the man knew it. He slowly unclenched hands that were fists, and he turned, still contained by the door. He bowed, a stiff, heavy bow. "Father," he said.

There was no reply.

After a moment, it became clear that none would be forthcoming, and he spun on his heels and strode to the desk. "Barston," he said coldly. "I require another *appointment*. My discussions with the right-kin are not yet done."

So, the man had a name. Barston. ATerafin? Teller thought he must be.

Barston nodded smoothly, as if such ill-tempered demands were common occurrences. For all Teller knew, they were.

"I would like to know," the angry man continued, "what business was so urgent that our meeting had to come to such an abrupt close."

"The Terafin's business," Barston replied smoothly. The lack of composure that he'd shown upon leaving the right-kin's office was completely absent; behind his desk, he seemed unflappable. He didn't look across the room at Teller.

Teller, in turn, tried very hard to disappear.

"Boy."

Apparently, given the utter lack of anyone else in the room, he hadn't done a very good job. He straightened his shoulders and turned.

"Rymark," Barston ATerafin said. Efficiency had given way to ice and had also surrendered the angry stranger's name.

The man failed to hear him. So much deliberate failure, today. Teller wondered whether he was going to have to develop the same failures in order to function in House Terafin. He thought so.

Even so, he could not ignore the single, sharp word.

Jay wants this, he reminded himself. He rose and offered Rymark ATerafin an almost perfect bow. That he could was due to the efforts of Ellerson.

"What urgent business brings you to the office of the right-kin?"

"Rymark," Barston said again, and this time he glanced, not at Teller or Rymark ATerafin, but at the Chosen who girded the doors as if they were so much furniture. To Teller's surprise, they moved away from those doors and toward Rymark ATerafin.

"It's a simple question," Rymark said, not to Barston but to the Chosen, who were now tight-lipped and silent. Teller wondered who they were; he didn't recognize them immediately. He'd have to ask Torvan, later.

Now? Now he faced Rymark, and he found his silence and held it.

"It is a question that is of no material concern to any save The Terafin and the right-kin," Barston replied.

Rymark lifted a hand; rings glinted in the magelights. Clearly, he was not a poor man. The rings were obviously gemmed; he meant them to convey something other than wealth. "He is not a child, Barston."

"He is due the respect that any guest of House Terafin is due. If you feel the need to question him, you will do it outside the confines of this office."

Teller was honestly surprised. Barston had not struck him as friendly in any way when he had first entered the room; when he had retreated from an office full of the right-kin and this angry man, he had almost slunk back to this desk. Yet he spoke now in Teller's defense, and he spoke with conviction.

Even Rymark could not fail to hear it, but he didn't move. The Chosen, however, did.

"ATerafin," one of them said.

Rymark looked at Teller. He lowered his hand. "Very well." The words were stiff and forced. He turned, the Chosen now to either side, and offered Barston a nod.

Barston returned to his chair; the Chosen, however, did not return to the doors. "You will meet him at your usual time?"

"I would like the earliest possible appointment that does not conflict with my studies in the Order of Knowledge."

"Very well. Two days hence, after the morning meal?"

The pause was long, but Teller could no longer see the man's expression. "Two days," he finally said. He turned on heel and he strode out of the room; the door slammed behind him.

Teller sat; his legs were shaking. The Chosen glanced at the door and at each other before returning to their silent, stiff positions.

"My apologies, Master Teller," Barston said quietly. He also glanced at the door. "Rymark ATerafin is generally an exemplar of House etiquette, but the right-kin is his father, and harsher words are often spoken between kin than between peers. I am sure," he added quietly, "he meant no harm by his disrespect. If you will wait but a moment," he said, rising, "the right-kin will see you."

Gabriel ATerafin was not a young man; he was not yet old, but Teller thought he and Rath were the same age. Or would have been. He wasn't certain what to expect when he was ushered, by Barston, to the open doorway and left there. The Chosen offered no help and no guidance; they were, once again, human statues.

"Teller?" the right-kin said quietly. "Please, come in. My apologies for keeping you waiting." He held out a hand toward the chairs in front of his desk. Teller wondered if every important official in the manse spent most of their days behind such a wooden bastion.

But he understood the quiet gesture, and he walked quickly to one of the chairs and took it, folding his hands in his lap.

"I see that you've been our guest for the last several weeks," the right-kin said quietly. "Ah, I forget myself. I am Gabriel ATerafin."

"ATerafin," Teller said, bowing his head briefly. He couldn't remember if he was to bow upon first entering the room, but it didn't matter; he'd already fluffed that.

This drew a smile from the older man. "In this House," he told Teller gravely, "most of its members are ATerafin. Please, call me Gabriel; I imagine the usual honorific would quickly become confusing otherwise."

Teller nodded. He didn't, on the other hand, use the right-kin's name. "It is confusing," he admitted.

"Has The Terafin spoken with you?"

"No."

"So you have no idea why you're here."

Ellerson had gotten him up, chosen appropriate clothing for him to wear, and sent him both to breakfast—early—and out the doors of the wing with a guide. That was all Teller knew. "No," he told Gabriel.

"It would appear," Gabriel said, "that The Terafin has been impressed by Jewel Markess, your effective sponsor." He waited for a moment, and when the words failed to have his intended effect, he smiled again.

It was a tired smile, but it had no harsh edges, and Teller found himself liking the man.

"Again, my apologies. The situation is somewhat unusual; Jewel Markess is not ATerafin and does not have the traditional right to sponsor. However, in this case, The Terafin has chosen to overlook the lack of House Name, and she has suggested that you might find the House less confusing if you were involved in some of its daily business."

Far from easing confusion, the words deepened it enough that Teller couldn't quite keep it off his face. "She wants me to work? But I have no—"

"Training?"

Teller nodded.

"Yes, we're aware of that," was the quiet reply. "It is felt that you would receive some training here. I am told that you can both read and write."

Teller's opinion of his own skills at either was not high. But as he wasn't certain who'd told Gabriel this, he simply nodded.

"Good. We will, of course, test this. No, Teller," Gabriel added, as Teller froze, "it is not a simple pass or fail test; you will not be asked to leave the House, and you will not in any way influence the opinion in which Jewel Markess is held." He glanced at the letter that lay between his hands on the desk's surface.

"The test is meant merely to gauge your abilities. No more, no less. What you will be asked to do during your stay will depend on those abilities. As you can see," he added, lifting the letter, "much of our communication is written. It is not simply a matter of formality, although that exists; we are very busy, and it is not always convenient to meet or to speak with the various Council members.

"I meet twice a week with The Terafin, but there are numerous concerns that are raised in each meeting; not all of the communication she sends to my office will be discussed in those meetings; we therefore require both the ability to write and the ability to read in order to prioritize."

Teller nodded.

"Of your reading skills, and possibly your writing—which would you consider stronger?"

"Reading," he replied, hesitantly.

"Very well. Should your reading skill be sufficient, you would work with Barston. Many of the external communications sent to House Terafin come to my office; Barston deals with them and passes on those which require my personal attention. Personal correspondence is generally marked as such, although most of my personal correspondence does not come to this office."

Teller opened his mouth and closed it again.

"Barston has been asking for an aide for the past several months," Gabriel told him. He rose, leaving the desk behind, and moved to the large, half-empty glass case that rested against one wall. From this, he took out a sheaf of papers, and, returning to his desk, he offered them to Teller.

They were—all of them—letters. Some were old, if you went by the dates in the corners.

"Pretend, for the moment, that you are Barston. No, that you are in his position. I am a very busy man," he added, with just the hint of a grimace, "and my time is not my own. Read that pile and sort it for me."

"Sort it how?"

"Place those letters that you feel are of immediate concern in one pile; in a second pile, place those that you feel require my attention. In the third, place those letters that you feel can be answered without my intervention. I will ask that you take them outside to do so; I do not want to pressure you or to limit the time you take, since I'm aware that this will all be new to you.

"Should you require assistance at all, I will instruct Barston to make himself available."

Taking the letters as if they weighed more than he did, Teller nodded. He reached the doors, and then remembering himself, turned and tendered the right-kin what he *hoped* was a perfect bow.

Gabriel smiled. "I should not say this," he told Teller, "but perhaps you will take some comfort from it. The House is indebted to your young leader. At the moment, there are very few in it who harbor any ill-will toward you."

Burton had said the same thing, what felt like years ago.

"The Terafin is, in my experienced opinion, a very worthy leader. We are lucky to have her, and if you work well and work hard, it is just possible that you will one day serve the House in her name."

Finch, like Teller, had been awakened early. Like Teller, she'd allowed Ellerson to choose her clothing. It was, unlike Teller's, a dress, and it chafed at her neck. He hadn't chosen House colors for her, although his choice in Teller's clothing had been more restricted; she wore a sunflower yellow with strands of black along both sleeves, which were long and cuffed at the wrist. The neck was high, the fabric thick, but it was the cool season, and in the early morning, it could be pretty damn chilly.

She had eaten breakfast in the nook with a bleary-eyed and silent Teller as a companion. They had done their best to consume what was put in front of them, but they were both nervous. It wasn't often that they were woken, alone, and sent to unknown corners of the manse, although if she were of a mind to be fair, they often *did* wake up early and go exploring if the servants didn't shoo them off.

This was different, and they both knew it.

Jay had said that it was time for them to act, to work. They'd been prepared for that. But this wasn't what they'd imagined.

When Teller had left at the side of Burton ATerafin, Ellerson had smiled down at her. "Neither of you have done anything wrong," he told her quietly. "The Terafin requested your presence, in two meetings. Teller has his; you have yours. You are expected," he added, handing her an overcoat that was tailored and fitted, and frowning slightly as she shrugged her sleeves into it, "to represent yourself as befits important guests of the most notable House on the Isle."

Four House Guards came to the wing, and Ellerson, straightening the back of her jacket and fussing at the collar, pushed her gently toward them. "ATerafin," he said, to one of the guards.

Finch breathed what might have been a sigh of relief, had it been audible. She recognized Torvan ATerafin.

Ellerson probably had as well, but he seldom lectured the den in front of anyone else, not even the servants. He saved his criticism for private use.

"Torvan!"

He did not, however, save all of his expressions. She grimaced, lowered her arm—which had been midwave—and tendered a more correct bow. This also produced a severe frown in the domicis.

She was never going to understand the patriciate. Ever.

Torvan, however, smiled. He didn't seem to be bothered by whatever she'd done that had disappointed the domicis. "Finch," he said. He bowed, but it was a shallow dip of motion, not stiff enough to be formal. "I've been given the privilege of escorting you to the mainland."

She fell in step beside him, and they began to walk down the hall, taking a corner. "Where are we going?"

"The Merchant Authority," he replied.

She frowned. "Oh, wait. The big, stone building that squats at the eastern end of the Common? Fancy stairs, fancy guards, lots of people with money and guards of their own?"

"The very same." he replied gravely.

If the other guards thought this out of place, they didn't appear to notice.

"Do you know why?"

"No."

"Oh."

"The House Guard doesn't question the orders given them," he replied as they approached the guardhouse that broke the line of gate. "Nor does it involve itself in the affairs of the House Council."

"This has to do with the House Council?" She almost missed a step.

"The orders were relayed by the Captain of the Chosen."

"I'm not—I'm not in trouble?"

He smiled. "No, Finch. You are not—yet—in trouble."

She didn't particularly like the sound of that *yet*. "What am *I* supposed to do at the Merchant Authority?"

This did produce a very rare grimace in response. "You have an appointment," he told her, "with one of the senior officials in the Merchant Authority. Ah, no," he added, lifting a hand before she could speak. "The woman works *for* House Terafin; she is, in fact, ATerafin. All of The Ten—and some of the other significant Merchant Houses—have permanent offices of varying sizes within the Authority complex.

"House Terafin employs perhaps a dozen people who work from, and through, those offices. The various merchants allied with the House, or of it, will do most of their business and request most of their paperwork through the Authority; only in the case of trade route grants do they approach the offices of the Trade Commission in *Avantari*."

Avantari. The Palace of the Twin Kings.

"You might meet members of other Houses at the Authority," he added.

"What do I say?"

"I have no doubt at all that you'll know."

She puzzled over his response as she walked.

Finch arrived for her meeting fifteen minutes early; Torvan took no detours, but then again, he didn't have to. He didn't need to dodge the magisterial guards, he didn't get out of the way of any obvious dens that roamed the streets with thuggish pride, and because he didn't, Finch's instinctive reactions were dampened. She followed in his shadow.

His shadow took her as far as the offices in the Merchant Authority. The fancy dress guards on the steps didn't stop him; they did nod, however, as he passed. The crowds—loud, often composed of angry, impatient people—didn't stop him, either; they didn't rush to get out of his way, but he didn't have to shove them to make room. Moving evenly and slowly, as if he owned any space his feet happened to land, he led her through the crowds on the open floor and into a hall; this he took, until he reached stairs.

Even these, he navigated with ease, but when he reached the closed doors that bore the Terafin House crest, he stopped. "We will wait for you here," he told her.

Finch had, like all of the street poor, daydreamed about living life in a grand palace on the Isle. As so often happened, daydreams—in which you could control every single thing that happened—had a way of being entirely unlike reality.

And reality greeted her bullishly in the form of the senior official she had been sent to meet. The woman wasn't as old as The Terafin, but she didn't really look like she'd ever been young; her hair was pulled back in a graying brown bun. It made her look very severe.

She was tall, but she was also wide, and her hands were square and blocky; her mouth had permanent lines in the corners of her lips that suggested a frown that didn't budge much. Her eyes were a shade of blue green that was almost shocking given the lack of much color in the rest of her face.

She sat behind a desk as if it were a battleship. It was cluttered with stacks of paper, but nothing about those stacks suggested a mess.

"Yes?" she said curtly, looking up.

Finch's throat dried instantly.

"I'm sorry," she said, because those words came easily, "to bother you. I'm here to speak with someone in the office."

" 'Someone?' "

Finch swallowed and looked around. Torvan was on the wrong side of the doors, and she had to get out of the way when a man in a hurry nearly shoved her to one side.

The woman slapped both of her palms across the desk and pushed herself out of her chair. "You!" she shouted.

Finch jumped.

It was not, however, at Finch that the single word was aimed.

The man in a hurry froze, then turned. He didn't look particularly happy, but then again, people in a hurry seldom did. "ATerafin?" he said.

"Watch where you're going if you want to set foot in this office again. You hear me? You almost ran that young girl over!"

He frowned, looked, and then reddened slightly. "Apologies," he told Finch quickly.

The woman behind the desk folded her arms across her chest and glared at him. Finch thought she was about to say more, but she pursed her lips. "I've an appointment in ten minutes," she told him, "or I'd have more to say. Don't just stand there, get out." She turned her glare on Finch.

Finch did her best not to cringe. "I'm sorry. I'm sure he didn't mean to hit me, I'm just in the way," she told that glare.

The woman clucked. Literally. Shaking her head, she said, "You'll need to do something about *that*, dear." The glare receded, but the frown that had accompanied it didn't. "I bet you apologize when you accidentally walk into a wall or a door. Well, come around the desk and let me look at you."

Finch, no fool, did as bid.

"Do you eat at all? Are they even remembering to feed you?"

"Yes, we eat well."

The woman snorted. "Not, clearly, well enough." She shook her head, and ran one blocky hand through her hair—none of which was in her eyes, it was pulled so tightly back. The gesture was comforting to Finch, who saw it so often. "You must be Finch, then."

Finch's eyes widened slightly.

"Yes," the woman told her, nodding toward a closed door. "I'm Lucille ATerafin. You have an appointment to see me."

They adjourned to a smaller—a much smaller—room. Like the doors to the large, outer office, the door to this room bore the Terafin House crest, but it was a single door, and it was a *normal* door. The window—such as it was—was closed, but it wouldn't have opened to sunlight in any case; it overlooked the crowded wickets and floor three stories down.

There were shelves on both of the walls that didn't boast door or window, but they were practical shelves, of a sturdy, dark wood that had clearly seen better—and less dusty—days. Papers lined those shelves, intermixed with lidded boxes and the occasional standing book.

Behind the desk was a chair; in front of the desk were two.

Lucille walked over to the desk and sat. On it. "You can sit if you'd like," she told Finch, waving a large hand. "We've got, what, two hours?"

Finch, who had not actually been told the name of the woman she was to meet, had no idea. She hesitated and then said, "I'm not sure."

"You're not sure?"

"I'm sorry—"

"Oh, stop it. I assure you, I don't bite." She paused, and then added, "Well, not much. And not polite, self-effacing children."

Finch nodded and carefully took a chair. Since Lucille was sitting on the desk, the chair wasn't that far from her.

"What, exactly, did they—whoever *they* are—tell you?"

"I was told I had a meeting at the Merchant Authority."

"That's it?"

Finch nodded.

"Did they happen to tell you what it was about?"

Finch shook her head.

"What a surprise. I swear, sometimes those people have their heads so far up their—" she stopped. "Never mind. Says here," she added, although what "here" referred to was entirely unclear, "that you can read. And write."

Finch cringed. "I can do a little of both," she told Lucille, "but I'm not very good at either one."

"How well do you handle numbers?"

Finch glanced at the window as if she might be able to run and jump out of it before she had to come up with an answer.

"I see. Is there anything else you think I should know?"

Something about the sentence felt wrong, but it wasn't until Finch answered that she realized what it was: Lucille was speaking Torra. Not Weston, not the language of the patriciate, but Torra.

"No," Finch told her, answering in the same language, although she didn't say as much.

"Well, that's a puzzle. You can't read or write much by your own admission, and you can't do math at all, but they taught you to speak Torra?"

Finch swallowed. The window looked more and more inviting. "No," she told Lucille, taking a breath and unconsciously squaring her shoulders. "No one taught me to speak Torra. I learned it, growing up. Where I grew up," she added, struggling to keep her voice even, because the subject was not one she talked about, ever, "we weren't taught to read or write—that came later."

"Later?"

"Later." Finch spoke quietly.

But Lucille, who was not, by any definition Finch knew, a quiet woman, understood what that particular hush meant. She nodded. "Where did you grow up?" When Finch didn't answer, she said, "I'd hazard somewhere in the inner holdings."

Finch nodded.

"And you made your way to House Terafin on the Isle?"

She nodded again, but this nod was clearly not enough of an answer. "I followed a—a friend." She knew better than to call Jay her den leader; that much at least Ellerson had drilled into all of their heads.

"A friend." Lucille's expression, which could not by any standard be considered friendly, darkened.

Finch nodded.

"This 'friend' took you to live with him in the manse? I'd like to know his name—his first name. I'll assume if he had the gall to promise you accommodations *in* the manse that he's ATerafin."

"Oh! No, no, it's not like that."

Lucille folded her arms across her chest, waiting. She'd lost her glare, but what was left in its place was almost worse; she was obviously suspicious.

"My friend—her name is Jewel, but everyone who likes their teeth calls her Jay. She found me," Finch said, the words coming out much faster than any of the others she'd spoken so far. "She saved my life, and she took me in. She's older than me, but only by a year and a bit."

"I . . . see. Saved your life?"

Finch nodded.

"And where was your family?"

And froze. But this question she would not answer, not coming from a stranger.

Lucille was big and loud, but she was also observant. "So the two of you lived together."

"No."

"No?"

"No. There were a lot of us crammed into a small space. I wasn't the only one she helped."

"And she was rich?"

Finch grimaced. "No. She was born in the holdings, same as us. Her mother and grandmother died one winter—she almost followed them. But that left her with her father, until the accident in the shipping ports. After that . . ." Finch shrugged.

Lucille nodded. It wasn't an unfamiliar story, after all.

"So your Jay?"

"She's doing some work for The Terafin. While she's working, The Terafin is letting us stay in the manse."

"Where?"

"Where?"

"Where in the manse?"

"Oh." Ellerson hadn't warned her about this. "Umm, I think in the West Wing."

"Let me get this straight. Your den leader—don't look so surprised; I may be old, but I'm not stupid—is working for The Terafin, and The Terafin *opened* the West Wing and deposited the rest of you in it?"

"More or less."

"When?"

"The twenty-second of Scaral."

Lucille whistled. "What have you been doing?"

Finch cringed. "Nothing. A whole lot of nothing."

"They probably forgot you were there until now; it's the type of thing they could overlook." Lucille slid off the desk surface. "But that nothing is about to change. No one who works in *this* office does nothing all day long, is that clear?"

Finch nodded.

"I'll see about your reading and your writing. The math is deplorable, but that can be corrected; if you've the brains and attention to pick up reading and writing, you can handle numbers. But the thing that will probably make you most useful here is that Torra. Is it street Torra?"

Finch nodded.

"Can't be helped. Follow me."

"Wait."

Lucille, who had somehow already reached the door while Finch sat feeling buffeted by the sudden change in direction her life had taken, paused. "What?"

"What did they tell you about me?"

For the first time that morning, Lucille smiled. The smile was almost shocking; it softened her face so much. There was no edge in it, no malice, none of the condescending glee that smiles often showed. "You'll do, dear," she told Finch. "You'll do.

"Come, let me show you the office. I can introduce you," she added, "to my boss."

The idea that Lucille could *have* a boss—could, in fact, answer to anyone—would never have occurred to Finch. The confusion must have shown, because Lucille laughed. The laugh, like the smile, was compelling; it made you want to stand closer, just to hear it better. "He's a good man," Lucille told Finch, "but a little on the old side, these days. He served House Terafin for all of his youth and all of his prime, and he increased efficiency and revenue in brilliant ways during that period; they wouldn't reward that service by removing him; it would be a humiliation and poor repayment for his accomplishments.

"But he has no edge now, and that's needed. I came to work for him fifteen years ago. I was older than you are now," she added, "And I was never a slip of a girl. But things needed sorting out, and badly. I sorted."

That, Finch could imagine.

"It's not *my* office," Lucille told her quietly. "I want you to remember that. Jarven is worth respect, and as long as I'm working here, he is going to get it."

Barston didn't stand over Teller's shoulder for more than an hour—but that hour was broken into distinct five-minute intervals. He had, after all, work to do, and that work would not wait. Teller knew this because he'd said it about a hundred times. He had also asked Teller, repeatedly, if there was anything he needed help with, and anything that required explanation. Given Teller's background, some flexibility in the testing was required, after all.

Teller found it bemusing. He had never, in his life, seen a grown man fuss so much. Not that he had that much experience with grown men, but still.

It wasn't that he thought Barston wanted him to fail, although it did occur to him sometime during his second hour seated at a small, plain desk in clear sight of the secretary, his stack of letters not appreciably smaller, that he would *not* be Barston's ideal of an aide. It wasn't even that Barston expected him to fail—although it was clear that he did. Barston, Teller thought, would expect everyone to fail. Even the right-kin.

But looking at these letters, Teller didn't think he would be much of an aide either, and that worried him. Some of the writing was almost impossible to read, although some was very, very clear. Some of what was written was so hostile, so obviously angry, it was a wonder that they'd kept it at all.

Still, he attempted to sort the letters, stacking them in three piles. He was hampered and frustrated by his complete lack of understanding of what Gabriel ATerafin *did*. Right-kin was his House title, and it clearly had some meaning for the House members, but that meaning was elusive and ultimately beyond his grasp.

He did what he could.

If Gabriel was the first point of contact in the House, all of the letters sent would come straight to his office. Given the stack, Teller understood—perhaps for the first time—that The Terafin could not possibly read and respond to everything it contained.

But neither, he thought, could Gabriel. No single person could. What, then, required Gabriel's attention, and what could be safely handled by someone else?

Barston hovered in the background until Teller was done. The moment the last of the letters left his hand—and the moment Bartson had finished speaking with another of Gabriel's appointments—he made his way to the small desk.

"You've finished?" he asked.

Teller looked dubiously at the three piles in front of him. "No," he told Barston, looking up and holding the older man's gaze. "But this is as close as I'm going to get. It's all complicated," he added.

For some reason, this didn't bother Barston. "Of course it is," the older man replied. "People often feel that the office of Secretary is really a glorified letter opener and obstacle. They don't appreciate either the subtleties or the initiative it requires."

As Teller was only barely aware that there was such an office, he made no comment. Not about that, at any rate. "Look," he said, taking a deep breath and holding it for a moment, "I don't think I'm the right person for this job."

To his surprise, Barston actually smiled. It was only a slight creasing of lip, but it was definitely there. "In my experience," Barston told him, reaching for the piles, "the less one feels up to this job, the better, in the end, one performs. If you are willing to admit you have limitations, it is much easier to mitigate them." After a moment, he added, "That is, if you're willing to admit you have something to learn, someone can teach you.

"Now, let's see how you've done."

"Can I ask a question?"

"You can, as I have said *several times* in the last few hours, ask a question any time you like. There are some sensitive House matters that I am not at liberty to discuss, but if I am unable to answer, I will make that clear."

"Why have you kept all these letters? They're all old, now; I think the most recent one was written thirty years ago."

Barston smiled. "Very good," he told Teller. "You can at least read and recognize dates. We keep these letters because there is very little that is currently sensitive in them. But when they were relevant, they required some discretion. Not all of them," he added, "but a fair number.

"Were you to view the letters that arrived this morning, for instance, they would be much less . . . incendiary. Like any other job, this one presents a fair amount of tedium. This pile is?"

"The one that Gabriel doesn't need to see."

"Good. It is fairly simple to determine whether or not an applicant for this position has rudimentary reading and comprehension skills. It is much less easy to determine whether or not they have the necessary instinct or discretion to handle the daily tasks of the right-kin's office." Barston began to sort through the letters.

Teller watched his expression as he did. He noted the frown, the slightly raised, graying eyebrows, and the brief, curt nods. It was the latter he wanted, but he saw few of those, and Barston did take five letters from the pile and set them aside. He did not, however, comment; instead, he reached for the second pile. Teller identified it, when asked, as the correspondence that would require the right-kin's eventual attention.

At one point, he paused and looked at Teller. "Are you familiar with the names of The Ten Houses?"

Teller nodded.

"And the names of the notable Houses among the patriciate?"

Silence.

"I see. To be expected, I suppose. It is a deficiency which you would be expected to correct at your earliest possible convenience." He set three letters aside. "This last would be those items that require immediate attention?" He leafed through these at speed, as if he knew them by heart, and removed only one letter. But this last caused a frown.

Teller kept his expression composed, and he folded his hands in his lap because otherwise he'd probably be signing to himself, which was always a bad thing.

"The others," he told Teller, waving at the letters he'd removed and placed into their own pile, "are misfiled. I will explain why at a later time. But this one," he told the boy, "is correctly filed. It is very seldom filed correctly. On the surface of things, it is an entirely harmless, even convivial piece of writing. Why did you place it in the pile that required immediate attention?"

He handed the letter itself to Teller.

"It's from one of The Ten," Teller said quietly. "It looks harmless, but almost none of the other letters are from one of The Ten. If you look—"

Barston raised a hand. "I know the letters quite well; I have been at this job, and evaluating hopeful applicants, for longer than you have been alive. Are you saying you chose to place this in the emergency pile simply because it was from one of The Ten? I note that you did not place the other two letters from similar Houses in that pile."

Teller swallowed. He had never been a person who liked tests; of the den, only Carver seemed to relish them. "No."

"Why this one?"

Teller hesitated. "I don't know. It just seemed strange. It was from the office of The Berrilya—"

"It was from The Berrilya himself. Continue."

This much grief over the *right* choice seemed unfair. "It was from The Berrilya," Teller said, obeying. "But it spoke about—about the right-kin's mother, and about The Berrilya's dogs, cats, and difficulty in garden arrangements."

"And his son, I believe, and the grandchild."

Teller nodded. "It's just that there was *nothing* in it that required any attention *at all*. The right-kin said he doesn't get personal letters through this office, but this one clearly came here. Whoever wrote it meant it to be read here."

"And?"

"I can't imagine The Terafin writing a letter like that and sending it as official correspondence by accident. I didn't think The Berrilya would either. So I thought it must be important."

"You didn't think it had been placed with the rest of the correspondence by accident? I assure you, it does happen."

"No."

Barston nodded. "You were correct, and for reasons I will not go into at this time. These others," he added, waving a hand over them, "were not correctly sorted. But as I said, I consider the sorting problem more a difficulty with your lack of education than with your lack of comprehension. Very well, Teller. For the moment, you are dismissed."

Teller rose and tendered Barston a perfect bow. When he rose, Barston nodded. "I will have to speak to the right-kin about a uniform more suited to this office. I will expect you tomorrow morning, after early breakfast. Punctuality," he added, in a more severe tone of voice, "is prized."

After the boy had left, Barston gathered the letters and knocked at Gabriel's door. It was a courtesy; he knew the schedule of appointments better than anyone, and he knew Gabriel was now alone. The right-kin preferred to deal with business in the earlier part of the day, when possible. Still, he waited to hear the muffled word that was almost certainly the command to enter before he opened the closed door.

"Well?" Gabriel asked, noting what Barston carried.

"He can obviously read," Barston replied. "That part, at least, was not an idle boast."

"His writing?"

"I did not have time to test that fully, but that is a matter of a few moment's work." He came and set the letters, in the piles that Teller had made, across the surface of the right-kin's desk. Gabriel took them and glanced through them briefly; he raised one brow. "Not terrible," he said at last. "His mistakes?"

Barston handed him the eight letters.

"I see."

Last, he handed him the one.

Gabriel chuckled. "They always get this one wrong."

"The boy did not."

"Pardon?"

"He sorted it into the pile demanding your immediate attention."

One gray brow rose. "He did, did he?"

"Yes. His reasoning was sound."

"Barston, I'm shocked. I think you liked him."

Barston frowned. "That is rather personal, Gabriel. I have spoken with the boy for a handful of minutes."

Rolling his eyes, Gabriel said, "Your pardon, Barston. Give me your impressions, then."

"He is too young to convey the proper authority of your office, of course. He is also—and perhaps this is more significant—severely undereducated; his experiences have not brought him into contact with the type of people who are prone to correspond with your office."

"And?"

Barston's frown deepened. Gabriel, face straight, appeared to be enjoying himself.

"Were his background to be known, I feel there are correspondents and visitors who would attempt to take advantage of that fact; they would feel that he would be more easily intimidated."

Gabriel nodded.

"However, he is polite enough, given his background. He is clearly honest, and while he was intimidated by the test itself, he was direct in his answers."

"You've been demanding an assistant for some time," Gabriel told his secretary, as he leaned back in his chair, stretching his arms over his head. "And gods know, I've tried to find you a suitable candidate. How many people have you walked through this office?"

"Seven. In two years," the secretary replied severely.

"None of the seven met with your approval. Does this boy?"

"I rather think that beside the point, ATerafin."

"How so?"

"The Terafin herself has requested that we find suitable employ for the child."

Gabriel laughed out loud, which further soured Barston's expression. "Oh no you don't, old friend. You are not allowed to hide behind The Terafin in this case. I am, in case it's escaped your attention, the right-kin. If I deem her request either unsuitable or detrimental to my duties—which depend upon the smooth functioning of this office—she won't blink."

Barston did not look overjoyed. "I trust you are enjoying this?"

"Immeasurably," Gabriel replied. "You haven't answered the question."

"The office requires a certain degree of care," Barston said. "I cannot fully answer your question without a trial period of some sort." He folded his arms across his chest.

"You have it, of course."

"But I feel, in spite of his mean birth, that the boy has potential. I also feel that because of that birth, he is far less likely to make demands of me, or the office, that are unreasonable or difficult. Very well, Gabriel, since it amuses you so much. Yes. I would like to take the boy on."

"I'll talk to The Terafin about his clothing."

It was Barston's turn to roll his eyes. "I'll bring you the letter to sign, shall I?"

"Lucille is," Jarven said, "a good girl."

Finch blinked. What she had expected, given Lucille's description, she couldn't remember. What she faced without those expectations was a man who was older than most of the people she saw in the inner holdings. His was a crisp and dignified age, to be sure, but it was evident in the lines and folds across his face, in the slender fragility of his hands, in the pale cast of his skin.

His hair was white, his beard thin, and his eyes a warm brown; his nose was slender and also slightly curved with age.

"Oh, I know she presents a very fierce front," he continued, his hands folded across his chest, as he leaned back into his chair. "And she can be quite ferocious." He said this last with a fond smile. It was almost as if he were talking about a child. "She says you've come to apprentice with her?"

Finch nodded, not caring to disagree with anything Lucille ATerafin had said.

"Well, you'll find the office interesting. It is certainly busy," he added. "Can you make a decent cup of tea?"

Tea was not a habitual drink of the den. Finch hesitated.

He may have been old, but he read it correctly. "I suppose it can't be helped; tea often seems out of fashion with young people, who are always in a hurry. But when Lucille makes tea," he added, for she had gone to do exactly that, "it can take thirty minutes."

Ellerson's tea took a good deal less time.

"It's not the tea itself, you understand," he confided. "It's the office business. She can't walk across the room without someone asking a question. Or ten."

"I don't think I'd dare."

"You'd be surprised," he told her. "There's always some fire that needs putting out, and Lucille, where such fires are concerned, is a walking bucket. She does have a bit of a temper, and she speaks her mind; usually, where there's been trouble, there's a good deal of mind to speak.

"But she appreciates hard work and effort. Give her both, and you'll do well here."

He didn't ask Finch about her qualifications; he didn't ask her about very much at all.

"The Merchant Authority," Jarven said, when Lucille failed to appear with his afternoon tea, "is an interesting place. It, like the outer office, is busy. There is probably more attempted crime in the Authority than there is in the rest of the holdings combined." His eyes twinkled, his lips curving in a smile framed by so many lines it must have been a common expression.

Finch doubted the truth of those words, but she refrained from argument. She was good at that.

"But it's a subtle crime," he continued, as if hearing what she didn't say. "It generally involves no swords and no obvious violence; what violence there is usually occurs well away from the Authority building itself. Money is here," he added. "Money is the foundation of power. Men—and women—want power. What they are willing to do to obtain it tells you everything about them that you need to know."

In spite of herself, she was interested. "If there's no violence and no threat of violence, what do you mean?"

"Robbery doesn't require a sword—or ten. Not here. It requires clever wits, steel will, and a very good eye for paperwork. Not more and not less. More can be won and lost over a desk such as this than exchanges hands anywhere else in the Empire. To such a desk, then, people bring their best. And their worst. They hide their desperation. They make their offers; they make their veiled threats.

"If violence is offered, it will be in support of those veiled threats, but the threats themselves are never explicit. Money is not romantic," he added. "It does not feature prominently in our legends or our stories. But without it, whole empires fall. Armies need to be paid and fed, after all."

She thought about this. "I don't think I understand."

"No, you probably don't. But you will. Come," he said, and rose. He didn't walk far, but he did walk to the shelves that seemed to be a feature of any Terafin office. He pulled a book from that shelf, and he returned to his desk, but this time he positioned his chair to one side, inviting Finch to join him.

He opened the book.

Finch paled. It wasn't full of words—it was full of numbers. Those numbers, written in a neat and tidy hand, went on for rows, separated by lines. "I'm sorry," she said, her disappointment clear. "I don't understand math very well."

He raised a pale brow. "Well, I imagine Lucille will do something about that," he said, as if her ignorance was, like any office fire, a thing that Lucille could launch herself against. "But you'll have to imagine, for a moment, that you do understand them, because numbers tell a story."

"A story?"

He nodded, and his smile reappeared. "At base, simple numbers tell what many would consider a simple story. For instance," he said, rising again and retrieving another book, "take these."

They were, to Finch's eye, more numbers. But there was something about Jarven at this moment that made her look more carefully.

"This tells you something. This column, you'll note, is marked."

She did. There were words there, on the left. She looked at them. Housing. Food. Clothing. There were a few words that she didn't recognize, but for the most part, the words there were fairly common.

Watching her, his smile deepened. "Yes! You see. These are the expenses without which you have a very difficult life. You require a roof over your head, food in your stomach, and clothing. At the very least. There is some mention here of education expenses, and some that are more social in function—but at base? These few are necessary.

"However," he continued, "this column and that one must balance. The expenses—the necessities—cannot be met without some form of income.

"These people? They lead a very wealthy life, at least on the surface. Yes, those are gold coin figures. But the income that went against those expenses was significantly less. What does that tell you?"

"They were going to starve sometime if they didn't stop spending money?"

"Very good." He closed the book. "It also tells you that they had at least one child—education expenses, and also that particular ball—and that they had a very elaborate house and a very elaborate set of grounds. As I said, this is simple."

To Finch, it didn't seem entirely simple, but she could grasp it. After all, what had the den struggled to do? Keep a roof over their heads. Clothing that fit on their backs. Food, when they could afford it.

"But this book," he said, turning back to the first, "tells an entirely different, and more subtle, story. It is complicated, and in the telling, many small things can be forgotten; it is in those small things that our crimes are often found."

The door opened. Lucille stood in its frame, a tea tray in her large hands. The man who had opened the door bowed to Jarven and then got out of the way.

Lucille snorted. "Jarven," she said.

He raised a brow.

"Don't confuse the girl before she even starts."

"I was hardly—"

"I recognize that book."

He grimaced. But he took the tea and said to Finch, "Perhaps another day, Finch, if you've time to keep an old man company."

Lucille snorted again. "All right, out you go, Finch; wait for me in the office."

"How long were you listening?" Jarven asked. "Oh, do sit down, Lucille."

Lucille, whose arms were folded across her chest now that the hazard of tea had been deposited with the senior Terafin official, said, "I'm fine on my feet. And I was listening for long enough. A good girl?"

Jarven laughed. "If you could only see your expression."

"I'm happy to know it's amusing to someone. Was that entirely necessary?"

"Not entirely, no. Sit, Lucille. A man of my age—"

"Stuff your age," Lucille replied. But she did take a chair. "What did you think?"

"I think the girl was born in, and of, the inner holdings," he replied. "But she didn't lie to you—she is living, with several other children her age, in the West Wing of the Terafin manse. They've caused a bit of a stir among the servants," he added.

"Snobbery?"

"Oh, tush, Lucille, you are so cynical." He waved a hand. "They have made a small network of friends among the serving class, and they confer with one of the Chosen from time to time. Finch also visits the healerie. What Finch failed to mention to you—and to me, I admit, but I think it due to the lack of understanding of its significance—is that The Terafin hired a domicis to attend them all."

Lucille whistled.

"If The Terafin hired a domicis for them," he added, "she is serious about at least their short-term future in Terafin."

"Which means we're going to have to take her."

"It would be advisable, in my opinion." He sipped tea noisily. "If it

were just a matter of idle hands and the need to keep them busy, I feel
The Terafin would have sent the girl to the healerie; she has the temperament for it."

Lucille, who had met Alowan in her time, nodded. "She does. But . . ."

"But?" Jarven's expression was sharp as a razor.

"They obviously sent her to here to toughen her up. That girl cringes as
often as she breathes, and 'I'm sorry' are the first words out of her mouth
when she opens it. She wouldn't get much toughening up in the healerie,
not under Alowan." She was silent for a moment. "She does live with her
den, then?"

"Yes. I think the girl capable of lying," he added, "when she feels the
need. I do not think, however, that she is adept at it. She does seem to
lack ambition," he continued, "but it is just possible, given the current
makeup of my office, that this lack is not the detriment it could be." He
raised a brow.

Lucille frowned. "Meaning?"

"She is unlikely to have any grand plans for the future that clash with
yours." He set the cup down. "She will fit in here, I think. If you can manage not to hover over her like a nervous mother."

At that, Lucille reddened slightly. "She's just a slip of a girl."

"Yes, a girl who is kind enough to listen to the babbling of dotards,"
he replied, grinning broadly. "What she needs to learn is not insignificant
if she is to function well, but she has passed any test I might offer her."

"She listened to your 'stories.'"

"Ah, no. That was pure self-indulgence. I think she will benefit from
her exposure to you, and I think her addition to the office staff will not
harm the overall tone. She will," he added, watching Lucille, "fit in."

Lucille snorted.

"Besides which, you liked her. Don't bother to deny it."

"I wasn't going to."

"Good. It is my suspicion that The Terafin intends for her to learn—by
this experience—some of the inner workings of the House finances. It will
certainly," he added with a grimace, "be demystifying."

"So you think she might be here for the long haul."

"I think it possible. With The Terafin things are not always predictable, but predictability is often dull and uninteresting. Let us accept her,
and see how she does; it may have good consequences for the office in the
future."

"Very well. I have one condition, however."

Jarven raised a white brow.

"You are *not* to continue to play the dotard, Jarven. Have a care for your dignity."

He laughed dryly. "I'll have you know," he told the woman on whom the office depended, "that I was enjoying our little chat. Besides which, it would be good to watch her and see how long it takes her to catch on." He raised a hand as Lucille's less than happy expression soured further. "I will, however, agree to your condition."

"You're in," Lucille told Finch when she at last left Jarven's inner office. Finch had found a seat for herself, tucking her legs beneath her to lessen the possibility that someone running from one end of the room to the other might trip over her feet.

"The pay's not much to start," she added. "And you start early tomorrow. I'll introduce you to everyone."

"What will I be doing?"

"Anything and everything that needs doing. I'll have a runner sent to the manse; you'll need to start learning some basic numbers there, and you'll have to do it on your own time." She held out her hand.

Finch stared at it for a moment and then offered up her own. Lucille's engulfed it.

"I'll send for a carriage," Lucille added. "It'll take you back to the manse."

"Oh."

"Oh?"

"I think Torvan's waiting outside."

Lucille frowned. "Torvan?"

"He's one of the Chosen. He was sent to escort me."

"Torvan. Torvan. Sounds familiar. Sent to escort you?" she added.

Finch nodded.

To her surprise, Lucille marched to the wide, doubled doors and opened them. "You!"

Leaping up from her chair, Finch scurried after her, remembering to close her mouth.

Torvan ATerafin, standing at the head of the other three men, tendered Lucille a bow. It wasn't even all that shallow. "ATerafin," he said.

"Don't start with me. You're responsible for our Finch, are you?"

"Yes, ma'am."

"And you walked here?"

"Yes, ma'am."

"They sent you here on foot?"

"Yes, ma'am."

Lucille frowned. "Well, take a carriage back."

"Lucille—" Finch began.

"Don't interrupt, dear. I don't intend for you to walk from the manse to the Common every day."

"But I—"

"Don't argue either." She glared at Torvan, who seemed as respectful and impassive as ever. "The carriage will meet you at the front steps," she told him.

He nodded.

"I'm due back in the office," she added to Finch. "I'll see you tomorrow." Having made whatever point she intended to make, she now retreated. The doors closed at her back.

Torvan turned to Finch. "Well," he said, looking down at her. "You seem to be unscathed."

Finch almost laughed.

"You won't have to worry about a misstep in that office," he added. "At least, not if that was anything to go by. She obviously thought well of you."

"She's—"

"And before you think her good opinion is all that common," he continued, "let me assure you it's not. Lucille ATerafin is famed throughout the House. Come on. Let's get you home."

But Finch cleared her throat. "Can we—can we take a detour?"

"A detour?"

She nodded.

"To do what?"

"I want to visit the farmers' market."

He glanced at the other guards and then shrugged. "It's my head she'll have when we fail to take her carriage."

"Carriages don't move all that fast in the Common," Finch pointed out.

"I don't think Lucille is going to care."

Chapter Eight

I F TORVAN WAS SURPRISED at the direction in which Finch
headed, he said nothing. Nor did the other House Guards; their formation altered only slightly, but they looked neither bored nor scandalized;
with the single exception of Torvan, not one of them had spoken to her
at all today.

The Merchant Authority became a fancy block of stone in the distance;
the merchant shops, with their expensive windows, their permanent signs,
and their private guards, slowly receded as well, passing windows becoming less ornate and less shiny as they walked. Finch had little experience in
shops of this kind; what they sold—and they sold a variety of things—the
den had never been able to afford.

It wasn't, therefore, this part of the Common that reminded her of
home, and if she had daydreamed of wealth, it had mysteriously come
hand-in-hand with leisure. With, she thought, as the roads narrowed,
becoming more crowded by the yard, acceptance.

Was that the point of the daydreams? Had she imagined that wealth
would somehow convey a sense of worthiness? Maybe. *You're not rich, not
yet*, she told herself firmly. It happened to be true.

But weeks spent in House Terafin had dulled the edge of hunger, and
the clothing that she now wore must have come from one of those very
fancy shops. Or at least the cloth did; all of the panels matched. All of the

time she'd spent standing while Helen ordered her about, taking measurements and chatting—or complaining about her son—had never produced a dress like this one; it had produced, instead, tunics and broad leggings. The fabrics were patchwork, the detritus of the various jobs that Helen had taken that paid real money.

Yet for all that, Finch had been at home in that clothing.

She'd been at home in the Common that now surrounded her, its open stalls, with faded flags and more faded canopies, peopled by merchants who'd probably learned at birth how to make themselves heard over the din of a crowd—and other like-minded merchants.

Glancing at Torvan, she said, "You've been here before?"

He chuckled. "Yes. I'm a guard."

"You're one of the Chosen."

"True. But the Chosen are part of the House Guard. We don't tend to have much custom for the fancy shops; we don't attend balls or events dressed in anything but our uniforms." He shrugged. "The food is pretty much the same, the market over. It's cheaper here."

"It's a lot more crowded, here."

He nodded. "Which, for someone with more money than time, is a distinct disadvantage. You're not shopping for food?" he asked, raising a brow.

"Well, if you listen to Lucille, I need it," she replied with a grimace. Then, realizing what had just fallen out of her mouth, she added, "She's nice, Torvan, and I liked her. But she's—"

"She makes a mother bear in cub season look calm and reasonable in comparison?" He laughed.

"She knows what she's thinking, and she shares."

He laughed again, and she thought she saw a faint grimace on the face of one of the other guards.

"But no, I'm not here to shop for food."

"What are you here for?"

She shook her head as they cleared the street and came into the wide circle around which farmers with varying levels of seniority had set up their wagons and portable stands. "I'm here," she told him, trying to see through the weaving wall of crowd, "to say hello to someone. Oh, there he is, and there's his daughter!"

She left him, then. The one advantage to being a size that clearly made Lucille worry about both her physical and mental health was that the crowds didn't really get in her way. She knew how to move through them, and even a month or two in the fancy manse on the Isle hadn't taken that from her.

"Finch!" Farmer Hanson's eyes widened. So did his hands, which was unfortunate, as he was holding a customer's rather full basket. He caught it before it fell; it would have fallen into his produce. Given the season, there wasn't much chance that the vegetables would be damaged by the fall, but people could be picky. She knew this because it was one of his common complaints.

"Girl, come around the back here, let me look at you!"

She smiled and instantly did as bid; his sons managed, although they were also busy, to get out of her way before their father could nag them. Even his daughter smiled, which was such a surprise Finch almost hesitated. You didn't see a smile on that woman's face every day. Or ever, really.

Farmer Hanson enfolded her in a bear hug before he pulled back to look at her. "That's a very pretty dress," he said. Something about the way he said it felt wrong.

"It's not mine," she told him quickly, and then, seeing that that wasn't quite the right thing to put him at his ease, added, "Jay's working for The Terafin."

His eyes, which had widened upon catching sight of her, rounded for just a second. But his face lost the odd expression. "For The Terafin?"

She nodded. "She's been so busy," she added, "we hardly ever see her."

"And she sent you the dress?"

"Oh, no. I'm supposed to start work tomorrow," she told him. "At the Merchant Authority."

He whistled. "Merchant Authority?"

She nodded.

"You're working there alone?"

"No."

"You came here alone?"

They never came to market alone. The streets weren't entirely safe for that. She shook her head. "But I'm not here with the others. I have an escort."

"An . . . escort."

She turned, and looked at the crowd. "See those guards?"

He nodded.

"Them."

"But . . . they're House Guards."

She nodded.

"I don't understand."

Smacking herself in the forehead, she said, "We're living in the manse on the Isle. In House Terafin."

He was silent for a moment, and then he smiled.

"I'm sorry we haven't come—we've been holed up there. Things got a bit crazy just before we had to leave our apartment. But I wanted to come and tell you that we're all okay."

"All of you are living there?"

Shadow crossed her smile, dampening it. "All of us but Duster and Lander," she said quietly. "They didn't . . . make it out."

"But Jay's all right?"

"Jay's fine. Just busy. She's not doing anything you'd disapprove of. I think."

He laughed. "You've done me the world of good, showing up here. I worried."

She caught his hand in hers and pressed it tightly. "I know," she told him softly. "I'm sorry. We didn't mean to make anyone worry; we just didn't *think*. And I have to get back—but I was here, I was so close . . ." She stopped for a moment and then said, "We all miss you."

"Live there long enough, miss, and you won't," he told her, still smiling broadly.

"You don't know Jay," she replied.

"Aye, maybe I don't. You tell her to take care of herself. And of the rest of you. Carver's behaving?"

"Like Carver," she grimaced. "But he hasn't gotten us all tossed out on our backsides yet, so that's something."

"What's Teller doing?"

"Umm, I think he's supposed to be given a job, too."

Someone shouted for the farmer's attention, and he snapped an order to one of his sons. "Can't they see I'm busy?"

Finch laughed. "You're always busy," she told him. She felt a deep and shining sense of affection for this man who had somehow managed to feed them more than they could afford to buy when things were at their worst. He wiped his eyes, mumbled something about dirt. She smiled.

"Tell your Jay to come down here herself."

"I will. Promise."

Arann sat in the breakfast nook in the wing, listening to Carver and Angel talk. Jester threw in as many words as he could wedge between theirs; in volume, the den didn't notice the absence of either Teller or Finch. Arann, on the other hand, valued the silence they often carried with them; there wasn't much of it here. Jay was still sleeping, and Ellerson had told them all she was not to be woken.

So it was with some relief that he looked up to see Ellerson standing in the open doorway. He noticed first. Had it not been for the domicis' loud and familiar clearing of his throat, he would probably have been the last to notice as well.

"Master Arann," Ellerson said. "Someone is here to see you."

"Me?"

Ellerson nodded.

"Unless there's some other Arann here we don't know about." The sarcasm came from Carver, but Arann ignored it. Carver could breathe sarcastically.

He rose and then looked down at his clothing.

"Your clothing," Ellerson told him, "is fine. It will offend no one— certainly not your visitor." He waited more or less patiently while Arann joined him and then led him out of the room and down the hall to the main doors and the visitor waiting room just in front of them.

To Arann's surprise, the visitor was Arrendas ATerafin. "My apologies if I've dragged you away from breakfast," he said, nodding.

"I was finished anyway." He looked at the Chosen, and then said, "Nothing's happened, has it? Nothing's wrong?"

Arrendas smiled. "Nothing is wrong."

"Why did you want to see me?"

Arann glanced at Ellerson; Ellerson returned the look, but his expression didn't shift at all. No help there, but the lack of any implied that Ellerson was content to let Arann handle the discussion on his own.

"I had word that you might be at loose ends today, with Finch and Teller gone. I'm not on duty," Arrendas added, although he was wearing his uniform. Seeing Arann's brow lift slightly, Arrendas added, "I'm due on duty in two hours."

"Oh."

"If you're otherwise occupied, I'll leave."

"No," Arann said quickly, as the raised voice of Carver drifted all the way down to the doors. "I'm free."

Arrendas lead him down the gallery halls, walking slowly. He paused in front of any painting, or any stretch of tapestry, that caught Arann's attention, and he offered a few words here and there.

"Do you like it here?" he asked, when they reached the end of the gallery.

Arann glanced at him and then looked away. After a long pause, he nodded. Then, aware that this could be misconstrued, he clenched his jaw and exhaled. "I like it here," he said quietly. "But I keep thinking of the people who didn't—didn't make it."

"Didn't make it?"

Arann couldn't tell if the question was genuine or not. After a moment, he shrugged. "Duster," he said quietly. "She died in the inner holdings so the rest of us could run. And—" He looked at the floor, "Lefty. He disappeared before we came here. Down in the maze.

"He would have liked it here. I mean, he would've been scared of it, but only at first. He would've liked the wing, and he would've liked the servants. I think he would've gotten used to Ellerson. He would really have liked the food."

Arrendas nodded attentively and began to walk, slowly, down one of the halls that branched off the gallery.

"I'd known him for so many years. He—he lost the fingers on his right hand. That was his good hand," he added. "We took care of each other. He was smarter than I was, but he was afraid of his own shadow."

"He wasn't afraid of yours, though."

It wasn't a question. Arann shook his head. "Not mine," he said, with a pained smile. "Which is good, because that's where he stood, most of the time. I told him I'd protect him," he added, his voice dropping. "I failed."

"It's not in the failure that such intent is measured," Arrendas told him.

But Arann, who was often accused of being slow, wasn't stupid. "Oh? And if The Terafin died while you were on watch?"

At that, Arrendas nodded, offering Arann a wry smile. "Your point," he told Arann. "Yes. I would consider that the ultimate failure."

"This failure is mine," Arann replied.

"And I'm not to try to take it from you?"

He nodded.

"Very well."

They walked in silence until they reached a set of double doors. These doors, unlike many of the others, seemed to be made of glass. On the other side of them, colors muted in the cool of Corvil, stood the Terafin grounds. "Have you been outside?"

He nodded. "Torvan brought me." He waited as Arrendas opened the doors and then slid outside, looking at the sun. It wasn't warm at this time of year, but it wasn't cold enough for snow. They'd seen snow; in the holdings, it was both beautiful and deadly.

But Teller had come to them in the snows.

Arrendas led him to the same pavillion that Torvan had led him to, but there was a marked difference: It was within sight of men. They were wielding practice swords of the type that Rath had sometimes made him pick up. "House Guard?" Arann asked.

Arrendas nodded.

"I've been thinking," Arann said, watching them drill. "About something Torvan said."

"Torvan talks a lot," Arrendas replied. But he said it with a smile; they were friends. Probably good friends.

"He told me I should consider—consider trying to get a job in the House Guard." Each word was spoken with care, because Arann wasn't certain how Arrendas would take this.

"And?"

Obviously, not badly. "I'm not—I don't know how to fight," he finally confessed. "Not well. Watching those guys drill, I know I'm not that good. I'm big," he added. "I can fight if I have to—but it's street fighting."

"You're old to start learning, yes. Have you ever held a sword?"

"Not a real one. Rath used to make us hold the practice ones. He taught me whatever I know." He grimaced. "Which was mostly how to get bruised a lot."

Arrendas laughed.

"You think I'm too old?"

"I didn't say that. You're older. It will be harder. But it won't be impossible, and if you make the decision to try, you'll work hard enough at it. Most of the House Guards don't come from the patriciate; it's not like they've spent money on swordmasters. They learn the hard way as well."

"Did you?"

"I came from a family of seven," Arrendas replied. "We lived on the edge of the inner holdings. I spent some time in the Kings' army before I applied here. I was perhaps two years younger than you are now when I started to train."

"How? The Kings' armies have age limits."

"I lied about mine," Arrendas replied with a grin. He stretched. In his armor, the cold wasn't piercing; in Arann's clothing, it was.

"I couldn't have taken Lefty into the Kings' army anyway," Arann replied. "But I want to protect them. The rest of my den."

"It won't just be the rest of your den you'll be protecting."

"I know. But I'd learn *how*."

Arrendas nodded. "Join the House Guard, Arann. I've reason to believe they'd take you."

Arann hesitated, and then, quietly, he nodded.

"Good," Arrendas replied, still grinning. "Come," he added, "and meet your captain."

Arann's eyes widened. "But—but—"

"You have to start sometime. I believe," he added, glancing up at the sun, "you're about two hours late. It'll be overlooked. Once." He paused, seeing Arann's expression, and relented. "The Terafin discussed this with your Jewel."

"She didn't say—"

"No, but The Terafin keeps her busy—and it's a necessity. Come."

And so, on the eve of the seventh of Corvil, the den gathered in the kitchen. Ellerson watched them. He listened to them talk, and he watched their leader listen. The energy level was high, higher than it had been at any other such meeting. It was also productive and focused. He smiled.

He did not entirely understand what had brought The Terafin to attempt this approach, but seeing its effects, he approved. He waited by the closed doors. If he was now tolerated in the kitchen, he was still not ordered to sit—and Jewel Markess was well capable of making such a curt and undignified demand.

Jewel was clearly enjoying herself, right up until Arann lifted his head and started to search for words.

"Jay?"

"What?"

"You told her you wanted me in with the guards."

"I told her," Jewel replied, "that I thought you would make a good House Guard; you've the size for it, and the strength—and what you lack in training, you make up for in loyalty. Even I didn't think she'd react so quickly. Why?"

"They'll count on me." The words, to Ellerson, were like the knelling of bells. He saw, from the subtle shift in Jewel's expression—and she was not given to subtlety—that she heard something of the same.

"They'll count on me to stand and fight, if we need to. To protect the House at all costs. Stuff like that," he added, slightly self-conscious. "And they don't care what I used to do. They don't care where I come from. They didn't even ask. They just asked me—" he drew a sharper breath now, "asked me to take up arms and take the—the oath."

As usual a small amount of bickering followed. Jewel didn't appear to hear it, although she did make them shut up. Ellerson did, but he dismissed it.

Jewel reached a hand across the table, and after a second, Arann took it. "What do you want to do?"

"I don't know." He dropped his gaze. "But—but they said, if I serve well, and if I—I distinguish myself, I can be ATerafin. And more than that—if I serve the House well enough, I might one day be one of the Chosen."

"Well, what's the problem anyway?" Angel finally said. "Take the god-frowned oath and—"

"Angel." He subsided. "Do you want to take the oath, Arann?"

"I don't know. I can't take it if I can't keep it. But if I take it—"

"You don't serve me anymore."

Ellerson watched and listened in a very careful, very still silence. This, he thought, was the first test that young Jewel Markess would face. How she passed it—or failed it—would define much that followed in the coming weeks, months, years.

"All right," she said softly—to the den at large. "Get out of here. Go back to watching. I have some things to think about myself."

It was not the best of answers; it was, however, better than Ellerson had feared. He watched the den file out, and he waited; Jewel collected a few miscellaneous household items that had mysteriously found their way into the wrong places.

But she wasn't angry, and they weren't ashamed; it was, to them, a game. He thought, at this point, that if they were to leave the manse, they would take nothing but what they had earned.

Would he be surprised if he turned out to be wrong? He thought about it, watching Jewel's curved back, her tense shoulders, the elbows she now placed on the surface of the kitchen table. Yes, he thought. Surprised and disappointed.

Morretz had given him a gift, late in life, that he had not thought of seeking for himself. And watching Jewel's silent struggle to be what she wanted to be, rather than what she now was, he understood that it was not a permanent gift; like so much that was beautiful, it was ephemeral.

He had watched the den for months, now, and he understood the role that Arann played—and perhaps had always played—in Jewel's mind. She was facing, squarely, the loss of that, and it was entirely due to the fact that he could be trusted. As she had trusted him. What he agreed to, he agreed to without frivolity.

"Well?" he said quietly, when she had failed to move for some minutes.

"What?"

"Can you take the street out of the den?"

"Why don't you go do something useful."

"At your command."

"Get lost."

"I will, of course, give you privacy should you desire it. But might I also say that there are members of Terafin who serve other organizations, just as The Terafin herself serves the Crowns?"

She nodded without looking up, and after a moment, he chose to leave her to her thoughts. He did not leave her with them for long, however.

"Go away."

He opened the door, but he paused in it as she called him.

"Jewel?"

"You said you serve me."

"That is my function."

"But you said you were chosen by The Terafin?"

"Indeed."

"And if The Terafin chose to order you to cease your service, would you do it?"

"I? No. But The Terafin understands that well enough. The only choice I have, besides the choice of vocation—that of service—is whether or not I will take a given master. I believe," he added, gentling his voice, "that

I underestimated both the master and the difficulty when I chose to accept you.

"However, once I have made my decision, it is made—and it is only unmade in the event of my death, your death, any unusual change in circumstance, or the expiration of any contractual period of time."

"What?"

It was hard, with Jewel, to know whether the language went above her head or not; she was at times deliberately obtuse. "Some people will ask for the service of a domicis for a period of time—say, three years—and at the end of that time, I would then be free to leave."

Her frown was slight; she was not, he judged, being deliberately obtuse now. "What about the change in circumstance?"

"If, for instance, you were somehow to become Terafin—or rather, to become The Terafin, that would warrant a shift of service."

"You mean, if I became more powerful, you'd leave?"

He nodded, seeing, for a moment, the future in the lines of her face, in the open surprise she offered. She was not, yet, what she would be. And what would she be? It was beyond him, in the end. "To serve a person of power is a difficult task, and it often requires power. Few of the domici understand the nature of power; it is brutal, gentle, and subtle. I do not, nor would I, claim it."

"I don't have any choice, do I?" She spoke, he knew, not of his own service but of Arann. In the end, it was not Ellerson's loss that she feared—not yet, and not truly—but the loss of her kin and her den. She had thought to protect herself from that loss by coming here. She would grow, he thought, to understand that loss was, like power, a subtler thing.

"You always have some choice," he replied with care. She looked exhausted.

"What?" Exhausted, he thought, and frightened—in the way one is frightened not of death but of the lingering, gray life that might precede it. "I can't keep him. I just can't. He doesn't want anything that I don't want. He wants to be ATerafin."

And it was you, Jewel, who gave him that option, that idea; it was you who encouraged the whole of your den to do what was asked of it so that they *might* one day become ATerafin. You understand, now, or are beginning to understand, that sometimes safety has its costs.

But, he thought, feeling some pride in her, you accept those costs; the other costs are too high. He cleared his throat. "Many, many boys dream of joining one of the great Houses."

She looked up at him.

"You don't have to lose him, you know." He turned doorward.

"What do you mean?"

"Many, many are those who dream of joining a great House. How many truly dream of leading one?" He left her then.

8th of Corvil, 410 A. A.
Terafin Manse, Averalaan Aramarelas

The day did not start as it ended. It didn't start like any other day for Teller, either; he was up for early breakfast, and his eyes were so bleary he couldn't quite tell whether it was dark because the sun had yet to clear the horizon or because he just couldn't open his eyes enough to really see light. Ellerson apologized for the state of his clothing and said within a week it would be "seen to," a prospect that didn't fill Teller's heart with joy.

Even less joyful, however, was the quiet reminder that Teller was there to represent the den—and the den's future—and in such a role, must consider himself an ambassador. He said nothing while Ellerson spoke, and to be fair, Ellerson didn't speak all that much—but he chose his words with the usual deliberation before delivering them.

He also made damn sure that Teller showed up in front of Gabriel ATerafin's office doors on time—where on time was, at Teller's best guess, a quarter hour early. The Chosen at the outer doors didn't really acknowledge his presence, but he was getting used to that. They also didn't stop him from entering the room.

Barston was seated at his desk. Teller wondered if the man ever left the office, or if there were a couple of large rooms, hidden behind a modest door, into which Barston retired at the end of the day.

Barston, unaware of this quiet musing, looked up at the sound of the doors. He actually smiled, although it was a stiff, mannered smile. "Very good, Teller. I am happy to note that at least on your first day here you practice some punctuality."

Teller nodded.

"We have yet to take delivery of any correspondence. You will find," Barston added, "over the course of the next few weeks, that *this* is the only truly quiet time of the day. Any work, any sorting, and any task that is not time-sensitive will be accomplished now." He rose. "I have a desk for you; it is not in sight of the doors. Many other applicants considered this lack of visibility a slight on their character and their aspirations." He raised a pale brow.

Teller tried not to look too openly confused; whatever he managed seemed to satisfy Barston.

"You are not very interested in visibility, are you?" Barston asked, as he led Teller around a corner and straight into a looming wall of shelves. Of many, many shelves. Some contained boxes, and some contained books; some contained stacks of open paper, all of which appeared to be letters, or at least written documents of some sort. He looked up, and up again, and then he looked in; he saw ladders, on bearings, leaning against some of those shelves.

"This is where we keep most of the House correspondence," Barston told him. He grimaced at the open piles. "We are, sadly, somewhat behind in the filing. That will be one of your jobs, if you prove yourself capable of handling it. The correspondence *must* be filed in a way that makes it accessible to those who come after you."

He led Teller past this. "The desk," he said, "is just behind these shelves. Anyone who needs to find you will, of course, have no problem."

Even Teller could understand that "anyone" meant Barston himself.

"Do you know how to handle a magelight?"

Teller nodded.

"Good. The desk is in view of windows; it was put in the back for that reason. But the light is not always good enough to work by. Certainly not at this time of year. There is, of course, an inkstand; there are quills, should you be required to annotate. If you should find that the case, you will use the blue ink. I do not need to tell you," he added, in a more severe tone, "to be careful. You are not to obscure any of the original writing, in any case—but the blue inks are the most expensive of the inks the House procures for our use. Keep it capped," he added.

Teller started toward the desk, and Barston cleared his throat. "You have nothing to *do* there, yet."

Teller nodded. It was going to be a long day.

"The first thing you do in this office," Lucille told Finch firmly, "is stop apologizing. I've half a mind to dock your pay for every incidence. Except in your case, I'm not sure it would be effective."

Finch bit her lip, and Lucille grimaced. "You were about to apologize to me, weren't you?"

Since there was no point in lying, Finch chose to say nothing. It was safest, but only by a small margin; for someone who liked to talk as much as Lucille did, she was surprisingly unwilling to accept someone else's silence.

She hadn't bothered to show Finch her desk—if Finch was to have one—and instead had insisted Finch pull up a chair behind hers. Which was the big bastion that greeted open doors. Finch might have felt too exposed there, but in the end it was hard to feel exposed when you were standing—or sitting—in Lucille's shadow. After the first three seconds, anyone coming through that door politely ignored Finch anyway.

One person was stupid enough to rudely ignore her. And, Finch had to admit, she took a little bit of pleasure in the severity of Lucille's response.

"People will treat you like some sort of servant if you let them," Lucille told her. "Look at the way they treat me."

"Abject fear?" Finch asked, before thought could shut her mouth.

Lucille raised a brow and then laughed. Which caused everyone in the office to glance toward them, but not with suspicion or even fear.

"Aye, well, there's probably truth in *that*. But that's now. When I first started to work here, people thought they could walk all over me. I think they thought intimidating me might somehow get their paperwork done more quickly.

"And there is urgency for some of it. You'll learn to know who to listen to and who to ignore. You'll even learn when to pay attention to people you usually ignore. That comes, with time, and with a sense of the business. But every single man or woman who comes through that door has an emergency, in his or her own mind, that must be dealt with now. They're all busy, they're all overworked—in their own opinions—and they all need things done on their schedule.

"We, however, need to do things on Terafin's schedule, and that schedule has to mesh with the Merchant Authority's." She turned as the door opened. "Back to work," she told Finch.

Finch nodded.

Although Barston had gone to the trouble of showing him the almost hidden workspace, Teller was tucked in a small corner of the office, away from Barston's desk, but in easy sight of it. Barston had—with slight hesitation—directed the mail delivery over to where Teller sat. It hadn't been too bad—a stack of letters a little less intimidating than the pile given him as a test.

Of course, that was just the *first* delivery. Letters arrived throughout the day. He opened them with care, read them, and then divided them into piles, which Barston would, of course, check later.

But, as it happened, one letter gave him pause. He hesitated for long enough that Barston noticed. Barston never looked as though he was watching, but he always did; he was one of those men who naturally had eyes in the back of his head. And probably both sides as well. "What is it, Teller? You've been working well—if a little slowly—all morning." He rose.

"I think this is—I think it's personal correspondence," Teller said.

"And you opened it?" Barston said, his voice dropping a few degrees.

"It's official correspondence from the Order of Knowledge," Teller began. "But I don't think—"

Barston held out his hand, and Teller gratefully deposited the letter into it. Barston read it quickly. He also appeared to read it only once.

"It is both official and personal," he told Teller, but the chill in his voice had eased considerably. "And as such, you can be forgiven for opening it. Oh, and that," he added, looking at the top of the sealed letters Teller had set aside as personal, "is actually official business. It's from Mordenel, who is somewhat old-fashioned and feels that a personal touch is helpful." Barston clearly did not appreciate this personal touch, but Teller didn't mind; he was watching carefully to see where Barston placed the letter he'd been handed.

Barston frowned, and then, with the slightest of smiles, he put it on the pile of correspondence that required Gabriel's eventual attention.

"Master Barston—"

"Barston, please."

"Barston, then. Are you certain that the right-kin shouldn't see that letter at once?" It was, from what Teller had been able to understand, a request for money for the tuition of his son, Rymark ATerafin, if his son did not wish to put his year in jeopardy.

Barston frowned and lifted a white brow. "I am certain," he finally said, "that if it is an issue, I will claim that I made the error. I am also certain that the right-kin personally delivered, to Rymark ATerafin, the sum equivalent to the year's tuition at the Order. If his tuition is in arrears, it is not through any oversight of the right-kin."

Teller still hesitated.

"What is the difficulty now, Teller?"

"I don't think his son will be pleased," he finally said.

"In all likelihood, he will not be pleased," Barston replied. "But if he doesn't learn that some actions have consequences, he is hardly likely to make the effort to correct them. If he comes to the office, direct him to speak with me. If he fails to take your direction," Barston added, "the Chosen will interfere."

"But—"

"The right-kin *is* his father. The office, however, is under *my* jurisdiction. I have never felt that personal affairs should interfere with the smooth running of the office, except in exceptional circumstances."

Teller nodded. It seemed safest.

"Finish with the rest," Barston added. "You've a few hours of work there yet, if I'm any judge."

"What are you doing?" Lucille asked Finch, in a tone of voice reserved in general for angry mothers whose children are embarrassing them in public.

"Guillarne ATerafin dropped these off. He wants them approved. By Jarven. Jarven told me to read them," she added, and she looked up at Lucille in despair.

"Remember what I told you about offering Jarven the respect his service is due?"

Finch nodded miserably.

"Forget it." Lucille grabbed the papers and scanned the first page very briefly. Her brows rose. "Did you understand one word of what you read?"

"Maybe one in three," was the equally miserable reply.

"Guillarne has some small stake in the mining concession granted Terafin by the Kings. This is not official trade business, but it affects some handling of that trade grant. The mines are important to Terafin, but they are not the only mines that Terafin owns. They're significant," she added, "because they produce emeralds and a handful of other gems of note." She flipped a page up. "There has been some questionable handling of gems in the Authority lately," Lucille added, lowering her voice, "which is under investigation. In the meantime, the mines have failed to produce a suitable quantity of gems."

"But what does this mean?" Finch asked, pointing at the documents.

"It is a trade agreement," Lucille replied, "between Guillarne, as a representative of Terafin, and a representative of House Cordufar."

Finch frowned. She stared at her hands for a long moment.

"Finch?"

"You said Cordufar?"

"I did." Lucille folded her arms. Her expression, when Finch looked up, was no longer thunderous; it was worse—Finch couldn't read it at all.

"What happens if Jarven signs this?" Finch asked.

"If Jarven signs this—and to my eye, it *is* urgent, but that's no excuse for his behavior—Guillarne will adjourn with a representative of Cordufar to have the document countersigned, witnessed, and entered in the Authority annals."

Finch's mouth was dry. "No," she said quietly. Her gaze drifted down to the desk as if it were anchored.

"No? Finch, what is the problem?"

Finch heard Lucille leafing, more slowly, through the trade agreement that had made no sense at all to her. "It's not the agreement," she said quietly. "I didn't understand most of it."

"What is it, then?"

"I'm not allowed to talk about it," was the miserable reply.

"You are going to need to talk about it," Lucille said firmly. "Come on." She touched Finch's shoulder; her hand was as firm as her words, but it was still gentle; it didn't cause a flinch.

"Where?"

"Jarven," Lucille replied, with a grimace.

"He's going to ask me what the document *said*." Finch's eyes rounded.

"If he does," Lucille replied, steering Finch toward the office, "I will personally break both of his legs."

Jarven looked up from his desk when the door opened; Lucille had failed to knock. Obviously this wasn't the first time she'd done it, and just as obviously, the lack of a knock meant something to the older man. He didn't speak. He waited.

Lucille propelled Finch toward one of the chairs in front of Jarven's desk; she avoided taking the other by leaning over the desk and dumping Guillarne ATerafin's precious set of contracts into Jarven's hands.

Jarven raised a brow.

"There might be trouble," Lucille told him quietly.

Frowning, he took the documents he had so casually told Finch to read. Clearly, the tongue-twisting Weston in which they were written gave him no difficulty. He raised a brow only once and glanced up at Lucille. Not, thank the gods, at Finch. "This, for House Cordufar, is a very, very generous set of trade concessions in the current market.

"Have you started making inquiries?"

Lucille snorted. "No. I barely had a chance to look them over myself." She glanced at Finch, and told her, "When an offer that looks too good on paper comes into the office, we generally tend to investigate it; what it usually means is that the man who made the offer is aware of some shift that will soon occur in the market itself. He might even be responsible for it.

"A very, very good deal can, in the end, be a very bad one."

Finch nodded. She could follow this.

"But," Lucille added, looking at Jarven again, "that's not why we're here."

"No? No, I don't suppose it would be."

"Have you heard anything about an upward trend?"

"Very little. But Cordufar's gem concerns are large, and he is not a man who is given to idle chatter."

"Finch doesn't think you should sign this."

Finch tried very hard not to squirm.

Jarven looked at her and then frowned. His friendly, if slightly distracted, smile failed utterly to come to his lips; he looked both old and suddenly severe. She glanced at Lucille, who didn't appear to notice the change in Jarven's demeanor. So, Finch thought.

"Finch," he said quietly, his voice steady and even, his gaze now piercing. "What about this contract has made you so nervous?"

"It's not the contract," she said, struggling not to either grovel or apologize. "I couldn't understand most of what it said. I didn't even *get* to the part that's a suspiciously good deal."

If the confession disappointed or annoyed him, it didn't show. Finch had a suspicion he'd expected it.

"If it is not the contents of the contract itself," he replied, "it is either the man who brought you the contracts—that would be young Guillarne, who is known for both his flashy style and the way his grasp on occasion exceeds his reach—or the House that negotiated it." He watched her expression carefully.

When she didn't answer, he turned to Lucille. "Lucille," he said quietly. "I would like any relevant information about House Cordufar brought to my office immediately. If suitable information is not within our files—"

"I know where to get it," Lucille replied grimly.

"Indeed. Do that now; we will assume that the rest of the usual emergencies can wait for an hour or two. Take an extended lunch."

Lucille nodded. She opened her mouth to speak, closed it again, and headed toward the door.

"No, not you, Finch," he told Finch as she rose to follow. "You are not nearly familiar enough with Lucille's arcane filing system to find anything in a suitable period of time; if you're lucky, it will only take you three days. We have less than one. Come. Sit. Wait."

Finch returned to her chair. Lucille was no longer standing between her and Jarven, and Finch already missed her.

Jarven watched her for a moment, and then, to Finch's surprise, he rose and headed toward the window. His window, unlike the window in the small rooms in which things were stored, shelved, or filed, overlooked street. The large trees that were famed throughout the Empire could be seen as rising trunks beyond his back; he faced Finch.

"I do not know if Lucille has informed you about my personal situation," he said quietly. "But I will tell you now that I live in the manse on the Isle."

"You live where we live?"

"Not precisely where you live, and I will add that I do not perhaps live in the same stately rooms. I have no servants who are watching anxiously to compensate for any misstep; at my age, I'm expected to make none."

She started to speak, and he raised a hand. "I know only a few things about your den. I know the name of your leader. Jewel Markess. I know that she has been seen in the company of a First Circle mage of some renown and that he treats her—to the great surprise of many—with some deference, and even respect."

"Respect?" she blurted out. "They scream at each other all the time!"

"That," was his dry reply, "would be a sign of Meralonne APhaniel's respect. More than that, however, I have not troubled myself to discover. However, one hears things, in a manse the size of House Terafin on the Isle.

"The most significant: On the day that Jewel Markess arrived, an assassination attempt was made upon The Terafin."

Finch nodded and swallowed.

"Jewel Markess apparently interfered in time to save The Terafin's life; she had the Chosen summon the mage, and the mage arrived in time. How accurate is this gossip?"

Finch felt he already knew, but he'd asked politely, and he waited for her reply. "It's true," she told him quietly.

"It is odd that the Chosen would seek the service of the magi in this case; it would take time, among other things. I have assumed—and again, I have not taken the trouble to confirm—that the assassin was either a mage or had some magical device that only a mage could counteract."

Finch said nothing.

Jarven smiled. It was not a friendly smile, but it was not a cruel one either. "I assume that you know very little of House Cordufar. It is a Merchant House. What you know, you did not learn in my office; you've not been here long enough. Let me then make an educated guess. You've heard of the House in your time at the manse, and you've heard of it solely through your den leader. Her business is not clearly known, but she works on matters of import to The Terafin.

"And if you have heard of House Cordufar, there is some suspicion that clouds it within the House." He lifted a hand. "Which does not entirely explain why you wish the contract signing to be delayed."

"I can't—I'm not supposed to—"

"Talk about it? You haven't."

This didn't make her feel better. Not when he watched her expression so closely.

"I am a man who has operated for many years on instinct," he told her at last. "I will devise some delay in the signing of these papers, because I feel—as you clearly do—that the timing must be an issue somehow. I do not believe that Lucille will find any hint of Cordufar's activities in gem concerns; I believe—as it is clear you do—that the offer is meant to invoke greed and bypass caution.

"But it is a pity. If I better understood what House Cordufar's intent is, we could make, as they call it, a killing." He stretched, briefly and returned to his chair. "Lucille will be some time yet, and I believe she has already sent a messenger—at speed—to The Terafin. Don't look so surprised," he added, frowning slightly. "Power in the Empire is often defined and supported by money. When matters appear sensitive, we don't have the time to route all requests through the regular—and somewhat slow—channels; we have means of making urgency clear."

He picked up the contracts, the unsigned contracts that had been delivered to Guillarne and, through him, to The Terafin offices in the Merchant Authority. "We have, it appears, less than a day to accept the offer." He looked up at her. "And as such, House Cordufar could not have approached a better member of House Terafin to advance any cause speed would serve; Guillarne is not old enough to be cautious, and he is both canny and—so far—successful. He has yet to learn a reason for caution."

"Have a care, Finch. When you return to the manse, speak with your den leader. I suspect that when the offer has expired, we will see some action from House Cordufar."

She paled.

"You must learn to guard your expression," he told her, his voice soft, his words shorn of the avuncular warmth she had first heard in it. "I meant merchant action." He rose again. "And I see that you have not taken it as such. Remain here for a moment. I must speak with Lucille."

"In the outer office?" she asked, her voice rising as he walked toward the door.

"In the outer office," he replied. He glanced once at her, his hand upon the door. "Finch," he finally asked quietly, "what do you fear?"

She swallowed. Closed her eyes briefly. "Demons."

He stared at her. "Demons," he finally replied. His eyes did not leave her face. She expected him to laugh or to say something—anything—to dismiss the single word she had offered him.

"One day," he told her, as he again reached for the door, "you will have to explain why. But no, not now." He opened it, and left her.

She remained in the office for more than an hour, although she didn't spend all of it confined to the chair. When Jarven failed to return, she rose and began to pace. Jarven's office wasn't small, and it wasn't tightly packed or crammed, the way so many of the other rooms were; it was spacious enough that she could stretch her legs; the carpet muffled the sound of her feet.

She reached the window and watched the traffic in the streets below. Here, the rich came, and carriages of all sizes and colors stopped at the foot of the stairs, while footmen brought stools or offered hands to the people within. She couldn't hear much, and while the windows did appear to open, she wasn't willing to risk touching them. They were glass; they weren't the open space that stood behind warped shutters.

Only when she heard shouting from the exterior office did she back away from the windows and return to her chair. She even managed to stay in it for a while, but the shouting, rather than diminishing, seemed to grow. At length, a mixture of curiosity and dread pulled her from her chair, and she approached the doors cautiously. They were damn solid doors.

Minutes passed before she forced herself to open them an inch or two, taking care to do so as silently as possible—not that she thought anyone would notice.

But at an inch, the voice was no longer muffled.

"Jarven, this is *outrageous*. You've had a chance to read and evaluate the contracts—"

"As I have already said, Guillarne."

"You haven't given me *any* reason for your refusal, and I tell you now, the House will never see as good an offer as the one Cordufar has put on the table. He doesn't bluff—he'll remove it if we delay."

"I am aware of his formidable reputation," Jarven replied mildly.

"You are *not* if you block or delay this."

Lucille was standing, arms folded, to one side of Jarven. To Finch's surprise, she hadn't yet spoken a word. But she glanced at Jarven.

"If you are going to ruin my chances to establish my own reputation," Guillarne said, his voice dropping in volume, "you will do me the courtesy of explaining why."

"Indeed, if I were to do that, I would."

Silence. Finch thought it might last. Guillarne, however, had other ideas.

"I will take this to the House Council!"

Lucille's arm's tightened, and her lips compressed. Finch waited for the explosion. To her surprise, there was none.

"If you can convene the Council in the appropriate time, be my guest," Jarven replied. "However, remember what I've told you in the past about possible gain."

Guillarne stared at him. "They'll have your job, for this. You'll be put out to pasture—"

Jarven lifted a hand as Lucille opened her mouth. It was Lucille's mouth that closed, but even from the office, Finch could hear the teeth snap.

"I may, indeed."

But Guillarne did not continue. Finch, on the other hand, would have fled the expression on Lucille's face.

Swallowing words, Guillarne studied Jarven's smooth expression for a moment. When he spoke again, his voice was quieter. "I would appreciate," he said stiffly, "if, when you are able to speak about this, you would explain your reasoning."

Jarven nodded. Then he smiled, and to Finch's surprise, it was a fond smile. "Guillarne, you are young, and you are brash, but of my students, you were always the most promising. You still are," he added. "And indeed, age addles me.

"I am not willing to allow you the end of these negotiations at this point. It is my suspicion that they would be far more costly for you than you could possibly imagine, and not even for information about House Cordufar would I be willing to take that risk. Ah," he added, as the doors to the outer office opened and a man in a nondescript uniform entered the room, "I believe that is our answer."

Lucille left him, looking only slightly less thunderous, and intercepted the messenger. He handed her a tube.

Guillarne, seeing it, glanced at Jarven. "You sent word to The Terafin," he finally said.

Jarven nodded.

"My apologies, Jarven. I—"

But Jarven shook his head. "Lucille?"

She walked back to him and handed him the tube; it glowed, like invoked magelight, when it touched his palm. Her anger was now muted. "It's serious," she said quietly. "I haven't seen that tube since—" she shook her head.

"Guillarne," Jarven said, "if at all possible, it is highly advisable that you avoid Lord Cordufar and his aides until later in the week. The risk," he added, "is yours to take."

But the sight of the tube had quelled Guillarne's fury, and what was left made him look much younger. He nodded.

Jarven turned back to the office, the tube in his hand. Finch, peering through the open door, had just enough time to step out of the way. He winked, and she reddened slightly. "I won't tell Lucille," he whispered.

"She probably saw me anyway."

"Sit, Finch. Lucille?"

Lucille stepped into the room and closed the doors. She gave Finch a look.

"I'm sorry—it's just that I heard the shouting, and I—"

"Half the Merchant Authority probably heard the shouting," Lucille snapped back. "And they had the brains not to try to crowd in through the doors."

"Lucille." Jarven said quietly.

"I don't think you should involve Finch—on her first day—in matters of the House," Lucille told Jarven stiffly.

"If I am not mistaken, she is already involved, and in ways that you and I are not," was the grave reply. Jarven spoke a word, and then he twisted the tube and pulled the top part free. The back of curled parchment lay exposed, and he withdrew this, handing the two halves of the container to Lucille.

He uncurled the letter, read it briefly, and nodded. "It is as I thought," he told them both. "Under no circumstance are we to allow these negotiations to take place. We are, however, free to attempt to extend the period the offer covers."

"There's more," Lucille said.

Jarven raised a brow. "There is, indeed, more. We are not, at this juncture, to allow private negotiations to take place between any House associated with Cordufar and *any* member of Terafin. This ban is in effect until explicitly revoked." He set the letter to one side on the pristine surface of the desk.

"What's happening, Jarven?" Lucille asked quietly.

"I'm not certain. But whatever it is, I fear you will have your answer soon." He turned to Finch. "You are to wait until an escort arrives from the manse. You are to return to the House with Torvan ATerafin, and if he does not accompany the escort, you are to remain in Lucille's care."

Finch nodded.

The rest of the day was quiet. Finch sat to one side of Lucille, behind Lucille's desk. She opened letters, and she stamped the time and date on the bottom; Lucille didn't expect her to read them all, but she no longer spent the time hovering over her new charge.

No, Lucille was busy writing letters for Jarven to sign. If Lucille spoke her mind as freely as any woman Finch had met in the inner holdings, she didn't write the same way, and Finch scuttled after paper that had been thrown or dropped on the floor as Lucille composed.

While she was on her knees trying to reach under the desk to retrieve one such discarded attempt, the doors opened. In and of itself, this wasn't surprising; they opened all the time. But the silence that spread across the office made it clear that this particular visitor was unexpected and possibly unwelcome.

Glancing up, she saw that Lucille had stiffened. She had also set aside her quill and the paper on which she was working. Some instinct made Finch's knees lock, and she stayed below the desk's surface, looking at feet. A man's feet, large and in expensive boots.

"Lord Cordufar," Lucille said. And then, after a pause, "I don't believe you have an appointment."

Feet were not terribly expressive. Silence, however, could be. This one went on for a while, and Lucille made no attempt to break it. But, eventually, Lord Cordufar did.

"I had hoped," he said, "since the port is closed, Patris Jarven's schedule would not be as unforgiving. I would like but a moment of his time."

"I'm afraid," Lucille replied, reaching for a book that sat between two marble horses on her desk's surface, "that won't be possible at this time of day. If you would like to make an appointment," she added, "I'm sure he would be delighted to speak with you at another time."

The silence stretched. Lord Cordufar's feet moved, and they moved toward the desk. In the office silence, the clear sound of armored feet could also be heard, but no one drew weapons.

"You may tell your lord," he finally said, "that she plays a very dangerous game."

"As you wish, Patris," Lucille replied.

He turned, then, and left the office, and only when the doors slammed—and they did— did Finch rise. She was shaking.

Lucille, pale, was not. She turned to Finch and said, "Go to your desk. I think it best, for the remainder of the day, that you work there."

Finch nodded. "It's probably better," she said, as she began to gather

her work, "than crouching on the floor behind your chair every time the door opens."

She stayed in that room until Torvan ATerafin showed up at the front doors, and she left while Lucille watched.

Chapter Nine

8th of Corvil, 410 A.A.
Terafin Manse, Averalaan Aramarelas

FINCH SAT UP IN BED with a start. She wasn't certain what had woken her, but sleep broke instantly, and she was already reaching for the comfort of a dagger's handle in the dark. Like many of the den, she divested herself of obvious weapons and obvious tools during the day, but night had always been different.

Holding the knife, she slid her legs off one side of the bed as the knock came at the door. It wasn't a gentle, nighttime intrusion of sound; it was a sharp, loud banging. She flung the blankets off, made her way to the door and threw it open.

Ellerson was standing in the frame. "The kitchen, please," he told her softly.

If she were still viscerally suspicious of nighttime visits by strangers, she would have failed to find that suspicion had she tried: His expression was grave, but the almost paternal gentleness that she so liked was still present. Seeing him in the darkness, a lamp in one hand, she said nothing. Instead, she fled to the closet to find clothing—any clothing at all—that would give her the freedom to move.

To run.

Night touched the Terafin manse. The halls were quiet; the servants, silent. The lamps were lit in the usual places, and the magelights shone at their lowest setting, but the silence was not peaceful.

It was broken by the steps of House Guards. Even those who were in theory off duty had been summoned and had made their way in haste to their posts. New guards and old, they stood in lines before their captains, waiting and receiving their orders to deploy.

The newest of the guards stood as tall as some of the oldest; he handled armor well, but he was not yet at home with the hilt of a sword. Not at home with its use. He knew that he was to look straight ahead while the captain addressed the guard, and he did as well as he could.

But he couldn't help looking over his shoulder at the sound of new footsteps, the arrival of new men—men who had, scant hours before, surrendered their shift and their duties and gone home. The young man with whom he'd been paired, who had been in the Guard for only two months, cleared his throat, and Arann snapped back to attention.

Claris was two inches shorter than Arann and not as broad, but he was better with a sword, and he talked more. He was red-haired, although his as wasn't as bright and unruly as Jester's; it was cropped in a regulation cut. Then again, so was Arann's. Were it not for his helmet, which he didn't like because it made his face feel as if it were in a cage, his ears would have been entirely exposed.

"We've word from The Terafin," the captain said. He'd had to repeat this several times, but the repetition didn't dull the words, couldn't make them boring. "We are to expect trouble, on a large scale, tonight. We've called the House Guard, and the Chosen are all deployed; The Terafin herself is preparing for war.

"We do *not* know what form the attack will take; nor do we know for certain when it will start. If the gods smile, our informant will be proved incorrect, and we will have lost sleep—but no lives."

Glancing at the man's bearded face, his pale skin, Arann thought that the gods would not smile, tonight. He didn't ask who the informant was. No one did. The Terafin trusted the information enough to call the House Guard; no guard needed to know more.

"We have visitors at the manse. Some, you are familiar with; some you are not. In the East Wing, there are two lords of note. They hail from the Western Kingdoms, beyond the Free Towns. The Terafin is concerned for their safety, and the heaviest of our patrols will therefore be outside the East Wing.

"The lords are not Essalieyanese, and they may, if they appear, have their animals with them. These will be dogs of various colors; they are almost all of a size. The dogs are reputed to be obedient and well trained, but they will do as their master orders; they will take no commands from anyone else. Do not attempt to interfere with the dogs, no matter what they do.

"The Hunter Lords, as they are called, may join us in battle if there is battle. The Terafin bids you to trust their instincts and to reinforce them if they require it. In all things, they are to be treated as if they are ATerafin. Is that clear?"

"Is it the Hunter Lords who are under attack, or is it Terafin?"

Arann couldn't see who spoke. He didn't recognize the voice. He did, however, recognize the captain's pinched expression. "In this case," he replied, "they are one and the same."

Arann was surprised he'd even answered.

"If intruders are detected, you are to sound the alarm. The runes on the walls at either end of each hall can be activated at need; if you cannot reach them safely, wind your horns."

Arann grimaced. Most of the sound he'd managed to pull from a horn wouldn't carry far enough to do anything but embarrass him.

"You picked a good day to start," Claris told him.

As Arann was thinking the exact opposite, he winced. "The horn—" he began.

Claris waved him off. "One of us'll sound it. First day—first week, if you don't get a chance to practice, and given *your* sword arm, you won't get much—you'll just come out sounding like a wet fart."

Claris was Arann's sparring partner. He looked less bruised, and in a good deal less pain, than Arann felt.

"What do you think's going to happen? Why do you think all the guard's been mobilized? It's got to be something big," he added. Arann's failure to answer hadn't slowed him down all shift.

He glanced at the back of Decarus Holloran, who was conferring with one of the Chosen; the urge to tell Claris to lower his voice and avoid the sergeant's attention was strong. But it was also pointless; Claris could start at a whisper; he just didn't stay that way.

"It's got to be something big."

Arann nodded as Holloran turned. They'd not impressed Holloran in either practice or drill, and judging from the look on the Decarus' face, impressing him was not going to be an option, at least not tonight.

"Cartan, Morris."

Or ever.

"I'm this close to suspending you for the action. You are here to watch and listen—and if necessary, to fight—not to jabber like off-duty servants. Is that understood?"

"Sir!"

"Good." He glared at them both. Since Arann rarely saw him do anything *but* glare, this was almost normal. But he didn't turn on heel and walk away, which was not. "Cartan."

It was what he called Arann. It was what he called anyone who arrived at the House Guard without a surname, which Arann had found both strange and comforting. Obviously, if the House Guard had some provision for cases like this, he wasn't the first off the streets.

"Sir!"

"You didn't come to Terafin on your own, did you? Just answer the question; when I want you to think, I'll tell you."

"No, sir."

"I see. And the person or persons that you traveled with also remain within the grounds of Terafin?"

"Yes, sir." It was clear that Holloran already knew this, but Arann had, over a single long and grueling day, become accustomed to questions that were in no way asked for the sake of actually gathering information.

"What can you tell me about your . . . leader?"

Oh, no. Arann stiffened, and looked instinctively to the door. He managed to drag his gaze back, but not quickly. *Jay,* he thought. *Jay, what's happening?*

But he thought he knew, now. Jay had set this in motion. She'd seen something. She'd seen something *big.*

Holloran was waiting, like an afterthought, and Arann shook himself. "What—what do you want to know?"

But Holloran shook his head in what was for him mild disapproval. "You've told me most of what the guard needs to know. Tell me this, then. Can we trust her?"

"Yes."

"You have no doubt?"

"None, sir. If she—if she's the one that says something's happening, then that's the way it is."

"Good. Because it doesn't appear we have any choice."

*   *   *

Across the House, in quiet rooms, sleep deserted House Terafin. In the healerie, Alowan and all of his assistants prepared the infirmary beds, cutting bandages, laying out disinfectants, and—where it was possible—praying. Alowan himself, roused from sleep, oversaw them. He was gentle in his insttructions because he was always gentle—but he was weary. In his early days at the side of the woman who now ruled Terafin, he had spent days, even weeks, in such preparations as these, and the end of the House War had brought with it the end of such funereal work.

At least that had been the hope.

"Will it be bad?" Maria asked him, her voice shaking only slightly.

He said nothing, but he touched her shoulder gently.

Arann's group was not the unit that sounded the alarm, but the alarm did sound. They were out in the West garden—as far from the East Halls as it was possible to be—when the horns blew. Claris froze, and Arann almost ran into him, but the man in charge—not, thank Kalliaris, the Decarus—did not notice.

What no one failed to notice was the single note, the lowing of that horn. They'd been tense and watchful for the better part of an hour, and Arann hadn't thought they could get any worse. He was wrong. Here, surrounded by the shadows of trees and the nimbus of light from the decorative standing stones in the garden, the men stiffened, froze, and then began to move as if—as if hunted. Not hunting.

But Decarus Mallan listened; the next horn call was three notes. He cursed once and then lifted his own horn and blew it, starting the relay. "They'll send orders," he told his troop. "Wait now, and watch."

"What's happening?" Claris asked, his voice a little higher than usual.

"We've intruders in the gardens," was the grim reply. "And if we're lucky, it's only the gardens."

But Mallan's voice didn't sound like the voice of a man who thought luck, if it came at all, would be good.

In the darkness of the halls, Jay stiffened.

"Jay?"

She cursed, a low string of blurred, hurried Torra.

"They found us," Finch heard herself whisper. A whisper was all she could force out of the tight walls of her throat. The only people in the halls that they'd seen so far were House Guards—and given the number of guards, it was clear that House Terafin was now preparing not for trouble, whatever that word meant, but for war.

"It's not us they're looking for," Jay replied. It should have been comforting. It wasn't. They were in the wrong place, now, for comfort. She lifted a hand and began to move more quickly, and they followed; no one asked her where she was going.

They'd been here for months now; they knew the halls as well as Jay did. Hells, Finch thought, given the time the den had spent in the manse while Jay searched through the dirt, they probably knew them better. Jay was driven by instinct; she crossed the small hall, turned into the largest of the galleries, and swept past the shadowed tapestries, the paintings, the glass cases.

Heading, Finch realized, not in, and not toward the rooms The Terafin occupied at the height of the manse, but out, toward the front doors, the gates, and the guardhouse. Out, on the other hand, was still a long distance away.

Horns sounded; lights flared at their backs; men's voices were raised, but, more ominous, their feet suddenly hit marble, and the cascading echoes of hard boots—as opposed to the den's more modest shoes—echoed like thunder as they hurried.

Amarais Handernesse ATerafin came down the stairs armed for war. She wore armor and carried a shield, but these were shiny and new; they had not seen any use that was not ceremonial since she had taken the House.

In and of itself, it was significant, but it was not the most significant thing she wore: She was girded with a sword. If she had not been raised to war, she had been, as many young women in ambitious houses, allowed to dally in the shadows of the weaponsmasters who had been hired for the sake of her brother.

Her dead brother.

Morretz walked behind and to one side; he would not leave her now, no matter what she said or did. She knew it; knew that the contract that she had signed so many years ago, which clearly delineated the roles of both master and domicis, was merely a simple guide to what was, in the end, a deceptively complex relationship. He was domicis, yes, and he served the Guild of Domicis—but he, as the House, was hers.

She let one hand rest against the cold hilt of a sword that she very seldom wore. She wore it now, not as an act of self-defense, but as a statement; the sword belonged to the House. It was the Terafin Sword, and it was older, by far, than she. It would be recognized. Was, she thought, as she saw the heavily armored men and women forming up in the heart of the foyer, already recognized.

They were too well trained to comment; they simply saw and acknowledged its presence in silence. She took the stairs as quickly as dignity allowed; she understood the importance of that dignity at this time. She was the House personified. All panic, all fear, all loss of control would be reflected. That knowledge was her armor, and she bore it as she made her way to the foyer in which the Chosen were now operating beneath the perpetual brilliance of the chandeliers.

Captain Alayra, the woman who ruled the Chosen in her name, was waiting. She raised mailed fist to chest and out in salute. "Terafin."

"Report."

"There are men in the West garden, near the House shrine."

"Ours?"

"No."

"And?"

"And down the road, perhaps half a mile, there's a large procession moving toward us. It may be coincidence, but they carry torches, not lamps, and the torchlight is glinting off steel."

Amarais was silent as she considered this.

Nothing could hide a large body of armed men moving, at speed, to House Terafin. Whatever secrecy, whatever subtlety, her enemies had employed, they had chosen to cast it aside. They could not now recover it, and they considered the loss worth the risk.

But risk, she thought bitterly, of what?

What did she know? What did she have? What threat was now in her possession that justified this public war, this public exposure? They were desperate, yes; she recognized the desperation in the boldness of the strike.

Alayra watched. "Terafin."

Amarais nodded, although she heard the word at a distance. Something had changed for her enemies. Could it be that they understood, fully, what Devon and Jewel Markess had discovered? It was a possibility. But . . . they had known, for almost two months, that someone was searching for some entry into the undercity of Jewel's description, and that search— with its attendant risks—had not provoked this frenzy of open activity.

No, she thought. Although it was just possible that they were afraid

of the weight of Devon's discovery, she thought it unlikely that it would
cause such a drastic change in their game. But if not that, what?

She glanced around the foyer, at her Chosen. Not for anything but
funerals had they gathered in such numbers in all of her years upon the
House Seat. The Captain of the Chosen conferred, briefly, with the Captain of the House Guard before they parted; the Chosen would remain
with The Terafin.

She did not interfere, did not speak. If not Devon and Jewel, it was
something else. Something had changed within Terafin.

The Hunter Lords, she thought. She had, within these walls, the
Hunter Lords. Devon had brought them here, to the safety of Terafin,
from the Halls of *Avantari*. He had said little, but he had made it clear
that they had already suffered one attack within the palace grounds.

It had not been, she thought, an attack composed of soldiery.

But perhaps there, it hadn't been necessary. In House Terafin, however,
they might have few agents, if any.

They might also succeed with force of arms in a way that they could
not, were the Hunter Lords in *Avantari*. If she had regret to spare for her
hospitality, she did not waste the time; the Hunter Lords were here, now,
and if their presence served no other purpose, it served one:

They had brought the game, at last, into the open.

The horns had stopped their winding cry, but the halls were now lit from
one end to another. It wasn't the magelights; those were always lit. It
was a different light. The paint itself seemed imbued with a gray, diffuse
nimbus. The glow had started when the alarm had been raised, and it had
spread. But it was an odd light; the glass in the windows didn't reflect it,
and as they crossed the gallery, moon's silver could be seen above the still,
dark shadows of the Terafin grounds.

If battle came to these halls, darkness wouldn't be an issue.

Angel nearly ran into Jay's back when she stopped short in the long
stretch of oddly lit hall. She froze, almost in midstep, and then she cursed
in the Torra that she used so often when things were bad.

Lifting an arm, signaling to her den, she began to run.

The ground shook.

Silence followed in the wake of its rumbling protest as men and women
looked up. They looked to Amarais.

"It's got to be the West Wing."

The Hunter Lords were in the East. Or had been.

"Where is the mage?" The Terafin asked softly.

"The mage," Meralonne APhaniel said, stepping into the foyer, "is here."

"Where is Torvan?"

"He could not travel in haste. Not armored and burdened as he was. I chose to travel ahead to the rendezvous. If that is acceptable to The Terafin?"

"It is acceptable." But barely, and only at need. His search through the inner holdings had taken all of his time—if his complaints and his reports were to be believed—and the enchantments laid upon the room the Chosen had used to summon him in emergencies had not been remade. She regretted that now, and bitterly.

But it was not the only error that she had made in her life.

"Good. What, by the dark court, is happening?"

"Torvan didn't brief you?"

"He said it was urgent that I meet you in the foyer as it was where you would be directing affairs. Or something similar; I confess that I don't remember his exact wording. When I attempted to discover what, exactly, it is that you expect to be—" his pause, as he glanced at the assembled guards was significant—"fighting, he didn't have a satisfactory answer."

"No. But I hope you do. If I'm not mistaken, our enemies—and I believe they are at the very least *Allasakari*—have just attacked our walls."

"Walls?" he said sharply. "The manse doesn't *have* walls. It barely has gates."

"Ah. I meant, of course, the walls of the mansion itself."

"Interesting."

Mages were the bane of the civilized Empire on a good day; they fussed, they preened, they demanded, and they carried a conversation as if speaking itself were a chore that had been invented to waste time. The Terafin, as any man or woman of power, was accustomed to their oddities.

This mage was different. His focus had sharpened, but he looked neither confused nor afraid. She thought, seeing the slow shift in his expression, that there was anticipation in it. She had spoken with him almost daily for two months, and he could barely manage civil; he was usually either bored or irritated.

He was neither, now.

The ground shook again, lending physical sensation to the sound of shattering glass and the short, but distinct, cries that followed. At this distance it wasn't possible to tell who shouted; it wasn't possible to tell what had been said.

The next sound: horns. They were close.

"The gatehouse," Alayra said. She spoke quietly, but the two words carried. The Terafin nodded and turned away from the mage.

Jay led them to the foyer. There, at the foot of the entrance, she paused, drawing one sharp breath. The foyer wasn't empty. The Chosen filled it, surrounding The Terafin. Angel almost failed to recognize her—she wore armor, although her helm was raised; she wore a long sword that trailed inches above the ground. But Morretz was by her side, and he stood beside no other in that fashion; he, however, wore his usual robes.

To one side of The Terafin stood the mage, Meralonne APhaniel. He, too, was robed, although his robes were strange; they seemed to shimmer in the fractured chandelier light, and it was hard to tell what color they were, the shade shifted so often. He wore no obvious weapons, and his hair was *way* too long, and unbound; he clearly hadn't been expecting to fight.

And yet.

Something about his expression, even at this distance, made a lie of that. Angel was not his father, not Terrick; he didn't think of himself as a warrior. But Meralonne, in that instant, was.

From across the hall, a man in armor entered the foyer at a run. He wore Terafin colors, and he headed directly to The Terafin; the Chosen must have recognized him, because they didn't stop him. He was already bending his knee before he had completely slowed, and he skidded on that knee as he struck his breastplate with a fist.

In the hall, the sound echoed as everyone turned to look at him, even the den.

"Report," The Terafin said calmly.

"The gate's being attacked. It won't last long. I think there's at least one mage out there. Probably two."

"Who is attacking?"

"It's—it's Darias."

"*Darias?*" The Terafin's expression didn't change, but her posture stiffened until she seemed the personification of the sword she bore.

"Darias colors," he replied. "Captain Jed'ra confirmed it."

"But that's *insane!*" Alayra said, speaking for every person who stood in the hall—everyone but the den, who had grown up in streets where den wars were always in the open. "They—they must be fighting under false colors."

"They aren't our friends and never have been," the young man countered. "Captain Jed'ra—Captain Jed'ra recognized some of the guards. The officers. Three of them. He says they're Darias all right. There are a hundred and fifty men, maybe two hundred. And that's only at the gate."

"Go back to the captain," The Terafin told him. "Resume your post. Alayra."

Alayra saluted. "Terafin."

"It's not just two hundred," a new voice said, as a man emerged from the doors that the messenger now made his way toward. Torvan ATerafin came from the small hall to the south into the foyer. "They've about forty men in the back. None of them are wearing any colors; they're in dark clothing. We spotted them early, and the archers were keeping them at bay."

"Were?"

"There's some sort of magery at work out back. Shadows," he added. "Darkness."

The Terafin glanced at the mage, and the mage nodded.

Before he could speak, the sounds of bells filled the distance, coming in from the gardens and the grounds.

Fire.

Angel glanced at Jay and then at the wide and open space of the foyer. All plans, he thought with a grimace, falter when you see the enemy. There was no enemy here, but the chance of hiding in the shadows, of waiting until they were needed, vanished; there was no damn place to hide. There were no shadows. The light cast by the chandeliers, cut into brilliant, hard shards, scattered across every surface: armor, carpet, tapestry, floor.

"Jay?" he said quietly.

"It's either here," she told them all, "on the landing, or there."

There: the stairs themselves. "You're crazy," Carver said flatly.

"Good. You come up with a better place. Now."

He looked. They all did. Then he shrugged. Here.

At least here had rails. You couldn't hide behind them, unless the fighting on the ground—which hadn't started—grew so ferocious no one thought to look up. The rails were marble, carved and polished so they reflected light only a little less harshly than the armor of the guards; they were, however, widely spaced. You could fit through them, in a pinch. Or at least the smaller members of the den could.

"Your pardon, Terafin," Meralonne APhaniel said, when the bells ceased their clamor. "But I believe you will find there has been some interference in the duties of your guards."

"Shall I?"

"Yes. I thought it best, after speaking with Torvan, to stop at the gates a moment. The fire that your servants are ringing is not exactly as it seems."

"What?"

He laughed. "I believe that my duty is at the gate; your young Sentrus seemed to feel that there was a 'mage or two' present—and it is strictly forbidden, by edict of the Magi, to practice magic of this nature in *Averalaan Aramarelas* without a writ of approval, signed in full.

"Which reminds me. Terafin, I give this into your keeping, as it may become necessary if I am not in a position to defend myself after this evening." He handed her a rolled scroll.

"And this?"

"A writ. Signed in full by the Council, of course."

She laughed. "Alayra. Accompany the mage."

"Is he to be in command?"

"He is to be an adviser. A valued adviser."

The Captain of the Chosen nodded. "Come along, then."

But Meralonne APhaniel was not—yet—done. He drew a sword— from where, it was not clear—and as he swung it through the air in a wide, clean arc, light followed its edge. He bowed once. "At your service, Terafin."

Finch didn't find the sound of a moving body of men much of a comfort; it came from beyond the foyer itself, and it grew. The den's silence grew as well; they were helpless here. The rails didn't protect them or hide them, but they sheltered behind them anyway, watching Jay, watching Carver, watching Angel.

Teller had chosen to climb to the edge of the landing above; he was flat against the ground, two daggers in his hands. He wasn't very good with them, but then again, neither was Finch, and she was also armed.

Jay drew one sharp breath and pointed to a set of doors; the foyer had a few of them. There *was* something there.

Shadows.

Slow, and short, like mist rolling into a valley, but darker and thicker.

The word *Darias*, which had been the sharpest, the harshest, of the words spoken below now faded, to be replaced by different words. Anger gave way to unease.

The den had faced demons. Only Duster had faced one full on; the rest had, by the grace of her action, fled. Arann had almost died. Lefty, Lander, and Fisher *had* died.

This, Finch thought, was what had killed them: this creeping, slow darkness, this sudden chill. It would suck light and warmth from the air, and finally life.

But before she could speak, The Terafin did. Her voice was clear and strong, and she drew her sword as she spoke.

"Terafin fought the *Allasakari* and their mage-born followers." She spoke clearly, cleanly. "And became one of The Ten, revered above all others save the god-born." She turned, then, to the foyer, and its slowly growing shadows. "Come! Your enmity began our road to greatness; let it continue that road, unhindered. We are ready!"

The first things through the door were . . . dogs. They were larger than any dog Finch had ever seen, and their coats, unlike the mangy coats of starving strays, gleamed in the light of the chandeliers. They did not look friendly, and even behind the rails of the stairs, with a row of armed men between her and their jaws, she tensed. Brown, black and white, black and gray, gray and brown, they growled as they searched the room.

But the dogs didn't attack anyone; instead, they turned and stood, waiting.

They didn't have to wait long, and if the dogs had been a surprise, what followed them was a bigger one: a woman, barely dressed, her hair wild and matted, unlike the coats of the dogs. She moved quickly and lightly on her feet, and every movement seemed deliberate; it was almost as if the lack of clothing were natural; it clearly didn't distress her. She glanced up at the stairs, and then she, too, stopped by the dogs, turning as if waiting.

The Chosen began to move, then, but they moved with care.

Following the dogs and the strange, wild woman came three people. The first, a man with hair that was golden to Angel's pale platinum; his face was red with exertion, and his eyes—even at this distance—were dark with lack of sleep or exhaustion. He was dressed in greens with a hint of brown, and he wore a sword; he wasn't armored. He half-led, half-dragged a woman at his side. She was shorter than the naked one and seemed more slender of build, but what was striking about her was her robes: They were a midnight blue, and they seemed to swirl at her feet as if her feet—and only her feet—were caught in a gale.

She looked up at the stairs, and her gaze caught Jay's. Finch knew it because Jay's breath was sharper, as if in recognition, although none of them had ever seen the stranger before.

Jay might have spoken; she looked as though she wanted to. But the last person through the open door was another man, and he was clearly the man the dogs and the naked woman had been waiting for. His hair was dark, his eyes were dark, and he wasn't troubled by the same lack of sleep as the fair-haired man; he walked with two dogs, one on either side—a gray dog and a white and black that seemed to be looking behind.

"Terafin," the fair-haired man now said, "We're—we're being pursued."

So, Jewel thought, watching.

Whatever was here was not here for the den. It wasn't here, she thought, looking at the distant face of the fair-haired Hunter—Stephen?—for The Terafin either. They had come, whoever they were, in force, and they had come for these men, this woman: foreigners from the Western Kingdoms that were barely a footnote in the history Rath had attempted to teach her, so many years ago.

"Let them through," The Terafin said. "Let them through and close ranks behind them."

Her Chosen moved at once, following her steady command; they didn't rush, but in spite of that, they moved damn fast. There was order in the way they walked, the way they stood; it was an order that was as foreign to Jewel as the lords The Terafin had ordered them, obliquely, to protect.

Stephen nodded and stumbled forward, holding onto his companion. But the Hunter Lord—Gilliam of Elseth—did not. He looked, instead, around the open space of the brightly lit foyer, his eyes sharp, his gaze piercing. Hawk's eyes. Bird of prey. An echo of hunting wolf.

The dogs gathered around him, as did the wild girl.

"Lord Elseth," The Terafin said, the words sharp. "Please."

Jewel wouldn't have dared to ignore her; she could feel her body stiffening at the command offered by a woman whose life had been defined by command. But Lord Elseth was born noble, bred noble; her command didn't interfere with his instincts. As if he didn't speak—or understand—Weston, he gestured, once, and the wild girl came running to his side, followed closely by those dogs.

Stephen of Elseth wasn't Gilliam; he flushed, glaring at Lord Gilliam's broad back. "Terafin," he said, striking his unmailed chest with the flat of his naked hand. He knelt, instantly, the reverence and obedience due The Terafin's rank reflected in every turn of limb. Which, given he wouldn't let go of the woman in blue robes, was an accomplishment.

What the first foreigner hadn't offered, The Terafin saw in the second, and she seemed, to Jewel's eye, to relax. "Speak," she replied.

"We—there is a demon-mage in pursuit."

"Demon-mage? What do you mean?"

"She—it—calls hereself Sor Na Shannen. She is a very powerful mage, but also one of the kin. The darkness follows her; she is Lord here."

"Who else?"

The question, the lack of surprise The Terafin showed, clearly surprised Lord Stephen. "Who else?"

"Besides this demon of whom you speak. Who else follows her?"

He frowned. Hesitated. He was not, Jewel thought, his lord's equal; his weariness allowed fear to show. Lord Gilliam? He stood like a living statue, a thing of graven stone; he *had* no fear to offer. Nothing but the burning intensity of his attention, his readiness. He had drawn his sword; when, Jewel couldn't say. She turned her attention back to Stephen, but he was now looking at the woman in midnight blue robes—the woman with the violet eyes, eyes that had, with ease, picked Jewel out of the crowded foyer, as if she could see through anything as inconsequential as stone, or wood. Or flesh.

"The—I think—the *Allasakari*," the woman said, and her voice surprised Jewel, it sounded so *young*.

"You think?" There was no youth in The Terafin's voice. No age. Nothing at that moment but steel.

The girl—woman?—hesitated, and then she squared her slender shoulders, pulling her wrist free, at last, of Stephen's hand. She slid equally slender hands into the moving folds of her robes, and when she withdrew them, she carried something in her hand. She cupped it with the other and held it out to The Terafin. There was defiance, in that gesture.

From her vantage on the stairs, Jewel could see what she held. It appeared to be a glass globe, of the type that could be seen throughout the Common during festivals. Appearances, Jewel thought, her own breath catching, her hands suddenly cold and tingling, were deceiving. She *knew* it. This was no cheap trick, no prop used to separate people from their money.

It was far, far worse.

Jewel could see it, for a moment, not as something separate from the young woman but as something integral and intrinsic, and she felt, watching, that a heart still beating would somehow *feel* like this if it were held in hands after you'd pulled it from your own chest. She had never stood so exposed, and hoped never, ever to do so.

And yet, exposed, the young woman seemed to shed her hesitance and her fear. The Terafin looked at what she held, and her brows lifted slightly, as if she knew it for what it was.

"*Allasakari*," the girl said, speaking without inflection. "They wear pendants; they bear the scars. They carry the darkness, Terafin; they barely contain it, and it will consume them if they do not find release."

"Numbers?" The Terafin asked, as if the words had no effect.

"Thirty. Maybe a few more or less. There is one other mage with them, and his signature is powerful." The girl continued to stare into the depths of what she held, but she fell silent; her brow creased in mild confusion, as if she could no longer understand all of what she was seeing.

And it *was* seeing, Jewel realized. The odd visions and nightmares that came to Jewel, this woman was somehow evoking—at will—through the crystal she held in her hands. Jewel had always desired that much control over her wild gift, but seeing it wielded, she swallowed. *The price*, she thought, although she didn't know why.

"Put it away, child," The Terafin said quietly. She turned away. "We have no more need of your sight now."

She lifted her head, and the Chosen stiffened.

Out of the Southern hall that had disgorged dogs and Hunter Lords and wild girl, there now came shadows, dense as night, and where they touched the light cast by chandeliers, the light grayed and dimmed.

"Stand back!" The young woman in midnight robes cried. Her voice was not The Terafin's voice; it was not—yet—a voice accustomed to command. But they heard her. "Get out of its way—it's deadly to you unless you're shielded!"

Even had she been accustomed to command, the Chosen wouldn't have moved. Jewel knew it, but she'd had months in House Terafin; nothing came between those men and women and the lord they had vowed to serve; nothing but death. Death approached.

"Evayne," Stephen of Elseth said, "The Terafin is no fool. Trust her."

So, Jewel thought. Evayne. The girl's name was Evayne.

"She doesn't know—no one does—"

"Trust her," he said again, and this time he caught her shoulders in his hands. He didn't move, didn't attempt to move her; he stood, just beyond the wall of the Chosen and their lord, and he watched as the shadows grew taller and denser.

What he saw didn't, in Jewel's estimation, surprise him.

But it did surprise her. A woman stepped into the foyer. She was tall and grand, and she wore power like a veil; she wore shadows like robes, but they didn't dim her light. Evayne had said there were thirty others, but they seemed unimportant, an afterthought: This woman was their lord, their leader.

She wore no armor, bore no arms, and barely bothered with clothing; her hair, spun long and fine and dark, trailed down her body. Her skin was the white of snow, her lips the red of new blood, wet and glistening. She was impossibly beautiful, and although her presence promised death—or worse—she was compelling. For the first time, Jewel understood what darkness offered and why men—and women—chose to give their lives to it.

But it was not that allure, not that invitation, that held her; it was the shock of recognition. She had seen this woman once before in a dream. In three dreams, when Rath had been alive and she could turn to him in terror for guidance or comfort.

The woman smiled. She glanced at The Terafin, at her Chosen, and at the people who stood beyond them in the hall.

"This is almost a worthy welcome," she said "A fitting beginning for what is to follow. Lay down your arms, turn over to me those three who are my rightful quarry, and you will come to me in peace. Fight me, and you will come in pain."

There was no doubt at all in her voice that they would, in the end, be hers. And for a moment, there was no doubt in Jewel's mind—and in the mind of her den—either.

*　　*　　*

"That is not much of a choice."

Jewel shook herself. She recognized the voice, but it was strangely distorted; it was as clear, as strong, and as compelling in its way as the woman's.

Meralonne APhaniel strode into the foyer, coming from the Northern halls, as the woman had come in her dark majesty from the South. His hair flew loose, white to her black, across his chest and back. He was neither light nor warmth to her cool and disturbing darkness, but something in him suggested moonlight or starlight, something born in darkness that still shines.

This, Jewel thought, as if waking from a slow, long dream, was the man at whom she'd shouted in her breakfast nook; this was the man whose endless smoking of pipe had been among his most notable characteristics. He wore a sword, and it shone, pale blue, reflecting no cast light.

And he looked young, Jewel thought; young and yet ancient.

"What is this?" The woman said softly, forgetting for a moment the three foreigners, the House Lord, and the Chosen.

His reply? He swung that sword in a wide arc. Light flared from its edge, and it was a light that cut and pierced her shadows. Those shadows lost power and menace, becoming once again the detritus of light, no more.

Her eyes widened. Her pale, perfect arms rose in an arc and the shadows in which she stood moved forward slowly, as if seeking to reclaim lost ground. "I do not know how you come to be here," she said, her voice cold, her fury like a winter storm. "But this is not your battle. I have chosen these as my own. Remember it, and you may walk from the field."

"It is not for one such as you to choose my battles for me. And as for these—surely they will decide their own fate." He laughed then, and the laughter was wild.

"Very well." Her hands fell, breaking the arc; the shadows faltered and shuddered, and when at last they parted, a man stood by her side. He was both taller and older than she, at least in appearance; his face was square and lined. Dark hair and dark beard had given way to time's passage, and silver streaked both, but for all that, he wasn't old. His wore simple, gray robes; they seemed almost out of place. He, like she, wore no armor and carried no weapons.

She turned to her companion, thus revealed. "Kill him."

He glanced at her and then away. Jewel thought she understood why; it was very, very hard to take her eyes off the woman. But he managed and turned to Meralonne.

"Well met, Member APhaniel." There was no friendliness at all in the greeting; there was barely grudging acknowledgment.

"Krysanthos," Meralonne said softly, after a long pause.

"Indeed."

"I believe you barely made Second Circle at the last ordination." These were the first words he'd spoken that made him sound as if he might just be the same mage that Jewel had worked beside for so damn long.

"Should I have revealed more of my powers to the Council? It was only barely worth the effort I did put in. But I am curious, APhaniel. Why do you play with the sorry sticks," he glanced at the sword in the mage's hand, "of lesser men when you have the power of the mage-born?"

Meralonne's only answer was a smile so slight it might have been a trick of the light.

"Very well. Let's get this over with." The mage he had called Krysanthos now raised his hands, his fingers weaving air as if it were the source of his power.

Around him, in front of the shadows, fire leaped from the marble floor, engulfing the Chosen and anyone else who stood between Krysanthos and Meralonne APhaniel.

Chapter Ten

FINCH CRIED OUT. It wasn't a warning, it was a rush of breath with sound attached.

The Chosen moved. They were, like Finch, surprised, but unlike Finch, their cries were pointed, directed, their words clear. They formed up and retreated from the flames; the flames, while obviously hot, didn't sear armor or the flesh beneath it, not yet.

But the flames weren't meant for the Chosen; they were meant, in their entirety, for Meralonne APhaniel, and as Finch turned back to watch him she saw that he was smiling. Just . . . smiling. It was as frightening, in its way, as the sudden appearance of fire had been—possibly more so, because fire, Finch knew, was a mage gift.

This fire? It didn't touch that mage. She'd seen him in the mornings; they all had. She'd certainly heard his raised voice and had been subjected to the stench of his pipe smoke. But *this* man? You couldn't imagine that he'd ever think of touching something as lowly as a pipe; you certainly couldn't imagine that he'd be shouting at a street child across a breakfast table.

He stepped *on* the fire, and when he did, it guttered. He didn't gesture, and he didn't pause; it just . . . went out.

She looked across the foyer and into the shadows that surrounded the other mage, the man who had called fire. Krysanthos was frowning. Fire leaped higher and brighter when he did, but when it came close to Meralonne, he sliced it with his sword and it fell.

The mage from the shadows threw his hands down, and the fires vanished. But Finch knew it wasn't over; even before he raised his hands again, palms upturned and splayed flat as if he were lifting something very heavy, she knew. She reached out blindly and caught Jester's hand, crushing it as she waited.

Waiting had always been hard, but it was harder now; she had no idea what they were waiting for, and even if they saw it, what good could they do? She glanced at Jay but saw almost nothing in her den leader's expression. Nothing but watchfulness and determination.

Finch took a deep breath and turned back.

The stairs *shook*.

And not just the stairs—the ground above which the stairs climbed. Marble cracked and rose in uneven chunks beneath the feet of the slowly walking Meralonne APhaniel. Gaps appeared beneath those feet, spreading to either side. Where they reached the Chosen, the Chosen, in their heavy armor, faltered and drew back, exchanging orders again.

But Meralonne?

He stepped across the growing divide. Where marble rose to strike him, he gestured—with his sword hand—and it fell back, clattering and lifeless. But he did this without looking, without appearing to *notice* that the ground itself seemed intent on swallowing or smashing him.

Finch had never seen a man she could honestly describe as beautiful before. She'd met this one. But not like this, never like this; her throat was dry, and her hands shook. Beauty, she thought, was death. She had never thought it before; she thought she would never think of it in any other way again.

And he did walk. He walked through the lightning that flared from the palms of the bearded mage; he walked through the brief rain of what seemed blood.

"Terafin!" Jay cried.

Finch, wide-eyed, looked at her; they all did.

But the woman to whom she shouted looked as well, Jay's voice cutting above the brief sound of crackling light, of falling water, of breaking stone.

Jay pointed up, and up again, and Finch followed the stretch of her extended arm until she saw what Jay meant: It was the grand chandelier above the double doors of the entry. Men stood beneath it; The Terafin herself was not far. She opened her mouth, but only slightly, and closed it again before words could escape.

But The Terafin did turn, and she did speak, and her Chosen pulled back. So, too, the foreigners, even the dark and grim one who appeared to have heard no other words or orders she'd given; the dogs followed him, although he gave no command. So did the near-naked girl, the blond man, and the woman in dark robes. They clustered closer to the walls and the entrance—or exit—to the Northern gallery.

As they moved, Krysanthos snarled. It was the first crack in his composure, but his composure was not Meralonne's; it was not, and would never be, perfect. His hands flew out and up, and Finch felt the hair on the back of her neck rise.

The cut-glass light shed by the chandelier began to shake and tremble, losing the clarity of its sharper edges. That light, reflected by the surface of marble that was no longer perfectly flat and unbroken, spun and twisted just before the chandelier fell.

It fell over the head of Meralonne APhaniel, who alone of all the men under The Terafin's command or protection had not heeded her sharp and sudden order to move. Nor did she call him.

Finch wouldn't have either.

Someone did—Chosen or House Guard, she couldn't tell—but those words didn't reach him. Neither did the chandelier. It fell, and it fell fast—but an inch above his head, it simply stopped. He walked out from under its shadow, and then, with a frown, turned for the first time. His sword rose, its tip touching the closest of the hanging, gold-trimmed, crystal shards.

It fell, slowly, to the broken ground at his back, and it fell without shattering or breaking. But in its way the chandelier was also beautiful, and Finch thought Meralonne may have protected it not because of the damage it might cause to the living, but because of its beauty.

He turned before it resumed its more stately descent and began once again to walk carefully and slowly toward the mage, who was now sweating. Heading, Finch thought, toward the other beautiful thing the room contained: the woman, in her dark glory.

The woman smiled, and her eyes? Her eyes seemed to have consumed the flame that Krysanthos had first called; they burned with a red brightness that could be seen clearly across the foyer. Her smile was cool and unkind when she offered it to Krysanthos. "So. Even this is beyond your ken."

"I would appreciate," was his brittle, swift reply, "your assistance."

"You will have it," she said, and she took a step forward. "And it will be costly. Never question me again, little mageling." She raised her hands, and for a moment the fire in her eyes dimmed as she closed them. But flames traveled down the length of her slender, perfect arms, gathering in her hands to become the solid essence of fire. She held a sword, a red, burning sword, and a shield of the same color.

Thus armed, she emerged from the folds of shadow that had served almost as a throne.

Meralonne APhaniel smiled. He lifted his right hand, and to it came a shield, silvered blue, etched with glowing, bright runes. His hair flew back, a pale, pale silver; hers rose, in strands of ebony. For a moment, they were the only two people in the hall.

But only for a moment.

The demon paused, glancing over her shoulder into the darkness she had momentarily forsaken. "This man," she said, and no one could mistake her meaning, "is mine. But now is the time. Take the others, leaving only the quarry I demand as my right."

She turned back to Meralonne.

But the shadows that had surrounded her moved, shifting and spreading as they opened the last of their folds.

Meralonne APhaniel raised his sword, straight in front of his chest, point to the ceiling, as if he were saluting her. She didn't respond in kind; instead, she leaped up, and up again, vaulting into the air as if gravity had no hold on her. She turned as she flew, her sword her pivot point, and fire flared from its edge.

Meralonne wasn't there to meet it.

Finch would have watched, *wanted* to watch, but the shadows had finally disgorged the last of their threats. Men came from them, armed with swords that were stripped of all light. They moved in utter silence toward the Chosen, who, unlike Finch, had never been so captivated by the mage and the woman that they were unaware.

But something was wrong with these men. They didn't wear armor, or at least nothing that caught light. They didn't wear helms. Because of this she could see their eyes: they were black. All black; there were no whites.

They made no sound. They didn't speak, and that was fine. But they made no *noise*. And as they moved, they absorbed all the little sounds that standing people made: breath, words.

The Chosen shouted orders. She saw them move. But silence enveloped them all, and no words escaped. They couldn't speak, and if they'd developed something like den-sign, it wasn't as complete. They lifted arms, waved hands, lifted swords, and braced to meet their attackers.

Armored or no, it was the Chosen who broke.

Jewel was frozen, silent. It was all she could do to breathe; the attempt to speak was beyond her.

The Chosen were dying. She'd expected death, but to *see* it, to see it like this, made the room a waking nightmare. There was no way to escape it; she could close her eyes no more. She could see the shadows, and she could see the men—and women—who fell to them, their training forgotten, their mouths open on the shape and the form of a scream that never followed.

The hair on her arms and the back of her neck rose. She caught the hesitant movement of hands out of the corner of her eyes. The den had had to operate in silence so often it *knew* how to speak when there was no other way. Her hands flew, but briefly. *Not yet. Not yet.*

And Carver asked *When.*

She had no answer. No answer she wanted to give him.

He stiffened, and she saw why.

Beneath the stairs, beneath the rails with their wide gaps, Lord Gilliam was fighting. He wasn't wearing armor, and his sword wasn't imbued with shadow or fire or light—but it ran red as he stood his ground against the *Allasakari.*

His dogs fought at his side, darting from side to side, worrying the enemy with their ample jaws, their prominent teeth. But they weren't as *fast* as the enemy they faced. One fell, his body severed in one stroke; another joined him, jaws still twitching around a leg.

The Hunter Lord *snarled* in fury, and his expression was so sudden, so intense, that Jewel could almost hear him in the unnatural silence. She couldn't see what happened to the bodies of his dogs because she realized with a slow and growing dread that the Alasakari hadn't so much come from the shadows as dragged the shadows with them, like a black mist.

That mist rolled over the bodies of the dogs on the ground. They rolled over the fallen Chosen, and Jewel did cry out then; she could. She could even scream because no one—not even her den—would hear the cry.

This was what they'd been searching for, Meralonne, Devon and she. This is what she had been trying so hard to find. That woman, these men, and the darkness that seemed to devour everything it touched.

This is what had killed Lefty and Lander and Fisher.

Only Duster had escaped that death, choosing a different one for herself.

The fear that held her began to burn away. It was not replaced by anger, although she felt some of its tug; it was replaced instead by a strange determination. Yes, damn it, she'd failed them. She'd failed them all.

But she wasn't going to fail again. Not here. Not now.

She stood, gaining height and visibility. Her movements seemed to alert no one. She saw the blond Hunter struggling with the Chosen as he sought to break their line, to reach Lord Gilliam. She put one hand on the rail to steady herself, as Stephen of Elseth fumbled a moment at his side, his movements—all movements—silent.

He drew from the folds of his tunic a simple bone horn. It was plain and unadorned, not the horn of a nobleman. But it was also, for a moment, the *only* thing she could see in a room that contained demons, *Allasakari*, and the Chosen of Terafin.

His hands shook. She tried to shout a warning—but to whom, she wasn't sure. It didn't matter; nothing emerged from her lips.

His lips pursed as he brought the horn to them. He drew breath, steadied his hand, and winded the horn. Silence was broken by a short, flat honk, a graceless, clumsy sound.

But she heard it. They *all* heard it. The *Allasakari* who froze or startled died; there was no quarter in this fight. As if the shadows that had taken and occupied their eyes were part of them, the darkness shuddered and rippled, flattening against the ground.

No other sound could be heard, and even that one bald note faded into memory, or possibly imagination, as the shadows regrouped and thickened, surging forward.

But Jewel knew, watching, that the waiting was almost done.

She saw the young woman in midnight blue hesitate, then grab Stephen's elbow, her hands tight against green fabric. What she said, if she spoke at all—and speech was a hard habit to break—could not be heard, not even by the man to whom she'd spoken.

But her words weren't necessary. Stephen of Elseth drew breath again, this time a longer, fuller breath. His hand still shook, and in the even glow of the magelights that flooded the ceiling above them all, he and the horn were of a color.

He winded the horn again.

But the sound he produced wasn't the faltering squawk of his previous attempt; it was a low, loud, resonant note. The shadows curled, and the *Allasakari* shouted, and for a moment, their shouts could be heard before silence once again engulfed every part of the foyer that didn't contain Stephen of Elseth.

The *Allasakari* began to move toward him; the Chosen, who stood in their way, intercepted them.

Stephen was unaware of his danger. Of anything but the horn. The second note was slightly higher, and it, like the first, was sure and even in tone. Jewel drew breath, held it, her hands tightening into fists.

At the sounding of the second note, the Chosen could be heard. The silence had never stopped them from speaking, only from communicating. It fell, and their voices rose in a familiar bark of sharp, harsh orders.

And his third note, the highest—and longest—of the three, allowed all noise, all movement, all clatter of boot against floor, to rush in as he held it.

"You did it!" the young woman in midnight blue shouted. "Whatever you did, it's—"

But Stephen didn't hear her, and Jewel didn't hear the rest of the words; they were lost, in that instant, to thunder and a different darkness. Yes, the hair on her neck stood on end, but so, too, the hair on her arms; her skin was nubbled with bumps.

She *knew* what she would see, if she could see it at all, because she'd seen it once before, in a dream that also contained the woman who now fought Meralonne APhaniel a few yards, and a world, away.

"What's—what's that?"

Stephen took Evayne's hand from his sleeve and set it firmly to one side. "Nothing that you need fear," he told her, speaking loudly enough for the words to carry.

Nothing, Jewel thought, that she need fear. But Stephen? He feared it. He was white.

"But what is it?"

The shadow on the ground grew frenzied, swirling as if caught by the edge of a storm. It struggled a moment near the entrance of the hall, enveloping the broken arch as it rose.

But against what? The shadows *were* shadows. They fell, in shreds; the light at last destroyed them where they lay. Above their slowly vanishing tendrils, something stepped into the hall.

The *Allasakari* cried out, as if they spoke with one voice, and they turned as one man.

Jewel was utterly silent.

A creature stepped through the last of the shadow, snarling, its long claws clattering against marble as its massive head swiveled from side to side. It was at once scaled and furred; it had a tail that cracked the stone at its back as it swung. Its massive head rose, and when it roared, the foyer shook. Long fangs glinted in the light.

"It is," Stephen said, "the Hunter's Death."

The *Allasakari* began to scream. And, Jewel thought grimly, to die. No silence absorbed their cries; no silence granted their deaths dignity. She knew they deserved it.

But she knew, as well, that she watched a god, and for the first time in her life, the gods were something to fear.

Lord Gilliam of Elseth raised his horn. He sounded the same three notes that Stephen had, but they were louder and more piercing; not even the fighting—and the fighting continued, even in the presence of the Hunter's Death—could mute it.

"Terafin!" he shouted. "Order your Chosen to retreat!" His dogs, the four left to him, withdrew; they gathered around him, steady and silent, as they looked at the great beast that was now destroying the *Allasakari*.

The Terafin froze for just a moment at the command. Jewel thought she would ignore him, and she knew, as well, that he wouldn't even notice.

But the Hunter Lord wasn't afraid. He was not—to Jewel's eye—even surprised. His face showed some of the fey strangeness that had so transformed Meralonne APhaniel in the eyes of the den.

He knew what he faced. Knew it and didn't fear it.

The Terafin turned to Torvan. "Signal a retreat to the Hall of the Lattan Moon."

He was bleeding, his sword was notched, and his expression as he received her orders was grim, but he saluted sharply and turned to carry out her command, his voice filling the foyer where hers had not.

The Chosen began to form up, retreating as the last of the *Allasakari* harried them. The *Allasakari* would die, Jewel thought, and they knew it. But they didn't care. They would kill until they dropped.

The Terafin's Chosen gathered at their lord's front and back before The Terafin began to move.

And then, time stopped, the way it did when something so horrible happened it was impossible to grasp anything else. The sounds of all fighting fell away, and Jewel watched—from the safety of the stairs—as Torvan turned, lifting his weapon arm. He brought his sword down and into the exposed back of his lord.

Carver leaped down the stairs, his hands already glinting, as The Terafin crumpled toward the floor. The Chosen were silent and unmoving, as frozen in their shock as Jay. He heard Angel follow, taking the stairs three at a time as he, too, headed toward the woman who had given them a home.

At their back, they heard Jay shout, "Stay where you are!"

It didn't matter; she wasn't talking to them.

But as they reached The Terafin, Torvan turned, moving slowly and stiffly. They stared at his face, at his expression, and they faltered, although Carver's weapons never fell.

"Why? *Why?*" It was Angel who shouted the single word that no one else found breath to utter. Horror and fury mingled in the two syllables; Carver thought Torvan flinched at the sound. He couldn't be sure.

Did it matter?

As if in answer to the angry, pointless question, Torvan looked up. It was not a brief glance; he threw his head back, his arms wide, as if, for a moment, demanding the judgment of gods. The cry that escaped his mouth destroyed silence, and more: It was a wail of loss and betrayal that seemed to go on forever.

Angel didn't move, but Carver stepped back as Torvan lowered his head and threw away his sword, exposing his chest. He meant to die.

Carver knew, at that moment, that he would die—but it wouldn't be Carver who killed him. Something was wrong here.

Something was wrong enough that Jay had to see it.

Jay would know.

There were no more *Allasakari* in the foyer. What remained of the force that had killed half the Chosen could barely be called corpses; they were so torn and rent. The shadows that had followed the *Allasakari*, both succoring and devouring them, slowed the great beast as it inched its way toward the light and those who still remained standing. The beast snarled and roared, its claws and teeth tearing at the darkness; the darkness, without an obvious corporeal form, returned those blows, rising and falling as if it were a cloud of tightly packed locusts.

Beyond the beast itself, to the west, lights flashed: some red, some blue, and some the brilliant white of lightning. The ground broke beneath Meralonne APhaniel and the woman who had commanded the *Allasakari*. The beast did not try to interrupt the odd dancing flight of their battle.

But the Hunter Lord, Gilliam of Elseth, stood sentinel; he did not take his gaze from the creature. Instead, he waited, calm now, his dogs still and alert at his feet. No doubt disturbed his expression; he expected the beast to reach them.

The shadows lessened inch by inch, until the broken and twisted columns that had once framed the southern arch could be seen. Night had fallen on Terafin; Night now gave way to the ugly uncertainty of dawn.

The creature that the Hunter Lords had somehow summoned roved among corpses as if seeking life; it found none.

And finding none, it turned at last toward the Chosen who had failed in their retreat. They stood in a wide circle around the body of their fallen lord.

"Call it off!" Alayra shouted. "We can't retreat—The Terafin's been injured. It's done what it was summoned for—call it off!"

Stephen of Elseth turned to look at her; he did not speak.

"CALL IT OFF!"

"We don't—we don't control it! It's—you've got to flee!"

Jay reached the foyer floor. Carver turned sideways to let her through. Angel, feet planted, knees bent, didn't move or give an inch. But, like Carver, he didn't attempt to end Torvan's life.

Carver lifted his hands, fingers dancing in den-sign. Jay didn't even look; if she was aware of him at all, it didn't show. He glanced at her expression as she moved toward Torvan ATerafin, and he flinched. They'd failed, he thought. The Terafin had, as Jay had seen, fallen.

But it wasn't to The Terafin that she looked, not for The Terafin that she reached.

"Don't kill him!" she shouted, raising her voice so that it carried above everything else that was happening in the foyer.

But if the Chosen faltered, if they halted at all, someone else didn't.

Lightning flew from the heights toward the ground on which Torvan, still weaponless, stood. It struck him, and smoke rose from his armor before his knees buckled.

"Stop it!" Jay shouted, louder now. "Stop it—you're just making it worse!"

Lightning struck again.

Carver thought there should have been rain, should have been thunder. And maybe there was—but it was all in Jay's voice. It didn't occur to him to tell her that Torvan had killed The Terafin; it didn't occur to him to argue with her at all. Whatever it was she'd seen in Torvan, she'd made her decision, and she was Jay.

She was their leader.

He took a deeper breath, felt a different type of tension in his arms and legs as he backed into Jay, turning his daggers out toward the world. Toward the Chosen. Toward the beast who was moving across what was left of the floor toward them.

Is this what Duster felt? Is this what she felt before she—

Four of the Chosen carried swords, shields; they closed with Torvan's back.

"Carver!"

He nodded. It was odd, to have Jay at his back; he was used to Duster. She touched his arm, and he spun.

"Where is it?"

He pulled the sheathed dagger out of the folds of his tunic; it caught on the threads of his shirt, and he yanked hard, dragging half of them out with it. He handed it to her.

"It's not Torvan, is it?" he asked, as softly as he could.

"It's not *just* Torvan—but he's there. In there."

Spitting to the side, he nodded. "What do you want us to do?"

"Nothing. Nothing at all. Just get the hell out of the halls, and take everyone else with you." She glanced over his shoulder at the great beast. Her eyes were a little too round, a little too wide. Whatever the creature was, Jay knew something about it that the rest of them didn't. And whatever it was she knew, she didn't like.

"What?"

"You heard me. Get out!" She turned away, not even waiting to see if he followed her orders.

Carver might not have obeyed, but Angel, silent until that moment, caught his elbow.

Carver signed like a madman.

"It doesn't matter," Angel said, pausing at the foot of the great stairs and signing to the rest of the den. "This is what she needs us to do, right now."

Carver swore. Angel, who hated to leave her side, was willing to leave it now. "Not down the damn stairs," he told Angel. "There are other, faster ways, and they're going to be a hell of a lot safer than that." He pointed at the beast.

"He's pulled down the arches and two pillars," Angel began.

"We're not crossing them. Trust me. I know where we're going." Because he knew, suddenly, where Angel intended to go. "Finch!"

She started to speak, then fell silent. "I can get us there," Carver told her. "You need to get him out because I'm not putting my weapons in his damn little box."

She knew he meant Alowan. She nodded, and Angel caught her hand. "We're not taking the main halls; if there's fighting, we should be able to bypass most of it."

"If there's shadow?"

"We're dead," he replied, with a grim smile.

Morretz had stayed his hand.

He could not say why. Torvan ATerafin now danced, moved, and fought—without weapons—and he had not yet fallen. Mage fire circled his feet, and mage shields rose around his chest like armor.

But Jewel Markess, street urchin and seer, had urged—had *ordered*—Morretz to stop. Even in his fury, even as shock had given way to something vastly darker and emptier, he had *obeyed*. The shock of obedience, in a man who owed obedience to only one woman while she lived, had taken him to the eye of the storm.

The Chosen faced someone with magical skill; Morretz should be among them. But he glanced at the girl who was trying to see her way through their moving ranks, and he cursed.

Jewel.

She looked up, but she did not look *to* him, and he cursed again. It had been years since he had used this particular skill; Amarais did not require it.

Jewel.

She looked around again, and this time, when he cursed, the words slipped into the realm of the spell used—at cost—to speak clearly and cleanly across distance. She heard the words he would never utter aloud; his professional dignity forbade it. Odd, to think of that now.

"Morretz!" She turned, then. "I need your help!"

We don't have a choice. We have to kill him.

"We have a choice, curse it—get me to him!"

He had only seconds to decide. Amarais had always trusted this girl's strange vision, her unusual instincts—instincts honed on the streets of the inner holdings and strengthened there. Gesturing, something that had irritated his teachers and mentors in his years in the Order of Knowledge, he caught her in the folds of one of his strongest spells.

She was slight of build, but he was not entirely used to lifting such unwieldy weight; had she struggled at all, he would have dropped her. As it was, she lurched in the air like a bird with three wings.

At your command, he told her.

The servants' halls were empty. The servants were either asleep—which Carver highly doubted—or someplace the servants gathered in an emergency; it was something that had never come up in his many conversations with Merry. He'd have to ask her later, if there was a later that allowed for simple things like speech.

But because the halls were empty, because there was no shadow, no guards who suddenly and unexpectedly turned into their worst nightmare, no locked doors, the den could *fly*. Or as close as feet allowed.

The manse was such a big damn place! But the den? It was *good* at running. Single file, taking corners without much of a slowdown because they could use the walls for balance, they ran at his back. No one asked questions, no one argued; if they talked at all, it was with their hands, and he couldn't see the gestures because he didn't look back.

He'd spent some time ranging these halls, first with Merry and then on his own. He'd met a lot of the servants that way, and while many of them were surprised to see him, no complaints had got back to the den.

He wasn't a servant—in Merry's opinion he lacked whatever it was that made a good one—but he wasn't, quite, a House member either; they'd let him wander between the two, turning a blind eye.

This, he thought, would repay that tolerance, that indulgence. If they made it. If they made it in time.

Morretz held her in place, moving her as if she were an ungainly, badly constructed puppet and he, a drunken street performer. He felt sweat bead his brow; he lost the ability to speak to her because he hadn't the skill to hold the two spells simultaneously.

Torvan—if the creature was Torvan, had been Torvan at all this eve— had not yet managed to down the Chosen who circled him, but they were caught in fire and sent rolling back in a clatter of plate and arms; had he been fighting only one or two, they would now be dead. Yet there was something about his magic, and his movements, that was ungainly, awkward. As if he were fighting against his will.

Was that what Jewel saw?

He couldn't ask. But he saw that she held a single weapon: a dagger. And he knew, suddenly, what that dagger was and what she intended. In the moving glimmer of fire, lightning, magestone, and shadow, it glowed, and it glowed like Summer sun. He was aware of the strange and ancient branch of magic that Meralonne APhaniel had used to save The Terafin's life from the first demon.

Morretz couldn't drop her near ground, and he couldn't deposit her before—or even directly behind—Torvan ATerafin; Jewel was no mage, and even the rudimentary protections that the least of mages learned were beyond her. He didn't think she could survive a few seconds of the fire. As if she were a sword, he watched, and he waited; she spun in the air, watching as well.

Entering the main halls again was like entering another world. The silence of the servants' halls, with their low ceilings, their unadorned walls, gave way to the distant sound of horns, of thunder, of the raised voices of men. Whether they were Terafin or Darias was impossible to say; what Finch knew, as her feet hit polished marble, was that they were *distant*. It was enough.

Teller was by her side, grim and pale; she glanced at him once and then headed straight to the single, simple door of the healerie. At its side, lid down, the box that Carver disliked so much stood mounted on the wall; she paused for a moment to deposit her daggers there.

She didn't knock on the door; she threw it wide. And she saw, beyond the aboretum and its quiet fountain, that the lights were on. Alowan was already approaching the door from the healing sanctum beyond, and at his back, some handful of his aides. They'd been prepared for injuries; they'd heard the alarm raised, had heard the bells on the grounds.

His expression wasn't so peaceful, and when he saw them—Teller, Finch—he closed his eyes briefly.

"Tell me," he said. "Quickly."

Finch shook her head. "We've no time," she told him. "You—we need you to come with us. It's The Terafin."

Morretz didn't speak another word to Jewel Markess. He was angry—at her, at himself—because they had both failed in their watch. But even angry, he'd done as she'd all but ordered; he carried her, her slight weight causing a strain that his duties to the House seldom offered. He was unaccustomed to carrying a weapon of any significant size, especially one that squirmed or gasped or struggled in spite of herself.

He looked for openings in the magical fires, the lightning, the raised and lowered shields. He looked for some way through the Terafin Chosen, as angered, as guilty, as he. When he found it, he wasn't gentle; he couldn't afford to be gentle. Nor could he afford to instruct or guide her.

If he had been thinking at all he would have taken the dagger from her. But he was not entirely certain that it would allow itself to be handled by raw magic; its glow was unlike any he'd studied in his years as a student of the Order of Knowledge.

Torvan—or whatever Torvan had become—was both swift and awkward; it was a compelling combination. Jewel would have once chance. He gave her that chance, now.

She held the blade, and he held her, and she brought it in and down.

Torvan turned before it struck him, wheeling instantly; he raised a palm and flame blossomed, long and fine, like a blade's edge. But he didn't try to kill her or cut her from the air; he tried to parry.

Instinctive reaction.

Had he attempted to kill Jewel, she would now be dead. As it was, the incidental damage singed her clothing and blackened her auburn hair. But the dagger? It passed untouched through the heart of the flame, its ornate blade penetrating the plates that protected Torvan's shoulder.

Morretz staggered, then, and let her go as Torvan screamed; the fires around him guttered, and he doubled over. Blood bubbled up, surrounded by shadow, the liquid and the essence of darkness entwined.

But the shadow? It burned. Even at this distance, free of the burden of Jewel Markess, Morretz could see this clearly. *So.*

It would have been cleaner, he thought dispassionately, had Torvan died the moment The Terafin fell. It would have simplified life in the future—if they were to have one at all. Not even Morretz in his deepest concentration could avoid the snarling roar of the creature that dominated the southern foyer.

But Jewel Markess was young. She wouldn't have understood.

And why, he thought, should that matter? He drew breath. Pulled some small power and used it to amplify his next words. "Chosen, in the name of The Terafin, stay your ground! Hold your arms!"

He was not their lord, and not their master; he was domicis. But . . . they obeyed. Thus, the relationship between the domicis and his master.

Jewel found her feet and crouched over Torvan's bent body; he could see the fall of her singed hair as it spilled into her eyes. She pushed it back. Her hand still held the dagger, but its metal was flat and cold; it no longer burned with golden light.

She didn't seem to notice that she was holding it as if it were still a dangerous weapon, that she was, in fact, holding it toward the Chosen, who had stopped their attacks. She wasn't snarling, but she looked, to Morretz, like a wild, feral child defending her kin.

Arrendas pushed his way through the standing Chosen. He had come from the front of the line that now faced the great beast, and he had come quickly.

Morretz descended the stairs, unnoticed.

"Jewel—what has happened?" Arrendas asked. His voice was not gentle.

"It's not his fault," she replied, the dagger pointed toward his chest as if it would do any good. "You sent him to get the mage alone—and he did—but he was—"

"The shadows were waiting." Torvan ATerafin lifted his head. His face was gray, and his voice was cracked and dry. But it was, Morretz thought, entirely his. "Arrendas, The Terafin—" He couldn't speak further, and in that moment, Morretz understood what it was about him that Jewel Markess, in her ignorance, had been unwilling to surrender.

One of the Chosen, a younger woman, pushed her way past Arrendas and knelt beside the body of her lord. Interesting, that Jewel allowed this. She touched The Terafin's throat, removing her gauntlet first, and then said, "I don't know. Call Alowan, now."

"We've—we've got him." Morretz looked to the north, and in spite of himself, he felt something like hope. It was quiet, and it was carried in the hands of Finch—a girl with no other name, no family other than the den of Jewel Markess.

Alowan Rowanson walked beside her. His hand was in hers.

The rest of the den? They were with her as well. Beside, behind, armed—except for Teller—they formed a rough escort for the healer. They had run, yes, at Jewel's command. He'd even heard the words she'd spoken.

But they had done what they had seen as necessary. They had run *to* Alowan. They had brought him back.

"Alowan—The Terafin—" Arrendas began.

But the old healer finally released the young girl's hand. He stepped gently but firmly between Jewel, with her pointed dagger, and the young Chosen, and he pushed them—again, gently and firmly—to either side. They went.

He knelt by The Terafin's side, and the Chosen drew breath, holding it. Waiting his judgment. The beast in the hall did not wait; it *roared*. The Chosen dropped hands to weapons, turning; Alowan didn't appear to notice.

"Let's move her," the woman that Jewel had allowed through said.

Alowan, eyes shut, said quietly, "She cannot be moved. Do not interrupt me. Do not allow anything to separate us."

The gods, Morretz thought, knew a strange, rough mercy. The Chosen drew swords and turned, united again in purpose, to face the last of the threats that the foyer held: the great beast.

All but two.

Arrendas ATerafin stood by Torvan's side. They had entered the House Guard at almost the same time, decades past; they had seen so many of the same battles, the same political squabbles, and they had survived the bloody contest that had been the House succession.

"Go to the north," Arrendas told Torvan. "You're injured. You can't fight here."

It was true. Torvan made no attempt to staunch the flow of blood from the wound Jewel Markess had made in his shoulder. But his pallor was not entirely due to blood loss.

"I cannot leave. If not for me—" Torvan bent, closing his eyes for a moment as he awkwardly approached the floor. But he forced them open, forced them to see clearly, and retrieved the sword he had flung away in the first shock of despair and horror.

The creature—the demon—that had ridden him had allowed him that much freedom. Pain. Despair. He raised his head and looked at the great beast. The demon had feared it. Torvan understood why; it was death. He didn't think he would ever fear death again.

The Hunter Lord—Lord Gilliam—somehow held the beast at bay, his dogs worrying its flank, the naked, wild girl growling as if she were one of them. But Stephen? He held, for a moment, the arms of the blue-robed woman, and he was as white as Torvan himself.

"Arrendas," Torvan said quietly.

Arrendas understood instantly what Torvan asked. Nor did he dissemble; it was one of the things they had in common. "I won't do it. I'll ready my weapon for battle, but not murder."

"Is it murder?" he said quietly. But he turned, then, and he met the wide-eyed gaze of Jewel Markess, who still knelt on the floor to one side of The Terafin. She was—almost—weeping; her eyes held tears at bay, but they could be seen. Her wound grazed his shoulder. A little lower, a little higher, and it would be over.

"You should have—" but he could not say it, not even now—not to her. He turned away. Turned back to Arrendas, who understood, in a way that was beyond Jewel, what had happened and what must follow. "We swore our oaths, Arrendas ATerafin. We are the Chosen. We pay the penalty for dishonoring her choice."

But Arrendas would not be moved, and his reply was colored by heat that could have been anger, had there not been some hint of desperation in it.

"And *she* decides whether or not that penalty is to be paid."

And will you spare our lord nothing? But he did not say it. Could not; it implied a weakness in The Terafin that he would not bring to light.

"It is not up to you—or me—to decide that for her."

If not us, Torvan thought, his own anger rising from the seeds of despair, *then who? We're the Chosen. We choose.* But he turned to look at the woman to whom he'd sworn his life, and the words would not come.

He turned away abruptly, seeing for a moment the fall of a sword he *could not prevent*, and he headed toward the front of the line; Arrendas, in a silence that was in its own way as angry, followed.

But they left off anger, they left off despair, and even thought, when the beast roared and charged, and the line of the Chosen broke.

We failed. And then: I failed again.

But she'd tried—that had to count for something. Maybe it would. Maybe it would, later, if there was one. She tried not to cry because crying was for children. She wasn't a child now. She was Jewel Markess, and she was the den leader.

If The Terafin survived, it wouldn't be because of Jewel or her den. It wouldn't be because they'd planned, they'd chosen a course of action, and they'd followed it. It had amounted to nothing.

Not nothing, she thought, and she looked at Torvan's back. But he faced the beast. And he wanted to die. Whatever she'd done for him, he didn't consider it a mercy.

Jewel sat by Alowan's side. Sat surrounded by the silence of her den. Even had they talked—and they didn't so much as lift hand, never mind voice—she wouldn't have heard them. All she could hear was the roar of the beast. The roar of a maddened god.

She didn't know how she knew it was a god, but she usually didn't; she accepted the knowledge as if it were fact. Because it was. Somehow, this beast was the Hunter God, and it was wild. It was death.

The Hunter's Death.

She couldn't speak. She didn't make a sound when the wild girl stopped in front of the beast's massive, slavering jaws and roared *at* it. Her voice was high, human, framed by fury and desperation; it contained nothing as simple as words. She glistened with sweat; her matted, lank hair flew around her face as she shook her head, snarling, the flat of normal, human teeth exposed.

Almost, he paused, this god, this creature. His eyes seemed to see the girl, and her voice seemed to touch him. He hesitated, lowering his head, and Jewel heard the intake of a dozen breaths—but hers wasn't one of them.

She *knew* that the creature would not kill the girl.

And she knew that no such compunction would stop it from doing what it did next: It leaped over both her and the Hunter Lord who had approached his death with such grim determination, and it crashed into the line of the Chosen, breaking it.

She flinched, closing her eyes, lifting her hands to her ears, as it found its first victim among those who defended the ground upon which their lord now lay. The fact that Jewel was right beside her signified nothing to either the Chosen or the god. Jewel, and her den, would never be that important.

But they could die just as if they were. The struggles of those who wielded power often crushed, first, those without any.

Her gaze was drawn to one of the Hunters. Not the dark-haired, angry one who seemed to command the dogs as if he could speak their language, and who even now was turning toward the back of the hungry god, but the other, the blond, the man who was polite, diffident, and adept with words. The man who had offered The Terafin her due and had demanded, in silence, that Lord Gilliam at least attempt to do the same.

He was white. He stood, horn in hand, watching, and he trembled. Jewel, who had lived with fear for most of her life, knew the feel and the taste of it. She'd daydreamed for most of that life of becoming so powerful that she never need to feel fear again. It had been a child's dream, a fool's dream.

The most powerful woman she had ever met lay near death beneath the hands of a healer. The most powerful man she had ever met fought a demon as if the foyer in the distance existed in an entirely different world.

The beast snarled and roared, and a higher snarl joined his in counterpoint; the wild girl, pale hair flying, had leaped somehow among the Chosen upon whom he was attempting to feed. Her throat shouldn't have been able to make a sound so loud and so furious—but this time, the beast noticed her, and when he leaped, he didn't leap to avoid her.

His jaws clipped her forearm, and even as the wild girl pulled back, Jewel could see that her arm was red—red and white. She staggered, but she made no sound.

Lord Gilliam did, as if he could somehow feel her pain. He moved, then, and moved quickly, wielding a long, heavy spear, with a very odd head. He jabbed the beast once with it, twice, and the beast deigned to notice the irritant; he turned the whole of his body from the girl—from the Chosen—and at last faced the only man who had raised weapon against him and drawn any blood at all.

"Stephen!" Lord Gilliam cried. "Take them to safety, now!"

She felt Stephen's fear ebb, shift, change, but it was still in Stephen, still governing his pallor. He moved to obey—no surprise, Jewel would have—grabbing two dogs, and nudging the wild girl to the north, behind the line of the Chosen assembled to protect their lord.

The Chosen themselves re-formed, men stepping into positions their comrades had occupied scant minutes before.

Stephen took a few steps, looking to the wild girl, the dogs. Jewel thought, Jewel *knew*, that this was somehow wrong. She couldn't breathe. She felt fear—her own, his, it didn't matter—and with that fear, a certainty that Stephen himself did not possess.

And then, face still pale, breath still shallow, Stephen of Elseth turned. She caught a glimpse of his face as he did; he didn't seem to see her, or The Terafin, or Alowan. He didn't see the Chosen who stood between him and Lord Gilliam. He saw the beast, and he flinched, but he held his ground.

"Evayne," he said, his voice unsteady.

She turned to him, her expression anxious, her violet eyes almost dark. "What?"

"Take care of them."

"What?"

"Take care of Gilliam and Espere and his stupid dogs."

The robes Evayne wore shifted at her feet, twisting round her legs, as if they were part of her, part of what she felt. As if, Jewel thought, almost numb, they could feel what Jewel herself could feel.

"Promise it," Stephen said. His voice did not rise. It did not grow steadier. The fear ate him, ate away at his ability to stand his ground. Jewel thought he would stop. She thought he would turn and flee, for she was absolutely certain she would have. "Promise it. Promise that you'll watch them no matter what age you travel in."

"But I—"

"Promise it."

Jewel didn't know him, but she understood that part of his fear. It was what she herself would have asked, although she would have used different names; the force of the desire for the safety of the people that she loved had guided her for most of her conscious life.

And it had led her to darkness, to loss, to death.

But it had never yet led to her own death. She started to rise, and her legs locked beneath her, her body denying her impulse to reach out, to touch Stephen of Elseth.

"I—I promise, Stephen. But—"

"Swear it by Bredan," he said, his voice lower now, although it was not notably steadier. "Swear it in his name."

"I—" Evayne hesitated, as if that name meant something to her. "I so swear. But—"

And Jewel knew. Knew what he would do. Even Evayne didn't seem to understand it. Or perhaps she was unwilling to do so; there was something about the way she sought Stephen's side that implied much. Had she known, she could have touched him; had she known, she could have grabbed his arm, or his tunic, or even his hair, which flew past in a golden blur.

But she stood, mouth half open, as he turned and ran. He ran *fast*. Almost as fast as Lord Gilliam had.

He didn't run to the north, to safety.

He didn't run toward Lord Gilliam, who had taken small wounds and who had offered them, but who had not—yet—fallen to the beast's great jaws. No, he ran into the shadowed wreckage to the south.

He stopped there, winded, his back against a partly crumbled wall. Jewel could see his face—even at this distance, although he stood beneath no magelights. She could see that he held the plain, bone horn in a shaking hand, and could see the way he lifted it to his lips. He drew a shallow breath.

She knew nothing about him, nothing at all. Nothing about his childhood, or his life, or the lands he had come from. But she didn't need to know any of that; she could see the way fear warred with determination and shame, and her breath caught when he lifted the horn again and sounded the first note. It was followed by another, both long; they were quiet and shaky. But the next two, two short notes were louder. Two long notes followed.

Jewel thought he would fail, then. *Knew* that somehow, if the horn stopped there, he would fail. She held her breath as he drew his.

He blew three notes.

She would remember the notes—all nine—for as long as she lived. And she *would* live, now.

As she *knew* it would, the great beast faltered, turning from Lord Gilliam and his spear as if they were no longer necessary, no longer of value. He raised his head, testing the air as if a breeze had followed the last of the dying notes, and then he turned toward the shadows, which held nothing now but corpses and Stephen of Elseth.

It was not the corpses he sought.

He sprang away from Lord Gilliam with a speed and a suppleness that his size and his weight should have made impossible, and he landed, cracking stone.

Lord Stephen didn't raise a weapon; he had no spear. He dropped the horn, and he met the gaze of the beast; he spoke no words at all. Made no plea. But he had time for none; perhaps, in their fashion, wild and savage gods could also be merciful.

He did scream, once.

Lord Gilliam of Elseth's answering scream was louder, longer. No new wounds suddenly erupted across his flesh; no shadow, no mage fire, and no lightning struck him. But had they, he would have made no sound.

His voice broke, and the scream trailed into something like animal keening; his dogs howled, and the wild girl, arm still bleeding, began to howl as well. Lord Gilliam staggered, dropped his spear, fell to one knee. The Chosen closed around him, their swords and shields facing out, toward the beast.

But the beast was done, Jewel knew, with killing. What was left?

Feeding.

Chapter Eleven

JEWEL'S KNEES LOCKED. She wasn't sure when she'd gained her feet, but all around her, her den was also standing. They waited, in loose formation, around Alowan, whose hands hadn't left The Terafin's face.

Jewel didn't want to watch the god feed, but she couldn't look away. And because she couldn't, she saw the glimmering of the magic that would transform the beast. Light, brief and brilliant, seemed to strike it—but the light came from within, sharp and harsh. It radiated outward, and as it did, it pulled at fur, at scale, at fang and claw, as if all of these things were no longer solid. But it pulled them *in*, as if light could devour.

As it did, the form of the beast, already shifting and pulsing, began to fall in on itself, the long tail shrinking and dwindling, the shoulders shedding armor, fur, and height. Even the massive head rose up from the ground, as if lifted, and began to condense.

Stephen had done this, somehow.

Jewel knew it, watching; the Chosen knew it as well. They saluted him, in ones and twos, their faces—where they could be seen at all beneath their helms—pale.

The foyer was utterly silent. Jewel glanced at the end of the hall that had once contained Sor Na Shannen and Meralonne; they were gone. Whether they were dead or not, she couldn't tell; she doubted it. But her certainty had deserted her, as it so often did. She felt tired.

Tired enough that she spoke no word to her den, not even in den-sign;

she didn't tell them to move, to leave, or to hide. She watched as the beast became, at last, something that could be called a god.

He was not, in appearance, human. His eyes were like gold, but brighter, warmer, as he turned away from Stephen's savaged corpse. There was no blood on his lips, no blood on his hands. There was, however, blood upon the antlers that rose from his forehead toward a ceiling that no longer held a chandelier.

He wore robes, but the color was hard to define; it was all colors, and no color, and it hung in loose folds from his shoulders and his arms, trailing over the upturned faces of the dead like a benison as he walked. He glanced at the living—Chosen, wild girl, healer-born, den. But he spoke to none of them; the lone Hunter Lord in the hall drew the brunt of his attention.

"Hunter," the god said.

Jewel had never heard a god speak. His voice wasn't a single voice; it was a multitude of voices, perfectly timed. Young, old, male, female, it shook the air, although it wasn't loud. "Hunter."

There was majesty in the single word, and in the voice, that both contained and *demanded* respect. Respect came in many forms. The Chosen stiffened. The den? Carver fell to his knees; Angel dropped to one, struggling. Finch, Teller, and Jester fell to the ground as well, but not to bow, not to offer respect; they sought shelter behind the mailed legs of the Chosen who still stood between their lord and the god.

Only Jewel remained on her feet, drawing her arms tight around her chest.

But if he noticed, this antlered god, he said nothing, did nothing. He didn't lift his gaze from Lord Gilliam's face. The wild girl stood to one side of Lord Gilliam. She didn't growl, didn't speak, and would not leave him as he stepped forward.

He wasn't afraid. He wasn't even angry, not yet—although Jewel thought it would come. But his face was wet, and if he wept silently, he still wept. He wasn't afraid of tears. He wasn't, Jewel thought, afraid of anything anymore.

The god watched Lord Gilliam for a long moment, and then he lifted his hands, in two fists, skyward, as if there were something in his grip and he had just pulled it, hard.

She felt the mists before she saw them, and she knew that everyone else could see what she saw; she could hear the intake of their breath. But they watched and waited while those mists rose up, until at last they enclosed the wild girl, the woman in midnight robes, and Lord Gilliam.

Only then did she breathe.

Meralonne APhaniel came from the north. He wasn't wounded, but he wasn't happy, and the light that had limned his face was guttered. He looked weary. He approached the Chosen, and they lowered their swords to allow him to pass.

"The demon?" Morretz asked, for The Terafin, lying beneath Alowan's hands, could not.

"She is gone," he replied, with a bitter twist of lips. "But not, alas, destroyed. And I am without my pipe."

Morretz's disdain for Meralonne's pipe was well known; he failed to hear the comment. "When did she leave?"

"Shortly after the god arrived," was his curt reply.

"And you let her escape?"

This question was met with a gaze that defined the word cold. "I have been long from the sword," was the reply. "But I will never be so long from it again." He gazed at the mist, as if he could see through it. "Do you understand what you see, Morretz?"

Morretz looked, pointedly, at The Terafin.

Meralonne shrugged. Jewel thought, for just a minute, that Morretz would hit him; the domicis' hands curled into sudden, hard fists. But he refrained. "You see a god," the mage said softly. "A god walking the world. You do not understand the significance."

But Morretz frowned. "A . . . god?"

Meralonne nodded. "A god long absent from the Council of Gods, and, I think, long missed."

"What god takes the form of a beast?"

"The Hunter God," Meralonne replied. He hesitated for a moment, and Jewel marked it because it was so unusual. Hesitation was not his style. "We have long theorized about the effect of the world on the gods as they exist now. I do not think that the god himself was, until the moment the Huntbrother died, aware of what, or who, he was."

"And the death somehow changed that."

"Not the death itself, no. But the feeding." He glanced at Jewel, as if he had always been aware of her presence. "Mark this, little urchin. Mark it well. It may be of significance to you in the years to come."

She tried hard not to bridle.

"Mortals are mortal—by definition. But there is about them some element that does not age or change, not easily. You would call it," he added, "a soul."

And what would you call it? she thought. She didn't ask. She didn't need to get into a bristling argument with the mage in this foyer, at this time.

"If he subsumes it, he touches the only element of the divine that is now natural in this world. I believe," he added softly, "that it sustains some part of his memory, for he *is* Bredan, now. He is the god who created the Covenant, and he has been long absent from the Heavens."

Morretz was silent for a moment. At length, he spoke. "The Covenant binds the gods to the Heavens."

"It binds those whose oath he took, yes."

"You are saying he did not take the same oath that the other gods did."

"He did not." Meralonne began to search through the folds of his robe—and he wore his robe, now, as if he had never been garbed in any other way. He cursed when his hands came up empty. "It is not much spoken of, and I believe," he added, nodding at the landscape of bodies, "that you must understand why.

"We have long theorized that the world itself was changed in the sundering. And there is proof." Having failed to find his pipe, he slumped against the banister, watching the mists that rolled in place.

"But I understand much, now. The Huntbrother, Stephen, is dead. He fulfilled his oath. The Hunter Lord is not, and he has yet to fulfill his.

"But the *Allasakari* were almost consumed by the shadows they carried, and the demon was strong." He straightened. "I will not argue with the servant while the master is absent," he told Morretz, "but there is no room for argument now; we are done with disagreements. The Terafin must go to the Kings, and the Kings to the Exalted.

"We face not demons and not rogue mages—although," he added, his lips twisting with contempt, "there are obviously rogue mages involved. Men are stupid; they seldom understand the cost of their desire for power until it destroys them." He glanced at Jewel.

Jewel, however, was looking at the mists. In their shifting gray and white, she could see the antlers of the god as if they were made of gold. Even the blood that adorned them glittered darkly. In a faraway voice, she said, "He will fight Allasakar."

She didn't seem to hear the sudden silence that followed her words.

But neither did Meralonne. "Yes," he said heavily. "If we have the time, little urchin, and if the god's long journey is not yet complete, Bredan will fight Allasakar." His voice gentled as he watched her face.

"But your role here is, I think, at an end. Where the god goes, you cannot—and will not—follow. The Terafin," he added, glancing at Alowan, "will rise, wake, and lead. But even The Terafin must accept the limitations of her role. She has been cautious and political, and her delay may well be costly in ways that the Empire cannot afford.

"But it is in the realm of human politics that the last of her duty lies."

"But—but—Allasakar—"

"And would you fight him? You, who can barely wield a weapon longer than a dagger?"

Stung, she pried her gaze from the god. "We'll do whatever we can—" she began.

"Yes. But not more." He paused and then said, quietly, "You cannot be everywhere. You cannot go everywhere. Not yet." He cursed, and released her. "You!" he shouted at the Chosen who had begun to approach their fallen comrades.

They stopped.

"You will not touch the bodies. Not the *Allasakari's* and not your own. Not until I tell you it is safe." He ran his hands over his eyes and cursed the lack of a pipe again. "My work," he told Jewel, "is not yet done this night. It has been long since the shadows swallowed so much life, and they linger wherever they can."

The god had come, the god had spoken with the strangers, and the god had gone. Evayne, too, seemed to have vanished. Lord Gilliam and the wild girl remained, along with those of his dogs that hadn't fallen in the fight. Meralonne didn't attempt to tell the Hunter Lord to stay away from the savaged corpse of Stephen of Elseth, the man he had called Hunt-brother, and Jewel thought it was a damn good thing.

Meralonne was *tired*. She had seen him peevish and annoyed—and bored—but exhausted? Only once, and he'd ended up in the healerie, where neither he nor the healer was comfortable.

Yet he traversed the foyer, examining all of the fallen, from both sides of the battle. Those he deemed safe were removed at his instruction. Those he did not, he labored over for some time, and Jewel watched the orange and gold light at the core of his palms as he did; she knew he worked magic and that he was skirting the edge of mage fevers to do it; he'd used *a lot* of magic this night.

But he wouldn't suffer a man present to touch any of the corpses until he'd done whatever it was he had to do, and even then, he bade the Chosen carry them to a room where they might lie undisturbed until a greater power than his could be called. They were not to be returned to their families, and they were not—yet—to be interred.

The den watched. Jester yawned, but he was embarrassed enough to at least cover his mouth when he did it. Only when Alowan rose, unsteadily, to his feet did they move. Finch had shouldered her way between Carver and Angel, dragging Teller in her wake. She had also shouldered her way between two of the Chosen, who startled but didn't force her back.

She wasn't there for The Terafin, after all.

She caught Alowan's hands in hers and then freed one so that Teller could take it. "Come," she said softly, as if she spoke to a child or a gravely injured man, "we'll take you home."

He attempted to pull his hands free, but she shook her head, her mousy hair falling into her eyes. "You can't stay here," she told him.

He managed to raise a white brow. "You listen," he said quietly. "Perhaps you failed to hear the rest. I cannot—I should not—be touched. Not yet. It is far, far too soon." He started to glance over his shoulder and then shuddered and turned away. The Terafin had not yet awakened.

Finch didn't ask him if he was all right. She didn't ask him if The Terafin was, either. She didn't say anything at all. But she didn't let go of his hand, and after a moment, his grip tightened.

"I'll be needed in the healerie," he told both Finch and Teller as he let them lead him away.

But Teller, gazing at the foyer, shook his head.

The rest of the den walked at a distance from the healer, escorting him as far as the healerie before they said their good-byes. Then they made their way in silence to the wing in which Ellerson waited.

"The Terafin's alive," Jewel told him bluntly. "No thanks to us, in the end." The words were bitter. Failure always was.

He was Ellerson; he understood what she meant, and he didn't press her for details. He did cast a significant glance at her tunic, and when she looked down, she saw that it was bloodied. "It's not mine," she told him softly. She didn't volunteer more, and, again, he didn't ask. But he did suggest that she bathe and change, and even at this hour—an hour at which almost anyone sane in the House would usually be asleep—the suggestion had appeal.

"Are you sure?" she asked him before she headed down the hall to the bathing rooms.

"I am. The servants will be available to heat water and have the baths filled; I think very, very few of the people who make the manse their home slept well—or possibly at all—this night. It will give them something to do," he added. "And action is often its own release."

Were it not for the hour, it would have felt normal. Jewel was tired enough to wonder how anything in the world could still be normal when so many people had died.

9th of Corvil, 410 A.A.
House Terafin, Averalaan Aramarelas

Morretz was silent. He was, in his fashion, grimly silent. But The Terafin failed to note the tenor of his actions. It was, of course, a deliberate failure, and he accepted it; he could not have labored at the side of this woman for so many years if he could not do so.

He did not remind her more than once of Alowan's advice. Nor would Alowan himself, were he here. The Terafin sought and accepted advice, but what she made of it was her decision, and no authority, no other information, overrode her. She would not stay abed for a week. She would not, Morretz thought, stay abed for *a day*.

It was not the first time they had argued like this, and Morretz knew he would have no success should he try now. Instead, he served breakfast, brought water, and made certain—inasmuch as he could—that she both ate and drank.

But she ate and drank, in the early hours of the morning, surrounded by the various symbols of her office: her seal, the wax in which it would be embedded, and the parchment upon which various letters and orders would be written; inkstands, quills, and blotters sat squarely beside cutlery.

It had been four hours. Four hours since she had woken with a start, pale as wax, in her own rooms. Four hours since she had commanded the presence of Captain Alayra. She sat, cushioned in bed, while Alayra answered her questions. What Morretz could not do, Alayra did not attempt. She knew—as well as he—that The Terafin would rise and would begin to see to the affairs of the House.

But in Alayra's case, Morretz thought, it was a relief.

And so she ate, wrote, and stamped, and when she was done, she rose.

"These must be delivered to the House Guard," she told him. He nodded; he knew what the letters contained.

She was still pale, but she was undeterred; she retreated to her personal quarters and asked Morretz to arrange for documents to be collected—immediately—for her perusal.

Only when he delivered them did she dismiss him. He knew why, but it pained him greatly. She had walked death's edge, and she had—once again—been summoned back by the power of Alowan. She did not demand his presence, and had she, Morretz would have disobeyed, which was always awkward between domicis and lord.

But she would ride out some of the bitterness of the desertion that healing always engendered in full and utter privacy; not even he was to bear witness. Or to offer comfort.

Arann came home in the afternoon, and not until he stepped through the doors did Jewel—or the rest of her den—relax. He saw them before he saw Ellerson, who was also waiting, and he grimaced. "Sorry," he told Jewel. "I couldn't get away, and things were so bad I didn't know how to send word."

Finch hugged him, and Jewel looked away for a moment, running the back of her hand across her eyes. When she turned to face him again, he was surrounded by the den with their endless questions.

"Have you seen the gardens?" Arann asked them, when he could slide a word in edgewise without having to shout.

Carver nodded. "We heard the fire bells, as well."

"Mage fire," Arann said. He shook his head. "Have you seen the foyer?"

"We were in it," Angel replied.

Arann whistled. "I heard there was fighting." The way his voice rose on the last word was an open invitation—but it was one that no one, for a long moment, took up. They glanced at Jewel.

She grimaced and nodded, and they began to talk. But even the talk was hushed—for the den.

"There'll be action," Arann told them quietly. "There *has* to be. Darias colors, Darias men—they were in the open streets. The Terafin will have to respond."

11th of Corvil, 410 A.A.
Order of Knowledge, Averalaan Aramarelas

Sigurne Mellifas sat, as she so often did, in the small office of her tower. She sat, as she also often did, surrounded by the letters and official documents that occupied so much of either her time or the time of the people who had thought it necessary to send them. She did not, however, feel the need to pretend a polite attention to their details, as the men and women who had penned them in various states of either irritation or distress were not there to take offense; she waited.

Nor did she wait long, in the end, although she felt each minute keenly. Time was now an hourglass that could not be turned: What was left was all they had. The wards around the door suddenly brightened in a curtain of orange and gray; she lifted a palm, turning it neatly and precisely in midair.

The door opened.

Meralonne APhaniel stood in its frame, studying her wards. He had never been the most trusting of men, and even now, he was cautious. "You did not bid me enter," he said quietly.

It was not—quite—a criticism, but it was an astute observation. She disliked obvious displays of magic, and although only the naive would assume that the guildmaster did not, in fact, use any, everything about her daily routine suggested it. When pressed for an explanation, she would tell the student—for it was invariably a student who asked—that using magic to do simple things like fill a glass or open a door was, to her, a trivialization of its mystery and its purpose.

Which was, of course, untrue. She did not use magic because she did not desire the attention it brought her. "An oversight," she replied.

"The Terafin has called a meeting of the full Council." He took the chair in front of her desk, but he did not withdraw his pipe from his robes; her mood did not allow it. "It was not worded as a request. They meet, as we speak, on the Isle."

Sigurne did not relax, although the news was good.

"My mages are in place around Cordufar," he added softly. "They observe, but they take no action."

"And?"

"There is very little to observe."

She hesitated and then said, "I have received word from the Kings."

His posture did not change, but his eyes were brighter and sharper than usual. "And that word?"

"An assassination attempt in *Avantari*. It failed; the Princess Royale is abed in the healerie, but she was not gravely injured in the fighting."

"The assassins?"

"Demons."

"They grow bold."

"Bold or desperate," Sigurne replied. "And we must hope it is the latter." She rose. "The time is almost come."

"Time?"

"Allasakar," she said softly, speaking a name that was seldom spoken within the tower, "is on the move. He must be. We do not know how long he has been in passage—but no other explanation now fits with the facts we do possess." She walked from one side of the tower to the other, as if caged by both age and walls. She looked, and felt, that age; she felt the frailty of years, for the strength of wisdom had all but deserted her.

"What will the Kings do now?"

"What they must," was her curt reply. "In this, the attempt upon their lives serves us. They will not shelter behind Imperial politics now—they cannot. The Ten are also well aware of this.

"You have not located Krysanthos?"

"No. I think there is some chance he will not survive the evening's work."

"They will kill him?"

"The demons? I think not. But he was not judicious in his use of power." A small smile played at the lips of Meralonne APhaniel; it was not a pleasant one.

"The Hunter Lord is ready," Meralonne told her, also rising. "But the death of his Huntbrother has unbalanced him."

"Will he fight?"

"It is all he is capable of now. He is not . . . entirely rational. I do not understand all of the Breodani lore, but Zareth Khan has answered some of our questions. The Hunters hunt the god once a year. That is their oath. He takes—he devours—one Hunter, and the lands in which the Breodani live continue to flourish. "Lord Gilliam will call the Hunt when it is needful."

"We will not have time to travel—"

"Ah, apologies, Sigurne. He will call the hunt in Averalaan, and he will

call it—and his god—when we at last locate the entry point to the summoning gate of the Lord of the Hells."

She nodded but did not relax. "Where is it, APhaniel?"

"I think you already know."

"The undercity."

He nodded. "The undercity, as Jewel Markess calls it."

"And you?"

"I think it was once called *Vexusa*."

He had said, in words, what she had been afraid to say. "You have no
doubts."

He said nothing. It was a peculiar nothing; the silence was charged.
He seemed young to her, then; young in a way that made youth a fey and
shining danger.

"What lies in the heart of Vexusa, Meralonne? What do you seek
there?"

But he shook his head slightly. "The god."

"Why?"

His smile, like his expression, was dangerous and bright.

"Moorelas fell in Vexusa," Sigurne told him softly. "Armed—and armored, if legend is to be believed—"

"It is not."

"—with a sword that could kill the gods themselves. He perished."

"The sword could kill gods. But it was never a guarantee; it was possibility, no more. Come, Sigurne. Gods, in their day, killed gods. Bredan
walks the plane, and if he is diminished, and he *is*—he is still a god. We
have no champion, and we have no sword, but where gods walk, none are
needed.

"I will speak with the Exalted." Meralonne rose.

"What will you say?"

"They will bespeak their parents." He turned toward the door, and then
back. "But if they do not have the information we seek, we will not bring
the Hunter God to the Lord of the Hells in time."

"We cannot enter Vexusa."

"That," he said softly, "is my suspicion. It is also my only fear."

11th of Corvil, 410 A.A.
The Hall of Wise Counsel, Avantari

The Terafin, accompanied by six of the Chosen, entered the Hall of Wise
Counsel in silence, Morretz to her left. To her right walked Gabriel AT-
erafin. He, like the Chosen, wore House colors and arms, and if a sword
on Gabriel looked strange to her, she had not asked him to set it aside; it
was his right to bear the weapon.

She herself did not. *Justice*, the House Sword, lay in its case at the heart
of her personal chambers, and she carried no other. She was aware that if
she were required to wield a sword in her own defense, she would likely
die. A weapon as stark and simple as a sword was not her strength; it was
not where her power lay. Nor did she find comfort in wearing one.

Morretz did not fuss. He did not speak. His silence in the carriage that
had brought them to *Avantari*, the palace of Kings was the loud silence
of a man who was forcing himself to say nothing. It was not, however, a
resentful silence. He had asked only that The Terafin consider a delay of a
week in which to recover from her brush with death.

As she had desired to act immediately, she considered the days she had
given him—the two—to be a compromise. He had pointed out that the
two days, in which she had written letters without pause from dawn to
dusk, were hardly days spent recovering; to force a meeting of The Ten
on a simple two days' notice required cunning, guile, and force of both
will and word.

But beyond that?

Amarais glanced at his shuttered expression. Beyond that, he had fallen
silent. Not even Morretz could demand that she ignore what had occurred
in the foyer of her House. Nor could he pretend that they had the luxury
of time.

The Terafin House runners, the messengers who could cross the Isle
from morning to night without pause, had earned their keep and deepened the respect granted them; they took her sealed scrolls, and they
traveled with speed, returning to her hand scrolls of a similar nature from
different Houses.

She had broken many seals that day.

Nor had her letters traveled strictly between House Terafin and the
rest of The Ten; they had gone out to Meralonne APhaniel in the Order
of Knowledge and to Sioban Glassen, the Bardmaster of Senniel college;

they had crossed the footbridge that led from the Isle to the hundred holdings, touching Merchant Houses of some renown and power along their way; they had also visited the temples of the gods, seeking counsel from the god-born, the children upon whom the gods themselves depended for their deeper knowledge of the affairs of the mortal realm. They had traveled, as well, to *Avantari* and even now sat in possession of the Queens Siodonay and Marieyan.

To the Kings, she had sent one letter.

But it was the letters from The Ten that were to be her chief concern on the ninth and tenth of Corvil. She intended to survive whatever was to follow the attack upon her House, and if the House did survive, she did not wish to weaken it. She was willing to take that risk, now—but she was Amarais; she would do her best to lessen the risk as much as she could.

Within The Ten, various Houses formed shifting alliances in order to broker influence and power; they might vote—in the unlikely event that a vote was called—in blocks. The Terafin, as the first among equals, had forged her own alliances, but they were tenuous at best; it was Terafin, after all, that had farthest to fall and least to gain; any other House might rise in influence if they could pick over the political remains of a divided House.

But it was The Ten, at the foundation of the Empire, who had ridden at the command of the first of the Twin Kings; they could rise, she thought, to the occasion when—and if—it could be proved necessary. She held this thought firmly in mind as she left the confines of her carriage and waited for the Chosen to join her. When they did, she proceeded through the inner gates of the courtyard in which carriages and horses were met and from there toward the grand hall that almost defined the outer castle. Beyond, in a garden that ringed the inner castle, she paused for a moment.

"Terafin?" Morretz said quietly.

She shook her head.

The dead were not here; the graves were not here. Nor were the charred ruins of large swathes of her own House gardens; instead, there were patches of indigo flowers, sheltering beneath the lazy but artful bend of willows. The breeze that came down from the height of the walls on either side carried, in its moving folds, the scent of roses, of lilac, of rowan.

But she had seen the newly turned earth into which the House Guard and almost a third of her Chosen had been laid. She had summoned the Exalted to House Terafin—and they had come—to bless and cleanse the dead of the taint of shadow; they had also performed the funeral rites, the last respects, over the fallen, while their attendants, full priests in their own right, had held braziers in which incense burned.

The presence of the god-born comforted the families in some small way, for the Exalted did not attend simple funerals or simple weddings; they seldom left their grand and glorious cathedrals at all. But for Amarais herself, there was no peace to be found in their presence.

Instead, she found anger, and she balanced between its ice and its fire as she stood beneath the shadow of willows in the lee of the palace of Kings. She had taken the oaths of the Chosen personally; they were *hers*. Hers to command, to lead. Hers to lose, to mourn, and to avenge.

"Terafin," Morretz said, speaking her title as if it were her name, the question shorn off its edge. "It is almost time."

She nodded. "Come," she told him quietly. "It is time to meet my peers."

The Hall of Wise Counsel was not empty when she arrived. It contained servants and the still figures, against the walls, of the Kings' Swords. She frowned a moment when she saw them, but she did not speak. It was seldom that the Kings' Swords were stationed within the Hall of Wise Counsel, but their presence was, in the end, a signal that even within *Avantari*, the Kings were now on alert.

Sweet water lay on a sideboard, near the table; there was no wine.

"Terafin."

She glanced at the Council seats and saw The Morriset rise.

"Morriset." She extended a hand as he approached, and he took it briefly. It was his wont to be informal in even the most formal of circumstances. She smiled as he bowed and held that smile as he rose. He was as far from imposing as a man of power could be: middle-aged, of middling height, his brown hair streaked with unruly silver, his beard a little ragged at the edges. He wore very fine cloth but in a way that suggested his tailor's measurements had somehow failed to keep up with the unfortunate passage of time.

She had always been cautious around a man who clearly made so much effort to appear harmless and ineffective. The latter, at least, was a lie; under his guidance, Morriset's fortunes had grown. To underscore this, he had arrived with Zandros AMorriset, the equivalent of the Terafin right-kin. Zandros, unlike The Morriset, was an imposing figure. His age and

The Morriset's were not far apart, but he wore age as if it were power. His hair was dark and his build almost military. He bowed, briefly, to The Terafin, but he did not otherwise approach her.

"We are, it appears, early," The Morriset said.

She nodded. The fact that he, like she, had chosen to arrive early was gratifying; it was a signal of support.

"The Tamalyn is also present. In *Avantari*," he added. "He arrived, I am told, some two hours past but repaired immediately to the court of Queen Marieyan."

"Did he arrive alone?"

"Ah, no. He arrived in the presence of the formidable and somewhat dour Michi ATamalyn; he arrived, however, without House Guards."

At least, Amarais thought, she would get him here on time. If any leader of a House could be said to be entirely unsuited to the governance of one, it was the current Tamalyn. His interests better suited the more esoteric branches of the Order of Knowledge; how he'd managed to take control of a House Council was beyond The Terafin's ken.

"We will wait, I think," The Terafin said dryly.

"And you will discuss nothing of the matters that drove you to summon a full Council meeting before the meeting is in session?"

"I would, but they are long and detailed." She glanced at Gabriel, who nodded briskly. He watched the doors, his glance straying to the Kings' Swords without comment.

Five minutes. Ten. When the doors opened, they opened to one of the youngest of The Ten: The Kalakar. She had taken the House Seat at the age of thirty-two, and she had held it for four years in her frequently mailed fist. She was tall for a woman, and her shoulders were broad; her hair was a pale yellow, her eyes a gray-blue. She had a wide, strong jaw, and she walked with none of the deliberate and stately elegance that Amarais had spent so much of her young life learning to achieve; nor did she require it.

She had made a name for herself in the skirmishes in the South, in the Kings' armies. There had been some fear that she would carry her military expertise into the council chambers in Kalakar; her advisers were frequently men who had served her in the army. She had certainly put her stamp upon the Kalakar House Guard—but she had done little else to interfere with the smooth running of the rest of the House's concerns.

She was, in all, a formidable and worthy rival; Amarais respected her greatly. There was nothing forced in the greeting she offered The Kalakar,and nothing perfunctory about The Kalakar's brief bow.

"Terafin," she said, rising, her expression grave. "I have had some word of events that occurred on the eighth of Corvil."

The Terafin nodded, unsurprised. She expected that eight of The Ten were aware, at least in part, of the events that had pushed her toward this meeting.

"I'm aware that there is always some element of competition among The Ten," the woman whose personal name was Ellora said. "But we all stand to lose much if that competition becomes open warfare in the streets of the Isle." Her gaze, as she met The Terafin's, was speculative. "You're not speaking," she said at last. "There's more to this."

"There always is," The Terafin replied, with a rare smile. "But when the Council is in full session—"

The doors opened, and The Berrilya entered the long hall.

If Darias was one of Terafin's natural rivals, The Berrilya was Kalakar's. But his concerns were not, as Darias or Terafin, political or economic in nature. Older and more severe than The Kalakar, The Berrilya had made his life the Kings' army. He was a man who not only abided by tradition but held it almost in reverence; he was also a man to whom responsibility came naturally, even if he took it reluctantly. That Ellora was young was not an issue; many of the men under his command were. But she was flexible in ways that he was not, and those under her command showed a loyalty that had nothing, in the end, to do with tradition.

Nor could she be safely ignored: she was one of The Ten. Women comprised a small percentage of the Kings' forces, but they did fight, and Devran accepted this. Fighting and command, however, were two different things; she could not, with the importance of her political position, be relegated to a minor role.

He had attempted, through argument and guile, to have her retired. She had responded with heat, more argument, and no guile whatsoever. She had won that battle. But The Terafin thought the war was not, by any means, over.

Two of The Ten, Amarais thought, were still actively engaged with, and in, the army; she was not aware of another historical period in which this could be said. The Kings allowed it without open hesitation; she was not certain, in their position, she would have.

But both were said to be good at what they did, and perhaps the Kings, in their wisdom, did not wish to deprive themselves of either. The situation in the South had always been delicate.

She nodded to The Berrilya, and he returned her nod. "Terafin," he said. After a longer—and more significant—pause, he nodded to The Kalakar. "Kalakar."

"Berrilya."

"We were not due to meet again until Advent; I am aware that the situation is almost inexplicable, but I have matters to which I must personally attend."

"We will begin in all haste when the Council is fully present," Amarais replied serenely.

Devran's frown could have frozen water. "Are we not, now, due to start?"

"We are. But the palace itself is in a heightened state of security; it is possible that the others have been delayed at the gates."

It was, of course, almost entirely impossible, but The Berrilya understood the value of polite fiction. He did not, however, extend that understanding to the value of equally polite social interaction; he and his adjutant removed themselves from the floor as he took his seat in the Hall and settled in stiffly to wait.

The Darias arrived five minutes later.

All eyes turned to the doors when he entered, and they did not leave; not even the most powerful of men or women were immune to curiosity.

"Terafin," The Darias said, without preamble. "This had better be good."

He was older than Amarais, but he wore his age the way Zandros AMorriset did; he was tall, and his build alone was imposing. His hair was dark, and his skin darker as well; he was not a man who feared sun or exposure. Not yet. The russet, brown, and gold of his House did not entirely suit his coloring, but he carried them off with aplomb; he could hardly change them for a meeting of this import. He also wore a long sword.

"I assure you," The Terafin replied, her voice cool, "that House Terafin does not press a meeting of this nature for trivial reasons."

"Trivial?" The Darias shrugged, an elegant motion that caused light to pool in the moving folds of his robes. "That, in the end, will be for the Council to decide. But I warn you—"

She lifted a hand. "We are surely not yet at the stage where bald warnings are now offered as veiled threats in *Avantari*." Her words were cool, her expression, chill.

It stopped him. "Very well," he said, after a slight pause. "Let the Council convene."

"We wait," she replied, "upon the rest of The Ten. You are not the only person who felt they had the luxury of time." She felt Gabriel grow tense at her side, but her right-kin did not choose to speak.

Nor did The Darias. He met her gaze and held it, but he did not attempt to otherwise engage; he understood, from the tone of her voice and the implied criticism she had just openly offered, that her anger was not slight.

And so, they gathered: The Ten. The men and women who, among the patriciate of the Empire, claimed some special privilege under the Kings' laws. They could not be unseated; they could not be deposed. Their names could not be bought or sold. They were not required to conform to the ancient laws that governed heredity; nor were they required to conform to the laws that governed the behavior of the rest of the Empire if their actions did not materially affect outsiders.

Fennesar came next, followed closely by Wayelyn, the least of The Ten in matters both political and monetary. Where The Fennesar was, in effect, similar to The Morriset, The Wayelyn was not: he was of the bard-born. Trained by Senniel, he had traveled much of the Empire in his youth, and his voice could still be used to good effect; it often was, in Council. It was difficult not to like him, and difficult not to trust him, although most of the Houses managed; he was not ambitious in any way that they understood.

His wife, however, the undisputed head of the Wayelyn Council, was cut from different cloth; *she* was a woman who understood the demands of power. Often frustrated by her husband, her hands held the reins of the House.

Garisar came next. Of the Council members, The Garisar was the elder statesman. He, like The Darias, was physically imposing; unlike The Darias his loyalties were undivided. It was not to his House that he looked, and not for his House that his intellect and his perception were honed: he served the Twin Kings.

Rumor—and rumor was, like any information that came without solid source, to be suspected—had it that he had spent some years working with, and for, the Astari. Amarais believed it. She did not care for The Garisar, and she did not trust his advice—but such advice was seldom offered. She thought, seeing the cast of his face this day, that he would speak, and for once, he would speak in concert with Terafin.

It was a disturbing thought.

The Korisamis came next. He came, as he often did, in the odd robes that Korisamis House Members wore. Silk, they fell from shoulder to ground in a fall interrupted by a sash with a complicated series of knots. Indigo sash, azure robe, gold hem. He looked more in keeping with the foreigners from the Dominion of Annagar than he did with the nobles of the various Courts; his head gleamed in magelight; it was bald. A deliberate baldness. Even his beard was a stylized drop of two graying lines that reached the midpoint of his chest.

He wasn't the last; that was reserved—with little surprise from the seated members of the Council—for the harried head of House Tamalyn, who managed to slide between the open doors before The Korisamis had fully deserted them. That he did not collide with The Korisamis was proof that *Kalliaris* smiled when amused. And that trivial things amused her.

Everyone took their seats, and silence descended, one voice at a time fading into stillness, upon the Hall. The servants who hovered, almost invisible, now exited the hall itself, robbing the room of their quiet and steady presence; this left the Council of The Ten to their privacy.

It was theoretical privacy, of course; the Astari would listen to every word spoken in this room. It was one of the chief reasons why so much of the daily business of The Ten was conducted outside of *Avantari*.

The Darias, who, like The Terafin, was adept at wading through the undercurrents in a politically charged room, clearly did not like what he sensed here. Had he been a different man, he would have waited. He was not, however. "Terafin," he said, standing. "You have summoned a full Council meeting with little notice and little explanation. We would hear your explanation for such a summons without preamble. Or delay."

"Are you truly unaware, Darias?" she replied softly. She watched his expression with care; for just that moment, they might have been the only two people in the almost cavernous room.

His eyes narrowed, but not in the way of a cornered man who is about to unleash the full force of his power in his own defense. It was, to The Terafin, a more familiar expression—one she frequently bore. He was trying to discern what her game was and how she might now maneuver to achieve its end.

It did not dampen the anger that had driven her here, but she felt the twinge of something that might become pity. She was not, had never been, a gentle woman; compassion, now, was beyond her reach.

"I am obviously unaware of the nature of your concerns," he replied quietly. "I seldom ask a question to hear myself speak."

It was true of both of them; questions, like any other words, could be expertly wielded weapons; they were seldom idle chatter.

"I spent the better part of yesterday burying almost a third of my Chosen," she replied starkly.

A ripple crossed the floor, a hint of words, hidden behind hand or cloaked in whisper.

"My sympathies for your loss," he replied, in a grave voice. "But surely that is an internal matter?"

"It might have been," she replied, "were it not for the fact that their losses were preceded by an unprecedented attack upon the manor grounds themselves. It was not a subtle attack," she continued, aware that she now had the attention of every man and woman in the room. "But an attack easily witnessed by anyone who happened to be in the streets of *Averalaan Aramarelas* at the time."

Had she not had the full attention of every member of the Council, the silence would have shattered. Words were building in the folds of that silence, and when they started to flow, they would continue unabated.

His eyes widened slightly; it was his only movement.

"Fully one hundred and fifty men—at our best estimate given the lateness of the hour—traversed the Isle's streets, bearing arms and armor. They came to bring war to my House, and they traveled under a House banner. One of The Ten Houses," she added, her voice sharpening even as it lowered.

Silence broke like a damn. She weathered it, catching the sharp words and questions, ignoring the demands and the arguments that were already beginning. She had eyes for The Darias, and only The Darias, and for the moment, he had eyes for her.

He knew, she thought. He knew, now, what she would say. But she was not certain that he had known it before he entered this chamber. It brought her a measure of peace.

"Who?" The Berrilya asked, his single, imperative word cutting through all other syllables. "Who do you accuse of this act?"

She nodded at Devran. "House Darias."

Chapter Twelve

The silence that descended as her words cut through the heat and ice of the raised voices of The Ten would not hold, but it could be—barely—ignored. The Darias' silence, however, could not; it demanded her attention. His eyes had widened for seconds before they narrowed; the magelight caught them as if they were the edge of a finely made weapon.

The first word he spoke was, "Impossible."

Had she been calm, had she been political, had she truly been seeking personal advantage or political advantage for her House, she would have done as she now did, when she was none of those things. "Impossible?"

"Not a single one of The Ten would risk the ire of Kings—and the loss of the privilege accorded us by Reymalyn and Cormalyn the First—in such an act. You have proof of this? You have witnesses?"

"I have," she replied, keeping the edge out of her voice with effort. The ice, however, remained. "I have more," she continued. "I have the bodies of several of the aggressors. They remain in the keeping of Terafin mages; they are preserved should the Kings inquire. They bear Darias tabards and ranks; they were recognized by some of my Chosen. It was not a simple matter of impersonation or false colors."

"Darias, explain yourself." The Berrilya rose.

"Explain *myself*?" The Darias replied. "I have already said that this is the act of a madman—and I assure you, I am not that. Terafin and Darias have had differences in the past and will no doubt continue to have them in the future, but I have *nothing* to gain by such an open attack."

"Nonetheless, they were your men," The Terafin said. "If you wish to verify this, it can easily be done. My House Guard has been instructed to allow duly appointed members of House Darias access to both the manse and the bodies.

"House Terafin will likewise entertain the appointed representatives of any of the rest of The Ten, should they also wish to ascertain the truth of my claim; we are not, however, accepting any other visitors at the moment. The manse," she added softly, "was much damaged in the attack; the foyer was all but destroyed."

His brows rose, and his expression changed.

The Kalakar rose. In truth, Amarais was slightly surprised she had remained seated for this long when The Berrilya was standing. "Much damaged, Terafin?"

Amarais nodded.

"Please expand."

"The floor, two of the walls, and three of the supporting pillars are now being rebuilt."

"This was not the action of one hundred and fifty of Darias' men." Ellora said, the words flat and certain.

"No." Amarais took a steadying breath, held it, and then glanced at the Darias. "They did not come alone."

"Will you insist on being coy?" The Berrilya said, clearly unamused.

"If The Berrilya believes that caution is somehow coy, yes. It is my belief, based on very little information, that regardless of what we now say or do, the Kings will involve themselves in this affair."

"Given one hundred and fifty armed guards, that is a given." The Berrilya looked at The Darias.

The Darias was staring at them all, and something about his expression almost gave The Terafin pause. Almost. "Darias," she continued gravely, "the Terafin mage was present during the attack; if we suffered grave losses, it is due to his presence that those losses were not tripled—or worse.

"And he bid me inform the Council that among the attackers was one rogue mage. The rogue mage is, of course, the responsibility of the Order of Knowledge; I mention it to inform you, no more. But the Terafin mage—"

"Which mage, Terafin?" The Morriset asked.

"Member APhaniel."

He nodded. "Continue."

"Also bid me to say that the attack was led, in his opinion, by a woman of your acquaintance."

"Of my acquaintance," The Darias replied, as if his search for words of his own had failed him utterly.

"Yes. She is seen, regularly, in the company of Lord Cordufar, one of your lieges."

He did not reply for a full moment. When he did, he addressed not The Terafin but the Council. "I will not," he said, "accuse The Terafin of lying, not in this." That he would like to was not in question. He was not, however, a fool. "But I will tell you now that any attack—*any* attack— that occurred upon Terafin grounds was carried out without my order and without my permission." He lifted a hand as The Berrilya began to speak. "Believe that I am aware of what this could cost; it affects not only your Houses but my own. My own," he added, "most of all. I . . . am not in full possession of the facts, and I must ask a recess."

"It is premature to demand a recess," The Garisar replied.

The Darias' jaw tensed. So, too, did Amarais. The Garisar rarely chose to speak in Council.

"Terafin," he continued. "You have strongly implied the presence of magic in the attack upon your House."

She said nothing.

"Given the nature of the attack, it cannot have been magic performed under writ."

"If the mage was called rogue by a Member of the Order's Council, no," she replied with just a trace of sarcasm.

"We will hear the rest of the details," he said, "before we call a recess, if indeed a recess is granted at all."

"Very well." She glanced at The Darias, and the glance offered him nothing at all. "You are all, no doubt, aware of rumors about an assassination attempt that took place upon the grounds of my manse some weeks ago. What was not made clear at that time, and for reasons that will become clear as I speak, was that the assassination was not attempted in the normal way. No poison, no dagger, no crossbow; it was entirely magical in nature."

"House Terafin has powerful enemies."

"As no doubt every House in the Empire does," she told The Morriset. "This one, however, was not deemed to be human."

The Garisar now rose. The Kalakar and The Berrilya had failed to resume their seats. "Be clearer," he said sharply.

"Clarity is in short supply at the moment; however Member APhaniel felt the attacker was, in fact, demonic in nature."

"And you *kept this to yourself?*"

"Would you have me go groveling in terror to the Kings?" she snapped back, her control unraveling.

"Terafin has always been arrogant," he replied, with some heat, "but not even Terafin can be so arrogant as to assume that demons and their interest would be focused on Terafin alone!"

It stung. It did worse. Amarais felt her throat constrict, but she met his fury head-on. It was an echo of her own, and it was aimed, in the end, in the same direction.

"I had reasons," she said, her voice low, "for that assumption, and while those reasons bear some scrutiny, in the end, I feel that my judgment was in error. I have therefore called this Council Meeting in haste.

"The second attack upon my House was *not*, in my opinion, about House Terafin at all. And it was only the second of the attacks that made this clear and rendered my previous assumption unworthy. I am here, now, Garisar. Any penalty to be paid for my caution will in the end be decided not by The Ten but by the Twin Kings."

He was not mollified. He did, however, grant her a stiff, furious nod. She half expected him to stride out of the Council doors and toward the Kings' Court.

"The second attack," she said quietly, "in which Darias men participated, was led by a demon. And the foyer," she continued, "was destroyed, in part, by that demon, and in part, by *Allasakari*." The silence that followed her final word sounded like thunder.

The Darias moved away from his seat. "I will not have my House maligned in this fashion," he said stiffly. "House Darias does not and has never worshiped the Lord of the Hells. I demand a recess. I will repair to my House, and I will return with whatever information I can find."

"Darias—" The Garisar began.

But The Darias lifted a hand. "Now," he said quietly. There was no request in the single word.

Amarais nodded.

*   *   *

"He did not know," Morretz said quietly.

"I concur." Amarais stared out the window of the moving carriage. The Darias had demanded a recess, and she had granted it. He had also remained to see that the recess did not devolve into a discussion of House Darias in his absence. It was, of course, wise; she would have done the same.

But she could not imagine that she could find herself in The Darias' position. The magnitude of his crime could not be excused by ignorance; he knew this. But if the attack was conducted without his awareness, his crime was his ignorance.

It was not a crime she herself could conceive of committing. She *was* the House. What occurred within the confines of her manse, she knew.

And yet, she had almost died within the confines of her manse. Treacherous thought, but truth often was; she shared it with no one. She had almost died; Torvan ATerafin had almost killed her.

She understood what had happened to Torvan, and she took some of the blame for that catastrophe upon her own shoulders. If something similar had happened within House Darias, could The Darias be held accountable?

Yes. In the end, yes. Because he *was* Darias, as she was Terafin.

Gabriel ATerafin reached back to massage his neck. "What will you do?"

"What I can," she replied. "Word has already reached the Kings, and we will no doubt find a summons to *Avantari* to discuss events awaiting us upon our return to the House. The Kings will wait," she added softly, "upon the Council of The Ten and the outcome of this meeting."

"You are certain?"

"As certain as one can be, given the Twin Kings." She glanced at his expression and then, once again, at the moving city. The air was crisp and chill, the sky a neutral shade of blue; it suggested clouds without actually producing any. "I do not know, old friend," she finally said, still watching as buildings moved past. "But if we have played the game of politics and power—and demonstrably, undeniably, we have—and the Empire suffers for it, we, too, will be judged.

"We have made our decisions. We will live—or die—by the consequences. More than that, we cannot do; we cannot unmake or reverse the past."

"It is not for the past that I am concerned," replied Gabriel gravely. "What will you do with Torvan ATerafin?"

She offered him a very slight, and very pained, smile. "You are unkind, Gabriel."

He did not respond in kind. He knew her, and knew her well.

"I have not yet decided," she finally replied. The answer was not to his liking, but he accepted it. "He did nothing wrong, in the end."

"If nearly killing you is considered nothing wrong—"

She lifted a hand. "You know, as well as I, why that occurred."

"And I know, as well as you do, that it doesn't matter. You have thrown all of your focus and will into the Council, and it is commendable, given your current state. But, Amarais, I have known you for years. You often choose the work that must be done to avoid other work that must *also* be done."

Morretz was silent throughout this discussion, and as it continued until the carriage drew up the Terafin road, he did not speak until they were once again ensconced within her quarters.

"The Chosen will accept your decision, regardless of what it is."

She was slightly surprised by this, but she nodded; it was simple truth. "I am not certain the rest of the House will do so—not easily. But Gabriel is right; I have avoided the issue."

"You cannot be faulted for that, given the current situation."

"I am," she said, glancing at the pile of missives that had been as neatly stacked upon her desk as a large pile can be, "faulted much, it seems." She lifted one letter and grimaced. "The cost of the repairs will be staggering."

"I believe the cost of the repairs can be left in the hands of the right-kin, Terafin."

She nodded, and then lifted her head. "I will let him choose," she told her domicis, her expression as open as it had ever been. "I will not execute him for treason or treachery; he deserves far, far more from me. But I chose him for a reason. He will understand the difficulties I face."

"Then you give him, in the end, little choice at all."

She closed her eyes. "Leave me," she said.

He did.

12th of Corvil, 410 A.A.
The Hall of Wise Counsel, Avantari

The halls of *Avantari* were now notably adorned with the Kings' Swords; The Terafin wondered if all of the reserves had been called. She had taken, in the late hours of night, her room illuminated by both magelight and grief, an early report that suggested the assassination attempt in *Avantari* had been conducted with or by demons. More than that, her sources had been unable to divulge, and she did not have the luxury of time; what they were certain of, and what she accepted as fact, was that the Princess Royale, Mirialyn ACormaris, lay abed in the Queens' healerie, recovering from unspecified injuries.

The Ten gathered in ones and twos as the hour of the meeting approached. They took no care to time their arrival; for once, they arrived early, and they arrived prepared. She wondered what information they now possessed about both the attack upon House Terafin and the attack within *Avantari*; no doubt some of it would come to light in the meeting itself.

But if The Ten gathered, there was one glaring and notable exception: The Darias himself.

Nine were gathered, and if they continued to speak among themselves, they watched the doors; the doors failed to open until fully an hour had passed. The Terafin nursed her anger and her grief as the minutes dragged on; she responded politely to questions directed at her, but she did not otherwise engage any of the Council members.

When the doors finally opened, they opened upon a stranger. A stranger who wore the colors of House Darias. She frowned, trying to place him; there were very few members of import in *any* House that she had not met, if only briefly. He was young, this man, and fair where Archon had been dark; he was tall, but his shoulders were curved inward, and he did not have the physical bearing of The Darias.

He glanced around the room at the seated heads of the other nine Houses and then swallowed almost audibly. She thought he might be a designated messenger, but no Terafin messenger would hesitate so openly to discharge his duty.

Nor was he a messenger, for he approached the last empty chair, the Council Seat reserved for House Darias since the founding of the Empire. He did not take it, but he touched the height of its curved back a moment, as if to derive strength from the contact.

"Forgive me," he said. "I am Parsus ADarias." He tendered a full and respectful bow to the room at large.

"ADarias?" The Morriset asked.

"The House Council of Darias has sent me to take the seat of Darias at this time. Were the circumstances different, the seat would be left vacant."

"What game are you playing?" The Terafin said, coolly.

"Terafin." He offered a second bow, and it was both exquisite and perfect. "We play no game. The nature of your accusation was made clear to us after the Council of The Ten met yesterday." He raised a hand. "We do not doubt your word. What you state must have happened the way you said it did; you are The Terafin—you know the cost better than any of The Ten, and you would not have brought news of this House altercation into royal play were the threat not so great.

"There is no defense that Archon ADarias can make for his actions."

Archon. He'd said Archon ADarias.

Amarais did not flinch, and she did not close her eyes, but some small part of the anger that she'd nurtured since the Exalted had come to both cleanse and bury her fallen eased. It wouldn't bring them back to life. Nothing would, save the long journey to the bridge of Mandaros, and the Halls of the Lord of Judgment.

"Yes," the man said softly. "Archon ADarias resigned in disgrace from the title of Darias and the seat." He lifted his face, his pale, beardless face, and for just a moment, Amarais saw a loss that was felt as deeply, as personally, as she felt her own. It did not humble her. "His wishes for the disposition of his lands and his title have been set aside; there is no longer an heir to the seat, and until such time as one is chosen, I will rule as regent."

"And the—and Archon ADarias?"

"The First Day rites have been observed by the priests of the House Chapel."

Archon had always favored Cartanis.

"Terafin," Parsus ADarias continued, "the assessment of your claim against Archon ADarias is under review. The House will reach its decision shortly."

She nodded, gracious in victory. It was difficult; something this hollow and painful was seldom considered victory.

"Very well," The Berrilya said, while Amarais absorbed this change of fortune, this unexpected end of an old and worthy adversary. "Now, we must come to a decision of our own. Let the meeting commence, Terafin. Tell us, now, what you know."

Quietly, she began to speak. She had, at hand, several documents prepared by Gabriel; she did not refer to them; she had no need. When objections were raised, she would find the relevant information and hand it to the person objecting. For this reason, the meeting was not brief.

She covered the question of Cordufar and its holdings, the possibility of disappearances—and deaths—occurring in the inner holdings for literally a decade, and the probability of a compromised Magisterium.

The Garisar did not object to this, but he did raise a hand.

"I am not now, nor have I ever been, involved in a procedural way with the Magisterium," The Terafin said, before he could speak. "What I bring to the table is observation, no more."

He nodded, and she handed him a report. But his glance across its pages was brief.

She spoke slowly, deliberately, and openly. And when, at last, she came to the matter of Rath, there was another silence as the implications hit home.

"You are saying the demons could be anyone."

She nodded. "Or so said Member APhaniel; in this, I would trust his opinion."

"You realize the panic that this could cause?"

She nodded again. "It is for that reason that this is not widely known. There are ways of detecting the kin," she added softly. "They are not without risk."

"Magical?"

"Of a sort. Talent, definitely. One foreigner, whom I have not yet mentioned, had a sensitivity to the demons; he resided for some small while in *Avantari* for this reason. He is," she added softly, "dead." So she came last to the battle that was closest: the god, the demon, the *Allasakari* and the sacrifice of one foreign Hunter.

After that, the Council sat in silence. They looked to Parsus ADarias, as did The Terafin, but they demanded no more of him while they absorbed the information.

"The Kings must know," The Kalakar finally said.

"That is now my belief," The Terafin replied. "And yes, Garisar, I am aware that I have come late to it. I believe we must inform them, we must inspect our own ranks carefully, and we must provide them with all public—and private—support in the actions they choose to take henceforth." She hesitated once more and then said, "I have not yet spoken of what I believe the demons intend."

They watched her now; if any resented the fact that she held all of the information of value, it did not show.

"I have in my employ a young woman and her companions. They lived for some time in the inner holdings; they are not old enough to have been suspicious of the magisterial guard in any way that was not natural to their station.

"Some of the information I received came from them. The most significant, to my mind, was the existence of what they call the maze, or the undercity. They spent some years combing through the ruins of ancient buildings in the dark, in secret.

"When the young woman came to work for me, however, she discovered that all of the entrances with which she was familiar had been closed. We've ascertained that the closure was magical in nature—and that it was a very powerful magic that is not in general practice."

"What do you mean, not in general practice?"

"Member APhaniel felt that it was impossible."

"Ah. That version." The Morriset waved a thick hand. "My apologies, Terafin. Continue."

"And no apologies to the rest of us?" The Wayelyn said, with a deep smile.

"I was hardly interrupting anything worthwhile from you."

The Wayelyn laughed. The Berrilya frowned. The Kalakar chuckled briefly.

"Be that as it may," Amarais said, her lips curving in the slightest of smiles, "the ways into that maze, that city-beneath-the-city, were closed. She spent some weeks in the company of Member APhaniel ascertaining just this fact. I believe that our greatest danger lies beneath the streets of the city. We cannot, obviously, simply lift a shovel and dig—and even were we to start, it is my belief that we would meet resistance. It is not the type of resistance that can be effectively countered without the aid of both the magi and the Exalted.

"I have therefore taken the liberty," she said, rising, "of preparing a document which would travel—immediately—to the Kings' Court. I have also requested the unencumbered aid of the Order of Knowledge. I have no doubt, however, that the Order will treat directly with the Kings.

"If you would read and review what is written, and sign and seal it should it meet your approval, we may adjourn and repair to our Houses to begin to deal with our enemies.

"ADarias," she said quietly.

"Terafin." He was pale, and he was new enough to his position that he could not dampen the fear her words had invoked. But it was not fear for himself and not, in the end, fear for his House; what further disgrace could his House now suffer?

"We require access to the estates of Lord Cordufar."

Parsus tensed, and his fair skin darkened slightly. "It is not," he finally said, "in my hands, Terafin. Nor is it—entirely—in the hands of the House Council."

"How so?"

"Cordufar was leige, but he was not encumbered; his lands were entirely his own."

She waited, sensing more to come; she waited patiently. Even during the worst of the war for her own seat, she had been patient.

"When The Dar—when Archon ADarias returned from *Avantari* yesterday, he called an immediate meeting of the House Council; it was brief. He summoned the House Mage to the Council Meeting; we expected there would be some delay."

She grimaced. Even the most highly paid Members of the Order of Knowledge were not known for their ability to arrive anywhere in haste, especially not when it involved a Council Meeting of *any* variety.

"The Member that serves House Darias arrived shortly after the last of the House Council had gathered; he arrived at the side of Guildmaster Mellifas. She was not expected; the House Council had no time to prepare for her presence.

"There was some internal difficulty that—" he paled, swallowed, and shook his head. "There was some difficulty, and in the end, the arrival of the House Mage and Member Mellifas put a stop to it. More than that is not relevant to the matters at hand. The Darias then put the emergency session on permanent hold; the subject that was to be discussed had been presented in a way that the remaining Council members could not ignore."

Remaining, Amarais thought. She was not the only member of The Ten to note the word.

"Words were exchanged—in haste—between the guildmaster and Archon ADarias, at the end of which, it was agreed that a small delegation would be sent to House Cordufar. Guildmaster Mellifas felt that speed was of the essence, for she felt it probable that Lord Cordufar now knew that The Darias was aware of some of his activities." He fell silent for a moment, his gaze resting on the spotless surface of the large, long table upon which documents of import were placed.

"The delegation was sent?" The Terafin asked.

He nodded, still staring at the table. "It was sent. Some handful of The Darias' personal guard, two members of the Council, and two members of the Order of Knowledge, Sigurne Mellifas and one other. She did not take the Darias House Mage, and it is our suspicion that he had no desire whatever to accompany her.

"I did not recognize the mage that she did choose," he added, and this time he did look up. "But I believe she called him APhaniel.

"They left. It is not far to the Cordufar estates from House Darias, although the estates themselves are situated on the mainland and not on the Isle. The Darias frequently discussed this with Lord Cordufar, for he felt that a merchant of Cordufar's obvious competence and power should own land on the Isle—and went so far as to offer some small parcel of Darias lands for that purpose.

"Lord Cordufar, however, declined."

She nodded, wondering how long to give him. He was not a man who was accustomed to either the role thrust upon him or the upheaval that had led to it, and whatever it was he was trying to say required this verbal equivalent of walking in tight, nervous circles. But that required time, and time, she felt keenly, was something they no longer had.

Because of her choice.

"ADarias," she said, speaking gently. "The results of the visit?"

He lifted his graying face, then. "All but the magi and one member of the Darias personal guard died there. There was, in theory, enough magic used to level the entire manse. Lord Cordufar is not, now, an issue."

Amarais felt the ground shift beneath her feet and wondered, briefly, if the shift would support her position or not.

"Any permission required to access the Cordufar estates now rests in the hands of the Order of Knowledge—and the Kings. I do not know," he added, shaking himself and straightening his back, "what you hope to discover there."

"What we hope, what the Kings will soon hope, is to discover some entrance into these tunnels and streets that lay beneath the city. If, as we now believe, Lord Cordufar was intimately acquainted with what occurred, it is inconceivable that he himself had no way to enter the maze.

"The estates, the lands on which they sit, are our best hope." She rose, then. "I will make my plea to the Kings, and I will speak with the guildmaster. I believe they will grant my petition." She glanced around the long Council table; there were no raised objections. "I have already begun discussions with the Exalted. They are . . . grim. I will, should the Council vote to do so, report upon the results of those discussions when we reconvene."

"What can you hope to achieve that they cannot achieve on their own?"

What answer could she give that did not expose more of her hand—good and bad—than was wise? "We must all do what we can," she replied. "And Terafin House resources encompass many people with many different skills."

14th of Corvil, 410 A.A.
Terafin Manse, Averalaan Aramarelas

Ellerson woke Jewel early on the morning of the fourteenth.

He had spent most of the night on a pallet by the wall farthest from her bed. He had taken the liberty of requesting the purchase of a magestone for her personal use; it had not yet arrived. Given the destruction of the gardens and the devastation of the foyer, it was likely to be very, very delayed; nor did he feel a great and pressing need to remind anyone of his trivial request.

Still, the duties that he had adopted for the long stretch of night made him feel the full weight of his age. He was no longer a young man. Even as a young man, he had seldom served anyone whose path crossed the paths of so many of the powerful.

Yet crossing those paths and making them were not, in the end, the same; Jewel Markess slept poorly and woke frequently, screaming or whimpering. Dreams did not break when she did; they withered slowly, clinging as they died. But the light helped, and he kept it burning. He tended a lamp, refilling it as the oil dwindled.

She did not stir when he walked across the floor, did not stir when he lifted the lamp; she did if the light receded significantly, as if aware, even in dream, of its absence. For this reason, he worked at her bedside.

Her dreams troubled him. She did not speak of them to the den except in a veiled, offhand way. As if they were not important. But he had seen enough of Jewel Markess and her den to know that they were.

When night faded into a slow dawn, she slept peacefully; at this time, he took his leave and returned to his own small rooms. They were not, in any way, the equal of hers—but the bed was vastly more comfortable than the unobtrusive pallet.

It was from this room that he was summoned at dawn.

He dressed quickly and efficiently, and he departed, heading toward the doors of the wing. There, he met a man who was by now more than passingly familiar: Meralonne APhaniel.

He bowed. "Member APhaniel."

"Wake Jewel Markess if she is, as I suspect, sleeping. I would speak with her."

Ellerson hesitated; the night had been long and severely broken. The Terafin had reached no decision about the fate of Torvan ATerafin in the wake of the attack, and he knew it troubled the entire den, adding to their tension and their lack of sleep. But he glanced once at Meralonne APhaniel, and he nodded instead. "I will bring her immediately," he replied.

Meralonne grimaced. "I have worked at her side for more than a month. I am well aware of what the word *immediately* entails. I will wait," he added, drawing his pipe from his robes, "in the usual room."

Jewel met Meralonne in a breakfast nook that was already thick with the haze of pipe smoke. She could have pretended to resent it, but instead she slid down onto the long bench on the wall side of the table. She had often spent mornings on a similar bench while her Oma smoked her pipe, and her Oma was often as difficult and ill tempered as this man. She had certainly been more terrifying.

Meralonne was in the process of emptying and refilling the pipe's bowl, and Jewel was still quiet with sleep; she watched his long and supple fingers as they worked. But his silence couldn't last; he didn't usually come to be silent at her.

"I am here," he told her quietly, "at the request of The Terafin. I am not, however, here in the capacity of the Terafin mage; I am here as a member of the Magi, the governing body of the Order of Knowledge."

She nodded as if this made sense. It didn't. She didn't particularly care why he was here, after all.

"After some deliberation," he said, following a pause in which she might insert any words she could find, "it was decided that The Terafin's request to be allowed access to the Cordufar estates within the city would be granted. You are to accompany Devon ATerafin to the Cordufar manse."

Her brows rose. "You mean Lord Cordufar's estate?" Sleep fled then, and she would have joined it had she dared.

His expression was distinctly unusual. Nor did he answer for a moment, although she expected the usual words that he dredged out of nowhere, dripping with sarcasm. But he lit his pipe as he watched her expression shift from half asleep to wide awake.

"Understand, Jewel Markess," he said, sounding more like Ellerson than he ever had, "that the time for games has passed."

She wasn't playing games and opened her mouth to say as much. Closed it. No point.

"Devon ATerafin is trusted by the Kings," he continued. "You are not known to them. You are, however, trusted by Devon ATerafin, or you would not be accompanying him. I did not think it entirely necessary."

"Did you think it entirely unnecessary?"

His lips curved in a slight smile, and he tipped the smoldering pipe in her direction. But the smile never quite reached his eyes. "You are not what I expected when I was first tasked with accompanying you. I see you as little more than a child."

She bridled. It was early in the morning, and she hadn't eaten anything but pipe smoke.

"But in this battle, it doesn't matter whether or not I see truly. Children will die." He paused. "You cannot prevent it," he added softly. "All that you do, all that you *can* do, will define in the end *how many*."

Her throat went dry.

He nodded. "What happened in the Terafin manse was not arranged in a matter of hours or days. It was the only warning we will be offered. If," he added softly, "we are fortunate. But it was offered because our enemies now feel we are almost out of time.

"What I fear, Jewel, is the coming of a god. You cannot imagine what a god upon the plane will do, but a city as simple and devoid of power as this one will not stand long against him.

"And *this* city," he added grimly, "is the only city they fear; can you imagine the fate of the others?"

As he'd just said she couldn't, she bit back a retort and waited. Ellerson took this moment to slide a plate between her stiff chin and the table. He said nothing; he didn't even throw her the usual warning glance.

"You—and your den—spent some months or years combing dark tunnels beneath this city. You personally spent six weeks failing to find any of them, and we well understand why." He hesitated and then said, "It is, however, imperative, Jewel, that you find *something*."

"But—" she hesitated. "You've been to Cordufar's mansion?"

He nodded. "We have."

"And you've searched?"

Silence.

"You *have* searched?"

"We have done some preliminary investigation. The manse—as you will see—is not, perhaps, as it once was. We have discovered—and triggered—some handful of traps; we have lost three in the process."

She swallowed.

"It is my suspicion that you will not likewise be lost. We have touched nothing," he added, "otherwise. Devon will accompany you to the manse; I will, with Sigurne's permission, meet you there. Search where you can," he added. "Find what you can. We have no time now, and anything of import, any hint of how we might reach this undercity in which you searched, we *need*."

He rose and headed toward the door, but he paused there while her untouched food cooled. He didn't turn back, but he did speak. "You are not a warrior," he said softly. "You are not a mage. You are not, in my opinion, a competent thief. You can lead children, and you have led as many as you can to the dubious safety of this House.

"We do not require you to face gods, Jewel. We in fact require the opposite. If there is to be a battle—and we hope for just that, because if there is no battle, it will be slaughter, pure and simple—there is no role for you in it.

"Your role, such as it is, is to give us that opportunity, no more and no less. Do you understand?"

She didn't answer.

Because she didn't, he continued. "If there is danger, flee it. If there is fighting, let Devon ATerafin handle it. Stay alive. Your only role—and it is, I believe, necessary—is to give us enough information that we can carry the fight to where the *Kialli* now dwell. Do that, and you will have earned any respect and any honor that the House, or the Kings, can possibly convey."

His tone of voice, however, made clear that he thought she would find little. "This is your task," he finally said, as if to belie that.

And so she went. Devon ATerafin was, as promised, waiting for her in the first chamber of the wing. He was seated, and he rose when she entered. His expression was completely shuttered, and he moved with a tense, bottled grace. He was armed; she saw that.

Saw, as well, what form the arms took: daggers, ornate and useless for throwing. Useless, as well, for any real cutting or stabbing. They would only offer harm to one thing.

He saw the direction of her gaze and shrugged. "You're ready?" he asked.

She nodded. Ellerson had chosen clothing for her and then set it aside, allowing her free run of her massive closet. She had chosen—as she did when she was going to be crawling through dirt and debris—clothing as close to the old holding clothing as she now owned.

If she really owned anything in House Terafin.

Devon handed her a dagger. After a brief hesitation, he handed her a second. He didn't tell her when to use them; he didn't tell her to handle them with care. She wondered if he would speak at all.

But he led her from the wing, and she followed. He took a route that didn't lead to the foyer; those doors and that entrance were still closed, and she had no desire to revisit—even in daylight—the wreckage.

But she wasn't used to this much silence. "Devon?"

He glanced back at her.

"Have you spoken with The Terafin?"

He nodded.

"Have you talked about anything other than the Cordufar estates?"

At that, he paused. He didn't stop, not exactly, but he did slow. "How so?"

It was her turn to hesitate, and she did. But it didn't last. "What is she going to do with Torvan?"

His expression did change, but it was a fleeting change; she understood it well enough to know that he wouldn't answer.

People in this part of the hundred holdings—which would be the wealthy damn part—had no brains, in Jewel's decided opinion. Most of that decision was based on the crowd that had gathered in front of the Cordufar mansion's very closed gates. They weren't poor, judging by their clothing. Then again, she thought with a grimace, neither was she.

But she could see smoke and a very distinct ragged hole in the upper level of the manse visible over the fence, and she knew that had this occurred anywhere in the twenty-fifth, people would have been taking alternate streets just to avoid coming anywhere close. Here they were gawking and gossiping in the open streets; they might as well have been holding mugs of steaming tea.

Devon made headway through the crowd, but it took time; he was unfailingly polite but spoke very few words. Jewel, had she spoken any at all, would have been rude; she let him do the talking. But she followed closely behind before the crowd could close the gap it so grudgingly made to allow Devon passage.

The gates were guarded, and the men who guarded it wore armor and swords that had definitely seen use. They also wore tabards, but she didn't recognize the colors; they were gray. As they approached Devon, she could see that they sported a rod crossed over a sword, and she understood belatedly that these were the Kings' Swords. Devon didn't even blink.

Instead, he handed them a sealed scroll and waited while they broke it open. The man who had done so read it all; it wasn't a cursory examination. When he looked up, his eyes glanced off Devon's face and found Jewel's a few inches down. His brows rose, and he turned back to the scroll, reading it again as if he were looking for some way to deny Jewel entry.

Devon said, "She is the appointed representative of House Terafin. Her name is Jewel Markess." He waited. "House Terafin is aware that there may be some present danger in this investigation, and all responsibility for any injuries sustained at the behest of House Terafin will, of course, be ours."

The Kings' Sword returned the scroll to Devon without comment. "ATerafin," he said. "You will find the magi on the grounds."

"They're expecting me?"

"I was told to inform you where they might be found."

Devon nodded as the Swords parted the gates to let them through.

The Cordufar manse, seen from the right side of the gates—or, Jewel thought, the wrong side, depending on your definition—was breathtaking. Literally.

She stopped on the path and stared, openmouthed, at the ruin. Not even the sloping, old buildings in the poor holdings, with their partial roofs and walls, compared to this. There were no windows; there were spaces where windows should have been—but even those were now bent or broken enough that the shape of the windows couldn't be seen. The glass that had once been in those windows glittered in the open, cold sun—but it glittered in shards all across the grounds around the building. So, too, did twisted brass knobs and frames, and things that looked like sconces. There were no doors.

If the attack on House Terafin had come, in the end, from Cordufar, they'd paid in kind.

Devon had glanced at the manse. He approached it, but he stopped when he'd passed the trees and shrubs that marked the midpoint of the front grounds. On the Isle, grounds were short because land was scarce; on the mainland, this wasn't an issue. Or so he'd said. It was, and would always be, an issue for people born where Jewel and the rest of her den had been born; she'd struggled not to say as much.

"Here," he said, pointing at shards of glittering glass. "This seems to be the outer circumference of the damage." He slid gloves out of his pockets and put them on.

"You're going to pick through glass?"

"Jewel, even Arann couldn't break a window with enough force to send glass flying this distance. This was not the result of an armed military action."

She remembered what Meralonne had told her and fell silent for a moment. "Should we go and find the magi?"

He straightened. "Yes."

Sigurne Mellifas was waiting at a remove from the debris. Another four or five robed men and women were doing something nearby; Jewel couldn't tell what, and she didn't ask. She trailed after Devon in silence. Meralonne was not present. Not yet.

"ATerafin," Guildmaster Mellifas said, offering Devon a curt and businesslike nod.

"Guildmaster," he replied, in kind. "May I introduce Jewel Markess? The Terafin felt that she would be of some aid in the investigation."

"Member APhaniel said as much," the older woman replied. Her gaze, as it fell briefly upon Jewel's face, was not unkind, but it lingered in silence for a little too long. Jewel had been raised by an old woman, and she knew steel when she saw it. "Where did he go?" She raised her voice, and one of the robed men came to stand by her side. "Matteos," she said, "Find Meralonne."

"He is by the east side of the manse," Matteos replied. He waited for a moment, and then shrugged into Sigurne's perfect silence.

Ten minutes later, he returned, Meralonne APhaniel by his side. Notably absent was Meralonne's pipe. He didn't bother to offer Sigurne a polite gesture of respect; he looked weary.

"Come," he told Jewel, as if they were once again embarking on a fruitless search of dirty basements throughout the holdings. She shoved her hands into her pockets and trailed after him.

They didn't approach what had once been front doors. "The floor there is of dubious structural integrity," he told her when she glanced at it. "The floor on the upper level is likewise unencumbered by reliable joists. Where we can, the magi are picking through the rooms and the contents that might have survived the inferno; several of our number can support their own weight when the flooring is tenuous. It is not the floors that have caused the difficulty," he added, as if it needed to be said.

"Where are we going?"

"To the east, the trade entrance."

Even around back, at an entrance that no one of any import would be expected to use, let alone see, there was evidence of damage. The small, high windows, like the large and impressive ones, had lost all their glass, and the small bars that held the panes had, mostly, gone with them. The door—and to her surprise, there was one—was half off its hinges and clung to the last of them like an injured child might cling to a dead parent.

"What happened here?" she asked him as she slid around the gaping door and peered in. The floor here looked solid enough. It was covered in fine dust, but most of that dust wasn't black. She took a step in. Waited. The floors here were wooden. After a few seconds she walked farther in, and away from the light at her back.

"A great deal of magic. It is not inconceivable that several First Circle magi working in concert could achieve the same effect—but it would take some time."

"We need light," she told him. Light appeared at her back. She'd gotten used to this in the weeks she'd worked at his side—or under his feet—but she still felt the lack of a magestone bitterly. If the floors were wood, the wood was superficial. The walls were solid stone. The sconces on those walls were mostly in place, but they held no torches; Jewel could see where torches had fallen; the floor was black. It was not charred.

She knelt.

"It was almost instant, from our initial reports. Those who would be more intimately acquainted had no report to make, and Sigurne is against summoning the Judgment-born to bespeak them."

It took Jewel a few minutes to catch up with what Meralonne was implying. When she did, she straightened. "I'm going first?" she asked him softly.

"I can lead, if you'd prefer."

She shook her head. The stonework at the trade entrance, as he'd called it, was not nearly as ornamental as the work that had been destroyed at the front of the manse. "Your mages didn't come in through here, did they?"

"No. I do not think it occurred to them. They were not fools," he added. "They took precautions. But the nature of their precautions did not require stealth."

There were two things that were immediately visible as they walked farther into the manse. One, a hall that led into the manse itself, and the other, an open door that contained darkness. "Cellar?"

"Possibly. There are old plans of the Cordufar manse in existence; the magi have at least two. The manse, however, was modified—several times—after its initial construction; we do not expect the maps to remain exact."

"Or even close."

"Or," he replied with a nod, "even close." He glanced at the darkened door, which did, as Jewel suggested, descend.

As she descended in the glow of his magical light, she frowned. Reaching out, she steadied herself on a wall that was cool and slightly damp. "Meralonne," she told him, the frown deepening, "douse the light."

There was a moment's hesitation and the sound of drawn breath that usually preceded argument. But argument, if it waited, was now carefully hoarded; he did as she asked. The light went out. All that illuminated the stairs now was the open door at their back, and that light receded as Jewel inched her way down the stairs.

She counted steps as she made her way down in darkness. It wasn't a comfortable way to move; everything was hesitant and strained. Every movement of foot, the transfer of hand from wall; she moved sideways, so that one hand was always touching it.

Above her, she heard the play of his shifting robes; it was a comfort.

"You couldn't sense the magic?" she asked, as she moved.

"Apparently not."

"Why?"

"There are concealing spells," he said after a pause.

"Most of those should throw off magic. I know the magestones do."

"The magestones, yes. And the privacy stones as well, if one knows what to look for. But one has to be looking."

"But if the magic was powerful enough to do *this*, how hard would you have to be looking?"

"Not hard," he conceded. "But if it was instant, or almost instant, it wouldn't matter." He was silent for a few steps and then added, "The magic of the *Allasakari* is not well-known; if, as I suspect, the god's power was invoked, we would have done better to send the god-born. The Exalted."

They hadn't.

"The light?" he asked her, and she could hear his impatience in the two words.

She shook her head. He couldn't see it, and she said, "They don't need to see. Or they don't need light to see, not in this kind of darkness. If something could trigger a trap—a magical trap—it could be something as simple as light."

"Jewel," he told her, "I'm almost impressed."

"Don't be."

As she said it, she felt her throat tighten. She didn't dwell on darkness when she had anything else to think about. She absolutely didn't dwell on the run through the tunnels beneath the Merchant Authority. Then, Devon had been at her back or by her side, guiding her, his silence grow-ing weighty and more urgent as they moved.

"Here," she said.

Meralonne moved past her. He didn't step on her feet, and he wasn't as slow as she was. But his hands passed over hers, and he felt what she felt;

the stone had given way to wood. The wood had not done as well as the stone; whatever had shaken the manse had caused it to crack and splinter. "Yes," he said, after a pause. "There is a door."

"I can't find a handle."

"There isn't one."

"How can you even tell—"

"It's the only thing that's left standing; it's the only panel that wasn't cracked or broken."

He whispered a single word, and Jewel raised her voice in a wordless shout, raising her hands and her arms to cover her face. Nothing covered her ears, though, and the sound of wood exploding almost deafened her.

But the debris itself—and there must have been debris—didn't strike her or touch her; she came out of it without so much as a splinter.

"My apologies," Meralonne said, in the darkness. "But you were, essentially, correct. There is a door here."

When the door had nothing left to hold onto, it fell backward. This might be because Meralonne had pushed it; it was hard to tell. But it clattered against stone. "May I chance light now?"

She started to say no but said yes instead; his light was bright enough that she had to squint to see past it. The door had struck a wall. The wall wasn't of interest. But to the left of the wall, descending just as the stairs she had already taken descended, were more stairs.

"It was not meant to kill us," he told her softly.

"It wasn't meant to kill someone like you," she replied sharply. "It would have killed me or any of mine."

He raised a pale brow, then nodded. "Perhaps. It was not like the traps that lay in wait for those of my Order."

"Why?"

"I would guess that there are things below ground that the former Lord Cordufar did not wish to chance destroying. It is promising," he added softly.

Promising. She'd remember that, later.

She didn't want to lead. She hovered at the small landing, and even with Meralonne's light at her back, she had a visceral urge to turn and leave. But she mastered it. He had already somehow protected her from flying splinters and wood debris, and he wouldn't be far behind.

"Jewel?"

She shook her head. "It's nothing," she finally said.

"You're not afraid of the dark?"

"Actually," she muttered, as she began to climb down much rougher hewn stairs, her hand still using the wall as a guide, "I don't like it, much."

"It's just the absence of light."

Yes, and death is just the absence of life. She bit her tongue. It took effort. It took more effort to accept the fact that he was right: she was afraid of *this* darkness. Not because of the magic. She knew, as she made her way down, that she had seen the last of it; the manse was guttered. There was safety, of a sort; she could run off and leave the mages to their work, and no more of them would die from anything but their own carelessness.

It was therefore with some relief that she came to the narrowed gap caused by fallen rock; whatever had shaken the manse had also shaken its foundation. "We can't get through," she began as she turned. She almost ran into Meralonne APhaniel's chest.

His eyes were slate gray, and his expression was cool. "Jewel."

"There's no way into the maze here," she said, voice thin.

He stared at her for a long moment, and then his voice softened. "What do you see, Jewel?" He pushed her gently aside and sent light through the leaning stones. "There is room enough, if the rest of the foundation is solid."

"The dead," she said softly and almost tonelessly. Her hands were shaking, and she bunched them into fists, which didn't help. "None of the servants made it out."

He raised a brow. He didn't, thank *Kalliaris*, ask her how she knew. Instead, he said, "Go find Devon. I will return to Sigurne to obtain a few necessary items."

It was a gift, and she took it, running up the stairs and out of the building as if her life depended on it.

Devon ATerafin came out of the manse with Meralonne APhaniel; Jewel watched them outside the odd circle composed of shards of glass, twisted brass, splinters of painted wood. They were silent, but they were grim. She wanted to loiter beside one of the unharmed trees, but it would have been too obvious; instead, she housed her nerves, her terrible fear, and she waited.

They came to her.

Devon said, "It is time for us to return to the manse." Just that.

But Meralonne lifted a hand. "ATerafin," he said quietly.

Devon turned. Jewel couldn't see his expression, but she knew he must have mouthed something, because Meralonne shook his head, once, in measured denial.

Devon did not turn back to her; he clearly hadn't finished.

"You cannot protect her," was Meralonne's reply. He looked beyond Devon's shoulder, and Devon shrugged and turned. "We found some part of what we seek."

She tensed, but she nodded.

Meralonne now began to speak as Devon fell silent. "There are rooms at the base of the stairs, and they extend some way in darkness. There is one, in particular, that looks like an altar room.

"I do not know what you know, Jewel Markess. But the dead were there. We believe that they are the servants who were in the manse at the time of Lord Cordufar's departure.

"I will not," he added, as she paled, "speak further on the subject; it is in the hands of the Magisterium and Mysterium now. But beyond those rooms, we found what we seek. The demons are not kind; they are deliberate in their cruelty." He did not appear particularly upset about it; it was a statement of fact, like weather. "There is an entrance to the maze of your experience beneath the Cordufar manse. It is not safely reached.

"It is also protected by a magical barrier of a type that the Order of Knowledge has no direct experience with. We cannot breach it. I believe the *Kialli* might have chosen to unmake this entrance had they desired to do so; they did not. I believe they left both their dead and the magical barrier as a statement."

She stared at him.

"We will work, as we are able, to break it."

She said, mouth dry, "You can't."

Devon's brows rose, but Meralonne nodded. "I suspect as much," he replied. "But at the moment, it is our only option. It is not, in my opinion, a good one." He offered her a little half bow. "Return to House Terafin; should you be required, we will send word there."

The return to the manse was quiet. Devon didn't speak at all. Nor did Jewel. The dead weighed heavily on her, and she wasn't even certain it wasn't because of the nightmares that had plagued her for what seemed weeks now. She wanted to hole up in her room with the lamps burning, even if it wasn't dark.

Devon, unfortunately, had other ideas. To be fair—and this was a struggle—the ideas weren't entirely his; The Terafin, it seemed, was waiting for their report.

Devon detailed, quickly, what he and Meralonne APhaniel had discovered. Jewel said nothing. "We suspect that the slaughter started a week ago—not more, but certainly not less. There were day servants who did not reside within Cordufar proper. We've spoken more at length, with those who survived the fall of the estate and we can ascertain that Lord and Lady Cordufar were not among the dead. Their children were, and recently dead."

The Terafin accepted this without comment. "The fires?"

"Were not responsible for any of the servant's death's."

Jewel hesitated, biting back words.

"The deaths occurred before the manse was destroyed."

"Jewel," The Terafin said quietly, "What do you think?"

Jewel looked up at the woman who ruled the House. "I think that they have to be stopped. They all have to be stopped."

Devon reached out and caught her hand, and she remembered that he would have spared her the knowledge. All of it. Her hand tightened around his for a moment, and then she let go, drawing breath. He would have spared her, yes, and she greatly desired the comfort of ignorance—but it wouldn't do them any good. It wouldn't help.

"And that," The Terafin said, rising, "is just what we cannot do. Were you not what you are, Jewel, I would not tell you this. But I value any insight that you might have, however and whenever it might come, and I wish you to feel free to interrupt any meeting I might have, should any insight of relevance arise.

"If we can make our way into the maze that your den used to travel, the mages of the Order—guided by Teos, Lord of Knowledge—believe that we would be able to stop the enemy from completing his ascent. But we have searched, and searched again, for a way into the undercity; we have the entire Order, from Fourth Circle up, attempting to break the barrier that the—that our enemy has imposed.

"Not even the combined power of the Exalted has been able to achieve the smallest rupture."

Jewel understood that the deaths in the Cordufar manse would be the start, and they would spread across the city—across the Empire—until very, very little was left alive. "Can't they call their gods, the same way the *Allasakari* have?"

"They can," The Terafin replied. "But at the best guess of the Lord of Wisdom, it would take twenty years for the gods to answer in a like fashion. And he believes that if we have twenty weeks before the Lord of the Hells takes Averalaan, we are very, very lucky."

Chapter Thirteen

IT WASN'T LATE. In fact, it was early enough that Jewel shouldn't have been sleeping. But Ellerson had implied—where in this case implied meant bluntly stated—that she looked peaked and exhausted. He had offered her dinner, which she couldn't touch, and then he had all but ordered her to bed. In his servile fashion.

"I'll try to sleep," she told him dubiously. It was easier than actually saying no. Or telling him, in any detail, about the day she was trying so desperately not to think about.

She wasn't sure how long the attempt lasted, but nightmares robbed sleep of any restfulness. She'd had enough. Ellerson didn't insist she try again. Nor did he insist that she remain caged in the wing when she finally rolled out of bed and grabbed for the nearest clothing.

"Jewel," he said, as she headed to the doors, "trust your instincts."

She stopped, hands on the handles beneath the dimmed magelights. And then she turned to face him. "To do *what?*" she demanded, voice low. "This is *too damn big* for me. For us. This House. This war. The magic—all of it. What do we know how to do, Ellerson? Pick a lock, pick a pocket, accept handouts when we need them—how is that going to help anyone?"

He was silent, and she thought her bitter, frightened words had warned him off. But she should have known better; he was Ellerson, after all. She wondered, then, as she often did, who else he had served in his long life. She'd never asked because she knew he'd never answer.

"How did it help Teller?" he asked, quietly. "How did it help Finch?"

And yes, she'd known he would say that. But she was prepared. "How did it help Duster or Lefty or Fisher or Lander? They're *dead*." And Duster haunted her dreams, sleeping and waking. She had haunted them now for weeks, with about as much mercy as you'd ever expect from Duster.

"You're young," he told her. "You think there's nothing worse than death. You think that death is just death; that the life that led up to it counts for little. Jewel, you will always know failure. But you will also always have success. There is no end to either. You choose how you define your life based on both of these things.

"But Teller and Finch—and Arann—are alive, now, because of you. They are not significant players in the political arena, I grant you that. But neither were the servants who were slaughtered in Cordufar. Neither are the men, women, and children who will be slaughtered in Averalaan if the demons cannot be stopped.

"Measure them as you measure your den: one life at a time. I ask you, again, to trust your instincts."

She had no further arguments and no desire to make any. She wrenched the doors open and fled into the hall, feeling the weight of his words as a burden that she literally didn't know how to carry. Den leading, yes. She understood that. What did it mean, after all? Being like Oma. Being like an older sister. Telling people what to do and remembering to listen when they had something to say. Counting the coins in a cold, metal box. Watching as clothing shrunk and thinned over time. Trying to keep a roof over their heads.

But none of that had prepared her for this.

Oh, Rath—and how long had it been since she'd truly thought of Rath?—had tried. She saw that now, as she walked—quickly—toward the gardens in the back of the House, with their damaged but functional shrines. He had taught her the names of The Ten and of most of the important noble houses that weren't part of The Ten. She'd had to memorize colors and standards and political things that had made little sense at the time.

All of which meant nothing to her now.

She felt as she'd felt the day her father had left her for the last time, except this time she couldn't see the end as clearly. It wasn't her fault. It wasn't her failure.

But Ellerson's words . . . No.

The halls at this time of night weren't crowded. They weren't entirely deserted, but no one attempted to stop her. Most of the servants and most of the House Guard knew the den well enough to nod a polite—and distant—greeting. She didn't want more.

What she wanted was to be outside. There were no streets here, and she'd seen the streets of the holdings for all of her waking life. But there were also no people. Nor did she expect to see any; the small army of distressed gardeners who had been working to restore the grounds in the wake of the attack had all turned in for the day several hours ago; they would be up just before the sun was.

She made her way to the shrine of the Lord of Wisdom and paused there, beneath the scorched emblem of the Eagle, rod in his claws. The god wasn't here, of course, nor could she call him. But she hesitated a moment, seeking wisdom. Hearing her Oma's voice as she did. *If you know what to ask for*, she'd said, *you have most of your answer.*

Her Oma didn't hold with Northern gods. The gods of the South had never demanded *coin* as proof of allegiance, after all. What use did gods have for coin? They demanded blood, and, one way or another, the Southerners paid. Jewel remembered the scars, her Oma's scars, worn openly the way jewelry might have been, had they been able to afford any.

And why think of that now? What wisdom was there in that?

The eagle was stone, and silent. The pillars were scorched, but they would be cleaned; some cleaning had already been done.

Don't make me pay in blood, she thought, head bowed by the gleaming brass bowl that lay beneath the eagle. And then, because she was Jewel, an angrier thought intruded. *I've already paid.*

Wisdom, however, eluded her; anger dislodged it.

She rose and moved—quickly—because she didn't want to share that anger with a god. Not when they needed the gods.

Three shrines. She visited the Mother's next and then the shrine of Reymaris, Lord of Justice. Her anger had not dimmed. But here, at least, it had focus: Men and women went to the temple of Reymaris seeking redress for wrongs done them all the time. Surely the god was used to anger?

But here? The anger was different. All those people had died. She'd *seen* them, briefly. She had sent Devon to do whatever it was he would do in The Terafin's name; she could not have stayed either sane or quiet had she descended with him. *What did they do to deserve that death*, she demanded of the absent Reymaris. *What did you do to help them?*

The wrong anger, yes. The wrong question. She should have prayed for Justice for those dead. But Justice? It was bent and broken, like a sword caught in an earthquake; twisted almost beyond use. What Justice truly existed in a world where the helpless could die so horribly? Was Justice just power?

Her Oma had believed that. Her father hadn't.

Her father was dead. Her Oma was dead. Her mother. And following them, leaving Jewel behind, so many of her den, the family she had *chosen*. But not just them. Not just them. It never ended.

She rose, angry that she had bent knee at all, and she fled, walking stiffly and quickly through the empty flower beds. It was cold now; they would remain empty.

She wasn't even sure where she was going, but she should have known. Angry or not, she had visited all of the shrines; she was, in her shaky fury, making the circuit. There was one shrine left, and the path, broken in places, and repaired in others, led there. She had followed it blindly, seeking escape from nightmare; she had retreated from each god's small shrine, seeking escape from anger. The nightmare had receded; the anger would not.

She was shaking.

Let it go. Her father's voice. Her father's voice almost never came back to her; it was always her Oma. Let what go? Ah, no. Her anger. He had never been a truly angry man. *Let it go, Jewel.*

How? It wasn't as if she'd picked it up and was struggling to shoulder its burden—it clung to her; it burrowed into her insides; it shredded her with claws that she couldn't even reach to remove. She didn't like being angry. She never had. But there it was: she was. She wanted to hit something. To slap the gods.

And so she made her way at last to the Terafin shrine, and there she stopped, because she could hear voices. She wasn't alone.

She should have left. She meant to. Because one of the voices was The Terafin's, and she'd seen enough of The Terafin in the last little while to last a long lifetime.

But the other voice was Torvan's.

And Torvan had carried Arann into the House, when the den couldn't. Torvan had listened to the words of a bunch of ratty street urchins, and he had let them *all* in. Torvan, she thought, had been the means by which the demons had almost killed The Terafin.

"Look at me," The Terafin was saying. "What am I to do with you?" There was a pause, as if she expected him to answer. He didn't, which was no surprise to Jewel. "Fully half of my Chosen are dead or dying, and were it not for the creature that possessed you, they might be standing with me today."

Jewel drew breath. It was sharp; it cut through the anger that had walked her this far. But it didn't allow her to shed it. Anger was primal; it existed. It could be changed or shifted more easily than it could be killed.

"Shall you be held responsible for the Lord of the Hells? Shall you be held responsible for the reavers? Shall you be held responsible for the *Allasakari*? I have been to the shrines that quarter my gardens; this is the last one. At the shrine of Cormaris, I knew that I must lose you—whether in disgrace or by your own hand, in honor. The Chosen know what you did. They know what drove your hand, but just as you, they believe that fighting harder might have somehow spared them your fate. To have you in their midst—

"Look at me!"

Jewel edged closer, holding her breath, her hands balled in fists.

"What they believe is wrong. It is simply not true. Were I to meet that darkness, it would consume me. Meralonne might have a chance against it. And even he is not so certain.

"Understand what I am saying, Torvan. I know that what you did was not your choice; I find no fault with you. But knowing it doesn't necessarily change the wise course of action." She lifted a hand as Torvan looked up.

Jewel could see them both now: Torvan, kneeling upon the grass, his sword awkward across his lap, The Terafin, standing, her back draped by an old cloak that was far too large for her shoulders.

"At the shrine of Reymaris," The Terafin continued, "I knew that I must keep you, that the action of the enemy should not deprive me of a man I know to be loyal—a man that I chose, and in choosing, did not err.

"This is what the Kings face," she added softly, "this terrible choice—between the wise and the just. If I keep you, it will weaken the Chosen who are the backbone of my House, and if I condemn you—and we both know it is death I speak of—I weaken myself.

"What would you give for the Chosen?" Her voice was hard, now. "Would you die to keep them whole?"

Jewel was frozen in shock. She was cold, but it was not the cold of fear; it was the cold of a slowly growing fury.

Torvan lifted his face and met the gaze of the woman to whom he had pledged his allegiance. He looked—at peace. He looked—and this enraged Jewel—grateful. *Grateful.* And he—he unsheathed his sword, still seated. It was awkward, not graceful.

She almost couldn't understand what it meant. Almost. She was stunned with the shock of it.

But The Terafin? Damn The Terafin. She bowed—to him—and her bow was low and perfect. "You have not failed me," she told him, as his sword caught torchlight from the shrine at his back. "And I will remember it well when this is over. I will send Arrendas to you for the aid that you require." She walked to where he sat, his gaze still upon her, and she touched his forehead with the tips of her fingers, pulling away as he raised his face.

And it was *too damn much*. It was too much, here, now. Jewel was on her feet, and moving. "*No!*"

"What-are-you-doing-here?" The words were sharp as stilettos and just as furious as Jewel's.

"I'm here to save him," Jewel spat back, pointing one shaking hand at Torvan, who stared at both of them with an expression of slowly growing horror.

"He doesn't need saving," he managed to say. He steadied the flat of his sword; he had grabbed it by the hilt when she had shouted. To protect The Terafin. To protect the woman who was throwing his life away. "Jewel—Jay—"

"Don't talk to me like that," Jewel replied, voice low and shaking with fury. "Don't look at me like that. How can you do this?"

"I serve Terafin."

"No, goddess curse you, you serve *The Terafin*." She spun on her feet, then, and she turned to face The Terafin, her hands clenched so tightly her nails were cutting her palms. "You're his leader. He follows you. He would die for you."

"Jewel, leave," The Terafin said, mastering a rage that Jewel realized was not that much weaker than her own. "This does not concern you."

"The hells it doesn't."

The Terafin paled; she now looked like the alabaster out of which so many statues were carved. But less friendly.

Jewel drew breath, closed her eyes, lowered her face a moment, struggling to control her words, her tone. "I'm not ATerafin, Terafin. I am not under your command."

"No, you are not." Spoken as if it were a doom or a threat.

But it wasn't. It was freedom. Jewel wasn't ATerafin. She was—as she had always been—Jewel Markess. She had wanted the House Name for herself and her den, and she had wanted it so badly she'd been working under fear's shadow for months.

She slid out from under it now. "I lost my den-kin to the demons," she told The Terafin, the words the beginning of an accusation. "But I never gave any of them up." It struck home; color returned to the cheeks of the near-flawless woman who had made all of Terafin her den.

"Terafin is not a small den in the middle of a poor holding."

"No. Terafin is a great House," was Jewel's equally bitter reply. "In the middle of *Averalaan Aramarelas*. Much too good for the likes of me, of us."

"Jay," Torvan tried again.

The word was unwelcome. Unwanted. But it was a reminder. She looked away from The Terafin. "I'm sorry," she finally managed. "You don't deserve that last part." She would be damned, however, if she recanted anything else. "You can't let him do this."

"I can't see the Chosen weakened."

"It's not her choice," Torvan said.

"You *will* see the Chosen weakened," Jewel snarled, as if he hadn't spoken. "Sure, maybe most of them think that Torvan should've been able to stop the demon somehow—but Arrendas, at least, knows the truth. Maybe Alayra knows it now, too. You think those two won't be hurt by this? You think they won't know that you've just given up on him?"

"I think," was the cool response, "that they will not question me."

"They won't. But *I* will. I understand that you don't want your den to look weak. I know that you can't afford to let the outsiders know what you've lost. You call it wise. Sure.

"But I also know that this isn't about a stolen loaf of bread—it's a *life*, and it's *his* life, and he'll throw it away because you don't want to take the risk." She turned then, unable to contain the rising fury, the sense of bitter betrayal. Years of arguing with Duster about Lefty had left its mark. Yes, she understood the cost of looking weak.

But the cost of not looking weak in this case was *too damn high*. She walked over to where Torvan knelt and before he could move, she kicked the sword off his lap and sent it skidding across the stones that comprised the path here.

"I'm tired to death of being polite and deferential and political. You don't want him? *I'll* take him."

"It seems that you have a champion, Torvan." The Terafin's lips curved in a smile. It would have killed a meeker person than Jewel had anyone seen it.

Torvan, at last, said nothing. His eyes were round with shock. Jewel wondered, briefly, if *anyone* had ever been this rude—this deliberately, furiously rude—to his lord. She doubted it. And she didn't care. Maybe later. Maybe when they were sent packing in the middle of the night, the wealth and comfort of the manse denied them, she would hate herself for it.

But The Terafin's next words were not the ones that would strand her den in the holdings again. "Why this one, Jewel? Why Torvan?"

"Because I owe him."

"Oh?"

"When we first came here, he could've thrown us out. He didn't. We'd've lost Arann without him—because we'd have had to play games with time that Arann didn't have."

"Is that all?"

All? Jewel thought, for just that moment, that she would never understand this woman. And that she would be happier in her ignorance. "Yes." And then, after a moment. "No. Because he made me understand, at my very first visit to the shrine of Terafin, that I had something to offer the House—and that I did understand power. Your power.

"And it's because I understand it that I can't let Torvan die—even if he wants to, even if you think it's best for the House."

Torvan cleared his throat. Jewel, who had spent so much of the discussion ignoring everything he'd said in favor of actually preserving the life he didn't seem to value enough, glanced at him.

"You must be mistaken," he said quietly. He looked as if he regretted having to say it. "My rounds do not bring me to the shrine of Terafin;

The Terafin does not come here with any of her guards except, on rare occasions, Morretz."

It was the first time Jewel had heard Morretz granted the title of guard, and it should have said something significant about the domicis' role in House Terafin. It didn't. She *knew* Torvan. She couldn't forget the face—or the voice—of the man who had saved Arann's life. Who had, in the end, saved all of them, simply by taking a risk.

"W-what?"

"I've never spoken with you at the shrine of Terafin."

Jewel could think of nothing to say. Her mouth was still open, but in want of words—any words. He wasn't accusing her of lying—that much, she could see on his face. It stopped her from accusing him of the same, but only barely. She felt her hands curve into fists, and she struggled to find any words, even the wrong ones, to break the silence left in the wake of his denial.

But The Terafin suddenly turned, as Jewel stared. She walked past them both, moving slowly and more hesitantly than Jewel had ever seen her move as she made her way up the concentric circular stairs toward the altar. She lifted the cloak she wore as she walked, and she walked without looking at either Jewel or Torvan.

Jewel turned to watch The Terafin as she knelt, pressing her forehead gently against the stone as if somehow confirming that it was real by touch alone.

Neither Jewel nor Torvan spoke; this much, they granted her. But neither did they leave. They waited. After a long, long pause, she rewarded their wait. She rose, and turned to face them.

"Jewel, you were right to come. It has been a long time since things were as clear for me as they are for you; a long time since risk was the only way of life, for me. I want safety; I want certainty—I had almost forgotten that in ruling there is neither.

"Torvan, I chose you, and I chose well; you have never disappointed me. If I have—almost—disappointed you, then you are free to leave. Any dishonor or disgrace will be mine alone to bear."

He was utterly still. So, too, was Jewel. Maybe even for the same reason.

"But if you would, I would have you remain as one of the Chosen of Terafin. You know how difficult it will be; you know the mistrust that you will suffer, probably better than I."

No question at all in Jewel's mind what his answer would be. None. But she was suddenly fine with that. The anger that had driven her, jumping from injustice to injustice in a growing frenzy, now drained out of her as if she were a cracked vessel.

Torvan stood, walking unsteadily, as if he'd spent all day sitting with his legs folded beneath him. He bent, retrieved the sword that Jewel had kicked from his lap and his hands. As he rose, sword in hands, he stood closest to Jewel, and he spoke, softly, to her.

"You owe me nothing, Jewel. I told you that the day you took us to confront the demon. But I—I am in your debt. Your interference here has saved my life," he continued, still speaking quietly, "but it has done more: It has saved her the pain of ending it."

She nodded, half embarrassed by the weight of his solid, fixed gaze. But he shifted it, and he walked past her, bearing the sword. He had not sheathed it. It was shining by the time he approached the shrine.

The Terafin waited, and then, aware that this was the whole of the answer he would offer, she bent slightly, extending the flats of both palms.

But he stumbled just as the sword was placed in those palms, and his breath cut the air in much the same way the edge cut her hands.

Jewel couldn't see his expression, but she could imagine what it was. The Terafin's, though, was strange. She smiled. It was a pained smile.

"Pride is such a necessary thing in power, and such a dangerous one," she told him. "What you have offered, I accept."

"Your hand."

"I know." She looked down at that hand and then returned his sword to him; she did not tend it. "It is . . . Terafin. Reminding me. I bleed. I don't need to be more than I am; I only need to be all that I can.

"Now go back to your post, but attire yourself appropriately first. I would speak with Jewel a moment in private; tell the Chosen."

He tendered her a perfect bow, which, given he was carrying his sword very awkwardly, said a lot about him. Then he wiped it clean of her blood, and he sheathed it. He offered her a sharp salute, and he turned and left the House shrine, following the only orders he cared to follow: The Terafin's.

"His name was Jonnas," The Terafin said softly, gazing at the lamps above them before she turned to face Jewel. "He was, of all things, a cook, and at that not the cook to The Terafin himself, but rather a cook to those who tended the affairs of the House in this manor. Common wisdom dictates that cooks are either too large or too thin, but he defied common wisdom in many ways; he had lived his early years in the free townships, and he retained many of their mannerisms. I'm not sure why he elected to serve at a big House.

"He kept the kitchen staff together as if it were a family and he an uncle distant enough to be allowed to dispense wisdom without the resentment that it usually brings. Dispensing wisdom was one of the things that he did.

"I met him on my eighth day in Terafin, and I liked him. We had little in common—I, noble-born and bred, and he a commoner with no ties, until Terafin, to the nobility, and little enough respect for it. I asked him once why he served a noble House—one of The Ten, no less. His answer was this:

"It's The Ten that're most uppity; they don't know how to get anything practical done. They need me. And a man's got to be needed, he's got to be useful."

Jewel wasn't completely certain where this story was going, but The Terafin's face had softened into a smile at the memory. It made her look younger. Less harsh.

"I wasn't The Terafin then. And not destined to become The Terafin in his life, either."

There was a pause as she turned from Jewel toward the altar.

"I discovered the shrine on my own, when difficulties in Handernesse—the family of my birth—arose. And Jonnas would come to me here, to speak with me and offer me advice on the responsibilities of both the House and its leader. On what is owed to the family one is born to and to the family one chooses. On the ties to both. He was known for his common wisdom, and it comforted me to hear it, because I respected the old man, even if I had never told him so in so many words.

"When he died, I was already struggling with the three other possible heirs to the title; there had been some savage politics and, in one case, a very messy death. Assassination was not the way that I wished to take Terafin, and I would not use it; I was not involved in it, yet it still left me one less rival.

"But the divisions in the House caused by the death of the man in question—and his young son—were terrible; the manner of death could

306 ♦ Michelle West

not be kept from the crowns should it occur again, and the other Houses were beginning to crowd like vultures at our step.

"And I came to the shrine, as I did when troubled, for it seemed to me that I was going to lose my bid for the House—and possibly my life—to the man who was most ruthless in his quest for power." She lifted her head, and light touched the contours of her face, as if she were part of the altar, not separate from it.

"And as I prayed, Jonnas came to me as he always had, and he sat, just there, cross-legged and at ease, waiting for what I had to say." Her lips turned up then, in a rare self-deprecating smile. "And I said, 'But you're dead.'"

Jewel grimaced to stop herself from smiling, but The Terafin knew. She beckoned Jewel forward, and Jewel took the stairs and came to stand beside her, in front of the altar. Her own hand, the cut one, she placed against the stone, spreading her fingers there, unmindful of stain.

"He said, very gravely, 'No, but I will be if Hellas becomes The Terafin.' Ah, I'm sorry. Hellas ATerafin was the man considered most likely to draw victory out of bloodshed. And most likely to cause bloodshed. We do not speak these names to outsiders.

"I realized then that he wasn't Jonnas, that he had never been Jonnas, and I understood at last what Jonnas—what *this* one—had said about Terafin, about the Spirit of Terafin. I was his Chosen, and I was to rule Terafin—with honor." She bent and bowed her head softly to stone, and then raised it, turning to catch Jewel's gaze. It wasn't hard; it hadn't strayed from her face at all as she'd spoken.

"Do you understand?" The Terafin asked her softly.

Jewel nodded. The Torvan that had taken the time to speak to her and to ease her out of her fears of insignificance hadn't been Torvan either; no wonder he'd looked so confused. "Do you still speak to him?"

"No. I have not seen him in many years. But if Terafin needs his guidance, and no one else can fulfill this role, he comes. Tonight, he called you."

Damn silent call, Jewel thought, but she didn't say it. Instead, she glanced at the shrine, and thought about The Terafin, and about the families you *choose* and *build*, rather than the ones that you're born into. When she spoke at last, she said, "I'm already ATerafin, aren't I?"

"Not yet," The Terafin replied, surprising her. Her words were not unkind, however. "For I am The Terafin; the living rule here, not the dead.

Come. It is dark, and we have missed the early dinner hour. Dine with me, if you will."

Late dinner hour.

Morretz raised a brow when The Terafin returned to her chambers with Jewel Markess. But that was all he did; when The Terafin told him that they would take late dinner together in her quarters, he nodded smoothly and held out his arms for her cloak. Jewel watched him take it and then glanced at The Terafin; the cloak, while fine—and Jewel was not, admittedly, a good judge of cloth—was far too large for her. It seemed to be a man's cloak, and one that had seen better years; it was faded, and even in the light of The Terafin's chambers, the original color was not entirely clear to Jewel.

They adjourned to the small dining room where The Terafin took most of her meals during the week. On the Mothersday, the large dining hall was open, and she ate there, flanked by Gabriel ATerafin and any of the House Council who happened to be resident in the manse at the time. Jewel, who was not ATerafin, had heard of the meal, but she had never attended one. Guests did, on occasion, but never uninvited guests, at least not those who did not wish to immediately overstay their welcome.

Jewel looked around the room before she took her seat. It wasn't that much different from the room in which her den ate most of its meals. Even the chairs were similar, although admittedly less scuffed.

"I will not tell you not to mention the House Spirit or the shrine," The Terafin told her, as Morretz moved her chair.

"Did you?"

"No. But I had the advantage of desiring stability."

When Jewel was silent for that little too long, The Terafin added, in a much drier tone of voice, "I value the appearance of sanity."

Morretz disappeared and reappeared with a bottle of dark wine. The Terafin nodded, and he poured for both of them. Jewel, whose experience with wine was limited, hid a grimace.

"But you are the only other person I know of who has spoken with the Spirit of Terafin. Or rather, with whom the Spirit has chosen to speak."

"What does it mean?"

"That, in some measure, you have already earned his respect. Not more, but not less—and, perhaps for reasons of vanity, I feel that it is an important measure of character." Again she smiled. The smile dimmed slowly as she drank, and after a pause, she said, "I want you to tell me about my brother." It wasn't a command. It was spoken almost like one, but Jewel knew that was just how The Terafin spoke.

"About Rath?"

"Ararath, yes."

The next pause was Jewel's. But she nodded. "I don't know if it will make you happy," she told the older woman. "But he saved my life. He saved *all* of our lives."

The Terafin nodded.

"He wasn't exactly happy about it at the time, though."

And smiled. "I do not require you to make him a saint," she told Jewel. "I shouldn't require you to speak of him at all, not now, when things are so grim. But we did not speak at all after I left Handernesse. I would have welcomed him," she added. "But he was always proud."

And you're not?

As if she could hear the question Jewel was wise enough not to ask, she said, "I, too, have some of the Handernesse pride; it has been both strength and liability. Over the years, I have attempted to discern which function it serves and to unentangle myself when it is the latter.

"You knew him. I did not. What he was willing to share with you— and if he did not change much, that would be little—I would have you share with me, if you are able."

This, Jewel could do. She began with the first day she'd seen him, because it was easiest, and because, in retrospect, it was funniest. She didn't tell it the way Jester would have, but she didn't need to—The Terafin's brow rose and her lips turned up at all the right places. She wasn't judgmental, but Jewel had, in the space of this angry and confusing night, lost her fear of that.

"You tried to rob him."

"No. I *did* rob him." She almost added, *I'm not proud of it*, but at the moment, she was.

"And he took you in."

"Not exactly." She apologized for the lack of clarity of the next memory, then spoke of her illness, of his care of her, and of her words to him the first night he left her in his apartment. She spoke openly of her peculiar and unpredictable gift, because she *knew* that Rath would forgive her, and even encourage her. If he hadn't overcome his pride and his bitter hurt at his sister's desertion, he had still sent the den—all of them—to House Terafin. And that sister had taken them in.

The Terafin asked questions as Jewel's story unfolded. She asked for clarification when Jewel got ahead of herself, which she did often. She asked about the maps, the burning brothel, and the demons. But she also offered small stories of her own in the spaces between Jewel's narrative, helping Jewel to understand some of the Rath she'd known better.

Morretz came with food and more wine; he brought sweet water and bread and cheese after the meal's end. He cleared the dishes himself, but he did not speak a single word that might interrupt them.

When Jewel spoke of his death—of her *certainty* that he would die—she spoke slowly and hesitantly for the first time.

But The Terafin didn't hold her responsible for his choice, and if her eyes teared, briefly, she seemed pleased in the end—proud—of that choice. She rose for a moment after Jewel had finished. Turning, she walked to the window that was as tall as she, and she looked out into the silent streets of *Averalaan Aramarelas*. "You don't understand," she said quietly, speaking to Jewel's transparent reflection in the panes of glass before her.

Jewel nodded. She felt no condescension in the offered words.

"He chose his death. He chose his death because in the end, it would give us the only warning he could offer that would be believed." She leaned her forehead against the window for another moment and then lifted it, straightening her shoulders. "I tarried." She turned.

"But if his death is not to be wasted, if his choice is to be honored at all, it is now. I will not—I cannot—speak of him openly. But we will know."

"Is that enough?"

"For me?" The Terafin was silent for a moment, and then she nodded. "I only wish my grandfather still lived. I would tell him. It would bring him a measure of peace." She returned to the table and took her chair without the help of her domicis. "We are bound, in the end, by both the families we were born to and the families we build. It is true of me; it is true, as well, of you.

"But we are also human. The youngest and the oldest, the most foolish and the most wise. We require, on occasion, people with whom we can share the experiences that matter; it will not always be the same people, because experiences vary. But for now, I have you; you have me. Ararath sent you to me, and in the end, we are what is left of him." She lifted her glass and held it up above the flickering candles that lay in the center of the table. "I understand that your work in the Cordufar manse was not pleasant."

"You're going to send me back." It wasn't a question.

"Unless you ask me not to, yes. I will send you with Devon. There is still work there that may prove important to us, and you might have some insight that could be of value. The shield that prevents our entry into the maze must have a weakness."

"I'm not a mage—"

"No. You are, if I understand my talents, seer-born. But what—and how—you see, I cannot predict. Will you go?"

How much worse could it get? Jewel nodded.

"Then return to your domicis and your den." She set the glass down without touching it. "Finch has impressed Lucille ATerafin, by all reports. You have not met Lucille; when you do, you will understand how difficult a task that is. Teller has likewise earned the approval of Gabriel. That is less difficult, for Gabriel is both patient and considerate. He has also, however, earned the approval of Gabriel's secretary, Barston. A man more particular in his choice of aides has yet to be found." The subtle grimace that accompanied these words made clear that she spoke from experience, but it faded.

"They will continue to do their work during this crisis. As will Arann." The Terafin hesitated for just a moment. "I do not know if you wish the others to be similarly employed, and I have some suspicion that at least one of them would find employment difficult."

Carver, of course.

"But you will need them. What they learn from the work they do, and what they teach others by doing it, will be essential to you in the future."

16th of Corvil, 410 A.A.
Terafin Manse, Averalaan

When Gabriel ATerafin returned to the office for the fourth time that afternoon, he met Barston's somewhat accusatory glare with a cringe. The accusation, of course, would never be couched in anything as uncouth as words; the entirety of the office staff, such as it was, understood well why Gabriel was not to be found within his inner chambers. The right-kin paused at the desk; it was less than an hour until early dinner in the Terafin hall, and there was no question whatsoever that either Gabriel or Barston would be in attendance.

Barston drew away from the desk as Gabriel approached it, forcing Gabriel to shift direction so as not to be offering a gesture of solidarity to what was, at that point, an empty chair. Barston glanced once over his shoulder, and Gabriel saw clearly the object of his concern: it was his new assistant, Teller. The boy with no known family name or connections.

Gabriel kept the cringe that was building firmly to himself. "Barston," he said, clearing his throat. Barston gestured briefly—and frantically, for Barston, although it wouldn't past muster as frantic anywhere else in the manse—and Gabriel lowered his voice. "This is perhaps not the ideal time to train an assistant," he began. "And if his work in this case is poor, it is not indicative—" Barston's glacial expression froze the flow of Gabriel's words.

"He has been here for a full week," Barston said, in clipped, clear common. "I assure you, if I felt the quality of his judgment was not sound, I would have given him a temporary leave during this crisis."

Gabriel relaxed. "What, then, is the problem?"

"We have been forced to work long hours in the past two days," Barston replied. After a pause for the expected comprehension, and a more significant pause for irritation when it didn't immediately follow, he said, "Letters and messages are arriving with alarming frequency at all hours of the day and well into the night."

"And?"

Barston frowned. "The boy works. He doesn't complain. He doesn't ask for a break of any sort."

"This is cause for concern? I believe the last three attempts at an assistant were—"

"Irrelevant to this discussion."

Clearly, Barston *had* been working too hard. "I find his odd insights valuable," he finally said. "And I am therefore reluctant to deprive myself of his assistance at this time. But he is not Terafin; he does not have access to the Terafin dining halls."

"He has the West Wing, and they are reputed to have—"

"Itinerant cooks."

"—Very fine cooks, if not dedicated night and day to that small kitchen. I cannot very well designate the boy Terafin for the simple expedient of feeding him."

Barston looking mildly shocked at even the suggestion. "I was suggesting nothing of the sort," he said, in case the shock was not clear enough. "But I feel, in this case, some of the rules pertaining to food in the office might be . . . relaxed. For the duration of the crisis."

"That's all?"

Barston nodded grimly.

"Very well. If you require it, you have my permission. Shall I write it all out?"

"No."

"Good. If you don't mind, I'm about to slink into my office in the vague hope that I will actually be able to attend to any of the correspondence that is only a normal emergency."

"You mistake me, right-kin," Barston replied. "*I* will write the permission; you merely have to sign it."

Gabriel sighed. "Then put it on top of whatever horror you're about to dump on my desk, or I'll never find it again."

Teller, absent until the tail end of this conversation, now appeared looking hesitant but not fearful. "Right-kin?" he asked, tentatively.

Gabriel smiled; it was weary but genuine. "Yes?"

"There's a message here for you."

"There are probably two hundred."

"This was delivered in person."

Gabriel turned toward the door and saw the familiar House livery waiting just to one side of it.

"It's bad, isn't it?" Teller said softly.

"Worse, I think, than you know." Gabriel started toward the messenger and then stopped and turned back. "Or perhaps not. What has your den leader had to say about her investigations?"

"Nothing," Teller replied. "She's not supposed to speak about them without The Terafin's permission."

It was not, Gabriel thought, the entire truth, but he was satisfied with the response. "Barston is concerned about your lack of food in the office," he said quietly, eyeing the waiting guard. "And while I considered the possibility of relaxing office rules for the duration of this crisis, I believe I will ask, instead, that a standing invitation to meals in the Hall be issued; you will lunch with him."

He could tell, to his quiet amusement, that perhaps Teller did not consider it the mercy that Barston would, but then again, the boy was bright.

"Before I am once again diverted from the office for the next hour—or several—is there any message of note or import that I should deal with?"

Teller hesitated. Gabriel marked the hesitation instantly for what it was, and he lifted a hand, signaling to the guard that he was both aware of his presence and of what the presence demanded and that it would have to wait a moment.

"I would have said it was personal," he began quietly. Gabriel lifted a hand.

"You have managed, against all odds, to survive a week of Barston's scrutiny, and I do not have the time for either meekness or nerves."

Teller's hesitation did not evaporate, but Gabriel's words had the desired effect: The boy produced a single letter. "It's from Devon ATerafin," he said quietly.

Gabriel did not blink or cringe—not outwardly. But he took the letter from Teller's hand and tucked it into his sash. "Thank you, Teller. And yes, as you guess, it is not Devon's way to send personal notes; he is a busy man. I will carry this with me; I am called by The Terafin, and she is even busier than I. With luck, you will be gone before I return."

Teller nodded, but Barston snorted quietly.

Finch, on the other hand, found the Terafin offices in the Merchant Authority very quiet. The quiet itself was not a problem, although Lucille often felt the need to fill it with words. Word of the fate of Lord Cordufar's estate had traveled throughout the Authority, and it had left a lot of hushed huddles of gossip in its wake.

Very little in the way of business-as-usual was being conducted. Not none, of course; Lucille said that the wheels of commerce would continue to spin if the Kings themselves suddenly died. Mail arrived, but messengers were sparse; the entire merchant population of the city seemed to be riveted by the information that gossip so distorted.

"How bad is this going to be?" Finch asked, as Lucille grimaced at the mail.

"For us?"

Finch nodded.

In response, Lucille handed Finch a stack of papers. "While I realize you've started during the quiet season—while the port is mainly closed—we still have work that needs doing. Manifests," she explained. "It's easy to assume that anything that shakes the Authority causes the world to grind to a halt—but most of the real work is done by men and women who don't live in the building and spend as little time in it as possible. They still have goods and cargo; the caravans, except the Northern ones, are still running. So we have work to do." Lucille smiled brightly. It looked hideous because it was so wrong for her face. One glance at Finch's expression made clear just how successful it had been, and Lucille snorted and discarded it. "It's not as bad as it could be—not for Terafin. One or two of our members were pursuing Cordufar's concerns with some interest, but the Darias connection made any negotiations both glacial and unpromising.

"It's why," she added, "the offer to Guillarne would have had to be so attractive. And," she added, with just a hint of regret, "it was. I wonder who Lord Cordufar angered so greatly; the House is gutted. We'll see Royal Intervention there, for sure."

"Royal Intervention?"

"You *cannot* use that much obvious magic—and it was clearly destruction caused by magic—in Averalaan unless you happen to be the Kings. And they can't. Mages who could are probably in short supply, at least according to Jarven. The mages didn't go to Cordufar with the Kings; the Kings would have made a public declaration very shortly after the event had the attack been done at their command.

"But as it clearly wasn't, they have no choice. There'll be writs. There'll be mage hunts. There are, if rumor is to be believed, members of the Order of Knowledge crawling all over the grounds."

Finch hesitated, and Lucille marked it. "More stuff you can't talk about?"

Finch nodded, but the hesitation remained. At last she said, "I think the Kings already know who was responsible."

"Who?"

"Lord Cordufar."

Silence. It wouldn't last. "Finch," Lucille said quietly, "I really do think this is firmly in the category of stuff you can't talk about."

Finch gazed out past the desk, at the set of closed doors that divided Lucille's territory from the rest of the Merchant Authority. "I know," she said miserably. "But I think everyone will know it soon." She felt an arm around her shoulders and startled slightly, but she didn't pull away. "Jay's there."

"Where, Finch?"

"At the Cordufar manse. With the mages. I've only ever seen her this afraid a handful of times."

"And those times?"

"We lost people."

Lucille didn't ask. Instead, she muttered something about sending children into the midst of dangerous lunatics—by which, Finch inferred she meant the mage-born. But after a few minutes, she shoved manifests under Finch's nose and told her to get to work; she went off to talk to Jarven.

Five minutes later, Lucille exited the office. "Jarven," she said, her voice heavy with irritation, "would like tea." As Finch rose, she added, "And it would not break my heart or stain your record if you told him what he could do with that tea."

Jarven was seated behind his desk; the windows, their curtains drawn, shed enough light that it was hard to see more than his outline. But his nod was clear. Finch, juggling the tray, which was heavy enough that it seemed unfair that the cups always seemed to be perched so precariously no matter where she set them, stepped into the office. Lucille had been kind enough to open and hold the door for her, and Finch had no doubt whatsoever that she was even now making a face at Jarven over her head.

She did not, however, look back to confirm her suspicion; instead she made straight for the nearly spotless surface of the desk and set the tray down. Lucille's desk never looked anywhere close to as spotless, and it wasn't because a tidy tray held most of Jarven's important mail—which remained as Finch had placed it earlier in the day.

She poured a cup of tea for Jarven and carried it behind the desk, placing it carefully in front of him. He glanced down at it but did not move his hands, and she shrank inwardly. She hoped that the cringe didn't actually reach her expression; weeks working with Lucille had made clear how important it was to mask or hide it.

"Yes," he told her, as she made her way back to the chair she habitually took when he asked for her, "this is not, as you suspect, about the tea. Was Lucille annoyed?"

"You saw her," Finch replied carefully. When this failed to engender a response, she added, "Not more than she usually is."

He nodded. As Finch's eyes acclimatized themselves to the brighter environs of his office, she caught the telltale lift of lips that meant a wry smile. "I am duly impressed," he told her softly, "with your ability to worm your way into Lucille's heart. There are rumors circulating within the manse that she doesn't actually have one."

Finch had learned to hide timidity or fear; shock, however, was still unschooled. Her jaw did not remain hanging open for long.

"Oh, tush," Jarven said, lifting the cup she'd set before him. "You've no doubt heard some of the opinions firsthand."

"They all say Lucille is very . . . direct."

"They should also say that Finch is very tactful."

She reddened.

"But Lucille is also very protective. She disapproves of today's tea."

"I know," was the quiet response.

"She doesn't feel I have any business involving you in Council matters. Not at 'your age.'" He set the cup down again. Finch noted he hadn't bothered to drink anything. "She has the misfortune, on occasion, of seeing with her heart. You are, of course, young. Young to be here, in this office. Young to be involved in matters of the House. But you are involved," he added softly.

"Not in any way that matters," she replied, without thinking.

He raised a pale brow and then rose. Which was bad. But he wandered as far as his fine shelves and began to peruse the spines of the books that were just above him. His hands were behind his back as he did.

"You understand, by this time, that my job requires a certain amount of information," he said, his back toward her, his robes rippling as he walked, slowly, across the floor for the length of the shelf. "The gathering of information is a bit of a hobby of mine; I find it endlessly amusing. Like all hobbies, it requires some care and some ability to cultivate people. Many of those people—like you, yourself—will be young and overlooked. Most will not remain that way."

She said nothing; there wasn't much to say.

"You might also understand that within House Terafin there are always competitions. Among the merchants, among the Council members. We are united only when seen from the outside. And let me warn you, young Finch, that that semblance of unity to outsiders is important.

"But within the House? We quarrel. We compete. We aid others as it suits our purposes or our whims. I am considered old by the House Council. Which is fair. I am. I am generally considered harmless, or toothless."

He grinned. "Which is less fair, but it suits me. Among the old or the harmless, things slip that might not otherwise slip.

"What has your Jewel seen that has so disturbed her?" He turned, then.

"I can't talk about it," she replied.

"No?"

She shook her head.

To her surprise, he smiled. "Information," he told her, as he made his way back to his chair, no book in hand, "is like any other coin. I offer you this: I will explain—in terms that perhaps would elude Lucille—who the merchants of significance in House Terafin currently are. I will also offer you some guidance about future members of note, about people I feel are prominent, or will become so, on the House Council. In return for this, you will offer me some temporary refuge from my deplorable ignorance."

"How long do I have to think about this?"

He raised one brow, and then, to her surprise, he laughed. "Lucille," he said, when he finished, "would be proud of you, child. Take a day. Take—at most—two. Return to me, and give me your answer then."

She nodded. Hesitated. "Can I ask a question?"

"Any question you like."

"What can you tell me about Rymark ATerafin?"

"That," he replied, after a signifcant pause, "is beyond the purview of what I have offered."

She nodded again.

"Why do you ask?"

"No one will talk much about him."

"You've asked others?"

"The servants. The Chosen."

"They are wise. Do not—"

"But it's questions like that that you'll need to answer for me."

He nodded slowly. Thoughtfully. "Take your day," he said again. And then he smiled.

Chapter Fourteen

FINCH WAS CURLED UP QUIETLY in a chair in the corner of the large sitting room when Ellerson walked in. He glanced about the room, and she expected him to leave, but his white brows rose slightly at the sight of her, and he made his way toward her chair. He was carrying, of all things, a tray—but instead of food or dishes, it contained rags and something that smelled like oil. He set them down on a side table before he approached her. "You haven't eaten," he said.

He made the mild words sound like a serious accusation. It was a trick that she thought it would be useful to learn. But she didn't have it in her today. "No. I'm waiting for Jay. And Teller."

"Jewel has not yet returned?"

Finch shook her head. "Teller?"

"No. But he has been working late in the office of the right-kin these past few days; I do not expect to see him before the end of the late dinner hour."

She grimaced and drew her legs up toward her chest, resting her chin on the tops of her knees. Ellerson frowned, but she let him. She was too tired to attempt to find manners; they were work. She waited for him to leave. He didn't.

When she realized he had no intention of leaving, she relented, unfolding her legs and shifting her position so that she looked like she was actually sitting. This did not, however, have the desired effect; he didn't retrieve his tray, and he didn't continue on his way to wherever he'd been going.

"Finch," he said quietly, surprising her. He took the chair closest to the one she occupied.

"Do I look so bad?" she asked, with a rueful smile.

"You appear to be worried. Is your work at the Merchant Authority not going well?"

"No, it's—it's going well. At least I think it is."

"Lucille ATerafin has, by all accounts, a formidable disposition, and she is prone to be somewhat demanding and judgmental."

"Lucille is fine," Finch replied, with just a little heat. Ellerson raised a brow. "No, she is. She does tend to shout a lot—but never at me. Mostly at the members of the House who visit and forget their manners. Which seems to be about half of them on any given day. It's not Lucille." She hesitated and then said, "How did you know it was work?"

He smiled. "I made an educated guess. If it is not Lucille, is it Jarven?"

"You—you know Jarven?"

"I know *of* Jarven ATerafin. He is nominally in charge of the Terafin operations within the Authority, and he is also nominally in charge of the merchanting concerns that are not entirely internal. He is not a young man, but in his youth, he was highly . . . respected."

"How do you know all this?"

"I consider it part of my duties to be informed about the various members of a House. My information is not particularly deep," he added quietly, "but depth is not required in this instance."

"Would it be in another?"

"Do you think that Morretz has a superficial understanding of the House Council and the members that are powerful within the House?"

It hadn't occurred to Finch to wonder at all. She did so now. "I guess he can't. He knows what The Terafin knows; I think he's always with her."

"He is, as his duty dictates, almost always by her side. And yes, he will observe what she observes. But he will also utilize other sources of information, and he will advise her when appropriate and when advice is requested."

"But—but she's The Terafin."

"Yes."

"And he's a—"

"Domicis. It is not, as is often suspected, a fancier term for servant, Finch. To serve a woman of power requires more from a domicis than mere housekeeping. It requires knowledge, cunning, a deep understanding of the political arena; it also requires other skills that might aid the domicis in preserving his master's life. It is not merely a job that requires passive obedience; it is a calling, and it carries with it a large responsibility."

She was silent for some time, digesting this. "So . . . even if he isn't ATerafin, he has to know these things?"

Ellerson nodded.

"And if I'm not, should I know them as well?"

At this, he smiled. His smile confirmed what she half suspected: He knew. "I think," he told her gently, "that you already know the answer to the question. Information," he added, "is like coin. It can be spent, and it can be hoarded. It is useful in an emergency. The difficulty with information is that you cannot always tell *which* knowledge will be useful beforehand, and there is much that can be learned that will seem, for years, to be a waste of your time."

But she held on to the certainty that he knew, and she shifted position again, leaning forward, her palms beneath her thighs. "You . . . expected that Jarven would say something to me, didn't you?"

"I suspected he *might*. He is not a man who likes to be on the outside, although he is not one who has schemed heavily to remain on the inside. What did he ask?"

"He wants to know what Jay's up to."

"And in return?"

"He'll tell me what other people are up to, more or less."

Ellerson nodded gravely.

"But I can't just tell him what Jay's doing. We're not allowed—"

Ellerson lifted a hand. It was a gentle gesture. "No," he said quietly. "And that, I must leave to your discretion. But, Finch, I ask you to think about one thing."

"What?"

"The Terafin arranged for you to work with Lucille ATerafin in the Merchant Authority. The Terafin is not a fool, and she is not a poor judge of character; she would know, before she made the request, that you would come into contact with Jarven—a man who is genial and unintimidating when he chooses to be."

"You think she *wants* us to—"

"I think she wishes you to learn how the House operates. Teller is now working in the office of the right-kin. Gabriel is not Jarven; he knows much more about external affairs than Jarven will know, and he knows, as well, that any question he has—any question at all—The Terafin will answer. He will not barter with Teller as if he were a merchant; that is not his job, and it is not his character.

"But Teller has already learned quite a bit from the daily correspondence filtered through Gabriel's office, if I am not mistaken. He knows—or would know, if he bothered to think about it—who, externally, is considered a friend and who is considered a threat. He knows which of the Council members seek advice from Gabriel and which appear in his office during times of crisis, secure enough in their power that they can dispense with 'manners' as Lucille calls them. Yes, he knows more, and separating the useful information from the useless takes work and familiarity.

"I feel that neither your placement nor Teller's was accidental. Make of that what you will."

Jay came home before the end of the late dinner hour, but she wouldn't eat. Ellerson asked her if she would take dinner, and she stared at him as if he were momentarily speaking a language other than Weston, and she couldn't understand a word of it. Finch rose instantly; Teller had still not returned.

But Angel intercepted Ellerson before Finch could reach Jay. Angel was like that; she had hardly been aware he was in the room, but he made his presence felt now. Jay glanced at him, the blank expression on her face clearing as if with great effort. "Kitchen," she told him, curtly.

He looked at Finch, who nodded and slipped out of the room to round up everyone else. When she had sent them all on their way, she hesitated for a moment at the closed double doors of the wing, and then, making a decision, she opened them and marched off into the halls.

Barston looked up. Because he did, Teller did the same; they had been reviewing some of the correspondence that Teller was not entirely certain about. Teller rose before Barston did, because the person who had caught Barston's attention was Finch.

"May I help you?" Barston said, in his usual less-than-friendly voice.

Finch froze for just a second and then cleared her throat. "No, actually," she replied, without apology. "I'm here to see Teller."

Barton's frown could have frozen water. Teller cringed, but he made his way out from behind the almost monolithic desk, its surface covered with various piles that were striving for tidy and failing badly. The magelights were bright enough that the office was well lit, but the lack of sunlight made the light seem dingy.

"What happened?" he asked, as he approached Finch.

"Jay's back," she replied. She hesitated, glancing over his shoulder at Barston, whose expression he could well imagine. "She's called kitchen."

He turned to get a good look at the familiar expression and then nodded. "Give me a minute," he told her. "But wait outside; we can run back together."

They were the last two to reach the kitchen, but they'd had a longer distance to travel. Jay was sitting quietly on the edge of a stool; she hadn't bothered to pull up one of the chairs with actual arms. Finch glanced at the table; there was a lamp—two—that flickered orange; there were no magelights. More significantly, no slates. Teller noticed the lack and turned back toward the swinging doors they'd entered, but Jay barked his name and he stopped.

"No slates," she told him. "I wasn't dreaming."

He froze for just a second before he came back to the table—but Finch almost missed it. They all had. Jay's voice was just . . . *wrong*. They glanced at each other, but no one spoke. Kitchen councils were familiar and oddly comforting most of the time. This one wasn't going to be. They all knew it.

Even Ellerson, who now stood to one side of the doors by the wall, a third lamp hanging loosely from one hand.

Chairs scraping floor were the only noises in the room for a good five minutes. But even that died; they listened to the sound of flames enclosed by glass and watched the odd shapes of shadows lamplight threw.

"Today," Jay said, her voice rough.

Teller watched her face closely; Finch knew, because she watched Teller's. In council, such as this was, he was the den's weathervane. In crisis—which for months had meant Carmenta and his den—Angel was better, but there were no drawn knives here, no physical danger. And Teller, Finch thought, was now afraid.

"I was at the Cordufar manse. With the magi. And Devon." She glanced at Ellerson, and in the poor light, the shadows beneath her eyes were almost black. Those eyes were wide; she was staring straight ahead. But she lifted her hands, briefly, as if to cover her ears, and as she did, her eyes closed tightly.

"Breathe," Teller whispered. He reached out, covered the back of one of her hands with the palms of his, pulling it gently toward the tabletop. She didn't even shrug him off. But he didn't ask her anything. He waited. Because he did, they all did, although Arann was now tense and pale.

"It—we were digging. They were digging," she added. "The magi can lift the damn dirt and most of the stones without touching anything." She tried to smile. It was sickly. "They'd been at it for most of the day." Her voice dropped slowly, syllable by syllable, until it was barely audible.

"That's when it started." She closed her eyes again. Opened them. Finch thought she might leave her chair and begin to pace—but she lowered her hands and gripped the rounded edges tightly instead. "We can hear—we could hear—voices. We thought—we thought they were there. Trapped in the manse. So they started using real magic." She paused, looking around the table.

This time, Teller did speak. "Did they find them?"

She looked away, but she didn't snap at him, didn't raise either voice or hand as she often did when she was afraid or worried. "They're not in the manse. They're not in the basement."

"Jay—"

"We think—we're not sure—but we think they're in the undercity."

Silence.

"How loud were the voices?"

"Not loud. Not loud at all. But—too damn loud to be heard from the undercity."

It was Angel who looked up as she said that. "Magic?" he asked quietly.

"They think so. They weren't talking to me," she added. "They were talking to each other. I might have missed something. I—" she glanced at Ellerson again. Swallowed. "I have to go back tomorrow. I think they're bringing in more of the Order and some people from the Kings' Court."

"Jay," Teller said.

She looked at him.

"These people—"

"Are dying," she replied. She stared at her hands. "Devon said they're not real voices. He thinks it's some sort of attack."

No one asked Jay whether or not she believed him. They already knew the answer.

*   *   *

Jay slept badly.

Teller wouldn't have known, but anxiety over his desertion of the desk from which Barston ruled, combined with the kitchen meeting, had destroyed even the faint hope of sleep. It did not, unfortunately, alleviate exhaustion. He had eaten—they had all eaten—a sparse meal that Ellerson himself prepared in the kitchen after Jay had left, and the food now sat like cold rocks in the pit of his stomach. He wore the sleeping gown he'd been given and, over it, a heavier wrap; he lay with his head dead center in the depths of a huge pillow, staring at the ceiling in the darkness.

Because he was awake, he heard Jay's scream, and he was out of bed almost before he was aware that he was moving. He managed to catch himself before he threw the door open, and it opened silently into the muted lights of the hall. A moment later, another door opened; he saw Finch peering around the crack of darkness that led from her room.

They didn't speak; instead, they waited.

When they heard Jay again, they nodded and began to move; only when they reached her closed door did they hesitate.

"Ellerson's there," Finch said quietly.

Teller nodded.

Neither of them retreated. Jay was still screaming, and they couldn't force themselves to go back to their rooms. Teller grimaced and then opened the door. Its hinges, like the hinges of all the doors in this huge suite of overfurnished rooms, were well oiled; the movement was almost silent.

But the doors were thick; the voice that reached out for them from the lamplit room was much, much louder than the voice that had drawn them from their separate darknesses.

Ellerson was beside the bed, lamp in hand; he turned as they entered. If they expected anger or disapproval—and they did—he offered neither. Instead, his eyes lined with dark circles, he nodded curtly and stepped aside, the lamplight swaying against the wall and the curtains as if it were drunk.

Jay was sitting up, and her eyes were wide and vacant; they were also bloodshot. Her knees were bunched together against her chest, and her hands were full of bedclothing; they were also shaking.

Dream? Finch signed.

Teller signed back, *Not sure.* But he approached the bed as Finch slipped away. "Jay."

She stared ahead, seeing darkness and whatever it contained. She spoke, but the words were so garbled that they made no sense. Teller could speak both street Torra and Weston, and the words weren't in either language. It troubled him more than he wanted to admit because he knew Jay didn't speak any other languages, either. Not when she was awake.

"Jay," he said again, keeping his voice even. She answered him the fourth time he tried, and after each attempt, he spent minutes in patient silence. It was hard.

Harder, in some ways, than the letters that were crowding Barston's desk—and Gabriel's as well. There he had Barston to guide—and correct—him. Any mistake he made was bound to be caught. Here? Just Jay, her words bleeding, at last, into silence.

"Teller."

He nodded. Was surprised when she reached out, with no warning, and threw her arms around his neck. For a moment he went rigid and stiff, the way she would have. Then he relaxed. Forced himself to relax.

"I don't want to go back," she told him. He could barely hear her words. But he understood what she meant.

You couldn't offer Jay comfort if the only way to do it was to lie. And he knew—as well as she did—that she couldn't avoid the Cordufar manse. If The Terafin ordered her there, it was where she would go. Devon would come for her at dawn. She would follow.

Although he would have bet any money he earned that it would have been impossible, Teller missed the mage—and the morning screaming matches between him and Jay—because with Devon, Jay was almost unnaturally silent.

She knew, and she didn't repeat her words. Neither did he. Nor would he. He glanced at Ellerson, but there was no warning in the look he gave the domicis; they all knew that nothing that could hurt Jay would leave his lips.

"Kitchen?" he asked after she had relaxed her death grip slightly.

She looked at him and then away. "No," she whispered, hopelessly. "It was just a nightmare."

He looked at her face, made golden by orange light and hollow by night. Had it been day, he would have argued; he almost argued now. But he didn't because in the end, it was her call.

Finch came back, carrying bedding and pillows. She gestured at the floor, and Teller nodded. "We'll stay," he told Ellerson.

"Master Barston is unlikely to appreciate the work you do when exhausted."

"No. But he often doesn't appreciate the work I do when I'm not; he probably won't be able to tell the difference."

Finch added, "And the Merchant Authority is quiet as a grave at this time of year." She didn't add that it was a damn noisy grave, because it was meant to be reassuring. Ellerson's raised brow was most of his reply; he was also tired. He waited for just a moment and then nodded.

Teller caught his eye before he turned to the door. *Wait outside.*

Ellerson lifted a brow, and then smiled. He did not lift his hand to sign acceptance; he was domicis, not den, and it was not his language. But Teller had been certain for weeks now that Ellerson could understand what they said to each other when they were word-shy.

"How many nights running has she woken like this?" Teller asked, keeping his voice low.

Ellerson was silent for long enough that Teller wondered if answering the question was somehow considered a domicis breach of etiquette. Etiquette, which had never been a part of the den's life, had become one of the most valuable lessons House Terafin had to impart—if you intended to remain in the House. In the streets of the twenty-fifth, Teller doubted it would be of much value. But they weren't in the twenty-fifth. They might get there, but not tonight.

"I have lost count," was the formal and stiff reply. Teller understood two things: Ellerson knew exactly how many nights, and he chose not to divulge the number, but he intended to clearly state that they were many.

"Does she always babble the way she did tonight?"

"No, Master Teller. On most nights she just screams."

"This was different, then?"

"It was not a substantially different waking; I believe that she is almost at the end of her physical endurance. She sleeps very little, and even at her age, some sleep is required. But if you refer to her odd speech, no."

Teller said nothing for at least as long as Ellerson had been silent. But in the end he chose to speak. "Jay's been off since the attack on the manse. I thought Torvan's release would change things. It did, but not enough. Whatever's happening in the undercity— Don't let her think it's her fault. She will," he added. "She's like that. It's hard to make Jay share anything bad."

When Ellerson lifted a brow, he reddened slightly. "Yes, she throws things and shouts a lot. But . . . right now she's thinking that if she'd moved *faster*, they'd've found the undercity in time."

"In time," Ellerson asked, "for what?"

"That's the question. We're going to get an answer. I think—I think she already has one."

"A fair request, Master Teller. I have one of my own in return."

Teller nodded.

"Make her speak. In this, whether you know it or not, she relies upon the den. She tends to isolate herself; do not allow her to do that."

Teller lifted both hands to sign his strong and immediate acceptance of terms, and then he blushed and lowered them. "Done," he said.

In the morning, Jay was gone before anyone woke. Teller and Finch, on the early morning shift, gazed, bleary-eyed, at each other across the narrow breakfast table. In this case 'narrow' meant larger than the only table their entire apartment had once boasted. Arann had already eaten and gone. He had said—as they—very, very little.

Finch told Teller about Jarven's offer as they pushed food around their plates, glancing furtively to see if Ellerson was watching them with That Look. "I wanted to ask Jay," she told him, when she had finished.

He nodded; he understood why she hadn't.

"What do you think I should do? We're not technically supposed to know anything. If it leaks at all, they'll assume it's Jay's fault."

"They'll assume that anyway."

She thought about that for a moment, then grimaced. "Point."

He folded bread into smaller and smaller balls. This did earn a loud clearing-of-throat from their domicis, and he stopped. Mostly. "What do you think?" he asked, clearly stalling.

Finch said, "Take it."

Teller lifted a hand, palm down.

Finch nodded.

18th of Corvil, 410 A.A.
Terafin Manse, Averalaan Aramarelas

Devon ATerafin had arrived at the manse with strong misgivings, and had requested an unusually early briefing with The Terafin. It was not often that such requests were granted before breakfast, but given the nature of current events unfolding within Averalaan, etiquette could be disregarded for the moment.

She met him, not in the lower offices in which she conducted much of her obvious, daily business, but in the library, which was the quiet pride of her personal rooms. In these chambers, she had one of the Chosen and Morretz; no other guards intruded.

As if, Devon thought, she knew what he had come to say and wished to limit its circulation. He took a chair at the long, empty table and watched her reflection across the gleaming wood grain as she did likewise.

"Your work in Cordufar," she said quietly, "is cause for some concern?"

"We have encountered no further magical difficulties." Frowning, he added, "Or rather, have encountered none that have caused losses."

"Jewel's intervention?"

He nodded. "The magi, fractious as they are, are more intimidated by Meralonne APhaniel than by the possible loss of dignity in granting the requests of an undereducated girl. Her . . . instincts . . . are solid."

"We have already discussed the voices that were heard yesterday."

She nodded. She was distant; she intended to give him no aid.

And where no aid was forthcoming, finesse and subtlety were not possible. "I have strong misgivings," he told her, coming to the point, "about Jewel Markess' continued presence at the site."

"She is unstable?"

"No."

"She is causing the House some political difficulty as its representative?"

"She is not there—as you are well aware—in an official capacity as a representative of House Terafin; that has been my privilege and I assure you that I am not a sixteen-year-old street urchin in that regard."

The Terafin's smile was shallow but genuine. "No, indeed." The smile slipped away. "She was notably silent at yesterday's meeting; it was, however, brief. How will the investigation cause difficulty for her?"

"At the end of yesterday, the constant stream of voices emanating from beneath the remains of the Cordufar manse had all but stifled hers. I understand that she has not lived a remarkably cozened or sheltered life, but her particular inclinations make the existence of those voices difficult. Were she a different person, she would be more easily protected from the effects, but . . . she understands that what she hears is both magical in nature and entirely real at the same time.

"She knows that people are dying, and they are dying in terror just at the edge of our reach. We cannot stifle the sound of those voices without also causing temporary deafness in those who might otherwise hear; the magi are working on it, but they are not always known for their subtle solutions to delicate problems."

"How widely has information about this difficulty spread?"

"Not widely. Not yet."

The Terafin nodded. "Devon," she said quietly, "are you asking me not to send Jewel Markess with you?"

He could not—not quite—bring himself to say that. Instead, he said, "I think it unwise."

The Terafin nodded. "I understand," she replied.

"And will you send her?"

"I will. I have misgivings, but they cannot be allowed to hold sway."

"She will—"

"Be marked by this? So, in the end, will we all. She is not a child; she cannot, for the sake of pity or squeamishness, be spared. She has a role to play; how is she to play it if we choose to hide her from events?"

Devon nodded stiffly and rose. He made it almost to the doors before he turned. "What future do you see for her, Terafin, that you are willing to drive her so harshly?"

"I see no future for her at all if she cannot, in the end, be so driven."

18th of Corvil, 410 A. A.
Cordufar Manse, Averalaan

As Devon had suspected, the grounds of the Cordufar manse had not miraculously grown silent over the passage of one evening. As he had half feared, the noise had grown substantially in volume, enough so that voices—screams dying into the sounds that men make when they've gone beyond the edge of sanity—could be heard in the streets that surrounded the gated grounds.

Those streets were now empty; not even the magisterial guards that had been summoned by the residents because of the sounds of tortured screaming stayed in them for long. They were good enough that they did attempt to gain entry to the grounds, but not so professional that relief at encountering the Kings' Swords and the magi could not be seen clearly in their expressions.

Jewel's shoulders had begun a subtle inward gathering as they approached the gatehouse, and the tension did not subside. But she greeted both Meralonne and Sigurne with quiet diffidence before inquiring of them where they wished her to be deployed.

Devon had attempted to confine Jewel to the highest reaches of the excavation. Over the passage of a handful of days, the excavation had yielded many things beneath the manse's grounds, among them whole rooms that the magi identified as laboratories. The scorch-marked stone of both floor and walls seemed to uphold this designation; for this reason, the magi worked through these rooms quickly. Because there were more than two mages in a space of less than a hundred yards, they did not work quietly, and arguments broke out, like the hissing spats between territorial cats, at regular intervals. Given the reaction of the guildmaster, these were neither unexpected nor a matter for concern; they were however, judging by her pinched expression, very irritating.

Jewel did not seem to notice. She answered few questions, and after the first hour and a half of exploration, Devon realized that whatever safety her presence offered the men and woman who were now involved in the bulk of this work had become almost entirely theoretical. Whatever inner voice she heard was subtle and quiet, and it was entirely swamped by the voices that now rose without pause from the ground beneath their feet.

Those voices affected everyone who worked in the bowels of the earth and stone beneath the once fine manse; those who labored in the labs of the mage they had now identified as Davash AMarkham, and those who labored, with a quieter and fiercer desperation, at the shield beyond which no digging could take place.

No digging, Devon thought with a grimace, and no fire, no lightning, no magical force known to the First Circle. Nothing at all could breach it. Nothing, he thought grimly, but sound.

By midday, they found the remains of what appeared to be Davash AMarkham. Those remains were nestled between links of heavy gold, in what appeared to be a necklace. How they had found them, Devon didn't know and didn't ask; nor did he ask if they were certain. He understood the abilities of the magi, and he understood, as well, that questioning the conclusions they had drawn was in fact their own job. He merely had to listen to them bicker to derive all the answers he required. The Astari expected some report of their activities.

As did The Terafin.

But it was neither the Astari nor The Terafin he thought of now; it was Jewel. He spoke, briefly, with Sigurne, and less briefly with Meralonne, before he led Jewel away from the manse itself.

"Wait here," he told her quietly. "I have some work that must be attended to, but I do not think it will require much time."

"It will," she told him, looking at the grass beneath her boots as if she could see through it.

He nodded. "It often does," he told her quietly. He glanced at the manse. The voices were loud, even here. And the victims of the torture that took place, heard but entirely unseen, were many and varied.

Two hours passed before he could tear himself away from the councils of the magi, and those hours were difficult, even for Devon, a man who had been trained to ignore both the pain he caused and the pain he might one day endure. Training, he thought, was theoretical. It was never the actual event.

The magi had drifted away from the shield in ones and twos; Sigurne sent them away. She herself did not leave. Nor, Devon noted, did Meralonne APhaniel. That member of the Order would have made Duvari proud had he been one of Duvari's students, for he was the only man present who seemed to be untouched by the screams of pain and primal terror that broke conversation, over and over, like acid waves against a bitter shore.

Here they had cleared enough of the fallen ruins of the mansion away that the sun's bleak rays could be seen; dust motes traveled through the beams that broke shadow in wide spokes. But the sun was cold at this time of the year, and the light brought little comfort.

"I must see to my—to Jewel," Devon finally said. He was not certain if she were an excuse to leave the area where the voices were clearest; if she was, it was a failure. Above ground, hundreds of yards from the shield itself, the voices were now just as loud, and sharp enough to cut.

He knew it before he caught sight of Jewel, and he walked quickly toward her—coming, as he did, toward the gate, and the periphery of the sealed grounds.

She didn't see him. She couldn't hear him. He could barely hear the fall of his own steps, no matter how heavy his tread. But in her case? Her hands were cupped over her ears; she was both bent and rigid, her pale face surrounded by flyaway strands of curled hair. She did not—as she so often did—attempt to push that hair out of her eyes; her eyes were closed, and closed tightly.

Before he reached her, she stiffened, straightened, her eyes opening and widening, her hands falling away from the sides of her face as if thrown. She spun on her heel, looking frantically for something, for anything—he recognized the look—and she fell upon a shovel. It was not an excavator's tool but a gardener's. Here, all things had been found and used.

She fell to the ground and began to dig.

And while she did, he heard, clearly, the whimpering of a child's voice. Above it, the sound of a woman's voice—the mother's voice—as she attempted to keep hysteria and fear from her words. For his sake. For all the good it would do.

Dirt flew as Jewel dug; it flew wildly, in a spray of green and brown. He could almost see the whites of her eyes, could see the rise and fall of her chest as she took in air and spit it out again. She did not scream. She did not cry. She dug.

"Put it down, Jewel."

And dug. He came to her side, then, but she didn't acknowledge him. Wasn't aware of his presence at all. Her hands were shaking. The small furrow just before her bent knees was growing.

"Put it down, Jewel!"

She looked up, then. Her hands, still shaking, had stilled—and she looked at them in confusion.

"Put it down," he said. He could not speak softly and be heard, but he gentled his voice as much as he could.

"They have to be stopped," she said, voice low and gravelly, as if she had swallowed the earth, and it had become the only part of her that could speak. "They have to *pay*."

He bent over her. Her hands still clung to the spade, and he had to work to remove it. "They will," he said, lips as close to her ears as he could bring them. "I swear it by the turning and by every life I will ever have." He pulled the shovel from her hands and tossed it to one side, and then, without a further thought for the magi, the Astari, or The Terafin, he gathered her in his arms and lifted her, the way he might have lifted a much smaller child. Her legs swung over the curve of his left arm, and he felt her weight; she was so rigid she might have been stone.

"Come, this is not the place for you."

He felt her arms tighten around his neck and felt the cool abrasion of her cheek as she pressed her face into his chest, eyes closing before they vanished from his view. He held her, looking for exits, listening for a silence that would not, and did not, come.

What came instead was a voice that could cut through the screaming and the terror without ever becoming a part of it: a strong, clear voice. A woman's voice. Anyone who had heard that voice could not forget it; it was the voice of the bardmaster, the woman who commanded the fractious, rebellious and much-loved bards of Senniel College.

Sioban Glassen.

Jewel lifted her head, and Devon let her; he walked toward the manse rather than away from it, for he followed the sound of the bardic voice as if it alone could provide safety and comfort for the girl in his arms. The child, he thought, although he did not say it.

She asked him who they were, as they at last came into view, for she now recognized most of the First Circle mages by name—and temper—and she did not recognize these strangers. Devon did.

The bards began to test their instruments—stringed lutes, mandolins, and small harps. They were tuning, but even in the act of tuning, they brought music to the spaces they occupied, and it was a music that nothing could break; that was the talent and the power of Senniel.

After a few moments, Jewel's hold around his neck eased and her legs moved as she attempted to climb out of his grip. He let her go.

She listened. He watched her expression, and he felt a measure of comfort, for she had lost both the look of wild-eyed, unseeing frenzy and the shut-eyed retreat of a panicked child; what remained was pale, and it hinted at quiet determination, although Jewel, in Devon's experience, was seldom quiet in practice.

The dying still screamed, but the tenor of those screams shifted, quieted—and Devon noted that sound, unlike magic, seemed to travel in both directions: in and out.

"That," he told her, "is Sioban Glassen. She is a friend to the Kings and the Queens, and she presides over the famous Senniel College."

334 ♦ Michelle West

"Are they all bards?"

"They are. They are all," he added, "Master Bards. Sioban has, I think, emptied the College. Only two are missing, and I think they are well outside the Empire at the moment, traveling from Court to foreign Court." He named them all, slowly, and she nodded as he did; he wasn't sure how much of it she would retain. It didn't matter.

"What—what will they do?" Jewel asked. The question was quiet, but it *was* a question; she was now firmly behind her eyes. Those eyes glanced away from his in momentary embarrassment, and he didn't tell her that she had no cause for it; she did. But he didn't chide her; he had the same cause, after all, and he was older and more experienced.

"Listen," he said quietly. "They cannot speak normally if they are to be heard; you will doubtless hear what they have to say."

"But the bards—"

"Can speak in whispers that span miles, yes—but in my experience, they can speak to *one* person that way, one at a time. They will not do so now."

"We can sing them to sleep," Sioban said. Her eyes were ringed with gray, and her skin was tinged green, but her expression was grave and focused; Devon had always admired her ability to work with the bard-born. She drew from them the discipline she required, no more—but she was wise enough not to ask for more.

"You're right," Master Bard Alleron snapped, running his hands through his hair. "It's not good."

"Then come up with something—anything—else." Sioban folded her arms across her chest and held tightly. They were, as Devon was, holding on to what they could. He glanced at Jewel; she was listening to the voice, and if her breath was shallow, it was now even.

He waited to see who would speak next and was slightly surprised when he received his answer. The youngest Master Bard that Senniel College had ever produced now lifted his golden head. Ringlets trailed the sides of his face; his expression was both grave, which was expected, and calm, which was not. He reminded Devon, for just that moment, of Member APhaniel; the screams and the pleas of the dying did not seem to touch him at all.

Who is Kallandras? Duvari had asked a decade ago.

The only answer anyone could give was Master Bard of Senniel; the unknown otherwise shrouded his past. Yet it was this bard, of all the bards at her disposal, that Sioban most frequently sent traveling into dangerous territory, and this bard who had always survived.

"Sioban Glassen has the right of it. If we drown out the screams, we aren't ending their pain, not even for a moment."

"And putting them to sleep will end it?" Alleron demanded. "They'll be woken again, sure as sunrise—it'll be that much worse; the hope and then more torture."

"Alleron." Ah, Devon thought. Tallos. Tallos AMorriset. One of the few Housed bards. "We do not think clearly. Kallandras, Sioban—forgive us. This is not the work that we thought to do when we first arrived.

"Let us weave a song of sleep, and let us make it *strong*. We have fifteen voices here; it will not be so easy to wake the sleepers while our voices still have strength. And after? After, we will know that we have done all that we can. The Triumvirate does not ask for more, and if we are to continue, we must not."

"Alleron." Master Bard Gilliane now spoke. She was of an age with Tallos; older than Sioban, although less careworn on most days. This was not one of them. "You tell this to your students time and again: The voice cannot force a man to do much against his nature. The voice cannot order a man to die. These we cannot save; accept it."

Jewel stiffened at Devon's side, and her face went white. He understood then that she had not yet faced the truth that the rest of the magi had already—bitterly—accepted. Those who were trapped beneath the city would die, and they would die horribly; those who labored above, working against the magic of the impenetrable shield, were not laboring under the illusion that they could somehow come to their rescue.

She looked up at him, and he nodded. She said nothing; her hands clenched into fists at her sides, as if by so doing they might be prevented from picking up shovels or picks or rocks.

The fire went out of Alleron, then. "I'd give them death if I could."

"Then you would study the lost arts. The dead arts. And you would make of us something other than what we are—if that possibility exists in the here and now."

"I know it," he said. "But it *must* be better than allowing that." The silence that followed his words was strong enough that he could feel it, although it was broken—always broken—by the sounds of the dying. "Sioban," he said, as he lowered his forehead to rest against the top edge of his harp, "Forgive me. I—I will speak sleep."

"It is already done," she replied, her voice loud enough to carry the compassion she meant to offer. "Come. Let us begin." She turned and lifted her hand, signaling not to the bard-born, but the mage-born.

They drifted out of the bowels of the manse as if relieved that they could leave their duties in her hands, if only for the moment. Devon understood the feeling too well to despise it.

Meralonne APhaniel came last, but before joining the members of the Order, he approached Sioban. "The field is yours," he said, and he tendered her a perfect, patrician bow. She didn't even notice.

She was, as she had often described it, finding her voice; her expression was troubled but focused; there was no doubt at all in it. She would find what she needed.

Devon, like most of the men and women born in Averalaan—or the breadth of its Empire—was talentless. He had none of the power that marked the talent-born and none of the peculiar and often singular drive. But he found it fascinating, and he watched—he had always watched—as they brought their talents to bear.

Sioban began to sing. Her voice carved a space for itself among all the other voices raised not in song but in terror, and her voice held that space, clear and free, demanding that the voices all around hers begin to conform to its subtle command.

She did not demand sleep; she cajoled it, taking the mother's voice, or the wife's, or the sister's: speaking of exhaustion after the long, hard day, of the weariness and pain that sleep alone might relieve.

Talos AMorisset joined her, twining harmony around her melody; he spoke of dreams, suggesting the ways in which they turned from the possible into the impossible, the probable into the improbable, the horrific into the sublimely beautiful; a place without sense from which all things might be drawn, and to which all things were.

Alleron's voice was lower, older, as was the man himself, and where the others spoke softly or gently, he was the stern parent, reminding his children that there were rules about bedtimes in his home, and he expected them to be obeyed. No forbidden lamplight, his voice suggested, would evade his notice; it was time, past time, for sleep.

One by one the other Master Bards joined their voices—and their power—to Sioban's, until only their voices could be heard at all.

Devon thought, listening to them, that wars could be brought to a halt should they ever convene for that purpose; what man, in the end, desires neither sleep nor peace? It might take time for the voice to reach that desire, for many desires crowded the minds of men—but he had no doubt at all that these voices would, in the end, sway giants.

And the victims below were not those.

They slept. Their silence was a blessing, and if it was broken—and it was, repeatedly—nothing could be done to stop the bard-born voices from compelling, again, what they had compelled the first time.

Instead, for the first time since the screams had started, Devon heard voices that were raised not in terror or pain but in frustration and anger, and he knew that those voices were not human.

Jewel's head was listing against his chest; she was young, and she did not have his schooling; the bardic voices touched her almost as strongly as they did the voices of those below. He felt her lean against him, and he slid an arm around her shoulders, to catch her if she fell.

It was time, he thought. Time, now, to leave. The bards would sing for as long as their power held out—perhaps longer, by the grim set of their lips and their jaws. The Isle was distant enough that the voices would not trouble her, and if she woke to the memory of screaming—as they would all now wake—let it be hours from now in the dim comfort of familiar surroundings.

But before he could lift her, the last of the Master Bards suddenly raised his chin, and what Devon heard when he opened his full lips and began to sing drove all thoughts of Jewel's comfort from him.

Kallandras did not sing, as his fellow bards did, of sleep. Sleep was not a worthy subject for the purity and ice of his voice, the sudden cold blue of his eyes. He sang of death.

It was a death song that Devon, who had never heard it and would never hear it again while he lived, knew more intimately than he knew sleep, and he felt—for just a second—that it was his own soul laid bare.

The Senniel bards sang of sleep and the dark of night in which sleep might rightfully take place; Kallandras of Senniel sang of a darkness and desire that had no room for sleep at all. His voice soared; his range was impressive. His power could almost be seen, Devon felt it so strongly.

He spoke of killing. He spoke of *how* to kill. He spoke of what might come from that act, that final intimacy, when all hope and all struggle, all ambition and all complacency, met their end and were revealed as ashes and daydream. His song touched all manner of death, brief and sweet, long and endless.

But it did more than that; for as the rest of the bards compelled the helpless to find peace, this one lone voice spoke not to the victims but to the torturers, and it spoke as strongly as the other fourteen combined.

Devon woke Jewel, then. It was hard, but he understood that Kallandras of Senniel, and Kallandras alone, had the ability to speak not to those who waited to spend their last hours—perhaps their last days—in torment and fear but to those who would end them.

Jewel stirred, her eyes fluttering open and closing again. Devon shook her as gently as he could. The third time, he succeeded. Or perhaps she heard what Devon himself could hear; she pulled back, and her gaze turned to Kallandras and became riveted there.

One child's voice stopped suddenly, almost at the same time as his mother's. They would never be heard again. A roar shook the broken stone—literally shook it, it was so strong—and that voice broke sleep for a moment, while the Master Bards strengthened their efforts without pause.

Abraxus-karathis! Stop!

The roar grew like the wave that becomes so large it can shatter walls. Human cries, confused and frightened, followed in its wake—but they, too, were brief. Wings beat, fire crackled.

And among the final voices some were strong enough to be heard offering thanks, as if it were a prayer. He understood it and understood why; Jewel, however, shook. Maybe one day she would understand that death was sometimes the only possible peace; now, it was just an end. The wrong end.

STOP! I COMMAND YOU!

What were demons, after all, but the impulse to kill and destroy? How much compulsion, in the end, did the bard-born need to lay on them? Devon heard the screaming fury of the command itself, and then he heard the leathery beat of wings—huge wings, by the sound of the storm that rose with them. He heard thunder, the clap of lightning striking stone, and the harsh, guttural snarl of fury so intense it could not be contained in words.

He heard death, but not a death without battle. The demons were fighting each other, now.

Kallandras continued to sing until the storm receded, and all roars and thunder had once again been replaced by silence. Only then did he stop and bow his head; his face was gray-tinged white. The bards quieted, but less suddenly; their work was not yet done, or if it was, they had received no signal from Sioban. Nor would they, Devon thought; she was watching her youngest Master Bard with an expression of concern that was marred only by a trace of primal fear.

So, he thought.

He turned to leave, and he heard in the darkness a distinctive, quiet chuckle.

Very clever.

Kallandras raised his head for a moment, and he gazed into the distance of stone and earth, as if searching for the visage of the speaker. He did not, however, speak—not in any way that Devon could perceive.

"Come, Jewel," he told his silent companion. "It is time to return to Terafin, and make our report."

Chapter Fifteen

19th of Corvil, 410 A.A.
Merchant Authority, Averalaan

FINCH TOOK A DEEP BREATH and let herself into Jarven's office, knocking first to let him know that she was coming. He was, at this very early hour of the morning, standing with his back toward her and his eyes toward the long window that faced into the heart of the Common. Beneath him, beneath them both, the Common was coming to life, as it did at every dawn, rain or sweltering heat notwithstanding.

"Finch," he said, gazing at her reflection in the window. "You are here early."

"Lucille is making your tea," Finch replied, implying that she was not the only one who had chosen to make their way to the Merchant Authority before the sun had fully crested the horizon.

Jarven nodded and then turned. His expression was grave, and he did not offer his usual smile. "Have you heard the news?" he asked her quietly. A knock answered before Finch did, which was just as well; she had rehearsed everything she meant to say while walking—beside Torvan, whose company after everything that had happened in the manse was an unexpected joy—and all the words were there—they just didn't make it out of her mouth.

"Come in, Lucille," Jarven said, raising his voice slightly.

Finch ran to open the door, and Lucille nodded brusquely as she passed, tray in her ample hands. She set the tray down on Jarven's desk and then met his gaze. Something passed between them; Lucille was either worried or annoyed—it was hard to tell because when she *was* worried, it annoyed her, and when she was annoyed, she shared.

Jarven offered her the smile he had withheld when Finch had entered the room. Lucille exhaled. "How bad is it?" she asked the man who in theory ruled these offices.

"Bad," he replied without preamble. "Would you care to join us? I intend to occupy some of Finch's time."

"It's not busy enough that it matters," was Lucille's terse reply. "But no. I don't want tea. I would like to strangle someone."

"Anyone in particular?"

Finch cringed, because usually if you asked Lucille a question like that, you got an earful of answer. Today, however, Lucille made a tight line of her lips and shook her head. "I'll be outside," she told Jarven. "Try not to get Finch in trouble."

"I assure you—"

"Save it. It's not me you're negotiating with."

He took his chair and lifted the teapot. "As you wish, Lucille. Finch, please, take a seat. You're standing like a rabbit that's ready to bound off at the mere hint of a human presence."

Finch did as bid. She even remembered how to sit properly, as it was one of the things Ellerson liked to explain any time he saw her sitting in a chair. The idea that there was a right way to sit and a wrong way had never occurred to Finch, and she thought it funny. Most of the time. Today, Jarven's mood dampened humor.

"Very well." Jarven lifted his cup; Finch found hers too hot to touch. "Have you heard the news?"

She cleared her throat. "Yes."

One brow rose, and his lips turned up in a very slight smile. It reminded Finch of Teller's cat, although she couldn't say why. "And we have a deal?" he asked her.

"Yes."

"Good. I would like to know—"

She held up one hand. Den-sign, but it passed muster as a general signal for silence as well, and she was comfortable using it here. "I want to know exactly what our terms are."

"Pardon?"

"When I give you information, how can I be certain I'll receive something of like value in return?"

His brows—both of them—rose in surprise, and then he laughed out loud. This was followed quickly by a grimace, as he'd been holding the cup that was too hot for Finch. "How would you suggest we go about this to ensure that I'm being fair to you?"

She couldn't shake the feeling that he was laughing at her. "I was hoping," she said, in a quiet voice, "that you had a suggestion. This isn't something I do very often."

"It is not necessarily something that *I* do very often, either. And the public suggestion that I do indulge in this type of barter would give Lucille enough outrage to last years. But yes, I am much older than you are, and I have had the advantage of a broader range of experiences, some of which will no doubt be seen to be of dubious value.

"I had no formal contract in mind, verbal or otherwise. Where I can be of aid to you, without compromising the House or my role in it, I will be of aid. I will answer your questions honestly; if I cannot do so, I will tell you that I cannot do so."

"And how will I know you're telling me the truth?"

He laughed again and shook his head. "My dear," he said, when all that was left of that laugh was a smile, "I do wish Lucille had stayed. She would be proud of you. Shocked, I think, but proud.

"You can never be certain that someone is telling you the truth. No, I am not saying that you can be certain they're lying; that is not the way truth works. Take me, as an example. If you were to describe me to your den-kin, you would no doubt tell them that I am old, or even ancient, and that I am somewhat absentminded. If Lucille were to describe me to her kin or to her peers, she would say that I was an older man who was as canny as the most cutthroat of our ambitious young merchants and that my demeanor of aged experience hides the youthful mind of a wastrel."

Finch's brows rose. "She would never say any of that—she respects and admires you greatly!"

"Oh, tush. You are too easy to outrage, Finch. What I have said is the truth. You would be describing the same person, and your words would be the truth *you* perceive. There is no one truth.

"What I tell you is not information that you will necessarily know. It is the product of observation and examination, as well as some education.

The information will not come from your observations, and they will not be derived from your experiences. The ways in which my experience and yours intersect will probably become clearer only as you, yourself, gain that experience.

"Do you understand?"

"Maybe."

"Good. You will, of course, attempt to verify the truth, where it is possible. You will, won't you?"

She nodded.

"Good, again." He sipped tea slowly, studying her face.

She wasn't afraid to study his in return. She didn't understand Jarven. He *was* ancient, to her. And he was clearly absentminded; Lucille always said he'd forget his head if it weren't attached. But he was also clearly important enough to run this office, and he had rooms in the manse on the Isle. He was good enough at what he did, Lucille had told Finch, that he could stop an entire trade deal with a single well-placed word—usually spoken directly to The Terafin. He had money. He had no wife and no children, according to Lucille, but he had everything else he wanted.

Yet what he didn't seem to want was either her fear or her groveling obedience. He didn't mind that she questioned him, although it often made him laugh.

She didn't have Jay's instincts; no one else did. But she had her own instincts, and at this moment, watching this old man, she knew she could trust him.

"Yes," she told him. "I've heard the news."

"And it's not good." It wasn't a question.

"No." She took a deep breath and let it out; she lost three inches of height as she did, and she put her hands on the edge of the armrest to stop herself from slouching into the comfort of the padded chair. She hadn't been getting much sleep the past few nights.

"How bad is it?"

"Jarven—we've seen demons," she replied. She expected him to laugh. When he didn't, she became as still as the rabbit he had compared her to when speaking with Lucille. "You've heard this already."

That did pull a slight smile from him. "I have," he conceded.

"You're trying to figure out how honest *I'll* be."

The smile deepened. "I am. You may not read well, Finch, and according to Lucille your understanding of numbers is . . . rudimentary. But you are not without cunning; you are just without guile. That can be useful, if you use it correctly.

"But I have interrupted you. My apologies."

She nodded. "We've seen demons," she repeated. "And we've lost some of our own to them. We've seen—more. But this is the first time I've seen Jay like this."

"Like this?"

She's afraid to go to sleep. She's afraid to go outside. She's so afraid for all of us she can hardly breathe sometimes. But none of those words came out. Finch was willing to trade what she knew—but only about certain things. She wasn't willing to expose Jay to a stranger. Not yet. Maybe not ever. "She's worried," she finally said. "More worried than we've ever seen her."

"She wasn't worried about the demons?" he asked, raising both brow and cup.

"Of course she was. But that was—it was different. I think—I think this is so much bigger that she doesn't have a way to express it." Finch took a breath and then touched the sides of her cup. It was on the edge of too hot, but she could lift it, and it gave her something to do with those hands instead of folding them into her lap. "You know about Lord Cordufar?"

"I have heard about his manse, if that is what you mean."

Finch nodded. "That's what I mean."

"It is cordoned off from public view. Jewel Markess has been given access to it?"

"Given is the wrong word," Finch said, lips twisting in a frown. "She's been ordered there, by The Terafin. She's gone there every day."

"May I ask why?"

"Yes, but you'll have to ask The Terafin."

"Fair enough."

"And you won't."

He smiled. "No, Finch, I will not ask her; that is not how the game is played."

Finch didn't ask, although she was curious about the rules of the game he thought he was playing. "I don't—I don't understand all of what's happening there; Jay doesn't talk about it much because she's not really supposed to. And she only talks to us," she added quickly. "But . . . there's some sort of magic. The Order of Knowledge is there, all the time. And the bards from Senniel came; Jay said there were fifteen of them."

Jarven nodded.

"There are voices," Finch said, her own dropping. "Jay said—she said that someone was killing people slowly and horribly and that it never stopped."

"They could see this?"

"No. That's the thing. They could *hear* it. They can't get to the people who are dying. They told Jay—the mages did, and I think Devon—"

Jarven lifted a hand. "Devon? Devon ATerafin?"

Finch nodded. "Do you know him?"

Jarven was silent for a long moment. "She is in the company of Devon ATerafin."

"Yes. Constantly."

"I see. I'm sorry for the interruption. Please, continue. Would you like a biscuit?"

"No, thank you. I ate."

"I was in a hurry and did not, if you'll forgive me."

Finch nodded. "Devon told Jay that the voices were magic. That they were an illusion, a trick being played by the demons to demoralize us."

Jarven closed his eyes for a moment. It looked like one long blink. "Your Jewel doesn't believe this."

"She's Jay," Finch replied. "Why do people have problems calling her that?"

"I can't imagine," Jarven replied dryly. "Does she believe it?"

"No. She knows he's lying. She knows those people are dying, for real, beneath the city and that we can't do a damn thing to save any of them." She hesitated for just a minute and then said, in a rush, "Three days ago, you could only hear the voices where the mages were digging. Yesterday, you could hear them from the streets outside the manse—the people who live there kept calling the magisterial guards. She says the voices are going to get even louder, Jarven. She says we'll be able to hear them, by the end, all over the hundred. Maybe even the Isle.

"And she's afraid that some of *our* lost are there, waiting to die without any hope of rescue or mercy."

"She said that?"

"No. She'd never say that. But that's what she's afraid of. It's what we're all afraid of, and it's making us crazy."

"Why are the demons doing this, Finch?"

"I don't know," Finch whispered, looking past him and toward the light that streamed through the cut-glass panes of his window. "I think it has something to do with gods."

He set his cup aside and rose. "Very well. You have work to do, and I have apologies to make to Lucille; she is not very patient with my desire for company, even when the office is not particularly busy."

"Jarven?"

"Yes?"

"Are you worried?"

He hesitated for a moment, and then he said, "Yes."

19th of Corvil, 410 A.A.
Terafin Manse, Averalaan Aramarelas

"The point is," Jewel said, watching the faces of her den in their council room, pots hanging from hooks and chains above their table's center, "we're looking—the mages are looking—at the coming of the Lord of the Hells. I don't know when—they don't know when—but they're afraid. Some of them are terrified, which makes them useless."

"Devon?"

"Is not useless." She grimaced. "I don't think we have much time, if we have any time at all. It's going to be so bad in the city, I wouldn't stay."

"You'd leave Averalaan?" Finch's eyes had widened in genuine surprise.

"It's going to be a burning building. I love my home—when I have one, that is—but we can always make another home. If we're alive." She glanced away. "I don't want to be here," she finally said, dropping her voice. "I don't want to be here when you can hear the dying no matter where you are in the city. I don't want to hear them—" She almost lifted her hands to cover her ears.

Teller touched her elbow gently, and she lowered those hands, forcing them to lie at rest in her lap. She was so damn tired. The dreams wouldn't leave her alone; they came, again and again, like a wyrd that she could make no sense of.

No, that wasn't true. She was afraid that she did understand them—that they were the voices of the dead that she had yet to hear, that she *would* hear them—Lefty, Fisher, Lander—and even distorted by continuous and unimaginable pain, she would recognize them. While she was here, in safety, and they were unreachable.

But . . . they were dead, in her dream. Duster was always there, always. She was the walking corpse that troubled Jewel the most, possibly because she had always been so cruel and so determined in her need for vengeance.

"The mages *think* the deaths are occurring as part of a ceremony; they get something—magic, power, I didn't really understand that part—from the suffering and the deaths themselves if the deaths occur in the right place. The ceremony," she continued, drawing breath, feeling it cut, "is meant to summon the Lord of the Hells from the Hells to our world. To our city. If he succeeds, the end of the world starts here.

"I can't leave," Jewel told them all, trying to shrug the image of Duster off, as if it were just a superficial cover and not something that had sunk roots so deep she would never extricate them. "But the usual offer is open."

She glanced at Ellerson, who had taken up his spot to one side of the door. He was a constant presence in the wing and in the life of the den— one of them, but not one of them. She saw a slight frown deepen some of the creases around the corners of his lips, where a slight smile would deepen different ones. No expression on his face was more than slight.

Teller watched Jay as she waited for their answer. Jay had always said they were free to walk, and she had always meant it. But it had never been an option for any of them. They watched her, waiting. She'd seen them through winter in Teller's case and certain death in Finch's. They'd eaten more or less at the same table for years if you counted the apartment floor, and if they'd taken to thieving, they'd never stolen from each other.

She'd brought them here.

It was here that they meant to stay as long as she did.

"Is there anything that anyone can do to stop him?" Teller asked quietly.

"*Yes.*" Jay's eyes widened slightly, and then the stiff line of her shoulders suddenly trembled. Teller nodded gravely. He knew what the single word, spoken in that tone of voice, meant. She was certain. She could *see* it.

But what she could see wasn't clear to anyone but Jay. Years of experience had shown that sometimes it wasn't clear to her, either. But . . . there was a way. There was something.

"It's the feeling," Jay told them after a few awkward minutes had passed. "Don't ask me what."

"Well, look at the bright side," Finch told her.

"What?"

"If things get much worse, we'll all be here when Moorelas rides again."

"Moorelas is a story," Angel told her, more curt that he usually was when speaking to Finch. "And we're going to need a helluvalot more than stories to save us."

"Well, Allasakar was supposed to be a story, too. And if he's here, Moorelas can't be far behind."

"Jay?" Teller had not taken his eyes from her face.

"When the Sleepers wake. When Moorelas rides again, the Sleepers wake." Her voice dropped into a whisper, and the awkward smile of joke-gone-wrong slowly drained from her face. "'To fulfill their broken oath and restore honor to their lines.'" Her eyes widened, then. Her chair couldn't contain her; she was almost hopping from foot to foot with something very like excitement but more hysterical.

"It's the crypt. Mother's blessing, it's the *crypt*."

"The what?" Angel asked, sharply.

"We were there. That's what they're trying to tell me."

Carver slapped the table with his palm to get her attention. It worked, but in this state, it might not have. "Can you explain it to the rest of us?"

"Back when we first started exploring the maze, Duster and I—we found one old tunnel that was, well, like a manor hall. It was made of big, wide cut-stone blocks—real high ceilings, pretty frilly engravings, stuff like that. There were magelights in the walls. We thought it'd be the perfect place for the den; we'd never have trouble with turf wars again, and we could live in style."

"But something was already living there."

"You never told us about it."

"If I'd told you, you'd've dragged Lander off on some crazy search for—" She stopped, remembering who had been with Lander the night he had disappeared. "Sorry," she said, the word rough but meant.

"Doesn't matter. Tell us now."

"You remember the old crypt in the Church of Cartanis?"

"Yeah. Plaques on the floor, engravings on the wall, bits and pieces of stone."

"Not those. The big, stone boxes, with the statues on top. The ones the really important people get."

"I believe," Ellerson said quietly, "that you are speaking of the sarcophagi. And it is not necessarily people of import that receive such treatment, but rather people whose generosity to the church is measured in appropriate funding. Usually after their death, when their last testament is made public in the Halls of Omaran."

"Ellerson," Angel snapped, "do you have to turn everything into a lecture?"

"Do forgive the interruption, Jewel. Continue."

"We didn't know what they were. We thought they were just statues, same as always. I didn't think we'd come out beneath a church—but you know how hard it is to figure out how the underground and the above match up. Anyway, we went to grab a torch—the room was lit—but there weren't any. It was magic, of course, and magic makes me nervous. Made Duster nervous, too."

Angel knew what that meant; they all did. But Duster had been gone for long enough that they didn't flinch or avert their eyes. They missed her, in their own way; flinching, drawing back—it would have meant she was *here*.

Jay knew it. Jay felt it, Teller thought, more strongly than any of them. "Right. You know what she was like when she was nervous."

Yes. Usually it was hard to distinguish between nerves and fury with Duster. Both had the same effect on her. "We had our own small light, and we went into the crypt. You couldn't see the ceiling. I don't understand why. It was like—like walking into another world. But you could see these three tombs, and on them, these three statues. The floor was stone, same as the walls, but around each of the tombs were three thin, black circles, and in each of the circles were words. At least I think they were words. Couldn't read them."

"Did you recognize the alphabet?" Ellerson asked. They all glanced at him. His usually quiet voice was slightly sharper, his eyes narrowed.

But Jay didn't seem to notice—she was staring at the table's surface, her brow furrowed as if she were chasing a vision and it was—barely—still in sight, but receding.

"No. It was more like pictures than anything else.

"But the words, or whatever they were, were in gold; Duster thought we could pick them out, maybe sell them. I thought we could try tracing a couple, maybe find out if Rath could read 'em. Duster got there first."

No surprise, Teller thought. It was Duster; they were hungry.

"She bent down, touched the first circle, and snap, she was flying across the room."

"That's where she got that burn!" Finch said, startling them all with the unexpected heat in her voice. As if she'd always wondered. Teller grimaced; she had. Finch wondered a lot but said little.

But so did he. Thing was, if you waited long enough, you usually got answers. They often weren't the answers you wanted, though.

"That's where. They were alive. The one that she'd gotten near—he moved. They were—they were asleep."

"The Crypt of the Sleepers," Ellerson whispered. "Blood of the Mother."

Teller was almost shocked. He had never heard Ellerson use the phrase, although it was common enough everywhere else in the manse. "You do not know how lucky you were, young Jewel; there is a god that watches you. I have heard stories . . ."

"Yeah. Me too. Like about where the Sleepers supposedly fell."

No one spoke. The Sleepers had fallen in the city of the Lord of the Hells; they had betrayed Moorelas, and they had paid the price for breaking their oath at the hands of their furious Queen.

"I thought they couldn't be—they couldn't be the Sleepers—but they weren't human, Ellerson. They weren't like anything I've ever seen. They were taller and thinner and paler; they wore armor that only an Artisan could've made. And—and—they were *so* beautiful." She made beauty sound like something vaguely terrifying and truly ancient.

"You didn't like them."

"How would I know? They were sleeping."

"Jay," Teller said.

"No. I didn't. I don't know how Moorelas could have chosen them to make his final stand with—Moorelas was as close to a god as any man's ever going to be, but even *I* wouldn't take 'em for my den. What is it, Ellerson?"

"Tell The Terafin," he said quietly. "Tell her all."

"But . . . we don't know what it means yet."

"Trust your instincts."

Jay stared at him for a long moment; no one else spoke. It sounded to Teller as though this was the second part—or the third, or fourth—of a conversation that Jay and Ellerson had already had.

"Do you know where it is?" Ellerson asked, when the silent stare had dragged on long past the point of comfort.

"Could I reach it again above ground, do you mean?"

He nodded.

Jay glanced around the table, looking momentarily like a hunted creature. Teller wanted to tell Ellerson to go away—but he couldn't. Tonight, Ellerson was asking all of the questions that Teller would have, and it would have taken Teller longer. But he understood Jay's hesitation. She'd spent weeks finding either packed dirt or, worse, demons; she'd spent weeks trying to guide Meralonne APhaniel into the maze that they'd taken for granted until it had started to devour their own. She'd spent weeks failing—and she hated failure.

Especially when the cost of that failure was writ so large in the horrible deaths of dozens—or more—of the helpless. It was too much. Hope—any hope—could be crushing because it would probably end the same damn way.

"Jewel?"

"I think so."

"This," he said, his voice crisp and clear, but softer than normal for all that, "is unlike you. Where?"

"Beneath the Sanctum of Moorelas."

Angel remembered the Sanctum. He remembered walking from the Port Authority along the seawall, leaving the docks of the harbor behind while the crowds—and the ill temper they displayed at having to wait in endless lines with their shaky paperwork—thinned. He had come to see the statue of Moorelas with Terrick, his father's friend.

He could not remember all that Terrick had said. But he knew the legend as well as any visitor to Averalaan might know it, and he knew what happened to those who fell under Moorelas' shadow. He had watched the small crowds at the statue's base move in the direction of the sun to avoid it.

He knew that every person in the room with the single exception of Ellerson was now experiencing the profound horror of that shadow, that whispered cradle story—as if Jewel's words had brought Moorelas' shadow to the here and now more forcefully than the presence of demons, magic, and the whispers of gods.

"I wasn't aware," Ellerson said, when it became clear that no one else would speak, "that that was possible."

It was a statue. It had no dirt, no doors, no obvious way in to the underground; it had, instead, carved pictures of the battles that comprised Moorelas' brief and fierce life. But Jay didn't lie. Carver said she couldn't; Angel was less certain. Now, however, he knew she believed what she had just told them.

He studied her expression, and any hope that she was wrong slowly drained from him.

But it was Carver who put into words the rest of the den's fear. "You fell under Moorelas' shadow," he said.

Ellerson snorted impatiently. "You speak like children at street games," he said, far more edge in the words than he usually reserved for their lack of decorum, their inability to dress themselves "appropriately," and their language. "Will you also not step across the cracks of the cobbled stones?"

Teller turned to face the domicis.

"Duster died," he said quietly.

21st of Corvil, 410 A.A.
Sanctum of Moorelas, Averalaan

"Well?" Jay said.

Carver shrugged. Angel, standing by her side, was watchful. He didn't have the same fear as the rest of them, but he hadn't been born in the city, and the statue itself hadn't been part of his childhood lore. It was early morning; the sun had crested the sea horizon, and the white cast of the statue's face was washed in pale pink and blue. The shadow he cast was long and thin, and no one was standing anywhere near it.

That wouldn't normally have been remarkable; at this time of the morning, no one should have been here. If Angel had any doubts about the effect of the Cordufar mansion's spreading shadow, they died instantly. People were already huddled here, across the surface of the carvings that depicted Moorelas' life; he could feel their fear.

Carver, watching, glanced at Jay and then at Angel; he said nothing. But he was first to leave Jay's side, sauntering toward the statue itself— and avoiding, as the others did, the long wedge of its shadow. It wasn't easy to examine the statue's base without clearing away either people or their offerings, so it took more time.

Jay watched in silence, seeing not Carver or Moorelas, but the fearful crowd. They were strangers, of course, and not all of them were from the lower holdings, which had been home to the rest of the den for all of their lives except the last few months; some were in fancier dress and had, as offerings, food that would have been at home in the Terafin kitchens. Some of that food went not to the statue—which couldn't reasonably be expected to eat it—but to the children huddled in various states of boredom beside their parents. This caused some tension, and Angel understood it well enough; no one wanted charity. Even the offer would have offended his father deeply.

But children were children everywhere; they didn't appear to notice any pity or condescension. They ate, and they chattered quietly enough that their parents hadn't the heart to shut them up.

Carver came back. "Nothing," he told them. "Jay?"

She nodded. "Angel, stay here." She navigated the crowds—which were steadily increasing as the minutes passed—with an ease that Angel envied; she could slide between the small gaps as easily as if she were one of the children. She examined—and this was harder—the carvings, but that was cursory; she examined the sides of the pedestal with more care. What she saw, Angel couldn't tell, but nothing shocked or surprised her; there was no momentary widening of eyes, no sudden absence of awareness.

There was, however, a brief exchange of prayers between Jay and the people who had come here; some words that Angel could see spoken, although he couldn't hear them.

In the end, she returned to them. "Nothing," she told them quietly.

"You're sure this is where you came out?" Angel asked.

"Unless there's another Moorelas somewhere near the seawall, yes."

"Jay—"

"I don't know. But I think—I think this is where. Somehow."

Carver snorted. "Good luck finding it," he said. "They'll have to clear the statue entirely."

Which, given the steady crowd, was going to be a problem. Luckily, it was someone else's problem.

22nd of Corvil, 410 A.A.
Terafin Manse, Averalaan Aramarelas

All the next day, Jewel paced in the confines of the kitchen. Sleep had eluded her, because knowledge or no, the nightmares didn't leave her alone. Now they were clearer and more focused. And the dead that rose were no longer just her dead; they were the fallen, the oathbreakers. They would bring the end of days.

She thought they could be awakened, and she feared it.

She also feared what she knew she must now do: Go to The Terafin, and tell her, as Ellerson had said, everything. What The Terafin could do with that information, Jewel couldn't do. But would The Terafin believe her? Or would she have, instead, the reaction that Ellerson had had?

Children, she thought, bitterly. At street games.

The den came and went, and she was glad of their company. Teller left before she woke, as did Finch; Arann's shift was at the end, not the start, of the day. But Angel, Carver, and Jester weren't tied to someone else's schedule, and they traveled with ease from one end of the manse to the other, as familiar with its halls as they had once been with the streets of the twenty-fifth.

Jewel was not nearly as comfortable with the layout; she'd spent so much of her time outside the manse that it still didn't feel like home. Maybe, she thought, it never would.

But when they sat down for dinner—in the large room, which Ellerson insisted on—missing only Teller, who was still hard at work in Gabriel ATerafin's office—Angel cleared his throat as he took his chair. He had gone out for the day, but only for four or five hours, and he had returned with a peculiar, grim expression.

When they were most of the way through dinner, he was willing to share the reasons for it. Which made dinner a lot shorter, at least for Jewel, than it would otherwise have been. "The voices," he told her—speaking to her, although everyone except Jester and Carver stopped to listen.

She didn't even pretend to misunderstand him. "They're louder?" It was a fool's question. It held hope.

He nodded.

"How much louder?"

"I could hear them," he told her, "on the way to the Port Authority."

"But that's—" Her eyes widened.

"I couldn't hear them in the Port. I could barely hear them on the way—but, Jay, I knew what I was listening for. I stopped to talk to a friend in the Authority. He told me the magisterians are stretched to breaking. There's some big investigation into the Magisterium at the moment, and they're not hiring new guards—but they're getting far more reports and far more 'incidents' in the past week than they've had in the last ten years.

"People are panicking." He had set his fork down, and he didn't touch it or the food on his plate again. "It's not going to go away on its own, is it?"

She shook her head.

"Is it going to keep getting louder?"

She nodded.

"It'll drive people insane," he said. "It almost drove me insane, and I had to strain to catch it all."

She also set her fork down. She pushed the food to one side. "I'll go," she told Angel.

The rest of the den, even Carver, were now watching her.

"Go where?" Carver asked.

It was Angel who answered. "To The Terafin." He rose. "Should I go with you?"

"No. You can't be armor against her mockery if she laughs, and if something is waiting to kill me, they'll take you down as well." She hesitated and then whispered something that no one could quite catch. "Hells with it," she said. "Yes. Come with me. I'm spending enough time alone in my own head."

"Empty place?" Carver asked, with a lopsided grin. She smacked the back of his head on the way out.

The only part of the manse that Jewel knew by heart was this one: the route to—and from—The Terafin's personal chambers. She knew that all inquiries and all requests for a meeting—or an audience, as Ellerson called it, gods knew why—were in theory to be routed through Gabriel's office. She also knew that Gabriel's office was regularly sidestepped by people who thought they were so important that they shouldn't have to deal with Barston, Gabriel's personal secretary. She hesitated for a minute at the junction between the halls that led to the right-kin's office and the halls that lead to The Terafin, and in the end she decided she could endure the wrath of a man she knew only from Teller's reports.

Angel didn't speak. He walked on her right, and he glanced from side to side in the long empty hall so often that Jewel wondered if he thought she really was going to be in any danger. She didn't ask. She was trying—and failing—to come up with some sort of speech that wouldn't make her look like a witless child.

Trying, in fact, to think like the woman whose responsibility was so vast it encompassed all of House Terafin. How would she hear the words Jewel had to say? How would she weigh them? What risk would the House face if she were to believe them and act on them?

And what would she do if she did?

The latter, she failed utterly to envision. But the former? The Terafin trusted her sight, inasmuch as she trusted anyone's. She had sent Jewel, at the side of Meralonne APhaniel and Devon ATerafin, to places she had sent no one else, not even a member of the House. She had taken all the risks that Jewel's vision had suggested.

She took a deeper breath, held it, and then expelled it loudly. She hated fear. *Hated* it. But it was hers anyway, and the trick was just to keep going, no matter how heavy it got.

Jewel did not immediately recognize the Chosen at the door; she'd been hoping for Torvan or Arrendas. But they recognized her. They stopped her anyway, and Angel pulled up the right rear, stopping when she stopped. They asked both her name and her business.

"Jewel Markess. I have a matter of import to discuss with The Terafin."

"It's urgent?"

No hesitation, not now. "Yes. I don't think we have any chance—"

The guard who had spoken lifted a mailed hand. "We are not The Terafin," he said gravely. "And this is a matter, if I am any judge, for The Terafin." He glanced at Angel. "Your guard?"

The question surprised her. "He's my den-kin. Angel," she added. "He's with me."

The guard gave her an odd look, but he nodded and turned to Angel. "Your purpose?"

Angel met the guard's eyes and said, "Her back."

The guard's reply was a very brief, very odd smile. "Very well. You may pass."

"No one's with her, are they?" Jewel asked nervously as they stepped to one side of the still closed doors.

"No one," he replied, "that can easily be ordered from her presence."

The Terafin always looked as if she were expecting someone. Morretz was behind her and to one side, as he usually was. She sat at the long table in the library rather than behind one of the desks that seemed to be scattered throughout the manse for her use, and her hands were empty.

But her eyes were shadowed, and she seemed pale. "Corrin told me that you had a matter of some urgency you wished to discuss."

"If I could borrow him, and he could speak for me, it'd probably make my job easier," Jewel replied. She was rewarded by a tired, but genuine, smile.

"He felt that your phrasing was appropriate," she replied gently. "He is my Chosen. Had Ellerson not had some effect on your use of language, he would have opened the doors nonetheless. He understands some of what we face and some of what we . . . hope for. Why have you come?"

"It's about the undercity," Jewel replied.

The Terafin stilled. She was not a woman who fidgeted, but the absolute lack of motion was telling anyway. Jewel understood it; they hoped, and they failed, hoped and failed. It had almost come to a point where the one led inevitably to the other, like sunrise to sunset, and in between, people died. She wanted to get up and leave, but The Terafin's expression pinned her to her chair.

"Continue."

"I think—" Jewel swallowed. "I'm not sure, and it's probably nothing, but I think there's a way in that we've missed."

"That you've missed? In your outings with Meralonne and with Devon?"

"Yes. I didn't—I didn't think of it, and I didn't try to take them with me." Mostly because there was nowhere to take them. There were no basements, no trapdoors, no comforting and comfortable tunnels.

"Jewel," The Terafin said, her voice on the edge of harsh. Morretz had come to stand by her side to the left, and he watched not his master but Jewel Markess. He didn't speak, but he didn't have to. His was a silence that could probably fell trees in the Common.

"Have you ever gone to the Sanctum of Moorelas?" Jewel asked, forcing a firmness into her words that was as much of a lie as she'd ever offered the Lord of the House.

"The Sanctum?" The Terafin's face rippled in confusion; this was not the direction she'd expected the conversation to take. Which was fair. "Yes, several times. At least once a year during the Gathering. Why?" Before Jewel could answer, her eyes widened slightly. "You think you have a way in that involves the Sanctum?"

Jewel nodded. "I think it's the only way in—the only way left. I don't think there *is* any other way in."

"And they could not have closed this from the inside, as they did the others?"

"I don't think they could get to it." Jewel drew a short breath. "Terafin, I don't know that *we* can. But we were there."

"We?"

"Duster and I."

"Duster is the girl who died so that the rest of your den could escape the holdings?"

"Yes."

"Tell me, Jewel. Tell me quickly."

Jewel did.

When the door had closed on Jewel Markess and her silent and stiff guard, The Terafin rose. Morretz had already left her side and had entered the stacks, searching for the information she required. It was not a short search, and during it, Amarais paced the carpeted floor like the much younger woman she had once been. She ordered the magelights to brightness as Morretz at last emerged, his sleeves covered in dust, his arms balancing books, scrolls, and the remnants of either that previous rulers had seen fit to preserve.

He laid them upon her table.

"What do you think?" she asked him before she had opened the cover of the first book she touched.

"She believes every word she has spoken is the truth." He glanced at her and added, "So do you."

"I believe she believes it," was The Terafin's guarded reply.

"You believe it, Amarais. What you know and what she knows, however, is not the same. You believe it because there are arcane and ancient writs and even laws governing the Sanctum; she is unlikely to know about them. Most of the House," he added, "is unlikely to know about them; they are not invoked."

"No. But there must be a reason for those laws, and I need to see them again before I approach the Council. Or the Kings."

"Start here," Morretz said. "You read Old Weston?"

"No."

"Start there," he said instead, grimacing. "Because I can get by in Old Weston. It brings back memories."

Judging by his shuttered expression, none of them were good. He had spent years in the halls of the Order of Knowledge as one of its students; why he had left, she did not know. Nor could she ask. But she was grateful for that departure, grateful that he'd survived it, and grateful—profoundly grateful—that he had chosen to serve the Guild of Domicis instead.

In the end, they found some of what they sought, and The Terafin summoned Meralonne APhaniel.

He was instantly wary, and the fact that this was noticeable said much about his state: he looked exhausted and worn. Amarais did not know his age; she knew it must be considerable, but he always seem to elude its weight. Today, he wore the full measure of years, and unlike those same years on the shoulders of Sigurne Mellifas, they suited him poorly.

"Terafin. I realize that I am a mage in the employ of your House, but at the moment the Crowns demand my attention and my diligence. It is not easy to come here, and my presence will be missed."

"I would not call you for a message of little import, and indeed I expect that you will see this information to the source that it will best serve." She spoke coolly and was rewarded by a formal bow—one he had to rise to make.

"Your pardon, Terafin."

"Accepted."

"How may I serve you, Terafin?"

She smiled; there was no expression upon his face. "It has come to my attention that there is a colloquial phrase used among the general populace. *When the Sleepers Wake*. It is used to mean—"

"That something will never come to pass. Yes. I've heard the phrase."

She watched his face as if it were geography that she could find her bearings by studying. "Good. It is not a phrase that is used in my presence and not one that I am familiar with, perhaps because I have studied some of the history of the Sleepers."

There it was: the tensing of lines around eyes and the corners of a thinning mouth. What she said had not pleased him, as his next words made clear. "You have studied childhood lore."

"And yet you would agree that the Sleepers do exist." She was not entirely certain which way this conversation would go, and she was willing—barely—to let it unfold naturally.

He surprised her. He smiled. It removed years from his face, but it made of that face something almost fey. "I would agree, yes. But I would not necessarily say that the bardic understanding of the Sleepers and the reality meet in any meaningful way."

"Are these Sleepers dangerous?"

Meralonne's gaze was both measured and sardonic. "Who would know? They have never awakened."

"Yet it is considered an act of treason to interfere with them at all—to even, if I understand the law correctly, attempt to see or study them." She lifted one treatise and let it fall again, as if tempting him to argue. He did not. "A very old law, upheld when the Kings took power. It is not in the records of the current magisterial courts, but rather the historical ones. Four hundred years ago. When the Sleepers were, in fact, considered myth."

"How—"

"I wished plans," she replied smoothly, her voice the practiced voice of reason that had held her in such good stead during her long years in Terafin. "Some lay of the ground that would indicate that the Sanctum of Moorelas had once been part of a building." She studied his face for some sign of expression or surprise; none could be seen. He was cautious now. "Have you heard the phrase 'under Moorelas' shadow'?"

What he had not offered her before, he offered her now; his brow rose and his complexion—which had started out poor—was suddenly white. The surprise did not last; it was transformed by a grimace that trod the narrow line between smile and pain into something like a concession. "Yes. It means, colloquially, that someone is doomed."

That phrase, she'd heard. It was more common than the previous one, in her experience. "So much history beneath the ground of Averalaan, of what was once AMarakas, and before that, Develonn. And before that? Vexusa, I think."

"Yes, the Dark League. I did not know how old these lands were, or how much history they contained; I feel, almost, that I walk in legend."

It was true. But it was also beside the point; who walked in legend and felt that they were doing so? Who had the time for anything but momentary awe and a sense that the universe was profoundly larger than one's self?

"The Sanctum." She looked at him, waiting.

He said nothing, and she silently cursed the way mages hoarded knowledge and information. It was their coin, and they were parsimonious. She rose. This often signaled an end to the interview, but Meralonne understood that she merely wished to leave the confines of chair and desk. She paced. Morretz frowned; she let him.

"It is a shrine," she said, "to the memory of Moorelas, a monument to the forces of justice, of courage, of sacrifice. Each year, upon the four quarters, wreaths are placed at the foot of the statue that guards the city's bay. There are no doors into it, no windows—until today, I did not realize that it could be entered, although perhaps I should have; it is called the Sanctum of Moorelas. Few, if any, know what lies beneath its facade. You know." It was an accusation, but she was graceful enough to make of it a statement, hiding its edges, but not its point.

He did not attempt to deny it. The lack of denial, the lack of even an attempt, calmed her. *Jewel*, she thought. *You were right*. She was aware that she, too, was vindicated in her belief.

"It is an edict that was decreed by Cormaris, Reymaris, and the Mother; those who serve Cartanis have also upheld the law, and I believe the Mandaros-born do so as well. In fact, if you take the time—"

"I will find that there is not a single god who does not wish the Sleepers to remain undisturbed."

His smile was sharper. "Indeed."

"In fact, I will find there is not a single god who will even make reference to the Sleepers without indelicately applied pressure."

He bowed his head to her, lifting his hands in a steeple beneath his chin. Had he a pipe, he would have lit it; he did not.

"If you'd like, Morretz will bring you a pipe."

"He will not bring me *my* pipe." But he nodded to her, acknowledging not her rank but her perception. "Terafin, you put us in a difficult position."

"How much does the Council of the Magi know?"

"The Council? I cannot say for certain. Krysanthos knew, although he was not one of the wise. The Kings know. The Exalted. Certainly," he added, with a wry smile, "the Astari."

"But not The Ten."

"It is not relevant to The Ten."

Had she desired to turn the discussion sharply, she would have laughed—but the laugh would have been brittle, an expression of anger at his casual dismissal of the body of men and women who were second only to the Kings in power.

"It is relevant to The Ten now. It is relevant to all of Averalaan."

Her tone caught him. "What do you mean?" His voice was casual, almost soft. She had heard him snap, snarl, and shout on many occasions. She preferred that to this, although she couldn't clearly say why.

But if she was The Terafin, she was also human. She desired—for just that moment—to show him that The Ten were relevant and necessary. "It is through the Sanctum—and the secret that the Sanctum contains—that we will find our way into the undercity."

He watched her in silence. It was a silence that drained him of color, of all the little things—breath, motion—that gave him the semblance of life. Stone was as still. Only his eyes, gray-silver and light enough in this setting that she found them disturbing, moved. He absorbed both her words and her certainty, and as he did, they widened. "Of course. We should have known it."

Gone were all arrogance and all condescension.

"Tell me, Meralonne—why do the gods fear the Sleepers?"

"I . . . do not know," he replied after some time had passed, and he could not—in The Terafin's considered opinion—fabricate a pleasing enough lie. "And I will not venture to guess; it would take years, and a better understanding of the relationship between the gods and their followers than you or I possess."

Not better than yours, she thought, watching him. Certain of it. Willing to trust the instincts that had guided her through one bitter and bloody House War to her current uncontested position. She wanted to know more about this man. But she had tried in the past, and his past was closed to Terafin. It was also rumored to be closed to the Astari, but thus far, Meralonne had survived.

"And is the fear of the gods for the Sleepers greater than the fear of Allasakar's coming?"

He rose, unfolding slowly and wearily. "I believe it is time to answer that question." He did not ask her permission to leave; had he, she was not entirely certain she would have granted it. But she owned only his contracted time, not his loyalty. She let him go.

He reached the door, and turned; he was Meralonne, and it was seldom in him to let anyone else have the last word.

"Terafin."

"Yes?"

"If you worship those gods, you might wish to pray that the Sleepers do not awaken."

Chapter Sixteen

23rd of Corvil, 410 A.A.
Terafin Manse, Averalaan Aramarelas

THE FACT THAT BARSTON had any hair left was almost a shock to Teller. Over the course of the past ten days, he had taken to pulling at his hair in frustration, while explaining that things were not normally this difficult. On the morning of the twenty-third, just past what civilized people—in Barston's words—would call breakfast, they arrived together at the closed and guarded doors of Gabriel's office to find they were not the first people to do so.

Sadly, the other people weren't guards; the guards were always there. No, these early arrivals were very oddly robed, very unfriendly looking older men and women. Teller habitually stayed behind Barston when anyone official entered the office; he pressed himself into the nearest wall as Barston came to a sudden stop.

Barston, as far as Teller was concerned, felt that manners were necessary—and that groveling was not. He cautioned Teller against overt obsequiousness, as he called it, when dealing with the members of the House, because some of those members felt the name gave them the right to be both demanding and rude. Teller had once asked Barston how it was that demanding and rude people were offered the House Name to begin with, and Barston grimaced.

"Politics," he'd replied briskly. "And I'll thank you not to repeat that."

Whoever these men and women were, they weren't Terafin; if it hadn't been obvious by their dress, it would have been by Barston's attitude; he immediately bowed—a formal, perfect bow—and he held it until the oldest man present ordered him to rise.

Teller thought they were priests. The only priests he had seen in his life in the holdings were the daughters and sons of the Mother—and none of the women were wearing the Mother's symbols—but something about the robes and the staves these men and women carried suggested the cathedrals that, alone among the buildings on the Isle, were taller than the spires of *Avantari*, where the Twin Kings lived.

"My pardon for our tardiness," Barston said, when he gained his full height and once again became the stiff and precise man that Teller had worked with almost nonstop for weeks now.

"You are not late," the man replied. He lifted his hands and lowered the cowl that hooded his face, and Teller's eyes rounded. The man's eyes were golden. "But the Exalted of Cormaris received an urgent missive from The Terafin and bade us come to speak with her."

"Someone—someone at the gates sent you *here*?" Barston said, his voice thinning.

"Ah, no. Your pardon. We are aware that Terafin House protocol requires all unannounced and unscheduled visitors to speak with Gabriel ATerafin. We merely asked directions to his office and waited."

"For how long?"

"Not more than an hour," was the quiet reply.

Barston produced keys instantly, and he motioned the Chosen who attended the doors like statues to either side. "The right-kin is not due in his office for another half hour," he told the priest. Then he turned to Teller and whispered, "Go to Gabriel's rooms at once and bring him here."

"But—"

"He has to be in his rooms; he did not choose to take breakfast in the hall, or we would have seen him. Go *now*, and tell him—tell him whatever you feel is best to get him out of his room, appropriately attired, and *here*."

It wasn't as difficult as Barston's severely worded command implied. He didn't have to knock on the door; the Chosen did that. Nor did he have to wait outside in the hall; Gabriel's quarters, much like the den's, had a large sitting room in which people could wait in comfort. The Chosen on duty indicated that he was to wait for Gabriel, and he told them both that Barston had said the situation "could not be more urgent." They nodded gravely, but they always did that when on duty. He wondered what they said when they were off duty.

But not for long. Gabriel, attired for a long day at the office—as all the days had been since this crisis had started—met him almost immediately.

"What seems to be the problem?" he asked, as Teller stood.

"I'm not exactly sure it's a problem, but there are god-born priests waiting outside your office door."

Gabriel raised a hand to his eyes. "Which church, and how long have they been waiting?"

"Cormaris, and they said not more than an hour."

"Well," the right-kin said as he headed for the door, motioning for Teller to follow, "that didn't take long at all. The Terafin, as usual, was correct."

"Should I be in the office?"

"Yes; they won't be. They will be escorted directly to The Terafin as soon as Barston completely clears her schedule."

Teller carefully stopped himself from cringing, which earned him a slight smile from Gabriel. "It is not only Barston who will bear the brunt of several people's displeasure; the schedule—such as it is—has been cleared frequently and without warning in the past few weeks, much to the annoyance of several influential and wealthy people.

"I appreciate your presence in the office at this time," he added, in a more serious voice. "This is not the usual training that most applicants for a job here will undergo, but you've weathered it well. I am of a mind to speak with The Terafin about the matter of your pay."

"Speak with Barston first."

"Oh, indeed. Even if I did not, the various letters that would accompany such a suggestion would pass through his hands. Come, Teller. These are not the only god-born priests we will see today. With luck, and with the blessing of not only the Triumvirate but of any god who watches the Empire, this will be over soon, and things will return to what passes for normal."

In all, three delegations came that morning from the churches, one each from Cormaris, Reymaris, and the Mother. Barston had warned Teller to be unfailingly helpful and utterly silent unless words were somehow demanded, and Teller had obeyed with the ease of a quiet person used to living in a house full of the louder variety.

But it was easy. The priests were not, like the rest of the angrier House Members, difficult or frustrating; had it not been for Barston's obvious nerves, Teller would have found them calming. Even the golden eyes, after the initial shock, seemed natural they were the color of warmth, not power. While Barston was going out of his way not to offend them— and acting as if breathing their air was cause for the offense he wished to avoid—Teller observed.

They were formal, the way The Terafin was formal and the way Gabriel could be when he so chose; they were not, however, chilly or condescending. They spoke to each other while they waited, and some mention of children, or the children, carried in the otherwise silent space. It came to him, as he watched them, that they were just people with unusual jobs and a slightly different language. He could have taken them to Helen in the Commons, and after she'd dressed them, they would have almost fit in.

But they were here as representatives of the Exalted, and if they spoke to each other about trivial things, their demeanor was grave. Teller wondered how he must appear to them; he didn't ask. Barston would have had him ejected—through a closed door.

But when the god-born son of Cormaris paused to look at Teller, when he paused to ask Teller a harmless question, Barston froze, and Teller said, "I'm not ATerafin." He spoke gravely. "But one day, I hope to earn the right to the House Name."

The man's gaze sharpened, and for a moment, he seemed to look not at Teller but into him. It was a long damn moment. But when he smiled, the moment broke cleanly, and Teller was through the other side. "You will, I think, be a significant addition to Terafin in the years to come."

A compliment, and it made Teller smile, both at the time and later, when he had space and time to dwell on it. Better to dwell, his mother had once said, on the happy things, if you must look back at all. But best to keep moving while moving's called for.

Dinner in the den's wing was quiet only in the context of the den; there was some talk, some chatter, some whining, and a bit of shouting; there was a tussle for the last roll, which Ellerson always hated; there was the usual skirmish for chairs, although there were at least half a dozen chairs too many.

Jay snapped and snarled, but she did it in a quiet way. Ever since she'd gone to speak with The Terafin, she'd been uneasy, as if waiting. Teller told her softly that she wouldn't have to wait for long, and when she asked why, he told her about his day. Which, if anything, made her more quiet, not less.

But before dinner was over—which is to say, the food was gone—Ellerson appeared and walked directly to Jay, bending over her right ear from behind her chair. She jumped when he started talking, but she eased herself into her chair and let him finish. Then she grimaced and pushed herself up from the table.

"I'm wanted," she told the den, "by The Terafin."

"Now?"

"She took late dinner tonight. I don't expect it'll be long."

Ellerson said something else, and her grimace deepened. "Strike that," she told them, looking queasy.

"What is it?" Angel asked, rising. She waved him down again.

"Morretz is waiting for me outside the doors."

"Morretz?"

Jay shrugged. "I think it's code for I want you right now, and you're to come alone."

It was Ellerson's turn to frown, but his frown was less theatric. "If you will take a word of advice," he said, as he began to usher her out through the doors, "you will refrain from second-guessing The Terafin."

Morretz didn't look particuarly happy to be sent off as a messenger, but Jewel wasn't quite certain how he was making that clear; his expression was neutral, and he was polite and almost deferential. He always was. Still, speed was required; Morretz was seldom far from The Terafin's side. He lead Jewel straight through the Chosen, who didn't even raise arms in formal salute or greeting; they simply stared through him, and through Jewel, until she passed between them.

The Terafin was waiting in her library. She was surrounded by piles of paper and teetering stacks of books—or what was left of books, they were often so old—and she appeared to be entirely absorbed in her studies.

But when Morretz approached, she looked up instantly, and she set aside the paper she'd been poring over. "Jewel," she said. She didn't rise. Jewel didn't bow. But she did take the chair The Terafin indicated.

"You will, perhaps, have heard about the visitors I received today." There was a question there, and Jewel hesitated before she nodded. "Good.

Your Teller did good work there; I think Barston was perhaps overly flus-tered; it is seldom that the god-born pay social visits, even upon the Isle.

"I have not called you to speak of Teller, however. The meetings with the various priests came about more quickly than I had expected."

You expected them to come to you, though. What kind of a woman expected the god-born to dance at her whim? Jewel shook her head, knowing the answer: this one. But the woman seated a corner of a table away didn't look terrifying or impressive; she looked damn tired.

"As a result, there is a final meeting tomorrow, and that meeting will decide many things."

Jewel waited until she realized The Terafin meant her to ask. "What meeting?"

"We have been granted an audience," The Terafin replied, "with the Twin Kings on the morrow. We will travel to *Avantari* just after breakfast; breakfast will be early. I have requested suitable attire for you; Ellerson will see to the details."

The words, when they sunk in, made the chair entirely necessary. "We?"

"You are to accompany me."

"But—"

"Yes?"

"They're *the Kings*."

"Ah." The Terafin's smile was genuine, and pained. "Yes. And you are not yet fully prepared to meet them."

Jewel nodded, grateful for the understatement.

"I would like to tell you that you will not be required to speak. I can-not. If what you have said is true—and I believe it true, Jewel Markess—they will have questions."

"But what should I say?"

"Duvari will be there." When Jewel failed to react to the name, The Terafin shook her head. "Forgive me, I am also weary, and I forget that you are not a part of my Council. Duvari is the Lord of the Compact, the Leader of the Astari; he is to the Kings what the Chosen are to Terafin. But there are differences, and the most significant of these is this: He seeks threat to the Kings and guards against it; where there is no obvious threat, he seeks the subtle, and where there is no threat, he often imagines it anyway. It is the latter that is cause for some grief, and he spreads that grief in equal measure among The Ten, the Order of Knowledge, and the richest of the Merchant Houses.

"He is not the law, and the laws bind him to some degree. Do not lie to him. Do not attempt to lie to him. If you must speak at all, speak clearly and cleanly; any lack of polish in your words will be forgiven at this juncture.

"If you are not directly addressed, do not speak at all." She paused, then, and said, "Forgive me again. Understand that the cares you have for your den are not in the end substantially different than the cares I have for my House or the cares the Kings have for their Empire.

"If we are to save any of the three, it is this way: by speaking, by trusting, by working together as we can. And I believe that we *can*. Because of you, Jewel. Whether or not the Kings will believe it, I cannot say."

"Well?" Amarais asked Morretz, when he'd seen Jewel to the door and closed it behind her. Morretz faced the door for a few seconds longer than necessary; it was almost answer enough.

The relationship between the Lord of the House and her domicis was complicated, complex; an answer was not, at this point, what she really desired. And he knew it, of course he knew it; he turned. But he didn't speak.

She rose, closing the books she'd been studying. She had scribes and scholars at her beck and call, but she had taken a personal interest in this matter, rediscovering as she did the fascination in poring over the words of dead men and women. This was, in its entirety, what they had left behind over the passage of centuries. It was not the immortality that she desired, if she desired it at all.

"Duvari will be present," Morretz said at last, when she let the silence stretch.

Amarais nodded. "Will she pass his inspection?"

"He is Duvari. Sense and reason are always subordinate to suspicion, and at this time, suspicion will naturally hold sway. I do not know."

Amarais nodded again. "I will speak with Gabriel now," she told him. "No, do not summon him; I will go in person. Tell my Chosen. Papers will have to be drawn and dated; they will be signed after the fact." A common practice.

Morretz nodded.

"Morretz."

"Terafin."

"Had I not been so cautious, had I not been so *political*, things might

have played out differently. Had I chosen to take the counsel of Sigurne
Mellifas, we might not now be at this pass, all roads to the undercity
closed to us but—possibly—one.

"But I am what I am. This girl, this Jewel, will bear the weight of my
mistakes. Will she bear it well?"

"Terafin." Morretz hesitated. It was unusual. "I do not know," he finally
said. "But I would say that she is both fragile and strong. She will give
what she can; she understands, perhaps better than most, what we stand
to lose if the Kings cannot be swayed. She has also made her mistakes, and
to her, they are no less costly than yours are to you.

"I feel, however, that she will be exposed in her entirety, if not during the meeting, then after; Duvari will understand what she is, and he
will—without doubt—attempt to secure her services for either the Kings
or the Astari."

"She could never work as Astari," was The Terafin's flat reply.

"No."

"Very well." She headed to the doors, which were now open, and paused
in them. "Thank you."

24th of Corvil, 410 A. A.
Avantari, Averalaan Aramarelas

The den was awake when Jewel woke; they were silent for all of five minutes. Jewel was going to *see the Twin Kings.* They had questions, and for
the den, they did a masterful job of keeping those questions to themselves.
Unfortunately, they didn't do as good a job at keeping their open shock to
themselves when they first caught sight of her.

Ellerson's work in the morning had taken two hours; it had started before the glimmer of sunlight had crested either horizon or window. As a
result, her hair now looked starched. "It will not fall into your eyes; if you
possibly can, avoid your habit of reaching up to push it away."

As if. Right now, she'd probably only cut her hands on it.

She wore a dress. It was the most expensive dress she'd ever been poured
into, and she resented it; its skirts were wide enough to run in, but the
waist was high and tight, and if she was cornered, it would hinder movement. The fabric itself was soft and shiny, and the colors were deep blues
and purples, with a trace of yellow that caught the eye.

It didn't fit perfectly; Ellerson was slightly frustrated by this fact, enough that he let it show.

"What?" she snapped, irritable. "I've been *eating*. I've gained weight."

The domicis did not answer. If, that is, not answering meant not lecturing her on other aspects of her behavior. He should have been a drillmaster.

"Ellerson," she finally said, when she'd had enough fussing to last a long damn lifetime, "I'm not going to speak unless someone speaks to me *first*. The Terafin told me I was to answer any questions as honestly as I could, period. There's not a lot of room to screw up in that, is there?"

"There is," he replied stiffly. "Duvari will be there."

"So will most of the important parts of the Court. What is he going to do? Clap me in chains and drag me off? I haven't *done anything wrong*. The Justice-born King will be standing right there—or sitting, or whatever it is Kings do—he can't exactly fabricate a crime and offer a judgment on the spot." She spoke with some heat, because she needed to; he let her for the same reason.

Likewise, he let the den speak, and fuss, and worry. He let Jewel tell Angel he was absolutely not coming with her, and he let Angel stew in silence at the answer. He let the den offer her advice, even when he cringed at the advice offered, and when the bells sounded in the outer hall, he silenced them with one hand and practically dragged Jewel from the room by her elbow.

But at the door, he paused. "You will do well," he told her firmly. "Because we cannot afford less. No one understands why some are born talented and some are not; no one understands why, in the talent-born, some are mage-born, some maker, some bard, and some healer.

"But we have not seen a seer for a very long time, Jewel Markess, and if it comes to that, I believe you are the right person to claim—and use— that talent wisely."

She gaped at him. After a moment, and to avoid the embarrassment that was sure to follow silence, she said, "I haven't done all that well up to now."

He smiled. It made his face look older, but it also made his face look kinder. "You have done as well as you can. You've failed, yes—but we all fail; it is how we continue after failure that defines us. Remember that.

"Now, go. Torvan should be with the Chosen."

"How do you know?"

He raised a white brow and then said, with the same smile, "Morretz was one of my students. One of the best," he added, "but he retains some habits developed in the Domicis Hall." When she frowned, he added, "I asked."

24th of Corvil, 410 A.A.
Avantari, Averalaan Aramarelas

Avantari. The Palace of Kings.

Jewel said nothing as she walked, sandwiched neatly between the Chosen and beside The Terafin. Morretz accompanied The Terafin, of course, but to Jewel's surprise, Devon ATerafin had also been given leave to accompany the Lord of his House. He walked behind that Lord, and therefore behind Jewel, and he didn't speak a word.

She looked at everything: the height of the ceilings, the tapestries, the glow of lamp-bound magestones; she looked at the colored glass that stood where windows in the manor houses might stand, she looked at gardens protected by more glass than existed in the entire twenty-fifth holding, in various states of blossom. Here and there, men and women worked, bristling with that aura of efficiency that made even the servants of the patriciate seem so intimidating. That, and their ability to gaze right through you as if you did not exist in their world. That was fine; she wasn't trying to catch their eyes.

On the other hand, they also failed to notice The Terafin and the rest of her guards, which took more effort.

Carver had said the servants gossiped and chattered about the goings-on in the manse; Jewel couldn't imagine that the royal servants did the same. She felt someone nudge her elbow gently and flushed, falling back into step.

They were met at last at the doors of a large and imposing hall. The architecture in no way differed from the halls they'd taken to reach this one—but something about it was chillier and more distant than even the servants had been.

The man who met them was dressed in blues that shaded from pale to a deep, deep indigo and grays; he wore the emblem of the crossed rod and sword, but it was emblazoned in gold upon his left shoulder rather than on a tabard. He was neither young nor comfortably old, and there was no indulgence at all in his expression.

"Terafin," he said. He tendered her a perfect bow.

She nodded in silence.

"They are waiting for you," the man replied, as if he expected her silence. There was an edge of implied criticism in the words; The Terafin failed to hear it. Jewel struggled to do the same; it wasn't that hard. She already knew she was entirely inadequate. Nothing he could say or do would make it any worse. She hoped.

But as he led them down a hall that was even more tightly packed with guards than the previous ones, she wrinkled her nose; she could smell, in the distance, the faint, sweet smell of something too pleasant to be pipe smoke.

"Something's burning," she said, without thinking.

The man in the lead paused and glanced over Jewel's head before turning to speak, briefly, with the Lord who had dragged her here. Jewel missed The Terafin's reply; it was brief and quiet.

"Incense," the man told Jewel.

The answer was not entirely satisfactory, but the questions that followed she managed to keep on the right side of her mouth; she nodded but said nothing. But his answer became significant almost immediately, for when he signaled the Swords who stood on either side of peaked, arched doors, those doors began to roll inward, gliding above carpet and the exposed stone that lay to either side of it to reveal a series of thrones.

None of the thrones were vacant; two were occupied by men and a woman was seated in the middle. The most easily noted characteristic they all shared was the color of their eyes: golden.

The Exalted.

The Terafin had already folded into a deep and reverent bow, as did her Chosen, although they made more noise while doing so. Jewel wasn't far behind; she might have been first had she not been on the edge of fascination. Or panic.

"Rise," the woman said. Jewel knew her as the Mother's Daughter—her literal daughter.

The Terafin rose first. The Terafin rose alone. Jewel, glancing from side to side, chose to utterly abase herself and remain as close to the floor as she could. The carpet was like a walkway; it was narrow, and it ended at the Mother's seat. Jewel found the stone of these floors very cold. But cold was a comfort because gold was burning, and if she stood in its path for long, she thought there would be nothing left of her.

It was daunting, this meeting with the Exalted. As The Terafin—as ATerafin—she had had cause to meet the Exalted only a handful of times. Meeting them one at a time in the privacy of the manse was difficult enough; they, like the Kings, had a gaze that pierced all armor and all defense. They seldom offered judgment, but one was always certain that they could—and that it would be both as unflattering as one feared and as deserved.

But unworthy of their attention or no, Amarais was here for a reason; it was that that she focused on now.

"Accept my gratitude," she told the daughter of the Mother, "for this meeting."

The woman nodded, as august and distant as any Emperor of a bygone age. "There has been some discussion, Terafin, about your request, both for information and for action."

Amarais inclined her head. She did not look away from the Exalted's face, but for just a moment, she wanted to. She sensed both fear and anger in the woman, and it was a fear and anger not unlike her own—but it did not provide her the usual comfort of empathy.

The Exalted's gaze was appraising, and it was not the only gaze upon her; it was the one she chose, for the moment, to meet. "You understood that this might cause some concern."

"I did. But I also understood that there are other concerns that would— that must—dwarf it."

At this, the woman's lips turned up in a brief smile. "Well answered, daughter. The young woman at your side is the one you spoke of?"

And this, of course, was the trickiest element of this meeting. Jewel Markess was not, in any way, a child raised in the confines of the patriciate. That such an upbringing was confining was not in question, but at times such prisons forced appropriate behavior so instinctively on a person they could not mis-step.

Jewel could, often just by opening her mouth.

She had, of course, been dressed, and groomed by her domicis, and she had managed—barely—an almost unbroken silence while within *Avantari*. But that silence could not last. It would be broken here, and if the

Exalted were satisfied, it would be broken again—and both times, her words would be measured against Terafin.

Against The Terafin, who had brought her here.

Are you ready, Jewel Markess? She glanced at the curve of Jewel's back and almost smiled. It was a grim smile, which was appropriate for these halls.

"Exalted," The Terafin said, "Exalted, Exalted." She bowed three times, according each of the god-born present the respect they were due. "I have asked for—and been granted—this unusual audience to offer information and to request permission to act upon it, in accordance with the ancient laws that bind all interference with the Sanctum of Moorelas."

She recognized the silence that followed her words, and she was prepared for the sudden chill that settled into the expressions of the Exalted. It was not, however, the Mother's Daughter who spoke next; it was the son of Cormaris, Lord of Wisdom.

"Why do you speak of that shrine, Terafin?"

"It is our only avenue into the city beneath the city," she replied, forcing the authority of her rank into the words. "In no other way will we reach the Lord of the Hells in time."

"In time?"

A flash of annoyance would have heated her words; she held them until it had cooled. "You've heard the voices of his servants. Everyone in the city has, by now. Do you think they labor with no goal in mind? They have been exposed, and it is my belief they were exposed early; they play this game—this deadly, ugly game—to distract and break us.

"House Terafin has searched for the hidden ways into the underground, as I have informed the priests you guide. We have found nothing; the ways have been closed against us. Against," she added softly, "the god-born and those who might bring an effective power to bear against the *Allasakari*.

"I have seen demons," she continued, aware that the use of the word was unwelcome and unwilling to apologize for it. "They wore the guise of a family member of the House of my birth in order to either destroy me—or worse, take over Terafin from within, with no one the wiser."

"Yet you came to us late."

"Yes. To my regret and my shame, I chose to hide what I had discovered, in order to better uncover the enemies of my House. We are all concerned with the responsibilities we have chosen, and at times, they become all we can see." She bowed her head.

"Well spoken," the god-born son of Justice said. "But it does not answer the greater question. What will you have us do with the shrine?" His voice was both warm and sharp.

"Open it," she replied.

"You would have us open a monument?"

Her eyes narrowed. He had not denied that it was possible, and that was all she now needed to know. "Were it a simple monument, a thing of stone, I would not. But it is more than that, Exalted. It was always more than that." She hesitated, and then said, "Jewel Markess has been on the other side of the shrine."

The silence that followed was chilly indeed compared to the mention of the shrine.

"Jewel Markess is talent-born," she told the Exalted. "And much of what I described to the men who were sent to treat with Terafin in these matters was from her direct experience. Should you desire it, she will now recount that experience in person, without any interference from House Terafin."

"Describe again the halls you traversed to reach this supposed crypt."

Jewel bowed low to ground every time the Exalted—any of the Exalted—spoke. The Terafin watched her with care, as did Morretz and the Chosen. They could not, of course, intervene, and reminding Jewel of something as simple as etiquette would deprive her of any semblance of authority over her own words.

Ararath, The Terafin thought, as the Mother's Daughter now left her throne and approached the supine form of the young street thief, *whatever you saw in this girl, you saw clearly.* Perhaps she believed it because she desired to do so; it didn't matter. Here and now, the argumentative, head-strong girl who was willing to clash verbally with the most intimidating of mages that the Order of Knowledge had produced had reined herself in completely.

She answered the question the Son of Cormaris had asked. Her voice was not entirely steady, but the lack of steadiness was not due to nerves or anger; her expression was shadowed by obvious loss. The companion that had witnessed her entry into the crypt of the Sleepers had died before she had brought her den to the Terafin manse.

The Exalted conferred briefly among themselves—and out of the hearing of the Terafin contingent—before returning to their thrones. They were not pleased, and had they been able to face Jewel Markess and deny the possibility of truth in her words, they would have.

But they understood—perhaps better than Amarais—the danger that now threatened Averalaan, and with it, the whole of the Empire of the Twin Kings; they would not, and could not, deny that truth when it was also hope.

Our only hope, Amarais thought bleakly. *And it rests upon the shoulders of a girl of sixteen years, by her own reckoning.* Slender shoulders, drawn tightly in.

"Remain here," the Son of Reymaris said, speaking for the first time. His hair, once red, was now streaked with the gray of age and care, and of the three he seemed angriest.

Amarais nodded.

They did not leave the room but retreated to the far wall; it was the only wall in the room that was not adorned with tapestries. Instead, reliefs depicting the gods had been carved into the stone. Given that this hall was intended for the use of the Twin Kings and the Exalted, this was not surprising.

But when the wall parted, the figures of Justice and Wisdom separating slowly to expose a hidden—and quite probably magical—door, Amarais understood that they had won some small concession.

The Kings had come.

They were not alone.

Accompanying them were the Queens—Marieyan the Wise and Siodonay the Fair. Queen Marieyan was robed in simple, midnight blue; Siodonay had chosen bold, unadorned white as her color. Mourning white. Queen Marieyan had chosen to wear a tiara, which lent gravity to the situation, but Siodonay had taken up her sword.

Like The Terafin's sword, it made a statement in the silence.

But two such notable women could not hold her attention for long, for even The Terafin was not immune to the light of the god-born, and she found her gaze pulled—and held—by the two men who ruled the Empire of Essalieyan. Cormalyn, dark-haired, golden-eyed, and grave, stood beside Reymalyn, whose red hair was now silvered by the dignity of age.

Neither man looked pleased; they were, as the Exalted, men who could speak with their fathers, and they carried the concerns of their fathers into the mortal world, as all god-born did.

The Terafin noted, belatedly, that the Princes were not in obvious sight;

nor was the Princess Royale, daughter of Marieyan and Cormalyn. She wondered if they were watching and listening at a safe distance, or if they were elsewhere in *Avantari*.

To either side of the Kings, the Astari walked. The Kings' personal defenders, they were not quite guards, but in times of grave danger, they served that function. They wore no armor, although they were armed; they dressed as functionaries that might be found in any of the offices through which the Royal businesses were governed.

But chief among them, and the last to walk into the room, was a man The Terafin recognized with distaste. Duvari. The leader of the Astari. He gestured, and the stone likenesses of the gods closed once again at the backs of their sons. Then he turned and performed what was, for Duvari, a very unusual obeisance; he bowed, low, to the Exalted.

When he rose, it was easy to forget that he was capable of the humility of respect; he approached Jewel Markess. "With your permission?" he said, although it was unclear to whom.

King Cormalyn nodded, however.

"Rise."

And now, The Terafin thought, *we are tested.* "Jewel," she added, in a soft voice. "Rise."

The questioning was sharp and harsh; Jewel weathered it as well as could be expected, given her background and the lack of formal lessons she'd received since she'd come to The Terafin manse bearing Ararath's message. That would have to change; had the situation not been so dire, and had Jewel not been so unusual, she would already have become more proficient.

Duvari was not the man to ease her into an exchange of information, and by the time he had asked her variations on the same set of questions for the fifth time, it was clear that Jewel's ability to withstand—with grace—his condescension and obvious disdain was coming to an end.

Devon stood slightly behind Jewel and slightly to one side; The Terafin watched him without concern. Inasmuch as he could, he cared for Jewel, and he did not wish her to fail whatever test Duvari was now conducting.

". . . and what makes you think this—this crypt is located beneath the Sanctum of Moorelas?"

A sixth round had begun.

"I don't know it for certain," Jewel replied, speaking calmly and softly, although her expression was now sharp.

"Yet you've told your Lord that this is the case."

"Yes." More edge in the word than in the previous sentence. *Jewel, be cautious.*

"Why?"

"Because I couldn't think of anywhere else it could be. The Sanctum stands alone. The library closest to it doesn't have a crypt."

"Who else have you told about this?" When she failed to answer, for this was a new question, he added, "I asked you a question." His voice had dropped several degrees.

Amarais knew the answer of course: her den. The den for whom she had risked so much. "I heard it," Jewel replied. She moved, then, turning away from him. Devon stepped closer to her, and she moved to one side; it was subtle, but it was clearly a refusal.

Duvari drew closer, and she stood her ground. But she spoke a single word, and it wasn't an answer to his question. "Terafin."

"Jewel."

"I've told them everything I can tell them. I serve the House." Her voice was low, and it sounded stretched with effort.

"You have not," Duvari said coldly, "told us everything we wish to know."

"I have told you all that I can."

"It is not for The Terafin to decide that; it is for me. The Crowns are not yet satisfied with your response. We would ask you to resume your place."

She did not move.

"Jewel Markess, sit."

Jewel drew breath then. It was enough.

"Hold." The Terafin glanced once at Jewel and then turned her attention to Duvari. "Astari, the girl is a member of my House. She answers to me by the covenant between The Ten and the Crowns, and I do not choose to press her."

It was petty to take any satisfaction from his obvious surprise and his obvious annoyance, but it had been a long, long week.

"We were not informed that this was the case."

"I was not aware," was her cool reply, "that the permission of the Astari—or the Crowns—was required in the granting of a House Name. Nor was I aware that prior knowledge was a legal imperative."

"It is—"

"It is not, of course, required," Queen Siodonay said. She was war's child, and she took the measure of the battlefield before she entered it. "But as a courtesy—to both ourselves and the young ATerafin—it would have been appreciated."

"It would have been impossible," Duvari said coldly. He looked, briefly, toward Devon; Amarais marked it. But she also marked the complete neutrality of Devon's expression and the lack of any obvious gesture.

"Lord of the Compact," Queen Marieyan lifted her voice slightly.

Duvari turned to face her; for a moment Amarais thought he might argue. But he understood the import of the office, and he managed an "As you say, Majesty," that was smooth and uninflected.

Jewel had stopped trying to speak or trying not to speak. She was trying to breathe. She was no fool, had never been a fool; she understood exactly what The Terafin's chilly words to the Lord of the Compact meant. She had declared—in front of the Kings themselves—that Jewel Markess was ATerafin.

ATerafin.

Jewel had daydreamed, while crawling through so much dirt nothing short of magic could get her fingernails clean, of the day when she would finally be offered the House Name. She'd dreamed of what she would say. On some days, the dream had been of humble, grateful Jewel, on others, of proud Jewel. In none of those dreams had she refused what she had been offered.

And in reality, even had she wanted to do so, she couldn't; it would have damaged House Terafin and its ruler. She couldn't accuse The Terafin of lying to the Kings. Even if she was.

The lie had bought Jewel breathing room and space.

She glanced at Devon, who seemed to be her sole support in the room, for Torvan was by the walls, stiff and as uncommunicative as the reliefs of the gods themselves. Devon, however, was watching the Lord of the Compact and the Lord of the House the way some small children watched burning fires.

The Queen—Marieyan the Wise, Jewel thought, for she was older and she looked the part—had clipped the Lord of the Compact's wings. But not for long.

"But, Terafin, you understand your responsibility in this matter. If this young girl's information were openly known—"

"Then what? I have heard nothing today that indicates—to me—that you have any idea whatever of what will happen. If history—that remote and sullied record of things past—is to be trusted, these Sleepers have existed as they are now since before the Empire's founding; they have not once woken, they have not once been disturbed. And there have been wars, and worse, that have played out above them and around them while empires rose and fell. Vexusa fell around their ears—and such a fall as that city faced woke the very dead; the Dark League did not disturb them.

"Therefore, unless your purpose is to intimidate a young girl, I believe your interview here is at an end. Is that clear?"

Jewel had heard The Terafin speak in anger before. But Devon's frozen expression made it clear that this outburst, this anger, was both unusual and dangerous.

"Terafin," Queen Marieyan said. "Lord of the Compact. Our grievance is not, and must not, be with each other. Terafin, you must forgive the Lord of the Compact; his purpose is the protection of the Crowns, and he is zealous in his pursuit."

"And arrogant. And ruthless."

Even Jewel understood how bold this was. She sidled slightly closer to Devon, who had not moved. At all. She almost wanted to poke him to see if he was still breathing.

"It seems to me," the Exalted of Cormaris said, as he joined the Crowns without any warning at all, "that history, both ancient and recent, plays its hand. Terafin. Lord of the Compact. You do not serve your best interests or ours by this. Cease."

What the Queen's more diplomatic words had failed to do, his did: The Terafin bowed with complete and sincere respect to the Exalted of Cormaris. The Lord of the Compact followed, but he clearly wasn't used to the simple physical act of bending in the middle. Or at all.

"Who knows now matters not; more will know than we could possibly deal with before this matter is closed. This does not grant dispensation for any further spread of this tale by anyone in this room—or in House Terafin." He turned to Jewel, then, his expression grave and remote. "Young one, we believe your story, although we wish it were otherwise. Son of Reymaris?"

"I concur," was the short reply.

"Daughter of the Mother?"

"I also concur." She looked at Jewel with something like sympathy, but it was marred by what might have been a hint of fear, a hint of anger. Jewel thought she might speak, but in the end she merely shook her head and turned to face the Kings.

"Your Majesties, I speak for the Triumvirate."

"As is your right," King Reymalyn said.

The Exalted of the Mother nodded; she did not bow or scrape to the Kings, then or ever. "What would you have of us?"

The Kings now exchanged a glance before King Reymalyn spoke. "If there were another way, we would ask nothing. But it seems to us that the crypt of the Sleepers must be disturbed if Allasakar," and here, all of the Exalted drew sharp breath; they did not, however, admonish this half brother, this scion of gods, "is not to walk again. We would ask that you open the Sanctum to our forces."

The Exalted daughter of the Mother now lowered her head. She was silent for a full minute. When she raised it, she said, "It will not be an easy task, and the Triumvirate alone cannot accomplish it; we must bespeak the Church of Cartanis and the Church of Mandaros, and their leaders must be in agreement.

"There are reasons why the very ground would deny a making or an unmaking, such as our enemies have done, that did not have the keys of the gods behind it. All keys."

King Reymalyn nodded, as if this information were not a surprise. "Let it be done," he said quietly.

"As you command."

Jewel watched the Kings depart. The Queens left with them, as did the Astari. The Terafin left the Exalted upon their thrones; they would not, it was clear, remain there for long. But she did not return immediately through the halls of *Avantari* to the Terafin carriages that waited; she followed Devon instead.

He led them through the large and beautiful halls seen by visiting dignitaries, passing through the almost awe-inspiring galleries as if they were beneath notice. Jewel struggled to do the same, but she was weary enough to let light's play catch her eyes as she walked. Devon showed no signs of impatience; he slowed his graceful walk, waiting and occasionally commenting on the history of whichever item caught her attention.

Eventually, he led them to a set of very fine doors, and he opened them. A man who looked much like any other intimidating official Jewel had ever met looked up from his desk—and if desks had a secret longing to be something dramatic, like a fortress, it was this one. But the man caught sight of Devon and resumed his seat with a precise nod that implied a certain amount of grudging respect.

Devon led them to a large office that was in keeping with the public offices of House Terafin. No one, however, was in it. He crossed the room to the much more subdued desk and sank into the chair behind it, indicating the three other chairs that faced him. "You took a risk," he said to his Lord.

"I was not the author of that risk."

Jewel winced. She had taken a chair and vacated it immediately; moving toward the tall, fine windows that hinted at escape. But The Terafin's expression wasn't severe; it didn't radiate disapproval or disappointment. Or maybe that was just wishful thinking on Jewel's part, because she very, very much wished that she hadn't backed herself into that corner with the cold and autocratic Lord of the Compact. "I'm sorry," she said, cheeks red. "But thanks for covering for me. I owe you."

The Terafin looked at her for longer than was comfortable and then glanced at Devon, who shrugged very slightly, his lips turning up in an odd smile. It was Devon who broke the silence. "I don't think you understand. Did you think she was merely trying to save you some time at the hands of the Lord of the Compact?"

Since that's exactly what The Terafin had done, Jewel stared at Devon in silence, trying to sift through his words to get at their meaning.

"The name ATerafin is not offered lightly, and it is never offered in jest or in subterfuge. You are ATerafin, Jewel. This is no game."

You are ATerafin, Jewel.

The words hung in the air as if the voice were ink and they were written there in a fine, strong hand. A hand, she thought, like Rath's. She looked at the woman who had been his sister, a woman who had betrayed him by becoming ATerafin, and a woman whom he had never forgiven.

But unforgiven, he had trusted her enough to write her the letter that had started Jewel's life in Terafin. That letter had led to this meeting, to all of the many meetings that had simultaneously terrified her and made her feel that her endeavors were useful, even necessary.

She had imagined—in daydreams and in the odd and debilitating nightmare—the day in which she would be called into The Terafin's presence and offered the House Name. She had assumed it would be offered only if she succeeded in whatever larger-than-life goal The Terafin had set, that the name was the symbol of passing the test.

She had imagined, as well, what she would tell her den when she accepted, because in her daydreams, she had always accepted. This was like none of those times.

Had she thought it a lie? Yes. But it had been a lie offered to protect her from the most intimidating man she had ever met. Now, looking at The Terafin's face, she understood what that assumption was: a small slap in the face. It was the *House Name*, and this woman was the House.

She had offered the House protection to Jewel because Jewel was finally, somehow, worthy of it.

But she didn't feel any different. In her daydreams, everything was shining and clear; she had proved her worth. She had earned a place, and she felt as if she belonged there.

Here, in clothing that chafed her neck, surrounded by the walls of the intimidating *Avantari*, she accepted that daydreams were just that. The truth was never all of one thing or all of the other. She had proved her worth to the House—she must have—but she still felt the same insignificant and helpless Jewel Markess that she was the day she'd tried to rob Rath.

No, she thought, the day she'd *succeeded*.

The Terafin had already begun to speak with Devon, as if the matter were decided. And it was: Jewel was no fool. Or not more of one than her Oma had often called her. She wanted the House Name; it meant safety for the den. Whatever else it meant, she'd leave to the future, because the conversation wasn't such that she could interrupt it with a frenzy of questions. Which was hard.

"Because," Devon was saying, "the Sleepers are history, and they have slept, unchanged and unchanging, forever. I do not believe that our enemies somehow missed this entrance into the undercity; I believe they unmade it, as they unmade the rest. But the Exalted believe that the unmaking was rejected, as all known attempts to change the Sleepers have been—in a slow and subtle reworking that a mage in haste would miss completely. It is almost as if time itself guards them."

"They unmade the way," Jewel said quietly, "and the protection around the Sleepers unmade their unmaking."

Devon nodded in quiet approval, but then again, everything he did suggested quiet. It was a good quiet. "Yes."

"Then . . . they don't know."

"That is our hope. And we believe that it is our only hope."

"No."

Jewel and The Terafin turned toward this new speaker; Devon's reaction was entirely different, and later, Jewel might find it funny. Now, she was shocked and silent as he threw himself out of his chair, rolling along the ground to the flat of his feet as if there were demons in the room. Both of his hands had sprouted daggers, which she saw for an eyeblink before they left his hands, flying in the direction of the stranger's face.

They never reached her. She didn't so much as lift a hand or move to stop them; they simply froze in the air an inch away from her open eyes and fell.

"Well met, Devon ATerafin," She raised her hands. "I come in peace; I mean no harm." She now removed the hood that obscured much of her face; the hood was a deep—and familiar—midnight blue.

Jewel had seen the exact robe once before, and recently, but the voice was wrong. So was the face that the fallen hood now exposed. This woman was older than The Terafin, although her hair was still raven black, shot through with one white streak. Her eyes were a striking violet, a color that Jewel could not remember seeing on anyone else; she was not lovely. She was, however, intimidating in a way that even The Terafin was not.

"I am Evayne."

"And I am The Terafin." The Terafin lifted two fingers, as if in design, and Devon resumed his seat. "I do not . . . recognize you."

"No? But we've met. A long, long time ago. I was a youth, Terafin, and you were a combatant."

The Terafin did not assume that this stranger was mistaken; she was silent for a moment. "The robes."

Evayne nodded.

"Seer. You are . . . much aged."

"Yes. I am." She turned then to look at Jewel, who did not shrink back, although it took effort. "Jewel. You have not yet made the pilgrimage, and if I am not mistaken and my memory does not fail me, you will."

So much for effort. Jewel didn't realize she'd stepped back until she felt the wall against her shoulder blades. There was a threat in the words the woman had spoken, even if the words hadn't been spoken to threaten. It was hard to believe that this woman had once been frightened enough to run, leading two foreigners to the protection of The Terafin Chosen.

How much could a person change?

How much could Jewel?

"You are young," Evayne continued. "Younger than I was when I was left upon that road." The faintest hint of what might have been either sympathy or pity transformed her features briefly. "But enough. My time is brief; if the Lord of the Path is willing, I will meet you ere this battle's fought."

"Put them away, Devon." The Terafin's voice was both soft and chilly. "I believe that if the seer wished us dead, we would be."

Evayne raised a dark brow, and offered just the faintest hint of disapproval. "I am no threat to the Crowns you defend, Astari."

The single word dropped into the room as if it were part of the ceiling.

Devon did not deny her. The Terafin had called her seer. But he said, "How did you know that I am Astari? It is not . . . common knowledge."

"I've met you many times, ATerafin, and in many situations. This is one of the most peaceful, and it may be the last; it is not given to me to know my future."

"I've never seen you before in my life."

"No. You have not." She turned from him. Unfortunately, she turned toward Jewel, and she reached into her robes. When she pulled her hand clear, it carried a globe that lit the room, although its light was laced with shadow, like the roiled light of brilliant clouds. "Jewel, or Jay if you prefer, I know who you are. Look at me carefully, and look at what I hold. Then tell them what it is."

They already knew, Jewel thought, glancing at The Terafin's expression. "It's a—it's a seer's ball."

"Very well. But what, exactly, is a seer's ball? A crystal? A globe of blown glass for use by charlatans? Come, Jewel." The words were compelling, although they were soft, almost quiet. Jewel looked to The Terafin, almost hiding behind the House Name that was now hers.

But this time The Terafin nodded. So she faced the orb in the seer's hand, as the room got colder. She did not want to look into the orb itself;

she was willing to glance at it, but her glance slid away, as if it were a captive bird in a new cage.

"Jewel."

A captive bird in a new cage with a new owner pressing her nose through the bars. She looked. Glanced away. And then she took a deep breath and looked at Evayne for permission, which was strange given that the order had come from her.

But Evayne seemed to understand Jewel's hesitation—which was impressive, because Jewel didn't—and for the first time, a small smile touched her lips. It was not a warm one, but it was better than nothing.

And there, in the heart of the folding, brilliant storm, she found the girl she had first seen, and she found, as well, the face of one of the two foreign lords; he looked friendly, and sympathetic, but he did not speak. She found the face of a man who had seen battle, judging by the scars; he was not young, but he, too, smiled, in the way the old smiled at those they thought much younger. She found no name for either man in the crystal itself, but she didn't need one; for a moment, she *knew* who they were.

Or who they were to Evayne. Evayne a'Nolan.

She saw a boy the age of Teller, with a broad face and a mischievous smile; she saw an older woman, face careworn the way her mother's had been before she died, and an older man, who smiled; she liked the sound of his voice, although she hadn't actually heard him speak. But he smoked a pipe, too.

She saw the Master Bard of Senniel College, his face twisted in rage and pain and made slender by time—for he was young, here. She saw him older as well, the man she had seen sing in the ruins of the Cordufar manse—that face, she would never forget. Older still, his voice unchanged by time, she saw him gentled and softened by age. Kallandras. She saw more, felt more.

Fear had no face, but it grew as she touched the lives of people she knew would die. The lives of people she wanted desperately to save—but whose death might bring the only hope the world might have in the face of the—the Lord of the Hells.

All her life was given to that fight, that war. All of their lives, given as well. There was no mercy left in her, but there was pain. Guilt. Jewel knew guilt better than anyone—or so she'd thought.

But there was hope as well, and if it was slender, if it demanded the sacrifice of almost everything, it remained, and it was in its way one of the most beautiful things that Jewel had ever touched; she couldn't see it, but she could feel its strength.

Even now, with Allasakar on the threshold, it did not dim.

At her back, Jewel heard Devon clear his throat as if at a great remove. She startled slightly and looked up from the orb in the seer's hands to meet the startling violet of the older woman's eyes. The face she saw was not the face of the woman who lived within the crystal; it was a mask, and it was meant for the inspection of others. But for a moment, it looked wrong. There was no weakness in that face, no doubt, no hesitation.

Yet Jewel had seen it; she knew it existed.

"Tell them," she said quietly, in a voice so low only Jewel could hear it. "Tell them what it is."

"I'm not even sure I—"

"Yes. You are. Find the words for the certainty."

Jewel nodded slowly and turned to face the woman who had given her the name of her House. "It's her heart."

Chapter Seventeen

IF SHE EXPECTED MOCKERY—and in her den, she would have received some—she was to be disappointed; The Terafin gave the slightest of nods and said nothing.

But Evayne reached out and caught Jewel's chin, turning it toward her with the tips of her fingers. "And can you read it?"

Jewel nodded and turned again to The Terafin. "I—I'd trust her. I already do." She looked at Evayne. "This—it was made by you."

But Evayne shook her head and offered a tired smile. Or a sad one. At her age, it was often the same thing. "No, Jewel. It was made *of* me. I walked the Oracle's path; I passed the Oracle's test. And she passed mine."

Jewel wanted to ask what test Evayne had set for the Oracle. It didn't occur to her to ask who the Oracle was; not then. But it was The Terafin who spoke, and Evayne had not opened herself—her heart—to The Terafin.

"The Oracle. You walked her path." She glanced at Jewel and then at Devon before her eyes returned to the glowing orb in Evayne's hand. What Jewel had seen, it was clear The Terafin could not. "They called this a soul-crystal, a soul-shard. I remember my grandfather's stories. Is it like all stories? Does it lose its romance and power as you approach its reality?"

"It loses none of its power," Evayne replied, with a bitter, sharp flash of a smile, "and all of its romance." She turned once again to Jewel. "I thank you, little sister. And I hope—although in truth, I fear there is little chance of it—that you will not bear a like burden in your day."

Jewel heard truth in every word. *I don't think I could. I don't think I have it in me to do what you've done. Even if the world would end tomorrow if I didn't.*

Evayne shook her head slightly, and then she curved her palms over the orb and enfolded it, once again, within her robes. Jewel found the robes hard to watch as they swallowed light, and she realized only then how very unnatural they were. She reached out and then pulled back as Evayne turned, drawing herself up to a height that Jewel saw was not much greater than her own.

"You have in your dwelling a foreign noble," she said to The Terafin.

"Yes. We believe he is of import."

"He is. But he is the weapon, not the swordsman; know how to wield him and when to let him fly. It matters little who else is chosen, but Lord Elseth must be sent to the Sanctum when the way is open." She turned, then, to Devon. "You have at court a young bard. Bring him as well."

"I see. She is to send, and I am to bring? You do not know The Terafin."

"It will not be easy, and it will not be simple, but the ways must be opened and the path must be walked. Jewel, you and I will meet again ere this long battle is over. But time is of the essence." She smiled, but it was a brief, strange smile. Jewel understood why only seconds later: Evayne took one step toward them and vanished. No sign of her presence remained.

10th of Henden, 410 A. A.
Terafin Manse, Averalaan Aramarelas

No one who lived and worked within the manse would leave it on their normal rounds of business. Business, such as it was, was *not* normal. Those who lived in the manse but were obliged for reasons of employ to leave, braved the streets. Finch was one of them. Before she had set foot out of the West Wing, she was surrounded by House Guards; Torvan had come to her quarters in person to escort her to the Merchant Authority.

Teller hugged her, briefly and fiercely, as she walked out the doors; she worked not to clench both her jaw and her shoulders, and she greeted Torvan with what she hoped was a smile. If it was, it was worn pretty thin around the edges.

"You're certain you're needed in the Authority today?" Torvan asked. It was almost a ritual, these days.

"Lucille told me she'd see me tomorrow."

He grimaced. But he didn't argue—not with Finch, at any rate. He had asked to have a few words with Lucille, and she had, in ill temper, told him she would clear time on her schedule for this morning. That had been four days ago.

"Very well," he said. "Come. At this rate, we'll be late."

The voices that poured out of the ground could now be heard almost as far as the bay; they could be heard in all of the lower holdings, and all of the middle ones as well. The Kings' men roved the streets in their bright armor and their tabards—with the prominently crossed rod and sword front and center—in an attempt to keep peace.

But peace was hard to find. The agony and the utter terror of disembodied voices made every turn of the corner the moment—in dreams—in which you enter nightmare and nothing is in your control anymore. Finch, like most of the den, knew those nightmares. Hers were almost always of the family that had deserted her, a kinder way of saying: sold.

These were worse. As Jay had said they would be.

There were only a few safe places in which the voices could not be heard, a few alcoves of sanity and reason, and given the masses that now huddled in each—or stood at their steps, waiting their turn to worship, pray, or breathe—sanity and reason were in terribly short supply. The screams of the dying, and those who were about to die, came at all hours of the day or night. They would stop for hours at a time, as if to tease hope into being just so they could crush it utterly.

It was into that city that Finch now went, as she went every day. The bridge that she took led to the street nearest the bay. It did not lead directly to the Common, although if you followed it for long enough, it led to the Port, and for that reason, it was usually sparsely populated.

It also, however, led to the Sanctum of Moorelas, and if you could—avoiding only the fall of his shadow—huddle at his feet, or around them, the voices dropped off into a blessed silence.

The crowd that huddled closest to Moorelas' imposing and unchanging statue now were definitely *not* silent, nor were they remotely peaceful. Men and women exchanged angry words in their attempt to reach what they now considered the Blessing of Moorelas; some of the boys closer to Finch's age were exchanging blows. Torvan caught her by the shoulder and pulled her squarely into the center of the formation of House Guards; his expression was grim.

People were not yet so insane with terror that they were willing to treat the House Guard the way they treated their neighbors, but it was close. Every single day, it was closer. Finch shut her eyes for just a moment, took a deep, deep breath, and straightened. It was chilly; the wind was strong, even with a wall of human bodies between much of it and her.

But she understood those people.

She could hear screaming. A young voice, young enough to be her own—if she were in the Hells. Someone was weeping in the background; you could hear it whenever the victim drew breath, because that was the only time there was even a bit of a lull.

Finch struggled not to cover her ears with her hands; it never worked, anyway. But it was hard. Closer to the Merchant Authority, the sound was stronger than a human voice in that much pain could possibly be; it bounced off walls, cobblestones, and windows, gaining strength the way wind did between tall buildings.

She was pale when she reached the Authority building, but so was anyone who had made the trek to their place of work; the floors were—for the Authority—all but deserted. The streets? Emptier, given it was the Common. But new people had made their homes on the various street corners—or in front of the closed stalls that merchants had abandoned for the duration—and they spoke of the End of the World in bright and livid language. One of them had the temerity to shout at Torvan and curse The Ten for their arrogance and their something-or-other. He spoke loudly—he had to—but even his loud and grating voice was often drowned out in midsyllable.

Still, it was the only other voice she could easily hear as she made her way up the stairs and onto the floor, moving toward the third floor office in which the merchant arm of House Terafin had taken up permanent residence. Their doors had been closed, but it didn't dim the noise of the dying at all. Nothing, Finch thought, would.

Elevation did nothing to dampen the screaming. They walked quickly down the hall and then up the stairs and reached the doors that bore the prominent Terafin crest.

Finch's escort didn't bother to knock; there was no point. Knocks couldn't be heard over the screams and the low, low moans. Lucille, who demanded manners, was nevertheless a practical woman.

Finch, however, went in first. Lucille was at her desk, her shoulders slightly slumped—but tense, as if she were pushing against something that was resisting. Her skin was the same pale color that Finch's probably was, and her lower lids were adorned with almost black semicircles. But she smiled—if tiredly—when she saw Finch. The smile froze in place when she saw Torvan standing behind her.

Torvan remained in the office for forty-five tight-lipped minutes before the screaming stopped. "We have," he said, when he could hear himself without shouting—and Finch knew he could make himself heard as easily as Lucille could, which meant he didn't want everything he said to *be* heard, "an appointment."

"We do. We can use Jarven's office," Lucille added, rising.

"Jarven's not in?"

"Of course he's in. He's downstairs talking to the skittish dolts in the Authority proper to avoid riots on the wrong damn sides of the wicket."

Torvan found the screaming as unbearable as Finch did, but when the voices at last fell silent, he felt the profound failure of those responsible for keeping people safe. As a House Guard, he was expected to keep this reaction to himself, and as a House Guard, he was second to none. "ATerafin," he said crisply.

Lucille raised a brow and sank into the chair that the absent Jarven usually claimed. "You wanted to speak with me?"

"I do."

"About?"

"Finch."

Lucille rose. Torvan was almost surprised. "What about Finch," she said, her back toward him as she inspected the windows.

He hesitated. Lucille and doubt were so far apart they might have waged war across Imperial borders. But at the moment, they seemed to have reached an armistice, and he felt some of his anger dissipate. "I don't think she should be here," he finally said.

"If what we hear—what we hear *every damn day*—is any indication, there's no safety. At all." Her hands reached out for the edges of the curtain and ran across the tassels.

"Agreed. But if there is no guarantee of safety, there is peace. The Isle has not—yet—been subject to the spells of the enemy."

"Spells of the enemy?" She spit the words out, as if they were so bitter she couldn't stand to have them in her mouth. "Is that what you call the last words of the dying?" She turned to him, then, and he saw the dark circles beneath her eyes as a frame for their sudden reddening.

"No."

"And you think she won't be aware of it, she won't think about it? Out of sight, out of mind, is that it? You think she's that kind of person?"

Torvan almost took a step back. It did not, however, help when dealing with Lucille ATerafin. "No. She is, however, human. She is not a fool; she knows the only peace those faceless voices will ever have now is death. And silence becomes that peace."

Lucille's shoulders stiffened as she drew breath. But it was not Lucille ATerafin who answered.

"It is not Lucille's decision," Jarven ATerafin said. "It is mine."

Torvan turned to see the older man standing in the doorway; he had not heard the door open.

"Jarven—" Lucille began as she turned to face her superior, but Jarven lifted a hand, his robes draping loosely at his wrist.

"You are not presenting any information that Lucille herself has not already brought forth, and, I might add, you are being much more circumspect in your concern." He raised a brow as Lucille's eyes narrowed. "It is not, however, her decision."

"So you've said," Torvan replied. "May I know why you made this choice?"

"You are not speaking for The Terafin, are you?"

"No. But I am—"

"Chosen, yes, yes. I'm aware of that." He moved past Torvan and took his chair. "Am I in enough trouble," he asked Lucille, "that I must do without tea?"

She rolled her eyes and headed toward the door.

"Please," Jarven said to Torvan, indicating a chair. "I'm not entirely comfortable with armed men towering above me in my own office."

It was not entirely comfortable to sit while kitted out for duty, but Torvan did manage. He knew Jarven's reputation, but aside from the occasional surprise that anyone would willingly share space with Lucille ATerafin, he did not otherwise have cause to think about him often.

"You've been with the House for several years now," Jarven said. "And you've served under the current Terafin for the duration. You are perhaps more aware than I of what she intends for the young unknown, Jewel Markess."

"She is no longer Markess," Terafin replied carefully.

"Pardon?"

"She is Jewel ATerafin."

This momentarily silenced Jarven, a man not known for his inability to find words at need. Lucille had time to arrive and set his tea tray down in front of him with a little more force than necessary before she retreated. She did not, however, slam the door.

"Is this fact known?" Jarven finally asked.

"It is not widely known," Torvan replied. "But if the name is offered directly by The Terafin, rather than through the right-kin and the general application process, the House Council is not required to—"

"Ratify it, yes. I am aware of that." He was silent while he stirred his tea. When he looked up, his gaze was sharper. "Is Finch aware of this change in status?"

It was not the question Torvan had expected. He considered it for a moment. It had never occurred to him that Jewel would keep the change a secret, but Jarven's question made the possibility suddenly seem probable. "I believe I begin to understand your reputation."

"Reputation can be useful," Jarven replied. "I note you haven't answered the question. I am, however, a merciful man. If I were a betting man, I would place a large sum on the fact that she does not, in fact, know. Which would imply that none of her friends do."

Torvan was silent.

"I have little acquaintance with Jewel Markess; I have observed her only briefly, and only at a distance. All of my knowledge is derived from my association with Finch, who takes no family name. I asked about her family's name, once," he added. "It is not a question I will repeat.

"But it cannot have escaped your notice, Chosen, that the guards assigned to Finch are not House Guards; they are Chosen. Finch was not sent here because we required aid or were short of possible employees; she was sent because The Terafin wished her to train in the Merchant Authority, to train, at best guess, under either myself, if I am egotistical, or Lucille, which I sadly think the more likely.

"Teller, also of Jewel's den, was sent to Barston in the right-kin's office. A stiffer, more formal man could not be found in the House. Both of these positions are, of course, quite junior—but it is impossible to work in either office without gaining an understanding of the machinations of House Terafin.

"Why do you suppose those would be of value to The Terafin? A gang of orphans and runaways attempting to conform to House standards? The answer must lie, in part, with the leader. The leader who is now ATerafin.

"But that same leader has apparently taken pains to either hide or ignore the name. She has certainly not seen fit to share her good news. Why would that be?" He waved a hand as Torvan opened his mouth, and Torvan sighed inwardly and shut up. "I believe she feels that the change in status would put distance between them. She doesn't want it. She trusts Finch and Teller—I would say she trusts them all, but I infer this from Finch's behavior.

"The Terafin is willing to give that trust absolute weight. She could have sent Jewel to work in either the Authority or the right-kin's office; she did not. She considered both Finch and Teller to be somehow crucial to Jewel. Thus, Finch is here.

"Am I to second guess The Terafin?"

"No, but when she sent Finch to the Authority, no one had any idea what would follow in this wretched month of Henden. She did not intend to place Finch in—" he bit back the word he had been about to offer.

"Yes, it is true," Jarven replied, almost serene. "She had no idea. But she has not seen fit to recall Finch. Finch arrives every day with her coterie of Chosen; Finch leaves every day with the same. If The Terafin were concerned for the girl's well-being, if she felt the girl incapable of handling the very stressful situation, she would have pulled her out."

"No," Torvan replied sharply. "She would have asked you for your assessment."

Jarven smiled and nodded once, as if Torvan had done something particularly clever. It was grating; Torvan, unlike Finch, was not a child. "She did, indeed. And I offered it." He had not drunk his tea, but he rose. "Finch will be Jewel's eyes and ears in the hundred holdings, albeit the richer ones at the moment.

"She is, as Lucille says, a good girl. She sees, hears, and in the end, reports. Jewel is now ATerafin, and at a very young age; what service she has already rendered the House is known. But The Terafin intends larger things for her; the placement of her den-kin makes this clear.

"I am fond of the girl—of Finch. But she has a spine; she is not skittish without cause. She is cautious, yes. If she is to serve Jewel ATerafin, she cannot afford to be sheltered or treated like a wilting flower. She is not that," he added. "No, she is not immune to the cries of the tortured and the dying. Neither is Lucille. You would never subject Lucille to this condescension.

"Let Finch remain," he added. "Let her see what occurs in the Authority in times of near panic. Or possibly times of total panic. It is an experience that will be a foundation for any other involvement she has in the House." He walked to the door and opened it. "I am still a busy man, and I appreciate your time and your concern. If, after you have considered my words, you still cling to your opinion, we can discuss it." He paused, then offered Torvan a pained smile. "I am also being somewhat selfish in this. Lucille finds the situation . . . difficult. She is not a woman who is accustomed to doing nothing; nor is she a woman for whom anything is completely impossible often.

"While Finch is here, she focuses her worry on Finch. Yes, she coddles the child too much, but the alternative, for Lucille, is to throw her considerable weight behind a problem that no one—perhaps not even the Exalted—can solve. And that," he added softly, "would not be to the benefit of the Merchant Authority offices."

"No luck?" Lucille asked Torvan when the doors had closed at his back.

He glanced at her and then grimaced, shaking his head. "I'll be back at the end of the day."

Finch was already seated to one side of Lucille's desk. She now had her own modest desk, but she was seldom to be found there. He found himself liking Lucille, which was almost shocking. "Keep an eye on her," he heard himself say. "Jarven was adamant that she remain."

Lucille nodded. "She's not well read," she said in a quiet voice, as if her exhaustion had loosened her tongue. "And when she came through those doors, she couldn't add two small numbers together. She had no understanding of the basics of finance and trading, and while she has those now, she slides off the complexities.

"But she works. She works hard. Jarven—although he won't admit it—is very fond of her, and she eases his daily routine. Mostly," she added sourly, "by giving him someone attentive to talk at. I wasn't certain about her."

Lucille wasn't certain about anyone; she was famed for her uncertainty.

"She comes from nowhere, she has nothing. But it doesn't slow her down. It also doesn't make her ambitious," she added, using the word as if it were the harshest of invective. "But this—"

"She would be suffering no matter where she was," Torvan replied. He surprised himself with what he said next. "Because had she not somehow made her way to the manse, she would hear it. She would hear it, likely, in the cold, with little to no food, no wood for fire, no fire for light."

"Jarven got to you, didn't he?"

Torvan grimaced. "Yes. I didn't understand the many ways in which he achieved the reputation he has; he is subtle." This seemed to please Lucille, who was still, however, annoyed with Jarven. People could often be contrary. "But here, she remembers what she would have had—or wouldn't have had—and she knows, better than you or I, exactly what the holdings suffer now. I think hiding her at the manse—my word, not Jarven's—might only add to the guilt she feels at her undeserved good fortune.

"And she has small shoulders for a burden of that size."

Lucille hesitated before exhaling loudly, which caused Finch to look up. "That's the first reasonable thing anyone has said about the situation," she finally told Torvan. "And coming from a House Guard. Who would have thought?"

Business, Torvan thought, with mild irritation, as usual.

11th of Henden, 410 A. A.
Merchant Authority, Averalaan

Finch worked.

When the silence broke—and it did, it always did—she froze, her hands on a quill, paper beneath it. She didn't close her eyes; she didn't cover her ears. The first day she'd heard the screaming, she had leaped up from the desk in panic, and she'd run to the windows. But so had everyone else. Everyone but Jarven ATerafin.

That had been what felt like years ago. It wasn't. If she really wanted to, she could count the actual number of days. In the days that had followed the first one, when people had begun to realize that the voices were not actually physically close—and certainly not close enough to receive the succor or the rescue they deserved—she had done both: closed her eyes, covered her ears. Dropped her quill or the papers she was stacking or the books she was carrying. She had almost dropped the tea service, but Lucille was there to steady her.

And, to be fair, to remind her just how much the dishes had cost the Authority offices, down to the last copper.

The days had passed, and the screams had grown louder—which Finch would have bet was impossible. Sometimes they were all she could hear. Even in the silence, they echoed. But she no longer attempted to plug her ears, mostly because it did nothing. She didn't close her eyes because in the darkness behind her lids, the voices were the *only* things in the world, and that made it worse.

She swallowed, she tensed, and then she kept moving.

There had been what Lucille called a small contingent of armed men patrolling the Common. Finch had gone to see, because they passed by the windows of the office, and she decided that the word *small* was obviously one that had a different meaning for Lucille than it would have had for the den. "Are they going to stop it?"

"Stop it? Oh. No, dear; if there were anything on earth that could have done that, it would be finished by now. They're here to keep the peace. Such as it is."

"But from what?"

"From us," was the quiet reply. "People are stupid when they're frightened. Stupid people forget consequences and costs; they're so caught up in their fear they can't think about the future." She hesitated and then said, "One of the Southern Offices was set on fire during the night. No one was there," she added, "so no one died. The Kings' Swords are here to make sure there's no repeat in any other office while people can die. Go back to the desk, dear. There's nothing to see here."

Here.

But what about the rest of the holdings? What about the twenty-fifth? Finch started to ask, but she stopped, because she thought she already knew the answer. Jay was the angry one, had always been the angry one—but Finch felt some of Jay's anger now. Maybe because she had someplace warm to sleep and enough food to eat. She shook herself and returned to the desk.

At the desk, she picked up her quill, centered the paper on which she was to write something. Anything. A report. She wrote the date and stopped. Henden. Of course it was Henden. The eleventh, yes; it was not yet a return to the six dark days that marked the end of the year.

That had marked the end of the year so long ago it had never felt real, although she, like any child born in Averalaan, had observed the Six Days. In the Common during the Six Days, business slowed to a trickle; it never completely halted. The foreigners continued their trade, and some of the ambitious merchants would hire them to work. But for most of the city, the banners and shrouds came out; the food became simple and sparse. Not that it wasn't usually simple and sparse in Finch's experience, or her previous experience. She hadn't thought about what it would be like, those six days, in House Terafin. Would the food stop?

If the screaming stopped, Finch thought, on the edge of a prayer, she would find a way to live without the food. It was the eleventh, not the twenty-third. If the Dark Days hadn't even arrived, how much worse would they be this year? The city would be consumed by them. The Kings' Swords couldn't stop fear from spreading; they would add to it, yes—becoming just another thing to fear.

"Lucille?"

Lucille was by her side like a looming shadow—but it was a shadow, conversely, made of light and warmth and solidity. Finch, like Jewel, didn't like to be touched or held, not by people she didn't absolutely trust. But she almost turned and threw herself into this woman's arms. Didn't, because she was in the office, and she had work to do.

"Yes, Finch. I'm here."

"The Dark Days." Finch looked up.

"Yes. Almost upon us, not that there's been much preparation for the celebration at their end." Lucille shook her head. "But they *did* end. Remember that, if you can. The darkness, the fear, the terror that gripped this poor city—it ended when Veralaan returned."

Veralaan had been the only heir to the Blood Baron who ruled the country that had not—quite—been an Empire. The Baron was mageborn, Finch recalled, although some stories placed him as the scion of demons. He'd died, and left one living child as heir. Every noble in the Barony had circled her like carrion creatures, demanding her hand—and through it, control of the Barony itself. But Veralaan had disappeared for *one night*, and when she returned, she brought two sons, two fifteen-year-old sons, and she had resigned her claim to the throne in their favor. And one look at either child might explain much: They had eyes of gold. God-born, both, and Veralaan greatly aged in her single night's absence.

The sons of her body, the first Twin Kings of the Empire, did not inherit in peace; they fought battle after battle to hold their mother's birthright. The first Wisdom-born King. The first Justice-born King. Cormalyn. Reymalyn. Sons of gods, they vowed to rule the Empire wisely and justly.

"There's no Veralaan now," Finch whispered.

"No. Maybe there never was; old stories are strange that way. But . . . the Kings are still god-born, and they still rule. While they live and rule, they fulfill their fathers' mandate. It isn't over, yet, Finch. It's dark, yes." Lucille turned her face away for a moment, but Finch saw the tightening of her mouth and the lines around the corners of her eyes; she swallowed her pain.

"It will get darker, gods know how. But the darkness ends, every Advent. We celebrate Veralaan's return. Hells, the city bears her name, and she was just as human, and just as talentless, as most of us. You, me. It's hard to hope," she added, lowering her voice. "And it hurts. But without it? We have riots, and we kill each other in terror and anger."

Finch tried a smile. It shattered on a sob—not hers, but the faceless sob of a dying man. Or a dying boy—it was hard to tell. He was screaming for his mother.

"It's hard to wait," Lucille added. "It's harder than anything I've ever done. Look at me. I'm used to getting things *done*, Finch. Just to stand back, to wait with the helpless as if I'm one of them—" She shook her head.

And for just a moment, Finch could see a familiar face, a familiar expression, in the lines of the older, stouter woman: Jay's face.

"Waiting is always hard. I sometimes think the fighting—and the dying that comes with it—would be easier because I'd be *doing* something. But I've learned how to wait. Hardest thing I've learned. How to wait, with grace. How to know when I *can* make a difference, and when I have to trust someone else—someone I can't see or damn well speak to or at—to make that difference for me."

"I want you to meet Jay," Finch said.

Lucille raised a brow.

"She could say that. What you said. I mean, she couldn't—but—" she shook her head. "But I think she needs to learn what you've learned. I think you could teach her."

Lucille surprised Finch with the gift of her open laughter. It played out against the shattered and shattering sobs. "That's not a lesson you can teach," she told Finch. "If the girl's anything at all like I was, she'd probably stab me for trying."

Finch looked shocked—because she was—and Lucille laughed harder. If there was an edge of hysteria to the laughter, it didn't matter; it had been so damn long since Lucille had laughed, and Finch wanted the anchor of that sound. "But I've a mind to meet this Jay of yours anyway. Not to give her advice she'd spit at, mind, but to thank her. She kept you safe, girl. And this office would be pretty bloody unbearable without you, at the moment."

Pain swallowed mirth, and the warmth guttered. The problem with the office was that there was hardly any business-as-usual; they were waiting here, in the safety of the Authority, with the guards lining the stairs in such numbers a normal merchant would be hard pressed to make his or her way through the thicket of their arms.

And all the while the man, or the boy pain had turned him into, begged and cried and screamed.

There was no silence coming; not for an hour or more. There was work, but Lucille called it make-work, which had seemed so odd to Finch in her first week but made so much sense now. But to work seemed almost an act of trivialization, to both of them, even though Lucille said sharply, "There's nothing we can do. At all. We might as well do *something*."

No wonder people were slowly going mad all across the hundred holdings. Finch, at the desk, might go mad if she had to endure another day of a stranger's untouchable pain.

But she swallowed. She thought that *every* day. And she came back *every* day. Because Lucille was counting on her. Because Jarven was happy to take tea with her and discuss the minutiae of the office in so much detail even Lucille couldn't keep up a polite facade—not that she was all that good at that anyway.

"Finch." Lucille bent and removed something from Finch's hand; it was the paper on which she'd been making notes. They were silent for a moment, facing each other, and then Lucille very carefully pulled Finch into her arms. Finch didn't even stiffen.

She let herself be held by this bear of a woman, this woman who terrified even the House Guard, and she bit her lip until it bled because it had been days and days and days and the voices were getting louder and there was no end in sight and any of those people, any one of them, could be her *own* kin: Lefty, Fisher, Lander. Gone to the undercity.

Jay hadn't said it. It didn't need to be said. They all knew it. All of them. There was no hope for any of the people who had obviously died so horribly below their damn feet. There was no—

Hope.

Finch heard it first, but not by much; she felt Lucille's arms stiffen and then fall way. "Lucille?"

"Aye," the older woman said. "I heard it, too."

And in case they didn't, it came again: The clear—the absolutely unmistakable—sound of horns being winded. It cut through the screaming for just a moment; it cut through the terror. It wasn't music; it was a call to arms, a call to war. But it was nonetheless possibly the most powerful single note that Finch had ever heard in her life, and she would remember it that way for as long as she lived.

Lucille drew her to the windows that overlooked the street as Jarven uncharacteristically came out of his office to join them.

"Who is it?" Finch asked. "Is it the Kings? Have the Kings come?"

Jarven's smile was gentle and rueful, which meant she was wrong.

"Listen. The horns draw closer. If I am not mistaken, Finch, you will see whose horns are being winded because you will see the standard carried." He frowned slightly and then added, "You *are* being taught to recognize the standards of the Houses—not just The Ten—as well as those of *Avantari*?"

When she looked at him with marked hesitation, he turned to Lucille and said, "That will not do. She will have to learn those as well; we cannot have her cause an incident because she failed to recognize the significance of the nobles she might deal with."

"As opposed to you, who cause incidents with full and total knowledge?"

"Lucille," he said, looking hurt. And then, "Ah. My eyes are not what they once were, Finch. Look, if you can, out the right bay—can you see them now?"

She glanced at Lucille, who said, "He's in charge. If he tells you to climb up into the window and press your face against the panes, I am not in a position to countermand his orders." She hesitated and then said, "Here, let me help."

To Finch's surprise, she did, and Lucille was strong enough to bear her weight as if it were nothing. She started to say something and stopped, because she could see them now: horsed riders, armor glinting in the cold winter sun. A banner flew; the wind in the city wasn't high, and it hung straight, the emblem of the rod and the sword gleaming in the sunlight like gold against a field of blue. Above the crossed symbols of the Justice-born King and the Wisdom-born King was a silver crown with three peaks, the largest of which contained what looked to Finch like a diamond, or like a diamond should look if the stories were true. The leader of the group—for there was one, even if she rode behind the banners—rode a large horse, and it was she who carried the horn, for she stopped in the center of the large semicircle over which the Merchant Authority ruled, and she winded it.

Her armor was like the armor in stories. It was perfect, perfectly shaped; it reflected light, and it seemed to bear writing that glowed, faintly, across its chest. The legs and the arms were in jointed pieces trimmed in gilt; the gauntlets seemed gold, although they couldn't be.

When she lifted her helm, she handed it to someone, and she shook her hair loose; it fell in white-gold plaits, and Finch knew, then, who this must be: Queen Siodonay the Fair, wife to King Reymalyn. The Queen lifted the horn to her lips, and when it sounded, it was the only thing that could be heard in the office. Finch wanted the note to go on forever.

Jarven said, "The Queen Siodonay."

Finch said nothing.

A smaller banner came to rest beside the Queen's banner; it was similar in color and in design, but instead of the Queen's crown, it bore a narrow circlet that glittered in the sun.

"Finch?"

"I don't know."

"Ah. The Princess Royale. The only child not god-born to be granted the Kings in this generation. Nevertheless, it is said she favors her grandfather, Cormaris, Lord of Wisdom. I would not be surprised in the end if this was her idea."

Last came a man in armor, astride a dark horse, who wore not a helmet but a . . . wreath. A golden wreath. No banner was brought for him, so she couldn't be expected to recognize him by his colors, but in this case, she didn't need them. No one who had lived in any part of Averalaan for all his or her life could fail to recognize the wreath. Even if they were so poor they never got to see any of the competitions that led to that wreath, they could line the streets at the height of summer to watch the victors on parade.

Finch said, pointing, "That man—he's won the Kings' Crown!"

"Aye," Lucille said, in an oddly quiet voice, "that he has. And twice. Jarven?"

Finch looked back. Jarven was studying the streets through the window; he appeared to be watching the Queen, but she could see the way his gaze flickered over the gathering crowd.

"Sivari is his name. Verrus Sivari," Jarven told her, without looking away from the streets. "What is the Princess Royale doing?"

Finch looked. She appeared to be standing to the right of the Queen Siodonay.

"Ah," he said softly. "They will speak, Finch. Would you care to accompany me?"

"Jarven," Lucille said sharply.

"It will be a long time before she has another opportunity to hear a Queen speak," he replied with gravity. "And on no other occasion—gods bless us—will the need be so grave. These are the Dark Days," he told her quietly, "upon us, early. And that—that is the face, and the *fact*, of hope. She is wife to King Reymalyn. And it was King Reymalyn and King Coramlyn who delivered us from the Blood Barons, and who built the Empire so that, wise and just, it could withstand its many enemies.

"Come. Siodonay was a warrior before she was a Queen, and you don't get to be called that if you aren't canny and strong-willed." He held out his arm, his elbow toward Finch, and she stared at it for a long moment before she flushed and placed her hand on it.

Lucille said, "I'll mind the office."

"Lucille—"

"I hate crowds, you know that. I'll open the window a sliver; I'll hear anything important. But Jarven—let anything bad happen to her—"

"Yes, yes," he said, but under his breath.

There were, of course, Kings' Swords. They lined the streets, and they watched as people began to gather, drawn at first by the only sound they could hear that was not pain and death, and held by the presence of the Queen and her two companions. Queen Siodonay was tall and fair; she wasn't young, but no one young could have been the Queen she was that day. Finch at once loved her and feared to disappoint her, and Jarven smiled as she slowed.

It was a brief smile.

Queen Siodonay had come, not to give orders, but to begin—early—

the recitation of the Dark Days, the rituals of which had not yet begun. But she did not speak immediately, for beneath the feet of the crowd, imprisoned by earth, stone, and magic, an unseen boy was dying. She didn't pretend he wasn't; she didn't ignore his pain. But she didn't quaver or weep or draw back; that was not why she had come.

As if pain and guilt were a storm, she stood in its center, and she bowed her head slightly, that was all. Her hands fell to her sides, one on the hilt of her sword, and she waited, with a grim and perfect patience that suggested respect for the dying. But if she did not cry out, as so many did, cringing or covering their ears, she did cry; the tears fell freely down her still face.

They were the tears of a Queen; they offered sorrow shorn of terror. People wept to see them, but their terror ebbed. At her side, the Princess Royale remained, head bowed. Her helm was in the crook of one arm; the other rested against the hilt of sheathed sword as if she, too, were ready for battle.

As if this dying, this terrible death, was the battleground.

Only when death offered silence did the Queen raise her horn again, and this time, the notes she blew were different. But Verrus Sivari fell to one knee, and so did the Princess Royale, as those notes played out. They remained kneeling as the Queen's voice rose in the silence. No one knew how long it would last, and this uncertainty made it easier to cling to the harsh clarity of her voice. Siodonay of the North. Siodonay the Fair.

She spoke of the Dark Days.

It was fitting.

The Common had not yet donned the black and white of Imperial Mourning, nor had it divested itself of the flags and the standing boards of the merchants who made it a second home—even if most of those merchants had failed to keep their regular hours for the past week or more. This year, it hardly seemed to matter; paying respects to the victims of past terrors, when the victims of the unknown enemies here and now were so much more real, was first in no one's mind.

But . . . when she spoke of the Dark Days, she *made them* these days. This terror, this fear of certain death, of armies of mages and bloody rains of fire, earth, and ice—these were the Dark Days. No cloth was necessary to mark it; no self-imposed privations were necessary to remind one of what the past might have been like. It had stepped forward to greet them, showing them the starkness of their fear.

She didn't ask them to embrace it. She asked them, instead, to accept it for what it was: the only way their unseen and undeclared enemy could attack them.

Murmurs filled the street around her words; she left pauses for them and picked up her speech again when they had traveled far enough. Her hand never once left the hilt of her sword.

"The heart and soul of man has always been the battleground of our enemies," she said, lifting her voice as if it were the horn that hung by her side. "They cannot storm the streets of our city; they don't have the power. But they can do the work of armies if you surrender to them.

"If you riot in the streets in your terror, no armies will be needed; you will fight—and kill—each other. They need no better weapon than that.

"Do not give it to them. Understand that you are the soldiers upon which Averalaan depends—and has always depended. If we are to win this war—and it is a war, make no mistake—it will be because you have frustrated their desire and their ambition to break the city without ever approaching its walls.

"And you will. They need your fear and your panic; they rely upon them. But your ancestors, your forefathers, faced the darkness, and we remember and honor them every year. This year you will be called upon to do more than honor those memories; you will live up to what they believed and what they hoped for.

"And when Veral returns—as it returns *every* year—the shadow will pass, and you will remember that what *they* fought for and what *they* believed in is, measure for measure, what *you* will now fight for and what you will struggle—in the darkness of hours—to believe in.

"That is what Averalaan is. A city named after a woman who was trained not to sword but to loom and who was expected, because of that lack, to choose a husband who would continue to break and destroy her people.

"The path she chose none foresaw—least of all those assured of their power and the fear it engendered. We are *all* her children; we live upon lands that proudly bear her name. War is not always fought upon horseback or in armor, and it is not always won by strength of arms.

"In less than a fortnight, you will find the banners and flags and curtains that have marked our traditions for centuries, and you will lay them out in the shadow of war; we will do likewise. But we will be here on the mainland, among you; we will wait, and we will fight, as we ask you to wait and fight.

"Trust yourselves, even when fear is strongest. We do."

Verrus Sivari and the Princess Royale rose, and they offered a salute very like the one that Torvan offered The Terafin. But they did not offer it to the Queen; they offered it instead, in respect of her words, to the crowd that watched and listened, to the people who had huddled behind closed doors and shuttered windows for most of the day, pretending to work, the way Finch had done, day in and day out since the voices had first spread to the Common.

And Finch felt pride in those attempts for the first time. They were more than just make-work; she understood that now. They were making *sanity*. They were trying to hold on to the motions of everyday life because *it mattered*. She looked up at Jarven, who placed a gentle hand on her shoulder and nodded as if she had spoken.

"Yes," he said, with a smile. It was a weary smile, but it was genuine. He looked back to the Queen, and his smile strengthened. "Yes. Come, Finch."

"Back to work?"

"Back," he said quietly, "to work. While we can, it is important to do so. And," he added, as the crowd began to slowly disperse, "I hope that some merciful god did indeed persuade Lucille to open a window and keep an ear out."

Finch laughed. "Has she been difficult?"

"My dear child, you have no idea." He stopped, and then shook his head. "Or perhaps I fool myself in my old age; it is quite likely that you do. We have a long day ahead of us."

She nodded, and they passed what appeared to be a phalanx of Merchant Authority guards to enter an almost palatially empty floor. Finch glanced at the empty wickets. They'd be filled, she thought. People would come.

And her chair would be filled. Lucille's desk. Jarven's. It wasn't going to win the war—no matter what the Queen implied—but lack of those people wasn't going to *lose* it. Finch swore it to herself, and that was the message she took for her den when she at last met Torvan at the front doors.

Chapter Eighteen

23rd of Henden, 410 A. A.
Terafin Manse, Averalaan Aramarelas

NOT ALL OF THE SERVANTS who worked within the manse itself lived there; many lived on the mainland. The servants' quarters in the Terafin manse were, for the most part, small, and very few were suited to families. But families now huddled in rooms that were not their own, on mattresses or bedrolls set against the walls; the Master of the Household Staff had chosen to overlook this breach of rules, and while little could make that formidable woman loved, this came close.

Merry was busy, of course, but most of the servants—on this side of the wall, where the halls were narrow enough to look normal—were used to the sight of Carver; they shooed him away when they were busy and nodded or exchanged a few polite words when they were on break or off shift. Helen, however, taking care of two very bored children, one of whom was almost walking, waved him into one such cramped room. It was normally hers, and her bed had been shoved as far into the corner as it could go without causing structural damage.

"Come help me," she said.

He held up his hands. "I'm not good with kids—"

"I don't care. In five more minutes, I won't be either."

He laughed and squeezed himself into the room. Merry came by fifteen minutes later and found him on the floor under the wriggling feet of two children; Helen had retreated to the corner for what passed for privacy in these parts. It was a privacy Carver understood; he'd spent most of his life living with that definition, and the manse, with its vast, empty rooms, seemed cold and silent as a crypt in comparison.

"What," Merry said, in a voice that made her name very inappropriate, "are you doing here now?"

"I was sent to help out," he replied.

"Liar."

"Well, yes, sometimes," he said, with a grin. That grin rushed head-on into her thin-lipped frown, and it was the frown that broke first.

"Help us with what?"

"Preparations. For the Dark Days."

"I'm not sure—" she began, and then, in a louder voice, "Helen, Ivyn's got the duster, and he's eating the feathers."

Carver laughed as Helen rolled out of bed, and he took that opportunity to end her needed break, sliding an arm around Merry. "Finch said there are banners and shrouds, and dark curtains for the windows."

"She knows this how?"

"I think she—I think she asked the Master of the Household Staff."

Merry blanched. You could threaten her with serious injury and she'd take a broom to your face—but the Master of the Household Staff was in a category of her own. Along with Lord of the Hells, Carver thought.

"We can't just take—"

"The groundskeepers have been at work," he added. "And the flags are down on the poles. I think they mean to do it."

"Now?"

He nodded. "Now. I'll miss the kitchen staff, though."

Merry grimaced. Food—such as it was during the Dark Days—was strictly rationed for anyone over the age of six, and what there was of it was unpleasant. Flat bread. Brown rice. Dried meat and hard cheese—if you were lucky. If you were unlucky? Same old food you always had. Which was often not much.

"We're not to do the manse," he added. "Just the servants' quarters."

"Most of us don't *have* windows."

He shrugged. "You're supposed to help us—and bring along anyone who's on break to do the same."

"Us?" she asked, with justifiable suspicion.

"The West Wing," he replied. "Ellerson said our choice of decoration is not in the hands of the Household Staff. He also said," Carver added, deepening his voice and sharpening his annunciation, "You may wish to seek aid in the handling of the drapes and the tapestries, Master Carver."

She tried very hard not to laugh and failed miserably. On this side of the wall, she always did. Carver smiled. It had become very hard to make her—or anyone—laugh in the past few weeks; he understood why.

But being grim changed nothing, and if they were all going to die anyway, they might as well try to enjoy the few days remaining. He caught her hand, squeezed it, let it go.

"Let me get changed," she said.

"Can I help?"

"No."

Ellerson watched the den work. Finch was absent, as was Teller. Arann was present, but as he had been on night patrol, he was sleeping. Jewel was absent, as she had been for many of the days, at The Terafin's whim. She left the Wing looking pinched and exhausted, and she returned looking more so; her sleep was, to be charitable, poor. She ate little, drank little, and spoke little, but when she thought the den wasn't watching, she watched them with something that looked like envy.

The kitchen, however, was in use every evening when Teller and Finch returned from work. It was there, listening to them talk about their days, that she relaxed—watching intently, and interrupting them for details.

For herself, she had little to report. Which was unfortunate; Ellerson knew that she was now ATerafin, and also knew that she had chosen to keep that information to herself.

Do you think they won't trust you, Jewel? Do you think they'll fear to be left behind after everything they've done and everything you've done? He said nothing. She had not informed him of the change in her status, and he had not yet decided to broach the subject. But she felt the weight of her secret, if he was any judge; she was not good at keeping her own counsel when she was among her kin.

She was, however, there to help with preparations for the Dark Days. She was strict about food, which caused Jester and Carver to grimace; she was strict about light—the lamps were forbidden, and she threatened to have them all removed—permanently, mind—if that prohibition was broken.

This extended, sadly, to her sleeping hours; given her mood, the domicis was disinclined to point out that lack of sleep might become an issue should she continue to be required to attend The Terafin. In most ways, Jewel was a pragmatic, practical girl. In this, she was not, and she made clear that her orders were not to be questioned.

For light, there were tallow candles, and they were to be used sparingly. For food, flat bread had been made—by whom, Ellerson was not entirely certain; there were also the traditional hard cheeses and dried meat. They had water, and water was all the drink they were to have. Her parents— one of them—had been a strict observer of the Six Days; Jewel followed that parent's lead as if, by so doing, she could somehow guarantee that the traditional end of those days would become, as well, the end of the ones the city now endured.

But the waiting was hard; he saw it in the sinking lines of her shoulders and the darkening circles beneath her eyes; for the last few weeks she had eaten as if the Dark Days were already being observed. He heard it in the way she woke in the darkness of the manse at night and saw it in the path she chose to take as she paced the rooms the den occupied.

Tonight, however, when she woke, she was silent; she dressed in the dark—and that, Ellerson could not help but hear; she was expressive when she stubbed her toes. He did not approach her in the hall, but he did observe.

She noticed him and turned to face him.

"Would it not be better," he said quietly, "to wait?"

"All I've *done* is wait," she replied, with enough heat to dispel sleep's tenuous grip. "All *we've* done is wait. The priests—even the Exalted— won't commit to this." She hesitated and then grudgingly added, "No, the Exalted will. But the Kings already have, so it'd be hard for them to argue. It's the other gods. Or the other god-born."

"Other?"

"Cartanis, Mandaros, Teos. I don't know who else," she added. "I don't think Kalliaris gets a vote."

As Kalliaris was the closest to a personal god that the den had, Ellerson kept his silence on the goddess of luck. "If the gods are concerned," he said quietly, "there is good reason for it."

"How good can it be, Ellerson? People are dying—horrible, horrible deaths that make slit throats and lopped off heads look good—every damn day. What else needs to happen? We can't reach them. We can't save them. We sit here—we *especially*—and do *nothing*!"

"What would you do, then?"

"I don't know! Anything. Anything at all." She looked around at the walls as if they were closing in on her.

Ellerson said, "Shall I send for an escort?"

Which stopped her short. "A what?"

"An escort, ATerafin."

Her eyes rounded slightly, and then she raised both hands in den-sign for *shut up now*.

He waited.

"I don't need an escort. I'm just going out."

"The Terafin has seen fit to require an escort—of Chosen—for Finch when she leaves the grounds. Finch is not—"

"I'm not leaving the damn grounds," she replied, but she'd lowered her voice, and her expression was one of resignation. "You know."

"Indeed. I am apprised of any change in situation which might affect the master I have understaken to serve."

"Don't tell them," she said softly. "I'll tell them. I will. But this is not the time."

He did not ask her what the time would be; he just nodded. "Where will you be traveling?"

"To the grounds."

He turned to the side table in the darkness and handed her a heavy bundle. "I thought that might be the case," he replied. "It is cold, to-night. You are not eating or sleeping."

"I am—"

"—And now would not be the time to fall ill. I will wait for you," he added.

"We're not eating—"

"With boiled water."

"We don't have the—"

"Jewel."

She bit back words and took the cloak.

She visited the Terafin shrine. As far as she knew, Ellerson had never come here, but he'd known where she was going the minute he'd heard the door creak; she'd've bet money on it, on any other day of the year but these six.

Torvan was waiting for her in the half-light of torches to one side of the altar that was spotless no matter what time of year it was. Even the leaves didn't dare to fall here. Jewel dared to walk, but only barely. She had not come to the shrine since the day she'd met the Twin Kings, if you could call total abasement and abject humility "meeting."

He nodded when she approached the shrine, and a half-smile changed his expression as she hesitated there.

"It's not you," she said in an awkward rush. "It's the torches. They're still burning."

A brow rose; his expression was entirely unlike Torvan's in that moment. "Torches? Ah, yes. The light. There is no symbolic extinguishing of these lights," he said gravely. "For they burned even during the Baronial wars, when mages ruled and demons were their assassins of choice.

"They burned in the days leading up to Veralaan's decision; they burned when she returned with the young Kings-to-be at her side. There are some lights that cannot be hidden."

"You don't observe the rites."

"No. I observe only Terafin." He turned then to look at the cloudless sky, as if he could appreciate its clarity. Jewel could barely acknowledge it.

"Acknowledge it," he said softly. "It is not less beautiful because there is ugliness in the world."

"I can't—I can't think of things like that now."

"Oh? Why?"

"Because there are people suffering and dying—"

"There will always be people suffering and dying; it is only your ignorance that affords you protection from their pain. It is real," he added. "I do not trivialize it. But it is not the entirety of the world, nor has it ever been." He paused, and then asked, "Have you come to reaffirm your chosen name?" And nodded at the shrine.

She stared at him as if he had spoken in Old Weston. And then she had the grace to redden.

"Are you not proud of the name that you bear?" he asked, his voice soft, the light in his eyes hard.

"I am—"

"And yet you hide it. You fail to mention it to those whose direct service you have taken."

She flinched, but she didn't argue.

"Why?"

"People are dying," she said quietly.

"People are dying. People are also being born. They breathe, they eat, they sleep; they know pain and joy and fear. The House Name changes neither fact. But it should mean enough to change something. Why are you here, Jewel Markess?"

She sat on the cold marble floor and lifted hands to her face. "I don't know," she said quietly. "I thought—I thought if we came here, if I could prove I was useful, we'd have a place here. We'd be safe."

He said nothing.

"And I've proved myself useful enough to The Terafin," she added, with a trace of defiance, as if she expected him to argue. He didn't. "But this House is hers. And the den is *mine*. I don't know how to be hers and theirs at the same time. And I won't give them up for the Name. If that was part of it, if that was the condition, we'd go back to stealing on the streets."

"You do not think them worthy of the House?"

She stiffened. Before she could speak any of the heated words that were tripping over each other in their rush to leave her mouth, the Terafin Spirit held up a hand.

"I judge as I judge," he said softly. "But I am not judging now; I am asking for *your* judgment."

"I don't judge them."

"You do, or you would not lead them. Each one of your den proved herself or himself to you somehow."

But it wasn't like that. She had rescued Finch because of a dream; she had found Teller in the snow beside his mother's corpse because of a waking vision. Angel had come to her the way Teller had. Arann. She'd practically tripped over Carver while avoiding a drunk den in the streets of the holdings. Jester, still alive somehow, had come with the freeing of Duster—and Duster was dead.

So many were dead. Or worse.

But she thought of Finch, who had never been any use in a fight, and she said, quietly, "Yes. Yes, they're worthy of any House that would take me."

His smile was almost weary; she didn't understand it.

"What will you give to my House, Jewel Markess?"

"What more can I give?" She spoke without anger, but she also spoke without desperation. Unfolding her legs, she rose and then walked to the House altar by which the Spirit—who still appeared as Torvan—was standing. "I've given The Terafin everything I can. Everything about myself I was supposed to keep hidden. The most loyal of my den, to her

House Guard. My two smartest to her right-kin and her official in the Merchant Authority. I've done everything she's asked——"

"Because she asked it?"

"Yes." After a pause, she looked away. "No." Her answer was almost inaudible, but she had a suspicion that wouldn't trouble the dead. "I would do it anyway. If I *knew* what to do—I'd do it." Looking beyond the shrine and the Spirit, she gazed toward the mainland, which was completely invisible in the night garden. "There are some things that are more important than just us." She hesitated, and then said, "Any of those people in the holdings could have been us. Some of them may be." She stopped speaking.

He nodded. "I know. You fear that your lost kin didn't die when they disappeared—but that they might be dying now, in unimaginable pain, out of your reach or the reach of anyone who might be able to bring them peace. Do you think it is not a fear I myself faced, when I ruled?"

She said nothing.

"Do you think it is not a fear The Terafin faces, now?"

"I *don't know.* She's so composed, she's so in control of almost everything—I don't understand why she can't make the god-born *listen.* People are dying, and their agreement is the *only* damn hope we have! But she says we have to *wait.* And every day—*every day*—more people are being tortured to death. Every day." The last words were once again almost inaudible, as if she'd spent what little energy she had left on the brief burst of emotional fury. "I sit beside her. We talk. She tells me to wait. Every day. We wait. We hardly plan. We don't know what the gods know——" She lifted her face to look at his, but it was unreadable. "I feel helpless here. I don't feel safe. I don't feel that there's any such thing as safety, anymore.

"And I can't tell them that. Not now."

"There is no such thing as safety," the Terafin Spirit replied softly. "And if it is for reassurance that you have come here, you will not find it."

She shook her head.

"Why did you come, Jewel?"

"I'm not sure I can be what you want me to be," Jewel replied. As she did, she felt something loosen in her chest; she wasn't sure what. She'd carried the words inside for days. Maybe for months, really—since she'd set foot on the grounds, Arann dying in Torvan's arms. "I can't do anything. The world could end tomorrow, and I'd be like the mice and strays, for all the good I'd do."

"And you believe that?"

"Shouldn't I?"

To her surprise, he smiled. It was a weary smile, but it was also open; it was not Torvan's easy smile, and it transformed the familiar features in a subtle way. "You are young," he said quietly. "And you measure yourself, always, by your failures. By your current failures. You do not see your successes. Tell me, Jewel Markess, do you count the lives of your den worth nothing?"

She bit back her first answer. Waited.

"Not everything you value will outlast you. Some of the things you build will be destroyed—by your oversight, the malice of others, or the simple passing of time."

"Unless I stick around after I'm dead to watch over it?" she asked.

He raised a brow, the corners of his mouth twitching slightly. But he said, "Not even then. But time gives perspective. With time, you come to understand that not everything is lost. When a fire scours the forest and destroys the lives within, new growth occurs in the open spaces left behind, and life returns. It is not the same life, but it offers some hope for the future.

"You take responsibility for your den; in their fashion, and as they can, they take responsibility for you. It is a characteristic that I seek. But many people who possess a sense of duty possess, as well, a crippling sense of guilt when they feel they have failed. The guilt, the inability to continue in the face of guilt, consumes them.

"Understand, Jewel Markess, that no one, man or woman, can be all things to all people; no single man or woman can be all things to House Terafin. Not even the Lord who rules it. What the Lord who rules it sees, is how best to leverage those men and women who can do what he or she cannot. She is not perfect. She will make mistakes. She will fail in some of her responsibilities because one does not always see them clearly, or in time."

"Has she?"

His smile was slight. "You may ask her. Perhaps she will even reply. What she does not say, I will not."

"Why are you telling me all of this?"

"Because if you allow guilt to paralyze or devour you, you will be able to shoulder no other burdens, and the House will demand that you shoulder a great many with both dignity and grace."

Jewel snorted. "Dignity and grace? Me?"

"Yes," was his grave reply.

She wondered if the dead had a sense of humor. Then again, she didn't have much of one, these days. It was hard. "How?"

"How?"

"How do I avoid the guilt?"

"Accept that there are things you cannot do."

"But if I don't try, how do I know what those things are?"

"You will know. Or you will learn. Sometimes it is hardest to wait and to trust. You must learn both."

"And what about knowing when to *act*?"

"I think," he said, in an entirely different tone, "that that will not be one of the problems you will have to face. Sometimes action is necessary, Jewel; it does not have to be *your* action."

She was silent, then. "My Oma taught me," she finally said, "that if a job needs doing, it's best to do it yourself; if you wait, you'll wait a long damn time, and you'll get mediocre work if it happens at all."

"That is only true when the work that needs doing is work you can do on your own. But in the larger world, that is almost never the case."

She hesitated before she spoke again. "So, The Terafin waiting for the god-born—"

"She cannot force the god-born to her will; not even the Kings could do that. Nor can she do what the god-born can do; could she, she would be at Moorelas' shrine now, surrounded by her Chosen and quite probably most of the magi. She waits with as much grace as she can, but she also applies as much pressure as she dares, and that pressure is exerted not only by House Terafin but also by the Council of The Ten.

"The god-born will come to understand that they must choose between their fear of the future and the threat they face now."

"But the people—"

He lifted a hand. "You are not killing them. It is not your will, your desire, or your hand that is torturing the helpless beneath Averalaan. What you can do, you have done, and without your words and your past experience, the city would not now have any hope at all. Do you understand?"

She waited for a long moment. At last, she nodded. "Do I have to like it?" she asked, with a bitter smile.

"No. In this, liking or not liking is not necessary." He glanced at the altar. "Will you place your hands upon the Altar of Terafin?"

She drew breath and walked to the altar's side. There she hesitated, her hands an inch above the stone. She finally withdrew it. "Not yet," she told him softly.

"Not yet?"

"I want them here with me."

"Your den?"

She nodded.

"I will wait for you, Jewel Markess. But be aware: I will not wait forever." His voice was soft and cool as he stepped back from the altar and became just another part of the cold night air.

When she returned to the wing, she was surprised to find Ellerson in conversation with Morretz.

"My apologies," he said, "for the hour of this visit, although I see I did not wake you."

She grimaced. "Sleep's been in short supply, anyway. I went for a walk." The grimace fell away. "Does The Terafin want me now?"

"She sent me with word. The Sons of Cartanis will come at dawn; they wish to speak with both The Terafin and her seer."

"Her . . . seer."

"They were explicit." He paused, and then added, "The Sons of Teos sent word; they will accede to the Kings' request."

Jewel was silent for a moment. "Then it's only Cartanis."

He nodded. "The waiting is almost over, Jewel. Ellerson will make certain you are prepared for your meeting in the morning. If it is at all possible, sleep."

She hesitated and then asked, "Is The Terafin sleeping?"

The slightest of smiles touched his face in the shadows. "She sent me here," he told Jewel. "And I believe she will sleep at least as well as you will."

26th of Henden, 410 A.A.
Terafin Manse, Averalaan Aramarelas

Sleep was ugly, fitful, and broken. It was also the type of sleep that felt like it had been all of five wretched minutes long, although more time than that had passed. Ellerson had laid out clothing for her, and she saw, as she pushed back curtains that let in a hue of blue that was not quite morning light, that it was a dress of white and black. The fabric was muted; it had no obvious sheen; it was simple enough she could put it on without help. But she hesitated as she lifted it by the shoulders and glanced at her domicis.

"Why these colors?" she asked. "Why now?"

"Are they not the colors of the season, Jewel?"

She shook her head. "Maybe among the rich," she finally said.

"And among the poor, if you must make that demarcation?"

"Mourning." She almost didn't answer the question; she knew he knew the answer just as well as she did.

"You feel this is inappropriate."

"No . . . but . . ." She shook herself.

"There are things that you cannot say to the god-born," Ellerson told her. "Not in so many words. This will make a statement, yes. But it is not a statement with which he can argue, and it is not a statement at which he might take offense.

"It is, however, a full explanation of your position, here, in the relative safety of the Terafin manse. Should you wish it, I will acquire other clothing that would also be considered suitable for a meeting of this significance."

But his words had pierced the fog of early morning, searing it away. "No," she said grimly. "I'll wear it."

He nodded, as if this had never been in doubt. "Remember, Jewel, he is not your enemy. He is a man whose concerns are not the same as yours, but not everyone who fails to do as you wish can be counted a foe."

She snorted. "Carver doesn't do half of what I tell him to do, and he's still one of mine. I think I already know that one."

Ellerson looked as if he would like to say more; he didn't. Instead, he helped her dress—which wasn't necessary—and led her to the breakfast nook. She went through the motions of eating while he waited by the wall; nothing she had ever said had convinced him that joining her at the table would make eating easier. Today she didn't try. She was careful not to spill anything on the wide, simple skirts, and when she was done, she found Torvan waiting at the doors to escort her to The Terafin's official meeting rooms.

Only when they were far enough away from the doors that she was certain Ellerson wouldn't hear her did she turn to Torvan. "How bad is it?"

"Bad?"

"I can't help but noticing the halls are full of guards."

"Cartanis is the Lord of Just War. It is a gesture of respect, not a response to threat," Torvan replied. "If it weren't for the time of year, there would be more; tapestries, and ancient weapons would now gird half the gallery walls, and the whole of the public face of this courtyard would appear martial in nature.

"Given the significance of the Dark Days this year, The Terafin did not feel such a display was appropriate or necessary. The captain, however, felt that a show of the House Guards' numbers would not be out of line with either the season or the visitor."

"So he's not here yet?"

Torvan grimaced. "Oh, he's here. He is now touring the reconstruction site, as he called it, inspecting the remnants of the damage done in the foyer. He was most insistent on it."

"The damage in the—oh. Is The Terafin with him?"

"Yes. Captain Alayra is also present."

"Is that where we're going now?"

"Yes."

The priests she had seen, and the god-born she had met had dressed in robes that were both stately and quietly authoritative; the colors they had worn in some way suggested their parentage.

The son of Cartanis did not wear robes. Nor was he surrounded by robed priests, their braziers hanging from carried poles. He wore armor. It wasn't even particularly shiny, although it had no obvious dents or wear to Jewel's admittedly untrained eye. He also carried a huge sword, strapped across his back; he wore no cape. His boots made a lot of noise as he strode across the new marble that had been laid across sections of the foyer. His silver-gray hair was long, and he wore it in a braid in the Northern Imperial style of the Queen Siodonay's people.

He wasn't a tall man. It didn't matter. Where he walked, everyone seemed to fall unconsciously into step either beside or behind him. Everyone except The Terafin.

But he turned first as Jewel approached, and she saw the color of his eyes and almost stopped walking. She couldn't even say why—it's not like she expected his eyes to be any other color; they were golden, of course, because he was god-born. But she missed a step, stumbled, and cursed the hem of the skirts that trailed just above the ground.

Torvan caught her, righted her, and said a very loud nothing before releasing her arm and offering his lord a perfect salute. He offered the god-born son of Cartanis a perfect bow immediately after, and he held that bow for much longer than people normally did. He rose only when the son of Cartanis bid him rise; The Terafin said nothing until Torvan was once again standing.

"Jewel," she said quietly.

Jewel separated herself from Torvan and came to stand beside The Terafin.

"This is Caras, son of Cartanis. Caras, this is Jewel ATerafin."

The gold of his eyes was bright and hard as Jewel extended a hand and froze. "This is your seer? She's a child."

Jewel said nothing. Having already let loose a very audible curse, she wasn't about to add to her social disgrace. She met his gaze and held it in silence. To her surprise, he laughed and took her hand; his was larger, and it was surprisingly warm. The same couldn't be said about the foyer.

"Not as young as you look, then," he said, when he let her hand go. "Come. Walk with us. The Terafin has been kind enough to relay events that occurred here on the eighth of Corvil. I would like to know what you saw."

"More or less what she saw," Jewel replied. She glanced at The Terafin.

"In the noise and confusion of any battle, no two people will see or hear the same thing; I do not accuse your Lord of attempting to hide any truth."

But Jewel frowned, and after a moment, she said, "You know what she saw. You believe it. You don't expect me to tell you anything you don't already know. You *did* come here to speak to me, though. What do you want from me, exactly?"

His eyes rounded, and he laughed again, but there was an edge to his smile, and his eyes were narrower, as if he were reassessing her, this time with care.

The Terafin, however, said, "If it would please you, Caras, I would be interested in your answer as well. I had assumed that your agreement to aid the others in the opening of the Sanctum was contingent upon—"

"Your assumption is not incorrect," Caras replied. The warmth and humor left his face. "You do not understand what you ask or what it presages, Terafin."

Before The Terafin could speak, Jewel did. "Is it worse than what we already understand? Will opening the Sanctum summon the Lord of the Hells to the city? Oh, wait—that's *already* happening. And we're *feeding him* our own damn people!"

The Terafin stiffened.

Caras, on the other hand, merely raised a brow. "You *are* young," he said at last. "But youth does not make you timid. These people who are dying, how many of them are yours, girl?"

"They're *all* mine," she said, voice low. "Because any one of them could have been me. Any one of them could have been my friends."

"A fair answer."

She should have stopped speaking. She knew it. But short of turning and storming out of the foyer, she couldn't stop her mouth; it was as if all the words she hadn't said for months were now fighting their way out. "It should be your damn answer! All of you! Some of these people worship at your churches and your altars. What can you possibly fear from the future that's worse?"

His brow rose again. One of the men at his side stepped forward, and Caras lifted a hand without otherwise turning to look at or acknowledge him. He stilled.

"Do you understand what sleeps in the Sanctum, Jewel ATerafin?"

She was silent for a moment. It didn't last. "Does it matter?" Her voice was quieter now. "I understand what's waking in the undercity. I understand what it's doing there, what it means to do everywhere. How much more of a danger can the Sleepers be?"

"Sleeping? They are no danger at all. But waking, they will be."

"How much *more* of a danger than a god?"

He was silent.

But in his silence, she heard his answer, the way she sometimes saw glimpses of the future. She went white, and her hands balled in tight fists at her sides because if they didn't, she would have slapped him. Or tried. She managed to turn to the The Terafin. "Terafin," she said, her voice a stretched whisper.

"Dismissed," was the whole of The Terafin's reply. "Torvan, see her to her quarters. We will speak later."

Torvan said nothing as they walked. Which was bad. She knew she'd disappointed him, and she tried very, very hard to care more. But it seemed as though so much of it was a game of waiting and pretending to act, and she wanted to scream against the injustice of it. Instead, she was silent, aware that if it was a game, it was a deadly serious one, and if they lost, more than money or a single life would be destroyed.

She'd never been good at this. She wondered if she ever would be.

Torvan left her at the doors of the wing, and she pushed them open. Ellerson raised a brow as she slid in, shoulders slumped. "Kitchen?" he asked softly.

"No, thanks. There's no news."

The white of that brow drew higher.

"I lost my temper," she told him.

"Please tell me you did not lose your temper at the head of the Church of Cartanis."

Carver slid around the doorframe and into view, followed by Angel. Arann was—no surprise—patrolling the halls and the grounds as a show of force to impress Caras. But Finch and Teller were also awake, as was Jester, and they gathered in the sitting room.

She hesitated and then gave up. "Kitchen," she told them, because they were milling around looking awkward, and at least there she could tell them all to sit the hell down.

There was a knock at the door. Or rather, something louder and more demanding. Jewel glanced at Ellerson, and flinched. "We're not expecting visitors, are we?" she said, without much hope.

"No. Exactly what did you say to the son of Cartanis, Jewel?"

"Exactly what I was thinking. We're going to the kitchen. If I've pissed off The Terafin enough that it's not our kitchen anymore, you can come and show us the door."

They crowded around the kitchen table, this den of hers.

"What did you say?" Teller asked her softly when Ellerson failed to return instantly to kick them all out.

Jewel grimaced. "I told him what I thought of his waiting. Something bad might happen if the Sleepers wake—it's why they're dragging their heels."

"He's god-born," Finch said, speaking just as quietly as Teller. "If it's something the gods fear—"

"They're just afraid of facing their own deaths. They don't care about ours!"

"If the gods die—"

"Only *one* of them has to die," she snapped.

"And the risk to the others?"

The problem with shouting is it drowns out the little noises. And a man in that much armor shouldn't have been able to walk making little noises. Jewel turned to face Caras. The Terafin was not with him, but neither were his honor guards, or whatever he called them. Ellerson was standing on the wrong side of the door, at a respectful distance.

Jewel stood instantly—almost everyone in the room did—and she flushed because he would *have* to walk in on this discussion. But she'd said it, she believed it, and she wasn't willing to apologize for either. They were *gods*. If the gods gave in to their fears, what chance did anyone else have?

"What would you sacrifice, little seer, in order to win this war? Would you sacrifice your friends? Would you see them die so that strangers might live?" He glanced around the room—and froze when his eyes reached Angel. His brows rose, revealing a little more of golden irises in a Winter face.

"So," he said, after a long pause. He lifted a hand. It was not, to Jewel's eyes, a salute; there was command in the gesture.

Angel didn't have Jay's temper, and he didn't have the depth of the fury that sometimes drove her—but like any of her den-kin, he'd benefited from it in his time.

"You are of Weyrdon," the man said quietly.

He knew the god-born had golden eyes. In some way, this man was brother to the only other that he'd met. He nodded.

"You are Garroc's son." It wasn't a question. Nor did Angel wonder how or why he knew.

"My father was Weyrdon. My mother was not. I was born in the Empire."

"Your father was sent into the Empire. Do you understand what he sought?"

"Yes." Angel spoke the word firmly, as if there were no doubt. There was; he didn't choose to share it.

"Your father did not complete his task before his death. It was a warrior's death," the man added, "and he was honored for it, and for undertaking his long exile from home and kin."

Angel said nothing. The silence extended, as if some answer were expected to fill it, although no question had been asked.

"What rite of passage did you undergo to be Weyrdon?"

After another pause, Angel said, "I am Angel, son of Garroc. Who questions me?"

A pale brow rose, and then the man chuckled. "I am Caras, son of Cartanis. Weyrdon is my brother and my father's son, and his fight is the long fight. Garroc's mission was known to me, although I met him but once. In truth, I did not think the time right for his exile.

"But I did not see the growing shadow until it was—almost—upon us. Night is coming," he added. "I ask again: What rite of passage marked you as man among your kin?"

"I survived." Angel hesitated for a moment, and then he slipped into Rendish. "If you question my worth to Weyrdon, you must question Weyrdon. I cannot speak for him."

"A fair answer," Caras replied—in Rendish. "Have you found what Weyrdon sought?"

"I don't know what Weyrdon sought. I know what he asked *me* to seek."

"And you will find it, or you will fail. Your failure will be costly in ways even I cannot perceive. I have lived in the Empire for most of my adult life; it is cold in ways that the North never was. I knew of Garroc's quest, as I said—but I had no aid and no advice to offer. I have met all of the leaders of note and power in this land, and I cannot see in them any end to Weyrdon's quest; I see their mortality."

"You came here tonight to meet me."

"I had some word that you might have arrived at this place," Caras replied. "And I had some pretext for visiting. Tell me, Angel, Garroc's son, do you serve The Terafin?"

"No."

"And is it your intent to offer her your oath? Is she the Lord you have chosen?"

"The Lord I serve," Angel said carefully, "is not Cartanis. Cartanis was my father's god, but he was not my father's Lord. I follow his tenets, but I do not owe him obedience."

"Which means you will not answer."

"I will answer because I choose to aid the son of Cartanis. I will not answer because I owe him more than that courtesy."

"The question of who holds your oath is a question most men will own, with pride, in public."

"Garroc was sent—in private, in apparent disgrace—from Weyrdon's side. There was nothing public about his quest, and in the end, I choose to believe there were reasons for his secrecy and his privacy."

"Or reasons for your anger on his behalf?" Caras asked softly. "He would not have desired it."

Angel didn't answer. When the pause was significant enough to indicate the end of that small part of the conversation, Angel said, "I will not offer my service to The Terafin."

"Why, then, are you here, son of Garroc?"

Angel was silent. Gold was the color of dreams and money, of wealth and power. It was also the color of war; he saw it in the eyes of the son of Cartanis, and he didn't flinch. War, little understood, had taken both his father and mother, and it had led Angel on the long, bitter road to this city, where despair and a certain sense of failure had almost destroyed him.

It hadn't, and he knew why.

He thought, as Caras watched, that he had always known. He had never put it into words, because words—for the men of Weyrdon—were a matter of life and death. But they were facing life and death now, across the breadth of Averalaan—and if they did not somehow succeed, that death would march across the lands to the North, South, and West. It would devour fields and farmers who labored in ignorance; it would kill old and young, warriors and those for whom, in the end, they chose to go to war.

But success wasn't in their hands. Jay had made that bitterly clear. Whatever they'd managed, they'd done by accident and in desperation, and what was left was now in the hands of the Kings, their soldiers, and the god-born. Caras.

What was in Angel's hands, what had always, in the end, been in his hands, was choice. It was a simple choice, really, because it felt like no choice at all; it just *was*. His glance flickered off Caras' face and to Ellerson's, who stood to one side of the swinging doors—doors that were now closed.

He thought Ellerson smiled. It was his usual stiff, minimal smile, but Angel took comfort from it.

He straightened his shoulders slightly. "I'm here," he said quietly, "because Jay is here. I go where she goes." He spoke in Rendish, only partly because it meant no one else in the room would understand the words, or question them.

Caras frowned, and then his eyes widened slightly. He turned to look at

Jay, who was watching him in an intent—and because it was Jay, angry—silence. "This one?" he said to Angel, although he didn't look away from her.

"Yes. I won't offer The Terafin my oath because it would be false the moment I did. Weyrdon didn't tell me to find a Lord that *he* would be willing to follow; he told me to find one that *I* would."

"She has not taken your oath."

"No. That's not—" he winced. "It's not what she's like. She wouldn't understand it, and she'd probably be embarrassed. It doesn't matter; my oath isn't about her, in the end; it's mine. I'm not her slave and I'm not her servant. But where she goes, I follow. She doesn't need a formal oath to understand that."

"She's a child."

"So am I, by that reckoning. But if it weren't for her, we'd have no hope at all; Allasakar would have remained undetected until it was too late."

Caras almost took a step back at Angel's bold use of the name.

"And if it weren't for your hesitation, we might have already saved lives," Angel continued. He spoke without Jay's heat or her obvious anger, as if he were merely making an observation. But he spoke, again, in Rendish.

Caras almost seemed not to have heard. He looked at Jay for a long moment, and she continued to hold his gaze.

To Angel's surprise, Caras bowed to her. Judging from Jay's expression, it surprised her even more.

In Weston, the son of Cartanis said, when he rose, "Very well, little seer. For good or ill, I will join the god-born and the Exalted before the Sanctum of Moorelas. If it eases you, there are reasons for the delay that have little to do with cowardice or our lack of desire for battle." His smile was grim, but there was humor in it, given his father. "If the Lord of the Hells is to be defeated in Averalaan—or beneath it—there is only one living force that can meet him on the field of battle with any hope of success.

"If what The Terafin said is accurate, you have already seen him once, and you have seen the death he brings—but he was not at his full strength when he was last summoned, and we believe it was costly in ways that the gods of old could not have conceived when they agreed to abide by the Covenant that bars them forever from walking these lands.

"Only three did not make the that binding oath, and among those three are the one we do not name, who rules in the Hells, and Bredan, the Lord of Oaths. It is Bredan who must be called, and in his full power, and there is but one day—by his own oath to an almost forgotten people—upon which that can occur.

"The Hunters of the Western Kingdoms call that day, which we call the first of Veral, the day of the Sacred Hunt."

"The first of Veral."

He nodded. "The ceremony is long and it is arduous, although to you it will look like simple words and gestures. But it will avail us little to open the Sanctum to any force at all if we do not open it at that time."

Her shoulders slumped a little. "Yes," she said quietly.

"Yes?"

"It eases me. To know that there's a reason. Even then—"

"You do not have a warrior's heart," he said softly. "But you will need it in the years to come. Honor your fallen; weep for them openly. But do not let the guilt of their loss destroy you. If it does, you have surrendered before the war has truly started; there is no better way for the enemy to harm us than that.

"Why do you think they kill and torture as they do? It is to break people who might otherwise have the will and the heart to stand against the darkness they bring."

The anger drained out of her face, and Angel missed it; what was left was almost painful to look at. "There must be something—"

"That you can do? Oh, ATerafin, there will be. But it is not, yet, your time, and if you are broken, bitter, and caught in the self-loathing of guilt, will you be able to do what must be done?"

"But I don't *know* what has to be done—"

"No. But you are seer-born; I know of only one other in the Empire."

"Evayne?" Jewel asked quietly.

"So. You've met; I should have known. Yes, I speak of Evayne. She has chosen the longest road, and the darkest one, and perhaps because she has, you will not be faced with the same choice. I do not know," he added. "She is mortal, and as all mortals, in time, she must fail or wither. Before you speak, understand that it is also *my* fate; I do not judge.

"It is my belief, ATerafin, that you will know what must be done when the time is right. Perhaps only then. Do not let your fear be your only guide."

"I'm not afraid—"

"Fear of the consequences of failure is still, in the end, fear." He bowed again. "This will not be the last time we meet. Perhaps the next time," he added, with a smile that was wry but warmer, "I may bring my men without fear of their justifiable reaction to your manners."

Chapter Nineteen

28th of Henden, 410 A. A.
The Sanctum of Moorelas, Averalaan Aramarelas

THE HUNTER LORD, Gilliam of Elseth, stood in silence. He wasn't alone; the dogs from which he refused to be separated—which had caused some difficulty among the servants, according to Carver—stood like sentinels by his side, and the woman, Espere, her hair still unkempt although she'd been wedged into clothing, wandered among them, nudging them from time to time. She glanced at Lord Gilliam as if she wanted to be beside him, but although she approached, she shied away just as quickly.

Jewel watched them. They weren't far from the Terafin House Guards, but they existed in their own little world. Lord Gilliam wore leather armor, no tabard, and a cloak that was both fine and worn. In the gray of this midnight hour, the colors were blurred and dark. The only thing that drew the eye was the spear he carried. To Jewel's eye, it shone faintly, like dampened moonlight; it was white, and it seemed to demand the whole of his attention.

He didn't speak. Not to The Terafin. Not to his sole living companion. He hadn't spoken more than a few words—sharp words, usually about the handling of his dogs—since Stephen had died. Carver had said the servants worried about him; he ate little, slept poorly, and paced the confines of any room he was trapped in. As if he were waiting.

He was. She saw it in his face, in the gaunt dark circles beneath his eyes. Those circles were visible even in the muted light. His brother was dead, and he meant to avenge that death and have peace. She understood his desire, and she felt a bitter, piercing envy, because, knuckles white on the haft of the spear, *he* was going to do it. He was important enough, old enough, skilled enough, that he would descend into the Sanctum at the side of Kings and mages—if the damn thing ever opened.

She would not.

She'd wait, like every other terrified person in the city, until dawn. If dawn came. And she *was* terrified. Watching Lord Gilliam, she couldn't doubt that he knew how to use the spear; having seen him once, in the ruins of the Terafin foyer, she knew damn well that he would use it against *anything*. Fear didn't paralyze him—he barely seemed to notice it at all.

She could daydream about being a hero. But her nightmares were different; in those, faced with the things she feared most, she ran. Or she froze. She didn't want to admit that she'd do the same damn thing in the undercity. Then again, no one had asked. The Terafin and Devon had discussed her role briefly. Jewel was to remain with The Terafin. Devon had pointed out that Jewel's intermittent and unpredictable visions might be of use; The Terafin had fixed him with a polite stare, after which he'd fallen silent. Neat trick, that; Jewel thought she'd have to learn it one day.

But not today. Not tonight, so close to the edge.

The god-born had gathered around the standing statue of Moorelas; in the moonlight, and the damp, cold wind that blew off the sea, they had set up their braziers, their small fires protected by lids or lesser priests. They had greeted each other formally and stiffly, and they had each in turn looked up at Moorelas' stone visage as if seeking a sign.

Gods might walk the earth again, but statues didn't. He looked beyond them, his expression as grave and graven as it had always been. And so they positioned themselves: the three Exalted, the sons of Mandaros, Cartanis, and Teos, Lord of Knowledge, and the two sons of Cormaris and Reymaris, who between them guided the whole of the Empire from its coastal cities to its inland holdings. That had been almost twelve hours ago, according to Morretz. At this time of night, it was hard for Jewel to gauge the passing of time, but she would have guessed longer. No one had asked her.

The god-born chanted, as Caras had said they would. And as he had said it would, it looked to her like a lot of almost singing—but the words they almost sang made no sense to her. The syllables were full and deep, and they were spoken with a perfect synchronicty—but they were in no language that she recognized. It wasn't Old Weston. She wondered, briefly, whether it was the spoken form of the rune that had girded the closed door through which she and Duster had prayed their way, or the runes that had adorned the floor, longer than she was tall. She couldn't ask, of course.

She could only watch the god-born for so long, and while Moorelas had always fascinated her, an hour staring at his unmoving face and stone hair was long enough.

She watched the gathered people instead, for they were many.

The Kings' Swords had closed off the streets, and only those carrying the Kings' writ were granted passage to the Sanctum. This had apparently caused a near riot, but the Kings' Swords seemed to expect that, and King Cormalyn himself had chosen to address the panicked, angry crowd.

"Tonight," he told them, "the Six Days draw to a close. It is now time for the Kings and their armies to go to battle, for our enemy has at last revealed himself, and there is a way, both ancient and dangerous, to approach him that did not exist before. The Sanctum of Moorelas will not be safe, for it is now entirely in his shadow. Go back to your families; go back to your homes. Await the dawn; it *will* come."

He spoke over the quivering screams of a dying man. They heard him. They went home. They didn't go silently, but it didn't matter; even terrified they weren't insane enough to attack the Kings' men or the Kings' banner while the Kings were present.

The guard on the road was heavy, however, and it did not diminish.

The Terafin, Devon ATerafin, and Jewel passed through the checkpoint, along with a select handful of the Terafin House Guard. Through that same checkpoint came members of the Order of Knowledge: Sigurne Mellifas, Meralonne APhaniel, and many others that Jewel didn't recognize. The Senniel bards came as well. The god-born were already in place by the time the Terafin contingent had reached the street closest to the Sanctum; they could not approach it—not without cutting through a large number of people.

There were no lights in the buildings that faced the Sanctum; the observation of the Six Days ruled here, in strength. The magelights had been doused as well. But the city wasn't dark; the moons were high and full, and the clouds were almost ethereal.

But the night was dark and cold; nothing remained of the passing day. Here, the voices of the god-born seemed to echo, as if the sea were a wall, as if the whole city were one great stone room, meant to trap and hoard all sound. Sometimes The Terafin spoke, because the god-born paused for five minutes of each hour, as if to gather breath to continue. They held hands when they chanted, closing their odd circle. Jewel thought she could see the glow of their eyes at this distance.

She could certainly smell the incense that wafted on the breeze from the sea.

But when the cadences of the voices shifted, she felt the hair on the back of her neck rise. Their voices weren't loud, or rather, the god-born weren't shouting—but she felt that their incomprehensible words must be heard across the whole of the city. It should have been comforting. It wasn't.

"Peace, Jewel."

She startled, turned, and bumped into Devon ATerafin. "They are almost done."

She nodded and turned away. "The Kings look like they're dressed for war."

"The Kings," he said quietly, his voice low and almost silent, "will ride to war."

"Ride?"

"It's a phrase." He glanced at her again and repeated the words.

Annoyed, even here, she said, "It doesn't work that way, Devon. You *know* that."

He didn't even have the grace to look embarrassed. "You yourself have said you've no idea when—or how—vision will come. If we lose either King at this time, we are in peril, and any insight at all, any hint, might well save—"

"Devon," The Terafin said coldly.

He drew breath as if to speak; he didn't.

But Jewel said, "You won't need me. Someone will be there to guide you." Jewel glanced at The Terafin, who said nothing. At all.

He left, then, and navigated his way through the crowd; when he reached the Kings' men, he stopped. She could see him, but only barely, and only because there was a lot of metal on the Kings' men that caught the light, reflecting it.

She was hungry, she was cold, and she was tired. She had been on her feet for over half the day. But it wasn't a picnic; they hadn't brought much in the way of food. She had the usual waterskin, which she was discreetly emptying.

But she kept her complaints to herself; she had watched the god-born since she had arrived, and except for those five minutes once an hour, they had not paused. They hadn't eaten. They drank water—at least she thought it was water—in the brief break granted them, and then they returned to their task.

As two of those god-born were Kings, no one else was going to be offered—or allowed—food.

She glanced at the face of the full moon and saw the second moon in shadow. Now, she thought.

The voices of the god-born built, each syllable carried by eight voices, each word louder than the last. The slow and steady drone of repetition was broken here; it was as if twelve hours of steady, constant pleading had built into this storm of sudden sound. There was beauty in it, although it was not quite song, but there was terror in it as well, for when it was over, they would have an answer.

She hadn't stopped to wonder what that answer would be, or what form it would take. Now, holding her breath, she waited as the raised voices suddenly stopped, and silence, deafening in contrast, took their place.

Then, syllables like hammer against anvil, the god-born spoke again. Eight words. Eight, one for each standing man and woman who formed the human chain around the base of the Sanctum's famous statue.

When the eighth word was finished, they were done with speaking. Jewel watched as they raised arms, hands still clasped, and lifted their tense, still faces, toward the heavens; toward the moon with its nimbus glow; toward the cold and icy glance of thousands of stars. Exalted, Sacred and Kings, they were supplicants here, mortals treading upon the ground the gods had forbidden them.

A second passed. Two. Maybe even a minute before they had their answer. The statue of Moorelas, hero of legend, moved.

His face was stone and nothing about that changed. Nothing about his grim visage changed much either, and his sword didn't magically become metal, nor his vestments cloth. But Jewel could see, as if he were the moon come down to earth, a nimbus of light surrounding his carved body; it was almost too bright too look at.

She looked anyway, squinting. It didn't matter; no one was watching her. No one, she thought, was watching anyone but Moorelas of Aston.

He, in turn, glanced down at the upturned faces of the eight who had somehow wakened him: The Exalted of the Mother, Cormaris and Reymaris. The Sacred of Mandaros and Cartanis. The son of Teos, Lord of Knowledge, a man wearing not the robes of a priest but the more familiar robes of the Order of Knowledge. Last, he looked at the first men in the Empire: King Cormalyn. King Reymalyn.

To each, he offered a single nod, and as he did, they stepped out of the circle, breaking it.

Beyond them, his gaze traveled to the assembled army. Jewel's traveled as well, as if drawn by his attention, by what he considered worthy of that attention. She saw the armored men who served Cartanis, Lord of Just War, the armed and armored men who likewise served Reymaris and Cormaris. But she saw, as well, the children of the Mother, and she recognized them because they weren't girded for war: they wore their usual workaday robes, and they carried not weapons but baskets; their hips were heavy with hanging skins that carried more, she thought, than simple water.

To one side, robed and unarmored, she saw mages from the Order of Knowledge, Meralonne APhaniel at their head. But *this* Meralonne she had seen only once before, in the foyer of the Terafin manse. His hair was long and white, and his skin was pale; he was Winter, to Jewel.

Moorelas nodded to each of them and then spoke.

"Well met."

They bent, then. Bowing or falling to one knee, they offered this statue respect. Even Jewel, who stood so far beneath him his gaze hadn't so much as grazed her forehead.

One man, however, failed to show the awe or the respect that was Moorelas' due. He stood, surrounded by his dogs, and he waited.

"Follower of Bredan," the statue said to him.

Lord Gilliam looked up and met the gaze of the statue in silence.

"Free your Lord, and you will have peace."

The Hunter Lord's grip on the spear shifted, and only then did he bow his head; he did not kneel. Jewel wondered if any force existed that would bend those knees.

But the statue seemed satisfied and turned once again to the assembled men and women who continued to offer the obvious, physical show of respect.

"The time is not yet, but the ways will be opened. Touch not what you see, and seek not to disturb it—or you will break the compact that your Lords—and mine—have made."

He bent, then—and he could, which should have been more of a shock, kneeling upon the dais that had supported him for, well, ever. He lifted his great stone sword in both hands, point toward the center of the pedestal. "Fare thee well, for ere this night is past, many of you will walk upon Mandaros' fields and in his halls. Walk in honor."

He, too, lifted his face toward the moons and the heavens, and then he closed his eyes and drove the point of his sword directly into the heart of the pedestal.

The light that flared from the contact point was not a single color, but all of them, and it was bright and harsh, as lightning would have been if the storm from which it came were gods themselves.

That light now ate away at the carved reliefs that surrounded the statue, the reliefs upon which the god-born had stood for most of the day. Details of Moorelas' life faded, losing shape and texture, until only smooth plates of flat light ringed the statue.

"Pass through," Moorelas said, his voice quieter. "And quickly. The time is short." He withdrew his sword as he spoke, and he rose once again and turned his face out toward the sea, which he always faced.

Life left him, but the light that circled him remained, and only when he was utterly still did the Kings begin to move.

Devon ATerafin gazed—once—at the woman whose name he bore. Terafin. She returned that gaze and held it, her own measured and without any hint of softness. Or regret. There was anger in her, and it burned her the way the much more obvious shame, desire, and rage made Jewel almost incandescent in her youth. That youth would dwindle, in time, if she survived.

He nodded, once, to The Terafin, for she was distant, and then he gave the whole of his attention to the monument. The familiar engraved depictions of a legendary hero's life had faded into smooth, even plates that glowed; moonlight was trapped there, and magic—magic made old and wild and utterly inexplicable by the voices and the touch of the god-born.

He touched the hilts of his daggers as if gesture were prayer, and then he moved to stand behind the armored Kings. He was now one of the many shadows they cast and would remain so, in silence, until the end of the journey, even if that journey brought him, at last, to the halls of Mandaros, as Moorelas' statue had suggested. These men, these Twin Kings, were the heart and mind of the Empire.

Devon had dedicated his life to their protection and preservation. But they did not directly command him; that was left to Duvari, the most hated man in the Empire.

"ATerafin," the leader of the Astari now said, and Devon nodded, his gaze never leaving the Kings. "You have what you require?"

"I do."

"The Terafin seer—"

"The Terafin has refused to surrender her, Duvari, and what the Kings will not compel, I cannot. But we will have another guide, if I am not mistaken."

"The mage?"

"No."

Duvari's silence was a thing to be dreaded, and many men filled it with stammering; Devon did not. He did not like Duvari—no one did—but he did not fear or despise him. Duvari, alone among the men and women who served, had made no compromise that had not been decreed by the Kings who were the sole focus of his life. Not for a man of Duvari's steel the double life of a man who served as a semidistinguished trade official in *Avantari*; not for Duvari the uneasy struggle between serving two masters and two causes.

But Duvari was pragmatic; he understood the need for men like Devon ATerafin. Inasmuch as he could, Duvari trusted Devon. "Who, then?"

"There is another seer in the Empire, but she is strange, and not without power."

"I do not see her."

"She has not yet arrived. You will see her, in due time."

The Kings began to speak, and Devon and Duvari fell silent to listen—although they listened for very different things. Duvari tested, always, the mood and tone of the gathered crowd. Today, in Devon's estimation, it was pointless. If the fractious and divided Empire ever worked together, they did so now; they were of one mind.

But if Duvari listened as the Kings gave their orders and addressed—possibly for the last time—their sons and Queens, he heard what Devon heard as the Kings were at last fully fitted with the Sword and the Rod: The Kings meant to *lead*.

One heartbeat of silence followed this simple declaration. Devon would not have spoken a word against it, and perhaps his training and his tenure in the House of a powerful Lord had instilled this instant acceptance of the whims of rulers. Duvari, however, was not Devon.

"Your Majesties," the Lord of the Compact said, his voice the only clear voice in the muted silence. "Nothing is known about the Sanctum or what lies beyond these glowing walls. The magi have done some preliminary investigation with the tools at hand, but we have received no word of what they have found."

"Indeed," King Cormalyn said. King Reymalyn did not speak a word. "Nor would we expect otherwise, Lord of the Compact. But the Sanctum was created by the living gods, and we are their scions in this mortal world.

"They have given us the sternest of their warnings, and they have allowed us, in their wisdom, to enter what has been long, long forbidden. We will not send our own to explore what we *must*, at need, explore. Where we command men to follow, we will lead."

"Let us precede you, Your Majesty, if you will not ask this of any others."

King Cormalyn's smile was bright, if weary, and his eyes were glowing gently, gold to the silver of the statue's base and pedestal. "I think we must deny that request." He glanced at King Reymalyn, the man who was commonly called his brother, although there were no actual blood ties between them.

Duvari opened his mouth, and King Reymalyn, silent until this moment, turned to face the Lord of the Compact fully. He did not speak, but his expression made clear that he was the son of the god of Justice, and the god's blood was strong in him this night. He was done with pragmatism and wisdom, and if King Cormalyn could accept this lapse, everyone else must also do so. Even Duvari.

Duvari was not fool enough to stand before the silent rage of Kings, and he fell silent at once, bowing fully before he stepped away.

King Reymalyn then turned to the Wisdom-born King, and King Cormalyn nodded. It was therefore King Reymalyn, sword in hand, who entered the Sanctum first. He walked directly toward the pale luminescent base of the statue, and as he did, his feet began to descend through what had once been carved rock. If he felt pain, he did not show it; nor would he. What he carried within was worse.

King Cormalyn did not wait until the Justice-born King had vanished from sight before he, too, followed. In his wake, the Kings' Swords began their descent, but they followed Duvari and Devon.

Jewel watched as the men and women who were meant to go to war began to move, following the orders that trickled back from the Kings. The Kings themselves were fussed over by other men and women, and they bore it silently, as if it were a fact of life. She thought she'd hate that.

But she wanted to follow them. She wanted to slip between the Terafin Chosen and dog their steps, to see for herself the battle, the end of the war—however it turned out. She wanted to see the demons die, and die horribly; they had—she knew—killed her kin. Killed Duster in the open streets, and beneath those streets killed Lefty and Fisher and Lander.

"We would not have come this far without you," The Terafin said quietly. "No dream would have led us to this place, and we would have no chance at all.

"You are ATerafin, Jewel. You must learn to think beyond the fist that strikes or the dagger that draws blood. Instead of one hand, you have called upon many. Where you have no hold on the fires or the elements, the mages have come; where you cannot heal or offer succor, the priests; where you cannot fight and stand against the force of demonic strength, the warriors." She lifted her hood and drew it above her shoulders; it was large for her face and framed it poorly. "Come."

Jewel swallowed and nodded as, one by one, the Kings' men stepped upon the plates of light and vanished from sight. She wanted to watch them leave; she wanted to wait until the last soldier had been swallowed by magic that was as old as the gods.

But The Terafin was waiting. Jewel cast one backward glance at Moorelas, who stood, once again, unmoved by anything as paltry as the living, and she bowed her head.

The Hunter Lord approached The Terafin as the men began their descent, and he bowed to her. It was a stiff bow, but everything about the man had been stiff since the death of his Huntbrother, and that would not change until either he or the god was dead. Jewel understood it better than she understood most things about nobles.

"Lord Elseth," The Terafin said, granting him his due. "Will you descend now in the wake of the Kings?"

"I will," was his grave reply. "But I ask a boon."

"If it is within my power, I will grant it."

"I wish to leave my dogs here."

The silence was not long, but it felt endless. The Hunter Lord looked away. "These are not," he finally said, picking the foreign words carefully, "the lands of my birth. They are not the lands in which my dogs were born. Here they are treated as animals."

They *were* animals, Jewel thought, but she was wise enough to say nothing.

"And I do not wish to lose them here, where they will die unremarked and ill-respected for their sacrifice."

The Terafin was silent until it became clear he would not say more. "Will you then hunt without your pack? I am not Breodanir, but even I am aware—"

"I will not lead them to certain death. Espere will accompany me, but we may fight in halls of stone; there are no forests, here."

She still did not accede.

"I have lost enough."

She nodded then. "I will speak with the Mother's children. But I fear that your dogs will not be parted from you."

"They will go where I tell them to go."

Devon, who had followed Jewel into the dirt and the darkness of tunnels that were, in theory, their entry into the ruins of an ancient city, felt the light envelop him as he walked. He, like Duvari—like any sane, rational man—was uneasy in the obvious presence of magic. Magestones and privacy stones aside, magic was a force best left to gods, and in the hands of mortals—even the god-born—it was a danger.

He therefore expected the passage to be difficult, and only in part because he wasn't certain where—or when—it would end. But the light itself was almost pleasant, and it was certainly warmer than the cold midnight of Henden air. He could hear, at a remove, the wind that wailed during the storm season; he could hear the thunder that rumbled in the clouds and the breaking of waves along the seawall. He could hear, as if they mimed wind, the muted voices of people; none of the voices were familiar, and he couldn't make out the individual words spoken; they were pressed together, unintelligible.

As if, he thought, they were some part of nature, the natural world, indistinct from waves or storm or wind or the growth of leaves on the trees that girded the Common; inevitable as sunrise and sunset, as moonrise and eclipse.

But the voices, like the break of waves or the rush of wind, passed into silence as Devon at last emerged. Gone were the glowing flat panes, and gone was the forbidding visage of Moorelas and the threat of his shadow: His eyes acclimatized themselves quickly to the dimly lit halls in which giants might once have walked. They were not whole; they had seen some cataclysm that had sheared their heights. But what was left was easily taller than Kings or god-born men, and it surrounded marble floors that bore long cracks but no other signs of wear. Here, gold was inlaid in large, circular patterns that suggested words; he could not read or recognize them.

"We will have more light," Duvari said, in his cool and entirely flat voice.

"*No.*"

And there she was. The mages turned, and in the scant light of the room, swords rose in the hands of the Kings' men; Duvari's weapons could not yet be seen. But Devon drew nothing; he recognized the voice. He wasn't bard-born, but voices, once heard, seldom escaped his memory.

He turned, as did the whole of the assembled force, but he waited. Duvari glanced briefly at him, and—as as much as he ever did—he also relaxed. He signaled a brief question; Devon returned only a nod. Two seers, he thought, and so different from one another that the only thing they appeared to share was a talent and a gender.

Evayne a'Nolan stood, robed in familiar blue, alone. A long moment passed, in which orders might have been given or followed; no one broke the silence until she herself stepped forward, toward where the Kings stood. She crossed marble, the hem of her robes brushing away the dust of centuries, and when she had approached as closely as Duvari would allow, she knelt before the Twin Kings and bowed her head.

Nor did she lift it until King Cormalyn spoke. "Rise. Rise and identify yourself."

"I am Evayne," she said, unfolding at his command. "Evayne a'Nolan."

"What are you, and what are you doing within these walls?"

"I am waiting for you, Majesty, for I have walked the hidden path, and in so doing, I have learned enough to be of service to you while our paths converge." Her robes shuddered and rose, as if stirred by a wind, a wind that touched no one else. Devon, who had seen her before, nevertheless found it disquieting. As was the orb she now drew from the folds of those robes; it sat, pulsing faintly, in her hands. If the healer-born wore the open palms, this was the only symbol of office a seer might bear.

"And why should we trust you?"

"Because, my Lord, no one living, no one sane, seeks the ascent of the darkness." Her voice was proud and cool, but without hesitation; she looked with ease into the eyes of the Wisdom-born King. She was not tall, but lack of height in no way diminished her presence. "Those who call themselves *Allasakari* have already been devoured, and those who delude themselves into thinking they will have power. . . . But I have not come to speak of that. I am seer-born, and the way to the undercity is treacherous. Will you accept my aid?"

"And who is Evayne a'Nolan that we should know her to be sane?" Duvari spoke now, and sharply, as was his wont.

She glanced at him as if he were barely of consequence, which caused Devon to stifle a smile. Duvari noticed, of course; he noticed everything.

"A friend," she replied.

"But friend to whom? It is a matter of ease to claim friendship—and often a matter of deceit."

"I will not force myself upon you. I cannot. If you will not have my aid, I will leave you."

Devon almost spoke, then. But one look at Duvari's expression was enough; he maintained silence. Nor did Evayne look to him for either succor or support. She looked to no one.

But help did follow. From out of the shadows behind the Kings a familiar bard appeared. He did not speak to Evayne a'Nolan, nor did he immediately acknowledge her presence. Instead, he knelt before the Twin Kings, his posture the posture of the supplicant. "Majesties, I am Master Bard Kallandras of Senniel; I have served the Crowns' circuit for my tenure. I bear this woman little love, but I will speak for her. You may trust her."

Devon was slightly surprised; Evayne, however, was motionless.

Nor was Kallandras the only man to speak on her behalf. Meralonne APhaniel now separated himself from the less than perfect precision of the ranks of the warrior-magi and joined Kallandras. He, too, adopted the posture of the supplicant, although he did it with far less practiced grace—or ease—than the bard.

"Majesties, I am Member Meralonne APhaniel of the Order of Knowledge and of the Council of the Magi, and of the Wise. This one was once . . . my student. I, too, will speak for her."

The third man who came to stand before the Kings did not abase himself; he made no gesture of allegiance—nor was one expected. "Your Majesties. I am not Essalieyanese, but I have fought demons and the darkness in my native lands—and you have granted me permission to hunt them here. If my word means anything to you—or to the man who speaks for you—I give it as well: I speak for Evayne."

"I do not speak for the King," Duvari said, his voice both cold and sharp.

"He speaks," the Justice-born King added, with the hint of a smile, "for the Kings' safety. We will accept your guarantees, gentlemen."

The Kings then retreated some small distance and spoke in tones so quiet only Duvari might catch all of their words; no other was allowed so close. But Devon didn't make the attempt; he watched Evayne, instead. She approached Meralonne, Kallandras, and Lord Gilliam of Elseth as they rose in the absence of Kings.

The Master Bard of Senniel, first to speak, was also first to turn away at her approach, and he turned in a silence so complete that no one watching could mistake it for anything but a rejection. She lifted a hand as he retreated, but she lowered it again and did not speak.

Meralonne APhaniel waited until she turned to him.

"I have not forgiven your silence," he said, in a cool voice.

"I know. But mark it well: The time is coming when my silence will be broken at your behest, and then we will both wish for the years in which I sat at your feet learning the arts."

"Is this a seeing?"

"Yes." She turned away from the mage but then stopped. "But not of the gift. Of the heart."

Meralonne, a man for whom discussions of the heart seemed out of place—at best—fell silent as she left him. But he watched her back and the moving folds of her robes, and it seemed to Devon that he watched with bitterness and, yes, hunger. Anger.

But to Lord Gilliam of Elseth, she tendered what she had tendered the Twin Kings: a perfect obeisance. She tried to fall to her knees, but he reached out and grabbed her arm; the cloth of her robes rustled and struggled against his grip, although he didn't seem to notice. "Don't," he told her roughly, drawing his hand away abruptly. "I didn't save him either. He always said the Hunter would take him. I always said—" words, which had never been his strength, deserted him, and he struggled with silence for a long moment.

"But tonight," he finally managed, hefting the spear, "it will all be over."

"Hunt well, Hunter Lord," Evayne said, rising. "And you, little sister," she added, for the wild girl now dogged Lord Gilliam's shadow, as close to his person as the dogs that would have followed him everywhere. "Hunt well."

The girl keened her wordless keen.

These were her friends, the men who trusted her. Devon shook his head; there was no affection at all, no sense of camaraderie, in any of the exchanges. There was history, yes, but the history seemed to be a thing of pain; no joy rose from it.

Evayne now returned to the Twin Kings. "Your Majesties, it is not safe to use magic within the great chamber. It has . . . unusual effects, not all of them pleasant. However, if someone should be so foolish, it will almost certainly be survived. But below, in the chamber where the Sleepers lay, any use of magic will destroy the caster. Once we are in the tunnels proper, the protections wane."

"Very well," King Cormalyn replied. "Member APhaniel, you had best impart this information to your mages."

Duvari was not pleased, and he did not scruple to hide this fact. Duvari, however, seldom looked pleased, and the tight rein of his anger was a simple fact of life for those who were forced, by the necessity of his role and his duties, to endure his presence. He kept as close to the Kings as possible, but as Evayne took the lead and the Kings followed closely behind, it was difficult to put himself between them. Devon traveled by Duvari's side. Only the unknown terrain troubled him; the scant light he could work with. The hall was long and wide and would present no difficulty in a fight; he could not, however, see ceilings; nor could he see the whole of the distant walls or what might lie in the shadows pooled there.

But he could hear the growing distress of the distant magi; the fools had heard advice that it was beyond their meager self-control to follow. As the Kings' assembled forces traversed the great hall with its golden symbols engraved upon marble floors, its broken pillars, loose rocks, and distant shadows, the mages stopped or cried out in an excitement they could not contain; that excitement turned quickly to bitter regret. He was certain that there had been some use of magic in the distance, but it was slight, subtle, and easily extinguished.

At last they paused at the top of stone stairs that lead in a wide spiral into darkness below.

"Here," Evayne told them, although her eyes did not leave those stairs, "we begin our descent. Light your lamps if you have them, or your torches—but do not rely on magery to guide your steps." It would have been almost insulting to add this reminder, except that the magi appeared to require it.

The stairs were disconcerting; they hit a note each time someone stepped on them. The notes, if approached one step at a time, might have sounded like music; as it was, it was cacophony, and if any subtlety in approach was required for the small force to survive its first contact with the denizens of the mysterious undercity of Jewel Markess, they were all doomed.

"It is the song of approach," Evayne told the Kings and a very tight-lipped Lord of the Compact. "And of departure. The stairs were built to chime it, by some magic or some craftsmanship that has long been forgotten. No one could approach those who waited above by stealth. No one could leave in secrecy."

"They'll hear us below," Devon said quietly.

She raised a brow. "I do not know. But I think not. The chamber of the Sleepers lies between us and our enemy."

"Lead," King Cormalyn told her quietly, as if even the mention of the *Sleepers* was disquieting and he intended, by this command, to stifle it instantly. It was . . . unusual. And, in Devon's opinion, entirely unnecessary; the cacophony of the hundreds of men and women who descended the stairs would have drowned out all but the shouted word, and Evayne did not shout or raise her voice.

Instead, she waited a little way off the last—or first—of the steps until there was once again silence. Here, they stood at the foot of an empty hall; it was long, and it was not so fine a hall as the one above. There were no windows, and the walls were visible; there was no obvious shearing of their height. But they were stone, not marble. This was not meant to impress but merely to convey. Nor was it a single hall. The ceilings above were vaulted, and the hall branched into tunnels to the right and left.

Devon had no other orientation; the journey through the Sanctum had made all other directions almost superfluous.

He would not have been particularly surprised to learn that some of the Order's mages had disappeared down one or another of those tunnels, for the magi knew that the ways were, and would remain, closed to them after. He would, however, have been annoyed.

They came to a full stop at a set of large doors. Large, in this case, was an understatement; not even in *Avantari*, a building with which Devon was intimately familiar, were doors of this height to be found. They were closed, and there was no sign of keyholes. In the place of keyholes or knockers, they carried a large seal, which seemed, at base, a spiral that turned uniformly from edge to center. It glowed gold, suggesting base metal. It was not, in Devon's opinion, any such thing.

"These," Evayne said, turning to the Kings, "are the last of the doors. There were three, but two have already been breached by the breaking of the earth and the sinking of the city. They were magicked once, but the source of their power has long since fled this world."

"Magic," Member APhaniel said, in a sharp, crisp voice, "does not flee when the caster dies." He spoke as master to pupil here, and with some disappointment.

"No. But it is weakened when the race dies. Or when the race leaves." She met his gaze, and she smiled—it was an odd smile. There was no triumph in it, and much weariness. "And if I gave you the impression that no magic remained here, please forgive me—for the magic is not one that you or I could easily break." She turned, then, to the Exalted, and they came.

"It offers warning," the Exalted of the Mother said, after a long pause spent in the study of the single rune.

"And promises danger," Evayne replied.

"You read the oldest tongue?"

Silence. When the pause had gone on for long enough, Evayne said, "Exalted, grace us; open the door that your ancestor barred. We have so little time."

The Mother's daughter approached the doors. She drew breath, lifted her arms, and began to chant. The chant sounded almost familiar to Devon, but it had been years since he had sat through a service in the Mother's temple, and even in his youth it had not been to the Mother that he had paid his most earnest respects. He was content to watch.

The sons of Cormaris and Reymaris came to stand beside her to the left and right, and they held torches aloft, although she didn't seem to require them. But they did not speak.

Devon had expected the doors to open, and in some fashion they did; but there was no clicking of lock or tumbling of bolt. Instead, the doors grew translucent as she chanted, losing shape and solidity until only the rune itself remained, cutting edges into vision that could still be seen when he closed his eyes.

At last, that single rune dimmed, and the stone frame stood empty.

Light flooded in through the opening.

There was no hall that led to the chamber; the door seemed part of what served as wall. Beyond it, Devon could see biers, stylized and pale, the engraving exact and sharp. Makers must have labored here—or gods— but their work did not receive its due, for upon those biers lay three men. Their hair was white, and they were unhelmed; they lay upon their backs, the perfect and precise lines of their profiles exposed to any witness. And witnesses came, in the hundreds, held back only by the Kings and the Exalted, for the Kings ceded their lead only to Evayne a'Nolan, and all others must wait.

Evayne stepped through the frame in which a door had once stood.

The Exalted of Cormaris turned to the Kings. "Do not approach them, and be wary of crossing any circle's path."

The circles were evident to Devon only once he had entered their chamber proper. The biers, like the three petals of a trifold flower, were surrounded by golden circles into which words had been engraved. He did not study them long; the language was not one he recognized. Instead, he studied the Sleepers themselves, for he had no doubt at all that these were they: even in sleep they radiated composure and power, and they were beautiful in the way that no statue, even one touched by Artisans, could be. Their skin was the white of alabaster, their lashes and hair were also white; their cheekbones were high and pronounced, and no wrinkles or lines marred their faces at all. No scars.

Mindful of the words of the Exalted, Devon followed the Kings lead; he did not linger for more than a moment, and that, almost against his will. Only Duvari seemed immune to the subtle demand for attention— possibly obeisance—from these three. He had not gotten far, however, for Meralonne APhaniel approached their silent guide.

"Did you always know where they were?" he asked. Even the mage was subdued.

"Not always."

"Did you know of it while I taught you?"

"No."

He had already turned away from her answer, and he now approached the bier farthest from the door. She lifted a hand, reached for his shoulder, and then let it fall without touching him; she did not speak.

"Mage," the son of Cormaris said sharply.

"If I could, I would not wake them," was the soft reply. "I understand what you vowed, Exalted, and I would not force you to defend that oath while there is a greater enemy—a mutual one—to face." He bowed; it was stiff, and slight, but in this room it had weight. The Exalted nodded grimly but did not relax, for the mage now skirted the edge of the circle around the bier, until he approached the Sleeper's face.

"What—what are they?" a younger man asked.

"They are the Princes of the Firstborn," was his soft reply.

"And what was their crime?" the Exalted of Cormaris asked, his voice just as soft.

"Did your Lord not tell you?"

The Exalted did not play the word games that often delighted fractious magi; he frowned, as if the question were impertinent. "Only that they were guilty of betrayal."

"But not what that betrayal was?" The mage smiled; it was a very bitter expression. "It was manifold, Exalted. And for it, they have lost their swords and their names—see, you cannot glance upon the device that was once the pride of their kin." He lifted a slender hand and pointed to the blank shield that now lay beneath the unworn helm across the Sleeper's armored chest.

"You know much, Meralonne."

"Legend Lord is one of my specialties. Come. The darkness is waiting, and it will wait neither peacefully nor long."

Evayne did not lead them through the building that Jewel had so accurately described. In silence, she led them through a crack or a fissure that lay beyond the Sleepers, and into the darkness.

"Why this way, Evayne?" Meralonne asked.

"The Sleepers are not our friends, but they are no more friend to our enemies; that way will be watched, and is watched now; it will be guarded by the most powerful of the servants that are available. This? It leads into the city as well, but it is narrow here, before it opens."

"Jewel—"

"Could not have reached the Sleepers were it not for her size; we would need to move rock and risk the collapse of more should we attempt to retrace the route she took. It is here," Evayne added, pointing.

The Kings nodded in silence; they were unsettled by the sight of the Sleepers, and momentarily humbled by it.

Chapter Twenty

28th of Scaral, 410 A.A.
Terafin Manse, Averalaan Aramarelas

THEY MADE THEIR WAY BACK to the manse in the silence past
midnight, and Jewel noted that it *was* silent. But it was a cold silence; neither she—nor anyone else on the walk—could be certain that it
would last. Sometimes it would stretch out like the promise of peace—or
worse, far worse, the hope of it—and then it would break, and the pain
would start again.

Only when she reached the bridge did Jewel frown. She turned back
to look at the ranks of the Terafin Chosen, bumping into Morretz who,
uncharacteristically, had continued to walk.

"Jewel?" The Terafin asked, as she too paused.

"Where's Devon?"

"Devon will not be returning to the manse with us."

"But—" Jewel's mouth caught up with her words and closed before
they could escape. The Terafin hadn't answered the question, but the
answer she did offer meant there'd be no further discussion. She nodded
and jogged quickly—and without any grace—back to The Terafin's side.

"They will be waiting for us," The Terafin told her.

Jewel could have pretended to misunderstand; she didn't. It was the
last day of Henden—the last night. In history, it was the darkest of the
nights, for the five previous had seen the slaughter of tens of thousands,
and their corpses lay where they had fallen in the open streets.

No, she thought. *That's story. That's legend.*

It didn't matter. This Henden and that Henden were, for a moment, the same. There were no Blood Barons; there was no war for succession. Instead, there were demons, and the dead lay not on the open streets but beneath them, their dying cries as sharp and painful as any mercenary's sword.

Then?

Veralaan, the heir to the throne, had returned with two young men at her side: King Reymalyn the First, and King Cormayln the First. Their eyes were golden, and they had been raised by their fathers in the lands that lay between the mortal realm and the lands the gods called home. They had come to rule.

They had come to show the people of this Empire that ruling, in and of itself, did not require a lack of wisdom or justice. They asked for followers, and people followed. People died as well, but in the stories those deaths were ennobling. Jewel had never been suspicious of that last part until now.

Dead was dead, wasn't it?

Her dead were dead. Noble death, ignoble death—it didn't matter. She'd seen Lord Gilliam's face, and she knew—*knew*—he felt the same. But . . . she wasn't Lord Gilliam. It wasn't for the dead that she burned, now; it wasn't for the dead that she lived. She *had* the living, and they were waiting, someplace in House Terafin, for her return.

She swallowed air; it was cold and biting. The night was still silent when she turned to The Terafin. "You'll speak to them?" she asked softly.

The Terafin's brow rose, and then she smiled. "You understand," she said quietly. "Yes. Where they wait, I will speak. And if you will it, you will speak as well. Tell them of what you witnessed here. Let that word spread: Moorelas of Aston spoke to the Kings and granted them passage into the darkness beyond. It is the Kings' ride, not Moorelas', but they ride, in the end, with the same purpose."

But if the people who lived within the manse did gather, they didn't gather in the foyer; they didn't gather in the galleries or the long halls. Jewel thought they might be huddling in the rooms behind the walls; Carver had mentioned that it was "more crowded than usual."

The Terafin didn't seem all that surprised when she entered the doors and the manse itself was empty. It was also darker than normal; the magelights had been whispered to darkness, and only candles flickered in their brass holders against the wall. She nodded; the windows were also shrouded; here, the moon's light was so heavily veiled it might not have existed at all.

Jewel started to head toward the West Wing, but The Terafin called her back. "Come," she said quietly. "Join me. Morretz will summon the household in my absence."

"But—"

"They will not sleep, Jewel. Not even Alowan will do that—perhaps especially not Alowan."

"He's not—"

"ATerafin? No. Not in name." The Terafin offered a rueful smile, and it stripped years off her face. "I have lost track of the number of times I have offered him the House Name. Each and every time he has politely refused. It's become a tradition between the two of us. But he will never accept it, and I will always desire his acceptance. It is a reminder to me that I cannot have all that I desire."

And what, Jewel thought, as she followed The Terafin up the winding stairs, do you want now? She didn't ask. She couldn't ask.

"There is a place I go," The Terafin told her quietly, "when I am troubled or when I seek privacy."

Given her huge and well-guarded chambers, which seemed to Jewel's admittedly inexperienced eye to be empty most of the time, this almost made no sense. But The Terafin entered those chambers, passing between two of the Chosen Jewel didn't recognize, and she shed the finery of her official outer clothing for a much more practical coat—and a long, large cape that had clearly been made for broader—and older—shoulders.

This, she wrapped about herself. Then she nodded to the Chosen. Torvan and Gordon returned the nod with a sharp salute and followed; the other four remained behind.

What must it be like to have men like Torvan live—and die—at your command? How hard was it to never disappoint them?

Jewel shook her head. She couldn't imagine The Terafin being capable of causing that disappointment. She seemed so controlled, so perfectly poised, so graceful in her power. Certainly, as she tripped over the skirts of the dress that Ellerson had chosen and cursed, compared to Jewel she was all of those things.

But what else was she?

A small ladder led, of all things, to the ceiling, and The Terafin climbed it with care. She unhinged something in the ceiling, and it fell slowly and heavily toward the ground. It was a staircase—a narrow, wooden staircase. It led into the darkness of the sky.

"We are not to be disturbed," The Terafin told Torvan, "by any save Morretz; he will come when it is time."

Torvan nodded.

Jewel followed her Lord into the night sky.

"This," The Terafin said, raising her face to the moons, "is my refuge." It was a small balcony on the roof of the manse itself; it was not large, and it was not—at least in this light—heavily decorated.

"The kitchen," Jewel said, because words seem to be expected, "was mine. But there were people in it."

The Terafin nodded and fell silent for several minutes. But she broke the silence. "They killed my brother," she said quietly. She glanced at Jewel, and then added, with a shadowed smile that was clear in the moonlight, "my baby brother." She now occupied her hands with folds of cloth, drawing the edges of the cape toward her cheeks as she inhaled.

Jewel wondered whose cape it had once been; she didn't ask. But she said, "They killed mine as well." Thinking of Lefty, in particular, although the faces of all those they'd lost in the undercity were clear to her. She drew a breath. Held it. Exhaled. "Terafin—"

"You wish to speak to me about your den."

As often happened when people were so damn right so unexpectedly, the rest of the words deserted Jewel. But she swallowed and nodded.

"You have not informed them of the change in your station." It wasn't a question.

"No."

"May I ask why?"

"If I can ask how you know. That I didn't tell them, I mean."

"They are no different. In Gabriel's office, Teller labors in relative silence, and in Lucille ATerafin's office, Finch does likewise. Believe," The Terafin added with a grimace, "that if Finch had mentioned your sudden elevation to Lucille half of Terafin would know. They don't, and therefore, you've said nothing. Why?"

Jewel hesitated and then folded her elbows and forearms so she could rest against them and stare out into the grounds below. "I want to be happy," she finally said. "It's something to be proud of. But . . . it seems wrong right now. To have good luck."

"You think it a matter of luck?"

"Isn't it?" She turned her head to look up at The Terafin. "If you're going to tell me I've earned it . . ." She shrugged. "I've earned it because I was born cursed, and that curse is useful to the House."

"It is more than useful and not only to the House. Some are born with the mage talent; some are born with the voice. Some are born with the hands of healers. Those are gifts, and they are as much a gift as those born with the talent for making music or creating works of beauty."

"But my den isn't any of those things. They're just mine. I trust them. I need them. I keep an eye out for them—and they watch my back. Always have, since I first found them. And I don't want to leave them behind. I don't want *them* to feel like I'm leaving them behind. We would never be here at all if we hadn't stuck it out together."

"You wish them to take the House Name."

"I want—" Jewel closed her eyes and rested her chin against her arms again. At last, she said, "Yes. But it's not mine to offer them."

"No."

"It's yours."

"Yes. And there is a procedure in place for applicants to the House."

"And what is this procedure?"

"It involves an interview, among other things. It involves a variety of tests, few of them written. It is hard to test character," The Terafin added.

"I've met some of the ATerafin. Hard to imagine they could take a test of character, let alone pass it."

"The House needs many things," The Terafin replied, after a long pause. "And not all of those things are simple. It needs men and women with ambition and the arrogance to achieve their goals. It needs, among other things, money, because money can be brokered into the power the patriciate best understands. It requires people canny enough, and experienced enough, to treat with wolves without freezing or fleeing.

"And yes, I can well imagine that many, many ATerafin who fill that role would not be to your liking. They are not to be trusted in the easy way you trust your den or the way I trust my Chosen."

"And if I tell them to apply, what are their chances?"

"What would you have said yours were, when you first arrived?"

Jewel nodded. It was a fair question. "Can I take the same test?"

"No."

"Why?"

"Because you are already ATerafin. You cannot pretend to be otherwise, although you can fail to mention it to your den." The Terafin's smile was weary. "You lack subtlety," she said. "And the skills with which to negotiate. You are a seer, Jewel ATerafin. There has not, to our knowledge, been one in the Empire for centuries."

"There's Evayne."

"Evayne is not . . . the same."

"What do you know about her?"

But The Terafin shook her head. "That she is not ATerafin. Let me return to the point. You are a seer. The fact that you were raised in the lower holdings does not change that. The fact that you come without money and with a very tattered education doesn't change that. You would, could you prove your claim—"

"I've never claimed—"

"—to the satisfaction of any House Leader, be entertained as a suitable candidate for House Membership. But you came to Terafin first, and it is in Terafin that you will live. You are—you were—Ararath's last gift." She turned, exposing the patrician length of her profile. "If you understood how valuable you are, you might demand that the den be offered what was offered you."

"And you'd grant it?"

The Terafin smiled. "I would agree to consider it," she said gravely. "Because I understand what your presence in my House might mean in future and because I see, clearly, what it might mean come dawn. But I would hide it, Jewel. Inasmuch as it is possible, I *will* hide it. I cannot, therefore, with ease go to my Council and invoke the specter of a seer's power and glory.

"But I expected no less from you than this; and I expected, in the end, that you would undervalue yourself enough that you would hesitate to make your acceptance of the House Name contingent upon theirs. It is . . . unusual to be offered the Name so quickly, when you have no proven track record in one area of expertise or another. Understand that."

"You can't do it?"

The Terafin surprised her, then. She laughed. "I *am* The Terafin, Jewel. I can, of course, as you say 'do it.' But understand that they will be mine, and they will be part of *my* House. What they are to you will become mixed with what they must be, to me. They will learn that loyalties bind them in unexpected ways. Are you sure this is what you wish, not for them, but for yourself? Think carefully."

In the darkness of the Sixth Day, Jewel did. She remembered, clearly, what she'd felt when Arann had told her he wanted to join the House Guard. He wasn't ATerafin, but she'd known what it had meant. He was going somewhere she couldn't follow, and he was going somewhere that might make it hard, in the end, to follow her.

"They're mine," she said quietly. "But they're not mine. I'm not the girl I was when Rath first found me; they're not the people they were when I first found them. It's hard to see it, sometimes, but it's there. What I want—for me—is to be big enough to accept that."

Silence. Moonlight.

"Are you?"

Jewel shrugged. "Not always. But right now, I could be, and I think that has to count for something. I don't want to lose them," she added. "But there are a lot of ways to lose people. I think they could be happy here."

"You want them to be happy."

"Yeah. But . . . I don't want them to be happy without me." She looked at the coal-dark shape of trees in the garden beneath the roof. "Is that bad?"

"It's human," The Terafin replied. "What do you want from them?"

"What they give me now. They listen. They think. They tell me. They're there for me when I need them."

"Very well."

"Are those the right answers?"

"I don't know. They are not, in my opinion, the wrong answers, but they are not, in the end, my den."

"And what do you want? From your people?"

"It amounts, in the end, to the same thing," The Terafin replied. "But it covers many more people; some of the people who bear my House Name I have met only a handful of times. They earned their name before I took power, and they work at a great remove from Averalaan."

"Jewel?"

Jewel rose at the sound of the familiar voice, and she saw that the trap had been lifted. Morretz glanced up. "Terafin."

The Terafin did not turn. "Is it time?"

"It is. The servants have gathered, and the family. They are many this year."

The Terafin nodded, and Jewel realized, not for the first time, that the whole of Terafin, all the people in this manse, and all the people beyond it, were in some ways The Terafin's den. To Jewel, she said, "Are you ready?"

But Jewel was frozen, on the rooftop terrace. The hair on the back of her neck had risen so suddenly she felt as if she'd been struck by some invisible lightning, some paralyzing force of nature. She spun on the roof and crossed the narrow terrace; she looked out, toward the old city across the bay. There, rising above the dark of moon-touched night, a shadow was rising, like a dark void. She opened her mouth, but no words escaped.

"What is it, Jewel? What do you see?"

She didn't answer. She couldn't. But the earth did: The ground shook beneath their feet.

"Terafin," Morretz said again, as if there had been no interruption. Jewel recognized the tone, and it startled her; it was almost like . . . Teller's.

And it had the same effect on the woman who ruled the House as Teller's might have had on Jewel. She rose, stiffening; you could see her don the mantle of office, although she spoke no other word, made no other gesture.

"Jewel, come. We must attend the family."

This time, Jewel rose, understanding the truth of those words. What she'd seen didn't matter. It changed nothing. They had their responsibilities, and at a time like this, those were the only things that counted.

She nodded, and together they made their way down from the open freedom of the roof, their words once again caged by the necessities of their chosen ranks.

But they didn't immediately join the rest of the House, and Jewel understood why only after a few moments of utter confusion. The Terafin dressed. Or rather, she changed. The finery appropriate for any meeting of import—even one at midnight in the cold sea winds by the Sanctum of Moorelas—was not appropriate for First Day rites. Historically, the First Day was the end of the reign of the Blood Barons. But people came to that end through the darkest of days the Baronies had ever known; they came hungry, and poor, and afraid.

It was hard to bear hope when hope itself seemed like deception.

The Terafin, like the people who now found shelter in her manse, understood the Six Days and their significance, and she emerged unadorned; she wore no rings, no necklace, no bracelets. She didn't even bear the House Sword.

Jewel had far less to shed. She waited, and when The Terafin signaled, she followed in her wake.

The servants have gathered, and the family. They are many, this year.

Morretz had given them warning. Clearly the warning had meant something to The Terafin; to Jewel, it just as clearly hadn't meant *enough*. As she approached the newly constructed stairs of the foyer, she saw . . . people. Not all of them were ATerafin; she knew that from Carver. She knew that the Master of the Household Staff, a woman more feared than admired, had chosen to turn a blind eye to the influx of families from the holdings.

Those families, small children attached to adult legs, smaller children borne in arms, were waiting in the foyer. So, too, the servants—cooks, gardeners, maids—who made the mansion run, day in and day out. Jewel recognized only one or two because there were *so many* people. Even market days weren't so damn crowded.

Only the children made any noise at all.

Glancing at The Terafin, Jewel saw that she'd expected this; she wasn't surprised, intimidated, or frightened. The den had learned that crowds, like daggers, had two edges; The Terafin had not. Here, it was The Terafin's experience that ruled. Jewel followed her like shadow.

She went down the stairs. Morretz spoke her name once, and she nodded, but didn't look back. Instead, she looked forward, and as she came into view, people began to make the noise that they'd held in.

"Terafin!"

"TERAFIN!"

She waited until they were quiet, which took some time; people approached her, and one man touched—or grabbed—her elbow. There were no Chosen who served as her guardians here. Jewel glanced at Morretz; he did not interfere. Because he didn't, she wouldn't.

But when there was as much silence and respect as fear allowed, The Terafin lifted her voice. She could be heard across the foyer, but it didn't sound as though she was shouting.

"Come to the shrine."

* * *

She led, and they followed. They passed through the dark and somber manse. The windows had been shrouded, but Jewel didn't expect much light would have come through anyway. Not tonight.

What they watched for, what they silently—or not so silently—prayed for, was dawn. Dawn, silence, and a lifting of the shadow. The grounds had seen damage, as had the foyer; the foyer had been repaired much more quickly—and if Teller's information was right, at far more expense. But the shrines to the three gods still stood, and to get to the shrine Jewel suspected The Terafin was leading her people toward, one had to pass the three.

Prayers were said at each as the line moved—slowly, and messily—but they came at last to the House shrine. The grass would be flattened, in the best case. No one, however, cared. They watched The Terafin. The Terafin, in turn, watched them. She promised them nothing, not in words—but there was a certainty to her movements, a certainty to her bearing, that brought calm just by force of presence.

She mounted the steps to the altar; no one joined her. Not even Morretz. When she reached the altar, she bent before it for a moment, offering her respect to the House she ruled, as if all rulership were a singular gesture of respect, no more. She did not, however, plead.

Instead, she rose and turned, the altar at her back, framed by the rounded dome of the shrine's roof, its ever-burning lights, and its pillars. Those lights were, in theory, forbidden during the Six Days, but Jewel understood why they burned; it was almost impossible to argue with a ghost.

"This," The Terafin said, "is the First Day as we have never seen it, and we wait—as our ancestors waited—for the coming of the Kings.

"I have been to the mainland, and tonight I have heard the voice of Moorelas. Through his Sanctum and his agency, the Kings have led the Exalted and the magi into the darkness that has festered and hidden beneath Averalaan.

"I was not given leave to join them; my sword was neither requested nor desired. Instead, I have returned to Terafin, and with you I wait the dawn, when we may pull the shrouds from windows and lamp and see light once more. I am grateful, and honored, to be here. I can think of no finer men—and women—with whom to wait out these late hours." She nodded to them, as regal in her fashion as the Queens, and then—to Jewel's surprise, she sat on the marble steps and motioned for Jewel to join her.

Jewel, however, was gazing into the gathered crowd for the people she hadn't automatically seen: her den. Her kin. Here, the servants had gathered as much of their families to them as they could; Jewel had only The Terafin and Morretz.

They were the heart of the House, it was true; but the House was not yet the whole of Jewel's life. Most of her life had been lived in the holdings. Her worth to the House was practically defined by them, or what now lay beneath them.

But she hadn't become valuable in isolation. She hadn't found the entrance to the undercity by any cleverness of her own. Rath had shown her. She hadn't made it on her own in the holdings; she'd had Rath and, later, the whole of her den. It was the Sixth Day. Come dawn, it would be the first of Veral, and the start of the new year.

Or it would be over.

She stared into the crowd, passing over unfamiliar faces that nonetheless *felt* familiar in their fear and their desire to protect those they cared about from that fear. On the Isle, the children didn't play in the streets, and their grandparents didn't watch from stairs or doors or porches; they played behind gates—if they played at all. Here, they huddled in the dark, sleeping or fitful or restless, but yes—even in the dark, in the edges of the light cast by the altar, some did play.

She remembered snow and snowballs, and Lefty, the day they found Teller. And she didn't resent the play or the joy in it, even here. She glanced at the altar, remembering the Terafin Spirit's words.

When she glanced back, she saw a ripple in the crowd, and in spite of herself, she smiled, because pushing their way through—the usual, subtle movements didn't work as well when densely packed people were still, and not on the move—was a spiral of white hair she would have recognized anywhere.

Angel was here. And beside him, or just behind, was Carver.

"Jay?" It was Carver who spoke. Angel just slid in beside her and offered silence and the hint of a smile. She couldn't see the others; she knew Arann must be on duty someplace in the manse, because he was junior enough to get all the crappy late shifts. But Finch, Teller, and Jester didn't follow Carver and Angel.

She thought about waiting for them, but she wasn't certain they'd show up, and if they did, they wouldn't shove their way through a crowd like this. A normal crowd, yes, but these people? No. Not just to stand a little closer to her.

"We started this together," she said to Carver.

"Yeah." He glanced at the crowd as well, as if seeking the rest of the den. "How's it going to end?"

"Wrong question," Angel said. He smacked Carver between the shoulder blades. "Are we going to win?"

She had no answer to give them; she wanted to say yes, but since it didn't slide out naturally, it would have been just a pathetically hopeful guess. She turned, started toward the steps she'd abandoned, and stopped. Froze there.

They knew what it meant.

But she gazed past them, past the crowd, pass the manse, as if these things had been rendered so insubstantial they were as transparent as ghosts in stories. She could see the waters of the ocean that surrounded the bay on which the Isle sat, and beyond it, the form and shape of the city's skyline, as translucent as the manor, the manse, and all its people.

There was only one thing that was solid, and it lay coiled beneath the city, growing and rising as she watched. It was not the shape of a man, not yet—but it struggled toward that solidity.

She could hear the screams of the dying in the distance, and she almost lifted her hands to cover her ears.

"What—what is it?" someone asked. Not one of hers. Not The Terafin, not Morretz.

"The Shining City," she said. "It's rising." But she had no strength for words; they came out so softly only those closest to her heard them, and no one repeated them.

28th of Henden, 410 A.A.
The Undercity, Averalaan

Isladar watched the standing arch. The keystone had taken much time and much effort to invest with the power it now held, and that time had been a concern to Lord Karathis and Sor Na Shannen. They had not challenged him openly; where their control was too poor to contain their displeasure, their underlings had suffered. Nor was he surprised; they had taken the form and shape of mortals, and they had purported to live as mortals for a mortal life span, but in the end, they were of the Hells; mortality was a lesser form of life, one stripped of power or majesty because it lacked eternity.

They had therefore learned little.

Oh, they had learned to exploit the weaknesses they found, and, in particular, Sor Na Shannen had become adroit—but she was honing an edge that already existed.

Soon, he thought, it would not matter. The darkness was growing; light was cast by fire or not at all, but they little required it. The Lord was almost upon this broken, crippled plane.

And yet. Isladar's smile was slight and subtle. He had always professed an interest in the brief ephemera that was mortal thought and mortal life, and he had seen the potential in it. The *Kialli* feared power, yes, but they did not understand the elusive ways in which the weak might become powerful.

But they would, he thought.

He did not turn or start when Karathis-Errakis appeared, bound by flame, upon the coliseum's floor. The kin abased himself instantly, his fire reflected by marble and gaze as Lord Karathis and Sor Na Shannen immediately turned their attention upon Karathis' servant.

"Lord."

Karathis was not pleased. Here, in the darkness, the sacrifices continued unabated, and the pain brought an almost meditative pleasure to those denied it for so many decades. He did not wish to be disturbed in the midst of the Contemplation. If Errakis was a kin of flame, it was candle to the bonfire of his Lord's power; that power literally burned.

But Isladar saw the appearance of the kin as a counter, a move in the long game, and he lifted a hand. "Enough, Karathis."

Between Lords, honorifics were not a necessity; they were not a matter of form. Karathis' fire burned a moment longer, as if he sought to make a point. He did; he did not, and would not, press it further. Not now. The Lord could hear all that was said, and done, without effort, he was now that close.

"Speak," Karathis told his servant.

"Strangers approach from the southeast."

Karathis' eyes burned brighter. "What is this?"

"We think—we think at least one hundred, at most three. Humans."

"Impossible." Karathis' claws began to grow darker, longer, and harder. They glinted in the guttering fire that surrounded the prone Errakis.

"From the southeast?" Isladar asked.

Errakis did not respond, which was wise, given the mood of his Lord. He had made his point.

"Answer him." Karathis said.

"Yes, Lord Isladar."

"Interesting. Were they armed?"

"Yes. But—the armed men have not been fighting in the tunnels. They move with speed and in complete silence."

"How were they discovered?"

"Arradis-Shannen was destroyed in the seeker's cavern. Before he died, he sent word."

Isladar glanced at Karathis, no more; he did not speak. He was not surprised.

"They have mages." The words were cold and flat.

"Yes, Lord."

Karathis nodded. Isladar waited for further comment and realized that none would be forthcoming. Ah, well. "Karathis, do not be a fool."

Karathis stiffened and turned from his servitor.

"Arradis-Shannen was *Kialli*. If he were brought down in battle by mere human mages, we would have felt the ground breaking beneath our feet."

Karathis still did not speak.

"No. They have Summer magic. They think to bring light with them into the Winter's haven." Isladar spoke in sharp, strong words, but he watched as he did. He was not angry.

Nor, he thought, was Karathis. The Duke of the Hells smiled. "Let them bring light. We lost many to the cursed bardic voices—let them supply the final sacrifices that our Lord requires."

And here it was: Isladar's opening. He had so few, and they had to be navigated with care. But care, among the *Kialli*, meant many things. "We cannot afford that. Think: The one who carries the Hunter's Horn may lead the human pack."

Karathis stilled. Isladar waited, wondering if wisdom would now undo this subtle, fragile web. Silence continued for a beat. Two.

But it was broken on the third as Karathis lifted his head and *roared*.

Isladar closed his eyes. In spite of himself, he felt the momentary wonder of Karathis' voice, unleashed; in its fashion, it was a thing of beauty, and it had endured the aeons. He remembered it. Their enemies might have horns or flags or light; this Lord had voice to raise above them all, and it might be heard in the farthest corner of conflict should he care to make it heard.

But Sor Na Shannen paid no head to the splendor of this unleashed echo of the past. "This is not possible." Her tone was soft, but it vibrated with her fury. "Karathis—"

"I closed the tunnels personally. I saw each unmaking. Or do you challenge this?"

She did not and would not. She was subtle, yes; her power was not one to break rock or physical body. Her method of destruction was slow and thorough, but it would not stand her in good stead here. "We cannot hold that tunnel," she said at last, and her eyes went to the arch and to what it contained. Her Lord for eternity.

"We have no choice."

"Look at it," she snapped, as she turned away. "There are no crawlways above it and none below; it is too low to properly shadow. If Isladar is correct, the strongest of our number will not be able to wield full power there."

Karathis snarled. "You are not required to hold it indefinitely. A few weeks—"

"You will not have weeks," Isladar said, speaking quietly now.

"How long?" The last syllable was an elongated growl, barely a syllable.

"Hours, I think." Isladar glanced at the arch. "And at that, few."

Karathis looked to the gate as well, and through it, to the heart of shadow, its motion elliptical, indefinite. Before it, altars had been erected, and they bore blood; around them, piled like the refuse they had become, bodies. There were not enough of them. He roared again, and as he did, wings unfurled between his shoulder blades; Karathis had ever been a Lord who disliked the dictates of gravity and the bindings of earth.

"Isladar, you know what must be done. Do it. I will attend to the intruders."

The Kings' forces had seen battle. Here, in the dark, uneven tunnels that led—that were said to lead—to the summoning stones of the *Allasakari*, they had found their first demons. And had been found by them. Among the priests, some fifteen would no longer fight, and five would no longer do anything.

Devon was armed with the ceremonial daggers of the Exalted, but he had not yet used them; the Exalted were armed with the magic that imbued those daggers, and it made the daggers the lesser weapon. The magi were gifted with fire, and to Devon's surprise, they could fight; they were silent; the fractious nature of the Order of Knowledge was utterly absent. They looked to Meralonne for their lead, when they sought it at all, and they were efficient.

Silence made efficiency seem cold-blooded.

The tunnels had narrowed and widened in places, as Jewel had described, but they at last opened into what appeared to be a hall. The ceiling above was obscured by shadows, which the Exalted indicated were natural.

Evayne, who had walked regardless of interruption, slowed now. Her glance took in the whole of the cavern; she lifted a hand, no more, and then turned to the Kings.

"Here," she said quietly, "we will face opposition."

Since they had already faced opposition, and enough opposition to leave five dead and fifteen incapacitated, Devon raised a brow. Evayne did not appear to notice.

Meralonne APhaniel said, "Opposition?"

She nodded. She said no more, and Devon, familiar with the erratic and incomplete nature of Jewel Markess' gift, did not expect it, even from a woman decades older and demonstrably more learned. But he readied himself, with a single nod at Duvari.

Duvari spoke briefly with the Kings. He was not pleased that their guide was a stranger. Nor would he have been pleased had it been otherwise. Duvari did not have more than a passing knowledge of joy, and inasmuch as he had retained that knowledge, it was always secondhand. But the Kings chose to examine the lay of the land, and this cavern, its heights momentarily—and carefully—illuminated by the magi, had the widest path, the most open area, in which to make a stand.

Nor did they doubt that they would have to do so; they gave their quiet orders while Evayne watched.

It was not long before Devon sensed movement, and it was the unsettling movement of the rock beneath his feet. In response, small pebbles fell from the heights of the rounded walls to either side of their momentary encampment, the sounds echoing in the sudden silence, as all men strained for a glimpse, in the shadowed light, of the danger they now faced.

The Kings, however, obeyed Duvari's "request" to retreat, and he sent the Astari forward to encircle them. Devon was one of those Astari; he watched and he listened. But unlike his compatriots, he watched the seer and waited. Her face was a mask, but the sounds and the movement didn't startle her. She was alert, aware—aware even of his gaze and his interest. It forced the hint of a smile from her lips, but it was a smile that would have been at home on Duvari's face.

Or rather, on Duvari's face at a different time.

"What is the cause of this?" Duvari demanded, as the ground once again heaved beneath their feet.

"Some sort of magic," Sigurne Mellifas replied, little liking his tone.

Were the Lord of the Compact a less literal man, his sarcasm might have reverberated in angry echoes down the length of the hall. He was, however, Duvari. "Can you counter it?"

"Not if we don't know it's type, no." She said more, but Devon lost her words as the floor of the cavern once again shifted beneath their feet. This time the shifting lasted longer, and the walls and the rock-riddled cavern above them shook as well, shedding splinters.

When the ground had stilled, Devon looked to the Kings; they were calm, their eyes a steady, unblinking gold that offered certainty, if it was required. He shifted his gaze to Evayne.

She stood alone in the darkness, and he saw that she now held the orb, the seer's crystal, between her curved palms. It cast a subtle, moving light across her features. She was not young, not close; her eyes were wide and unblinking, her pupils so enlarged her irises seemed to be all black. They reflected nothing at this distance, but he thought—and why, he wasn't certain—of a child momentarily captivated by the corpse of a dog or a cat in the market, her expression turned from concern and horror to confusion. She wasn't Jewel, but he saw something that bound the two, young woman and older.

"Evayne?" Kallandras of Senniel now spoke. His concern was cool; his own expression was almost haggard, which was shocking in the smooth and cool features of one of Senniel's most famous bards.

"I cannot say for certain," she told him, tearing her gaze away from what she held. "I feared it might be the elemental magics—but it seems that they are too wild for our enemies."

"They are not too wild," Meralonne APhaniel told her quietly. "But they are not appropriate here. If what you have said is true—if what you have seen is true—we are on the road to the Cathedral that once stood at the heart of Vexusa. If you look at the ground here, and here, I would say we are almost upon it. Call the elemental earth magics, call the Old Earth, and it is quite likely that not only the tunnels but also the Cathedral would be destroyed. And the caster, for that matter, if old tales are true.

"Never bargain with the Old Earth when you have nothing of value to give it. The demon-kin have nothing at all of interest to the earth." He spoke casually, dismissing the demonic as if it were only barely worthy of consideration.

"Not to the earth, little brother," a voice said in the darkness. "But come. Let there be *fire*."

With fire came light; it was an orange light that shed heat and twisted the air as it moved. In its wake, Devon thought, mouth drying, legend walked, cloaked in flame. It was not human, nor had it ever been; no one could mistake the creature for anything but demonic. It was taller than the tallest man present, perhaps double the height, and wings of flame, with hearts of ebony, spread from either side of its back, its large shoulders. It stood like a man—like a giant—on two legs, and its arms, burning as its wings burned, rested a moment at its sides.

It had no eyes but fire, and when it opened its mouth, fire flew as well.

"This is ill news," Meralonne whispered softly; had he not moved to stand so close to Evayne, Devon might have missed the words; they did not carry far over the crackle of flame. The mage gestured; it was a brief movement of fingers in warm air. Yards from the creature, an opalescent and opaque wall suddenly grew from floor to ceiling; it shielded the Kings and those who followed.

"You know what it is?" Evayne asked.

"Oh, yes," he replied, master to student, as if for this moment that relationship had never been broken. "He is—or was—one of the Dukes of the Hells.

"Tell me," Meralonne said to Evayne, although his gaze did not leave the winged fire. "You learned the Winter rites—did you ever learn the wild ones?"

"No mortal can contain the wild ways. How can you test me at a time like this?"

"It was not a test. It was a very, very strong hope. I do not know everything about you or your kin—and those mortals born of immortal blood, no matter how tainted, can sometimes bear the wild weight a moment or two.

"How important is this mission, Evayne? At what cost must we succeed?"

The seer did not answer. Meralonne grimaced as fire hit the wall he had created; he did not gesture again, and Devon saw, as clearly as any man watching, that the wall would not hold. "Answer me; we do not have much time."

The seer's eyes widened. "Not at that cost," was her sharp, cold reply.

Devon would have found it more interesting if the barrier had not crumpled so easily. The Exalted—and the Kings themselves—now stepped in, and a gold light shadowed the mage's protection, strengthening it for a moment.

But it was not—Devon saw this clearly—enough. Nor would it be.

"We will never reach the Cathedral if a price is not paid. Do you not understand what you have seen this day? This was Vexusa, yes—but before that it was something far worse, far darker; the Sleepers fell at the heart of a god's dominion. There are places upon the world that still hold the ghosts of the things that have passed within them; there are places, dark and deep, that hold *more*. This is one."

He might have said more, but the wall folded, and he took two steps back as if he'd been struck. When he spoke again, it was no longer in any language that Devon understood: three words. Three sharp words that had the feel and texture of thunder.

Lightning, when it followed, was a sword. A blue sword, and with it, a shield, limned in a light that was almost painful to look upon. He raised both and stepped forward beyond the periphery of the line marked now by the Astari and the Exalted. The Kings exchanged only a glance, but they did not speak or attempt to call him back.

Nor did Sigurne Mellifas, for Meralonne APhaniel had become as strange, and as terrifying in his own fashion, as the creature they now faced.

And the creature acknowledged it. "Well met," he said.

Meralonne did not reply. Instead, he said, "Evayne, tell the mages to use spells of defense—and only those spells."

"But—"

"Do it." He stepped forward into the darkness.

"You are already too late," the creature said, stepping farther into the hall.

"If we were too late, we would face the god and not the lackey," Meralonne replied, his words cool and dismissive.

The creature snarled, then. "You will wish, before this is over, that you *had*."

Evayne did not deliver the commands of Meralonne APhaniel, but those commands did carry—Devon thought the Master Bard responsible, in the end, for their conveyance. Thus the mages threw up more familiar shields; the Kings retreated, but only a few yards; they could not easily retreat farther.

Fire bathed the ground as if it were torrential rain. What it touched, it burned, and the rock beneath both the feet of the demon and the feet of the mage reddened and whitened before it was done. The demon gestured, and his fury produced more fire, more rain, and the rocks above began to melt.

But the mages were prepared for this, and when rock fell in molten drops, it touched mage shields and slid to one side of the group or the other.

"You will wish it," Meralonne replied, his voice cold and clear. "Your Lord is not known to suffer failure gladly."

"You are beginning to bore me." As he spoke, a red, red sword came to his hand, just as the mage's sword had come to his.

Sigurne Mellifas watched. She was pale, and the weight of years across her shoulders had never felt so heavy, so immobilizing. Around her, Matteos had martialed the magi, and they worked now against the molten rock that dripped from stalactites above.

She left that work—worthy and necessary work—in his hands. She had seen *Kialli* in her youth, and she understood; better than any present save perhaps Meralonne himself, what they were capable of. But she had *never* seen a creature to rival the one Meralonne now faced, and she was afraid for him.

Afraid for them all. She cast, as she had once been taught; it was forbidden art, forbidden magic, all. Her hands shook; she remembered the cold condescension of her first master's words: *Only the weak require foci to force magic to their will.*

Aye, but in his world weakness had defined her life. She cared about the city, its Kings and its people; she cared about the Empire. She cared about the fates of the people she might never know or see. What matter, then, that she required the foci of movement and gesture to concentrate? His was a ghost's voice, a dead voice, a much-loathed voice.

And he had never taught her this. No mortal had, or could.

This had been a gift, an almost casual gift, from a fellow captive. A *Kialli* Lord.

She watched, for a moment, as that Lord might have watched. And what she saw made her close her eyes and whisper a single name. *Meralonne.*

She did not speak the name aloud, and as the sounds of combat were displaced by the cries of the magi over whom she presided, she withdrew almost gratefully from the act of witnessing the battle, for she now had no doubt whatsoever what its outcome must be.

Karathis was indeed powerful enough to be worthy of the title Duke of Hell. It was a title that was not in use in the Empire, although it had once been before the Twin Kings. The falling rock—which would kill if it landed upon the gathered men and women here—would be a mercy, in the end.

But she did not say it; where there was life, there was hope.

Hope faltered as she heard one cry above the many now raised in alarm. Meralonne's. She turned, then, to see the enigmatic, pipe-smoking companion of decades; he had fallen to one knee, and his shield arm dangled by his side; his shield had shattered.

Flame rose. Rock didn't burn; it melted, and it melted slowly—but the fires rose anyway, consuming nothing natural. The magi, bound by falling, molten rock, were now hemmed in by flame, and it was a wild thing; it slammed against their shields, and although it touched no one, it was close. The area that the magi could protect dwindled, shrinking by inches until the whole of the Kings' forces were surrounded by walls of flame.

Only one man rose, and only one man attempted anything at all: Kallandras, the Master Bard of Senniel College. Sigurne knew him. Alone among the bards, he merited Duvari's attention and suspicion in the same way that the patriciate did: simply by breathing.

He lifted one hand, palm out, as if in denial.

Sigurne frowned, watching. She felt, but could not identify, the magic he now summoned. But she heard the roar of wind in the hall, and it was a wind that came from no sky; the flames were flattened a moment at the force of its passage, and the demon roared in fury.

But the fires did not gutter, although the wind harried them; the demon was strong.

The Exalted and the Kings did more than merely witness. They worked in the silence of concentration. They had lost one archer to the demon's casual magic, and no more arrows flew in the halls, although naked blades reflected the fire's light in an ugly orange.

That light changed slowly, but it did change, turning at last from orange to gold: a gold that implied harvest, that implied the fruition of promise and not its hope.

Lord Karathis looked up from Meralonne APhaniel, who was also rising. "Summer magic," he said, his voice a strong, loud rumble, its syllables like the breaking of the earth itself. "How quaint. But you face no mere Winter."

"No? We faced one of the *Kialli*, and he fell taking only a handful with him." The golden light that had come at the exhortations of the god-born seemed to suffuse Meralonne, strengthening him. His shield arm still hung by his side, and he did not move it, but he raised sword, and he once again faced Karathis.

"You did not face one of the ducal lords." The words were cold; the fires grew. "I do not know why you chose to interfere in this battle—but for you, it no longer matters."

The magi attempted to shout a warning, but the warning was given another way: three of the Astari who stood between the Kings and their enemy were instantly ash, the shields of the magi and the subtle glow of Summer magic notwithstanding.

They were not the first of the Astari that Devon had seen fall; they were the first he had seen fall so instantly; there was literally nothing left of them, not even their weapons. The demon, this ducal lord, was toying with them.

Duvari was frozen for a second—as frozen as Devon, himself.

Into the silence, however, came a stranger's voice, half-forgotten until this moment. Devon turned to see the half-naked woman who had accompanied Lord Gilliam of Elseth on his descent. She had one hand on his arm; he was stiff. But her eyes, her eyes were golden, as golden as Summer light, as golden as the god-born.

Devon, who had met her now on a number of occasions, realized that he had never heard her speak.

"Set me free," she said. She spoke only to Lord Gilliam; she didn't seem to notice that anyone else existed.

The Hunter Lord stared at her as if she spoke a language that was beyond him.

"Lord, set me free. I would stay with you, but if we are to fight, we must be equal—and we must be separate. Please."

He was utterly silent; he might have been stone. He did not—Devon thought he could not—speak, although, for the first time, she had. What, he thought, was her name?

Espere. Espere, the wild.

The Hunter Lord still did not speak, but something must have passed between these two. Devon had spoken to innumerable Breodani diplomats in his time, and he felt that he understood most of their customs and their strange existence. This was beyond him.

Espere began to change.

"Do not panic," Evayne a'Nolan said, her voice strong and clear. "She is one of ours."

And panic, Devon thought, might otherwise have occurred. Espere began to keen, and her voice was the voice of a beast; her limbs thickened and lengthened, the straight of her back curving as those limbs reached for earth to better support the sudden mass of her weight. She was both furred and scaled, and she was not small.

Espere's face grew in size, the jaws elongating, nose becoming snout and flat, human teeth becoming long, sharp fangs. She had a tail, and it twitched only slightly because were it to swing, it would knock men and women into the fires that surrounded them.

She touched Lord Gilliam of Elseth with the point of her muzzle, dropping it—dropping it—to his shoulder.

And then she lifted her head, and she turned to face Lord Karathis, whose battle with Meralonne APhaniel, solitary soldier, had continued, even though the mage no longer held his shield.

Opening her jaws, she roared so loudly it should have brought the rest of the ceiling down upon their heads.

And then she leaped.

Chapter Twenty-one

THE DEMON LORD was not expecting this new combatant; that much was instantly clear. She crashed into him, and he moved at a speed it was almost impossible to track with the eye—the mortal eye. Her jaws slammed shut on nothing. But her tail caught his thigh, and the flames that threatened the Kings' forces banked again.

Devon, however, did not watch. Not the Kings, not the mages, not the Exalted. He moved instinctively—and quickly—through the boundaries inscribed by fire and magical ice toward Meralonne APhaniel. He didn't reach him first; Kallandras of Senniel, moving just as quickly and just as unerringly, did.

But not by much.

The moment Espere—or what was left of her—had entered the fray, Meralonne had withdrawn. He had not retreated to the main body of the small army but rather toward the wall damaged by the magic of the fight itself. There, the curved rock at his back, he sat.

"Meralonne," the bard said, crouching in a way that didn't expose his back to the conflict.

Meralonne APhaniel's shield arm was almost cradled against his chest. He looked up at the sound of his name—as if the sounds of battle yards away were so distant they could not disturb him—and his face twisted in a bitter, pained grimace. It surprised Devon. Meralonne was not Duvari; he was not as controlled or self-contained as the Lord of the Compact. But his expressions tended to irritation, annoyance, and arrogant condescension. Devon had never seen him express pain such as this.

But Kallandras seemed neither surprised nor perturbed.

"What a pair we make, we two," Meralonne finally said softly.

"Yes." The bard glanced at the slowly melting rock beneath the blurred frenzy of beast and demon. "Will it be enough?"

"I am no seer. But the Oathbinder is very near, and while he is here, his half-blood child is in her element. I would not choose this battle were I a ducal lord."

Devon did not give Kallandras time to answer. "Kallandras, take him to the healers."

Kallandras agreed, and Devon withdrew. But he noted, with mild irritation, that while Kallandras did lead Meralonne toward the healers, the mage did not actually allow himself to be tended. Not only that, but, after a conversation that was too quiet for Devon to catch, the mage actually had the gall, in the midst of the magic, the fire, and the roar of giants, to light his *pipe*.

The smell of the tobacco permeated the air.

Devon shook his head and turned away.

The beast that had, moments ago, been an almost witless human woman roared. The demon roared as well, although syllables lay in the depths of his ancient voice. Twice the edge of his sword struck her; twice it slid off something that must be scale, scraping as it slid. His whip, with its multiple tongues of flame, struck her tail, and the scent of burning hair joined the scent of mage's pipe. That and the much stronger smell of burned flesh, where the Astari had once stood.

But blood was drawn by fanged jaw and long, ebon claws, and the demon lord rose, his wings carrying him above her. It should have given him the advantage, but her form took little damage from his fire and his shadow, and it seemed to Devon that the demon's most effective weapon was . . . his sword.

It was not, of course, a normal sword; Devon suspected that it was not actually a sword at all, although it looked like a great sword with deep, red edges. He came to ground again, his wings like the wings of angry, threatened swans; Devon had no doubt they could break limbs if the demon were so inclined.

She lifted her head; it was horned. It had not been horned before she made her charge. She parried the sword and staggered, but she held her ground, roaring, growling, snapping, as if that were the whole of her necessary conversation.

But so, too, the demon lord.

"My Lord, the archers?" Devon asked softly.

But the Kings, who had lost one man to the sudden and swift reversal of his arrow's flight, did not speak to allow it. She fought alone, and they bore witness. The magi still struggled with the demonic fires, although no new ones came; the god-born still chanted in their quiet, intense voices.

Devon shadowed the Kings; the Kings watched the battle. No one spoke, or if they did, their words didn't carry. But in the stillness of the two raised, inhuman voices, one sound did: A horn.

The first note was long, and for a moment, when winded, it was the *only* sound in the hall. The second note was, beat for beat, as long as the first, but the third was shorter, sharper, rising at the tail end as if in either supplication or demand.

The demon lord looked up, looked, for a moment, past the Kings' line to the man who had winded the horn; who was, even now, lowering it to adjust his grip on the haft of his spear: Lord Gilliam of Elseth.

Even at this distance, Devon saw clearly the smile that transformed the demonic features. He lifted his wings, driving the beast back with the force of their battering; he also lifted the sword—but this he drove into the very rock upon which he stood and fought. It cracked at the force of that single blow, and a crevice, hemming in the fury of red fire, opened; it traveled with speed and certainty toward where the Hunter Lord stood.

But the fires did not reach him, although they breached the mages' shields. He had moved. He had moved, Devon thought, at least as fast as a trained Astari in his prime might have moved.

And then they were *all* moving. Evayne didn't attempt to clear the area; she stood, her hands spread, palms down, as if to stabilize the rock beneath their feet before it threw them or melted.

But there was no second strike against the Hunter Lord because he leaped out of the circle inscribed by magical boundaries and into the fray itself.

"What is that fool doing?" Meralonne's voice was not the only one to be heard, but it was loud with scorn and disbelief. Devon knew this man. The mage pointed, although it was hardly necessary; the beast could stand

and fight no matter what the state of the ground beneath its feet—but the Hunter Lord was wearing leather, and Devon had no doubt that it was normal, sturdy, and expensive; it wasn't magical. Patches of rock began to glow red; the ground around the Hunter was fast melting. He could dodge, yes, but sooner or later, there would be no place to stand.

Devon had no answer to give.

Meralonne APhaniel, injured, set his pipe aside and once again summoned his sword. The shield, however, did not materialize, and his shield arm still hung limply at his side. He could flex the fingers, however, and at the moment, they were curved in a fist.

Evayne's voice was low enough that Devon didn't catch her words, but the mage did not likewise speak softly.

"No?" He laughed; it was a bitter, heated sound. "Evayne, it is not for the student to choose the master's battles."

"I am *not* your student, nor have I been for—" heat now lent volume to her words.

"Evayne." Kallandras spoke deceptively softly; his voice carried.

"What?"

"If Lord Elseth dies, who will wind the horn? And if the horn is not winded, who will face the god?"

A moment's stillness, and then Evayne turned, the midnight folds of her robes moving as if in a gale, although the winds had long since died. Her eyes were narrow, and anger colored her cheeks. "I have lived my life in this cause. Do you think to remind *me*—"

Her words were lost to the sudden roar of demonic pain. It was a blessed sound, and Devon, as the Kings he served, forgot all else as he turned.

Gilliam, Lord Elseth, had resolved the issue of molten stone in a particularly savage way; he now hung from the haft of a spear which was embedded too far into the demon's back to be easily dislodged by frenzied movement. He clung to it without grace but with a determination that allowed for no fear.

And as the demon struggled with the weight of the Hunter Lord, he exposed himself to the savage and certain attack of the beast. Her great jaws snapped so quickly they could not be easily avoided by one encumbered with the weight of that spear.

It was not an elegant death; it was messy and bloody, and it came only slowly as the demon's cries were severed, with its throat.

"It seems," Meralonne said, "that this discussion is at an end."

*　　*　　*

Isladar watched the roiling shadows framed by arch and crowned by key-stone. The solitary keystone produced the only light in the coliseum, and it was now dim and pale. The voice of the Lord of the Hells could be more felt than heard. No one interrupted it.

But Karathis' final cry could not be ignored, and it could not be diminished; it was a short and visceral statement, to which Sor Na Shannen's sharp intake of breath was final punctuation. The shadows condensed and coiled as Lord Isladar watched.

It was too soon.

Too soon, he thought. In two months—for Ariane had damaged the arch, and the god's passage had been slowed—Allasakar might emerge from the portal and walk the earth in possession of all his power and strength, the bridge between this world and the Hells complete and solid.

But Lord Karathis was—had been—the most powerful of the *Kialli* present, and none doubted that he was now dwindling to ash. Two months was beyond them, even with the power of their god to sustain them in their defense of this last stronghold.

What will you do, Lord? Not even Isladar was unwise enough to ask. He watched, as even the least of the kin present now watched. By his side, Sor Na Shannen, architect of Allasakar's return, watched as well. *The plane is almost open to you. Will you walk it lessened, Lord? Will you leave some part of your power behind, and enter the world early? Or will you wait in the Hells for another such opportunity?*

There had been only one, in all the years of the long sundering.

This is not the world it once was; then, the world conformed to your will and the will of your brethren; now it is wild and untended and it heeds its own will. Without the whole of your power, it might never clearly hear your voice, and what it cannot hear, it will not obey.

The demon lord dissolved into a fine, pale ash as it crumpled. Devon was not surprised; he had seen it before, albeit always with lesser creatures, lesser dangers. The ash itself did not remain undisturbed; as it fell, the beast's jaws finally closed entirely, and she fell with him, across the orange ground.

The mages were prepared; they caught Lord Elseth before he could likewise touch the inimical stone, and they would have carried him above it to safety, but he demurred. Meralonne, not Sigurne, ordered the magi to obey the Hunter Lord, and they acquiesced; they understood that they were in his debt. They carried him as he bent above the invisible floor of their magic, and he gathered the beast in his arms.

Even as he began this ludicrous attempt, the beast shifted. She did not dissolve, as the demon had done, but her form dwindled, losing scale and singed fur and ridged horns; losing, as well, the prehensile tail and the long, curved claws. It was not as disturbing to watch as her first transformation had been. She stirred as he lifted her, but she didn't open her eyes, and as he finally carried her into the heart of the Kings' small army, the injuries she had sustained in her battle became apparent; she bled, and the wounds themselves were not clean.

The spear lay where it had fallen, and if Devon had wondered whether it was magical, the answer was immediately apparent; the hot, red rock didn't burn it or otherwise touch it at all. Nor could the mages; the Hunter Lord, however, seemed unconcerned. The wild girl, naked now, her hair a tangled mess, her limbs bruised and bleeding, occupied the whole of his attention.

One man approached: Dantallon, the Queens' healer. They spoke briefly, and after an obvious pause, the Hunter Lord very gently handed the wild girl into the healer's keeping. He then turned and began to walk back toward the spear.

The mages had done what they could to make the passage possible; the city beyond the hall now waited. Gilliam retrieved the spear and paused as Evayne asked a question that Devon could not quite catch. The answer, however, was clear.

"I trust Dantallon," he said softly, "and while she is part of me, not even I would force a child to hunt—and kill—her father."

Devon frowned. The Hunter Lord's quarry was not, in the end, the Lord of the Hells; it was his *own* god. He remembered that the Huntbrother had died a very traditional Breodanir death in the foyer of the Terafin manse; clearly, the Hunter Lord desired the elusive peace of vengeance.

It was not what the Kings desired.

They left the damaged hall behind, and as they did, the magi began to summon more light. It was dim light, and when it was brought to bear in silence, they discovered that were some shadows and some pockets of darkness that such simple light did not pierce. So the Exalted joined the Kings and brought a different light with them; that light was strong enough, although it was gentle. Devon, walking almost directly behind the men whose protection was his most significant duty, could see what the Kings saw.

The hall opened into another hall, shorter than the one in which they had met the demon. Its roof, like the roof of the first, was rounded and rough, suggesting cavern in a way that was at odds with the walls. Even these changed abruptly as they walked, walls giving way to rough stone and hard-packed dirt. It was not over, however.

There was no movement of moon to mark the passage of time in this unnatural night sky; it was broken instead by small whispers and truncated conversations as people noted the architecture or its lack. Devon didn't speak. He listened, and he watched. Some of the magi did the same, but they trusted the Exalted, and their curious guide, to note any real danger.

Devon, trained by Duvari himself, did not, of course. Trust was almost a foreign concept. But there were no more demons to harry their forces, no opposition against which they must fight to gain their goal.

He made way only once, when Evayne approached the Kings. Her face was pale, her jaw set.

"Your Majesties, we are almost upon the Cathedral. Follow me now, and quickly."

She led them without hesitation and without further pause.

The tunnel twisted sharply to the left, narrowing until it was barely two men wide. This caused only a brief pause, and an almost inaudible conversation between Duvari and the Kings, before they continued through the gap. Evayne moved as if the conversation had not taken place, and given the dark color of her robes, she was almost lost to sight as the roughness of these particular walls fell away, opening at last into a less well-girded darkness.

Their quiet voices no longer rebounded off tunnel walls; they vanished into the heights or the distance that the darkness did not easily allow them to penetrate. The Exalted once again began their tired chant, but Evayne now waved them to silence, the nicety of respect due their station irrelevant. She pulled the edges of her hood from around her face, exposing it in that instant: She was a woman in her prime, and time had worn distinct lines around the corners of her eyes and mouth; her eyes, in the poor light, seemed violet. Lifting her hands, turning her back to the darkness that waited, she said, "So that you will see and remember. Father!"

Her cloak roiled at her feet, struggling against her as if it were a caged creature. From out of the folds of that robe, the seer's crystal rose. She did not, and had not, touched it; her hands were still lifted and her face up-turned as if to catch its rising light. In its wake, light fell, and it fell like a rain of fire, but where it passed, color followed in its wake, and the whole of the unnatural night was, for a moment, stripped away and denied. As if the orange sparks were the brushstrokes of a frenzied artist, the bands of color grew until the whole of the cavern was revealed.

Here, they finally saw a literally fallen city: the facades of huge build-ings, broken at the heights; the bases of statues in the center of open streets, and the rock and rubble that might once have been standing struc-tures; the streets themselves, wider than the streets of the city above, but fronted entirely by buildings, and not the large grounds which character-ized so much of Averalaan. Those streets extended for miles.

They were almost silent, even the mages, although that particular si-lence was certain not to last.

In the darkness of the coliseum, the keystone was now flickering as if light, suddenly understanding the severity of its peril, was desperately battering the rock in a final attempt to escape—and survive. It was almost done.

"My Lord," someone said, "they are in the city." It was not immediately clear who spoke, nor for whom the words were intended. The silence was thick and tense, but it was colored in all ways by anticipation. An era was about to end, or to begin, and they were to witness it.

"Lord Isladar, should we—"

Isladar lifted his hand. He did not kill the speaker. "No. Stand ready. He is almost nigh."

"Now is the time," Evayne said, lifting her voice. Only one part of the city her light had exposed was still dark, and that darkness rose from the ground to the sky like a pillar of glittering obsidian. It was to this that she now directed their attention.

"Kings, Exalted, Sacred; Members of the Order of the profound; As-tari, Defenders, Priests—to the heart of a history that you could not have made, I have brought you.

"The Darkness rises; beneath the shadows that light cannot pierce, the citadel is waking. Allaksakar takes the last steps upon his path to this world. Let us meet him, as Moorelas met him; let us tender no less an answer."

Light answered the words, and this time, Evayne did not tell the mages to guide or guard their magic. Nor did she still the sound of swords clashing against shields; that, Devon thought, would be the Northern contingent, although those born and raised closer to Averalaan soon joined them.

King Reymalyn lifted his voice not in command but in song—and that song was taken up, by bard and by soldier, and carried. Devon understood why men marched to song; had he not, he would have learned something by watching, by bearing witness.

Evayne lifted her voice to be heard; she had not finished, but she did not demand the quelling of those voices. "Lord Elseth, the time has come. It is the first of Veral. The sun is breaking across the horizon in Breodanir." She lifted her seer's crystal high enough that he might see it; Devon had not seen it return to her hand. From its heart, dawn's light shone for a moment upon the form of Gilliam, Lord Elseth. He held his spear ready in grim silence, but his hand fell now to the horn by his side.

"Call the Hunt, Hunter Lord, and join it."

After a marked hesitation, he did.

The horn's music was unlike any horn call that Devon had ever heard in his life. It was not song, but like music, it invoked imagery, and this imagery was so at odds with what the seer's light had revealed that he— and all of the Kings' forces—were thrust, for a moment into the darkness not of stone and enclosed space but of nighttime forests. Those forests, ancient, bore trees thrice the width of a grown man; their roots ran deeper than this hidden city.

And in the heart of that forest, all manner of life existed, but only one thing now answered the call. It lumbered, huge, ancient, toward the dying notes, as if summoned, at last, to the Hunt.

To the Hunt of the stricken Lord Elseth, who desired the peace of his god's death to still his own voices of loss. But it was more, much more, than that.

There was a god upon the plane. The Hunter God. And he had come from his forests to the streets below Averalaan, as promised.

*   *   *

In the ancient city of Vexusa, in the heartland of his greatest enemy, the Hunter God tendered his answer.

And in the center of a Cathedral lost to shadow and magic, before the waiting eyes of demon-kin who stood at rigid, silent attention, the darkness finally became *perfect*.

Devon had been in the Between, the misty place in which man might meet his gods, at the behest of their children. He had therefore seen gods and heard their endless chorus of voices. But no god had come to his world; no god had walked the streets or the parlors.

This was, therefore, the first god he had met in the flesh.

They fell, slowly, to knee, excepting only Duvari.

The god came through the vanished forest. As he walked, his form shifted, losing bulk and the gait of a giant beast. He straightened, stiffened, and at last stood as a man might stand, although his feet were bare and unencumbered.

He didn't wear armor; he was neither too tall, nor too short. His hair was becoming fair, as he walked, and his cheekbones were high. He looked, or would have looked, entirely mortal, were it not for the color of his eyes. Devon recognized him instantly: he was, except for those eyes, the very likeness of Lord Elseth's dead Huntbrother.

Lord Elseth's knuckles grew white around the haft of the spear; he lifted it. What he might have done next, no one knew; Evayne reached to the side to grip his shoulder so tightly that her knuckles blanched the same color as his. "Lord Elseth," she said, the softness of her voice at odds with the apparent strength of her grip, "peace."

But Lord Elseth had seen enough; he rose.

Evayne rose with him; it was that, or release him. "Lord Elseth," she said again. "Now is not the time to use the spear."

He hesitated; he understood the weight of both her words and their situation. But he was on edge now. Devon moved carefully, calculating. He understood that the spear in Lord Elseth's hands could injure the god. Could possibly kill him. In the time before gods had deserted the world, weapons had been made that could. Moorelas of Aston had wielded the most famous, and the most effective, of those.

But the god—if indeed god it was—neither knew nor cared. As he walked, it became clear that he approached only his follower. His face grew lined, his expression exhausted. Only the eyes, which now seemed to be all colors—or none—marked him as Other. He carried the weapons and the characteristic horn of the Breodani Hunters.

"Gil?" he said, almost hesitantly, as he came to a stop perhaps fifteen feet away from the Hunter Lord.

The expression on the face of Lord Elseth cracked the moment the word left his lips.

"I told him this was a bad idea. I told him you'd think it was an insult. Did he listen? I can understand why he's called the *Hunter* God."

Silence. A beat. No one moved or spoke. "*Stephen?*"

The distance between them disappeared seconds later.

"Gil, I'm not—I'm not alive. But he—Bredan—told me I should speak with you."

"I'll get you out."

"I'm not the important one. I was the last one taken; I still have some . . . solidity." He turned, half turned, as his Hunter still held him, toward the pillar of darkness. "He's stepped across, Gil—but he came too quickly—you forced him. Bredan asks your leave to Hunt once more before—before you do."

"My leave?" The words were bitter, stark.

Stephen shook his Hunter. "This isn't about your loss—or mine— Hunter Lord. This is about the fate of man. If Bredan doesn't kill the Avatar of the darkness—"

"I know." Lord Elseth's words were almost a growl. But he accepted—as he so often had—the correction of his Huntbrother, and he released him slowly. "Stephen, I—"

"I know." He smiled. It was a weary smile, but it offered Gilliam some small peace. "He doesn't have much power. The fight with the enemy will drain it all—and more."

"What does it—"

"It means that all that'll be left is the Hunter's Death. The beast, not the Oathbinder." He paused. "That's when the Hunt starts. But, Gil—he says that it will be as if the Hunt hasn't been called in years." He stepped back, and his features began to shift. But they hardened again as he shook his head, as if grasping at one final moment.

"We—he—" He shook his head. "In Mandaros' Hall."

"Swear it," was the intense reply.

"I swear it." A crackle of blue light laced air as the God of Oaths witnessed, and accepted. Only after this was done did Stephen grimace and turn away as quickly as possible, running in long Hunter strides toward the darkness ahead. His body lost the shape and the form of the familiar Huntbrother, gaining width, height, bulk; becoming, at last, the beast at the heart of the forest. The god.

That god now lifted his head and *roared*.

"Lord Elseth," Meralonne APhaniel said, "what did he mean?" He stood to one side of the Hunter Lord; Devon had literally failed to see him move.

Gilliam did not answer; he watched his god lope toward the shadow in a silence that was grim and terrible with both longing and fury.

"He meant," Evayne said, when it had become clear that he would not answer at all, "that the Hunter's Death will kill anything in sight until its need is satiated."

Devon understood. Only one sworn to the Hunter God of the Breodani could satiate that hunger. Bredan had been a God of Oaths, and it was the sworn oath of his Hunters—and their brothers—to serve the god in his time of need.

"Hunt well, Lord Elseth," the mage said softly.

All existence was a game. All of it, a gamble.

Lord Isladar stood a moment in perfect darkness, his eyes closed. He could feel the earth beneath the marble; it was rumbling as if it meant to create new fissures and new breaks into which anything might fall. Old Earth, he thought, and knew it as truth. The earth was almost waking, and he well knew why: the Lord of the Covenant was here.

The Lord of the Covenant, who, against all wisdom, had himself followed a path similar to the one the Lord of the Hells had traced, crawling and struggling toward the forbidden world of Man. Of Man. Once, the gods had ruled here. The gods, their wild children, their firstborn.

The Arianni. The Allasiani.

The earth had obeyed when they spoke; the water would part and the air would carry them, wingless, into the skies. And the fires? He smiled, but it was a bitter, unseen smile. They could still touch the fires.

But fire had never been Isladar's element. He could command it, but it was not to fire that he went for either peace or comfort, where comfort might be found at all; there was nothing for him here now.

Nothing but his Lord.

He turned at the sound of paws striking marble. Not even the strongest of shadows could bind the creature that made that noise, for he was a god, in form and shape. Were it not for his weakness and his folly, he would have been more powerful than the Lord of the Hells, for nothing had impeded his progress, and nothing had forced him to come early into the world, stripped of a portion of his essential power.

He was more beast than god now, diminished by his choice.

Allasakar was also, more regrettably, diminished by the choice forced upon him.

And in the end, it was for neither that Lord Isladar listened. For one god still traversed the mortal realm; he was certain of it. He had listened, he had studied, and he had searched for some proof; he had come away with nothing.

But Lord Isladar had come to the Hells with nothing; all promise turned, in the instant of his arrival, to ash and death.

All existence was a game, yes. But this long, long game had started, in the end, at the bidding, the tortuous and opaque bidding, of one god. Nameless god. Sometimes called Mystery and sometimes called the God of Man. An odd god, to be worshiped by none, revered by none, obeyed, in the end, by none.

No cathedrals were built in his name because he had no name, although the existence of such mundane, mortal buildings was possible *only* because of his intervention and his cunning. He therefore owned no part of the souls of Man, the flimsy and fleeting shards of a greater, shattered divinity that formed the transient, moving battlefield over which the last great war of the gods would be fought.

Allasakar had no god-born children. No woman had survived a pregnancy, and although the gods sometimes bore children from their own flesh, no child had survived such a birthing either—no *mortal* child. A god could, yes. But the gods were gone.

All but three.

Will you show your hand, here? Will you, nameless one?

The beast god answered with a roar.

All existence was a game, a war, a battle. Isladar watched, waited, and smiled. *You have waited long; here, at last, is my Lord's opening move.*

The great beast ran toward the rising column of a darkness that seemed impregnable to light. Its form had become almost familiar to Devon, and he cast a backward glance at the healers and the Mother-born priestesses but caught no glimpse of the wild girl. But he saw the kinship between the form she had donned for her battle with a demon lord and the form of the beast that now ran, unerring, toward his enemy.

His fur was a subtle silver, and it shed a pale, pale light—moonlight, for the darkness, not the radiance of the sun. Yet it was a strong, pervasive light, and when it met the rising pillar of darkness, it was not engulfed. Instead, the darkness cracked, falling away to either side of the moving god as if it were forming reluctant walls at his command. Those walls, limned in the same silver as the great beast's fur, remained, and the Kings' forces now passed between them, following not the seer who had led them this far but the god who might see them to victory.

Or to death.

Nine had already been lost in the passage to the city. No one expected that they were the last of the casualties. But the only ones that mattered now to Devon were the Kings.

At the heart of the column itself stood a single, vast building. Evayne had called it the Dark Cathedral, and it was clear, in the scant light that followed the wake of the living god, why. It rose at least four stories, and it rested atop the flats of large, semicircular stairs that had not been built with the small in mind. Although it was striking in the bold clarity of its initial lines, it looked as if it had been composed of slate and gold. It could not, of course, be slate. The gold itself reflected light as if light were repulsive. And yet, it was beautiful in its fashion.

The god paused for the first time at the foot of those stairs and looked up to their heights. Standing before the five recessed arches that formed the complicated architrave of the entry was a man. It was hard, in the dim light, to tell what colors he wore; his face was shrouded by the edges of a hood. He stood between the carved ebony of winged gargoyles, each much larger than a man; their claws gleamed in the light of torches and burning braziers, carried by the priests in this last procession. They moved, flexing wings as they turned unblinking eyes upon the small force beneath them.

The god did not speak; he roared.

And the man, in response, laughed. "You are too late. Our Lord has come." He raised a staff in the light cast by both god and mortal, and he summoned darkness. "Prepare, sacrists. Prepare, exultants. Allasakar—" The rest of the sentence was lost with his throat as the the god leaped, in one muscular movement, up the stairs. Nor did the demons come to his aid; they flew up, as quickly as possible, beyond the reach of the god. But they did not move fast enough or far enough. As if they were simple sparrows and he a hunting cat, his claws clipped and shredded their wings before he passed them by.

The Kings followed; not even the magi spared the demons a second glance. They had heard and understood the *Allasakari's* claim: the Lord of the Hells had arrived.

But so, too, had Bredan, the Lord of the Covenant.

The god ran on. The Kings did not immediately follow. They turned to the Exalted and then to the men under their command. Those men now checked their sword knots. No song left their lips, and they did not strike their shields or otherwise speak, but there was no terror in this silence; there was the simple weight of determination. They may have prayed; prayers were often unvoiced.

Devon knew; his were. He didn't pray often, but when he did, it was not in fear or supplication. His own gods were distant this day.

The Lord of the Compact, however, was not. He no longer asked the Kings to stay back; nor did he attempt to exert the authority his role as their protector had always granted him. Even Duvari understood that the time for such protection had passed. They had walked, as Moorelas had once ridden, into the shadow, and in such a shadow as this, there was no safety, no nicety of rigid form or protocol.

There were gods. There was death.

But perhaps the gods had always heralded death when they had once walked. It was a new, and unwelcome, thought; Devon slid out from under it. If there were no protocols and no forms, there was the simple truth of a vow: He was the Kings' man. He didn't inspect his sword knots; he checked, instead, for the weapons blessed by the Exalted. Here, they offered little comfort.

The Exalted nodded, and the Kings, nodding instead of bowing, turned. But they turned to Evayne, who had remained silent for most of the passage. She nodded as well and began to lead.

The god could not, now, be seen, and the seeress did not forbid the magi to use magic; the glow of magelight, absent its familiar, containing stones, now flooded every nook, every corner, of the grand hall they entered. It was a light that was heavy with shadow; it could not, and did not, mimic the welcome clarity of day. But it left nothing hidden, which was its intent.

Avantari did not boast halls of these majestic heights; nor did it boast the complicated vaulting of the ceilings so high above. Devon understood that power and beauty were not disparate. He understood, as well, that power did not preclude art. This Cathedral was proof of that fact.

"Seeress," Duvari said. Duvari alone seemed immune to the towering heights and the impressive architecture the magelight revealed. It was irrelevant in all ways to the Lord of the Compact.

"The halls round here," she told him, her voice cool, "into small apartments and offices for lesser dignitaries. Ignore them; follow the hall to its end."

What offices and what lesser dignitaries did the Lord of the Hells require? Devon's thoughts drifted to the concept of a bureaucracy in the Hells, and he smiled at the thought. It was brief and bitter. "The Cathedral here has no nave—it has a coliseum. The halls we are traveling form the interior wall to the pens. The coliseum itself is four stories high, and in its day—" she shook her head, as if aware that she sounded like a guide. "We must enter as the—as the combatants did."

The stone of the halls trembled as the beast roared in the darkness; the men and women who walked it shook as the darkness answered.

They were the combatants now. As Evayne had suggested, they followed—swiftly—as she led them through the longer, darker enclosure in which the slaves must have walked before they met their end in the coliseum. They might have been armed and armored, as the Kings' men were; they might have been without so much as a club. Very little history remained of this city—or the one that lay beneath its foundations.

But the Kings' men followed this inner corridor until they came, at last, to a closed gate. It was not stone, and it was not so fine in design as the grand, first halls had been.

Which was good. The beast had reached the gates. He lifted his head, and he crashed through it, leaving splintered wood and twisted metal in his wake. He did not look to see if they followed, nor would he; Devon understood that to the shining beast, there was only one worthy foe, only one enemy, upon the field he now approached. All others were insignificant.

*   *   *

Meralonne APhaniel uttered a brief phrase, an alien phrase, to Devon's right, and Devon turned a fraction. But the mage said nothing else. Instead, he drew his sword—from where, Devon did not see. He shed pain, as he did; he shed the infirmity of an arm that should have been broken when his shield was riven. He stood tall, and if there was no wind to dissipate the heavy stench of death, wind nonetheless flew through the strands of his unbound hair.

"Look well," he said softly, speaking now in the language of the Empire. "You will see what no living men—or women—have seen for millennia: gods walking the world."

Devon looked as if compelled.

The beast, shining as if he were the moon made flesh, approached a darkness that was in all ways solid; it suggested height, and strength, and—disturbingly—a midnight beauty that could stop breath by the force of the awe it evoked. For a moment, these two were the only living things the world contained; all else was shadow and ash.

It was the Kings who forced themselves to look away first. Not even the Exalted were immune to the unexpected power of the gods' presence.

"There is a reason," King Cormalyn said, his voice weak and thin compared to even the mage's, "that the gods are no longer welcome to walk the face of the world, and it is to be found here."

He lifted an arm, and he pointed, and although his voice lacked the surprising and unlooked for majesty of Meralonne APhaniel's, the men and women had been trained to its sound, and they now obeyed the Wisdom-born King: they looked. They looked through the gap left by the sundering of the gate; its jagged boards, its twisted, broken bars, formed a frame.

And it was a fitting frame, in the end. At the feet of gods who walked the world for the first time in millennia, if Meralonne APhaniel was correct, were the bodies of people who would never walk again.

It was not the gods that now drew—and held—the Kings' attention, not the gods that awed or silenced them. It was the faceless, nameless dead, for these dead were their failures writ large, and in them, the promise of the same death, the same failure, waited for the Empire should the Kings and their companions now falter.

King Reymalyn drew his sword; King Cormalyn did likewise, although he carried the rod in his shield hand. It was both symbol of office and artifact, and not even Duvari was bold enough to comment on its use. They walked, with purpose, through the shattered gate and toward the center of the coliseum, where the demons attended the gods with the same reverent silence as Meralonne APhaniel had.

Devon closed his eyes a moment, remembering—as if it was ever in doubt—why he served these men and why, in time, he would serve their heirs.

The gods met, like lightning and earth, like tidal wave and shore. In their wake, their followers, lesser and insignificant, followed. They shouted, yes; they raised voices in the war cries of their people. But even the Kings' voices were lost to the roar and the fury of a language that defied comprehension.

Shorn of heralds or horns, the Kings' men carried the banners of Wisdom and Justice into the shadows and darkness, where they were quickly lost to sight. The god did not cleave to shadow but produced it—as Bredan produced moon's light. They were both night creatures, and they were both terrifying in their way.

But their voices quickly became as natural as earthquakes or the storms that threatened all ships in harbor; the Kings' men were left to stand against them. They readied weapons as they moved, and they moved slowly.

The humans arrayed against them—and they were here, in number—were not so reluctant; they were robed, but glints of chain could be seen as their robes moved and parted at the length of their stride. Where their demon masters waited, ringed in fire and shadow, they charged toward the fray, as if war were a child's toy, and they were afraid any hesitation might take it from them.

Their feet crushed the faces and limbs of the dead, and the dead, in their cumbersome piles gave those feet uneven purchase; some stumbled, righting themselves with difficulty. They kicked the corpses that had dared to inconvenience them, and some alchemy of spirit transformed the horror that the Kings' men felt into an instant, growing rage.

Although enraged, they were cautious, and they moved only to the outer edge of where the bodies lay piled, like an awkward mountain of refuse. They wished, even in the preservation of their own lives, to cause no more indignity to the dead.

Even, Devon thought grimly, if the dead were now beyond caring and beyond the sting of such indignities. He moved forward, unsheathing one dagger and holding it in his left hand; in his right, he had his favored sword.

Sigurne watched Meralonne APhaniel.

Matteos stood by her side, the signature of his power so clear she could almost touch it, although she could see no sign of it at all. "Sigurne," he said quietly, as the Kings' men began their slow convergence on the lesser army of the Lord of the Hells.

She nodded. She could see the *Kialli*; they numbered perhaps half a dozen, surrounded by their servitors, their immortal slaves. Not since her captivity and her apprenticeship in the frozen lands of the North had she seen such a gathering of creatures, and there? They had been at the beck and call of a mortal mage. They had loathed him, yes, but no more than she herself had loathed him, and they had served him, in the end, just as faithfully as she. They had merely been less effective.

"Sigurne?"

She shook her head. "A moment, Matteos." She turned to watch Meralonne APhaniel. For decades she had worked by his side, often under his rough tutelage. He had seldom asked her what she had learned from her first master, and she had been grateful for his lack of curiosity. Or for his certainty that there was nothing she could, in turn, teach him. In a youth long gone, she had never been certain which of the two it was. But she *had* been certain, on the first day she had seen him, before she had learned either his name or her own fate.

On that day, she had thought him angelae, some lost scion of the gods sent, at last, into the folds of the world to free it from the grip of the kin.

He had been—he *was*—so profoundly free, so unfettered in his savage joy; he was without mercy and without fear. She had not even been able to envy him; she had recognized him as something above, and beyond, her ken.

Years had dimmed that perception, but it lay waiting. He had walked toward a Duke of the Hells without that savage joy, and he had lost, in the process, the shield that he had carried on that bright, clear, azure day, when he had been a thing of wind and light.

She thought the loss of the shield meant the loss of the use of the arm, but she was wrong; he had drawn his sword, and as he walked abreast of the Kings' men, the wind that touched nothing else began to fray the blanketing edge of his hair, teasing it toward the unseen sky.

She couldn't see his expression, for the magi were not here to fight on the front lines, and he did not face her. But it was not his words that returned to her now, not the words of her long-ago savior.

It was the words of a fellow captive, kin to the creatures that had slaughtered countless innocents in pursuit of this moment: the moment when their Lord might again walk the face of the world.

Watch, Sigurne. Watch. You will be the only witness, in the end, of any worth, for you have seen and you have understood enough to give this battle context. Watch it, for I suspect you will see an echo of the ancient days in its unfolding.

She watched, and she witnessed, but she was no longer young, and she was no longer trapped within the confines of a tower overlooking a battle she could not affect.

As Meralonne closed with Sor Na Shannen, she shook herself and turned to Matteos. "My apologies," she said, in as soft a voice as the noise in the coliseum would permit. "Look now to the Kings and the Exalted; the kin have used fire as their predominant form of attack, and that is what our first line of defense must concentrate on. The Exalted will—must—deal with the Shadow and the Winter magics on their own."

But even speaking, her gaze was drawn again to the demons, and to this particular one, the woman who had danced with Ararath in the former glory of the Cordufar manse. Even here, surrounded by fire, a red sword in her hand, her movements implied both dance and pleasure because they were so graceful, so powerful, and so joyful.

Do you exist simply for war? Sigurne thought. *Is battle the only joy you know in your existence?*

But no. The answer lay at her feet: the dead. Their corpses had been tossed like refuse in piles around the arch but one final indignity remained to them. They rose.

Rising, they were still obviously dead; they lumbered to their feet like a poorly made, teetering wall, their broken or missing limbs dictating their gait and their stability. Their eyes—where eyes existed—were sightless, their jaws slack and open. They didn't speak, but they weren't silent; speech was denied them, but low, animal grunts were not. Tall, short, young, old, they shambled into place before the *Allasakari*, standing between them and the forces of the Kings. They held no weapons; they needed none. Their deaths had the force of accusation, and it was turned wholly toward the people who had failed them.

Only the dead nearest the *Allasakari* themselves remained in place, but they linked arms, with no concern for height or comfort, and they planted their feet, broken or whole, against the floor. Those that rose on the farthest edges of the loose formation turned toward the Kings' men and began to walk.

Will you cut us down again? They seemed to ask.

Sigurne became as motionless as they could no longer be.

"Sigurne—" Matteos' voice was unsteady. Even Matteos.

She shook her head, not in horror but to convey the answer to the question he could not quite bring himself to ask. "No. There is no magic I recognize in this. I cannot detect anything that we could work against; this is in the hands of the Exalted."

But if the Exalted bore the blood of gods, they were, in the end, as mortal as Sigurne. Like Matteos, the sight of the moving dead struck them—and the demons knew it. Of course they knew; pain was their study, their only area of expertise, and they were capable, at need, of subtlety.

"They are *not* alive, Matteos. They are not trapped here. They are not aware of us at all."

As if to deny the truth of her words, the dead turned their gaze to the armed and armored men; the look seemed to sweep the coliseum like a scythe. Matteos stiffened; he did not, however, take a step back. Others, less fortunate, did.

Sigurne, however, did not. Not even when the dead—those who had throat for it—began to wail and keen, as if they were already damned and might never escape.

The Astari were the first to recover.

The fact that Duvari seemed entirely unmoved might have been worthy of comment, but Sigurne, likewise, seemed unaffected. In Sigurne, however, it surprised, because Sigurne Mellifas cultivated the appearance of affectionate and slightly feeble age. Those who knew her well knew the story of how she'd come to the Order of Knowlege—but the story, like so many stories of wild, impatient youth, had no strength, no edge. They forgot that she had been born in a land where simple exposure to the air could kill. Death was guaranteed. Survival was not; one had to work to earn it, day in and day out, often in the face of creatures that were likewise caught up in the simple struggle to do the same. In the winter, that left little room for either joy or guilt.

She had walked into a winter night. She had entered a nightmare that not even the tower of the mage in the frozen North had given her. She gestured, sharply, and the ground around the feet of the magi shifted; it was subtle.

"Tell the Kings to be wary; there are kin hidden among the dead, and they are by far the greater danger."

Matteos nodded; he lifted his voice, cloaked it in magic, and sent the words to where they might do the most good; he could not tell, at this distance and in this light, how well they were heeded—but that was true of most advice he offered.

Devon ATerafin stood beside Duvari; on his far side was a woman whose name Sigurne did not immediately know. All three now carried daggers in both hands; they had surrendered the greater damage and reach they might have achieved by using their swords. It was odd to see them at the side of the Kings, armed with nothing but ceremonial daggers; odd to see them sheathe swords in favor of the lesser weapon.

Sigurne was, however, intimately familiar with the daggers, and it made their choice entirely sound. She had given such weapons, time and again, to Ararath Handernesse; she had taken them from his hands and returned them to the cathedrals upon the Isle, where they might once again be imbued with a moment of Summer.

Against a god, they would be of little use. But against the kin, and against these teetering corpses, they might be.

But Sigurne—even Sigurne—flinched, for the first of the undead to reach the front lines of the Kings' men, and with them, Devon ATerafin, was not, or had not been, adult. There was always tragedy in the simple fact of a child's corpse. This was far, far worse.

Her suspicion about Devon's presence at the side of the Kings hardened into certainty as she watched him. *Amarais*, she thought, *you are canny.*

The child wailed piteously as it approached the line, arms stretched as if seeking parental embrace and the comfort it would provide. The soldiers shuddered, although the line held. Devon, however, did not; he might have been chiseled from the same quarry that had produced Duvari. Moving, the two daggers in his hand shedding a faint and uneasy light in the shadows, he brought the blades to bear against the smallest and slightest of the lumbering undead.

The child shuddered as the blades bit into his flesh, but he did not stop moving; his arms were still open, still held wide. Devon knelt, his blades still, and he lifted the dead child in his arms, as if offering comfort. The knives pierced the dead flesh of the child's back, and it screamed.

It was almost too much for Sigurne. But she had endured worse in her time: she had seen the slaughter of the living. There was no soul for this child, no spirit, nothing that gave it the spark of life. Life would never return to its limbs.

Devon lifted the child as it finally stilled, and he threw its corpse into the moving line of its undead brethren.

Chapter Twenty-two

IN THE DARKNESS THEY FOUGHT. The *Allasakari*, shielded by the moving dead more effectively than the Kings' men by simple armor, drew their swords. They weren't encumbered by heavier armor, but neither were their blades encumbered by natural law. The dead didn't trouble or concern them; they moved among them without guilt or fear.

They were not, however, proof against the mage-born. And if the mage-born warriors had offered only protection and witness to this point, they were now unleashed, and they responded as if driven. Sigurne did not direct them; Meralonne, in theory, did. But Meralonne was dancing—in a deadly, compelling way—with the former Lord Cordufar's mistress. He had not yet died by her fire or her sword, and she used both; nor had he managed to kill her. There would be no quarter offered here; she would die, or he would; nothing else would end their combat.

Sigurne therefore left Matteos in charge of the magical shields and protections the Kings and the Exalted required; the Exalted, even now, limned in golden, weak light, were slowing the progress of the dead. The dead, cumbersome, and slow, were both the least significant of the dangers and the worst. If they could be laid, at last, to rest, it no longer mattered where or how; their keening was almost soul-destroying in its justified rage and fear.

She turned to the warrior-magi, young and harsh. They were few; they had always been few. Of the Order's many mages, they were the least trusted and the most foreign, for they did not bend their power or their intellect to discovery; they bent it to the application of the discoveries of others. And Duvari feared them, for they were the open face of what the magi could become: weapons. The weapons by which whole battles might be fought and won.

They were not Duvari; they were pale. But they were also determined, and when she ordered them to fire into the ranks of the undead, the undead burned. The light from that burning was both horrifying and welcome, for it exposed the darker-clad *Allasakari*, and the mages began to kill them; the Kings' men did their work there as well.

But above the battle, which was even now consuming life and time, the din of the voices of gods raged; not even Meralonne's dance of death could drown it out.

Beauty was not often something that terrified, but here, it did, for the gods, *both* gods, were beautiful, and they were almost paralyzing to gaze upon. Sigurne kept her focus as tight and as narrow as possible.

The wind came.

A breeze, at first, it stirred even the dead, as if it were a reminder of all they had lost and would never know again. This was artifice; she knew it. But she felt the same, and she would, if she were standing at the close of this battle, emerge into sun and sea wind and open skies once more. It was welcome.

But in this dark and twisted place, what was welcome, what was natural, could not remain so. The breeze grew stronger, and stray bits of debris were caught in its folds. Matteos shouted her name, and she glanced back at him. The wind passed through the shields erected by the magi, where the fires of the enemy did not.

And the wind grew. And grew, until words and shouts no longer traveled in a predictable direction; they had bards who could bespeak the Kings and their men, but there were few indeed of those.

She glanced and saw one. But Kallandras of Senniel? He was nowhere to be found among the Kings' men, and she could not clearly see him in the chaos of the unfolding battle.

But she heard the seer curse, and curse loudly, before her voice was also lost. Turning, she could see that Evayne a'Nolan held her seer's crystal between her palms; she could not clearly see her expression because the light the ball now shed was too bright in this dark place. Beside her, almost aloof from the battle that had unfolded, stood the lone Hunter Lord, his hand upon his spear, his expression shadowed and remote. He watched the gods; no one else dared.

He waited.

Once more the wind parted, capricious; it tugged at the Kings' standard, twisting the weighted fabric and distorting what was embroidered there. Sigurne cast, quickly, to succor the man whose sole task was to see that it did not fall.

And she heard, as she did, the seer's shocked voice: "*Kallandras, no!*"

The wind came.

One man heard its voice as clearly as the Master Bard who had summoned it and unleashed its delighted fury in the darkness. One man understood what it signified. No mortal could call the wild elements; no mortal could—alone—control them. This was wisdom and, in its fashion, truth. But it was not the whole of the truth.

The wind's voice was strong and wild, yes; it found fire, and the fires around Sor Na Shannen banked at the ferocity of its attack. Had it attacked only fire, it would have been a benison. But it was sightless and confined in these tunnels, this cavern. A city had once stood here; the heights had been utterly destroyed by the fall of a god. Would that he had died.

Meralonne parried and danced, and the wind touched his cloak and his sword, pulling at his hair. He did not try to contain it; it did not try to harm him. Open his mouth and he might speak, for a moment, the language it spoke.

Sor Na Shannen was not what she had been on the night he had first encountered her in the Terafin manse; nor was she what she had been in her role as Lord Cordufar's very bold, very desirable mistress. She stood in her Lord's shadow, and she spoke with the edge of his voice; his power infused her. She was not, and would never be, Karathis' equal—but she was more, much more, than she had been.

Meralonne APhaniel was sundered in both space and time from his Lord; he might never again hear his Lord's voice or feel the privilege and honor of his Lord's power. His shield was riven; all that was left him was his sword. His sword and the experience with which he wielded it. The wind tugged him. It shredded the fires. Sor Na Shannen barely seemed to notice their absence; their voices were now too small.

But she felt the wind, even she.

"What is this?" The wind was fickle in its fashion; it was drawn to power that was not immediately inimical to its nature. Her hair, ebon to his platinum, the wind also caressed, drawing it up and around her face in fine strands.

Do you not know? he thought, putting his sword up for a moment. She had done the same, and he watched her expression, her confusion. *Do you not understand what it is that you hear? Has the long sundering diminished you so much that you must walk, deaf, across the face of the world?*

He might have asked. It would have wounded her. But before he could speak, wind did: The stone balcony that overlooked the arena splintered against the far wall.

She understood then. The wild wind had been called, and it had come. It carried shards of the balcony across the whole coliseum.

Meralonne called, and wind replied; he rode its currents, felt them solidify, briefly, like Artisan's steps beneath his feet. He longed for the absence of boots and greaves and armor, but this was not the place, not the time.

Sor Na Shannen was shadowed and darkened by the grace of her Lord; Meralonne's was absent. But unlooked for—always unlooked for—was the wilderness, the wild. The wind had come, and he did not care, not yet, who had called it, who had been fool enough, crazed enough, *desperate* enough, to call it.

He used the power it gave him.

But he did not surrender to it; he was old enough and wise enough to understand the cost of consorting with the wild element on its own terms. Instead, he teased its attention, and he slowed Sor Na Shannen just enough in her parry that he might strike home with his own blade.

She was not so slow, not so addled as all that; he drew blood but claimed no victory.

They felled demons. The Kings. Their Astari. Even their men. They felled the walking dead to reach their enemy, but the dead rose, legless or armless, again and again. The demons, however, did not; they became ash in the endless, bitter wind.

The standards could no longer be seen. Voices could not be heard above the wind's roar. Sand, grit, and stone caught in eyes, mouths, and ears. But the demons were also troubled by the wind; Devon thought the wind could not be in their hands. Whose, then?

* * *

The Lord fought; Sor Na Shannen could feel his presence. It was different here than it had been in the Hells, where she had finally made the long climb—and survived its dangers—to present herself at his feet. At his feet, not by his side. His side was reserved for those who, over countless centuries, had proved themselves worthy. Against a Duke of the Hells, Sor Na Shannen had never been counted.

Nor would she be if she returned again to the Hells; that was not, and could never be, her fight to win. But *this?* This was. This world. This gate. This opportunity and this freedom. These were things that not even Dukes, in the countless centuries, had been able to give her Lord. She had come *so close.* The Lord had gifted her, blessed her, almost revered her for what she, and she alone, had accomplished in his name.

He was here. He was here, and he was beseiged; he could no more grant her what she desired than she could now ask. And she would ask it.

Yes, he wore the mantle of the Hells, the final gift from his estranged and much-loathed brethren. His will, by dint of that gift, was her will, for in a battle between the two, he would—always—win. The other kinlords, the other *Kialli*, might rage against it; not so Sor Na Shannen. For in any contest of note, with the whole of his will and intent bearing down upon her, she would lose. Did the details matter?

She had chosen to follow her Lord to the Hells, forsaking the open sky and the boundless water and the endless earth for love of Allasakar. It was a love that burned and scoured; it destroyed the weak. She was not weak, had never been weak.

She wanted this.

She turned, once, and received a blade's edge for her carelessness.

She summoned fire in her rage at this interference, this unwanted intrusion. Nor did she worry about its control; the wind was here, and it would recognize its ancient enemy. What fire now burned, loose and wild, was no longer a concern; it could not harm Allasakar, and everything else was inconsequential.

Or so it seemed, in her towering rage.

But the winds, free to roam, suddenly banked, and their attention focused not upon the combatants and the insignificant architecture of the coliseum—for they would build, here, and they would build a city to rival the Shining City at the height of her power—but upon the only important standing structure in the whole of this fallen city: the arch itself.

She turned in flight, her sword tracing a red arc across the air; she cried out a warning, for she knew that the Lord had come early into this world and that he was tethered to power that had not yet fully emerged. If the arch collapsed early, it would *never* emerge, and he would be lessened greatly.

He heard her; he must have heard her. But the roars of the Lord of the Covenant shattered both warning and attention, and he could not yet do as she had done: turn from the fray.

Nor could she, in safety. She sought a glimpse of the face of Allasakar as the winds carried stones and dirt toward her eyes.

It was folly, and she paid. Her enemy's sword buried itself in her flesh.

She was a denizen of the Hells; she had made her choice. The Hells, as their Lord, knew no mercy and no kindness. His beauty was a thing of power, and it was, in the end, for the powerful; the glimpse of him that she sought was denied as ice and Winter doused all fire and all movement.

Meralonne APhaniel, putting up his sword, felt the ashes of his enemy brush his cheek and his hair.

It was not a victory that filled him with either joy or pride; it had not come about because of his own skill but rather her lack. Even had it been a moment of triumph, he would have been forced to set it aside, for the voice of the wind was sharp and clear. He did not bespeak it in any obvious way but instead stepped, naturally, into its folds and climbed as if it were an edifice.

The wind was its own music, its own instrument. It had no fingers, no weapons but its voice; it was very like the bard-born in that way. Unlike the bard-born, however, it was not forced to be subtle.

Meralonne!

He glanced at Evayne. She was much aged since she had last come to his rooms in the Order of Knowledge. Where she had gained those years, and when, was a bitter mystery, but with the years, she had also gained power and stature such as mortals rarely achieved. He turned to face her, yards above the ground over which the dead and the dying now fought for supremacy.

Speak to it. Calm it. It is wild, now; it will kill them all.

Them, he thought. Not us.

It was true. Even now, the ranks of the living were being tossed about like so much debris, tilted off their feet and spun in the act of either killing or defending. The shambling dead were likewise disturbed, but unlike the living, they felt no alarm, no loss of composure. No fear.

Fear, of course, fed the *Kialli*, strengthening them in their own battles.

He did not bespeak Evayne. He was not kind enough, nor forgiving enough, in the end. But if she watched—and she was a seer, he did not doubt that she could—she would be comforted in some small measure. He lifted his head, and his hair splayed out in the palms wind made of nothing. He spoke to it—to its ancient anger at confinement and to its exultation at this unexpected and momentary freedom. But he did not attempt to gentle its force, not yet. Instead, he spoke of fire and earth. The wind roared like a young dragon in response.

It swept in toward the fires, tearing them from their moorings; the fire—the only element over which the *Kialli* had any control—fought back.

But the wind also continued its assault on the standing arch. It was the arch that was the goal of the Kings' men and of Meralonne APhaniel.

Can you not see how it resists you? It has no voice; it does not speak. But you cannot destroy it.

His words angered the wind; they were meant to do so. But the anger of the wild was a fine, fine edge to walk.

Across the coliseum, the dead faltered in a single wave. Their gait was slow and stumbling; this, however, was different. They stiffened at once, no matter what they were doing, as if in the rictus of early death. And then they fell.

With them fell the unnatural shadow that absorbed or devoured light; it was as if the whole of the darkness was being pulled back, inch by inch, toward its source: Allasakar. His roar, unlike the wind's, was deep and clear, and even those who had never heard his voice knew it for what it was: a god, in anger.

By some strange alchemy of the divine, darkness was light: the Lord of the Hells was clothed in it, as if it were raiment or armor, and he shone with it. He sent his enemy—his only worthy foe—staggering backward as he raised his arms in both fury and denial.

The trembling stones of the arch stilled instantly as the god bespoke the wind.

*   *   *

But the wind was wild. Of all the elements, it was the hardest to contain, the most capricious. It could be controlled, yes—but only for so
long, and always harboring at least as much resentment as the summoned and chained demon-kin themselves. To cajole was better—to
flatter; to coax.

But the gods were as they were. Allasakar did not cajole or coax; he
commanded, and he was obeyed.

To pit one's will against the will of a god was a fool's sport. But it was
not the will of the god that Meralonne now contested: It was the whim of
the wild air. He had not yet bent his will against it; he had merely conversed. Nor did he attempt to forcibly wrest it from the Lord of the Hells.

Instead, he whispered the names of its ancient enemies: Fire. Earth.

It was enough. The wind slipped free of Allasakar's grasp, and it re-
newed its ancient attack on the standing arch—focusing its fury on the
keystone that glimmered at its height.

The Lord of the Hells turned.

He turned toward the embattled arch, exposing his back to the Hunter
God. There were no rules of honor and engagement in this fight; between
gods, there had never been rules. The Hunter Lord leaped at his exposed
back.

Wings unfurled from that back, an expanse of shadow that glittered
like obsidian in its outward rush; the gods crashed together like lightning
and earth. But the Hunter God in his bestial form clung; the beating of
wings could not dislodge him.

The Lord of the Hells did not fall.

"Sigurne!" Matteos shouted.

He was not four feet from her, but without aid of magic—a magic
that was almost entirely focused on the protection of the Kings and the
Exalted—he had to strain merely to be heard at all. She glanced at him,
and he lifted his arm, pointing into the rising clouds of debris that blew
across the whole of the confined front.

Or at least that's what she thought; she narrowed her eyes and looked
more carefully. Matteos could be protective, but he would not attempt to
point out clouds that no one not dead could miss. Nor was she wrong.
Through the clouds, through the debris, through the ranks of literally

flying—if briefly, and painfully—combatants, she saw at last what he intended her to see: the wings of a god.

The god, besieged by the bestial form of his enemy and the force of wild wind unleashed, was not weakening; he was growing stronger, the depths of his shadow darker and longer.

They could not win.

She saw it clearly, and for a moment, she faltered. She had heard the stories of the time when gods had walked the earth. She had not heard them in the laps of her parents or grandparents, aunts or uncles, for her people seldom spoke of the business of gods. No, she had heard them from the lips of a *Kialli* lord who had walked the earth in the shadows cast by gods. He had spoken of the splintering of the ground, the rising of the seas, the changing shapes of whole coasts. He had spoken of the power of the gods, and power was revered.

The Hunter God was no match for the Lord of the Hells; Sigurne could see this clearly.

She looked at the Lord of the Hells. Looked as she had been taught, not by the mage who had taken her from her village, turning her by command and teaching into something, someone, who would never be allowed to return, but by another captive: a demon. A lord. Velvet voiced, tall, slender, and human in appearance, he had knelt by her side, his lips almost brushing her ear.

You must learn to see, if you mean to understand us at all.

"Show me."

Then, as now, she paid the *Kialli* Lord's price. She accepted the truth of her own desire, and she *looked*.

Mortality was a taint. An unforgiving weakness. Those in its grip were condemned to die, no matter how they lived, because mortal life was not for the worthy. It simply was. Therefore the untainted, the untouched, the unenfeebled were the immortals, wherever they might be.

The search for immortality had driven Sigurne's first master. Demons, of course, lived forever. How else could their names exist for hundreds or thousand of years and still be of use? But the summoning of demons was forbidden to the mages of the Order of Knowledge. Therefore, to look for immortality, he must have freedom in his researches. To have freedom, he must escape the watchful eye of the Magi. To escape their notice, he must kill the god-born, for what they saw, their parents could see.

All of it, useless to think of now.

But it came, wordless, *certain* knowledge: she gazed upon gods, and she was *not worthy*.

Allasakar's power was almost numbing in its glory.

Sigurne was not—had never been—interested in glory, except perhaps in the dim and inaccessible reaches of childhood. What she loved was small and dingy in comparison, but it was hers to defend. She looked— with effort—past the beauty of the Lord of the Hells and acknowledged the fact of her grim desire for him as she did. It, like breathing, was a natural consequence of mortality.

She could see that the god's power was anchored, and it was the anchor she now sought. She found it; she found it because she had been taught to see those shadows and to search for their majesty. Somewhere, her second teacher now rested in the plains of the Hells. Did he know, as he stood, or served, or suffered, what she now did with what he had taught her?

Did it matter?

It was the arch. The standing arch that seemed so out of place. The arch was his gate, and the gate. He had emerged from it, but it was not closed. He was not fully here; he could draw the power that was his by his very nature, but he drew it from the arch, from the Hells; without the arch itself, without the gate, he would be lessened, diminished.

She snapped her eyes shut. Always, *always*, in the darkest of hours hope was both blessing and bane, burden and relief. She could not do what needed to be done; she didn't have the power, and even at the cost of her life, she could not contain enough of it.

But she turned to look for Evayne a'Nolan, knowing, as if she too were momentarily cursed by the gift of sight, who might be able to accomplish the task.

The seer had already turned toward the gods. Sigurne didn't try to catch her attention; it wasn't necessary. As if she could, without effort, see what Sigurne had so laboriously learned so many decades past, her violet eyes widened.

And then her lips turned up briefly, not in joy or amusement, but in involuntary relief. She began to run, her robes swirling around her feet against the dictates of the roaring wind. Nor did the wind strike or touch her. But she stopped just short of where the gods raged; not even she dared more.

Her arms rose in an arc, sharp and slender, her palms flat and extended.

Between their mounds, light grew, crackling and burning the vision. Sigurne *felt* it. Had she not been watching, however, she would not have known the source of the magic; so much magic was being used in this small, confined space. She waited for the lightning to fly from the seer's hands; instead, it grew.

And it grew.

Faced with the magic of gods and demons, it shouldn't have been impressive—but it was. It was mortal will, made manifest, in the middle of battle; it was not casual, and it was not a simple fact of life: It was choice. It would be costly.

But failure would be profoundly worse.

When the light flew at last, the seer shuddered, and her arms fell at once to her sides, trembling there a moment before her knees also buckled beneath her sudden weight. Sigurne trembled for entirely different reasons.

In the distance made of the flesh of gods and the wings and claws of demons, the keystone *shattered*.

Three things happened then.

The seer vanished.

The wind roared.

The Lord of the Hells screamed.

Of these three, it was the last sound that struck Sigurne the most deeply, although in the end it was not the most dangerous. She heard pain, shock, and an abiding fury in the single sound the god made before he turned the whole of his attention—at last—upon his bestial foe. It was the sound of hope, inverted. She closed her eyes.

The wind almost tore her off her feet.

It was enraged.

Meralonne's voice, Meralonne's cajoling, could no longer reach the wind; the keystone in the arch had shattered, and the wind was now left with no obstacle, no resistance. Nor had the wind destroyed it; had it, it might have been satiated for a moment and open to suggestion.

Now? It raged as only wild wind could; it had been deprived of its quarry.

People could be controlled in their rage; the wild elements could not. Their rage was the heart of their existence; it was primal. It could, with will, be confined, but it was a contest and a struggle.

He smiled as the wind pulled his hair. The smile dimmed. For he could hear, at last, twined with the wind's rage, the keening of a familiar voice: wordless, bereft.

It was the voice of Kallandras of Senniel College, the mortal who had unleashed the wind.

"Hold!" King Cormayln cried. By the power of birth and blood, he was *heard*. Above the wind. Above the roar of gods. Above the threats and the rage of demons. His standard had not—by miracle and the grace of human desperation—fallen, but while he spoke, it wasn't necessary.

Devon paused. There had been some forward momentum when the ranks of the animate dead had faltered and slowly collapsed in on itself, but it was a scattered movement; the Kings' forces now coalesced, retreating with intelligence where possible until they formed one body.

The demons—what few remained—had also regrouped. Their numbers were lessened; in particular, the striking and compelling woman was nowhere to be seen. He would have the story later, if there were any left alive to tell it. But now, the gods raged.

If they spoke at all it was a guttural, visceral language that could not be contained by the civility of words; they spoke in blood and talons, in sword and claw. Wings rose and fell, not in flight but in fury. But so, too, did tails; there was nothing remotely human about this combat.

The tenor of the battle shifted as they watched. Not all could put up swords and bear witness; not all of the *Allasakari* were dead. But they, like the corpses, seemed bereft of shadow and power; they were not, in the end, a match for the Kings' forces.

But they were evenly matched, the Lord of the Hells and the Hunter God. Something had changed; Devon was not certain what. He shouted; he was not King Cormayln. The words were taken by wind, torn by them; he could not be certain who might hear them. Nor did it matter now.

They watched.

They waited. As much as they could around flying debris, they bore witness.

Isladar watched. Veiled not by shadow but by lesser magics, he stood aside, his lips curved in the faintest hint of a smile. His brethren fought, but they fought poorly, for they had seen the destruction of the standing arch, the shattering of the keystone, and they understood what it meant: Immortality availed nothing, now. Time was suddenly consequential.

Sor Na Shannen's last cry did not linger or echo. But Isladar bowed to the ashes the wind carried. She had played her part and played it well; no matter that she had also played it with blind devotion and adoration. She had given him the gift of her fear. Such a gift might once have succored gods, but only one now remained who could draw strength from pain, and he fought for his life.

The Hunter God was strong. He had taken a form rooted to earth; there was no such sustenance for Allasakar.

The wind howled its endless, bitter rage. Isladar could not calm it and could not control more of it than this: He hid from it, dampening and silencing the presence of his power. The wind, however, was no one's ally. It was caprice defined. It sought destruction now, and death, and it harried two gods, tearing chunks of stone edifices from the coliseum and throwing them.

One struck the wings of the god.

One struck the tail of the beast.

Neither flinched; neither noticed.

In their own way, they were as elemental, as wild, as the wind itself; the only thing that mattered, until the combat was done, was the presence of the enemy.

Isladar smiled. Allasakar fought with one wing. It was almost time to end it. He was here now; his feet touched mortal rock and mortal soil. He was diminished, yes—but so, too, was the world; the ancient wonders were buried or destroyed.

My Lord, he said, forcing his voice to carry by dint of magic.

There was no answer; he expected none. He had often waited decades for some sign of his Lord's response while he shadowed the throne of the Hells. But he could not wait decades here.

My Lord, he said again, strengthening his voice. It was risky. *This is but a battle. You are new to the plane; the Lord of the Covenant is old. He has waited throughout the centuries of his people's ignorance.*

Stay and fight, and there is a chance that the work of decades is undone. This, too, was risky. It was truth, but the *Kialli* understood that truth was no excuse and no shield. The wrong truth uttered at the right moment might reach the Lord, yet still doom the fool who dared utter it. But if Allasakar fell here, it was over.

He is bestial, now. He is much diminished, yes. But he is primal, and the wild earth has his ear. His cunning is animal cunning; it is direct, and brutish. He will detect no subterfuge, no subtlety.

Again, there was no response.

But look, Lord: the Hunter is waiting. Can you not see what he carries? It is bane to the Hunter God; bane to the Lord of the Covenant. He will Hunt, if the battle is over. He will send the Lord of the Covenant back to the bridge beyond, where he has long been absent from his See.

They cannot stand against you, without the aid of a god. There is no other god but this one; if you fall here, in seeming, Bredan will finally return to the heavens; if he tries to return to the mortal world, he will return far too late to prevent your subjugation of the plane. Retreat, and plan in glory, and the gods—all the gods— will know, and they will be helpless in the face of your strength.

This time, the shadows twisted against the wind. The Lord of the Covenant's jaws snapped shut on the conceit of wing, and the wing tore.

Very well. Very well, Isladar. I will play this game, and they will pay.

Isladar smiled.

The Lord of the Hells did not throw down his sword or expose his throat, and it seemed that very little about the combat changed. But that was the way of the Lord; where subterfuge was required, it was crafted with care. He could lie, of course; he had, in the past. But his lies were imbued with the force and strength of belief, of believability; they were the truth that his audience desired, and they were glorious lies, larger in all ways than most truths. This lie was no exception.

The Lord's enemies—his many enemies—wanted triumph; they wanted victory. To play into that desire and that hope was not difficult. They saw, in the end, what they both feared and desired: the death of a god. Even the *Kialli* paused a moment to stare and to witness.

They saw what Isladar saw; they took from it something different. Lord Isladar of no demesne had returned to the world at last; he had no need to breathe, or eat, or sleep, and he did not therefore hold breath. But had he required it, he would have.

Almost. The first step. The first move in the long game was almost complete. It was a game that could occupy the rest of eternity, but it had begun at the foot of the Lord's throne in the Hells, and one day, it would end there.

The Lord of the Hells wielded a sword of flame, kin to the weapons of the *Kialli* in the way that the man in his prime is kin to the infant he cuddles. His sword met bone, pierced flesh; the wound closed, as it had closed so many times in this combat.

But the Lord took wounds as well, and they were slower, now, to heal. He hoarded his power.

Go North, he told his leige. *Take those that survive, if they will follow. Go North, and await me there.*

Isladar bowed. It would not be seen.

Meralonne felt the battle's turn. He saw it in the breaking of wings that were conceit and unnecessary power, and his smile was a slender edge. Thus, the arrogance of gods gave way to fury, for the arch by which the Lord of the Hells had traveled to, and attained, the plane itself was now scattered debris. What power he might gather now was scattered, and it would take time.

The immortals seldom worried about time; it was one of the few advantages given those who toiled the whole of their short span in their desperate attempt to give lie to the fact of death. Mortals struggled with both time and death daily, and they were struggling now, in the shadows of gods. The earth broke, and broke again; cracks took marble, and the force of Allasakar's sudden strike unanchored great slabs of rock.

His sword, however, cleaved marble, missing the Lord of the Covenant, and in the slowed rise of its fire-edged blade, the Lord of the Covenant was there, jaws snapping at exposed forearm almost too quickly to be seen. But not to be heard. Even above the wind.

And the wind harried them all.

The Lord of the Covenant was driven back by shadow, driven into splintered marble that moved as he moved, clinging to rent flesh. He, too, was harried by wild air, but it did not move or stop him; it did not injure him. Where he bled, it was always from the sword of the god.

It was not a battle that could be joined with ease by Meralonne or any mortal mage.

Nor did the fighting between the remnants of Allasakar's mortal forces and the Kings' hold his interest long; the magi were harrying them, where the wind allowed them any safe purchase. There was only one fight left, and he braced himself and turned his face into the winds.

There he heard keening. It was not the wind's voice, although it was so twined with its rage it was difficult to separate the two. But if there was rage in the second voice, it was the rage caused by pain, by one's own choices. It sought no revenge, no justice; it did not speak of that kind of loss.

But it spoke of *loss*, and Meralonne was stunned by it, silent in an entirely different way. He felt young again, but this youth was not the absent youth of ferocious delight, when glory was as yet untarnished. It was farther back, and deeper, than that.

Once, he had had no colleagues, those fractious and oft-whining mages that cluttered the grounds of the Order of Knowledge on the Isle. He had had *kin*. Once, he had had a home in a distant Court and a Lord whom he revered and loved, as one loves those things that are terrible and glorious.

His shield was riven, and he felt the pain of it, although his arm, by magic's artifice, was whole. His sword came to his hand with no conscious effort on his part; it was what was left to him.

Nothing was left to the other. Nothing: no kin, no weapon, no legacy. He had knowledge and the bitter pain of memory, and he had—he still had—hope. Meralonne had at least divested himself of that folly. But it returned to him now—the wages of hope, not the strength.

Meralonne lifted his face, then; his hair streamed across it like a shroud. But he was not dead, not yet, and he *would not die here*. Not here. Not in the shadow of old battles and older glories. Not when new battles such as this one awaited. Nor would he fight them alone.

He would meet them at the side of Sigurne Mellifas, while she held fast against the indignity of age; he would meet them at the side of the Kings, Reymalyn and Cormaylyn, or their untried sons. He would meet them in spite of the interference of Duvari of the Astari.

And to do that, they too must survive.

"Kallandras!"

For he had heard the bard's voice and knew it. And knew, as well, the how and the why of the wind's power and freedom.

In his youth, he had heard the wind's voice. Clearer and sweeter than water or the harsh crackle of fire, quicker and lighter than the ponderous, slow syllables offered by earth, it had offered him the world. It was not a constant refrain, but it was there. Sometimes he rode the wind and saw, from the vantage of height, the whole of the world made small and insignificant. To the wind, height signified nothing, of course; the world *was* small and insignificant.

But the wind's voice was soothing, and it was, if one practiced a little caution, all-encompassing. Only the wind could achieve that with ease; all of the other wild elements would crush or kill in the attempt. The bard heard the wind's voice. Meralonne thought, given the wild, rising fury of the wind, that he might no longer be able to separate it from his own.

He called again, using magic husbanded until this moment. "Kallandras!"

There was no shift in the wind. Nothing that indicated that the bard had even heard him. Meralonne closed his eyes.

There was nothing to be done, then—nothing but to kill the bard; he could not take the reins of the wind while the bard's will sustained it.

The Lord of the Hells screamed in mingled pain and fury. Sigurne shook with the force of his cry, and it sickened her in almost the same way as the pleading of the unseen, torture victims had. Her own reaction both surprised and enraged her. Was she, then, a young child, to be terrified into pity and empathy at the simple *sound* of pain?

Yet it was not the sound alone.

She could see the Lord of the Hells. Hate him, fight him, dedicate her life to the frustration of his goals and desires—these she could do while she watched. But she could not despise him; she could not look away from him, could not think him anything but beautiful. This was the strength of the darkness: It was beautiful, it was desirable. It was night.

She blanched when the jaws of the Lord of the Covenant snapped bone; she stifled a cry—with both hands—when the Lord of the Hells fell to one knee, sword slowly raised. The power that had sustained him was gone, the arch destroyed.

All that was left now was to send him back to the Hells, to destroy the avatar, the physical embodiment. She was grateful, in the end, that the Hunter God was present and ashamed for the gratitude because it came from the wrong place. She could not have easily lifted hand against this god, and had she overcome that compulsion? She could not have destroyed him.

And his death was necessary.

She watched it. She watched the Hunter God—as beautiful, as terrible, in his own way—as he descended upon the fallen god at last; the winds flew around their forms, both obscuring them and parting like an artless veil.

*   *   *

Meralonne approached, sword in hand. He could not control the whole of the wind, but he could barter with it for his purposes; he could move between its raging refrains and retain his balance in the air. Around him, rocks flew, and smaller pieces of metal—armor or weapons, he wasn't certain—but they did not strike him or force him to ground.

Instead, they rose to the heights of the cavern, and great, stone chunks crashed into the marble below and into the columns that girded the coliseum itself. The Kings' men would not last, not even with the magi to protect them.

He moved above them, separated from their fate, and only one thing gave him pause: the cry of the Lord of the Hells. Not even the triumphant sound of the Lord of the Covenant had the same effect.

He bowed his head. It was over.

And yet it was not. Lifting his gaze, he caught sight of Kallandras of Senniel, and he froze. The bard was *singing*. He was singing into the wind; his lips moved, his head rose, in utter silence. Bardic voice. Bardic audience. No one else would hear what Kallandras now sang save the person for whom it was intended—if he was within the range of his power.

Seeing him now, Meralonne could not doubt it. His gold hair was wild, unkempt, the ringlets stretched and tangled by their contact with the air. He had thought the bard enspelled—charmed by the power and the compulsion of the wild element. He revised that opinion as he gazed at the bard's face.

Upon his thumb—not the ring finger that was the conceit of the Empire—a ring blazed with white fire; it burned both vision and flesh, and were it not for the roaring movement of wind, the charred scent would linger everywhere.

What have you done? What have you done to yourself?

Meralonne raised his sword and then put it up; it vanished as his will to cause the bard's death wavered. It had been a long, long time—too long since the power of one man's pain and loss had moved him, speaking to his own.

Kill him, he told himself, dispassionately. *Kill him, and have done.*

But there was no anger, no heat, in the words; they were empty. Almost before he had made the conscious decision, he reached out to touch the bard's stiff, outstretched arms, avoiding the ring hand, the ring arm, as he did.

He spoke words he had not spoken since his youth. Quick words, fierce words. They were unnecessary; the bard couldn't hear them. He could fight what lay behind them, of course. He could fight what was a momentary binding; he had the will.

Or would have, had the wind not absorbed so much of his attention. So it seemed, until the binding spell took effect.

It cut. It cut the mage. The bard's pain and loss were strong enough that he didn't even notice. They had to be. The song that he sang, the words that he spoke in silence, could have been Meralonne's words.

But he knew how to call him, then. Not by name—not by *that* name. Lifting his voice, forcing it to be heard in spite of the wind, he shouted a single word.

Brother.

The god was gone. Their enemy had fallen.

Only the Hunter God remained, and it turned, now, into the ranks of those closest: the demons. The *Allasakari*. Meralonne's report—where was he?—had made clear that the god had killed friend and foe alike in the Terafin manse, and Sigurne sent urgent word to the Kings and to those men she could reach, all but ordering them to withdraw, to retreat where they could in safety do so.

She turned then to see the distant Northern Lord for a moment, no more; he had joined in the battle against the demons that remained, and he wielded the only weapon that had any hope of injuring his god. It was his, now; the battle was his.

The Hunter Lord struggled, as they all did, with the unnatural storm's fury. One man approached him as he stood, his gaze fixed upon the Hunter God.

"Lord Elseth! Lord Elseth!" Devon ATerafin shouted. He had to shout simply to be heard. If Lord Elseth spoke at all, his words were lost. Devon's, however, were not; he, like so many of the men and women who served the Kings in their various guises, had been trained to pitch his voice a great distance at need.

"The beast is at our flank."

The foreign Lord nodded grimly. "Get out! All of you, get out!"

"We can't! The wind blocks the exits—we've lost four mages against it."

"Then stop the wind!"

*　　*　　*

Assassin. *Kovaschaii*. Sworn and bound to the Dark Lady. This was the Master Bard who had been sent, time and again, by the Bardmaster of Senniel into the thick of war and intrigue; this was the man who against all hope always returned to her side, bearing the word she desired or the word the Kings sought.

No wonder, then. No wonder that he had been able to sing a song of death and killing so compelling that the torture of innocents had become, for moments, the mercy of their painless, quick slaughter.

Meralonne felt no horror and no disgust. Had he not, in his youth, done the same?

Kallandras turned to face him, his eyes pale and shining, his lips turned up in a smile that was so open, so uncharacteristically *joyful*, Meralonne almost turned away. The wind did not tear him down or drive him forward, and Meralonne, understanding some part of the why, chose to mirror his stance: He spread his arms, slowly, to either side, and his hair, long and unbound, swirled around them both.

But the smile the bard offered dimmed and changed. What was left was bitter self-knowledge.

Meralonne, however, shook his head; what his own expression now exposed, he could not clearly see. He had known that the word would draw the bard's attention when no other word could. But he had spoken the single word as if it encompassed his own longing, his own loss.

One could hide from the bard-born, with practice. One could even lie. But it took effort, the deliberate placement of syllables and their nuances. Meralonne had not even tried.

"Kallandras! Call the wind back. Call it, or you will do the work of the kin."

Kallandras' eyes widened, losing their glow, their wind-infused power. He glanced at his hand, at the ring that now burned flesh. Wincing, he curled that hand into a fist, and he lifted it.

And I am spent, Meralonne thought. But he, too, bent will toward the leashing of the wild air.

Chapter Twenty-three

EMBATTLED BY WIND AND DEATH, Lord Elseth lowered his spear.

Devon watched as he could. Lord Elseth had come to this dark, shadowed remnant of an ancient city with a single purpose: vengeance. Not for something as simple as wind and the ferocity of a maddened god would he abandon the fight; nor was he abandoning it now.

No, this sudden stillness was some part of his purpose. The Hunter's hand dropped to his side, and when it rose again, it carried a horn. He planted his feet firmly apart, lifted the horn to his lips and blew three notes.

The wind did not carry them away; it didn't disturb them at all; they were clearer than speech or screaming would have been.

Reaching out, Meralonne gripped the ringless hand of the bard. He had not intended to touch him at all.

"Its voice—" Kallandras said, his own broken, as if he'd sung at full power for hours.

"I know," Meralonne said, his voice both loud and soft. "Hold tight, little brother. Hold long. The wind is about to realize it is angry."

"Meralonne, I don't know how to let it go. I don't want to lose it—"

"I know. But we are fated to have and to lose, you and I. Walk the path bravely."

Together, they began to call back the gale.

*   *   *

There was a cost, a price to be paid. It could be paid in life's blood, and so often it was. The mage and the bard, locked by Meralonne's grip, began to spin in the air, like the outer spokes of a broken wheel. They fought the movement, and they lived through their sudden descent, forcing the air to bear them in an arc that did not end in broken stone or their own broken flesh.

Meralonne snarled in fury, meeting the wind's rage with his own. Kallandras offered the wind his loss, his pain, and his guilt. Of the two, it was the bard the wind now attacked, because it sensed certain weakness there. And it *was* there. Meralonne could not speak, could not divide the focus of his will; he could not argue with the bard or demand that he rise above his own pain.

He could see that the ring now glowed so brightly it was painful to look upon. What Myrddion had made so many centuries ago was now being pressed to its utmost limits; it had never been tested until now. If it did not hold, the wind would destroy them all.

But Kallandras lifted his face; his hair, wild and unkempt, now trailed blood—but from what wound, it was not clear. He opened his cracked lips, and he began—again—to sing.

The storm stopped abruptly at the force of his voice. But the wind was not yet finished; it switched tactics, and Meralonne heard its voice raised, for the first time, in harmony with the bard's. His eyes stung, not from sand or dirt or shards of bitter rock but from something else he did not care to name, for the wind sang of freedom.

It sang of companionship, kinship, unity.

It offered these as gifts to a merely mortal man, and that man smiled bitterly, painfully, blood adorning his phrasing like punctuation. He wanted to lose himself to the wind's voice and be done; Meralonne, bound to him for moments longer, knew this as certainly as if it were his own desire.

But more than that, he wanted the safety of what was lost to him forever. He sang the wind home, and the wind, crying, came.

Silence.

It was broken by the roar of a wild god. That roar was no different in effect than the roar of the angered element; where it was heard, it froze the unwary, and they met their deaths.

The Kings' standards, by some grace of magic and determination, stood; they were still now, but the embroidery of their emblems could be seen in the darkness. Even had there been no light, they would have shone; the magi had labored over them. The Kings' forces still stood, and they made their way toward those banners; but they moved slowly, awkwardly, as if the sudden silence had deafened them. They did not look to the Kings. Indeed, they did not look to the standards, except by instinct. The whole of their battered attention now rested upon one man's shoulders: Lord Gilliam of Elseth.

And his whole attention was absorbed by the Lord of the Covenant, whose pale coat was now darkened by blood. They watched each other so intently they might have been statues carved by an Artisan to commemorate this moment.

The Exalted were busy; the children of the Mother had already begun the work that would not wait: They attempted to save the fallen whose spirits had not passed across the bridge in the beyond that led to the Halls of Mandaros. They fought death here, as if they were life's soldiers.

The air was still. No wind came to lift the banners; no breeze came to cool the foreheads of men who now lay aground. There was no sun, no movement of cloud, no glimpse of true light—nor would there be here. Only those who made the ascent to the city above would see it, and many who had made the journey into the darkness would not.

But the horn had been sounded. The Sacred Hunt of the Western Kingdom of Breodanir had finally been called. The raging, bestial god turned as the last note died into utter stillness, all other prey forgotten. He rose on hind legs, and he roared; the ground shook with it. What had they called him? The Hunter's Death. The Hunter's inevitable death.

Sigurne, who had studied some of the notes and papers that had come out of Breodanir via the Order of which she was head, knew some of the customs of the Breodani. Once a year, during the Sacred Hunt, the god hunted his people. One noble, or his Huntbrother, would die. Always. That death, like the seasons, could not be prevented.

The man who faced him was mortal. He held a spear that had been crafted for this Hunt, but he stood alone, and in the shadow of a god's glory, he looked too small and too frail to withstand the onslaught of his god. Yet upon his shoulders, their lives now rested.

"Matteos," Sigurne said, still watching, "retrieve those who can be retrieved. Stay as far from the god as you did when the Lord of the Hells was upon the field."

Meralonne carried Kallandras as the wind guttered and the stillness took hold. He carried Kallandras through the roar of a god, and he spared only a glimpse for the solitary figure who faced the beast. Once, in bygone years, he had carried the fallen with just such grace, and he had been gentle with them, he who was known only for his ferocity.

The bard reached up to tug at the edge of his robes, for he wore robes now that the battle was over. Meralonne, witness to the destruction of part of the Terafin manse, knew better than the Exalted or the magi what must follow the fall of the Hunter Lord.

"What is it?" he asked softly. He spoke an old tongue; the bard did not appear to notice the difference in the language at all.

But Kallandras attempted to stand, to leave the haven of the only support he was offered. Meralonne ceased all motion, but he did not release the bard to the earth, upon which the dead lay scattered like interlocking sculptures.

Instead, he held him upright, and he watched as the bard's lips began to move. He could not hear what the bard said, but given his expression, he did not expect to; nor did he offer the necessary warning about the use of talent-born power. Kallandras had passed his limits and hovered on the brink of mage fevers so strong they might consume him.

He knew it; he must know it. But if he did not care, Meralonne would not. He granted the bard choice, and the dignity of the cost of that choice; and he waited while the bard's cracked lips moved, with effort, over thirteen words.

Only when he was done did the bard sag, as if all strings had been cut, into the comfort and strength of a stranger's arms. He wept there, and he did not care who bore witness.

Meralonne APhaniel did, but he was the only person who was allowed to do so, for he used his own magic, as unwisely as Kallandras had just done, to shield him from the view of all others.

Silence.

Hunter God and Hunter now existed in a forest of broken stone and natural shadow. Only the Hunter God's light illuminated them at all, and it was not a conscious choice on his part.

Lord Gilliam of Elseth lowered the horn. He raised the spear in both hands, as if in salute. He was pale in the light the god shed, but there was no fear in him. The god began to move, and the Hunter Lord smiled.

He was a foreigner, in a foreign city; he had seen demons and he had seen gods and he had seen the death of his closest friend, in the span of weeks. The only thing that moved him to black rage had been the treatment of the dogs that had died in the battle at the Terafin manse, for he had expected—demanded—that they be accorded the funeral rites of heroes.

Devon, better than any man present, knew the truth of these things, especially the last. And so, to Devon, the young Hunter Lord looked isolated, standing alone, and it seemed wrong to him. But he was Astari, and he had his orders: to stand by the Kings now. To wait.

There should be trumpets, he thought, as the spear was slowly lowered. There should be heralds; there should be hushed praise. Anything but this silence, this held breath, this empty waiting.

Devon followed the gods, but he seldom prayed, and this close to the Exalted, there wasn't much point; if the gods couldn't hear the prayers of the Exalted, they would hear no one's. Surrounded by death, and only death, the Hunter Lord squared his shoulders, lowered his spear, and froze.

The silence was broken by the baying of hounds.

They came against his orders and against his command; they came against the wishes of the slightly frightened priests who had been given their care. They came through the unlit caverns and the unlit, broken streets, and they came in silence until they had all but reached their Hunter's side: three dogs, their colors almost indistinguishable in the muted light.

He did not turn; he did not otherwise acknowledge their presence.

But Devon smiled. It was a slight smile, and it acknowledged pain and the possibility of fresh loss, but it was also right: They were his, and they existed for the hunt. Even this one.

The lone Hunter from the Kingdom of Breodanir straightened. He watched, the dogs ready at his side, as the god began, at last, to move.

He lumbered, too bulky to seem swift, too powerful to be anything else. The Hunter Lord seemed as enspelled as the rest of the witnesses, and he moved slowly, and late; the god's claws tore through his cloak and his tunic in one easy motion. Blood welled across Breodani thigh, dark against green, seen by the god's moving, internal light.

Lord Gilliam of Elseth turned, leaped, rolled; the cloak fell away from his shoulders, its clasp snapped. He was on his feet before the god had reached the spot where he had fallen, and he was away, once again in control.

The dogs harried the god's flank, snapping and leaping clear, even as their Hunter had. The spear was not a light or quick weapon, and although its head was edged, it was meant for point, not slash. Lord Gilliam made no attempt to do the latter. He kept the point between himself and the god as he navigated broken stone and pillars as if they were the geography of an ancient forest.

As Meralonne, burdened, approached the gathering of the Kings' men, he saw that they were already in motion as the Hunter and the god faced each other. He was weary, but not so much so that he could not spare an idle thought for the folly and vanity of men. It soured a mood that was already melancholy; he longed for his pipe and the comfort of his personal clutter and spells.

"Stand your ground," he told them curtly, raising his voice only slightly to be heard.

A Kings' Sword the magi recognized as Verrus Sivari—oft decorated and well thought of by the Kings—turned. "It is not our way to stand idle while our allies face death."

"And it is your way, of course, to commit to death your own people. Stand your ground." There was no pipe, no office, no confined—and empty—space, and his arms ached with the weight of the bard—a weight that at one time would have been insignificant. Nor did the Kings' men rush now to his side to offer the fallen the respect that was his due, and this, too, irked the mage. He had not the time to argue with idiots while Kallandras bled in silence.

But he took the time, cursing it.

"The Kings' Swords," was the even reply, "take their orders from the Kings."

It was cumbersome to bow. Meralonne first knelt, setting aside the bard. When he rose, he offered a gesture of respect that was so perfect it was leavened with sarcasm. Which fell flat.

"Member APhaniel." It was King Reymalyn who now spoke. "What would you have of us?"

"I would have you save the lives of your servitors. They are gathering to intervene in the struggle." It took effort not to curse them as idiots, but he made the effort, wondering at the same time, why. "There is only one weapon in the city that can affect the creature you see before us. That man wields it, as he is oathsworn to do. Neither he nor the creature would benefit from the aid that you seek to offer—but neither he, nor the creature, would be injured by it either. Your men will break like a single wave against the seawall." He spoke mildly as if stating simple fact; he was.

Nor did the King question him.

The Lord of the Compact, however, turned to the King. "My Lord, heed him."

King Reymalyn took the magi's measure with his piercing, golden gaze, and then he lifted his hand and gave the order.

They had seen gods fight; they had seen a god fall, and they knew there was only one possible outcome. They had not raised a hand against the Lord of the Hells and could not now raise hand against the Lord of the Hunt. Lord Gilliam of Elseth was no god, to fight upon even ground. No god, to survive the wrath and the fury of gods.

But he dared what they did not dare, bound in some way to a god the magi had once sworn could not be genuine. The god turned, briefly, to lunge at one of the darker of the dogs; his great paw clipped the dog's legs, and the smaller creature flew. He was low enough to ground to skid, claws scrabbling against marble that had not been broken or cracked.

Here and there the stone did shine; the wind had removed both debris and corpses. The dog gained traction and wheeled, arrowing again toward the fight.

But the dogs had harried the beast enough; it roared. Because of its shape and its size, it was possible to see it as a creature, no more. It was not. It knew who commanded the dogs, and it knew—who better?—that to kill Lord Gilliam was to destroy all resistance.

It turned toward the Hunter Lord, who now waited, spear shaft in both hands, legs slightly bent as he braced himself for the god's approach.

And as they watched, hands on swords, breath held, the world shifted, and where columns stood, trees formed in their stead, wide trunked and thick branched. The scattered stone shards, the sharp new edges of broken marble, were caught in the same transformation, becoming, in light that was already scant, the undergrowth that might grace such trees.

It was dark in the forest.

The beast did not charge, although its movements, sleek and fast, implied one. The dogs harried it from the left and the right, but they stayed well clear of the jaws of the beast, and they ranged the reach of his neck. They could not, however, outrange the beast's paws, and when their small jaws grazed flesh, it turned and batted them away, as if they were small vermin.

Devon, aware of what the dogs meant to Lord Gilliam, held his breath, but the dogs were stunned for only a few seconds on landing; the blows had not been fatal.

The Hunter Lord looked up to meet the eyes of the approaching god, and he froze, staring at something that no one else could see, and everyone watching could comprehend: divinity made, for a moment, flesh.

It almost cost him his life.

The god leaped, all the while holding fast to Lord Gilliam's gaze. It was a heavy, cumbersome leap, and it fell just short; jaws that should have removed the arm that held the spear tore cloth and skin in a loud snap. Lord Gilliam grunted and shook off the pain as his dogs snarled in fury and sprang, harrying the god at a distance that was entirely unsafe. They did not try to annoy or tire now; they tried to protect. They drew blood, and if their teeth and their jaws were in no way the equal of a god's, they angered the beast enough that Lord Gilliam could pull back and steady himself.

The god's claws raked the side of one dog, exposing ribs. But the dog, like its master, did not fall. Lord Gilliam shifted his grip on the spear, and as the god turned to snap again at the hounds that attempted to stay just beyond the reach of his jaws, the Hunter Lord drove the spear he wielded into the beast's flesh, just below and to one side of the line of its jaw.

The god roared, and if dragons had ever truly existed, their legendary voices were an echo of his rage and his pain. His voice was the only voice in the coliseum, and the ghostly trees shuddered with its force, as if it were a gale. Not so the men and women who bore witness; they froze or flinched, forcing themselves to hold steady as the Hunter Lord was lifted off his feet.

He held fast to the spear the god attempted to dislodge by thrashing. He held fast when the god snapped his head, side to side, and he was born aloft in a wide arc, his feet kicking air. His weight drove the tip further home.

The beast's jaws could not reach the Hunter Lord; nor could his claws, although he did try to dislodge the Hunter with the force of their blows. It seemed impossible to Devon that the god would retain this form, that he would anchor himself to the structure and shape of a beast, no matter how bizarre or otherworldly. It was not, now, to his advantage, and if he shed shape—as gods were said to be able to do—he might escape the deepening wound the spear caused.

He thrashed instead; he lashed out, claws raking whatever they could reach. The Hunter Lord seemed—for a moment—to be scion of the Hunt itself; he was bleeding, that much could be seen even at this distance, and he *must* be tiring, but he did not release the spear. Nor did he seem to notice anything but the God of the Hunt and the Hunt itself.

The Breodanir belief was that the god decreed *this* Hunt. It was the first day of Veral across the Empire, and across the Western Kingdoms as well, and it was upon the first of that month that the Sacred Hunt, in the Sacred Woods of The Breodanir King's forests, was called. It was the first day of spring. Of renewal.

It was said that one Hunter Lord or one Huntbrother—or sometimes both—always fell during the Hunt, and they fell, it had been said, to the God Breodan, who on this one day turned the tables on his followers, chose his prey, and hunted them to ground.

Devon, watching, understood the visceral truth of this ritual now. The Hunter Lords met their death at the hands of this visage of their god. And they knew it. They knew they faced this death, once a year, and that without it, there was no true spring, no crops, no growth in the land. They faced it, they hunted, and they fought.

As Gilliam of Elseth now fought—blooded, weakening, but unwilling or merely incapable of acknowledging failure until death was simple, unadorned fact. He was not yet dead. But his grip was weaker, and he was slipping.

But the spear was no normal spear; it had been given to Lord Gilliam for this hunt, and it bit deeply, drawing blood, weakening the struggles of the god as the god weakened his follower. This was a battle of attrition. They both seemed to understand it and to accept its terms, and perhaps those terms had been agreed to not only by followers but by the god himself.

The god could not toss the spear—and its bearer—forever; when Lord Gilliam failed to loose his grip on the spear's shaft, the beast lowered his chest, and the Hunter Lord fell with it, feet once again planted on the ground. Trees surrounded them, spaced like columns. The god roared.

His follower bared bloody teeth in silence.

They faced each other, and Devon lost sight of the merely mortal man as the Hunter tried to rise; the god's fur and his form were a pale shroud that obscured the Breodanir Lord, momentarily, from the sight of the witnesses. The intruders.

The god roared once more.

And then Lord Gilliam of Elseth, unseen, found the strength to push the spear home.

The god fell silent; for a moment he looked like an Artisan's rendition of himself; every hair on his body, every scale, the twisting lash of tail and the hard, downward curve of claws, made larger, in all ways, than life. Above it.

Silence.

The form of the god grew less solid as they watched, turning from sculpted stone to blown glass that held, at its center, a radiant light. Through his wavering body they could see the bloodied face of Lord Gilliam of Elseth, the widening of his eyes.

He collapsed slowly to the ground.

Wind came, then. Wind as unlike the storms that had torn rock from its masonry as it was possible to be. Wind touched the trees that had sprung up at the will of the god, and wind bore the leaves from the branches, spreading their green shadows across the whole of the coliseum's floor like a benediction.

Light came, as well, as if the cavernous heights above had broken to allow the entry of dawn. It felt like the first dawn, a significant one—and why wouldn't it? It was the first of Veral. It was the day of Ascent. From out of the shrouded homes of the patriciate, from out of the shrouded hovels of the commoners, people would now be emerging from the shadows in the streets high above.

But they would do so, in the end, because of one Hunter and the sacrifice of his brother. And his dogs, who had abandoned the dignity of the battle itself for something that made them look ridiculously young: They leaped up on their Hunter, knocking him flat, and they took turns pushing each other off the rise of his chest.

The Exalted of the Mother now departed the guard she'd been given, for if there was cause for celebration—and there was, and men's voices were raised a moment in the songs that sustained them on the long marches to and from a war—there were those who lay aground, injured but not yet dead.

She went to Gilliam of Elseth, and she tended his wounds, although his expression—seen, admittedly, at a distance—made her attentions seem less welcome and more fearsome than the jaws and the claws of a bestial god. Devon, who had seen many, many poor patients in his time, had to turn to hide a broadening smile.

He could now look away from Lord Elseth and his foe, and he saw, in the distance, Meralonne APhaniel, cradling the body of one of the fallen to his chest. It was an odd gesture for the mage to make, and Devon marked it. He marked, as well, the moment the mage simply ceased to be present.

To travel at will was a singular magical gift, not because it was difficult but because it took so much power. Meralonne revealed himself by that action as one of the truly powerful of his Order, for he had twice fought the kin, had taken his injuries, and still had enough in reserve to return to the city above—without the weary and long journey back through the caverns.

But it would not be so wearying a journey as all that. The caverns were silent. The dead were at peace. The living? They would mourn. They would remember, and their memories would wake them from sleep in the quiet of the night. But they *lived*. The Kings lived. The threat of the Lord of the Hells was now lessened.

It never completely ended, though; how could it? The gods might be defeated in their physical form, but they were eternal. What could truly kill gods? Bredan was merely free, now, of the mortal plane.

But if the gods could be killed after all, who would be willing, and who capable, of such an act?

Duvari spoke, coldly and curtly, as was his wont; Devon's sudden brief burst of laughter at his comment passed unremarked.

1st of Veral, 411 A. A.
Sanctum of Moorelas, Averalaan

The Kings appeared at the foot of the Sanctum of Moorelas as the sun fully crested the horizon. They did not, perhaps, arrive with their usual dignity and decorum, for they appeared six feet above ground in midair. But they didn't fall into the shadow cast by the statue, and when they gained their feet—quickly, by all reports, and given gossip and the speed and accuracy at which it traveled, reports varied widely—they turned toward Moorelas, and they tendered him a bow such as Kings never tendered anyone.

Duvari and the rest of the Astari were not, of course, far behind; it was small wonder that they didn't land *on* the Kings. Devon, however, had had some warning of what their exit would entail. The rest of the Kings' forces followed.

When they were at last assembled, when they were, in fact, looking across the bay at the spires of the Exalted and the towers of *Avantari*, the night left them. The Kings waited until their standards were once again properly positioned before they gave the signal. Horns were lifted and winded to herald the day. The first day.

They progressed slowly toward the bridge that led to the isle, and there they made another departure from accepted protocols. The Kings did not turn toward the bridge; instead, they turned toward the holdings. The black shrouds of the Six Days still remained in some windows, but even as they watched, they were removed. So, too, the dark ribbons that adorned the poles in the Common. Fewer bakers and farmers had dared to travel to Averalaan for the first of Veral this year than in any year in living memory, but they were there, and their signs, bright, gaudy, and ofttimes greedy, were small flecks of brilliant color lining the street, just as certainly as flower beds lined the walks of the patriciate.

Sigurne Mellifas, supported in part—and not for show—by Matteos, watched wearily as the surviving members of this necessary expedition were unceremoniously dropped on their behinds near the Sanctum. She was exhausted enough that she did not direct her mages to intervene in any of these landings where there were no injuries. However, the healthy fell first and warned those bringing the injured. The dead would come last. The Kings would not leave them in the open grave of the hidden city; nor would they leave them to shadows and the straggling remnants of their enemies, greater and lesser. The fact that their spirits had already fled to the peace—and the blessed forgetfulness—of Mandaros' long halls would not sway them in this decree, nor did most of the living make the attempt.

But, Sigurne thought, gazing once again at the few brave—or foolish—farmers who had made their trek to the city, this is how the dead, in the end, were respected: this life, this normal, everyday life, with its little greeds, its little customs, its little necessities. Sometimes it took strength to live that life. No one now knew this better than the people in the holdings.

"Sigurne?"

She glanced at Matteos. "I'll stay."

"You're exhausted." His tone was accusatory, and she smiled in spite of the truth of the words.

"I am," she said serenely. "But so are we all. This is the first dawn, Matteos; do not, in your severity, seek to deprive me of it. I thought it might never come again in this fashion, and it does not—quite—feel real to me yet.

"It is good to see it. It is good," she added, her smile gentling, "to see it at your side. We lost many, there. But," she added with a grimace, as three familiar voices now carried to her ears, "it appears that the ones we didn't lose are engaging in unflattering public debate. Which may force me to strangle them myself."

1st of Veral, 411 A. A.
Averalaan

Finch stood at the edge of the footbridge that led to both *Averalaan Aramarelas* and the Terafin manse. She could not *quite* think of it as home yet. But the twenty-fifth holding was no longer home, either.

She'd chosen this bridge, which, while guarded, was less well traveled, not because she wished anonymity; if you crossed over to the Isle or from it, you obviously had wealth and access to power. No. This bridge, the footbridge, had been built at the command of the first Twin Kings, Reymalyn and Cormalyn. On this day, centuries ago—this very day—Veralaan had returned from the Between, where men might meet their gods if they had the will, with two young men by her side.

And those two men were the sons of gods: Cormaris, Lord of Wisdom, and Reymaris, Lord of Justice.

At the foot of this bridge, perhaps as a reminder—to themselves or to the people who lived in the city that now bore their mother's name—they had ordered statues built. Three gods therefore stood not on the Isle but the holdings, two on one side of the bridge and one on the other. The two who stood on the side closest to Finch, Jester, and Teller, were the sons of Wisdom and Justice: Cormalyn the First and Reymalyn the First. Across from them, and watching them as carefully as any mother watches her sons, stood Veralaan.

Finch sat between Jester and Teller, her knees drawn up and tucked beneath her chin, her arms wrapped around her legs. She was silent because the city itself was—blessedly—silent. There were no screams, no sobs, no pleas; only the gulls cried, and if they sounded hungrier than usual, there was a reason for that: There was very little food to be scavenged from the bustling streets of Averalaan during the Six Dark Days.

The shadows that had covered the city now broke as if they were simple clouds, and dawn, in purple, pink, and orange, heralded the new day. First Day had come, as it had once come during the life of Veralaan, the woman after whom the city was named.

It was a blessed day. Finch, more than any of the den except Jay, had had to endure the endless, tormented deaths of people she couldn't name and didn't know. She had hardened herself, and she had gone to work, day in and day out, hoping for silence. Praying for mercy—whether for herself or the dying, in the end she couldn't say. That hardness now cracked like a shell, and she closed her eyes and lowered her head until she could feel her knees.

In the silence and the, fading darkness, she heard the sounds of horns, and she lifted her head immediately.

Teller and Jester were watching the holdings. No, not the holdings: the Sanctum.

"The Kings," Teller said to her, uncertain whether or not she also watched. "The Kings have returned."

"How can you even see them?"

"I can't. But the standards are there. Look."

She did. And then she looked down at her feet. Or rather, at Jester's. Between his boots—his heavy, well-made, Terafin-bought boots—lay a wreath of flowers. They had been twined with care around a wire frame, and they were still new enough that their petals hadn't begun to wilt or droop. White roses. Orchids.

Ellerson had given them to her. Because, he had said, the customs of the Six Days must be observed. She had stared at him as if he'd finally lost his mind, although his expression was the familiar, starched expression she'd grown to love.

"Where did these come from?"

"Does it matter?"

"Yes. The gardens haven't really recovered; the Master Gardener will have our hides—if only that—if these flowers came from the Terafin grounds."

Ellerson had raised a brow. "I am not," he said stiffly, "in the habit of stealing flowers from the grounds; nor am I in the habit of misrepresenting the needs of this wing when speaking with the gardeners."

She started to tell him that wasn't what she meant but fell silent, because it was, in fact, what she'd meant.

He waited, because he often waited, and Finch said, at last, "What do you want me to do with them?" They were very fine, very beautiful flowers. When Finch had been a smaller child, and she had still had a family she believed in, they had found daisies or other small weeds that had weathered the colder clime with which to celebrate the end of the Six Days; in truth, in most years, there had been none.

"Make a wreath," he replied.

It was her turn to wait, and after a moment, he said, "I am a fool. You've never made one." He pinched the bridge of his nose and then said, "Come, then, help me. I will show you how."

White was for loss. Color was for the living; white, the color of shrouds and death; the color of snow. She worked by Ellerson's side with the flowers he had brought.

And the work had been good, although the roses had thorns and her fingers looked like pincushions at the end of it. He was better at this than she was, and she wondered where he had learned it, and why; she didn't ask. Ellerson never spoke of anything personal.

When they were done, he set the wreath on the table and rose.

"The Kings have gone," he told her gravely, "and the Kings will return."

She nodded. She'd told herself this on and off for hours, in a desperate hope that repetition would become belief.

"When they do, Finch, my days here are numbered."

They weren't in the kitchen now because Jay wasn't here. She was with The Terafin. But Jay *should* be here for this.

"They wouldn't fire you—"

He smiled. It was a pained smile. "No," he said gravely, his words at odds with his expression. "They would not and will not. But I am an old man, Finch. And the life I chose as domicis is not the life of a man who serves the powerful. Morretz's choice was not mine, in the end."

"But—but you don't! You serve us!"

"Yes. And I will not lie. It has been challenging to do so. Challenging, but infinitely rewarding. I repent of every unkind thought I have directed at Morretz since I came out of retirement to serve your den; I would do it again, were the situation different.

"But there will be no service if the Kings fail. I speak not of their failure but their success. Is that clear?"

She nodded.

"If they succeed, it will be in large part because of the efforts of Jewel Markess. What she has done for the House is now known to the Kings, and will it or not, she will become a significant power."

"But she can't—she's not even an adult! She's from the holdings—"

Ellerson lifted a hand. "I cannot serve her. She will be known as a seer before the year is out, if she even has a year. Not all Houses will be happy to have her input into the affairs of Terafin, and those who are pragmatic will desire her death."

"They couldn't—"

"Not with ease, no, and not without some repercussions if they are foolish enough to be caught. But it will start, Finch, and I cannot protect her if it does."

"That's not your job—"

"No. It is not. And because it is not, I cannot remain. She would not ask me to leave," he added. "But I cannot serve her in good conscience. At the very best, I can hope not to hobble her. But at worst?" He didn't feel the need to expand on the worst, but Finch understood him.

"I will tell her," he added. "But . . . I wished to give you some warning. I understand that she accepts me, and I understand that she has allowed herself to rely on me. I will do what I can to see to her replacement."

"Someone else will come?"

"Yes, Finch. The Terafin will not allow Jewel to be without a domicis." He lifted the wreath, then, and handed it to her. "Take it. Place it wherever in the city seems appropriate to you and your den." He rose then; he had allowed himself the unheard of luxury of actually sitting in the presence of one of the den in order to show her how to twine stems around the wire frame he'd provided.

"And in truth, I tell you this because I will miss you, your tea—which has become somewhat better of late—and the way in which you also care for your den, and I am not certain I will have any other opportunity to convey the depth of my regret."

When they had finished, Finch found Jester and Teller in the wing; the others were gone. She bore the wreath Ellerson had made with her help. Teller looked at it, but Jester was the one who nodded. How much, in the end, did she really know about him?

"We'll take it to the Sanctum," he said.

But Teller shook his head. "We won't be able to get anywhere near the Sanctum. They'll have the streets closed at every possible approach."

Teller, who worked in the office of the right-kin, had information sources that were now considered by the den to be beyond reproach. So they had walked the streets of the Isle, and in the clothing of Terafin, they were not stopped or treated with suspicion. But even the High Market was not the right place, and the cathedrals of the Triumvirate were so finely accoutred the wreath seemed almost too humble for their steps or their gates.

So at last they decided to return to the holdings, crossing the bridge that—whether it was intended or not—separated the moneyed from the moneyless, because the people who had died in this undeclared war had come from the poorest of streets and had gone to their deaths without comfort or any hope of rescue.

White was for loss.

Those losses, faceless and nameless, would haunt Finch for the rest of her life. Day in and day out, she had come to the holdings to work—in the gray and silent Terafin offices in the Merchant Authority—because to work, as the Queen had said, was to defy the insanity and frenzied fear the demons hoped to cause.

She rose and lifted the wreath with care. And then she gazed up at the stone faces of Kings. She had never claimed to understand Justice and had long since given up asking for it; she made her peace with Reymaris by attempting to cause no injustices. She looked toward Veralaan; the determined and isolated Baroness-in-waiting she did understand.

But if she had prayed for one thing during these bitter, bitter days, it had been the strength Cormaris provided: Wisdom. She looked at the statue and then turned back to Jester and Teller. Jester raised one brow and then nodded and shrugged. Teller raised a brow in an entirely different way, but she didn't want to leave the wreath at the foot of the statue; she wanted to make more of a statement with this wreath on this First Day. Jester lent her hand, boosting her up so she could gain the wobbly advantage of height—the statues were larger than man-size, even a large man.

Men of power would have worn gold and jewels and the insignias of their Houses or their Orders. Men of power would have had far too much dignity for such an obvious sign of mourning. But Cormdyn was the son of Wisdom. Cormalyn would understand, if anyone would.

She used the stone chest of the King to balance herself as she lifted her hands—clutching the wreath—and placed the flowers firmly over the head of the statue.

She clambered down, brushed petals from her palms, and then turned to Jester and Teller. "Home?" she asked, looking out toward the holdings. Neither of them misunderstood her. Home meant, and had meant for years now, that-place-where-Jay-is. "Not yet," Jester said. "Let's go see if Farmer Hanson made it to the Common."

1st of Veral, 411 A.A.
Terafin Manse, Averalaan Aramarelas

Dawn broke in the Terafin gardens. Dawn touched the heads and the shoulders of the men and women who had gathered here. They weren't on their feet; they had found patches of grass to sit on, and they often held children in their laps or over their shoulders. Their voices drew back, as if they were curtains, when the sky began its shift from the darkness of night—a night that had seemed, for hours, endless—to the purple and blues of early morn. People raised heads, squinting or shading their eyes as they watched the slow change.

Jewel knew why; she almost pinched herself. Almost. But if this was a dream or an illusion, it was a *good* dream; she'd had nothing but nightmares in the last few months, and she didn't want to wake up.

Carver exhaled slowly; Angel, who'd been sitting one step above her, guarding her back, lowered his face into his hands in silence. When he raised it again, he let them drop, exposing silent tears; they were framed by a smile that was both weary and so deeply felt Jewel had to smile in response; it was that or cry herself.

He rose. He hadn't quite finished. He looked at the gathered crowd; they obscured the footpath to the shrine entirely. Then he turned back to her. "Duster should have seen this," he said. It wasn't an accusation; he looked . . . peaceful.

Carver nodded, although he signed a quick *shut up* in Angel's direction. Angel affected not to notice—or perhaps he truly didn't. Of the den, his sign was still the slowest.

"She would have hated all these people," Jewel replied, her words soft and muted so they wouldn't carry. "She would have hated their fear."

"She would have," Angel agreed. "But if not for her, they wouldn't be here."

Jay reddened. She would have argued with him, but she wanted to give Duster this moment because she deserved it. So she accepted the unspoken reasoning that led from Duster to these people: Duster had died so they could escape the twenty-fifth alive, and because they did, Jewel had been here, where there were enough people with power who could act on what she could sometimes see.

His smile deepened, and his tears started again. It was a striking combination. "She loved you and she hated that she loved you. But she wanted to save you. If she'd survived, I'm not sure how she'd've explained it."

Jewel winced. She knew exactly how Duster would have explained it. But wincing, she also laughed.

Sometimes, her Oma said quietly, *it's the people who are hardest to love who need it the most.* Her voice was as contemplative as it ever got, at least in memory, and Jewel turned toward Carver and Angel, who had come to stand shoulder to shoulder.

Haunt me, Duster. Haunt me. Don't let me forget you. I'll take the bad. I'll live with it. But let me remember the parts that were good.

"I loved her, too," she said out loud; Carver looked at his feet; Angel, however, looked at her. He wasn't embarrassed by a word she seldom spoke out loud. "And if you think her reaction to her birthday present was bad, don't try to picture what it would've been if she'd heard me say *that*."

Neither answered, and she realized, belatedly, that they were on their feet for a reason: The Terafin had moved. Finally, after hours on her feet, gazing out at the back of the manse in which all of her visible House huddled, she had moved. Morretz stood quietly to one side of his lord. He was never the most visible of men, but he was never absent anywhere except for her personal chambers.

There, and one other time that Jewel could think of, which had led, in the end to this First Day: the meeting with her so-called brother, Ararath of Handernesse. Rath.

They looked nothing alike, this slender, elegant woman and Rath, aged by life in the streets and in the North or on the ships he seldom spoke about. She didn't understand what had happened between them. But she thought that in the end Rath would also be, if not happy, then satisfied with the way things had turned out.

She missed him.

She missed Duster. And Lefty, and Lander, and Fisher. She'd been so crazy with the fear of losing anyone else that she hadn't really stopped much to think about the loss and what it meant. She glanced at Angel; Angel was crying, or had been, and he didn't turn his face away; he didn't try to hide it. She wanted to ask him why.

But . . . she didn't think less of *him* for the tears that her Oma had always hated.

And maybe it was time, now. Maybe she could cry, just once. Other people already were, in joy or relief or gratitude. Her tears wouldn't be noticed if she shed them. She looked up at The Terafin's face. The Terafin, who had stood at the height of the House shrine, leaving her Chosen behind. She had not cried; she spoke from time to time, but it was speech meant to comfort or succor. She asked nothing for herself.

Jewel's throat tightened. It was true; no one else would note the tears for what they were. But . . . The Terafin didn't cry. She didn't shout or throw up her arms or turn and hug the person next to her—which, given it was Morretz, would have been really awkward.

She didn't, on the other hand, threaten to give those people something to cry about either. It had been one of her Oma's favorite phrases, and Jewel had only once been foolish enough to say, *I have something to cry about already or I wouldn't be crying.*

As if her Oma were standing beside her, she kept her tears to herself.

Instead of crying, Jewel waited beside her den-kin, feeling her legs begin to shake as the reality of First Day continued to make itself felt. The sun was rising, and it was glorious, and it spread light across manse and shrine and crowd alike.

Five minutes passed. Ten. Only then did The Terafin lift her chin and step forward. The House altar was at her back; she didn't touch it, didn't look at it. Here and now that made sense; she sustained the House.

Her smile was slight, and it was the first expression that allowed some hint of emotion to color her face. "First Day has come," she said, pitching her voice so that it carried. It didn't sound as though she was shouting, either. "And there is now much to be done; we have lived through the Dark Days, as our ancestors once did.

"When Veralaan returned from the Between with her grown sons, they sought the throne. They were newly come from the homes of their fathers, and they did not arrive with strength of arms; they arrived, the scions of Wisdom and Justice, without armies or subjects. Veralaan was heir to the Empire, but she abdicated her rule in favor of her sons—both of her sons.

"Terafin was among the first of the Houses to join the cause of the Kings. They approached the Kings at the bridge that even now marks the Isle, and in the name of Wisdom and Justice, The Terafin offered the Kings—the first Kings—his sword. When he offered his sword," she continued, for this was a story that all knew well, even Jewel, who'd been born and bred in the poor holdings, "he did not offer a single weapon.

"He offered the whole of House Terafin. In offering the House, he offered the lives of each and every man and woman who bore the Terafin name—his name. He offered their allegiance, their obedience, and their determination. Did they stand at his side? No. Did they stand in his wake? No.

"But they stood where you have stood for these Dark Days: In the manse. In its halls. I am The Terafin," she said. "And I, just as the first Terafin to serve the Twin Kings, understand the power of the House: it resides in you. Not singly; no single one of us can carry the burden of a House, just as no single one of us can carry the burden of Empires.

"But for the dream of Justice, for the hope of Wisdom, and in the name of Mercy, the Mother's mercy, I, too, have committed you to the Kings and to the Empire.

"And you have not failed me. Nor has the dream of those three things.

We have faced the risk of madness and death for this First Day, and we see it as perhaps only one generation has seen it before.

"It is time, now, to celebrate. Acknowledge that the risk is never done, the service is never finished—but that there is joy in the service. Take down the shrouds, return the candles and the lamps and the magelights to their former brilliance; return to the kitchens and the halls of Terafin, and as you can, rejoice. Return to the life that the Kings' rule makes possible.

"It is for this that we have fought, and even our dead might smile and know a moment's peace, were they here.

"Terafin has always been served by men and women of principle and honor. They are not always young, and they are not all masters of arms."

There was some laughter at this, but it was in and of the crowd as people poked and prodded one another.

"But if arms were the only measure of value, there would be no Empire. Even those whose skill *is* arms may sometimes set them aside; set them aside now. I will join you for the first meal in the dining halls in two hours."

That caused a ripple of conversation and possibly some panic—but it was a good panic, really. The Terafin then nodded once, a clear indication that she had finished speaking. The children didn't really notice—the ones that were still awake—but the adults that minded them did.

The grounds began to clear, and Jewel started to follow the crowd.

"Jewel."

She turned to The Terafin.

"I would have you join me at the high table for breakfast." The Terafin's smile acknowledged just how much of a reward this was for Jewel; it was almost a grimace.

Jewel froze. "Terafin—"

"It is a request, not a command." She looked beyond Jewel's shoulders to where Angel and Carver stood waiting. "Gentlemen, if you would return to your quarters, I will send Jewel back with my Chosen."

Carver glanced at Jay, signed. *Go?*

She signed a very hasty *yes* in reply. Angel, however, signed *no*. Jewel wasn't used to instant obedience; she wasn't The Terafin, after all. But most of her den wouldn't argue while The Terafin was standing a few yards away, and Jewel wasn't of a mind to have an argument in front of the woman who was, technically, her lord.

"Can I just have a minute?" she asked The Terafin.

The Terafin nodded. "They are not mine," she added, "and they are therefore not required to instantly obey *me*."

Jewel approached Carver and Angel; they hadn't stopped signing, although at this point they were signing—vehemently—at each other.

"Angel," she said, without preamble. "The Terafin asked you to leave. I *agreed*. Why are you still here?"

"It wasn't a request," he said quietly. "And I don't take orders from her."

"We're living under her roof. She's one of the most powerful people in the Empire. We've scuttled like roaches at the sound of magisterians before—why pick *now* to start a fight?"

"I wasn't starting a fight—"

"*She* asked you to go. *I* told you to listen. You're not picking a fight with her—you're picking a fight *with me*."

He shrugged, and his hands stilled. But he wasn't backing down.

Angel could be *quiet*. This one was a loud quiet, totally unlike Teller's or Finch's. She understood their quiet; she didn't understand Angel's. He was angry; that much was clear. She was heading that way, herself.

Carver caught his shoulder; Angel shrugged it off in a way that suggested any further attempt to move him or turn him would end in violence—in front of the Terafin shrine, and ten yards away from the woman who ruled the House.

"She told me to go," he said, not even glancing at Carver. "And I want her to understand that I don't serve her. She's not *my* lord."

Jewel raised her hands to her face. It had been a long night. It had been *nothing* but long nights—and days—since she'd arrived at the manse. Clearly, she wasn't the only one who was close to the edge of insanity. She lowered her hands, where they settled on her hips in a way that her Oma would have instantly recognized. "She owns the place we're living in," she finally said, in a dead-quiet voice. "And pissing her off is like spitting at the landlord. Remember him? Big guy with the keys?"

"And the bad breath and the drinking habit and the scary wife." He glanced over her shoulder at The Terafin and then back, having made his point; he'd lost some of the tension around his jaw, and his fists had relaxed slightly. He hesitated as if he wanted to say more, and then lifted both hands, palm up, in surrender.

"What the hell was that about?" she heard Carver say as they headed down the now deserted path.

She didn't hear Angel's reply, and she wanted to. Instead, she fixed what she hoped was a neutral expression across her face before turning back to The Terafin. Aside from Morretz and the Chosen, they were alone in the garden. And that *was* as alone as one could get with The Terafin.

The Terafin was gazing up at the sky, which was growing paler and clearer as the minutes passed. She began to speak without looking away from this distant glimpse of the heavens.

"He is young," she said. It took Jewel a moment to realize who she was speaking about.

"Angel?" she asked, just to be certain.

"Yes. Although it is true of all of your den; it is true, as well, of you." Her hands slid behind her back as she continued to gaze at some point well above the manse. "Honesty is a rare commodity among those who practice politics, but there is an art to it; it is not an art you are yet conversant with, if you will ever be.

"Your life here will not be easy. It will be easy in some ways compared to the life you once led in the lower holdings—but in some ways, vastly more difficult. You will study here. You will learn. You will be forced to move among the powerful, and you must know enough about them to survive, because once it is clear who and what you are—and we will attempt to hide it, but it is too large a secret—there are Houses that will consider you an . . . unfair advantage. They will sacrifice much to have you removed.

"I'm not sure if Ararath ever told you what you were, or what you are; I am certain he never told you how valuable you would be—untrained and uneducated—to any House."

"He implied that I wouldn't have the freedom of choice if it was known."

"He wasn't entirely correct, but close enough. He sent you to me," she added softly. This time she did look down. Jewel wasn't certain this favored her.

"No," she surprised herself by saying. "He sent me to *you.*"

Her smile was thin; it held pain. But it held pain; it didn't release it. "We are a gift to each other, then?"

"I—I think so."

They were silent for a moment. Morretz was well away, although Jewel suspected he was listening anyway.

"You will keep the House Name." It wasn't a question, but it wasn't an order.

Jewel held breath and then released it. "Yes. You knew I would," she added. "You knew I wanted it."

"I did. But I knew why."

"And?" Jewel turned to face The Terafin, struggling to keep her arms loose at her sides. She failed; her hands rose to push hair out of her eyes, repeatedly.

"Come to breakfast," was the quiet reply. "I will make the announcement there."

Jewel's eyes widened. "B-breakfast? Announcement?"

The Terafin raised one brow and then said, gently, "You will have to tell them sometime."

"Y-you'll take them, then? You'll take them as well?"

"I will, as you say, take them as well. One is already a member of my House Guard, and two are in key positions within the House's general operations, albeit junior positions. Barston is actually grudgingly satisfied with Teller's work—and when you meet Barston officially, you will understand just how much of a compliment that is. Lucille ATerafin has said very little about Finch's work, but if Finch did *poor* work, believe that she would have much, much more to share. Jarven ATerafin, however, has spoken favorably of her."

Jewel knew of all three, but she said nothing.

"If we wait," The Terafin continued, "it will be more difficult to make a case for the rest of your den. At the moment, the House is aware of what Terafin owes you, and I will face little opposition in Council if I choose to both nominate and grant the House Name to your den. You, of course, will not be questioned."

"What will you tell them if you *are* questioned? About the others, I mean?"

The Terafin's smile was slight. "I will tell them that exposure to the magi and the Kings has made you aware of your singular value, and you will not remain in the House without this concession. They will accept it as necessary, even if they find it distasteful; I would. They will also see it as a sign of your knowledge of your worth, which will be expected.

"I will make the announcement at breakfast."

"Wait."

The Terafin nodded.

"Can you make it at tomorrow's breakfast?"

"No. I do not normally join the House for breakfast. Today is an exception, and the reasons for it is obvious. If you will wait until tomorrow, it will be in the evening."

"I'll live with it," Jewel said, almost without thinking. "I need to talk to them all first." She hesitated again, and then said, "Does it have to be public?"

At this, The Terafin frowned. "Yes. The House Name is a matter of both pride and achievement; it is not an embarrassment or a humiliation, and gaining the House Name will never be treated as a guilty secret." Her voice softened. "And it must be now, Jewel. It is now, or years from now. The House is not aware of all of the details of your involvement—or your den's—in this bitter season; they are, however, aware that you were in some ways critical to our survival.

"This is a fitting reward, a fitting gesture of gratitude. No one will gainsay it; no one will question it. Wait a month, wait two, and gratitude will fade. If you intend to hide the House Name to save your den from the resentment of those who must approach it more slowly, time is not your friend."

Jewel nodded because it *was* what she was afraid of. She knew they were the outsiders here. "I'll tell them."

Chapter Twenty-four

ENDINGS WERE ALWAYS DIFFICULT.

Ellerson, who had weathered many, still found them painful. But without endings, there were no new beginnings. He reminded himself of this, seated as he was before The Terafin, because he required the reminder.

"You are certain of your decision?" The Terafin asked quietly. Her hand held a quill, and before her, on an otherwise spotless desk, lay his contract.

Because she was not his master, he felt no need to dissemble. "I am," he replied. "As certain, Terafin, as you yourself are."

She lifted a brow. "I am less certain," she finally said. "It has not escaped my attention that your interactions with the den itself were more numerous than your interactions with its leader; they will miss your guidance."

"I will miss offering it," he replied. "But I cannot now be what Jewel requires." He glanced up at Morretz, who stood to one side of his lord, and raised a white brow at his former student.

Morretz, of course, noticed, as did The Terafin. But he nodded. "I concur," he said, stiffly. If he was not pleased, his anger was still secondary to his chosen vocation. But only barely, Ellerson thought.

"The guildmaster and I could come up with no alternative," he told Morretz. "In all the lists of possible candidates, who would you have chosen to replace me? She is a seer, Morretz. She is ATerafin. There is a very real chance that in spite of the domicis we have selected, she will not survive. Had she been surrendered to the Kings and the Kings' service, she would be safer—but in truth, not by much, and it is likely that she would spend her days and years surrounded by the Astari."

"I see little difference, at the moment."

"Morretz," The Terafin said softly but coolly. He subsided. She waited. Into the awkward silence, one of the Chosen walked.

"The new domicis has arrived."

She was silent for a moment longer, and then she moved; she signed the papers and rose. "If you will wait," she told Ellerson.

He nodded.

Torvan ATerafin joined his lord in the library. He offered her the salute their respective ranks demanded, and she indicated, by gesture, that kneeling was neither required nor desired; he stood. Morretz was restless, although his movements were minimal and silent.

"Torvan," The Terafin said, "you are aware that Jewel is ATerafin, in a way that most of the House is not."

He nodded.

"Were it not for your intervention, she would not, I think, be a House member; were it not for your intervention, her sense of debt and obligation to the House I rule would be minimal."

He nodded again, but now he was watchful.

"Were it not for her intervention, you would not now be standing before me. I am grateful for both her intervention and your continued service." She waited.

After a long pause, Torvan said, "What do you intend her role in the House to be?"

She rewarded the question with a nod and the faintest of smiles. "I will, in the near future, nominate her to the House Council."

Both of his brows rose. "She is young," he finally said.

"Yes. But it is impossible that the Council will not know of her abilities; they will accede to the request because it will give them easy exposure and access to her. They will not, however, accede without argument.

"During this period of transition, she will require guards. House Guards are assigned duties to Council Members, as you are aware. As you are also no doubt aware, the House Guards so assigned often have . . . stretched loyalties." He opened his mouth, and closed it when she lifted a hand. "I require no defense of the House Guard."

"Terafin."

"She will not require many guards; I want at most eight, in rotation. But of those eight, I want at least one whom I consider to be beyond reproach."

Torvan was not, and had never been, a fool. "You mean for me to join her detail." His words were even and flat.

She inclined her head. "I've spoken with Alayra."

Torvan's grimace was brief. Alayra had not—quite—forgiven him for the attempted assassination. In time, perhaps. "She was relieved?"

"She had no objections. She has not, however, reassigned you."

"Oh?"

"You are Chosen, Torvan. Were it not for your intervention, the first demon to enter the manse would have achieved what the second failed to achieve; I had divested myself of even Morretz for that meeting." She hesitated and then added, "I did not fail to remind Alayra of this fact. She will come around. You know her as well as I."

"My life is not her life's work," he replied, after a pause. "Trusting me is an unnecessary risk."

"I trust you."

He was silent for a moment. "You mean to leave the choice to me."

"It will be seen as a punishment, or perhaps a display of doubt on my part. But I will not make—or force—that choice on you; I have already erred once, and I will not repeat the mistake, even if the consequences are not immediately as dire.

"Jewel does not understand protocol; she will learn, but it will never come as naturally to her as it does to the rest of the House Council. She's cautious, and she'll continue to be cautious, but in ways that will do nothing to preserve her life should it be threatened now; it is for that reason that the guard is not a simple formality.

"You understand her value to the House. Everyone on the Council will do the same. But no one on the Council will have your history with her."

Torvan was silent for another moment. "If I do not accept the reassignment, who will you install in my place?"

"I will confer with Alayra. I will also take your suggestions under consideration."

He shook his head, and the slightest of smiles shaded his expression. "If House Guards are assigned, enterprising members of your Council may seek to influence the guards in question."

"You see the difficulty."

"I do. She is not capable of the rigid protocols of formality that separate her life from the lives of the people she must depend on. She would be easy to influence in one way or another, if there was any subtlety involved."

The Terafin nodded.

"She would not, however, be easy to browbeat or threaten."

"No. But they will have some exposure to her in the months—and years—to come; they aren't fools."

He cleared his throat. "I've served as Chosen for years, Terafin."

She waited.

"I've attended House Council meetings; I've attended important trade overtures. I've even attended sessions of the full Council of Ten. She'll have her domicis?"

"She will. It will not, however, be Ellerson."

"No, it couldn't be." He hesitated and then began to pace. As he was not, in fact, on duty, he could—but it was unusual. "The domicis is not currently in residence in the manse?"

"No. In this case, the domicis would be required to accept a permanent position rather than a contracted term."

He raised a brow and lowered it again quickly. "My experience within the House and with the Council could prove useful in that case."

"Invaluable. The domicis will, of course, come up to speed as quickly as his service requires—but you would, if you accept, be part of how that speed is achieved."

"How much leeway would I be given?"

"In what sense?"

"May I choose the guards?"

"Within reason."

"There will be no other Chosen?"

"There will be eyebrows raised at the presence of one of my Chosen; more, I cannot grant, although I would not begrudge it."

"Pay?"

"They will, of course, be House Guards; their schedule of pay will reflect that."

He nodded again, and she had to stop herself from smiling.

"I realize there are protocols involved, but if I accept this assignment—"

"As you clearly mean to do?"

He had the grace to redden slightly. "She is not what you are, Terafin," he said gravely.

"No. But in time, she may well be what I am now. If she survives. What concession did you intend to ask of me?"

"Only that I be able to inform her myself."

"The relationship her guards will have with her will of necessity be slightly unusual. Yes," The Terafin added. "Granted."

"Then I will depart. I will inform the Captain of the House Guard and seek his advice."

She watched him go. Everything she had said was, of course, the truth—but it was not the whole truth; she offered Torvan the detail because she thought, in the end, it would suit him; he had grown attached to the den and its fortunes in the House, and he owed Jewel Markess his life. Jewel, conversely, owed him a life she valued more than her own; they had, between them, the solid foundation of an abiding trust.

Morretz cleared his throat. "Terafin," he said.

"Is it time?"

"We are to meet with the applicant from the Guild of the Domicis within the quarter hour."

Amarais was curious. She was long past the age where curiosity could not be contained by silence, but she glanced once at Morretz before she made her way out of the office and into the library of her personal quarters. Morretz, as her personal domicis, was expected both to have opinions and to make them known with discretion; she was accustomed to the small and almost invisible signs of his disapproval. Nor did she often disagree with his appraisal.

But in his years as her domicis, she had never seen such obvious, barely concealed hostility. He walked stiffly, and his silence was so thin she expected it to break at any time. She had, however, asked what it was about the candidate that he disliked, and he had fallen utterly silent.

She was therefore to be left to her own devices in his evaluation.

Four of her Chosen were in the library as she entered. The room's fifth occupant was a tall, dark-haired man. He glanced at her as she entered, and his glance strayed—briefly—to Morretz. Without pausing to look back at her domicis, she couldn't see his reaction.

The man was standing to one side of the large, long table at which she habitually worked when she did not have pressing engagements. He stood beneath the glassed windows set into the ceilings above; the evening had already dimmed the natural light enough that magical light had begun its timed glow.

She took a chair and motioned for her visitor to do likewise; he seemed to miss the gesture. Interesting. He did, however, offer her a perfect, if stiff bow.

"I am Avandar Gallais," he told her quietly. "I have come from the Guild of Domicis to meet with the ATerafin."

She raised a brow. His voice was both deep and clear; he was not nervous in the presence of power. Nor had she expected he would be, but there was something about his stance that implied that he was accustomed to *being* a power. He had not come to the manse in the robes of the guildhall with which she was familiar; he wore red and black robes, which suited his coloring. His eyes were dark enough in the evening light to seem black. He was not a young man. Neither was he old; he defied age, as only one other she had met could: Meralonne APhaniel. They were not, this man and the mage, alike in any obvious way, but as she took the measure of the domicis, she thought they were like night and Winter.

Morretz took his place to one side of her chair in utter silence.

The doors opened to allow Gabriel entrance; he glanced at the new domicis and then walked straight across the carpets to The Terafin's side; he also took the seat she indicated and then handed her a small sheaf of papers. It was a much more complicated contract than Ellerson's had been, and he had looked so dismayed when she'd asked that he personally see to its contents, she had almost repented. He was understaffed, given the day, and had he not been, the weeks that had led to it ensured no escape from the duties of his office in the foreseeable future.

But he understood the need, and he had done as she'd asked. She glanced without concern at the first of many pages and then turned again to face the standing domicis. To her surprise, it was the domicis who spoke.

"I have not yet accepted this assignment."

She raised a brow.

"It was not my intent to waste service in pursuit of children," he continued. "I am aware of the duties of the previous domicis."

His obvious arrogance caused her brow to rise further; she glanced at Gabriel, whose barely concealed astonishment amused her. She set the contract aside on the table's surface.

"I would therefore hear more about this girl before I make my decision."

Were it up to Gabriel, the decision would no longer be in his hands; that much was clear. Add to it Morretz's obvious animosity, and Avandar Gallais did not seem, in any way, to be an appropriate candidate. She inclined her head, however.

"This conversation is, of course, under the guildhall rules," she told the domicis.

"Indeed. If, in the end, she is not of significance to me, I will have no desire to speak of her at all."

The Terafin raised a brow. "Very well. Jewel Markess ATerafin is sixteen years of age, as far as we know. She was born in the lower hundred holdings; she was both raised and orphaned there."

One black brow rose.

"She can speak passable Torra; she can read and write."

It rose further, and the lines of man's lips compressed. "You test my patience," he finally said.

"Indeed," she replied, with a cool smile.

The contours of his brow changed, and the smile he offered in return was a match for hers. "Forgive my impatience," he said. "I have lingered in the guildhall for what feels an interminable length waiting for a suitable lord to whom I might offer my service."

"Jewel is in no way a traditional member of the patriciate. Her understanding of the subtleties of power is entirely in keeping with her background."

"But she is valuable enough—to you—that you seek a permanent contract in her stead."

"She is."

"May I ask why?"

"You may. It is relevant to your decision." But Amarais hesitated for a moment. The man was a noble, or had been born to the nobility. He had not learned his carriage or bearing in any other way. He was, she thought, younger than she—but not by much. She glanced at Gabriel, who was frowning. Morretz, however, was stone.

"You are aware of the difficulties that occurred in the city in the past few weeks?"

He surprised her then. He shrugged. "I am." The way he spoke the two words made it clear that he thought he understood the whole of what had occurred—something she herself could not easily say. His arrogance was astonishing; it was either refreshing or irritating, or some blend of both.

"Oh?" The single spoken word was cool.

"The *Kialli* play their games," he replied. "As do the gods, in their time. Neither are of much concern to me."

Gabriel rose, his left palm splayed against the surface of the table.

"Gabriel," she said. "Please, be seated." She turned her attention back to the domicis. "It appears that your understanding is more . . . complete . . . than one would except from a member of the Guild of Domicis."

He said nothing.

In her fashion, she conceded ground. "Were it not for her intervention, the *Kialli* . . . would have won the games they played, to the detriment of our Empire."

At this, he inclined his head. He did not, however, speak.

"She is seer-born."

If The Terafin had hoped for a stronger reaction, she was to be disappointed; he did, however, pause.

"You are certain." It wasn't really a question.

"Yes."

"The Empire does not contain many seers."

"It does not, as you are well aware," Gabriel broke in.

Amarais again lifted a hand. "Gabriel, he is not here as an applicant to the House; it is not as ATerafin that he will serve. To our knowledge," she added, speaking again to the domicis, "there are none except Jewel. The one other seer with whom we have any experience is not, in my opinion, an Imperial citizen."

"And he?"

"Is not a matter of concern."

"Very well. You have in your House a child of the streets who has the talent of a seer and no training whatsoever."

"I do."

"And my role?"

"Your role," she replied, rising, "is to see that she survives as a member of this House. She is not well versed in the political; you would be responsible for some of her education. She has some experience, at this point, with the magi; her early work for House Terafin involved close cooperation with the Order of Knowledge."

"I . . . see."

The Terafin frowned. "Avandar Gallais," she said quietly.

He met her gaze and held it.

"Why do you labor in the guildhall?"

"For reasons of my own."

"You were not born to a life of service."

"No. It does not come naturally to me."

"My understanding, from those I have met and worked with, is that a life of service is a vocation. It is not—"

He lifted a hand. "Believe, Terafin, that I have heard it all. The guild-master is satisfied that I am both serious and capable. If you are not, you are, of course, free to dismiss me." He hesitated, and then said, "She is untrained."

"She is."

"And yet she was instrumental in the unraveling of Allasakar's plans?" He spoke the name of the Lord of the Hells so casually he might have been talking about a political opponent.

"She was."

He nodded to himself. "And she is likely, in your opinion, to have or make enemies?"

"She is. If for no other reason than her talent; she will be seen as too much of an advantage to my House, and my rivals may well attempt to level the field."

He was silent for a long moment, and then he glanced at Morretz. "I will meet her," he said, at last.

"It will take some small time to arrange for her presence," The Terafin replied. "If it is convenient for you to remain here, remain here; if it is not, we will arrange a meeting on a different day."

"I will wait," he replied.

In the quiet of the smallest of offices within her personal chambers, Amarais bent and touched a magestone before she rose and turned to her domicis. "Who is he?"

Morretz met The Terafin's gaze with utter silence. She did him the kindness of turning away, her gaze seeking the Isle beyond the glass of uncurtained windows.

"Will he keep her safe?"

"He is capable of it."

"He was not trained by the Order of Knowledge, according to the brief sent by the guildmaster."

"He did not require it."

"There are very few mages who are not required to at least pay lip service to the Order; the threat of being marked as a rogue mage is not negligible."

"He is clearly unconcerned."

Silence. "Morretz," she finally said, softly.

He closed his eyes. "Yes, Amarais," he replied. "If you allow this, he is capable of protecting Jewel. Not even the *Allasakari* could have touched her had he been present, in my opinion."

She waited.

After a long pause, he said, "Ellerson is not against it, although he has reservations; the guildmaster is not against it. Any misgivings I have are entirely personal."

"Thank you. I will send the Chosen for Jewel."

Amarais chose to take a desk that seldom saw use within the confines of her personal library. She spoke to the magestones and received light as her reply; the day—the First Day, in all its fragile glory—was drawing to a close, and the light that illuminated the library from the ceilings above had gradually dimmed as it donned evening colors. She was weary, and when weary, she found meetings of this particular nature difficult; she knew what to expect from the young Jewel Markess.

If she hoped for disappointment, she was not to receive it; Jewel arrived, looking tense and particularly young, in the wake of Arrendas ATerafin. The young den leader glanced at the room's occupants, and her whole face stiffened when she saw Gabriel and the stranger, Avandar Gallais. She had been in the manse long enough that the Chosen failed to catch her attention, although her gaze did linger upon Morretz.

It was, however, Avandar Gallais who commanded the brunt of her attention; her eyes, ringed with lack of sleep, narrowed. She did not, sadly, look impressed, and curiosity gave way to the underpinnings of instant suspicion. She folded her arms across her chest as she stood.

"Jewel," The Terafin said. "Please. Be seated."

Amarais thought she would refuse; she had clearly heard the order. But she acquiesced—slowly and awkwardly, to be certain—and found a chair. It was, of course, the chair farthest from the stranger and closest to the standing shelves that housed the most obvious of The Terafin's personal collection.

Amarais glanced at Morretz. *Did I*, she thought, *trust you, when we first met? Did I evaluate you accurately at all?* She couldn't ask, but had she, he would have answered honestly. No.

But she had felt no visceral dislike of him, no instant suspicion. She lifted her head briefly, and Morretz nodded. A moment later, Ellerson departed the more enclosed office and entered the room, disturbing what was an almost funereal tableau.

Jewel frowned when she saw him.

"Ellerson, please be seated."

He nodded stiffly, and he chose a chair that was some distance from the young woman he had served. Jewel was not a fool; she understood what it meant. That understanding was written across her expression like first heartbreak in the young. She mastered it, but with obvious difficulty, and faced Amarais.

"Yes," Amarais said quietly, answering the question that Jewel was wise enough not to ask.

But to her surprise, Ellerson now turned to face the girl, and his expression—so shuttered and so proper—cracked, as if the openness of Jewel's demanded a like honesty.

"Jewel."

What she could contain in silence for the sake of dignity began to break free of her control then. "You told me—only if you died, or if I died—"

He didn't flinch. Instead, he said, "Or if the contract expired. Or if there was a great change in circumstance."

"But there hasn't—"

He lifted a hand, a gesture that was clearly familiar to Jewel, who fell silent. But his voice belied the imperiousness of that gesture. "I am not your lord. It is not my place to tell you things that you obviously have not considered carefully enough for yourself." He cleared his throat. "Think, Jewel, born Markess; think carefully."

But Amarais understood that Jewel could not, at this moment, do what he requested. "Ellerson of the domicis," she said, "you have served well; the House of Terafin is pleased with your effort." She turned to Jewel, whose expression was far, far too clear. "Understand that it is not at my request that Ellerson has removed himself from your service."

"But . . . *why?*"

"Because," Ellerson said, interrupting Amarais before she could speak again, "I am not the right domicis for a young woman who will—someday—be a person of great power. Remember what I told you. To serve a person of power, one must *be* a person of power. I am not that. I have never been that. And to serve in that capacity would be, ultimately, a failure of service so profound that I could not contemplate it seriously.

"You are not what I thought you would be, young Jewel, and I have served many in my time. Had circumstances remained what they were, it would have been my honor to serve." His voice was the softest it had been, and the regret was genuine.

In his fashion, he was kind. He rose, he offered her a bow—a deep one—and he turned away from her and headed toward the doors at which the Chosen stood guard. Jewel lifted a hand, opened her mouth, and then snapped it shut, watching and learning, as she watched, that not all loss involved death. All of her previous losses, Amarais knew, had. Death could not be argued with; there was no negotiation, no plea, no offerings that could stay it.

She saw some of Ararath in the way the girl stiffened, and it almost hurt. Jewel said nothing. Forced herself to say nothing, although her expression obviated the need for words.

Into this silence Avandar Gallais now strode. To The Terafin, he said, "This is the one?"

Amarais bit back the deep sarcasm that was her first response. She, like Jewel, was tired. "Yes." The single word was clipped. But as she gathered the strands of her own fraying temper, Avandar responded.

"Good."

He didn't so much as raise his hand; his expression gave nothing away.

But Jewel leaped up and hit the ground, rolling toward the stacks as lightning enfolded her chair.

Morretz cried out, gesturing sharply in the wake of the obvious and unexpected magical attack. The Chosen drew their swords, breaking the silence with the sound of steel against steel and the brevity of spoken order. Gabriel left his chair, with less grace and speed than Jewel had left hers, turning toward Avandar Gallais as he did.

Avandar Gallais, however, seemed not to notice; he was watching as Jewel slowly levered herself to her feet, her hands gripping the edges of shelves to do so. The faintest edge of a smile touched his lips; it was a cold smile. Amarais almost dismissed him.

Almost. But she had seldom seen such an open display of power, and never in such casual circumstances as this. It was now clear, if she had wished for some small demonstration of his abilities, that he was capable. What remained in the wake of the brief and unexpected attack—and it was that—was Jewel Markess' response.

Amarais did not expect Jewel's relationship with a domicis to mirror her own interactions with Morretz. She knew that Jewel lacked any of the political knowledge that she herself had been born to, and her early life had also denied her the experience of observation. If circumstances were different, she would have forgone a domicis, relying instead upon interactions with the members of the House and the House Council to supply what she lacked. She did not have that luxury; nor did Jewel.

In her search for suitable servitors for House Terafin, she had interviewed a number of the domicis, and she had yet to meet one with the force of personality and the aura of casual power that Avandar Gallais displayed.

Power of this nature could be—was—intimidating, however; it could easily overwhelm. What Jewel said next would be decisive.

She lifted her hand as the Chosen converged, gesturing, as well, to Gabriel to resume his seat. Morretz, bristling at her side, had not moved.

"That was unnecessary." Her voice held the ice of her expression.

"For you, yes," Avandar replied. "But it is not you who will devote your life to the service of this one." As Jewel gained her feet and her expression folded into a glare, he added, "My apologies."

Morretz spoke then. "Avandar, you go too far." His voice was low, the words sharp and hard.

Avandar turned to The Terafin's domicis. "Oh?"

But The Terafin, aware of the tension that underlay the sparse words, watched neither man; she watched, instead, the newest member of House Terafin. *He will serve you, Jewel. How will you handle this?*

Jewel's answer was not, Amarais thought, an answer she herself could have tendered; the young woman slid a book off the shelf she had used to support her weight when she rose from her forced roll. Her movements were both economical and silent; she had spoken no word. She watched the two domicis, locked in their own private struggle, and her lips folded in as predatory a smile as The Terafin had ever seen on her face.

She then threw the slender volume; its gilt words and edging caught light as it flew. She had clearly been taught to throw; the book collided with Avandar's shoulder, breaking the tension that existed between him and Morretz.

She had wondered if anything besides violence would; the answer was no, but it was violence from a quarter that she had not expected. Nor, clearly, had Avandar Gallais.

"It seems that you are not the only one to test, Avandar," The Terafin said, watching his expression with care.

He raised a brow, and then he shrugged, Morretz apparently forgotten. "No, just the only one to fail." He turned fully to Jewel then, and he bowed; it was an exaggerated sweep of motion. "Your pardon, little one."

Amarais almost winced, but she said nothing.

"Terafin, I accept your contract. I will this one."

The Terafin nodded. "This," she told Jewel qiuetly, "is Avandar Gallais. He is of the domici, and he has come to fulfill the obligation that Ellerson felt he could not."

"W-what?"

"I am your domicis," Avandar replied.

Jewel, however, was staring at The Terafin as if she'd finally lost her mind. "I won't have him!"

Amarais now rose. "You will," she said. "This interview is at an end."

Only when she had left Jewel—and her domicis, Avandar—did she turn to Morretz. He was characteristically silent. But his silences, like his gestures and his spare movements, could be read if one had the experience of decades. She did.

"She is not capable of dealing with the subtle, Morretz. Ellerson was many things, but subtle—with the den—was not one of them."

"He could have killed her," Morretz replied.

"Understood. But he did not."

Morretz raised a brow. "And had he?"

She did not reply; nor did he expect it. After a pause, she said, "It is Avandar Gallais who will walk away bruised. He is a man who is accustomed to power and the wielding of power; she is a girl who is not. Nor am I entirely certain that she will ever wield power in the way that it is customarily wielded."

Morretz nodded stiffly.

"But in her ignorance she held her own against Meralonne APhaniel, and in her ignorance she held her own against Devon ATerafin. She is not easily cowed."

"She held her tongue with you."

"Yes. But only with me, and that is fitting; I am The Terafin." Amarais' smile was thin. "And she did not, in truth, hold her tongue in all circumstances. If anything she views as her own is threatened, she is capable, Morretz. You did not hear her on the night I went to Torvan ATerafin."

"No."

"Trust her."

"It is not Jewel that I mistrust."

It was almost dark by the time Jewel reached the familiar doors of the West Wing. She'd forgotten to ask The Terafin if this was to be her permanent home in the House, but it didn't matter. She'd come home to the fact that she'd lost Ellerson. He wasn't dead. But living, he'd chosen to leave. She'd heard all his reasons. The Terafin even seemed to think they'd made sense.

But they made no sense to Jewel, and she didn't want to try to make sense of them now; Avandar Gallais trailed her like an unwelcome, unwanted shadow. She stopped in front of the closed doors, wanted to rest her forehead against their surface. She wouldn't, because he was watching.

"Understand," he said, in his forbidding and unfamiliar voice, "that I am here to serve you and to see to your needs."

"What I *need*," she snapped, showing him her back because she was too damn tired to school her expression, "is privacy. I need to be at home, where I can relax."

"And I am not yet part of that home."

She wanted to tell him he would *never* be part of her home. She was certain she still had splinters of chair attached to her clothing, and he'd destroyed the chair without warning while she was almost still in it. But she was also certain that refusing to accept him meant that she was obliquely refusing to accept the House Name, somehow—and she had only barely gotten The Terafin's quiet word that the den would be ATerafin. She struggled with her temper, and she won—but it was close.

"No," she managed.

"Then let us see this home, Jewel."

"I'm not called Jewel," she told him, her palm resting against the

closed door. She took a deep breath. *He comes with the House. Remember that.*
"I'm called Jay."

"Jay? May I ask why?"

She turned and stared at him; he met her gaze without the stiff sense of propriety that had always characterized Ellerson. "How would you like to be called *Jewel* every day of your life?"

"I am not particularly troubled by what others call me. If you dislike the name, you are of course free to choose another. It signifies little. What you are called, and what you *are*, are not the same. But if you must choose a name more to your liking, Jay seems . . . insignificant."

"It's what I'm called," she repeated.

He shrugged. It was not a casual shrug; it was too minimal a motion for that. But it was familiar in some way she couldn't quite put a finger on. She glanced at the closed door. "Why are you doing this?" she finally asked.

He raised a black brow.

"This. This domicis thing. Serving someone."

He had not, in her brief hour of acquaintance, appeared to be a friendly man. Then again, if she was trying to be fair—and she *was* trying—neither had Ellerson. But Ellerson's age had suited his stiffness, and beneath the entirely proper words she had always had some sense of his affection and his approval. Avandar Gallais was about as warm and giving as stone in winter, but infinitely more dangerous. She couldn't imagine someone like Avandar serving anyone.

He was silent for a moment, staring not at the closed door but at her upturned face; she had to look up. He was tall. "Did you," he finally asked, his voice as cold as the outside air, "interrogate Ellerson in a like fashion?"

Her turn to shrug. "No. But he never tried to kill me."

Avandar lifted a brow. "Claims were made," he finally said, "about your abilities. I wished to ascertain their veracity."

"And you couldn't think of a better way?"

"Not as convenient a way, no. I have had some experience with the seer-born in my time; when they are trained, they are powerful. You, however, have had no training; what you can or cannot do is not as easily determined. If I was not brought here under false pretenses, there was no threat to your life."

"And if you had been?"

He said nothing.

"How much did they tell you about me? Besides that?"

"Very little. You are . . . den leader . . . to a small group of people your own age. You are to be schooled in etiquette; your reading and writing, in the two languages you speak, are to be tested, and if they are found wanting—" and his tone of voice made it clear he thought it likely, "your education in both is to be furthered.

"I am aware, however, that your value to the House is determined by your unusual talent; that your value *to* the House is a direct threat to the power of any other ambitious House. And I am confident that I can preserve your life. *If* you heed my warnings."

"I don't see that your warnings are going to be better than *mine*," she said, and she looked pointedly at the shoulder that she'd hit with the book. She'd been aiming, on the other hand, for the side of his head.

His smile was cool. "Very clever." He looked pointedly at the closed door.

She grimaced, slid her hands to her hips, and faced him squarely, keeping her voice as low and even as possible. "Everything I value is behind these doors. Everything."

He raised a brow. "That is a dangerous admission to make," he told her softly.

"Does it matter? It's true."

"Behind these doors, as you call them, is your den?"

She nodded. "I trust them. I trust them with my life."

"Trust," he continued, in his cool, distant voice, "is a luxury."

"No. It's a necessity. I don't care what you're watching out for. I don't care what you do to protect me—The Terafin might, but I didn't choose you, so that's her problem. But *these* people are mine, Avandar. I'd rather have no domicis and no House Name than lose them, and if you can't treat them as part of *me*, I will. That's my unbreakable rule. Understand? We would never have made it this far without each other."

He didn't speak for a minute; she thought he meant to turn and walk away. It would have been a relief.

"You are weak," he finally said. It wasn't what she expected. But it didn't sting.

"Yes," she replied, shrugging. "I am. I've always been weak. So have they, in their own way. It's what we are *together* that makes us strong.

They're my friends; they're all the family I have. They're not my servants, and they're not my subordinates; you're not to interfere with them."

"Understood. But Jewel . . . Jay, understand that as you come to prominence, they will become targets. If it is known that they are of such significance, they *will* be used against you."

"How?"

His brows rose, and then, to her surprise, the slightest of smiles shifted the corners of his lips. "My experience is not, it appears, to be wasted here. Come, let us enter the rooms that will be my home while you live."

She hesitated, and then she pushed the doors open.

2nd of Veral, 411 A.A.
Terafin Manse, Averalaan Aramarelas

It was strange to enter the kitchen without Ellerson. Avandar had been introduced to the den; Angel and Carver were still watching him with vague suspicion. Arann was present because he'd been given the night off—but no one had told him why. Jewel had taken a few moments to assure him in the strongest possible terms—and language—that it wasn't because they weren't satisfied with his work.

"I need to tell you all something," she finally said, when the silence of Ellerson's absence and the ambivalence of Avandar's presence had been dispensed with.

They waited. Everyone but Finch and Teller had slept for most of the day; the First of Veral was, of course, a holiday—but the second, not so much. Teller had spent most of the daylight hours beside Barston; Finch had gone into a blessedly silent Merchant Authority. They were both home now, and they'd been fed.

"Kitchen," Jewel told them.

They rose and filed out of the dining room. Avandar Gallais watched them leave; he waited for Jewel. She waited for as much silence as she was going to get before she turned to him, hating his expression. It was clear he didn't think much of her den. To be fair—and she wasn't trying very hard—it was also clear they didn't think much of him. But this was their home; he was the stranger. Had it been up to Jewel, he would have been last on her list of possible choices.

"We meet in the kitchen. It's enclosed. There's one window; there's no way anyone can actually get in. Your services are *not* required in the kitchen."

He raised a brow.

"And you probably want to look around, anyway. To see where everything is. To—I don't know. Move your stuff in." It occurred to her that she had never seen Ellerson move his stuff, as she called it, either in—or out.

Avandar raised a brow. "I will absent myself from this meeting," he told her. "I will, however, observe."

"You will *not* spy on us."

"Then I will be present."

She folded her arms across her chest. "No, you won't be."

Silence.

As he met her even gaze, she had a sense of familiarity that had nothing to do with the past; it went forward, into the future. It wasn't vision, not precisely, but she was utterly certain that this argument was familiar; that sometime in the near—or far—future, she could hold it in her sleep, it would become so ingrained. So, too, the arguments that she and Avandar had not yet had about clothing, carriage, bearing; the arguments about language and the use of language; the arguments about morality and political context, about expedience and the conflicting desire to do the *right* thing. Half sentences came and fled until she'd almost lost track of what she had just started.

He would be chilly. Arrogant. Condescending. He would be galling, infuriating, and so pragmatic she would have to combat the useless desire to push him through the nearest high window.

He would push her and push her and push her, demanding that she become a *power*. Whatever the hell that meant. She *knew* this. And . . . he would be there. Beside her. He would save her life, although from what, she couldn't say. He would remain aloof and distant and in need of nothing until . . .

Until he didn't.

His gaze narrowed as she took a step back, lifting a hand instinctively to ward him off. He remained motionless. She shook her head to clear it.

"What," he said softly, "did you see?"

She shook her head again, for an entirely different reason. "Nothing," she added, to the immediate and silent lift of one brow. "I have to talk to my den. I *don't* want you spying on them. If you have to, do what Ellerson did."

"And that?" He clearly didn't like being compared to the gentle, older man.

"Stand near the door by the wall; observe if you must, but don't interfere." It wasn't strictly true; in the end, from his vantage by the wall, Ellerson *had* joined the den. And . . . he'd left it, as well.

She shook herself, turned, and entered the kitchen's swinging door, not much caring if Avandar got hit by it as he followed. Maybe she would, when she'd recovered from the destruction of the chair in The Terafin's library. She didn't intend to tell any of her den about that part.

She took a seat they'd left empty at the head of the table; Teller had even dragged a lamp in, because while it wasn't dark, if the conversation took a while, it would be by its end. Tonight, they couldn't afford to go on forever.

But when she sat, she placed her hands palm down on the table's surface and stared at her own knuckles for a while.

"Jay?" Teller said quietly. Teller, always Teller.

She looked up, then. "I have something to tell you all."

They were tense because she was tense—and why in the Hells was she tense? This was good news, wasn't it? This was the *very best* thing they could have dreamed of having when they'd first arrived at the forbidding front gates.

They waited. She left her chair. "The Terafin offered me the House Name."

Their silence was colored by confusion.

"And this is somehow bad?" Carver finally asked.

"No."

"Something we should feel guilty about?"

"No."

"Something *you* should feel guilty about?"

She grimaced. "Maybe."

Teller said, "How long ago did this happen?" He was Teller, and he could be counted on to understand the singular cloud on a beautiful, clear horizon. It was to Teller she now looked.

"A month," she finally said. "Maybe more."

"A *month*?" Even his brows rose. She couldn't bear more than a glance around the rest of the table.

"It was on the day I went to *Avantari*, to speak with the Kings. The . . . man in charge of their . . . bodyguards . . . started to question me, and he asked me something I didn't want to answer. The Terafin made him stop by invoking House Law."

"She told him you were ATerafin?"

Jewel nodded. "I couldn't argue. I couldn't disagree. I thought—I thought she was lying to protect me."

Teller said, after a long pause, "Even if she were—and technically, she was—she couldn't rescind the Name; you could revoke it, but it would embarrass her."

Jewel nodded.

"But—but why didn't you say anything? Isn't this what you wanted?" It was Finch who asked, and Jewel pulled her gaze away from Teller.

"Yes," she said. It was so quiet it almost sounded like no.

"Did you think we wouldn't trust you? Did you think we'd think you'd just leave us behind?"

"No! I just—everything was *so bad*, Finch. *Everything*. People were dying every hour of every damn day. I couldn't just be *happy*. Having the House Name—when we could *all* be dying like that at any minute— didn't seem so important." She turned to them, lifting her chin and facing them fully. "I wanted the House," she said, "so we would be *safe*. So we'd have a place where there was food, and guards, and protection." She grimaced. "I think the rebuilding of the foyer is almost finished."

They were silent; Henden had passed, but it had left invisible scars, or ghosts; they would feel them, in the darkness and the midnight hours. They'd remember what Jewel remembered: the savage, unapproachable beauty that reigned even in the midst of inexplicable horrors. When they did, they'd be humbled; they'd feel as small and insignificant as they actually were.

"Coming here saved Arann," Finch said at last.

Jewel nodded, and the line of her shoulders relaxed. "It did," she said softly. "But what about the rest? The people who couldn't somehow cross the bridge?"

Teller said, "You brought word. Without that word, it wouldn't matter where they lived. It wouldn't matter that we live *here*. It doesn't matter why she gave you the House Name—you earned it."

"I didn't do it alone," she said. "I've *never* done it alone."

Teller smiled; it was brief but clear. Jewel felt something unknot, then—although she couldn't have said for all the money in the world what exactly had been knotted, what she'd been afraid of.

"And I can't do this alone."

"What's 'this?'"

She threw out an arm, encompassing the kitchen, the windows, the door that led to the rest of the wing—and the domicis. "This," she said.

Finch asked quietly, "Will we be able to stay?"

Jewel smiled then. "Yes. And not because you're my den—not just because of that. You'll be—you'll all be—ATerafin."

Silence.

"I mean, if you want. If you want it."

It was noisy, then. Overlapping noise. Hands flew, some in den-sign and some in excitement. Jester whistled; it was a piercing—and annoying—sound. Carver slapped his back, sending him into the table; he didn't do it on purpose, and it didn't matter. The dignity that Ellerson so prized was entirely discarded; they lost years and fear in their chaotic and unplanned celebration.

All of them except Angel.

He listened as the noise grew around him, gaining distance by the simple expedient of silence, until he had—sitting still—moved so far away from them that someone noticed.

"Angel?" Jay said. She said it quietly; he saw it as a familiar movement of lips, the sound of the syllables lost in the noise, because he was watching her so carefully.

He stood abruptly; his chair teetered and fell. The sound broke the rhythm of celebration in the kitchen, spreading his silence outward until it touched even Jester.

This time, when Jay said his name, he could hear it. Hear the question in it, and see a shadow of uncertainty drop like a heavy stone into the well of the den's joy. He wanted to break it and hated himself for doing so at the same time. But it wasn't about them, not really. He let his hands drop, with effort, to his sides, but he left the chair where it had fallen.

"Angel?" This time, everyone could hear her.

Angel swallowed and nodded. He spoke stiffly because it was the only way to wedge the words between his clenched teeth. "The House Name."

"For all of us," she said, not quite divining the reason for his unhappiness.

"What does it mean?"

She was confused.

"To have the House Name. To accept it."

Carver was staring at the side of his face so intently Angel could practically feel it. "It means we'll be ATerafin."

"And you'll still be an idiot," Angel said quietly, turning to face him. "What does it *mean* to be ATerafin?"

"Means we live here."

Angel didn't hit him; it was close. "You think that's *all* it means? We live here now; we're not ATerafin. We don't *have to be* ATerafin to live here."

"Means we've a better chance of *staying*."

"Carver, shut up," Jay said. To Angel she said, "You know what it means. We give The Terafin our oath to serve Terafin. We protect House Terafin's interests." She glanced at Arann. Arann, who was already a House Guard and had already offered an oath of his own in pursuit of the duties he'd accepted. "We don't half-ass it. We mean it."

Angel nodded grimly. "You can all do it without me." His voice was flat and hard.

"Angel."

"I mean it. I won't swear an oath to The Terafin."

"Angel—"

He caught her in the middle of a long breath. "I can't."

"Why?" Carver demanded. "What difference does it make?"

"I can't serve more than one person," he replied.

"So? Don't. It's not like she's going to ask you to leave us."

"It's not about her. It's about the den."

But it wasn't.

"It's not like you've sworn an oath to serve anyone else."

It was true. And if he agreed, it was also a lie. His breath was shorter, sharper; in spite of himself, he was getting angry. The kitchen felt smaller than any kitchen had ever felt at any time—even at the old apartment in the twenty-fifth, where they were practically sitting in each other's laps.

Jewel was pale.

"We've—we're expected in the House Dining Hall. Tonight. She's going to announce it."

"And it's all or nothing?" he asked. He managed to keep his voice even. He didn't manage to keep it quiet.

Jewel was clearly off-balance. Part of him wanted to help, to make things easier for her. Part of him was so viscerally *angry* that he couldn't even try. "It's not. It's you and whoever you bring with you. And I'm *not* going." He turned, then, and he left the room, pushing the doors so hard they hit the outer wall before they bounced back.

Carver said, "I'll go after him."

"Don't."

"The hells."

"Carver—" But he was already out the door. The room was now full of mostly awkward silence. Jewel shoved her hair out of her eyes.

"We're supposed to go to dinner?"

She nodded, distracted. "Dinner, yes. Dress for it," she added, because there was no Ellerson to hound them anymore. Avandar had remained silent throughout, as she'd ordered, and she looked across the room to where he now stood. Like Ellerson, he was still; he didn't fidget. But unlike Ellerson, he radiated a disapproval that he hadn't earned the right to feel.

She ignored him and turned back to what remained of her den. "We might as well start getting ready. Carver'll be back soon."

Finch winced; she'd seen Angel's expression, and didn't expect that "soon" and "unbruised" meant the same thing.

Chapter Twenty-five

IT WAS DARK, and it was now late enough that the Port Authority would be closed for business, something that wasn't true in the summer season. Angel hesitated at the foot of the bridge between the Isle and the holdings. He had the necessary identification to cross it—which required none—and come back, which was trickier. The Port, however, held very few flagged ships, and he decided that he would be most likely to find Terrick at home above the blacksmith in the Common; this was perhaps the one time of year in which living over the sweltering heat the blacksmith produced would be welcome; it still wasn't warm.

But anger provided all the warmth he needed, and it was turned both outward and inward. He had never formalized anything with Jay; she'd never asked for his service, never taken his oath, never demanded much—except, perhaps, that he not eat all the available food. He'd never offered. He hadn't asked to serve her, because it would have been embarrassing. She'd have stared at him as if he were trying to grow two heads, and if he wasn't lucky, she'd've smacked one of them as well.

He might never have made the conscious choice if it weren't for the son of Cartanis. Even if he had, it might not have had the significance it now did if it weren't for his father's duty, the burden that Angel himself had inherited so cautiously. He *was* part of her den. The newcomer, yes—but she was important to him in the same ways that she was important to the rest: Teller, Arann, Finch, Carver, and Jester. Even Jester. But she was important to him also in ways that she wasn't to the rest of the den.

And it was a burden, he understood that. But it was *his* burden, not hers.

Tonight he felt its weight, its awkwardness, its pretentiousness. He couldn't share that—not with them. Not with Jay. He shouldn't have felt the need to share it at all. But here he was, in the Common, the blacksmith's forge not a block away.

He made his way to the first of two doors, fished out the keys that he still had, and entered. It was dark in the narrow stairway, but he could see the faint gleam of muted light at its height; Terrick was home. Terrick, home, would hear the door; he would hear the creak of the warped, wooden steps. He would, of course, hear the key in the lock if Angel tried to unlock the second door.

He didn't; he knocked.

Beyond the door, the floor creaked in a familiar way; Angel had lived with Terrick for months, and he knew the sound and the rhythm of his steps. He waited.

Terrick appeared in the open door, looking entirely unsurprised to see him. "You've eaten?" he asked.

Angel nodded.

"You've eaten enough?" He smiled.

Angel grimaced, ducking his head, heavy with its spire of hair, as he did.

Terrick stepped out of the way, and Angel walked into the darkened room. A candle burned here; in the small stove, wood burned as well. Terrick's eyes were circled and dark, but they would be; he'd been sleeping—and working—in the holdings. Two days of silence wouldn't keep nightmares or memories at bay.

"First Day arrived," Terrick said gravely.

Angel nodded.

"And the silence, at last, of the grave. If you have ever wondered why that silence is peaceful," the Rendish man added, his voice dropping, "you will never wonder again." He lifted his hands to his face for a moment and then shook once and gained a couple of inches of height. "Will you tell me how it ended?"

Angel hesitated, and Terrick smiled; it was pained. "I can tell you that it did. I wasn't there for the end; I don't know all the details."

"This was accomplished by your Terafin?"

"No. But without her . . ." He shrugged.

"Come, then. Sit. Tell me why you are angry enough to run from the Isle to the Common and the company of a Port Authority clerk."

Angel looked at the floor. "It's not the Port Authority clerk I came for," he finally said.

"Ah. Tell me."

"Have you met a priest named Caras?"

Terrick became very still, not that he fidgeted much to begin with. "Yes."

"Is that where you go, now? The Cathedral of Cartanis?"

"Cartanis does not require cathedrals, as you well know. Or perhaps you don't; at times I forget you spent your youth in the warmth of the open fields of the Free Towns. The church was part of your life?"

"The Mother's church, yes." The Mother's church belonged in a different lifetime. Averalaan had become his home, and he knew why. But as he fell silent, he remembered the church, with its wooden benches, its pale walls, its candles and the baskets into which the villagers placed food and tallow and wool for the priests' use. He remembered his mother lighting a candle; remembered the way the orange flame seemed too meager, too insubstantial, for the strength of her quiet devotions. He could not, at this remove, hear her voice, and he didn't remember her words—but her expression, he hoarded.

"Angel."

Shaking his head, he looked up at Terrick.

"Sit. I've not eaten yet; keep me company."

"You'll only complain when I touch your food," Angel replied, forcing a smile to lift his pale lips. Terrick responded with the silent lift of a brow, and they took chairs facing each other. Terrick lost appetite easily; very little destroyed Angel's. The Rendish man ate slowly and deliberately, waiting.

"I met Caras," Angel finally said, as if this could be neutral.

Terrick nodded. "I'd guessed as much from the question. And?"

"He's god-born."

Terrick had an almost natural lack of sarcasm, which made the comment safe; in the den it would have elicited derision from at least Carver and Jester. But it was a comfortable derision. Angel had no brothers; he'd been, to his mother's sorrow, an only child. He wondered what his mother would make of Carver and Jester; he knew she would've liked Teller and Arann.

"He's Cartanis' son. So is Weyrdon."

The larger man could make his stillness almost graceful. "He spoke to you of Weyrdon." It wasn't a question.

Angel nodded, fidgeting a moment with the cuffs of a much finer shirt than Terrick's. "He came to the Terafin manse," he finally said, lifting his head and becoming as still as Terrick now was. The stillness, rather than being confining, brought a measure of peace. "He came, in theory, to speak with The Terafin."

"And in truth?"

"To see my den leader."

"The girl? Jewel Markess?"

Angel swallowed. "She's Jewel ATerafin, now." And she'd been ATerafin for a month, in secret. Jay, who couldn't lie to save her life, still knew—as they all did—how to hide.

Terrick's brows rose slightly. "She's young for it, for an outsider." His tone, not his words, asked Angel why this was a problem. But he'd always been good at waiting. Sometimes Angel could outwait him, forcing him to speak first if there was to be any conversation at all; this wasn't one of those times.

"When Garroc chose to serve Weyrdon," he finally said, "what did you do?"

"You know what I did; I continued to serve Garroc."

"But—what did you do at the time? When you found out?"

"An odd question." Terrick's smile was slim but genuine. "I was angry. I knew Garroc. I knew when he was smitten and when he was awed. I knew that Weyrdon had impressed him in a way that no other man had, before or after. But even knowing what would happen, what would have to happen . . . I was angry."

"Why?"

Terrick's eyes narrowed. "Why do you ask me this now, boy?"

"Because I'm angry," Angel replied. "I'm angry and it makes no sense." His hands curled to fists and he levered himself off his chair. He almost never paced; he never needed the comfort of the motion. Angel didn't feel caged or confined in his own body.

But now? He was. He was trapped inside an anger that he hated and couldn't shed. *Maybe this is why Jay could never keep still.*

Terrick watched Angel pace, examining the boy's words, his gestures, the thin line of his lips, the white knuckles of hands that would, whether he desired it or not, form fists at his sides.

He understood then. "You are angry at Jewel," he said, "because she has taken an oath to serve another lord."

"To serve The Terafin, yes. It comes with the House Name," Angel added bleakly. "She's wanted it all along. I *knew* she wanted it. We *all* knew. We knew *why*. She's worth it. She's earned it. More than earned it. If it weren't for Jay's intervention, the Lord of the Hells would be walking the streets of the city now. There would be no First Day; no end to Henden and the Darkness.

"She's worthy," he added, his voice lower, the circle he traced across the kitchen floor growing slightly smaller as he walked.

Terrick nodded. He fished out a pipe and set about lining its bowl. While he worked, he talked. "When Garroc chose to offer his service to Weyrdon, he had already accepted mine. Has Jewel?"

Angel stiffened. Swallowed. "No."

"No?"

"I've never offered it. Not formally. Not in so many words."

"Ah. And you feel that because you haven't, you've no right to feel abandoned?"

"I don't feel abandoned." He stopped walking. Took a deep breath. Examined the words he had just spoken in that quiet and critical way the boy sometimes could. Then he left off pacing and circling and returned to the table. "I feel abandoned."

"Aye. Garroc never left me. He never intended to leave me. He was as true to our friendship as it is possible to be while still having outside goals. This is what your Jewel is?"

Angel nodded.

"But the whole of *my* life, until Garroc made his choice, *was* that service, that relationship. Garroc fulfilled his role, and I, mine. Stepping outside of it, adding a man who would demand at least as much from Garroc—if not more—than I did or could was a change. It was large. And it was, of course, a change made—a change decided upon—by Garroc, and Garroc alone; he didn't even ask what I wanted."

As he had known they would, the words calmed Angel; they were, with a slight change of names, what the boy was feeling. "I told you, we fought often, Garroc and I. I did not bend knee to him."

"Did you fight, then?"

"In a manner of speaking. But I accepted it, in the end. I'd made my choice, years before, and I had no desire to walk away from the life or the lord I had chosen. I wanted things to remain as they were; it was a younger man's desire."

"And I'm young?"

"You are. Younger by far than I was when Garroc made his choice. And Garroc knew what I offered, what I had always offered, him. Your Jewel, if I understand what you've said correctly, does not."

"It's—you have to understand, Terrick," Angel finally said, spreading his hands, palm up, across the table. "Averalaan isn't Arrend. They're not—*we're* not—soldiers or warriors. We're not forced to defend our homes and our lives against raiders; we're not raised to sword or—or ax. In the city, they're not even raised to grow most of their own food.

"We—the den—look out for each other. We do what we can to keep ourselves going. One of the things that *doesn't* involve is hefting a weapon and cutting off someone's head. Or threatening to. It's different here." He grimaced. "There are no vows or oaths."

"But there are Names."

"House Names. Terafin is—"

"One of The Ten, yes. A powerful House."

"I don't even know if she'd understand."

Terrick raised a brow.

"My choice," Angel added. "I don't know if I could explain it in a way that didn't make it sound—wrong."

"You will tell her." It wasn't a question.

Angel exhaled inches of height and nodded.

"Good. She's made her choice, for good or ill. But her choice is not yours, boy. Your choice must stand on its own." He hesitated. "Caras knows?"

"Yes. He came to see Jewel, and he saw me as well. I told him. But I told him in Rendish; no one else could understand what we said. He asked me if I had found what Garroc sought.

"And I haven't. But what I've found is important to me, and I'm not Garroc. I'm not Weyrdon. I'm Angel." As he spoke, the boy unfolded, gaining height and losing the restlessness that had robbed him of his center.

"What did Caras say?"

"It doesn't matter."

Terrick's smile was slow to unfold, but that was as it should be; it crossed years, touching the distant past, and the pain of it, before it landed in the present. "Serve her. Guard her. Guide her when she can bear to take any advice but her own."

The boy's grimace was more familiar.

"And when you are ready, boy, when you know what must happen, come to me. I have waited almost two decades in this place, and I will go where you go."

"I'm not going anywhere. If she does this—no, when she does it—I'll be anchored to House Terafin."

"Tell her," Terrick said again.

He nodded, the white of his Rendish hair dipping slightly forward, as if it might fall.

He left Terrick's when the moon indicated the late dinner hour had passed. Whatever ceremony The Terafin required to elevate the rest of the den was—should be—finished. He'd missed it, but even if that proved awkward, he'd had no choice. Living in the manse? Angel could do that. But swearing an oath to another lord? Not while he breathed.

His mother wouldn't have cared. In fact, he was certain his mother would have boxed his ears in outrage. He'd been offered a *House Name*. He'd been offered the *Terafin* House Name. His mother had not been from a fine family, and her experience with the patriciate had involved servant's duties at best, but everyone who lived in the city knew the names of The Ten.

His father would have attempted to distract her from her disappointment.

Or would he? He'd served in the Kalakar House Guard. He couldn't have served in House Kalakar without swearing an oath of allegiance, could he?

Unsettled, Angel's brisk walk slowed to a crawl, and he looked up at the graven face of Moorelas. This wasn't where he'd intended to walk, but that suited the whole of his life at this moment. Moorelas faced not the city, where men and women congregated around his statue as if he were—almost—a god himself, but the seawall.

"Who did you serve?" Angel asked him, although he expected no answer.

Why did it matter? Maybe Moorelas had never willingly served anyone specific. He'd ridden to war, wielding a sword that could kill even the gods, and maybe he'd needed to serve no single man or woman to do so; maybe he could see purpose in every wandering stranger, every child, every ancient man or woman across the breadth of this Empire. Or this world. Maybe that's why he'd made his choice. Maybe not. It had certainly ended his life, regardless.

But he'd had a purpose.

Maybe he'd had doubts. Maybe doubt had never touched him because there were no other alternatives, no other way to live, to stay alive. Angel wasn't Moorelas. He wasn't a hero. He wasn't a warrior, not yet—and he might never become one. He'd been, until the death of his parents, a farmer's son.

But Jewel wasn't a warrior either.

She was just . . . Jay.

Jewel turns. "You," she says. "What's your name?"

"Angel."

She raises an auburn brow, and shoves her hair out of her eyes. "Are you an idiot?" Half-smile on her lips, and in her appraising glance.

He shrugs. He knows what she's talking about. The old woman, on the ground. Six of Carmenta's den. One boy. "Seemed like a good idea at the time."

"I'm sure that's what all the suicides say in Mandaros' Hall." She shakes her head, adds, "My kind of idiot. You have some place to stay?"

He has Terrick's.

But he shakes his head. No.

"You have one now, if you want it."

And maybe, he thought, sliding effortlessly into the past and back, that was all it came down to. Jay was home. His father—and his mother—had defended their home with their lives, and Angel got that. He understood it so viscerally he'd never needed words for it. He was their son; he'd found, and made, his home. Nothing would destroy it while he lived. The farmhouse hadn't always been easy, and it hadn't always been peaceful—although it'd been months before he could remember that clearly through his homesickness—but it had been *home*.

It didn't matter what Jay called herself. Markess. ATerafin. She was Jay. Angel was Angel.

He drew a deep breath and turned toward the bridge, stopping only once to offer Moorelas' statue an almost perfect bow.

When he finally reached the den's wing, he was surprised to see Torvan ATerafin standing at the doors. The halls were the type of dark they got when guests were no longer rushing to and from various meetings; the magelights were a soft, even glow that adorned the halls for as far as the eye could see. Angel hesitated, and then he approached the closed doors, which were behind Torvan's back.

Torvan nodded. "I was asked to wait here," he told Angel.

"For me?"

"For you."

"I was at the Common, visiting a friend."

Torvan raised a brow. "You weren't present at dinner."

"No."

"You are aware of the significance of this particular dinner?"

"Yes."

Torvan watched him carefully. "Carver didn't actually run into a door, did he?"

The anger that had driven Angel to Terrick's side had evaporated enough that the thought of Carver with a swollen eye being presented to the rest of the House as a newly anointed member of Terafin made him wince. "No," he finally said, looking away. "Was it bad?"

"It's Carver. He's well known, and he performs no obvious official function; I believe it was both embarrassing and survivable." Torvan hadn't moved, and by this time, it was clear to Angel that he wasn't going to, either.

"Jay's not in, is she?"

"No. The wing is empty. But your presence has been requested in the garden."

"The garden?"

"At the shrine."

Angel hesitated and then shook his head.

Torvan, however, didn't move. "You don't intend to take the House Name."

"No."

"May I ask why?"

Angel was silent; he was good at that. But Torvan had always been perceptive. Instead of asking again, he changed tack. "You understand that it's important to Jewel."

"Yes."

"Then come, Angel. If you will not accept the House Name, you will not accept it. But she intends to make her oath to the House, and if you can't support her by joining Terafin, support her as you can."

Angel glanced at the floor for a moment, and then he straightened his shoulders. "She won't leave it at that," he warned Torvan.

"Oh, probably not. She is who she is. But you, as well, are who you are. You'll both have to learn to accept it."

He nodded, and Torvan began to lead.

The last time Angel had seen the Terafin shrine, it had been surrounded by people of all ages, all stations. He almost didn't recognize it as he and Torvan approached. It was small, although well lit, and it was surrounded by rather bruised and flattened grass. But on the steps were the people he had come to think of, slowly, as family.

Arann was uniformed as a House Guard, and everyone else was also finely dressed; Finch looked almost uncomfortable in a deep, deep purple drape of cloth; she kept lifting her skirts so the hems didn't touch anything. But in less brilliant colors, Jester, Teller, and Carver looked about as comfortable as she did; they just didn't have anything to fidget with. Jay was wearing white and black and gold. The gold was a statement of a sort; mourning in the Empire among the patriciate had slightly different rules than mourning for anyone else.

She had accepted the House Name and, with it, the burden of rank; she made a statement.

Gabriel ATerafin was present, as were The Terafin and Morretz. The only Chosen, however, was Torvan himself, and he made his presence known simply by approaching the den—and his lord. He saluted The Terafin sharply; it was also loud, given how silent everyone was.

Jay looked at Angel. She was angry but also confused; the two blended across her features and formed something like apprehension. It made him feel guilty.

She stepped down from the side of the altar and made her way—quickly—toward him. He knew she wanted to put as much distance as possible between them and The Terafin, who seemed content to wait. He let her approach. Her dress was long and fine, and it made her seem for a moment like a younger version of the woman who ruled the House. But strands of her hair had escaped their bindings and crowded her eyes in curls; she shoved them back and up, dislodging more.

He lifted a hand as she opened her mouth. "I'm sorry I missed the dinner," he told her. "I should have been there." Her expression shifted, and he grimaced. "I couldn't because I would have spoiled everything. I *want* to be happy for you. I want to be happy for *them*. I know you wanted this, and I know you worked for it. But don't want it for *me*. I don't."

"But *why?*"

He struggled with anger and glanced at Carver. It wasn't just the fact that Jay was ATerafin that bothered him. It was that they all wanted it. They were all willing to move, to leave her, although that's not the way any of them saw it.

But Angel had seen her face the night that Arann had come to the kitchen to tell them all—to tell her—that he wanted to be a House Guard. Being a House Guard would compromise him. Angel had understood exactly what she'd felt—both parts: the desire to hold on to her den, especially Arann, and the desire to let them go, to let them find things that might be bigger, and more important, than she could be.

Jay didn't understand, had never understood, how important she was to them. She thought of herself as the person who could be there in emergencies, the person you could come to when things were tough. She never envisioned herself as the person you'd come to when things were flush and people were happy. They could come to her starving. They could come to her surrounded by six members of Carmenta's den. They could come beside their mother's snow-covered corpse; they could come fleeing for their lives, with death on their heels.

They could come to her, Angel thought, when they had nothing and knew it. Because Jay knew she was better than nothing; she didn't trust herself to be better than something good. So Arann had become a House Guard, and she had swallowed and accepted it. And now everyone—everyone but Angel—had chosen to become not den but ATerafin, part of the most powerful House in the Empire.

He wanted to tell her all of these things, but it wouldn't have helped.

"I don't want it."

"Angel—"

Angel exhaled. Again. He was willing to do almost anything that Jay asked. That had been true from the moment he'd laid eyes on her. Nothing that had happened since then—nothing—had changed that. Nothing could.

But this, he couldn't do.

He looked past the tense and down-turned shoulders of his den leader, and he saw her den. *His* den. Yes, Duster was gone; Lefty, Lander, and Fisher were gone. What was left was all the home he had, and it didn't matter where they actually lived, in the end. But they could do this. They could do this because to them, it was the same as obeying any of her other commands: Go to the Common. Go to the well. *Run. Hide.*

It wasn't a matter of trust; he trusted Jay, same as the rest. But, he thought, taking a deep breath, she had to trust him, as well. She had to trust him to do more than just follow.

"Why do you want me to take the House Name? It's *not* my name. It's never been my name. I'd wear it, and I'd wear it badly, because it's *not me*." He lifted an arm, pointing to the den, who still stood at a distance. "They'll take it because they think it'll change nothing. But you know that's not true. You knew it when Arann joined the House Guard, and that meant less than the name.

"You don't care what it costs *you*. You don't want to be selfish; you don't want to hold on to us if something better happens to come along. Something better than you. You're willing to take that risk, Jay, because you think it's the right thing, the only right thing, to do. But you're afraid of it." He stopped speaking for a moment, gathering words, and he stopped pacing—when had he started?—to look at his den leader. To really look at her.

The grounds this far from the shrine were dark, but the moon was clear, and her face was the gray of night; her expression was one that he didn't actually want to name, not even in the privacy of thought. She wasn't crying. Jay didn't.

"I get all that," he said, softening his voice and his words, trying to bleed the heat from them. "I understand what you want it to mean and what you think, in the end, it will mean. But I'm not willing to be AT-erafin. Not just to make you feel better. I don't need—I don't *want*—the opportunities we'll have because of the House Name. I'm not going to leave you. I'm not going to change—and I might be the only person here who won't.

"I don't have those dreams, Jay. Never did. I don't daydream that I'm a lord or a King or a Commander. I don't wish I'd been talent-born. I never have."

Carver had come down the stairs, and Angel winced; his eye was almost swollen shut. He hadn't meant to hit Carver so hard. Finch trailed behind him like shadow, the purple of her skirts seeping out into the greater darkness. Teller remained by Gabriel ATerafin's side, watching without apparent worry. Jester had come down the steps behind Finch; Arann had come as far as Torvan, but Torvan's lifted hand had stopped him dead.

Torvan's. Not Jay's.

They didn't see it, or maybe they just didn't understand what they saw. Even if they had, they wouldn't have cared much.

"What do you want?" Jay asked, her voice low.

He shrugged. "What I have. I'll need work. I won't have the House behind me. But if you leave the House, I'm leaving with you. I won't be bound by an oath I didn't want to take and don't mean."

She didn't speak for a long moment; he thought she was done—for now. Jay was never completely done; she just regrouped and started over. He knew that. Watching her shove hair out of her eyes—and there wasn't much there—he could see by the way her brows furrowed he'd been wrong.

He lifted a hand.

"There's only one way I'll ever be ATerafin," he told her.

She was Jay. He was about to give her a problem; she was good with those. Not always happy with them, but if she understood what the problem was, she could sort it out. She waited.

He straightened up to his full height, letting—forcing—his shoulder blades to slide down his back. He lifted his chin and, with it, the rise of his hair: Weyrdon's mark. His father's burden. "You become The Terafin. You become the leader of the House, and I'll take the name—because it'll be *your* name, Jay."

Her eyes widened. Her lips, however, thinned. The hands that had been half-curved now bunched into familiar fists. She could use them when she was angry; they all knew it. Angel wouldn't have cared if she'd taken a swing at him—but The Terafin would.

Jewel was ATerafin. Her hands shook, but they stayed where they were. Her eyes—he turned his face away. And then he turned back. "My father was from Arrend," he said. He hadn't meant to say it. He didn't mean to say what he said next, either. "He served Weyrdon, and he came to the Empire on Weyrdon's mission. He left his lord, and he never returned—he couldn't until he found what he sought. He died without finding it.

"I'm what's left, Jay. I'm *all* that's left. But I'm not my father. I could never be my father. In Arrend, in the North, men *serve*. They're not like the domicis. They're like the Chosen." He turned to where Torvan loitered. Torvan was looking at neither of them, but Angel knew that he was listening.

"Torvan."

The guard turned.

"You gave your oath to serve The Terafin and only The Terafin."

Torvan nodded.

"What would convince you to offer your oath to any other master?"

"Nothing."

Angel turned back to Jewel, who was staring at him. At his hair. At his face. "I'm not Rendish. And I *am*. I'll serve, Jay. But I'll serve you and only you."

Jewel lowered her hands. They were still bunched in fists, but they were loose now—the aftereffects of the anger and confusion that had suddenly deserted her. Angel didn't blink. His anger, like hers but so different in expression, had also been shed. In its place, determination took root, and with it, peace, as if he'd been struggling with a decision that finally made sense to him, now that he'd spoken it aloud.

It made no sense to her.

She stared at him in silence as Carver and Finch came to stand by her side.

"What if I'm not here?" she finally said, her voice low. "What if something happens *to me*?"

"Such as?"

"I get sick and die. Someone gets lucky and kills me."

Angel shrugged.

"If you have the Name," she said, in the same low tone, "it won't matter. They can't—they *won't*—take it from you. You'll be covered."

"I didn't say I don't understand why you want them to have the Name."

"And you don't think I want the same thing for you?"

"Oh, I think you want the same thing for me. But it's not always about what you want or what you need; sometimes it's about what *I* want and what *I* need."

She fell silent, then; he knew her well enough to know it wouldn't last, and he waited until she found the words she'd been scrambling for. "You were the only one who was stupid enough to go up against six of Carmenta's den on your own." Not the words he'd expected, and he didn't expect the half smile that changed the shape of her mouth, either.

"It seemed like a good idea, at the time."

"So does refusing the House Name."

He smiled, then, an echo of hers. Nodded.

"Then be that stupid," she said, her voice dropping. "Be that stupid, Angel. I'll keep you." She turned and almost ran into Finch, but she managed to stop before they collided. Finch whispered something to her, and she lifted a hand in den-sign. But she turned back.

"It's not you I don't trust," she told him quietly. "It's never been you. It's me. I don't understand why you want to do this, and I don't know that I'm worth it. I'm selfish, Angel. I know it. And because I know it, I try to—try to do things that limit the damage I can do."

He nodded, because he did understand.

"But . . . thank you. You're right. I know things will change. I *know* it, and sometimes I'm afraid of it. But I also know things always change, sometimes for the better—and if I don't take the risk, I lose that chance. If you don't take the risk, you'll lose it as well."

He shook his head. "I understand that I'm taking a different risk," he said. "But every choice is risky."

"You come up with that yourself?"

He laughed, and it hurt, but it was still a good laugh. "No. My father did. When he was training us in the Free Towns."

She hesitated and then said, "Will you come and watch? We're to swear our oaths to the House at the shrine."

"I'll watch," he said. He could, now. He joined her; Finch made room for him, looking as concerned as Jay but swallowing the words that Jay could never swallow. Carver hit him once between the shoulder blades, which caused him to stumble, narrowly avoiding the train of Jay's gown. He also signed, and the sign was curt and rude—but his expression, when Angel drew himself up and turned to face him, wasn't an angry one. The side of his face made Angel wince.

Sorry.

Wait for it.

Idiot.

They met Arann and joined Teller at the height of the stairs. Throughout the discussion, The Terafin had watched, her expression as neutral as a statue's. But when Angel came to stand among the den at the shrine, she looked at him. It wasn't a glance, and she said nothing, but her gaze was even and thoughtful.

He knew what he would say to her if she asked him to accept the House Name; he knew what he'd say when she asked him why he refused. But she did neither. Instead, she turned to the den as a whole.

"There is no ceremony to mark your adoption," she said quietly. "And while an oath is required, it can be entirely personal; there are no wrong words if your intent is sincere. Finch," she said, inclining her head. "Will you join my House?"

"Yes." Angel could hardy hear Finch's reply.

"Will you be ATerafin, forsaking the responsibility that comes with blood ties to all other family?"

The second yes was far more audible and far more definite than the first.

"And will you obey me, and The Terafin who comes after, for the benefit and the furtherance of House Terafin?"

"Yes."

"Then be ATerafin, Finch. We are honored to have you join us." The Terafin nodded to Gabriel, who had not spoken once, and he took from a satchel at his side one rolled and sealed scroll. This he gave to Finch.

"ATerafin," he said gravely.

Her hands shook, and she curtsied, but she didn't break the seal.

The Terafin than turned to Teller and asked exactly the same questions. But Gabriel smiled and added, "Remember that the House contains Barston and his very, very particular scheduling and notions of propriety."

Teller looked slightly offended on Barston's behalf, which deepened Gabriel's smile.

"You had best accept; if you were to continue your tutelage under Barston after refusing the honor of the name you've been offered, I fear that you would never hear the end of it."

At that, Teller smiled, and he also took the scroll that Gabriel handed him.

To Carver, The Terafin said, "You are not suitably trained to be a servant, however the servants have taken up your cause, and this is no small thing in a House of this size or this nature. You will find that you hear much, much more than the rest of your den; mark it, Carver. Learn to tease the strands of truth from the strands of speculation."

One of his eyes was hidden under the fall of his long, distinctive bangs; he brushed them, momentarily, to one side.

To Arann, The Terafin said, "You have, as expected, done well in the House Guards. Decarus Holloran has set aside his usual caution when it comes to those newly recruited; he is pleased with your dedication and the seriousness with which you approach your work. It is his wish, however, that you attempt to impress upon the other newer recruits some of your own attitude." She smiled as she said it.

Arann, as usual, didn't say a word. But he looked as if he thought he should. In the end, he simply offered her a perfect bow.

"What you want for and from the House depends in full measure upon what you can give the House, but I am confident that if you do not feel you are large enough for the Name now, you will grow into it."

She paused in front of Jester, and after she had taken his simple answer, she said, "I do not know what you will do in or for House Terafin, Jester, and it is seldom indeed that the House Name is offered in ignorance. You frequently laugh, and your words and gestures invoke laughter in those around you, which is not, in the end, a small thing. But you do not, in turn, join the House; you do not let it touch you. The rest of your kin have made their tentative, hesitant connections with the people who also serve; you stand back, always. You watch."

Jester was unusually silent.

"What do you see when you watch?" she asked.

He shrugged. He was the only one of the den who'd dared. "People."

Gabriel frowned. The Terafin did not. "And what will you do with the knowledge you gain from your observation?"

He shrugged again; this time, Jay signaled, moving a hand by her side without lifting it. She might as well have kicked him in the shins; The Terafin noticed everything.

"I don't know. I don't know when it'll be useful." He shoved his thumbs into the waist of his pants. "Most of what I notice, someone else sees first. I don't need to look smart. I don't want—" he shook his head. "If you need more from me—"

"No. I have chosen to trust that you are necessary to your den and that in a similar way, you will become necessary to my House."

Gabriel handed Jester the last of the scrolls. There wasn't one for Jay; she'd been ATerafin for a month. But clearly, ATerafin or no, there was something she'd left undone, and it was important to the woman who ruled the House. The Terafin turned, fully, to Jay, as if everyone else was now simple backdrop.

Jewel met The Terafin's gaze and held it. She had watched as the right-kin had handed out the official sealed scrolls to every member of her den except Angel. She'd watched Angel each time, as well, glancing briefly at the side of his face to see if there was any hint of regret or resentment. There wasn't.

But none of her den had been asked to do what Jewel now *knew* she would be asked to do: make an oath to the House.

The Terafin walked to the side of the altar. "I will not ask for a formal oath, because in the end, we have no ceremony that is personal enough. What you offer, and the ways in which you offer it, will be personal. But you, Jewel, have seen more clearly than all but I what lies at the heart of Terafin. You have come, at last, to the Terafin shrine, and you will leave it as a member of this House.

"We do not come to the shrine with any other House Members except the Chosen; the Chosen come, but they have all, without exception, already been granted the House Name. It is not to earn the name that they stand beside the altar. It is not to be judged worthy of the name that they kneel."

"Has the House ever rejected someone you've Chosen?"

"No."

"But you come anyway."

"Yes." She nodded toward the flat, empty surface of the altar. "Sometimes it . . . reminds me."

They shared a brief smile, The Terafin's tinged with regret.

Jewel knelt by the altar's side, remembering Torvan—her Torvan, not the real one, who stood down the steps, watching and waiting. She wondered if the Spirit would come to her tonight, and if he did, whose face he would wear. She had traversed the gallery of paintings that depicted the various rulers of the House from its founding, but there was no painting of the founder or his successor. Instead, there was a painting of the House Sword, and in this painting, the single word engraved in the blade glowed like sunlight on the clearest of days.

She had no idea what he had looked like in life. In death, it didn't matter. He was fluid; he took the shape he required, donning it as if it were clothing.

She placed her right hand on the altar's stone surface and almost jerked it back; the altar was warm to the touch, although there was no visible source of heat. It should have been cold; the night was, and it was now dark enough that no sun provided any lingering warmth. She left her hand where she'd placed it, but she glanced once at The Terafin, who nodded.

There was only one thing she could offer at this altar; that had been made clear to her the first time she'd found it. She had some taste of what life in House Terafin would be like: Avandar, not Ellerson; Meralonne, not Farmer Hanson; demons instead of rival dens. There would be days, weeks, and months when sleep was elusive, either because she woke so damn early to work and report to The Terafin, where she would be grilled for hours, or because her nightmares wouldn't leave her alone.

The demons were gone, but she *knew*, as she knelt by the altar, that death wore many guises and that sooner or later, she would face them all: human, inhuman, and indifferent force of nature. She couldn't prevent that. But if fear of starvation and death had driven her here, if it had ruled the whole of her life in the manse, it hadn't been the whole of her life. And if she hadn't been here, in the end, the warning that had brought the Exalted and the Kings to the foot of Moorelas would have arrived far too late. She couldn't have carried that word on her own; no one would have listened. No one would have believed.

But The Terafin could, and had.

The future waited. Lessons very like the ones Rath had undertaken loomed and, with them, the responsibilities that knowledge would allow her to fulfill. She would face them with her den—with those who'd survived—by her side.

She bowed her head, drew breath to speak, and then closed her eyes; she was shaking, which was stupid.

"Did I not tell you that you are not to touch the altar unless you have something to offer?"

Jewel looked up then, and as she did, The Terafin turned as well; they both froze for a moment at the face that the Terafin Spirit had chosen for his own this eve. It was Rath's.

He wore, as he sometimes did, his velvet jacket, the slightly ruffled sleeves peering out from the edge of its cuffs. His hair was drawn back, and he wore no hat; he wore his finest boots, and upon his finger a ring that Jewel had never seen. He meant to imply wealth, or perhaps significant birth.

No, she thought, rising. Rath, dressed like this, would have meant that. But this wasn't Rath.

"Indeed," he said, divining her thought and quenching, in the process, the sudden surge of her anger. "But it seemed appropriate, Jewel. Tonight." He glanced at the still form of The Terafin, and added, with a very familiar dip of chin, "Amarais."

The Terafin didn't speak a word. But he had shaken her; Jewel saw that in a glance. He waited in silence, and then, to her surprise—and she thought, to The Terafin's—he broke it. "Amarais," he said again, and this time his voice was gentler. "It has been many, many years since I have come to you."

"And both times clothed in the forms of the dead."

"Clothed, indeed, in the forms of your dead. But this one," he added, "is also Jewel's. He binds you to each other."

Jewel glanced from one to the other: Rath. The Terafin. And then, taking one sharp breath, she inserted herself forcibly between them, and placing her hands against the chest of the Spirit, she *pushed*. "You're wrong," she said, letting familiar heat envelop her words. "The House binds us to each other. House Terafin and what we've accomplished—so far—together. We don't need to be bound by *pain*."

"You mistake me, Jewel," he replied. "There is pain, yes. But beyond pain, there are other memories and other strengths, which also serve as a bridge; it is narrow and it is private." He bowed, then, to The Terafin. "Amarais," he said, wearing Rath's face, speaking with Rath's voice.

Still The Terafin said nothing, did nothing. It was more than Jewel could bear. She turned and she placed both of her hands against the altar. "Here," she spit out. It wasn't enough. She climbed the altar, pulling herself up until she was sitting on the strange warmth of its surface. "This is it. This is what I offer. Take it or leave it."

He raised a brow.

"She is," The Terafin said softly, "what she is. She will learn to clothe and hide it, but it will remain. I understand—and accept—what she offers; there is strength in it, even when fear is at its strongest.

"Can you do less?"

"I, Amarais? No. I will accept what she offers because I know in the end what she will give—and what it will cost."

Jewel tensed at the words; she couldn't help it. He nodded.

"Yes. It is one of the dichotomies of life, Jewel. Without care, without concern, without a sense of duty and the affection it inspires, there is very, very little that one can give. But you will always be exposed because there will always be something that you can lose. Loss, when it does come, is always unexpected, and it always cuts.

"But there is no protection against it."

She stared at him, and then she said, "Is that why you're Rath?"

"Yes. And it is not for you, alone, but also for Amarais." He bowed, then, to The Terafin. "You have done well. You will do well. I am watching, and as I can, I will guide and guard. Teach Jewel what you can; it is up to Jewel to decide how much of it she can learn."

He turned then, and he looked not toward the House but toward the gardens beyond the shrine. "I am weary," he said. "And it is almost my time. But I linger." He lifted a hand, as if he were reaching for something, and then let it fall, slowly, to his side. "I linger, still.

"ATerafin. Terafin. What you offer, I accept. Go back to your House and make it as strong as you can." He walked away then and became, in an instant, both a memory and a part of the night.

They were silent, watching him, lost for a moment in the memories he had invoked. Morretz broke the silence, and he did it by simple movement; his feet had weight and texture against the cold stone.

The Terafin closed her eyes, drew breath, straightened her shoulders, and turned. "Morretz," she said softly. "We are done here. Let us repair to the manse."

Epilogue

8th of Veral, 411 A. A.
Terafin Manse, Averalaan Aramarelas

THERE WERE NO SECRETS in the manse. There was the pretense of secrecy, and people who were highly skilled in various forms of polite social deception could easily pretend not to have the offending information—but truly, secrecy was scarce. This was nowhere more true than it was among the servants, and, in particular, among those who had been assigned the task of caring for the unusual occupants of the West Wing. Since they weren't actually supposed to speak with those occupants, however, their social deception skills were somewhat lacking.

Carver had slid into the cramped, narrow halls used by the servants. He was fond of them, and over the months, he'd become as familiar with their layout as he'd been with any of the streetside entrances into the undercity. The farther away he got from the West Wing, the cooler the reception he received; no one, however, called either the guards, which would have been bad, or the Master of the Household Staff, which would have been worse.

He'd considered applying—as Merry called it—for a job as a servant in the manse; her reaction had made him reconsider, quickly. Servants in this manse were held to the highest of standards, and apparently, House Name or no, Carver would fail to reach them. Merry did say, in an attempt to cushion the blow, that she privately doubted that even The Terafin herself would meet the Master of the Household Staff's very exacting demands.

The Terafin, on the other hand, had no desire to find a job.

But it wasn't for a job that Carver had taken to the halls today; it was in part to get out of the wing, and in part to find Merry. He hadn't seen her for most of the week, and while it was true she was busier than she had been, it had been a long—and boring—week.

He did run into a few of the servants he knew on sight, and they greeted him by his newly acquired Name, which, given how many ATerafin there were within these walls, was funny. One or two of them even hugged him, but they were older, and they were also the same women who ruffled his hair or complained about its length, depending on how harried they were by their own duties at the time.

He stopped one. "Vera, have you seen Merry?"

"She was off on break. Why?" Vera could sharpen a single syllable into a very uncomfortable point. "You two aren't having troubles, are you?"

He shrugged. "I don't know. I haven't seen her in a week."

She pursed her lips and nodded. "Not that it's my business," she said, "but I'll give you a bit of advice."

Most of her advice had to do with his hair, his language, or his presence in the servants' hallways. He nodded anyway.

"Give her a bit of time."

"Time? For what?"

Vera raised an iron brow. "Your new status?"

Carver raised both of his, although the effect was probably the same, since only one was ever visible. "What does that have to do with anything?"

"You're ATerafin now."

"Yes—but so is she."

"Aye, and young for it, and the pride of her parents, too. She knows what she had to do to earn the Name and, more important, knows how long it took. But her life and your life are different. She wants to be happy for you; give her time and she will be. But—it's harder now, and she's smart enough to try to avoid you until she's sorted it."

"Smart?"

"She doesn't want to say what she's afraid she'll say."

"Given some of the stuff she *has* said, I don't know why she thinks I'll care."

Vera's smile was careworn. "Aye, there's that. But we all want to be our best when we're talking to people we like, and right now, she's not going to be that. Can you just let lie for a while longer?"

"Well, no."

Vera was almost done with friendly advice, given the set of her chin. "Have you considered what your role in the House will be?"

He shrugged. "I don't see it changing much."

"No, you probably don't. My break is almost done, Carver. I have to get back to work."

"Vera—can you just give her something for me if you won't tell me where she is?"

"Depends."

"On what?"

"Whether or not it'll get me fired."

"It won't get you fired." He handed her an envelope, which was sealed.

"What is it, then?"

"We're having a party."

"Beg pardon?"

"We're having a party."

"I heard that. What do you mean by 'party' and who is 'we?'"

Carver was, given Avandar's imperious insistence on any number of things, no longer certain exactly what was meant by "party." "The den is having a party in the wing," he finally said. "To celebrate the fact that we've been given the House Name." Before words could fall out of her open mouth, he added, "Jay checked it out first. The wing is ours, The Terafin agreed, and we have money for it. We can invite whomever we want as guests. Doesn't matter what they do or where they're from."

"And this?" Vera asked, waving the envelope in front of his face.

"It's an invitation. Apparently we need 'em. Jay and Avandar discussed it." They'd had a screaming row about it, but Carver kept that to himself. "Asking people to come by and telling them when apparently isn't good enough."

Vera looked down at the envelope and then back at Carver. "You realize the Master of the Household Staff isn't going to look kindly on this?"

He shrugged again. "The Terafin does."

The older woman took a deep breath, expelled it, and then gave the envelope back to Carver. "Come with me," she said.

She led Carver up a familiar set of narrow steps and down an equally familiar set of halls. The narrow doors that girded this hall on either side were where the servants who lived in the manse called home; Merry was one of them. It was, in fact, to Merry's closed door that Vera walked. She held a finger to her lips for a second and then knocked on the door.

Merry's distinctive "hello" filtered through the wood.

"It's Vera."

The floors creaked toward the door, which opened to reveal Merry's face. She was pale and looked distinctly unhappy. Unhappiness drifted into shock as she looked beyond Vera—indisputably present—to see Carver looming behind her. To no one's surprise, the door slammed shut.

"I told you," Vera muttered. She began banging on the door with her surprisingly ample fists. "Merry, open the door."

"No!"

"Merry, if you've given up on the boy, just let him know now."

Silence.

"And if you haven't, I'm off break in five minutes, and I can't spend much more time standing between the two of you."

Creaking. The door opened maybe an inch—not enough for Carver to slide a foot in, not that he tried. He would have had to shove Vera out of the way to do it, which would have been suicidal. "I'm not well," she said, speaking mostly to the door, although it was clear she meant the words for Carver.

"And if you've not given up on the boy," Vera continued, as if the muted words hadn't been spoken, "you'll need to talk to him sometime. He's a right pain," Vera added, "as I've told you a hundred times. But for all that, I don't *entirely* disapprove. He asked me to give you something," she added with a sniff, "and I'm *not* on the West Wing; I may be a servant, but I'm not his messenger. Go on, Merry. I've got my shift to make." So saying, she moved away from the door, leaving Carver and Merry alone.

Carver looked at his feet. Which was fine, because Merry was looking at his feet as well. The gap between door and frame widened, and he looked up. Merry was still standing in it, but he could see all of her now. She didn't look well. She was pale, her eyes ringed with dark circles, her lips cracked.

He felt suddenly awkward; this wasn't the Merry he knew. She wasn't always happy to see him, but she usually smacked him or cursed under her breath if he'd annoyed her; this was worse. It was awkward.

"I—I wanted you to have this," he finally said. He held out the envelope, and she stared at it as if she'd forgotten how to read.

"What is it?"

"It's an invitation. To a party."

She didn't break the seal. Instead she looked at him and then turned away and walked into the room. He was almost afraid to follow her, which annoyed him enough that he did. He closed the door quietly behind him, hating the awkwardness. It had been easier to run through the manse in the dark of night on the heels of demons, which was stupid—no one's life was depending on this.

There were no windows in the room, and the room itself was small enough that it would have fit right in in the twenty-fifth holding. Or the thirty-second, or even the thirty-fifth. It was tiny compared to the room he now called his own.

"What party?" she said, tonelessly.

He wanted to hold her; he didn't dare touch her. "The Terafin's given us her blessing to throw a party in our wing." He studied her expression.

"For what?"

"To celebrate."

"The House Name?"

He nodded. Her expression rippled, but it didn't shift much. And she didn't swear or throw the invitation away, which might—at this point— have been better. "You're inviting me."

"Yes. We can invite whoever we want."

She examined the invitation and picked at the seal. "We've heard rumors," she finally said, her voice flat and hard.

The servants always heard rumors. "So?"

"Do you know what The Terafin wants from Jewel?"

He shrugged. "Does it matter?"

Her hands tightened into fists, crumpling the unopened letter. "Yes, it matters."

"Then tell me."

"She wants to put her on the House Council."

"Oh. That."

Red brows rose as her eyes widened; he'd annoyed her and surprised her, both of which were better than wherever it was she'd been. "What do you *mean*, 'oh, that?'"

"It's not like she's there to do anything or make any decisions. Not yet. It's just a—job."

Merry's eyes widened further, and this time she did wheel and smack him hard on the chest. "You don't understand the House, Carver! You don't understand how it works!" One of her fists now held a bunched and crumpled invitation, and the wax had cracked and crumbled. "Do you think *House Council* members just spend their days hanging out with *servants?*"

"You're ATerafin."

"It *doesn't matter.*"

"Why? Burton said—"

"I don't give a damn what Burton said. Yes, I'm ATerafin. Yes, he's ATerafin. But do you really think that makes us equal to someone like Gabriel?"

"I—"

"Do you think that Gabriel—or any of the House Council—spend their time with the servants?"

Carver didn't understand Merry half the time. Mostly, it amused her; on one or two occasions it had enraged her. But never like this. He understood then. He understood that what Vera had said was wrong; it wasn't the Name.

"*I'm* not on the House Council," he said, voice low, his hands somehow dangerously perched on either of her shaking shoulders. "*I'm* not Jay."

She laughed. It was the least happy laugh he'd ever heard. "You're one of hers. Everyone knows it, Carver. You go where she goes. If she rises, you're going with her. And she can't afford to have supporters who are— who are—"

"Who are *what?*"

Merry turned away, or tried to. He tightened his grip.

"Merry, who are what?"

"Me," she whispered. And then she tore herself free and turned toward the far wall. "*Me!*"

He would have laughed, it was so stupid. But *Kalliaris* was watching, and laughter wasn't the first thing he did. He walked to where she was standing, back to him; he knew she was crying. "Why didn't you say something?"

She spun in that quick, startling way she sometimes could, her hands still bunched in fists, her knuckles white, her eyes red and wet. She even opened her mouth to speak. But the words didn't come for a few minutes, and when they did, they were broken by more unhappy laughter. "Carver—it never occurred to me there was anything *to* say."

"I don't think there is," he replied, keeping his voice low and quiet.

"No one asked me to stop being myself in exchange for the House Name. No one made me promise to avoid . . . the wrong people."

"And what would you have said? It's the *House Name*, Carver."

"I—"

"And Jewel wanted it. She's *earned* it. You don't know what's said about her. You don't know how important she could be."

"Uh—"

"You're important to her, the whole House gets that. But what she's going to be, and what I am—they're not in the same world."

"But I'm *not her*!"

"And if you were told that she needed you, and needed you to be part of the patriciate? Properly, not in your half-assed way? Would you have said no?"

"It *doesn't matter*. I *wasn't* told that. I'm *not Jay,* and I can do whatever I want!"

She stared at him, and then, shaking her head, she looked down at the creased invitation, its wax cracked.

"It's not a fancy party," he told her. "I think."

"In the wing, in the *manse*, and you think it's not going to be fancy?" She shook her head, tears still running down her cheeks as something that was almost a smile changed the shape of her mouth. "I—I like you, Carver. I really do. You're kind of stupid, you're kind of silly, you don't pay attention to any of the rules. You don't want much for yourself. You don't." She looked at him, then. "You'll learn."

He shrugged. "I'll learn. Maybe I'll learn. Maybe you will." Awkwardly, he added, "Will you come?"

She just stared.

"We're inviting everyone. Not only people we met here," he added, "although I think Finch is inviting Lucille and Jarven."

She stared.

"Merry—we didn't get here on our own. We had each other, but we had help. You helped," he added, voice lower. "You helped me. You let me tag along everywhere."

"I told you to get lost."

"Well, yeah, but not like you meant it."

She laughed; it was wobbly but genuine.

"If you hadn't," he added, "The Terafin might not have survived the night the demons came. When we went to get Alowan, we went through the servants halls because I knew them." He caught her hands, crunching the letter further. "Yes, Jay earned her name. But you've earned at least this much as well.

"Jay says—well, her Oma used to say—we can't count on the future. We just have now. I want you to come."

"I have nothing to wear—"

"Didn't you see us when we first arrived?"

She had, of course.

"If you're worried about clothing, that's easy."

"It's not—it's not just the clothing. The Master of the Household Staff won't like it."

"All the more reason to come. Please," he added. "We want the people who helped us all along."

She opened the invitation, then. "Carver—"

"Just say yes."

"But I—"

"Yes."

She hesitated and then asked, "Can I bring Mira?"

"Why?"

"I won't have anyone to talk to, and I—"

"You can talk to me." But as her request now offered more hope than he'd had for a week, he added, "Yes, if you want, you can bring Mira."

Jewel walked through the Common as if she'd finally come home. It was crowded, and as usual the stronger scents of the various stalls hit her nose in a rush; she had to turn sideways to avoid the moving wall of people, but she was used to that. Avandar, by her side, was not—but he was larger, and he was more forbidding; he didn't have to get out of the way.

"Is this absolutely necessary?" the domicis asked. He was, for Avandar, in a reasonable mood; on anyone except Meralonne APhaniel, it would have been considered foul. He had a sharp, patrician nose, which was useful for him, as he looked down it so often.

She didn't bother to answer, since she'd answered the same damn question a dozen times. But she made her way to the poorest section of the Common, and there she found Helen, wrapped in wool, her hands red with the chill of the season. She was, nonetheless, working. Jewel cleared her throat, avoiding Helen's son, who for once didn't look pissed off to see her.

Then again, he clearly didn't recognize her. "Can I help you, miss?"

She stared at him suspiciously and then glanced down at her clothing. It wasn't fancy compared to the stuff she was forced to wear for formal meetings, but it *was* fancy compared to the clothing that he and his mother generally sold.

"No, I'm here to speak to Helen."

He turned instantly, and with such alarming speed Jewel was half-afraid his mother would die of shock. But Helen rose. Moving at her usual speed, and with about as suspicious an expression as Jewel had ever seen on her face, she made her way to the front of the stall.

There she stopped, and her mouth slowly opened and stayed that way.

Jewel flushed. "Helen?" she asked, almost nervously. "Do you recognize me?"

"Jay?"

Jewel nodded. "I'm—I have something for you." She held out a hand, and Avandar, who had almost insisted she use the normal Terafin messengers, placed an invitation into it.

"Well, don't just stand there," Helen said to her useless son, "get out of the way and let her come in. Come here," she said to Jewel. "I want to look at you! What are you wearing?" she added.

"Oh, clothing. It's—I'm—" she pushed her way into the stall, leaving Avandar behind. "I'm living on the Isle, Helen."

"On the Isle?" Helen's brows rose. She reached out and gathered handfuls of cloth, pausing to examine the seams. "This is good work," she finally said.

"I hope so. I think whoever made it charges a lot." She held out the envelope, and Helen took it, turning it over. There was an awkward pause while she examined the seal, and she finally said, in an old, flat voice, "you'll have to read this for me. My eyes aren't what they used to be."

Her eyes, Jewel knew, were still good. But she didn't hesitate; she opened the envelope, cursing Avandar under her breath; if it had been up to her, there wouldn't have been any stupid invitations.

"We'd like to invite you to our place on the Isle. We're—we're having a party, and we want all our old friends to join us."

"Where is your place on the Isle?"

"We're living—" Jewel hadn't realized until this moment how awkward this would be, but she brazened ahead anyway. "We're living in the Terafin manse. We've arranged for all the tolls to be paid, for anyone who wants to come, and if you want, we can send a carriage. I asked," she said quickly. "The Terafin manse has a lot of carriages." She drew another nervous breath and then added, "If you want to bring your son, he can come too, if you think he'll be helpful."

Helen snorted, and the sound was so familiar, Jewel wanted—briefly—to hug her. Hugging Helen, who wore pins and needles all over her clothing, was always a mixed blessing. "He won't be," the old woman said. "Henry, where's my pipe?"

Henry, however, was speechless for once; his mouth had dropped open and been left hanging, as if he'd forgotten it was attached to his face. Jewel had never particularly liked him, and he'd certainly had no use for her den, but she understood that he was all the family Helen had.

"*Henry*," Helen said. She didn't like to have to ask something once; repeating it usually made her angry. But her son had failed to hear the imperious use of his name; he was staring at Jewel as if she'd grown two heads. On top of the one that she already had. Jewel almost laughed, but she felt sorry for him, because he was now embarrassing his mother in public.

Helen was much like her Oma, for a woman with no ties to the South; Jewel knew he'd suffer for it later. But later was later, and Jewel wouldn't be here to see it, with any luck; she still had a few places to visit before she returned to the manse. She caught Helen's still-pipeless hands in hers. "Please come," she said.

"I don't have a thing to wear," the old woman replied.

"We showed up on our first day there in the clothing you made for us," Jewel countered. "That was good enough for The Terafin. It was good enough for us, Helen; if we didn't have better, we didn't have nothing, thanks to you."

Helen grimaced. "You went there in those clothes?" Shaking her head, she added, "I don't know, Jay."

Avandar waited until the small stall was well behind them before he said, "The son will make certain his mother arrives."

"Good. I won't let him in without her."

"I believe he is aware of that. Are you certain this is wise?"

Jewel shrugged. Avandar, as a servant, was vastly more intimidating than most of the nobles she'd met. She didn't like him much; she was almost certain she never would. "Define wise."

"You are about to host a gathering at the Terafin manse; it will be your first official gathering."

"That's kind of the point."

He frowned.

"Look. I haven't agreed with you the last hundred times we've discussed this. I'm not going to agree now. Just drop it."

"As you say."

Since it was the way he'd ended each of the previous arguments, Jewel snorted. She walked quickly enough to put distance between them; he walked quickly enough to close it. She did not want him looming over her shoulder looking condescending while she talked to Farmer Hanson.

She could see the farmer in the distance. At this time of year, he sold far fewer things—but not nothing, unless the weather was bitter, in which case he didn't leave his farm. He wouldn't be here for as long as he would during the warmer months, but she could also see his daughter, with her famously dour expression, and at least two of his sons. She almost tripped over her feet—and did, in fact, trip over other people's—in her sudden rush to reach his stall.

The kind of angry ripples that rush of clumsiness produced in the Common meant he was aware that something was happening, and he was watching the crowd as she emerged from it. His eyes widened at that same time as his lined face broke into a grin—a wider grin than she was used to seeing on that familiar and much-missed face.

She reached the side of his stall as he was opening the small, swinging gate to allow her entry, and she didn't even stiffen when he enveloped her, instantly, in a hug.

But she did laugh when he finally set her away at arm's length and gave her the once-over. "Have you grown?" he asked.

"Not me. Teller has, if that helps."

He chuckled. "Finch came by to see me last month."

"She told me—I was jealous. I was crawling around in the dirt, or worse, with a really, really grouchy overseer." She'd decided against using the word mage, because while it was accurate, it failed to convey any of the experience. And it made people nervous.

"Well, you don't look dirty now. Things are going well for you?"

"Things are. I don't know how long it'll last," she added.

He laughed again. "Always the cautious one, you were." He shouted something at one of his sons—and even this made Jewel smile, because he *always* shouted at his sons, and they always accepted it with good grace. "Tell me what you've been up to."

She did. She skipped most of the bits that were, in theory, never to be mentioned to anyone; she also failed to use the word "god-born." She did tell him a bit about the Terafin foyer's destruction because everyone in the city had heard something about that. He was impressed by it, but even impressed, he still paused to ask questions about the rest of her den; she asked him about his wife, his daughter, and—yes—his useless sons.

"You won't be needing much from me now, will you?" the farmer asked, smile lines still deep around the corners of his eyes and mouth, although he was no longer chuckling.

It was true. Of course it was true. Jewel shook her head. She had daydreamed about the day when she wouldn't need to take things from Farmer Hanson. And the day when she could come to him in triumph and give him enough money that he could, in his quiet way, feed other kids who, like her, were in need. She wasn't even sure that this wasn't that day, but she felt no triumph.

It hadn't occurred to her, in that long ago daydream, that being that woman meant that she would no longer see him every day.

She no longer came to the market. She didn't do the den's shopping; no one in the den did. Food appeared in their dining room and breakfast nook as if by magic; it was cooked in the wing, but she had no idea where it had come from originally. She had no idea where laundry was done, or how; The Terafin's servants didn't go to a well to get water; they'd have needed an army's worth of buckets.

She shook herself, returning to Farmer Hanson.

"No," she said softly, because she wasn't good at lying, and even had she been, this man didn't deserve it. "But . . . we did. We needed you."

"You'll be the only one of my children to rise so far," he replied. "House Terafin. Arann's good?"

"He's good. Or better than he was. But I'm gabbing and forgetting why I came—you can see him for yourself." She handed the farmer the invitation.

He looked at it with some consternation, as if it were notification of a new tax or arrears from an old one. It was the seal, she thought. He didn't get much that had wax affixed to it.

"It's an invitation," she told him. She wanted to ask him if he could read it, but she bit the words back. "We're having a bit of a party at the manse. We want you—and all your family—to come join us. I'm sorry about the seal," she added. "It wasn't my idea, but someone insisted on it."

"Who?"

"My domicis."

"Your what?"

"He's a—a fancy servant. And a bodyguard. And a master of etiquette and political squabbling. And—"

The farmer held out a hand, laughing. "I surrender. So he told you you needed a fancy seal?"

"Yes. Apparently so my old friends could look at the invitation as if it were a legal writ."

"Maybe he knows best."

"Gods, I hope not."

The farmer's frown was brief. "But he serves you, right? You get to decide?"

She laughed; it was not an entirely happy laugh. "That's what I keep telling him." More anxiously, she asked, "Will you come?"

He broke the seal carefully and pulled out the invitation. "That's a lot of words for a 'come to my party.'" Before she could say another word, he looked up and smiled. "Yes, we'll come. We'd be proud, and frankly, my daughter would likely never forgive me if I said no."

Since this was easily the most believeable thing Farmer Hanson had ever said about his daughter, Jewel relaxed. She even hugged him again. "I have to go."

"Back to the manse?"

"Oh, no. Not yet. I need to find a dressmaker."

"Well, this is the right place for it—unless you want the High Market."

Jewel couldn't imagine a day would come when she'd want the High Market over the Common, and she said so, remembering to curb the rude words only half a second before they were leaving her mouth.

The farmer, notably, didn't mention the fact that *he'd* have nothing to wear, and Jewel decided to retreat before he spoke to his daughter about the party, because she was pretty certain the daughter would speak volumes on the subject.

Avandar had done her the "ill-advised" favor of allowing her to speak with Farmer Hanson alone; she returned the courtesy. She didn't try to lose him in the crowd for the rest of the afternoon. She had one invitation that would take her into the twenty-fifth holding itself; it would be her last visit before returning home.

But it wasn't the last planned visit; she now headed into the actual storefronts nearer the Merchant Authority. Avandar didn't stick out quite as much there, or at least not in theory; he did, however, still get much more room on the open street than size or arms—he wasn't wearing any—should have granted him.

"Here," she told him, pointing at the familiar windows of Haval's legitimate business.

"This is where you wish to commission clothing?"

"That too."

"Very well. At least it's not Helen's."

She had considered asking Helen to make her a dress, and she didn't appreciate Avandar's tone. But she thought Helen, instead of being proud, would feel inadequate and distressed, and she knew Haval would have no such issues. She also wanted to know what Haval thought of Avandar, and therefore gave neither man any warning, if you didn't count the bell that sounded every time the front door opened.

Haval was working, as he usually was, behind the counter closest to both the window and the door; he worked almost entirely in the natural light of the afternoon, and one of his eyes was occupied by the glass he often wore for detail work. In spite of the slowness with which he shed both work and glass, Jewel knew he was aware she was there. She watched his posture with care, attempting for a moment to ignore his expression.

It was hard, because he was, at the moment, smiling broadly. "Jewel." He never raised his voice except to call his wife. He set aside the material in a very careful bundle and then stepped out from behind the counter, glancing once—briefly—at Avandar. His expression, however, didn't shift. At all. Given that Avandar caused most people to move out of the way just by walking, this told Jewel something—but because it was Haval, she wasn't certain *what*.

She realized that she had been standing there in silence for just that little bit too long, and she shook herself. "I'm sorry," she said.

"Because?" He lifted a brow. "You are rescuing me from the tedium of my daily work."

"Well . . . not exactly."

"Not exactly? Hannerle!" He added, lifting his voice. "Jewel has come to pay us a visit, if you aren't terribly busy."

His wife, who was generally busy, nonetheless came out of the back rooms, wiping her hands on her apron as she entered the storefront. She looked, as usual, slightly harried—but she didn't look at all suspicious until her eyes glanced off Avandar, who was standing by the wall. She did, however, come to greet Jewel and to offer her a hand, which Jewel took. "We've not seen you since—"

"No," Jewel said, too quickly. "But I've been both busy and well, and I'm actually in need of a dress. I wanted Haval to make it."

"You see, Hannerle? My time and devotion to the young lady has paid off handsomely. Assuming," he added, with a broad smile, "that the expense of the dress is to be paid by House Terafin?"

"It is."

"Good, good. Come into the back room for a moment; I can take your measurements again; you look as if you've grown slightly *and* lost weight."

Jewel raised a brow. "Is there enough room for me in the back right now?"

"I'm sure there is," Hannerle said, before Haval could speak. "As long as you don't plan to sit on anything." Instead of retreating as she often did, she began to walk slowly past the various bolts of uncut cloth that the shop contained. "Go on, dear. I've a few ideas of what might be appropriate."

Hannerle hadn't exaggerated, but then again, it wasn't required; Haval's back room looked like the usual cluttered disaster. He clearly hadn't been doing much work of his own in the back room, because even his chair was completely invisible. There was, however, a clear patch of floor, which implied that, if he desired it, he could do work there. He did not, however, head to his chair, and since Jewel was following him, she ran into his back when he stopped. She managed not to stumble, because she didn't trust the floor not to be pin and needle strewn.

"At my age," Haval said, from somewhere above her head, "that posture would cause serious injury."

She snorted and straightened up. "Aren't I supposed to at least choose the cloth or the possible cut before you need measurements?"

"That is the theory, yes," he replied. His face had lost all trace of satisfaction—or greed—and was as smooth as a mask.

Jewel held up a hand before he could speak. "Let me guess. You don't like my domicis."

He raised one brow, and he raised it slowly enough to indicate that he'd chosen to be surprised by her words. Or chosen to reveal his surprise. With Haval, it was impossible to tell. "Your domicis?"

"Yes. The man who accompanied me into your store. The one you failed to look at or greet."

At that, he smiled; it was slight in both form and duration. "Very good, Jewel. I failed to acknowledge his presence because I understood that he was there to serve you; a servant of any worth expects to remain unacknowledged until and unless his master does so."

"But?"

The brow rose again. "I see you expected me to have reservations. Forcing me to enact them in this fashion seems slightly dishonest, Jewel. I believe I am almost proud of you."

"Thanks. I think. If it makes you feel any better, I don't like him much."

"No?"

"No. But he comes with the House Name."

Haval nodded. "ATerafin," he added, with a bow.

"You already knew."

"You needn't take that accusatory tone, Jewel. I should think you would expect word of your good fortune to have traveled by this late date."

"You've known for a while."

He smiled at that.

"You know about the domicis."

"I knew that you had one. I did not, however, foresee the difficulty the one you now have represents."

"Difficulty? What do you know about him?"

"Very little."

"Honestly?"

"Oh, tush, Jewel. That's beneath you." He reached into a pile on his desk and came up with a tape measure. "If you would lift your arms?"

"I will. But don't come near me with pins."

"When is the event?"

"In two weeks."

"*Two weeks?*" For the first time in her life, Jewel thought Haval was genuinely shocked.

"That's not enough?"

"Is it a significant event?"

"To us, yes."

"Who is 'us?'"

"My den. We're having a party," she added, and before he could actually wrap the tape measure around her, she dropped her arms and fished an invitation out of her satchel. "Here. Oh, no, wait—that's the wrong one. This one is yours."

Haval took it with care, examined the seal, and broke it; the wax fell on one of the clear parts of the floor. He read the letter with care. "So, you intend not only to ask me to attire you in a fashion appropriate to your newly acquired station but also to attire myself and my wife in a similar fashion as well, within a paltry two weeks?"

"Something like that. I don't need anything fancy. In fact, I'd be grateful if you made something simple and comfortable."

"And my reputation is to benefit from that how?" He shook his head. "This is vastly more alarming than the man you walked into the store with, I'll have you know. Lift your arms, Jewel. No, *do not* gesture unless you can do it with your exposed armpits."

"Can we get back to the man?"

"Perhaps. What do you wish to know?"

"I want your impression of him."

"Surely you can infer some of that while I work?"

She snorted.

"Very well. I am not entirely familiar with him. His name?"

"The name he goes by is Avandar Gallais."

"I see. You don't feel it is a genuine name?"

"No."

"Why?"

"I don't know."

"Very well. You are certain that he is what he claims he is?"

"A domicis? He came from the guildhall, and The Terafin's domicis certainly recognized him."

"He is, in my considered opinion, dangerous."

"To me or in general?"

"At the moment? They are not disparate." He frowned as Jewel sucked in air. "You might as well ask the question, Jewel; I would hate to see you suffocate."

"Do you know much about the Terafin House Council?"

"What an odd question for so junior a member of the House to ask. I am not ATerafin, why should I know?"

She made a face but otherwise stood still while he measured.

"I hope that your facial expressions are better contained while you are in the House. Very well. Arms down and turn around please."

She did as bid. There wasn't much lost because even staring at Haval's expression didn't give her much information.

"It happens that I am familiar with some—not all—of the House Council. Please tell me that you will not be in a position to interact with them in the very near future."

"If you promise not to lecture me about my ability to lie."

"Your *in*ability. And as I am incapable of making that promise at the moment, I will take your condition as the answer to my question. Let me then ask you to tell me that you will not *be* on the House Council at your age and with your obvious lack of experience."

"Same condition applies."

"And you give me *two weeks*."

"Haval—we're only inviting our old friends. Not that we *had* a lot of them, but we did have them. Farmer Hanson will be there. Helen, if her son can actually push her into and out of the carriage. You. A few others, some of whom I've never met. It's *not* a party for the patriciate."

"Ah. And you feel that your gathering will, in fact, play host to no people of any significance, politically speaking?"

Jewel's brows gathered as she frowned. It was her thinking expression.

"Let me hazard a guess. You are uncertain as to the political import—or acumen—of all of your guests."

"I think you'd call most of them insignificant," she finally said.

"Ah. And the rest?"

"I invited Meralonne APhaniel. I don't know if he'll come, but I doubt it. The Terafin may come for a bit, though—she's not insignificant."

"I . . . see. The depth of your understatement almost robs me of the ability to speak sensible words. Two weeks," he added. "Very well. We will head back to the store to see what Hannerle has chosen as suitable; she may well revise her opinion when she hears of at least the last of the guests you mentioned."

There was one more stop, and this took Jewel to the twenty-fifth holding. Speaking with Farmer Hanson had reminded her of the beginnings of her den; it had been Farmer Hanson who had sent her to Arann. And Lefty, she thought, gazing at the river as she slowed for a moment. Lefty, with his missing finger, his constant jumpiness, and his unexpected sarcasm. All she wanted for him now was that he be at peace, waiting no doubt in the shadows cast by the pillars of Mandaros' great hall, for Arann to finally join him. Arann had said—to Finch, not to Jewel, although Finch had mentioned it quietly afterward—that he'd seen Lefty when he'd almost crossed the bridge that divided the living, however tenuously life clung, from the dead.

He hadn't mentioned Lander or Fisher, but then neither had ever relied on him as completely as Lefty had.

"Jewel?"

She shook herself, retreating from thoughts of the dead. It was harder here. The tavern came into view, and with it, the ghostly image of a much younger Finch running down the street, a demon in pursuit. And it had been a demon; they hadn't understood that then. In restrospect she thought Rath might have.

But Finch, they'd saved. She'd found Carver the very night she'd come, seeking the slender girl whose flight had haunted her dreams. Here.

She paused in the recessed doorway and placed a palm against the door itself.

"Jewel." Avandar again, his unwelcome voice an intrusion that reminded her that the past was gone, closed, untouchable. She hated to expose herself to his arrogant condescension, and if she had to endure one more lecture, she was going to stab him. Somehow. She squared her shoulders and raised her chin, then pushed the door open.

It was now late enough in the afternoon that the tavern was dotted with people who were eating an early dinner. She glanced at the bar, and behind it, in his familiar and dirty apron, was Taverson. He glanced up, a cleaning rag in one hand, a large mug in the other. The air wasn't yet hazy with smoke, although that would come; fire was burning in the fireplace farther into the tavern.

He frowned as he saw her.

She wanted to sit down and eat dinner, to be served the stew that seared the mouth if you didn't wait for the damn thing to cool, to eat his wife's bread while around the table people got louder and louder. She had felt safe here, in spite of the press of bodies and the very real danger drunk men presented.

But she didn't want her only companion to be Avandar. The first several times she'd come here, she'd come with Rath. Rath had been, in his own way, as intimidating as Avandar—but only when he wanted to be. She couldn't imagine that she could ever love Avandar; she could barely tolerate him now.

Rath, she had loved. She rubbed her eyes and muttered something about the smoke, in case Avandar had noticed, and then marched up to the bar, standing between two empty stools and lifting herself up onto her toes. "Taverson," she said, raising her voice. "Do you remember me?"

The frown deepened. Taverson wasn't a small man. He'd removed a drunk more than a time or two, often by way of a door he hadn't bothered to open first. But he'd never thrown her, or any of her kin, out that door, and she didn't expect he'd try now; the worst she'd get was a curt bark.

His eyes rounded a bit, and his frown eased; he didn't generally smile. "You're Rath's little girl," he said. "Old Rath."

"Yes," she said. "I am."

"You're a damn sight more fancy than you were last I set eyes on you." He lifted his voice, shouted a name, and one of the girls who was waiting tables came out of the small crowd.

"You bellowed?" she said.

"Tell my wife that Rath's Jewel is here." He looked Jewel up and down again, and his glance shifted completely when he laid eyes on Avandar. "That one a friend of yours?"

She compromised. "He's with me."

"You're not with him?" he asked pointedly, knowing the difference.

She could feel her jaw fall and snapped it back into place. "*No*."

He shook his head. "Worse things happen, Jewel."

"Oh, I know. I know."

"You here to eat?"

"I'd love to, but I'm expected back. I just came to—"

"Jewel!"

Marla, Taverson's wife, had come out of the kitchen; she, like her husband, was wiping her hands on her apron. The apron had clearly seen a few days of solid wear. Before Jewel could say anything, strong and slightly sweaty arms enfolded her. She didn't bother to try to say more than hello because there wouldn't have been much point; it would have been hard to get more than a single word through the volley from Marla.

"We heard about Rath," she finally said, as she pulled Jewel toward a table. Beside it, limp and slightly discolored, was a plant in a cracked pot. "Come and sit," she added. "Tell us what you've been up to. We'll feed you," she added, pointing an unnecessary glare at her husband. "Sit."

All of the reasons she'd intended *not* to eat at the tavern withered; she sat.

Avandar joined her after Marla had retreated a safe distance—in this case, the kitchen. "You ate here often?"

"Not often enough." She glanced around the large room, with its half flight of stairs and its very dirty fireplace. It was cold enough that fire was needed when the tavern was still half-empty; at the end of the night, when it was packed so tight you had to step on people to get them to move out of the way, air was more of a problem. The doors were often pegged open at that point, and the sounds of the tavern would blend with the quiet rush of river and the silence of night streets.

He looked dubious, but Jewel expected that. "It was . . . safe?"

"I was with Rath. Or my den. But yeah, it was safe. If things got ugly, Taverson or his help would interfere. His wife once dropped a chair on someone's head."

"I doubt it was only a one-time occurrence." But he surprised her; he smiled slightly as he said it. "This is not a place I would have assumed you could find a comfort."

"Place?" She glanced at the low, rough beams of a ceiling that wasn't all that impressive and from there to what could be seen of the scuffed and slightly warped wooden floors. "Oh."

Taverson's wife returned, and with her came two steaming bowls of stew, a large basket of bread, and one—only one—mug. She put the mug down squarely in front of Avandar, and ale spilled over its lip. "You'll have water," she told Jewel firmly. Jewel almost laughed. It was only Marla who insisted on that, but no one argued with her much; if you wanted to drink, you waited until she'd gone for the night.

Cutlery was also placed on the table, but almost as an afterthought; the warning that the stew was hot certainly was.

Avandar lifted the dented spoon and examined it in the candlelight. Shaking his head, he pulled a magestone out of his robes and set it on the table, then spoke one curt word to brighten it. The word was not in a language Jewel understood. She frowned. "What did you say?"

He raised one brow. "Light."

"That's not what you said."

"It is; your lack of comprehension is the issue, and no, I feel no need to educate you in that regard."

Steam rose from the two bowls between them. Jewel, who liked the roof of her mouth, reached for the bread as Avandar inspected the contents of his mug. She waited for some comment about the quality of the food, but none was forthcoming. His expression shifted, softening into a totally unfamiliar smile; his gaze was distant enough that she knew she had nothing to do with it.

Not for the first time, she wondered where he'd come from and what he'd done to become a domicis, because in spite of his position, she couldn't imagine that he'd ever served anyone. But . . . he ate. He drank. He seemed, for the half hour, to be comfortable in this loud and slightly run-down room. He didn't speak much, but then again, neither did Jewel; she waited until the stew was cool enough to eat—which meant it was just on the edge of painful.

But it was good. It was tangy and warm; there was less meat in it than she was now used to eating at most dinners, and more potato. The bread was as good as anything she got at home, though. Home. Taverson's wife came and went as the bar grew more crowded, not because she was waiting at tables—she wasn't—but because she was in theory overseeing the kitchen. The ghosts of memory here were kinder than they had been on the walk.

Even the memory of Carver burning his mouth that first night made her smile.

She looked up; Avandar was watching her; the light made his eyes seem paler, somehow. "Who is Rath?" he asked. She hadn't expected the question.

"A friend."

"A friend?"

She nodded stiffly and looked away. Then she looked back, almost defiantly. "Everything I have now, I have because of him."

Avandar lifted a hand. "I require no confession." His voice was cool, clipped. "Will he be at your gathering?"

"Only in spirit. Knowing Rath, probably not even then." Restless, she pushed herself out of her chair and almost ran into Marla, who was not, after all, in the kitchen. Her arms were folded, and she looked worried. Worried was generally followed by angry, which was generally followed by violent, although that violence had never been fatal.

"No, I'm fine," Jewel said quickly, raising both hands to fend off the suspicious words that were about to be spoken. "He's here to—" she stopped, realizing that Taverson's wife was not, in fact, looking directly at her. She was looking into the tavern itself, at one particular table. She glanced at Jewel, offered a perfunctory smile, and then once again looked past her.

Jewel turned as well; she could hear the voices of men who had already had too much to drink. In and of itself, this wasn't a problem. But drinking peeled away different layers of skin depending on the drinker; in some cases, it peeled away the parts that were sane and cautious.

"Stay here," Marla said firmly. "Stay with your friend." She walked toward the bar, and Jewel, watching, saw that she approached her husband. Taverson was looking the table as well, and his expression—never the friendliest—had frozen in place. He wasn't angry—anger was normal, because stupidity was, in his words, *everywhere*, and he didn't much care for stupid. He was grim. He set aside everything and fished about under the bar, coming up with a truncheon.

Jewel returned to the table, since she wasn't that far from it, but she couldn't bring herself to sit. This was the point at which anyone with half a brain would be slinking out the front doors—and her den would have been among them.

But the problem that had drawn the tavern owner's wife became clear as Jewel watched; it wasn't that the men were drunk or belligerent; it was their target: one of the barmaids. She was still trying to be friendly, but in a tight-lipped way, and it was not going well; the whole situation was now balancing on an edge that was getting sharper and thinner as the sentences continued.

"Jewel."

She jumped when Avandar touched her shoulder. The bar was loud and noisy, and looming disaster had always been compelling and unsettling, but she hadn't been aware that he'd left his seat and had come to stand behind her. She expected him to tell her that it was time to leave; she even expected him to say something enraging about the tavern itself.

He did neither. He did shake his head in a very familiar and resigned way, but that was all. Taverson waved at Lorry, who had already left off any pretense of work; he, like Taverson, was not a small man—and like Taverson, not drunk.

But the table was crowded with men who were also not small, and they weren't yet drunk enough, in Jewel's opinion, to be pushovers. She drew a sharp breath as one of them—finally—grabbed the barmaid. This happened a lot, but usually the barmaids had practice in disengaging without taking—or causing—offense. Jewel knew that this wasn't going to be one of those times.

Avandar said, "This is not the work I envisioned when I accepted the position. Take the woman's advice: *Stay here*. Do not attempt to interfere." He even pushed her, firmly, back into her chair, and then he headed, more quickly than either Taverson or Lorry, toward the table in the back of the room.

"Gentlemen," he said. The word sounded quiet. Soft-spoken. But Jewel could hear it clearly over all the rest of the conversation in the tavern. That conversation began to dry up as people turned to look. At Avandar. At her domicis. Of all of the things she had expected from him, this wasn't even on the list.

"Avandar!" she shouted.

Her voice, unlike his, wasn't pitched to carry. But because the room had gotten quieter in the wake of his, it did. He didn't turn.

"We don't have a writ!"

He said, in the same quiet voice, "A writ will not be required. *Gentlemen*." There was something in the way he spoke the last word that pierced drunken malice and ugly self-indulgence. At least some of it. The barmaid's wrist and elbow were still wedged between two pairs of hands, and the tray she had been balancing had already been removed by a third pair.

Even the barmaid looked up at the sound of Avandar's voice.

Taverson had stopped about five feet from Avandar's back because Avandar was, frankly, in the way; he occupied the small set of steps that led into the larger back area, and he clearly had no intention of moving to allow them to pass. Taverson didn't try to push clear, either; he just waited for Avandar to move.

"Let the girl go," the domicis said, in the same even tone.

The two men whose backs were toward the stairs now turned in their chairs. They weren't young men, but they were, she thought, slightly younger than Avandar. They were more scarred, and they'd clearly seen their share of labor or fighting. If his voice had drawn their attention, his clothing dispelled the part of it that might have been based in fear.

"Girl wants to stay and visit," one of the two said. He wasn't, on the other hand, one of the two who was holding her. He rose, shoving his chair out of the way by kicking it over. It clattered, but it didn't break; the chairs here were damn heavy.

"Your lack of perception is stupendous," Avandar replied. "And, gentlemen, it was not a request."

One of the two men actually sniggered.

One of the two men that were holding the barmaid's arm let go; the other did not. Avandar shook his head and then walked down the stairs. His pace was measured and slow; Taverson and Lorry followed, but at a distance.

Knives appeared around the table. Long knives, at least three. Probably more. They were joined by derisive laughter, a couple of pointless insults that only people who'd drunk enough could think were clever. But something about Avandar made the men cautious enough to fan out between the barmaid and the domicis, knives in hand.

Avandar didn't appear to care, and Jewel found herself holding her breath. He didn't intend to stop either. He kept walking until he was within striking distance of the man in the center. And then he continued to walk. Jewel shouted his name, but Avandar now demonstrated that he had the same selective deafness that she often used on him.

The man with the knife backed up half a step and then snarled something that didn't travel the distance. It didn't have to—she could see the flash of his knife as he drove it home.

It *snapped*.

It snapped, and the blade bounced and fell, skittering across the floor in a much less boisterous room. The four men who were split to either side of Avandar froze for a second as the event pierced the haze of alcohol. It didn't appear to make them any smarter, though. Two more blades snapped as Avandar reached out and caught the first man, whose lower jaw looked unhinged as it hung there, by the throat.

He lifted the man with an ease that even Torvan couldn't have mastered and then tossed him carelessly into two of his friends, clearing a path for himself. He'd slowed—not stopped—to get rid of the obstacle, and he now faced the man who was still holding the girl. That man had drawn a knife as well, and it wavered in the air between Avandar and the barmaid before it flew to the underside of her jaw, its threat clear.

"If I see blood," Avandar said, in the same detached voice, "you are dead."

The two men he hadn't bowled over had backed away from the table, shaking their heads; one still carried a knife. Unfortunately—for them—they backed into Taverson and Lorry, neither of whom was feeling all that charitable.

The table was now deserted; only one man remained. His knife, however, meant that things were not yet over, and Jewel found herself whispering a prayer to *Kalliaris*. Smile, Lady. Smile. The barmaid was still; she didn't struggle, and she didn't speak. She looked at Avandar.

Avandar's back was to Jewel; she couldn't see his expression. She wasn't even sure she wanted to see it now. It wasn't that his voice was cool—she'd heard that before. But she *knew* he'd kill the man without a second thought—without even a first one. Maybe he even deserved it. But the barmaid didn't.

"*Avandar*!" she shouted, cupping her hands to either side of her mouth to gain volume.

He paused and turned to look at the young woman who was, in theory, his master. She understood, then, the difference between theory and fact. But understanding it or no, she walked toward him, shrugging off someone's hand to do so.

"I believe I told you to remain seated."

"You did."

"Return to the table. I will deal with this."

"I do not want her hurt."

He raised a brow, but his face was otherwise impassive.

"I mean it, Avandar. I don't want her hurt. I don't care what you do to *him*."

The brow rose slightly higher, and then his eyes narrowed. "Very well." He turned, lifted a hand, and gestured; the dagger fell, still attached to the man's hand.

The man's hand, however, was no longer attached to his arm. The barmaid turned a shade of white that reminded Jewel of milk; the floor and a large part of the man's shirt turned a shade of red that reminded her of death. He screamed; the barmaid, pale or no, pulled herself out of reach and ran toward Marla. The older woman's arms closed around her instantly, like a shield wall made of care and flesh and ferocity.

Avandar then turned back to Jewel, his lips thinned in something that had the shape of a smile, but none of its warmth. "Are we finished here?" he asked softly.

She wanted to slap him; she had never wanted to slap someone so badly in her life. But her hands stayed by her sides, and she looked to Taverson's wife, just as the barmaid had done but without the running. Marla was pale, the set of her mouth grim, and the look she gave Avandar was a mixture of grateful and frightened. But fear didn't last long. Then again, neither did gratitude.

Jewel understood two things as she watched the slow transformation of this familiar and comforting woman's face: that Avandar would be allowed across the threshold again, but he'd never be welcome; and that Jewel, tied to him in ways she was only beginning to understand, would likewise be less and less welcome. *This isn't my world, anymore*, she thought. She would never have said it; not here, not now.

But she walked to Taverson's wife, and said, in a quiet voice, "I'm sorry."

Marla, arms still around the barmaid's now invisible shoulders, looked down at Jewel, and her expression eased, although Jewel wasn't certain what she saw there. "Don't be. It would've gotten ugly. Uglier," she added with a grimace.

"How?" Jewel glanced at the man, who was cradling his wrist against his chest and keening in shock and pain.

"Six men, knives. We can usually talk them down, but when we can't, everyone gets hurt some. At least it wasn't one of mine." But she, too, looked at the man, and she shuddered once. "Don't worry about dinner. It's on us."

Jewel had forgotten about the dinner entirely. Avandar approached them, handed Jewel something, and then said, "It would be best if I remain outside."

No one argued.

"Where did you meet him?" Taverson asked, once the door had stopped swinging at Avandar's back.

Jewel looked at the tavern owner; he looked . . . tired. Just tired. Lorry had already gone to help their erstwhile customer up and out of the bar. Jewel had a suspicion that this was entirely pragmatic; most people had lost all appetite for food or drink, and they weren't likely to get it back while he was sitting at the otherwise empty table, bleeding on himself and the floor.

She drew a slow breath, exhaled, and then looked at what she now held in her hand: the invitation. Avandar had placed it there without a word. "At House Terafin," she told Taverson.

He frowned. "You'll have to speak up, Jay. What did you say?"

Raising her voice, which now trembled slightly, she repeated the words.

He stared at her, shook his head, and asked her to repeat the words again, because he clearly didn't think he'd heard them right the second time, either.

"He's a—one of the things he's supposed to be is a—a really fancy guard." She took a deeper breath and added, "I'm Jewel ATerafin now."

Taverson's eyes rounded, and he stared at her as if she, and not the men in the back of the bar, had had far too much to drink.

But she met and held his gaze, and as she did, she held out the envelope. He took it slowly, setting the truncheon down on the nearest table. The table had been, until about two minutes ago, occupied, and the truncheon nestled between bowls and mugs like an afterthought. He then looked down at the envelope. Unlike Farmer Hanson, his brows didn't fold into immediate suspicion; she thought he was examining the admittedly clumsy seal.

He didn't open the envelope; instead he looked at her, everything about his expression different. He looked at her clothing, at her hands—which weren't yet adorned by rings—at her boots; he looked at her hair. Her hair hadn't changed. Then, quietly, he looked down at the envelope again. "What's this, then?"

She didn't know how to begin. She looked at the bloody floor and the silent, shocked—and much emptier—tavern, and then she looked down at the envelope, thinking of the den's anticipation and joy. It had been hers as well. She was angry at herself for feeling the weight of this guilt. But it didn't matter; she couldn't shrug it off.

"It's an—" It was nothing to be embarrassed about. She forced herself to remember that. "It's an invitation. To a party," she added quickly.

One of his brows rose, and his expression became less guarded; he still looked damn tired. "A party, is it? And will your guard be there?" His smile was slight, but it was genuine.

She cringed. "I'm sorry," she said. "But—yes. He's also a servant."

"A . . . guard. And a servant. What is he, girl?"

"A domicis."

To her surprise, Taverson recognized the word. "You have a domicis? Or is he contracted to the House?" He glanced at the seal again, as if reminding himself that this was a real conversation, not an alcohol-induced illusion.

"He's mine. Until he dies. Or until I do."

"And you're thinking your death is the more likely, are you?"

"Not at the moment," she replied, with more of her normal heat and one venomous glance at the closed door.

The tavern owner chuckled, and the line of his shoulders also relaxed. "So you're having a party, then. Where?"

"Ummm."

One brow rose. Taverson turned to his wife, opened his mouth, and shut it again; she was still speaking softly to the barmaid. Jewel was almost certain that it was the method of her salvation that had caused the shock, not the need for rescue in the first place.

"Ummm?"

"It's at the Terafin manse. On the Isle."

At this, Taverson's brows did finally recede up and into his hairline, and he broke the seal, tearing the envelope open and pulling the letter out. He didn't accuse her of lying but he needed to see the letter because he'd just wandered so far out of his daily routine he was no longer sure of his bearings.

She waited.

"On the Isle," he whispered, shaking his head. "And you're ATerafin *and* you live in the manse."

She swallowed and nodded.

"Girl, I'm going to wake up tomorrow and if there's no blood on that floor, I'll think I was dreaming. I think I'm dreaming now." He raised his voice and called his wife. She frowned, but he waved her over anyway. When she opened her mouth, he handed her the letter; she frowned, because she wasn't used to interruption. Certainly not written interruption.

But she glanced once at Jewel, and then she read the letter itself. Her brows furrowed, and her eyes narrowed in concern. They eventually widened, but this time she really looked at Jewel.

"You're ATerafin? You're ATerafin and *on the Isle?*"

Jewel nodded, trying not to look self-conscious. Because there was no reason that she should be—and she felt as if she should be *apologizing*.

"And your friend?"

"He's a—"

"Domicis," Taverson told his wife.

"I guess that would explain the fancy clothing." She didn't say what else it might explain, but that hung, unsaid, between them. She looked back down at the letter. "You're having a party."

Jewel nodded, feeling funereal rather than celebratory.

"And you want *us* to come?" Before Jewel could answer—which would have been a nod, anyway, she turned to her husband. "Did you read this?" she asked, shaking the letter in front of his face.

He nodded and picked up his truncheon, which he carried back to the very quiet bar. His wife snorted the word *men* under her breath and turned back to Jewel. "You're certain?" she said, sounding more uncertain than she'd ever sounded.

This is what the name was worth in the twenty-fifth holding.

And what had she expected? If someone from House Terafin had ever approached her, she'd've been afraid—of making a fool of herself, of being suddenly unworthy. Funny how daydreams didn't take any of this into account.

"I'm certain. And if you tell me you have nothing to wear, I'll either cry or swear. Or both."

There was a moment of silence, and then a familiar—if weary—smile graced the older woman's lips and the corners of her eyes. "You've been inviting all your old friends, haven't you? Never mind. The guests—you get to choose them?"

"All of us do. Me, my den. It's our party, not House Terafin's. We get to choose." She turned away. "I just didn't think—"

Large hands caught her shoulders and turned her around. "You thought well enough. And we're going. You really want *all* of us?"

"We've got a lot of room. And we'll have a lot of food. Ummm, I'm not sure we'll have much to drink, though."

"Just as well, dear, just as well. We'll be there."

23rd of Veral, 411 A. A.
Terafin Manse, Averalaan Aramarelas

The West Wing was not the first set of rooms that guests arriving at the manse encountered, and while the manse boasted several exits and entrances, only one of those was considered appropriate for guests. That, of course, was fronted by the prominent steps, the huge doors, the intimidatingly perfect floors of the newly reconstructed foyer, and the chandelier.

The chandelier had suffered some damage when the demons and the *Allasakari* had attacked, but Meralonne's intervention had prevented it from being destroyed.

This had, according to Teller's information, mollified some members of the household who were less than entirely pleased with the destruction of the Terafin's mantel. Jewel, whose appreciation for what was, after all, a frame for a fireplace, didn't really understand why it had caused so much fuss, but Teller said Barston had been "upset." The chandelier, on the other hand, would have been marginally more expensive to replace. Given that the mantel was deemed irreplaceable, this also made no sense.

Jewel, however, had decided that sense would come with experience. Which would, if she survived the evening, come with time.

Guests were to enter by the front doors. They were, she was informed, to be greeted by both the guards and the Majordomo—a title she had not heard before, and wondered about—and from there, they were to be conveyed by the appropriate servants to the appropriate door—hers—having passed through the galleries that were now lit for night viewing.

Thinking of Helen, Jewel fretted. When Jewel fretted, pretty much everyone did; the den was supposed to sit here and play host. Jewel was pretty sure everyone else would be fine because they expected the Terafin manse to be fancy and intimidating; Helen expected it to be terrifying.

"Jay. *Jay.*"

Jewel looked up; Carver was leaning against the wall, arms folded. The usually invisible servants in the wing were anything but, tonight, and they looked possibly as nervous as most of the den felt. Or worse.

"What?"

"I'll go keep an eye out for Helen. You're sure she's coming?"

Avandar said, before Jewel could, "Yes. She will, however, be with her son. Since her son will be escorting her, I fail to see why she is such a cause for concern, and it is at least an hour before the first guest will arrive in any case."

"Helen is old," Jewel replied promptly.

"Yes?"

"She'll arrive early."

"Pardon?"

"She'll be afraid to arrive late, so she'll arrive early."

"I . . . see."

Jewel nodded, and Carver pushed himself off the wall and headed into the back of the wing. This left Jewel with Finch, Teller, and her anxiety; Jester, Angel, and Arann were off somewhere else. Possibly, she thought uncharitably, hiding. Teller was calm; Finch, however, was as settled and cheery as Jewel. She'd invited both Jarven and the formidable Lucille ATerafin to the party; given Lucille's frequently dim views on those who lived in the manse—anyone associated with the Merchant Authority offices, of course, excluded—Finch hadn't expected Lucille to actually accept. But she had.

Jarven, of course, had accepted, but Finch wasn't nearly as nervous about him; for one, he knew the manse as well as Carver did; she wouldn't have been surprised if he was just as familiar with the servants' halls as Carver. He wasn't likely to get lost unless he wanted to.

They would have both busied themselves tidying, but the servants were already doing that, and they'd made it clear—in their polite and utterly silent way—that help was not required. And not really helpful, either. Even the kitchen was entirely off-limits, because it was being used—and being used by people who could, by Terafin standards, actually *cook*.

Which left them with . . . nothing to do. They paced. And fiddled with their skirts. The only small consolation afforded them by any of these activities was the way they annoyed Avandar, who seemed to feel they should be able to treat the entire evening as something normal.

Helen was, as Jewel predicted, the first guest to arrive, and she arrived half an hour early. She was, as Avandar had predicted, accompanied by her son, who in spite of his obvious desire to be notable enough to be a guest at the Terafin manse, was clearly nervous. Carver, who had found Helen, was walking to her left while she made herself comfortable—inasmuch as she could—by talking his ear off. He was relieved of this duty when Helen finally laid eyes on both Jewel and Finch, who were loitering by the door in an attempt to stay out of everyone else's way. Jewel, remembering the days when her parents—and Oma—had hosted their gatherings, found it almost traumatizing to be allowed to do so little.

Helen, however, relaxed once she entered the wing. She had a lot to say—about the carpets, the curtains, the paintings, the size of the tables, the weight of the chairs—and she paused beside every bit of hanging cloth to actually look at its weave or guess at the dyes used to make it. It was, in her words, far too fancy for her little stall to afford—but she nonetheless viewed it all with a critical eye.

She had been forbidden her pipe, she told Jewel, casting a sideways glance at her son, who was not—since there were no other guests—far from her side. Jewel, remembering her Oma, grimaced. "Later," she told Helen.

Helen was then led on a tour of the den's various rooms, since the rooms, no matter who occupied them, were all tidy and clean. The farther away she got from her memory of the front entrance of the manse, the more at home she felt. Jewel and Finch showed her more drapes and opened their closets for her inspection; they also, after a hurried discussion, opened Teller's to the same. While they were thus busy, the next guests began to arrive, and noise slowly filled the cavernous rooms and halls of the West Wing, making them seem—for the first time since they'd been opened for the den's use—like a home and not another part of the intimidating and fancy mansion.

Home, for Jewel, would always be that noisy place that was full of people she loved—even if she sometimes wanted to smack them. She left Finch with Helen and headed back to the larger, more public rooms. There, she met Farmer Hanson, his daughter, his four sons, and his wife. Teller and Carver were already with them, and Jewel paused to send Avandar in search of Angel, Jester, and Arann before she tapped the farmer on the shoulder and hugged him tightly.

Even his daughter, whose name Jewel didn't actually know, looked far less forbidding—and therefore far more unnatural—when she wasn't on the lookout for thieves or, worse, idiots who mishandled her produce. The farmer's wife looked as nervous as Helen. But Jewel rescued a tray of drinks from a servant—where in this case rescue looked a lot like pleading and scuffling—and with care, passed them around the large room, and if the glasses were thinner and finer than the farmer and his family were accustomed to using, it didn't take them long to relax. Servants did insist on carrying the food, but that was fine, although one of the sons looked at the small wrapped pieces of ham and something-else very suspiciously before his mother kicked him, more or less quietly.

Taverson and his wife, Lorry and his wife, and Taverson's three daughters arrived next, and standing behind them, a tall, reserved man Jewel had never seen before. She said to Marla, "I lied; apparently we can't have a party and not have wine. It's against the House rules," and wine arrived as the guests' outer clothing was carefully removed and conveyed to gods only knew where.

The stranger entered shortly after the bottleneck in the door had cleared, and he turned to Jewel. "You are Jewel ATerafin?"

She nodded.

"My manners," he said. "I am Terrick Dumarr." He bowed.

No one else had bowed upon entry, which was good; Jewel thought she would die if any of her old friends bowed upon seeing her. She held out a hand and waited until he rose, which took some time. But he did at least shake her hand, and when he did, he smiled. It made his face seem less severe, but not by much.

"You're Angel's friend?" she asked.

He nodded. "You have not yet had a gathering of significance—in a political sense—in your home, have you?"

"No. And with luck, I'll never have to."

He chuckled. "Some people would ask luck to turn the other edge." He glanced past her shoulder—well, over her head, really—and into the large room at their backs. "Angel is not present?"

"He's probably hiding in his room. I sent Avandar to find him and dig him out."

"And, of course, my master's wishes are instantly obeyed," the domicis said. He stood behind Jester, Arann, and Angel. Only Angel had the grace to look embarrassed, because Angel instantly recognized the man who stood in front of his den leader.

Terrick lifted a broad hand. "I've been chatting with Jewel ATerafin," he told Angel.

Angel looked ill at ease. "Hopefully not embarrassing me while you're doing it."

"Not yet," the man said with a grin. "Although I meant to ask after The Terafin's finances, as it appears the House manages to keep up with the expense of feeding you." He laughed as Angel winced, and his laugh was a good sound; it bounced off the ceiling and the walls, shattering his reserve. Since he was a friend of Angel's, Jewel was predisposed to like him, but she felt, watching him with Angel, that she would have liked him regardless.

Angel led him to the far corner of the large room, in the obvious hope of failing to be further mocked.

Finch returned with Helen in time to meet Jarven and Lucille, who arrived at the wing together. Lucille was fussing in pretty much exactly the way Finch described, and Jarven weathered it with the affectionate patience she had also described. Lucille did hug Finch, but only after setting her at arm's length—which involved hands on her shoulders—to look at what she was wearing. She then turned to Jewel, as Finch said, "Lucille, this is Jay."

Jarven helpfully added, "She is referred to as Jewel by The Terafin."

Lucille reminded Jewel of her Oma, although she was younger, her build was wrong, and she wasn't cupping a pipe. Nothing about her coloring suggested a Southern heritage, either, but she held out a hand almost instantly. Jewel took it and found—no surprise—that Lucille's grip was strong. It was also warm.

"I hear you've joined the House proper," the older woman said, as she relinquished Jewel's hand. "Do you know what your duties will be?"

"Not yet. I think I'm eventually to learn about the merchant arm."

"Arm? Arm? There's more than one, my dear. And at least two of those so-called arms are run by the—"

"What she means to say," Jarven interjected, "is that they are run by members of standing—quite high standing—in the patriciate."

Jewel wasn't interested in what Jarven meant Lucille to say; she was, however, quite interested in what Lucille had intended to say before the interruption. She therefore led Lucille away from Jarven, on the pretext of finding her something to drink.

Jarven shook his head as they left. "That girl," he told Finch, with a small frown, "will need to develop some subtlety if she's to serve in any branch of the merchant arm."

"You can add it to the list of things she already has to learn," Finch replied diffidently. "But when you do, please keep in mind that the rest of us are going to have to take the same lessons."

"My dear, you wound me. Have I ever accused you of a lack of subtlety?"

Finch took a moment to think. "Not that I recall," she replied, which was safest.

He smiled and rescued a passing glass of wine from a servant who seemed to be able to navigate any crowd, no matter how densely packed it was. "I see the House cellars have been opened for your use this eve. You have quite an assortment of friends," he added, glancing around the room. "But I am not as young as I used to be."

It was one of his most frequently used phrases, his polite and particular code for *I would like to sit down*. Finch dropped quietly into the role that Lucille generally fulfilled and led him to an unoccupied chair. "Oh, neither am I."

One pale brow rose, but her smile was mild enough that he allowed any possibility of sarcasm to pass unremarked. "You, on the other hand, my dear, have developed a much more refined sense of subtlety. And you appear to be an entirely harmless young girl, in need of the care and the watchful eye of women like Lucille. Or," he added, inclining his head, "your Jay."

She took the chair by his side and gave him a look, which caused him to laugh. "I'm not accusing you of lying, dear Finch. But the way in which you choose to present your particular truths are more thoughtful and less . . . explosive."

She nodded. "You'll meet Teller," she said. "You'll like him. I think."

"I like almost everyone I meet," was his diffident reply. Since it was more or less true, she didn't argue. But she did watch his brows rise an inch before he turned to study the glass in his hand. "Interesting," he said, in as neutral a tone as he ever used. Interesting, in Jarven's use, was often bad.

She looked up and noted that two new people had joined the gathering. They were led into the room, and now surveyed it. One was a man who was younger than Jarven and somewhat slimmer; he was with a woman who was about his age and somewhat rounder. She was beaming. He was smiling. They both held glasses—it was impossible to get past the servants without taking something—and they headed toward the fireplace, around which chairs had also been placed.

Jay, dragging Lucille, intercepted them there. She threw her arms around the woman and then disentangled herself, remembering her duties, and introduced her to Lucille.

"Do you know who they are?" Jarven asked quietly, rising.

"Friends of Jay's. Haval and his wife, Hannerle."

"Haval?"

"He owns a shop in the Common. He made this dress," she added. "And the one Jay's wearing, as well."

"Did he, indeed?" Jarven paused to examine the dress with more attention to detail. "And Jewel knows him well?"

Finch frowned.

"Oh, tush, Finch. There's no need to look suspicious."

"There's no need to pretend I'm hurting your feelings either, but you do it anyway."

He chuckled. "Very well. I should like to be introduced to these friends." He added, when she hesitated, "As this gathering is short on the expected protocols and formalities, I'm perfectly willing to commit a social gaffe with regard to manners in this case."

Bowing to fact, Finch led Jarven to Lucille, Jay, and her two newest guests. Some conversational space was instantly made by Lucille for introductions, but Jay had to be nudged. Finch, therefore, introduced Jarven and Lucille and waited while Jay did the same for Haval and his wife, Hannerle.

Hannerle, of course, examined the cut of both Lucille's dark dress and Jarven's suit; she made no attempt to be subtle, but her curiosity was so straightforward only someone who wanted to take offense would have. But Haval seemed content to let his wife do the fussing, and given the fittings Finch had had to endure, it seemed a bit odd.

"Finch, dear, do stop fussing with the skirts," Haval said, as if he could read her mind.

Since she was, in fact, fussing with the skirt—and why, she didn't know—she grimaced and stopped. Lucille bristled, but only slightly.

"So, Haval, I'm curious," Jarven said, leaning slightly against the wall nearest the fireplace. "How did you meet young Jewel?"

Lucille glanced sharply at Jarven and then, more sharply, at Haval himself. Hannerle did the same, but in reverse order.

Haval, however, smiled benignly. "We had a mutual friend who was aware of Jewel's situation. I am not a High Market merchant, but—and I say this with no little pride—my skill with the needle is not less than one would expect of High Market clothiers. He introduced us."

"Ah. Well, you may display, as you say, no little pride—but I feel that your assessment in this case is accurate. The dresses are both very fine and also very appropriate to both age and new station."

"Thank you. I hope your word will carry weight with future clients." He turned to his wife as Jarven spoke again.

"How long have you been a clothier?"

"Oh, any number of years too long to count," was the pleasant reply.

"Indeed. I myself have sometimes felt that about my current career; there was more freedom in youth, if less wealth."

Finch looked between these two polite, friendly older men and then glanced at Lucille. Lucille's expression was now carved in stone, which meant something was up.

Lifting her hand in den-sign, she asked Jay what it was.

Jewel's hand flew quicky—and briefly—in response; she had no idea either. But she was worried. The two men didn't seem angry or hostile; she wasn't concerned about an incident, as it was sometimes called by the more genteel. "Jarven," she said, "do you know Haval?"

It was, from the silence that eddied between the two men, the wrong question. The right question, however, had failed to materialize.

"That is an interesting question, because I would swear that I've never met a clothier named Haval before in my life. Yet he does seem familiar, for all that."

"I often remind people of other people they know; it's a fault of a lack of distinctive features," was the bland and somewhat apologetic reply. "I assure you that I would have remembered any first meeting with the man in charge of the entire Terafin merchant operations, saving only those that involve Royal Charters."

"And speaking of Royal Charters," Jarven said, with a smile, "I believe that there are rumors that one of the attending guests will be a man who works very closely with Patris Larkasir in the Trade Commission office in *Avantari*."

"I have very little familiarity with trade in either form," Haval replied. "And surely such an illustrious guest, or guests, including yourself, will have far more valuable things to do at a gathering of this nature than spend time speaking with a humble clothier who cannot even approach the High Market."

"Nonsense, nonsense. If Jewel's experience and presence here teaches us nothing else, my dear Haval, it is that we are indeed far too inflexible. Look at the people gathered here; this is not, in any way, the usual politically motivated social gathering. Here, we might consider ourselves among friends."

"Friends, is it?" Haval's smile was cool and utterly neutral.

Jewel was almost transfixed. "Haval?"

He raised a brow and then grimaced mildly at her expression.

Jarven, standing not five feet from him, glanced at Jewel and did likewise.

A whole series of lectures was implied in those grimaces, which meant that silence should have been valued. It wasn't; it was long enough, and awkward enough, that lectures would have been better. But neither Lucille nor Hannerle seemed interested in running interference, and, in fact, they glanced at each other and then drew closer to the fire, where they spoke in low voices. Lucille very pointedly took Finch with her.

Which left Jewel with Haval and Jarven. And silence.

She folded her arms tightly across her chest. "So," she said, in a tone of voice she might have used on Carver when he was being particularly stubborn, "I'm guessing you two *do* know each other?"

Haval opened his mouth, and Jewel lifted a hand. "Yes, you can deny it, and yes, I'll believe almost anything you say—but not when he's standing right there denying all of it."

"I have not uttered a single word of either accusation or denial," Jarven said, in a mildly hurt tone.

She looked at him and raised a brow. Or both of them.

"Nor have I indicated that I am familiar with the clothier, although I must say his work is not shoddy."

The eyes narrowed.

Jarven actually laughed, shaking his head as the sound—which attracted attention—died into a chuckle. "You know, my dear, Finch has often said that Lucille reminds her of you, and I can now see why."

Haval, casting a brief glance at his wife, looked at Jewel rather sourly. "The young ATerafin has some studying to do," he told Jarven. "She was under the impression that no people of significance or power—other than The Terafin—were to be present this eve."

"And so you thought it safe to venture into the patriciate's heartland?"

"I wished the advantage of clothing both she and Finch ATerafin, as The Terafin herself would be present," was the clipped reply. "I in no way assumed that one of the unillustrious guests would be Jarven ATerafin, a man known for his—"

"Agile mind, at this age," was the serene reply.

"And I suppose she thinks that you dodder around your office drinking tea and playing chess badly?"

"I have given up on the bad chess," Jarven replied. "It is hard not to become involved in the outcome, and I win rather more than most people would like. It makes them too cautious."

"And we can't have that."

"Well, caution is to be generally encouraged, especially in the young, but it is not always advantageous to a man of my standing. Said standing," he added, "comes with a burden of notoriety of exactly the wrong type."

"It is seldom that a man of your station confuses notoriety with respect," Haval replied.

"Ah. And a man of your station, Haval the dressmaker?"

"A man of my station typically has neither and aspires to neither."

"Truly?"

"Truly. I am interested, ATerafin, in the making of fine dresses for ladies—and the odd gentleman—of worth."

"Ah. Because custom of worth would fail to make the mistake of assuming I'm a nonentity?"

"Among other things." Haval walked across the room to the painting that hung on the wall opposite the fire; it was closest to the very fine windows, which were curtained against the darkness of the season. He moved from the painting, which he regarded with no expression whatsoever to the drapery, which he regarded with an expression that gave the advantage to neutrality.

"Haval," Jarven said, for both he and Jewel had followed.

Without turning, Haval said, "There are games, ATerafin, that a man of my stature has no interest whatever in playing."

"A man of your stature. I see. Yet you strike me as a man against whom one might play chess, and with whom one might drink tea, were the moment right."

"I drink tea," Haval replied. "I no longer play chess."

"Ah."

"But perhaps Jewel might find a chessboard at which we might sit. It is, indeed, an unusual gathering, and such activities might even be encouraged here."

They both turned to look at Jewel, and Haval said, "Jewel please. You are destroying the fall of the fabric."

She unbunched her hands from folds of cloth and ran off to find a chessboard; she had no idea if there was one in the wing, since none of the den played.

Avandar found both a chessboard and a room in which the two older men might play. He set the board up and pulled out both chairs. As he did, he glanced at Jewel. Three men with faces this impassive shouldn't have been allowed to inhabit the same room. Or the same life, if it happened to be Jewel's. None of them spoke until it came to choosing sides; Avandar palmed a black and a white queen, and after some dextrous movement, he asked Jarven—not Haval—to choose a hand. He drew the black queen.

The two men then sat. They discarded the drinks in their hands—which is to say, they set them down carelessly and without further thought to imbibing. Avandar then withdrew, but only as far as the door.

"ATerafin," he said, when Jewel failed to move with him.

She glanced back.

"I do not believe your guests require an audience for this match."

This was probably true; Jewel, however, wanted to be the audience, regardless. She had never seen Haval's very superior exposure crack before; Jarven was, as Finch had suggested, more open—but not by much. Whatever lay in the past between these two, Jarven owned. Haval? Not so much.

"You realize," Haval said, contemplating the board with apparent care, "that my wife is unlikely to be pleased at my absence."

"Ah, well, wives."

Haval glance pointedly at Jarven. "Spoken like a man who has never acquired one."

"Indeed, indeed. For some reason, I have failed entirely to appeal to anyone sensible enough to want as a wife. The closest I have managed to come is Lucille, who runs the Terafin offices in the Merchant Authority. You did meet Lucille?" Jarven added. "She is definitely and obviously ill pleased; there is no 'unlikely' about the state of her happiness."

"And she is capable of ruining the overall state of your own happiness?"

"What do you think?"

"I think, at the moment, our stakes in this venture our similar." Haval turned to Jewel. "ATerafin, if you will excuse us?"

Jewel blinked, and Jarven chuckled. "You are the premiere host at this gathering, ATerafin. It would be both unseemly and inconvenient for you to remain in this room, keeping the company of two old men such as we."

She snorted. Loudly.

"Speaking of unseemly," Haval added, his gaze now firmly fixed upon a board on which neither man had yet moved a piece. "You needn't worry, Jewel. It is unlikely that a man as illustrious and well known as Jarven ATerafin would disgrace himself by causing difficulty at such a gathering."

"Perhaps it is not my behavior that concerns her, Haval."

"Perhaps she has not had a long enough acquaintance."

"Nonsense. I am exactly as I appear."

Haval lifted a pawn and plunked it down, heavily, on the board.

"Jewel," Avandar said. "Come. Your guests will be waiting."

She pulled herself, reluctantly, from the open door. Haval was generally a test of patience, a curiosity, and though she instinctively trusted him, she did not know much about him. This was the first thing he had done that had completely surprised her.

But Avandar's expression was smooth and cool, and it was clear that he intended to stare her into appropriate behavior. She left.

It was more crowded when Jewel returned to the main rooms in which guests now chatted. Food seemed in endless supply, as did wine, but so far no one had gotten so drunk that the latter was a problem. Barston ATerafin was in one corner, chatting with Teller, and Devon ATerafin had arrived. To Jewel's surprise, he appeared to be in very serious discussion with Lucille, enough so that discussion formed an invisible wall between the two and the rest of the gathering.

Torvan ATerafin arrived beside Arrendas and apologized for his tardiness, blaming it on work; he carried, of all things, flowers, which in this season were expensive. He gave them to Jewel as Arann intercepted them both. Arann's friend from the House Guard had also arrived, and if he'd been a little overawed at the splendor of Arann's situation on first arrival, drink and food had mellowed him considerably. Given the company he was about to keep, Jewel hoped for his sake that "considerably" wasn't too damn much.

And Carver's friends arrived as well: Merry and Mira. Carver didn't exactly bowl Jewel over to reach them, but it was close enough that Avandar aimed a distinctly chilly frown between Carver's shoulder blades as he passed them. Jewel hadn't met Merry before, and she waited for Carver to introduce them. When waiting failed to produce the introduction, she grimaced and introduced herself.

She'd seen Merry a handful of times, but always at a distance. Merry clearly knew who Jewel was; she also clearly knew who everyone else in the wing was. Jewel decided, then and there, that she wanted to stay on the right side of the servants.

Only Jester had failed to invite anyone of his "own" to the gathering. Jewel glanced across the room, but there were now enough standing bodies that it wasn't easy to find most of her den. She did, though. She saw Jester speaking with the Farmer Hanson's daughter; the farmer's severe daughter was actually laughing, which meant her face didn't crack when she smiled.

Her brothers had moved away from their parents—mostly following the winding path the food was taking—and they didn't seem self-conscious when talking to anyone, although they didn't immediately figure out what the difference between the servants and the guests was. Their father was, after the first few moments of uncertainty, chatting with Haval's wife and, to Jewel's surprise, with Devon.

But his wife and daughter had taken a seat together; they'd been silent and still, exchanging words with each other and falling silent when the servants offered them anything, as if afraid to touch. They weren't afraid of Jester, though. He knew.

His face was flushed; the color clashed with his hair. His hands flew, and a glimpse of his expression told her he was impersonating someone; she hoped for his sake—and hers—that that someone wasn't present.

As she approached them, he stopped. With a reckless smile, he said, "I hate rich people."

The farmer's wife chuckled. "You'll be hating yourself, then?"

His smile was a bitter, bitter one. "Looks like."

The farmer's wife now frowned. "Don't," she said, curtly. She didn't catch his hand, which had tightened, although she did start to reach for it. "You've got a place here; doesn't mean you have to be rich."

The daughter's frown was different, and it was aimed at her mother. "If he's to stay here," she finally said, "he'll have to fit in."

But Jewel shook her head. "He only has to fit in with us, same as always."

The daughter, whose name Jewel didn't recall ever knowing, raised a brow. She'd never been friendly, but if she hadn't been kind, she hadn't been cruel. "Same as always?" she said, in cool mimicry. "That's why we never see you anymore?"

It was true, and Jewel had learned from her Oma that only fools and whiny idiots argued with truth, no matter how much they hated it. The farmer's wife, on the other hand gave her daughter a look that made clear who the daughter favored.

"He misses you, it's true," she said, in a quieter voice. "But not the way he misses some of his other orphans. He knows what happened to you; he knows where you are. This," she added, looking around the obvious finery of the House on display, "wasn't even in his dreams for you. It's hard; he worries. Always has. It's one less thing to worry about." She raised a brow and added, "And some unidentified person has been sending him money.

"He doesn't hold with charity," she added severely.

"He should, he's given so much—"

She held up a hand. "He gives to those as needs. He doesn't want to be one of them."

Jewel laughed, remembering her prickly, proud Oma. "It's not for him, and he knows it; it's for us. The us that we were. The other kids like us that he'll find. For winter shirts, for boots—things he might want to give but can't afford for strangers."

The farmer's wife said, "So it was you!"

Jewel had the grace to redden. It hadn't honestly occurred to her that he'd think that money with those instructions would come from anyone else. "Yes," she told the farmer's daughter, "we're rich. And we aim to stay that way. But what's the point of being rich if we can't share a bit?"

"Not starving," was the pointed reply.

Jewel couldn't argue with that and didn't try. "I miss the Common. I know there are some who wouldn't believe it—but I miss it. I miss the morning runs. I miss my farmer. I miss Helen. I don't *want* to change."

Jester was watching her. She was aware that in silence, in a total lack of mockery, he'd joined the conversation that she'd never intended to have at a party. Meeting his gaze squarely, hands sliding down to her hips in a way her Oma would have recognized, she said, "Have I?"

He was trying to decide on an answer, but she wanted a serious one, not a joke, and made it clear in emphatic den-sign.

He shrugged. "I'm ATerafin."

"That's you, not me."

"If you'd changed much, I wouldn't be. Maybe Finch, maybe Teller—they're bright and they don't hate much. Maybe Arann, because he's always been big. But not me, Jay. Not me, not Carver. Not Angel. Well, he isn't anyway, but that's his choice." He turned to look out the nearest window. "She'd've taken 'em all: Duster, Fisher. Even Lander, who hated to talk, and Lefty with his crippled hand." He grimaced. "I don't know how long she'd've kept Duster; Duster would have hated this."

It was true. "Duster hated everything."

Jester laughed. "Almost everything," he agreed. "You could count yourself lucky if she hated you less than most things, but she'd've worked her way through them to you sooner or later."

Jewel laughed. Was surprised she could. The laugh broke for both of them at almost the same time.

Jester said, "We ran."

Jewel said, "She hated us enough to die for us."

Jester's laugh was raw; it was a testament to Duster. "For *us*? Jay—" He shook his head. "Only thing she didn't hate most of the time was you. You weren't afraid of her."

"I was—"

"Nah. You were afraid of what she might *do*, but it's not the same; you weren't afraid of what she'd do to *you*. She'd've come here, if she lived. She'd've hated this place because she didn't belong, and she'd be afraid of failing you. That's it. That's all."

Jewel looked at the window. "Lefty was waiting," she finally said. It wasn't, clearly, what Jester had been expecting. "When Arann almost died—Lefty was waiting for him.

"You think Duster'll wait?"

"Duster? I think Duster'll be at the foot of the bridge because she'll be afraid of entering the Halls of Mandaros and standing in his judgment. And she'll never admit it, because it's fear, and she's like that. I don't think she'll be *waiting* for us. But she'll be there, and if no one laughs, she'll follow."

"And you're not to rush there, yourselves," the farmer's wife said, in a voice that managed to be both gentle and severe at the same time. "You're young. I don't know all of what happened," she added, "but if Duster died to save you, she wanted you to *live*. Outlive us," she added. "Because if you don't, it'll break my husband's heart." She glanced at her daughter and sighed. "You'll change, of course." Before Jewel could interrupt, she lifted a hand. "We *all* change, Jay. We change in ways we could never see. I'm not the girl I was when I was your age. I'm not the woman I thought I'd be, either, but I'm good where I am.

"If anyone had told us you'd be ATerafin, we'd have chuckled—if we liked them. Or we'd've thought they were mad or scheming. We can't see our way to the end from the beginning, and that's the way it should be. Figure out what you value, girl. Cling to it, be true to it; it'll grow with you. It won't look the same to me or my husband, maybe—but it'll be there.

"And come and see him when you can. Not for the food—you'll have far finer here, no doubt, and far more dear—but to remind him."

"Remind him?"

"It's not all starvation and death and loss. Some of you make it out, or at least survive." She ran a hand across her eyes. "And listen to me, going on like this at your party. We're happy for you, Jay. There's going to be some envy, always is. But it doesn't mean the happiness isn't there."

And so she mingled, moving from group to group, from past to present and back, as if for one moment, all time could be measured this way, as if it overlapped, always, in unexpected ways. What she missed was her dead, or even their ghosts; she'd been haunted by the ghosts of the future for most of her life, so the ghosts of the dead held little terror.

This room, with its fireplace, its many chairs, and its circulating plates of food and drinks, was loud, and her thoughts were soft and attenuated, so she moved away from the noise that on most days she craved, leaving the great room for the smaller rooms and heading toward the kitchen, where she stopped before she touched the door, reversing her steps. The kitchen might define the den on most days, but this one wasn't one of them; it wasn't their kitchen, tonight. It belonged to the servants and the cooks, each of whom also had something to prove.

She reversed course, but instead of heading back into the thick of things, she turned toward the entrance, bumping into Avandar along the way. His raised brow clearly said, "Where are you going?" and her shrug, which was awkward and half-embarrassed, was as much of an answer as he needed. He fell into step beside her.

"I'm just—I'm stepping out for air."

"Yes."

"Avandar—"

"I am stepping out for air with you, as you appear to have shed your guard." When she opened her mouth, he grimaced. "I will not lecture you on your obvious desire for solitude. The Terafin, however, has yet to make an appearance, and if she happens to make one while you're wandering— alone—in the halls . . ."

Jewel gave up with as much grace as she could muster. She exited the doors, knowing that this made her the worst of hostesses, and headed into the external halls, which were apallingly well lit tonight. Avandar shadowed her every move.

She didn't get far before she found what she was looking for, although had anyone asked, she would have said, until this moment, she'd been looking for nothing, and lots of it.

Evayne a'Nolan stood beneath the steady glow of magelights, beside a standing urn that had cracked and faded with age. She wore what she'd worn every time Jewel had seen her: long, dark robes that rustled in the nonexistent breeze. Shadow pooled at her feet and, more alarmingly, in her eyes, tainting the whites.

But even so, she wasn't a threat. Jewel knew that much.

The seer's hands were empty and her face was partly hooded; she lifted those hands and removed the hood, as if it were an act of exposure. It wasn't. She was The Terafin's age, and she had The Terafin's composure; her expression was so guarded an army couldn't have got past it to what lay beneath.

"Jewel," she said.

"Evayne," Jewel replied. Avandar, by her side, said nothing. But Evayne looked at Avandar and her brows rose slightly.

"Viandaran," she whispered.

Jewel glanced from one to the other. Avandar was about as open as Evayne; nothing escaped. But she'd grown to recognize all the little signs of irritation or grievance that marked his daily interactions, and they were entirely absent. He said, after a moment, "Why are you here?" and his voice was Winter cold.

"I am not here to threaten or to cause harm," was the seer's even reply. "But Jewel ATerafin is the only seer born into the Empire in this generation; there is one other who is not yet born, but when she is, she will be born in the Free Towns to the west of the Empire."

"And that other?"

"Me." She turned to Jewel. "You have a question?"

"Yes."

"Ask. If I can answer, I will."

"Your age—that's not part of the talent, is it?"

"No. I age as you age, but I wander a path that travels between years as easily as the halls here travel between rooms."

"The crystal—"

"Yes. It is why I have come. You have vision, and that vision has led you here, but it will not, in the end, be enough. The crystal," she said, "comes from me, it is *of* me. It is the gift made physical, made manifest. What I see in it, what I *can* see in it, is deeper, wider; it is not a glimpse, not an accident, not a strike of lightning or luck or fate.

"Have you not dreamed of this?"

Jewel looked at the seer. "Yes," she finally whispered. It sounded a lot like no.

"There is only one teacher who can give you the skill you need to create the crystal, and that teacher must decide whether or not she finds you worthy. It is not a simple task, and her assessment is unpredictable; she is not human."

Jewel's brows rose.

"But you must make the trek, sooner or later, to her. When you are ready, Jewel, call me; I will come, and I will lead you there."

But Avandar now raised a hand. "It will not be necessary." His voice was cool.

"Oh?"

"I know the way, and I know of whom you speak. But you are not entirely truthful, Evayne; the trek itself is no guarantee of success, and the cost of failure is high; it scars, where it does not kill. Come, Jewel. It is time that we returned."

But Jewel asked, "Why did you take the test, Evayne?"

"Pardon?"

"You said you were—will be—born in the Free Towns. That wasn't a lie. What made you go to—to whoever this person is—and run the risk of ripping out your heart?"

Evayne's lips twisted in a bitter grimace. "I seldom meet seers," she said, at last. "And although I do not owe you an answer, not yet, I will give you one: my father."

"Your father?"

"I am god-born, Jewel Markess ATerafin. I do not know who my mother was; I know only who my father is. I took the test of the Oracle, and I walked the Oracle's path, because I was young. Oh, my father had told me of the war—of the gods and the kin and the monsters that would rise in the breaking of the ways—but I was then fifteen years of age, almost sixteen, and I had lived my life as a blacksmith's daughter. I neither knew of these things or, truth be told, cared; they frightened me. He frightened me then.

"I was a strange child, and I had few friends in the village, but those friends were all I valued. It has not happened yet," she added softly. "But

I will grow there, and I will walk a normal path, following in the wake of days, until the day my father makes himself known.

"There is war," she added softly. "And he tells me of it, of what it presages, of what it might mean." She shook her head. "But it isn't until I see the demons approach the village, it isn't until I see the slaughter begin, that I understand." Her violet eyes closed, and she grimaced again. It made her seem younger. "It was then, and only then, that I made my choice, because I understood that I would be sundered from my friends and from the village itself. But if I did as he asked, if I did *all* I could, I might, in the end, lead those who could stand against the demons to the town itself.

"And I have waited, Jewel."

Jewel stared at the seer for a long, silent moment, and then she said, "What happens to your friends?"

"I don't know."

"You can't see it?"

"One is not yet born, and the other? He will go to war in the South long before he makes Callenton his home."

"But you—you were sixteen?"

"Yes."

"And if you—if you win somehow, if *we* win, when you go home, will you be sixteen again?"

"No. I will be even older than I am now, and they will neither recognize nor understand me. I will never be the blacksmith's adopted daughter again, and I will never be at home in the primitive confines of a Free Town. They are lost to me; they were lost to me the minute I took my first step on the Oracle's path. But they would have been lost to me—and to themselves—regardless." She lifted a hand. "Has this answered your question?"

"Yes."

"Then I give you this. You have made all of your choices, if I recall correctly, to date to bring your friends and your family to this House, and they are with you now. You will not desert them easily, or perhaps at all; you cannot walk the paths I have walked because you weren't born to them, and I think—I think it impossible. Even with the crystal in your hands, you will be human and mortal; you will not be able to walk through time as if it were a mansion.

"Go back to your friends. Have what I cannot have, for a while longer. But remember me, and remember what I have said." She bowed then.

Jewel didn't. She waited until Evayne rose, her violet eyes glittering in the magelight, her expression once more serene and composed.

"I don't—I'm not—I'm not as strong as you are," she finally said.

"You are not *yet* as strong as I have become," was the soft reply. "But strength oft comes from necessity, and from the burden of both responsibility and love. Both of these you have, Jewel, and we have time yet—although it has, at last, begun to dwindle." She might have said more—she even opened her mouth—but the isolation of the empty halls had now ended; from the east, with a sparse guard of four, walked two familiar figures: The Terafin and her domicis.

"Much of your strength will come from the challenge of the House itself," Evayne continued, her voice soft. "But when it is time, you will know. Before then, you will walk paths that have not been walked since the gods left the world; you will see war and death and magics older than man; you will fight to hold everything that you have not yet won in the House tonight.

"You will gather allies, Jewel; you have already started. You will leave this House only once, and when you do, you will walk at the side of the enspelled, and you will ride on the backs of Kings; you will be served by the scions of Winter. You will see the dead and the living, and you will return to death and to war.

"I envy you," she added, her voice dipping slightly. "I envy what you will have before you face a choice whose end I cannot yet see. But often it is those who have much to lose who find the strength to preserve it, even if they cannot preserve it for themselves alone." She turned, the edges of her cloak billowing.

Jewel watched as she took one step forward and vanished.

The Terafin, down the hall, had seen, but she didn't stop, and she didn't rush forward; Evayne might, like any other troubling work of art, have been a part of the galleries themselves. Jewel waited.

"You are not in the West Wing," The Terafin said, as she drew closer. The guards were Chosen, although Jewel didn't know their names yet.

"No—it was loud and I . . . I wanted air." She glanced at the spot that had moments ago contained the only other seer Jewel had ever met.

"Ah. Well, perhaps you have never before held an event of this significance; you will learn with time. The dress," she added, "is very fine."

"This?"

"Indeed. Who made it?"

"Haval. He works in the Common, but he makes dresses for women of noble birth, as he calls them. Do you want to meet him?"

"I would, if he is a friend of yours, be most pleased to make his acquaintance. Come, Jewel. You will not have a night like this again, and if you can, you must enjoy it. Without joy, there is only burden, and the burdens will be heavy indeed."

Jewel nodded and fell into the space the Chosen had made for her.

They came at length to the West Wing and the gathering that continued within, unaware of the absence of one of its hosts. They could not remain unaware of the presence of The Terafin, however, and silence descended—if slowly—as her name spread across the crowd. She'd chosen to dress simply, although nothing she wore could ever be called inexpensive, and her hair was bound—as it had been the first day Jewel had laid eyes on her—in a fine net that seemed to sparkle slightly when she turned her head.

Haval and Jarven had finished their game—or abandoned it, at any rate—and had rejoined the gathering, and they looked up as The Terafin approached, led by Jewel.

"Terafin," she said, "this is Haval and his wife, Hannerle. Haval is my dressmaker."

Haval, who could manufacture any expression he chose, chose delight—and humility—for this first meeting.

"You've met Jarven?" Jewel asked.

"I have, indeed, met Jarven ATerafin," was the slightly amused reply. "And I trust that he is enjoying himself in an entirely appropriate fashion this eve."

"Oh, he is," Lucille replied a little grimly.

To Jewel's surprise, The Terafin laughed. "I did not promise it would be an easy job, Lucille—merely a rewarding one, in the end. It has been that?"

Lucille raised a brow and then, as if she were playing cards, folded; she smiled. "It's definitely been that, Terafin."

Jarven, unruffled, offered The Terafin a perfect bow. "You will mingle, of course," he said. "I would be interested to hear what you observe while you do."

"That is hardly playing by the rules, Jarven. You are a master of observation; you cannot expect such information to be simply given as if it were of little value."

Jarven chuckled. "Oh, indeed, indeed. May I join you?"

*   *   *

Jewel retreated to the fireplace and to Teller, who seemed to be waiting for her.

"Breathe," he told her.

She laughed. "I'm happy, Teller."

He waited, and she added, "I'm just not sure how long it will all last."

"For at least tonight," he replied firmly. He glanced at her expression and shook his head. "You really did have an Oma, didn't you?"

"That obvious?"

"She told you all we have is now—and *this* now is a good one. Stay in it, don't leave it until it's passed. None of us can see the future—" he held up a hand, den-sign, "ugh. You get the idea."

"You'd be a terrible Oma," Jewel replied with an affectionate grin.

"It's not one of my life's ambitions."

"Your *what*?"

"Barston says I'm to have 'life ambitions,' " was the rueful reply. "He says we're all to have them, especially you."

"Good damn thing I'm not the one working for him, then."

"No. You work directly for The Terafin—I think he thinks that's harder."

"It's not harder than starving," she said quietly. "It's not harder than freezing. It's not harder than—" she stopped, grimacing. "I'm not good at being happy," she finally said. "I'm afraid of it, sometimes."

"You and Duster," he replied, relenting, giving her the breadth of loss.

"What about Duster?" Finch asked, joining them in the momentary quiet of crackling wood and distant conversation.

"I miss her," Jewel said. "I miss her anger and her contempt and the dagger that never left her hand, even while she was sleeping." Finch put an arm around Jewel's shoulders, in part because she could without causing Jewel to flinch. "I miss Lefty. I miss Fisher and Lander. I wish they were here; they were part of it, in the beginning, but they never got to see the end."

"No," Teller replied. "But we'll see them again, at least once; we can tell them all about it then."

"If it's all the same to you, I want that to be a long, *long* time in the future."

Teller, serious, said, "So do I—but at least death will give us *something* if we've got no choice. We all miss them," he added softly. "I can't even say that Duster would've been happy for us—she'd probably be reminding us that we owed it all to her, that we'd never have made it without her. It's true, we wouldn't. Doesn't make it easier.

"But it's not supposed to be easy, losing someone. If it were, we wouldn't care enough to try to keep them. Best we can do is try."

"So we can feel less guilty?"

"So we're not afraid to care about each other."

Jewel said, "I've never been afraid of that." She glanced at the window and shook herself.

Finch, understanding, said, "Is it time?"

"I'm not sure how long she'll stay," Jewel replied. "But she's here now."

"You're sure you still want to give it to her here?"

She had been, until the actual party had arrived. Now she felt far less certain. Hesitating, she looked to Teller, and he nodded slowly. "I don't know how she'll explain it," he said. "But she's The Terafin—she doesn't have to. You're sure you don't want to keep it?"

"For what? I'll never, ever be able to use it."

"Neither will she," Teller pointed out.

"We don't know that. And anyway, that's not the point."

He didn't ask what the point was; he knew. "Go and get it," he told his den leader. "We'll try to clear a little space."

Jewel walked quickly to her room; Avandar stopped her once, but when she told him why she was leaving—and promised to return promptly without meeting any more powerful, mysterious visitors—he chose not to dog her steps. He was watching the crowd, and he paid attention to only a handful of the men and women present: The Terafin, but everyone did that; Devon ATerafin, Haval, Jarven. He'd glanced at Gabriel once or twice, but Gabriel's position as right-kin failed to engage his interest; he'd done more than glance at Angel's friend, Terrick. He didn't, however, speak to anyone.

Jewel entered her room and took a deep breath, leaning back against the door as she tilted her chin toward the ceiling. She was happy to have everyone here; she was happy to be able to feed them and offer them the hospitality of one of the most renowned Houses on the Isle. But she was, as usual, afraid that something would go wrong, and she knew she wouldn't relax, wouldn't let herself truly be joyful, until everyone had actually gone home.

She walked over to the bed and knelt by its side, reaching beneath it, which was awkward given the cut of her sleeves. There, out of the chest that had been its home for so many years in the fiefs, lay a sword in a scabbard. It was neither small nor light, and Jewel had seen it only a handful of times. It was one of the few items that Rath had kept from his early life in a manse that had once included the woman who was now The Terafin.

Jewel had taken it from his apartment, with the tacit permission of Meralonne APhaniel, which in the case of the mage meant his total disregard for the nonmagical detritus of a dead man. She was honest enough with herself to remember that some of the reason she'd wanted the sword was the weapon's obvious worth; the den could sell it if things didn't work out and they ended up back in the streets.

That fear was gone, nor had it been the only reason she'd taken it. Rath had hated his old life—but hate it or no, he had never quite managed to toss this away. Or to sell it, when money was needed. She had no doubt that money had been tight for him at various times—at least until he'd discovered the undercity—but still, the sword remained hidden beneath his bed. He'd carried it—and wielded it—to save Arann in the streets of the holdings.

Her hands tightened around the scabbard as she remembered Lefty's face on that day: He'd run *to her* to save Arann.

Shaking herself, she carried the sword out into the hall. It was heavy and long, and she handled it as if it were a narrow plank, not a weapon.

Finch and Teller, against all odds, had managed to—as they put it— clear space; the only person who occupied its center was The Terafin herself, although her domicis wasn't far behind. She looked up as Jewel entered the room and began to push herself, as politely as possible, through the small circle of onlookers, some of whom she *really* didn't want to offend.

"Jewel?" The Terafin raised a brow.

"I kept this for you," Jewel replied.

The smooth, austere face of the older woman rippled briefly as her brows drew together. "A sword?"

"It's not mine," was the quick reply. "I mean, it was never mine." Her hands shook because everyone was watching. Even the servants, who would no doubt spread word in the back halls the minute the party was over. Or sooner.

The Terafin held out both hands, and Jewel relieved herself of the burden, holding her breath as she did, and wondering what the sword would mean to The Terafin—if it meant anything at all.

The Terafin's hands closed around the scabbard for a moment, and then she gestured people back so that she could draw the sword itself. It shone in the brilliance of magelights; someone had whispered them to full light. She might never have been a soldier, but it was clear she'd been taught how to at least handle a sword.

Jewel had prepared an explanation, but as she watched, she knew it wouldn't be required.

"Where did you find this?" The Terafin asked, her voice strangely subdued, her expression almost vulnerable.

"Where he kept it, always."

"He kept it."

"He used to tell me to mind my own business when I asked. I saw him use it once."

"And you mean for me to keep it."

"It's not—" Jewel hesitated and then said, "I think he would have been happier to leave it in your hands than mine."

"I would have argued that point, once." The Terafin lifted her chin and met Jewel's gaze. "He was not a man who ever espoused forgiveness—neither in the giving nor the receiving. But . . . he sent you to me, Jewel. And if he was not forgiving, I think he must have understood what we might, in time, mean to each other. It was as much a gift as he had in him, and it reminds me that I—" She shook her head. "You do not wish to keep it?"

"No. But I want it to *be* kept."

The Terafin nodded. "It was a gift to my brother from my grandfather, both of whom were to be so bitterly disappointed in the choices I made—and both of whom I loved."

The last word caused a stir in the room; not speech, not exactly, but the sudden intake of breath, or the lack of breath. The Terafin couldn't have missed it, but she could have chosen to ignore it as she so often did.

Instead she raised a brow. "And am I not to speak of love at all, even in such a gathering as this? There are no contracts to be signed, no delicate—or difficult—political negotiations, no delegations of possibly hostile visitors; there are no priests, no magi, no Kings."

No one answered the question; Jewel thought no one would, although she did see Gabriel's brief, pained expression before he looked away. Without thinking, Jewel stepped forward and caught The Terafin's hand; Morretz and the Chosen allowed this.

"Yes," Jewel said, speaking loudly and clearly. "If you feel it, if you honor it. We're ATerafin; we're the kin of your choice, and if we can't hear it, who can?"

"Safely? No one," The Terafin said, in a much softer voice. She looked rueful, if steel could. "But . . . thank you, Jewel." She sheathed the sword. "Thank you, ATerafin. I have no like gift to offer."

But Jewel shook her head, her eyes filming with tears that she would never shed. "You already have," she whispered. "Terafin." She forced herself to smile, and was surprised at how strongly she felt the expression take root. "Come," she said, still holding the older woman's hand in hers. "I want you to meet everyone."